Gene Stratton-Porter Collection

Vol :1

A Daughter of the Land,

A Girl of the Limberlost,

At The Foot Of The Rainbow.

(3 Novels)

CONTENTS

BOOK ONE

CHAPTER I

THE WINGS OF MORNING

"TAKE the wings of Morning."

Kate Bates followed the narrow footpath rounding the corner of the small country church, as the old minister raised his voice slowly and impressively to repeat the command he had selected for his text. Fearing that her head would be level with the windows, she bent and walked swiftly past the church; but the words went with her, iterating and reiterating themselves in her brain. Once she paused to glance back toward the church, wondering what the minister would say in expounding that text. She had a fleeting thought of slipping in, taking the back seat and listening to the sermon. The remembrance that she had not dressed for church deterred her; then her face twisted grimly as she again turned to the path, for it occurred to her that she had nothing else to wear if she had started to attend church instead of going to see her brother.

As usual, she had left her bed at four o'clock; for seven hours she had cooked, washed dishes, made beds, swept, dusted, milked, churned, following the usual routine of a big family in the country. Then she had gone upstairs, dressed in clean gingham and confronted her mother.

"I think I have done my share for to-day," she said. "Suppose you call on our lady school-mistress for help with dinner. I'm going to Adam's."

Mrs. Bates lifted her gaunt form to very close six feet of height, looking narrowly at her daughter.

"Well, what the nation are you going to Adam's at this time a-Sunday for?" she demanded.

"Oh, I have a curiosity to learn if there is one of the eighteen members of this family who gives a cent what becomes of me!" answered Kate, her eyes meeting and looking clearly into her mother's.

"You are not letting yourself think he would 'give a cent' to send you to that fool normal-thing, are you?"

"I am not! But it wasn't a 'fool thing' when Mary and Nancy Ellen, and the older girls wanted to go. You even let Mary go to college two years."

"Mary had exceptional ability," said Mrs. Bates.

"I wonder how she convinced you of it. None of the rest of us can discover it," said Kate.

"What you need is a good strapping, Miss."

"I know it; but considering the facts that I am larger than you, and was eighteen in September, I shouldn't advise you to attempt it. What is the difference whether I was born in '62 or '42? Give me the chance you gave Mary, and I'll prove to you that I can do anything she has done, without having 'exceptional ability!'"

"The difference is that I am past sixty now. I was stout as an ox when Mary wanted to go to school. It is your duty and your job to stay here and do this work."

"To pay for having been born last? Not a bit more than if I had been born first. Any girl in the family owes you as much for life as I do; it is up to the others to pay back in service, after they are of age, if it is to me. I have done my share. If Father were not the richest farmer in the county, and one of the richest men, it would be different. He can afford to hire help for you, quite as well as he can for himself."

"Hire help! Who would I get to do the work here?"

"You'd have to double your assistants. You could not hire two women who would come here and do so much work as I do in a day. That is why I decline to give up teaching, and stay here to slave at your option, for gingham dresses and cowhide shoes, of your selection. If I were a boy, I'd work three years more and then I would be given two hundred acres of land, have a house and barn built for me, and a start of stock given me, as every boy in this family has had at twenty-one."

"A man is a man! He founds a family, he runs the Government! It is a different matter," said Mrs. Bates.

"It surely is; in this family. But I think, even with us, a man would have rather a difficult proposition on his hands to found a family without a woman; or to run the Government either."

"All right! Go on to Adam and see what you get."

"I'll have the satisfaction of knowing that Nancy Ellen gets dinner, anyway," said Kate as she passed through the door and followed the long path to the gate, from there walking beside the road in the direction of her brother's home. There were many horses in the pasture and single and double buggies in the barn; but it never occurred to Kate that she might ride: it was Sunday and the horses were resting. So she followed the path beside the fences, rounded the corner of the church and went on her way with the text from which the pastor was preaching, hammering in her brain. She became so absorbed in thought that she scarcely saw the footpath she followed, while June flowered, and perfumed, and sang all around her.

She was so intent upon the words she had heard that her feet unconsciously followed a well-defined branch from the main path leading into the woods, from the bridge, where she sat on a log, and for the unnumbered time, reviewed her problem. She had worked ever since she could remember. Never in her life had she gotten to school before noon on Monday, because of the large washings. After the other work was finished she had spent nights and mornings ironing, when she longed to study, seldom finishing before Saturday. Summer brought an endless round of harvesting, canning, drying; winter brought butchering, heaps of sewing, and postponed summer work. School began late in the fall and closed early in spring, with teachers often inefficient; yet because she was a close student and kept her books where she could take a peep and memorize and think as she washed dishes and cooked, she had thoroughly mastered all the country school near her home could teach her. With six weeks of a summer Normal course she would be as well prepared to teach as any of her sisters were, with the exception of Mary, who had been able to convince her parents that she possessed two college years' worth of "ability."

Kate laid no claim to "ability," herself; but she knew she was as strong as most men, had an ordinary brain that could be trained, and while she was far from beautiful she was equally as far from being ugly, for her skin was smooth and pink, her eyes large and blue-gray, her teeth even and white. She missed beauty because her cheekbones were high, her mouth large, her nose barely escaping a pug; but she had a real "crown of glory" in her hair, which was silken fine, long and heavy, of sunshine-gold in colour, curling naturally around her face and neck. Given pure blood to paint such a skin with varying emotions, enough wind to ravel out a few locks of such hair, the proportions of a Venus and perfect health, any girl could rest very well assured of being looked at twice, if not oftener.

Kate sat on a log, a most unusual occurrence for her, for she was familiar only with bare, hot houses, furnished with meagre necessities; reeking stables, barnyards and vegetable gardens. She knew less of the woods than the average city girl; but there was a soothing wind, a sweet perfume, a calming silence that quieted her tense mood and enabled her to think clearly; so the review went on over years of work and petty economies, amounting to one grand aggregate that gave to each of seven sons house, stock, and land at twenty-one; and to each of nine daughters a bolt of muslin and a fairly decent dress when she married, as the seven older ones did speedily, for they were fine, large, upstanding girls, some having real beauty, all exceptionally well-trained economists and workers. Because her mother had the younger daughters to help in the absence of the elder, each girl had been allowed the time and money to prepare herself to teach a country school; all of them had taught until they married. Nancy Ellen, the beauty of the family, the girl next older than Kate, had taken the home school for the second winter. Going to school to Nancy Ellen had been the greatest trial of Kate's life, until the possibility of not going to Normal had confronted her.

Nancy Ellen was almost as large as Kate, quite as pink, her features assembled in a manner that made all the difference, her jet-black hair as curly as Kate's, her eyes big and dark, her lips red. As for looking at Kate twice, no one ever looked at her at all if Nancy Ellen happened to be walking beside her. Kate bore that without protest; it would have wounded her pride to rebel openly; she did Nancy Ellen's share of the work to allow her to study and have her Normal course; she remained at home plainly clothed to loan Nancy Ellen her best dress when she attended Normal; but when she found that she was doomed to finish her last year at school under Nancy Ellen, to work double so that her sister might go to school early and remain late, coming home tired and with lessons to prepare for the morrow, some of the spontaneity left Kate's efforts.

She had a worse grievance when Nancy Ellen hung several new dresses and a wrapper on her side of the closet after her first pay-day, and furnished her end of the bureau with a white hair brush and a brass box filled with pink powder, with a swan's-down puff for its application. For three months Kate had waited and hoped that at least "thank you" would be vouchsafed her; when it failed for that length of time she did two things: she studied so diligently that her father called her into the barn and told her that if before the school, she asked Nancy Ellen another question she could not answer, he would use the buggy whip on her to within an inch of her life. The buggy whip always had been a familiar implement to Kate, so she stopped asking slippery questions, worked harder than ever, and spent her spare time planning what she would hang in the closet and put on her end of the bureau when she had finished her Normal course, and was teaching her first term of school.

Now she had learned all that Nancy Ellen could teach her, and much that Nancy Ellen never knew: it was time for Kate to be starting away to school. Because it was so self-evident that she should have what the others had had, she said nothing about it until the time came; then she found her father determined that she should remain at home to do the housework, for no compensation other than her board and such clothes as she always had worn, her mother wholly in accord with him, and marvel of all, Nancy Ellen quite enthusiastic on the subject.

Her father always had driven himself and his family like slaves, while her mother had ably seconded his efforts. Money from the sale of chickens, turkeys, butter, eggs, and garden truck that other women of the neighbourhood used for extra clothing for themselves and their daughters and to prettify their homes, Mrs. Bates handed to her husband to increase the amount necessary to purchase the two hundred acres of land for each son when he came of age. The youngest son had farmed his land with comfortable profit and started a bank account, while his parents and two sisters were still saving and working to finish the last payment. Kate thought with bitterness that if this final payment had been made possibly there would have been money to spare for her; but with that thought came the knowledge that her father had numerous investments on which he could have realized and made the payments had he not preferred that they should be a burden on his family.

"Take the wings of morning," repeated Kate, with all the emphasis the old minister had used. "Hummm! I wonder what kind of wings. Those of a peewee would scarcely do for me; I'd need the wings of an eagle to get me anywhere, and anyway it wasn't the wings of a bird I was to take, it was the wings of morning. I wonder what the wings of morning are, and how I go about taking them. God knows where my wings come in; by the ache in my feet I seem to have walked, mostly. Oh, what ARE the wings of morning?"

Kate stared straight before her, sitting absorbed and motionless. Close in front of her a little white moth fluttered over the twigs and grasses. A kingbird sailed into view and perched on a brush-heap preparatory to darting after the moth. While the bird measured the distance and waited for the moth to rise above the entangling grasses, with a sweep and a snap a smaller bird, very similar in shape and colouring, flashed down, catching the moth and flying high among the branches of a big tree.

"Aha! You missed your opportunity!" said Kate to the kingbird.

She sat straighter suddenly. "Opportunity," she repeated. "Here is where I am threatened with missing mine. Opportunity! I wonder now if that might not be another name for 'the wings of morning.' Morning is winging its way past me, the question is: do I sit still and let it pass, or do I take its wings and fly away?"

Kate brooded on that awhile, then her thought formulated into words again.

"It isn't as if Mother were sick or poor, she is perfectly well and stronger than nine women out of ten of her age; Father can afford to hire all the help she needs; there is nothing cruel or unkind in leaving her; and as for Nancy Ellen, why does the fact that I am a few years younger than she, make me her servant? Why do I cook for her, and make her bed, and wash her clothes, while she earns money to spend on herself? And she is doing everything in her power to keep me at it, because she likes what she is doing and what it brings her, and she doesn't give a tinker whether I like what I am doing or not; or whether I get anything I want out of it or not; or whether I miss getting off to Normal on time or not. She is blame selfish, that's what she is, so she won't like the jolt she's going to get; but it will benefit her soul, her soul that her pretty face keeps her from developing, so I shall give her a little valuable assistance. Mother will be furious and Father will have the buggy whip convenient; but I am going! I don't know how, or when, but I am GOING.

"Who has a thirst for knowledge, in Helicon may slake it,

If he has still, the Roman will, to find a way, or make it."

Kate arose tall and straight and addressed the surrounding woods. "Now you just watch me 'find a way or make it,'" she said. "I am 'taking the wings of morning,' observe my flight! See me cut curves and circles and sail and soar around all the other Bates girls the Lord ever made, one named Nancy Ellen in particular. It must be far past noon, and I've much to do to get ready. I fly!"

Kate walked back to the highway, but instead of going on she turned toward home. When she reached the gate she saw Nancy Ellen, dressed her prettiest, sitting beneath a cherry tree reading a book, in very plain view from the road. As Kate came up the path: "Hello!" said Nancy Ellen. "Wasn't Adam at home?"

"I don't know," answered Kate. "I was not there."

"You weren't? Why, where were you?" asked Nancy Ellen.

"Oh, I just took a walk!" answered Kate.

"Right at dinner time on Sunday? Well, I'll be switched!" cried Nancy Ellen.

"Pity you weren't oftener, when you most needed it," said Kate, passing up the walk and entering the door. Her mother asked the same questions so Kate answered them.

"Well, I am glad you came home," said Mrs. Bates. "There was no use tagging to Adam with a sorry story, when your father said flatly that you couldn't go."

"But I must go!" urged Kate. "I have as good a right to my chance as the others. If you put your foot down and say so, Mother, Father will let me go. Why shouldn't I have the same chance as Nancy Ellen? Please Mother, let me go!"

"You stay right where you are. There is an awful summer's work before us," said Mrs. Bates.

"There always is," answered Kate. "But now is just my chance while you have Nancy Ellen here to help you."

"She has some special studying to do, and you very well know that she has to attend the County Institute, and take the summer course of training for teachers."

"So do I," said Kate, stubbornly. "You really will not help me, Mother?"

"I've said my say! Your place is here! Here you stay!" answered her mother.

"All right," said Kate, "I'll cross you off the docket of my hopes, and try Father."

"Well, I warn you, you had better not! He has been nagged until his patience is lost," said Mrs. Bates.

Kate closed her lips and started in search of her father. She found him leaning on the pig pen watching pigs grow into money, one of his most favoured occupations. He scowled at her, drawing his huge frame to full height.

"I don't want to hear a word you have to say," he said. "You are the youngest, and your place is in the kitchen helping your mother. We have got the last installment to pay on Hiram's land this summer. March back to the house and busy yourself with something useful!"

Kate looked at him, from his big-boned, weather-beaten face, to his heavy shoes, then turned without a word and went back toward the house. She went around it to the cherry tree and with no preliminaries said to her sister: "Nancy Ellen, I want you to lend me enough money to fix my clothes a little and pay my way to Normal this summer. I can pay it all back this winter. I'll pay every cent with interest, before I spend any on anything else."

"Why, you must be crazy!" said Nancy Ellen.

"Would I be any crazier than you, when you wanted to go?" asked Kate.

"But you were here to help Mother," said Nancy Ellen.

"And you are here to help her now," persisted Kate.

"But I've got to fix up my clothes for the County Institute," said Nancy Ellen, "I'll be gone most of the summer."

"I have just as much right to go as you had," said Kate.

"Father and Mother both say you shall not go," answered her sister.

"I suppose there is no use to remind you that I did all in my power to help you to your chance."

"You did no more than you should have done," said Nancy Ellen.

"And this is no more than you should do for me, in the circumstances," said Kate.

"You very well know I can't! Father and Mother would turn me out of the house," said Nancy Ellen.

"I'd be only too glad if they would turn me out," said Kate. "You can let me have the money if you like. Mother wouldn't do anything but talk; and Father would not strike you, or make you go, he always favours you."

"He does nothing of the sort! I can't, and I won't, so there!" cried Nancy Ellen.

"'Won't,' is the real answer, 'so there,'" said Kate.

She went into the cellar and ate some cold food from the cupboard and drank a cup of milk. Then she went to her room and looked over all of her scanty stock of clothing, laying in a heap the pieces that needed mending. She took the clothes basket to the wash room, which was the front of the woodhouse, in summer; built a fire, heated water, and while making it appear that she was putting the clothes to soak, as usual, she washed everything she had that was fit to use, hanging the pieces to dry in the building.

"Watch me fly!" muttered Kate. "I don't seem to be cutting those curves so very fast; but I'm moving. I believe now, having exhausted all home resources, that Adam is my next objective. He is the only one in the family who ever paid the slightest attention to me, maybe he cares a trifle what becomes of me, but Oh, how I dread Agatha! However, watch me take wing! If Adam fails me I have six remaining prospects among my loving brothers, and if none of them has any feeling for me or faith in me there yet remain my seven dear brothers-in-law, before I appeal to the tender mercies of the neighbours; but how I dread Agatha! Yet I fly!"

CHAPTER II

AN EMBRYO MIND READER

KATE was far from physical flight as she pounded the indignation of her soul into the path with her substantial feet. Baffled and angry, she kept reviewing the situation as she went swiftly on her way, regardless of dust and heat. She could see no justice in being forced into a position that promised to end in further humiliation and defeat of her hopes. If she only could find Adam at the stable, as she passed, and talk with him alone! Secretly, she well knew that the chief source of her dread of meeting her sister-in-law was that to her Agatha was so funny that ridiculing her had been regarded as perfectly legitimate pastime. For Agatha WAS funny; but she had no idea of it, and could no more avoid it than a bee could avoid being buzzy, so the manner in which her sisters-in-law imitated her and laughed at her, none too secretly, was far from kind. While she never guessed what was going on, she realized the antagonism in their attitude and stoutly resented it.

Adam was his father's favourite son, a stalwart, fine-appearing, big man, silent, honest, and forceful; the son most after the desires of the father's heart, yet Adam was the one son of the seven who had ignored his father's law that all of his boys were to marry strong, healthy young women, poor women, working women. Each of the others at coming of age had contracted this prescribed marriage as speedily as possible, first asking father Bates, the girl afterward. If father Bates disapproved, the girl was never asked at all. And the reason for this docility on the part of these big, matured men, lay wholly in the methods of father Bates. He gave those two hundred acres of land to each of them on coming of age, and the same sum to each for the building of a house and barn and the purchase of stock; gave it to them in words, and with the fullest assurance that it was theirs to improve, to live on, to add to. Each of them had seen and handled his deed, each had to admit he never had known his father to tell a lie or deviate the least from fairness in a deal of any kind, each had been compelled to go in the way indicated by his father for years; but not a man of them held his own deed. These precious bits of paper remained locked in the big wooden chest beside the father's bed, while the land stood on the records in his name; the taxes they paid him each year he, himself, carried to the county clerk; so that he was the largest landholder in the county and one of the very richest men. It must have been extreme unction to his soul to enter the county office and ask for the assessment on those "little parcels of land of mine." Men treated him very deferentially, and so did his sons. Those documents carefully locked away had the effect of obtaining ever-ready help to harvest his hay and wheat whenever he desired, to make his least wish quickly deferred to, to give him authority and the power for which he lived and worked earlier, later, and harder than any other man of his day and locality.

Adam was like him as possible up to the time he married, yet Adam was the only one of his sons who disobeyed him; but there was a redeeming feature. Adam married a slender tall slip of a woman, four years his senior, who had been teaching in the Hartley schools when he began courting her. She was a prim, fussy woman, born of a prim father and a fussy mother, so what was to be expected? Her face was narrow and set, her body and her movements almost rigid, her hair, always parted, lifted from each side and tied on the crown, fell in stiff little curls, the back part hanging free. Her speech, as precise as her movements, was formed into set habit through long study of the dictionary. She was born antagonistic to whatever existed, no matter what it was. So surely as every other woman agreed on a dress, a recipe, a house, anything whatever, so surely Agatha thought out and followed a different method, the disconcerting thing about her being that she usually finished any undertaking with less exertion, ahead of time, and having saved considerable money.

She could have written a fine book of synonyms, for as certainly as any one said anything in her presence that she had occasion to repeat, she changed the wording to six-syllabled mouthfuls, delivered with ponderous circumlocution. She subscribed to papers and magazines, which she read and remembered. And she danced! When other women thought even a waltz immoral and shocking; perfectly stiff, her curls exactly in place, Agatha could be seen, and frequently was seen, waltzing on the front porch in the arms of, and to a tune whistled by young Adam, whose full name was Adam Alcibiades Bates. In his younger days, when discipline had been required, Kate once had heard her say to the little fellow: "Adam Alcibiades ascend these steps and proceed immediately to your maternal ancestor."

Kate thought of this with a dry smile as she plodded on toward Agatha's home hoping she could see her brother at the barn, but she knew that most probably she would "ascend the steps and proceed to the maternal ancestor," of Adam Bates 3d. Then she would be forced to explain her visit and combat both Adam and his wife; for Agatha was not a nonentity like her collection of healthful, hard-working sisters-in-law. Agatha worked if she chose, and she did not work if she did not choose. Mostly she worked and worked harder than any one ever thought. She had a habit of keeping her house always immaculate, finishing her cleaning very early and then reading in a conspicuous spot on the veranda when other women were busy with their most tiresome tasks. Such was Agatha, whom Kate dreaded meeting, with every reason, for Agatha, despite curls, bony structure, language, and dance, was the most powerful factor in the whole Bates family with her father-in-law; and all because when he purchased the original two hundred acres for Adam, and made the first allowance for buildings and stock, Agatha slipped the money from Adam's fingers in some inexplainable way, and spent it all for stock; because forsooth! Agatha was an only child, and her prim father endowed her, she said so herself, with three hundred acres of land, better in location and more fertile than that given to Adam, land having on it a roomy and comfortable brick house, completely furnished, a large barn and also stock; so that her place could be used to live on and farm, while Adam's could be given over to grazing herds of cattle which he bought cheaply, fattened and sold at the top of the market.

If each had brought such a farm into the family with her, father Bates could have endured six more prim, angular, becurled daughters-in-law, very well indeed, for land was his one and only God. His respect for Agatha was markedly very high, for in addition to her farm he secretly admired her independence of thought and action, and was amazed by the fact that she was about her work when several of the blooming girls he had selected for wives for his sons were confined to the sofa with a pain, while not one of them schemed, planned, connived with her husband and piled up the money as Agatha did, therefore she stood at the head of the women of the Bates family; while she was considered to have worked miracles in the heart of Adam Bates, for with his exception no man of the family ever had been seen to touch a woman, either publicly or privately, to offer the slightest form of endearment, assistance or courtesy. "Women are to work and to bear children," said the elder Bates. "Put them at the first job when they are born, and at the second at eighteen, and keep them hard at it."

At their rate of progression several of the Bates sons and daughters would produce families that, with a couple of pairs of twins, would equal the sixteen of the elder Bates; but not so Agatha. She had one son of fifteen and one daughter of ten, and she said that was all she intended to have, certainly it was all she did have; but she further aggravated matters by announcing that she had had them because she wanted them; at such times as she intended to; and that she had the boy first and five years the older, so that he could look after his sister when they went into company. Also she walked up and sat upon Adam's lap whenever she chose, ruffled his hair, pulled his ears, and kissed him squarely on the mouth, with every appearance of having help, while the dance on the front porch with her son or daughter was of daily occurrence. And anything funnier than Agatha, prim and angular with never a hair out of place, stiffly hopping "Money Musk" and "Turkey In The Straw," or the "Blue Danube" waltz, anything funnier than that, never happened. But the two Adams, Jr. and 3d, watched with reverent and adoring eyes, for she was MOTHER, and no one else on earth rested so high in their respect as the inflexible woman they lived with. That she was different from all the other women of her time and location was hard on the other women. Had they been exactly right, they would have been exactly like her.

So Kate, thinking all these things over, her own problem acutely "advanced and proceeded." She advanced past the closed barn, and stock in the pasture, past the garden flaming June, past the dooryard, up the steps, down the hall, into the screened back porch dining room and "proceeded" to take a chair, while the family finished the Sunday night supper, at which they were seated. Kate was not hungry and she did not wish to trouble her sister-in-law to set another place, so she took the remaining chair, against the wall, behind Agatha, facing Adam, 3d, across the table, and with Adam Jr., in profile at the head, and little Susan at the foot. Then she waited her chance. Being tired and aggressive she did not wait long.

"I might as well tell you why I came," she said bluntly. "Father won't give me money to go to Normal, as he has all the others. He says I have got to stay at home and help Mother."

"Well, Mother is getting so old she needs help," said Adam, Jr., as he continued his supper.

"Of course she is," said Kate. "We all know that. But what is the matter with Nancy Ellen helping her, while I take my turn at Normal? There wasn't a thing I could do last summer to help her off that I didn't do, even to lending her my best dress and staying at home for six Sundays because I had nothing else fit to wear where I'd be seen."

No one said a word. Kate continued: "Then Father secured our home school for her and I had to spend the winter going to school to her, when you very well know that I always studied harder, and was ahead of her, even after she'd been to Normal. And I got up early and worked late, and cooked, and washed, and waited on her, while she got her lessons and reports ready, and fixed up her nice new clothes, and now she won't touch the work, and she is doing all she can to help Father keep me from going."

"I never knew Father to need much help on anything he made up his mind to," said Adam.

Kate sat very tense. She looked steadily at her brother, but he looked quite as steadily at his plate. The back of her sister-in-law was fully as expressive as her face. Her head was very erect, her shoulders stiff and still, not a curl moved as she poured Adam's tea and Susan's milk. Only Adam, 3d, looked at Kate with companionable eyes, as if he might feel a slight degree of interest or sympathy, so she found herself explaining directly to him.

"Things are blame unfair in our family, anyway!" she said, bitterly. "You have got to be born a boy to have any chance worth while; if you are a girl it is mighty small, and if you are the youngest, by any mischance, you have none at all. I don't want to harp things over; but I wish you would explain to me why having been born a few years after Nancy Ellen makes me her slave, and cuts me out of my chance to teach, and to have some freedom and clothes. They might as well have told Hiram he was not to have any land and stay at home and help Father because he was the youngest boy; it would have been quite as fair; but nothing like that happens to the boys of this family, it is always the girls who get left. I have worked for years, knowing every cent I saved and earned above barely enough to cover me, would go to help pay for Hiram's land and house and stock; but he wouldn't turn a hand to help me, neither will any of the rest of you."

"Then what are you here for?" asked Adam.

"Because I am going to give you, and every other brother and sister I have, the chance to REFUSE to loan me enough to buy a few clothes and pay my way to Normal, so I can pass the examinations, and teach this fall. And when you have all refused, I am going to the neighbours, until I find someone who will loan me the money I need. A hundred dollars would be plenty. I could pay it back with two months' teaching, with any interest you say."

Kate paused, short of breath, her eyes blazing, her cheeks red. Adam went steadily on with his supper. Agatha appeared stiffer and more uncompromising in the back than before, which Kate had not thought possible. But the same dull red on the girl's cheeks had begun to burn on the face of young Adam. Suddenly he broke into a clear laugh.

"Oh, Ma, you're too funny!" he cried. "I can read your face like a book. I bet you ten dollars I can tell you just word for word what you are going to say. I dare you let me! You know I can!" Still laughing, his eyes dancing, a picture to see, he stretched his arm across the table toward her, and his mother adored him, however she strove to conceal the fact from him.

"Ten dollars!" she scoffed. "When did we become so wealthy? I'll give you one dollar if you tell me exactly what I was going to say."

The boy glanced at his father. "Oh this is too easy!" he cried. "It's like robbing the baby's bank!" And then to his mother: "You were just opening your lips to say: 'Give it to her! If you don't, I will!' And you are even a little bit more of a brick than usual to do it. It's a darned shame the way all of them impose on Kate."

There was a complete change in Agatha's back. Adam, Jr., laid down his fork and stared at his wife in deep amazement. Adam, 3d, stretched his hand farther toward his mother. "Give me that dollar!" he cajoled.

"Well, I am not concealing it in the sleeve of my garments," she said. "If I have one, it is reposing in my purse, in juxtaposition to the other articles that belong there, and if you receive it, it will be bestowed upon you when I deem the occasion suitable."

Young Adam's fist came down with a smash. "I get the dollar!" he triumphed. "I TOLD you so! I KNEW she was going to say it! Ain't I a dandy mind reader though? But it is bully for you, Father, because of course, if Mother wouldn't let Kate have it, you'd HAVE to; but if you DID it might make trouble with your paternal land-grabber, and endanger your precious deed that you hope to get in the sweet by-and-by. But if Mother loans the money, Grandfather can't say a word, because it is her very own, and didn't cost him anything, and he always agrees with her anyway! Hurrah for hurrah, Kate! Nancy Ellen may wash her own petticoat in the morning, while I take you to the train. You'll let me, Father? You did let me go to Hartley alone, once. I'll be careful! I won't let a thing happen. I'll come straight home. And oh, my dollar, you and me; I'll put you in the bank and let you grow to three!"

"You may go," said his father, promptly.

"You shall proceed according to your Aunt Katherine's instructions," said his mother, at the same time.

"Katie, get your carpet-sack! When do we start?" demanded young Adam.

"Morning will be all right with me, you blessed youngun," said Kate, "but I don't own a telescope or anything to put what little I have in, and Nancy Ellen never would spare hers; she will want to go to County Institute before I get back."

"You may have mine," said Agatha. "You are perfectly welcome to take it wherever your peregrinations lead you, and return it when you please. I shall proceed to my chamber and formulate your check immediately. You are also welcome to my best hat and cape, and any of my clothing or personal adornments you can use to advantage."

"Oh, Agatha, I wish you were as big as a house, like me," said Kate, joyfully. "I couldn't possibly crowd into anything you wear, but it would almost tickle me to death to have Nancy Ellen know you let me take your things, when she won't even offer me a dud of her old stuff; I never remotely hoped for any of the new."

"You shall have my cape and hat, anyway. The cape is new and very fashionable. Come upstairs and try the hat," said Agatha.

The cape was new and fashionable as Agatha had said; it would not fasten at the neck, but there would be no necessity that it should during July and August, while it would improve any dress it was worn with on a cool evening. The hat Kate could not possibly use with her large, broad face and mass of hair, but she was almost as pleased with the offer as if the hat had been most becoming. Then Agatha brought out her telescope, in which Kate laid the cape while Agatha wrote her a check for one hundred and twenty dollars, and told her where and how to cash it. The extra twenty was to buy a pair of new walking shoes, some hose, and a hat, before she went to her train. When they went downstairs Adam, Jr., had a horse hitched and Adam, 3d, drove her to her home, where, at the foot of the garden, they took one long survey of the landscape and hid the telescope behind the privet bush. Then Adam drove away quietly, Kate entered the dooryard from the garden, and soon afterward went to the wash room and hastily ironed her clothing.

Nancy Ellen had gone to visit a neighbour girl, so Kate risked her remaining until after church in the evening. She hurried to their room and mended all her own clothing she had laid out. Then she deliberately went over Nancy Ellen's and helped herself to a pair of pretty nightdresses, such as she had never owned, a white embroidered petticoat, the second best white dress, and a most becoming sailor hat. These she made into a parcel and carried to the wash room, brought in the telescope and packed it, hiding it under a workbench and covering it with shavings. After that she went to her room and wrote a note, and then slept deeply until the morning call. She arose at once and went to the wash room but instead of washing the family clothing, she took a bath in the largest tub, and washed her hair to a state resembling spun gold. During breakfast she kept sharp watch down the road. When she saw Adam, 3d, coming she stuck her note under the hook on which she had seen her father hang his hat all her life, and carrying the telescope in the clothes basket covered with a rumpled sheet, she passed across the yard and handed it over the fence to Adam, climbed that same fence, and they started toward Hartley.

Kate put the sailor hat on her head, and sat very straight, an anxious line crossing her forehead. She was running away, and if discovered, there was the barest chance that her father might follow, and make a most disagreeable scene, before the train pulled out. He had gone to a far field to plow corn and Kate fervently hoped he would plow until noon, which he did. Nancy Ellen washed the dishes, and went into the front room to study, while Mrs. Bates put on her sunbonnet and began hoeing the potatoes. Not one of the family noticed that Monday's wash was not on the clothes line as usual. Kate and Adam drove as fast as they dared, and on reaching town, cashed the check, decided that Nancy Ellen's hat would serve, thus saving the price of a new one for emergencies that might arise, bought the shoes, and went to the depot, where they had an anxious hour to wait.

"I expect Grandpa will be pretty mad," said Adam.

"I am sure there is not the slightest chance but that he will be," said Kate.

"Dare you go back home when school is over?" he asked.

"Probably not," she answered.

"What will you do?" he questioned.

"When I investigated sister Nancy Ellen's bureau I found a list of the School Supervisors of the county, so I am going to put in my spare time writing them about my qualifications to teach their schools this winter. All the other girls did well and taught first-class schools, I shall also. I am not a bit afraid but that I may take my choice of several. When I finish it will be only a few days until school begins, so I can go hunt my boarding place and stay there."

"Mother would let you stay at our house," said Adam.

"Yes, I think she would, after yesterday; but I don't want to make trouble that might extend to Father and your father. I had better keep away."

"Yes, I guess you had," said Adam. "If Grandfather rows, he raises a racket. But maybe he won't!"

"Maybe! Wouldn't you like to see what happens when Mother come in from the potatoes and Nancy Ellen comes out from the living room, and Father comes to dinner, all about the same time?"

Adam laughed appreciatively.

"Wouldn't I just!" he cried. "Kate, you like my mother, don't you?"

"I certainly do! She has been splendid. I never dreamed of such a thing as getting the money from her."

"I didn't either," said Adam, "until—I became a mind reader."

Kate looked straight into his eyes.

"How about that, Adam?" she asked.

Adam chuckled. "She didn't intend to say a word. She was going to let the Bateses fight it out among themselves. Her mouth was shut so tight it didn't look as if she could open it if she wanted to. I thought it would be better for you to borrow the money from her, so Father wouldn't get into a mess, and I knew how fine she was, so I just SUGGESTED it to her. That's all!"

"Adam, you're a dandy!" cried Kate.

"I am having a whole buggy load of fun, and you ought to go," said he. "It's all right! Don't you worry! I'll take care of you."

"Why, thank you, Adam!" said Kate. "That is the first time any one ever offered to take care of me in my life. With me it always has been pretty much of a 'go-it-alone' proposition."

"What of Nancy Ellen's did you take?" he asked. "Why didn't you get some gloves? Your hands are so red and work-worn. Mother's never look that way."

"Your mother never has done the rough field work I do, and I haven't taken time to be careful. They do look badly. I wish I had taken a pair of the lady's gloves; but I doubt if she would have survived that. I understand that one of the unpardonable sins is putting on gloves belonging to any one else."

Then the train came and Kate climbed aboard with Adam's parting injunction in her ears: "Sit beside an open window on this side!"

So she looked for and found the window and as she seated herself she saw Adam on the outside and leaned to speak to him again. Just as the train started he thrust his hand inside, dropped his dollar on her lap, and in a tense whisper commanded her: "Get yourself some gloves!" Then he ran.

Kate picked up the dollar, while her eyes dimmed with tears.

"Why, the fine youngster!" she said. "The Jim-dandy fine youngster!"

Adam could not remember when he ever had been so happy as he was driving home. He found his mother singing, his father in a genial mood, so he concluded that the greatest thing in the world to make a whole family happy was to do something kind for someone else. But he reflected that there would be far from a happy family at his grandfather's; and he was right. Grandmother Bates came in from her hoeing at eleven o'clock tired and hungry, expecting to find the wash dry and dinner almost ready. There was no wash and no odour of food. She went to the wood-shed and stared unbelievingly at the cold stove, the tubs of soaking clothes.

She turned and went into the kitchen, where she saw no signs of Kate or of dinner, then she lifted up her voice and shouted: "Nancy Ellen!"

Nancy Ellen came in a hurry. "Why, Mother, what is the matter?" she cried.

"Matter, yourself!" exclaimed Mrs. Bates. "Look in the wash room! Why aren't the clothes on the line? Where is that good-for-nothing Kate?"

Nancy Ellen went to the wash room and looked. She came back pale and amazed. "Maybe she is sick," she ventured. "She never has been; but she might be! Maybe she has lain down."

"On Monday morning! And the wash not out! You simpleton!" cried Mrs. Bates.

Nancy Ellen hurried upstairs and came back with bulging eyes.

"Every scrap of her clothing is gone, and half of mine!"

"She's gone to that fool Normal-thing! Where did she get the money?" cried Mrs. Bates.

"I don't know!" said Nancy Ellen. "She asked me yesterday, but of course I told her that so long as you and Father decided she was not to go, I couldn't possibly lend her the money."

"Did you look if she had taken it?"

Nancy Ellen straightened. "Mother! I didn't need do that!"

"You said she took your clothes," said Mrs. Bates.

"I had hers this time last year. She'll bring back clothes."

"Not here, she won't! Father will see that she never darkens these doors again. This is the first time in his life that a child of his has disobeyed him."

"Except Adam, when he married Agatha; and he strutted like a fighting cock about that."

"Well, he won't 'strut' about this, and you won't either, even if you are showing signs of standing up for her. Go at that wash, while I get dinner."

Dinner was on the table when Adam Bates hung his hat on its hook and saw the note for him. He took it down and read:

> FATHER: I have gone to Normal. I borrowed the money of a woman who was willing to trust me to pay it back as soon as I earned it. Not Nancy Ellen, of course. She would not even loan me a pocket handkerchief, though you remember I stayed at home six weeks last summer to let her take what she wanted of mine. Mother: I think you can get Sally Whistler to help you as cheaply as any one and that she will do very well. Nancy Ellen: I have taken your second best hat and a few of your things, but not half so many as I loaned you. I hope it makes you mad enough to burst. I hope you get as mad and stay as mad as I have been most of this year while you taught me

things you didn't know yourself; and I cooked and washed for you so you could wear fine clothes and play the lady. KATE

Adam Bates read that note to himself, stretching every inch of his six feet six, his face a dull red, his eyes glaring. Then he turned to his wife and daughter.

"Is Kate gone? Without proper clothing and on borrowed money," he demanded.

"I don't know," said Mrs. Bates. "I was hoeing potatoes all forenoon."

"Listen to this," he thundered. Then he slowly read the note aloud. But someway the spoken words did not have the same effect as when he read them mentally in the first shock of anger. When he heard his own voice read off the line, "I hope it makes you mad enough to burst," there was a catch and a queer gurgle in his throat. Mrs. Bates gazed at him anxiously. Was he so surprised and angry he was choking? Might it be a stroke? It was! It was a master stroke. He got no farther than "taught me things you didn't know yourself," when he lowered the sheet, threw back his head and laughed as none of his family ever had seen him laugh in his life; laughed and laughed until his frame was shaken and the tears rolled. Finally he looked at the dazed Nancy Ellen. "Get Sally Whistler, nothing!" he said. "You hustle your stumps and do for your mother what Kate did while you were away last summer. And if you have any common decency send your sister as many of your best things as you had of hers, at least. Do you hear me?"

CHAPTER III

PEREGRINATIONS

"PEREGRINATIONS," laughed Kate, turning to the window to hide her face. "Oh, Agatha, you are a dear, but you are too funny! Even a Fourth of July orator would not have used that word. I never heard it before in all of my life outside spelling-school."

Then she looked at the dollar she was gripping and ceased to laugh.

"The dear lad," she whispered. "He did the whole thing. She was going to let us 'fight it out'; I could tell by her back, and Adam wouldn't have helped me a cent, quite as much because he didn't want to as because Father wouldn't have liked it. Fancy the little chap knowing he can wheedle his mother into anything, and exactly how to go about it! I won't spend a penny on myself until she is paid, and then I'll make her a present of something nice, just to let her and Nancy Ellen see that I appreciate being helped to my chance, for I had reached that point where I would have walked to school and worked in somebody's kitchen, before I'd have missed my opportunity. I could have done it; but this will be far pleasanter and give me a much better showing."

Then Kate began watching the people in the car with eager curiosity, for she had been on a train only twice before in her life. She decided that she was in a company of young people and some even of middle age, going to Normal. She also noticed that most of them were looking at her with probably the same interest she found in them. Then at one of the stations a girl asked to sit with her and explained that she was going to Normal, so Kate said she was also. The girl seemed to have several acquaintances on the car, for she left her seat to speak with them and when the train stopped at a very pleasant city and the car began to empty itself, on the platform Kate was introduced by this girl to several young women and men near her age. A party of four, going to board close the school, with a woman they knew about, invited Kate to go with them and because she was strange and shaken by her experiences she agreed. All of them piled their luggage on a wagon to be delivered, so Kate let hers go also. Then they walked down a long shady street, and entered a dainty and comfortable residence, a place that seemed to Kate to be the home of people of wealth. She was assigned a room with another girl, such a pleasant girl; but a vague uneasiness had begun to make itself felt, so before she unpacked she went back to the sitting room and learned that the price of board was eight dollars a week. Forty-eight dollars for six weeks! She would not have enough for books and tuition. Besides, Nancy Ellen had boarded with a family on Butler Street whose charge was only five-fifty. Kate was eager to stay where these very agreeable young people did, she imagined herself going to classes with them and having association that to her would be a great treat, but she never would dare ask for more money. She thought swiftly a minute, and then made her first mistake.

Instead of going to the other girls and frankly confessing that she could not afford the prices they were paying, she watched her chance, picked up her telescope and hurried down the street, walking swiftly until she was out of sight of the house. Then she began inquiring her way to Butler Street and after a long, hot walk, found the place. The rooms and board were very poor, but Kate felt that she could endure whatever Nancy Ellen had, so she unpacked, and went to the Normal School to register and learn what she would need. On coming from the building she saw that she would be forced to pass close by the group of girls she had deserted and this was made doubly difficult because she could see that they were talking about her. Then she understood how foolish she had been and as she was struggling to summon courage to explain to them she caught these words plainly:

"Who is going to ask her for it?"

"I am," said the girl who had sat beside Kate on the train. "I don't propose to pay it myself!"

Then she came directly to Kate and said briefly: "Fifty cents, please!"

"For what?" stammered Kate.

"Your luggage. You changed your boarding place in such a hurry you forgot to settle, and as I made the arrangement, I had to pay it."

"Do please excuse me," said Kate. "I was so bewildered, I forgot."

"Certainly!" said the girl and Kate dropped the money into the extended hand and hurried past, her face scorched red with shame, for one of them had said: "That's a good one! I wouldn't have thought it of her."

Kate went back to her hot, stuffy room and tried to study, but she succeeded only in being miserable, for she realized that she had lost her second chance to have either companions or friends, by not saying the few words of explanation that would have righted her in the opinion of those she would meet each day for six weeks. It was not a good beginning, while the end was what might have been expected. A young man from her neighbourhood spoke to her and the girls seeing, asked him about Kate, learning thereby that her father was worth more money than all of theirs put together. Some of them had accepted the explanation that Kate was "bewildered" and had acted hastily; but when the young man finished Bates history, they merely thought her mean, and left her severely to herself, so her only recourse was to study so diligently, and recite so perfectly that none of them could equal her, and this she did.

In acute discomfort and with a sore heart, Kate passed her first six weeks away from home. She wrote to each man on the list of school directors she had taken from Nancy Ellen's desk. Some answered that they had their teachers already engaged, others made no reply. One bright spot was the receipt of a letter from Nancy Ellen saying she was sending her best dress, to be very careful of it, and if Kate would let her know the day she would be home she would meet her at the station. Kate sent her thanks, wore the dress to two lectures, and wrote the letter telling when she would return.

As the time drew nearer she became sickeningly anxious about a school. What if she failed in securing one? What if she could not pay back Agatha's money? What if she had taken "the wings of morning," and fallen in her flight? In desperation she went to the Superintendent of the Normal and told him her trouble. He wrote her a fine letter of recommendation and she sent it to one of the men from whom she had not heard, the director of a school in the village of Walden, seven miles east of Hartley, being seventeen miles from her home, thus seeming to Kate a desirable location, also she knew the village to be pretty and the school one that paid well. Then she finished her work the best she could, and disappointed and anxious, entered the train for home.

When the engine whistled at the bridge outside Hartley Kate arose, lifted her telescope from the rack overhead, and made her way to the door, so that she was the first person to leave the car when it stopped. As she stepped to the platform she had a distinct shock, for her father reached for the telescope, while his greeting and his face were decidedly friendly, for him. As they walked down the street Kate was trying wildly to think of the best thing to say when he asked if she had a school. But he did not ask. Then she saw in the pocket of his light summer coat a packet of letters folded inside a newspaper, and there was one long, official-looking envelope that stood above the others far enough that she could see "Miss K—" of the address. Instantly she decided that it was her answer from the School Director of Walden and she was tremblingly eager to see it. She thought an instant and then asked: "Have you been to the post office?"

"Yes, I got the mail," he answered.

"Will you please see if there are any letters for me?" she asked.

"When we get home," he said. "I am in a hurry now. Here's a list of things Ma wants, and don't be all day about getting them."

Kate's lips closed to a thin line and her eyes began to grow steel coloured and big. She dragged back a step and looked at the loosely swaying pocket again. She thought intently a second. As they passed several people on the walk she stepped back of her father and gently raised the letter enough to see that the address was to her. Instantly she lifted it from the others, slipped it up her dress sleeve, and again took her place beside her father until they reached the store where her mother did her shopping. Then he waited outside while Kate hurried in, and ripping open the letter, found a contract ready for her to sign for the Walden school. The salary was twenty dollars a month more than Nancy Ellen had received for their country school the previous winter and the term four months longer.

Kate was so delighted she could have shouted. Instead she went with all speed to the stationery counter and bought an envelope to fit the contract, which she signed, and writing a hasty note of thanks she mailed the letter in the store mail box, then began her mother's purchases. This took so much time that her father came into the store before she had finished, demanding that she hurry, so in feverish haste she bought what was wanted and followed to the buggy. On the road home she began to study her father; she could see that he was well pleased over something but she had no idea what could have happened; she had expected anything from verbal wrath to the buggy whip, so she was surprised, but so happy over having secured such a good school, at higher wages than Nancy Ellen's, that she spent most of her time thinking of herself and planning as to when she would go to Walden, where she would stay, how she would teach, and Oh, bliss unspeakable, what she would do with so much money; for two month's pay would more than wipe out her indebtedness to Agatha, and by getting the very cheapest board she could endure, after that she would have over three fourths of her money to spend each month for books and clothes. She was intently engaged with her side of the closet and her end of the bureau, when she had her first glimpse of home; even preoccupied as she was, she saw a difference. Several loose pickets in the fence had been nailed in place. The lilac beside the door and the cabbage roses had been trimmed, so that they did not drag over the walk, while the yard had been gone over with a lawn-mower.

Kate turned to her father. "Well, for land's sake!" she said. "I wanted a lawn-mower all last summer, and you wouldn't buy it for me. I wonder why you got it the minute I was gone."

"I got it because Nancy Ellen especially wanted it, and she has been a mighty good girl all summer," he said.

"If that is the case, then she should be rewarded with the privilege of running a lawn-mower," said Kate.

Her father looked at her sharply; but her face was so pleasant he decided she did not intend to be saucy, so he said: "No doubt she will be willing to let you help her all you want to."

"Not the ghost of a doubt about that," laughed Kate, "and I always wanted to try running one, too. They look so nice in pictures, and how one improves a place! I hardly know this is home. Now if we only had a fresh coat of white paint we could line up with the neighbours."

"I have been thinking about that," said Mr. Bates, and Kate glanced at him, doubting her hearing.

He noticed her surprise and added in explanation: "Paint every so often saves a building. It's good economy."

"Then let's economize immediately," said Kate. "And on the barn, too. It is even more weather-beaten than the house."

"I'll see about it the next time I go to town," said Mr. Bates; so Kate entered the house prepared for anything and wondering what it all meant for wherever she looked everything was shining the brightest that scrubbing and scouring could make it shine, the best of everything was out and in use; not that it was much, but it made a noticeable difference. Her mother greeted her pleasantly, with a new tone of voice, while Nancy Ellen was transformed. Kate noticed that, immediately. She always had been a pretty girl, now she was beautiful, radiantly beautiful, with a new shining beauty that dazzled Kate as she looked at her. No one offered any explanation while Kate could see none. At last she asked: "What on earth has happened? I don't understand."

"Of course you don't," laughed Nancy Ellen. "You thought you ran the whole place and did everything yourself, so I thought I'd just show you how things look when I run them."

"You are a top-notcher," said Kate. "Figuratively and literally, I offer you the palm. Let the good work go on! I highly approve; but I don't see how you found time to do all this and go to Institute."

"I didn't go to Institute," said Nancy Ellen.

"You didn't! But you must!" cried Kate.

"Oh must I? Well, since you have decided to run your affairs as you please, in spite of all of us, just suppose you let me run mine the same way. Only, I rather enjoy having Father and Mother approve of what I do."

Kate climbed the stairs with this to digest as she went; so while she put away her clothing she thought things over, but saw no light. She would go to Adam's to return the telescope to-morrow, possibly he could tell her. As she hung her dresses in the closet and returned Nancy Ellen's to their places she was still more amazed, for there hung three pretty new wash dresses, one of a rosy pink that would make Nancy Ellen appear very lovely.

What was the reason, Kate wondered. The Bates family never did anything unless there was some purpose in it, what was the purpose in this? And Nancy Ellen had not gone to Institute. She evidently had worked constantly and hard, yet she was in much sweeter frame of mind than usual. She must have spent almost all she had saved from her school on new clothes. Kate could not solve the problem, so she decided to watch and wait. She also waited for someone to say something about her plans, but no one said a word, so after waiting all evening Kate decided that they would ask before they learned anything from her. She took her place as usual, and the work went on as if she had not been away; but she was happy, even in her bewilderment.

If her father noticed the absence of the letter she had slipped from his pocket he said nothing about it as he drew the paper and letters forth and laid them on the table. Kate had a few bad minutes while this was going on, she was sure he hesitated an instant and looked closely at the letters he sorted; but when he said nothing, she breathed deeply in relief and went on being joyous. It seemed to her that never had the family been in such a good-natured state since Adam had married Agatha and her three hundred acres with house, furniture, and stock. She went on in ignorance of what had happened until after Sunday dinner the following day. Then she had planned to visit Agatha and Adam. It was very probable that it was because she was dressing for this visit that Nancy Ellen decided on Kate's enlightenment, for she could not have helped seeing that her sister was almost stunned at times.

Kate gave her a fine opening. As she stood brushing her wealth of gold with full-length sweeps of her arm, she was at an angle that brought her facing the mirror before which Nancy Ellen sat training waves and pinning up loose braids. Her hair was beautiful and she slowly smiled at her image as she tried different effects of wave, loose curl, braids high piled or flat. Across her bed lay a dress that was a reproduction of one that she had worn for three years, but a glorified reproduction. The original dress had been Nancy Ellen's first departure from the brown and gray gingham which her mother always had purchased because it would wear well, and when from constant washing it faded to an exact dirt colour it had the advantage of providing a background that did not show the dirt. Nancy Ellen had earned the money for a new dress by raising turkeys, so when the turkeys went to town to be sold, for the first time in her life Nancy Ellen went along to select the dress. No one told her what kind of dress to get, because no one imagined that she would dare buy any startling variation from what always had been provided for her.

But Nancy Ellen had stood facing a narrow mirror when she reached the gingham counter and the clerk, taking one look at her fresh, beautiful face with its sharp contrasts of black eyes and hair, rose-tinted skin that refused to tan, and red cheeks and lips, began shaking out delicate blues, pale pinks, golden yellows. He called them chambray; insisted that they wore for ever, and were fadeless, which was practically the truth. On the day that dress was like to burst its waist seams, it was the same warm rosy pink that transformed Nancy Ellen from the disfiguration of dirt-brown to apple and peach bloom, wild roses and swamp mallow, a girl quite as pretty as a girl ever grows, and much prettier than any girl ever has any business to be. The instant Nancy Ellen held the chambray under her chin and in an oblique glance saw the face of the clerk, the material was hers no matter what the cost, which does not refer to the price, by any means. Knowing that the dress would be an innovation that would set her mother storming and fill Kate with envy, which would probably culminate in the demand that the goods be returned and exchanged for dirt-brown, when she reached home Nancy Ellen climbed from the wagon and told her father that she was going on to Adam's to have Agatha cut out her dress so that she could begin to sew on it that night. Such commendable industry met his hearty approval, so he told her to go and he would see that Kate did her share of the work. Wise Nancy Ellen came home and sat her down to sew on her gorgeous frock, while the storm she had feared raged in all its fury; but the goods was cut, and could not be returned. Yet, through it, a miracle happened: Nancy Ellen so appreciated herself in pink that the extreme care she used with that dress saved it from half the trips of a dirt-brown one to the wash board and the ironing table; while, marvel of marvels, it did not shrink, it did not fade, also it wore like buckskin. The result was that before the season had passed Kate was allowed to purchase a pale blue, which improved her appearance quite as much in proportion as pink had Nancy Ellen's; neither did the blue fade nor shrink nor require so much washing, for the same reason. Three years the pink dress had been Nancy Ellen's PIECE DE RESISTANCE; now she had a new one, much the same, yet conspicuously different. This was a daring rose colour, full and wide, peeping white embroidery trimming, and big pearl buttons, really a beautiful dress, made in a becoming manner. Kate looked at it in cheerful envy. Never mind! The coming summer she would have a blue that would make that pink look silly. From the dress she turned to Nancy Ellen, barely in time to see her bend her head and smirk, broadly, smilingly, approvingly, at her reflection in the glass.

"For mercy sake, what IS the matter with you?" demanded Kate, ripping a strand of hair in sudden irritation.

"Oh, something lovely!" answered her sister, knowing that this was her chance to impart the glad tidings herself; if she lost it, Agatha would get the thrill of Kate's surprise. So Nancy Ellen opened her drawer and slowly produced and set upon her bureau a cabinet photograph of a remarkably strong-featured, handsome young man. Then she turned to Kate and smiled a slow, challenging smile. Kate walked over and picked up the picture, studying it intently but in growing amazement.

"Who is he?" she asked finally.

"My man!" answered Nancy Ellen, possessively, triumphantly.

Kate stared at her. "Honest to God?" she cried in wonderment.

"Honest!" said Nancy Ellen.

"Where on earth did you find him?" demanded Kate.

"Picked him out of the blackberry patch," said Nancy Ellen.

"Those darn blackberries are always late," said Kate, throwing the picture back on the bureau. "Ain't that just my luck! You wouldn't touch the raspberries. I had to pick them every one myself. But the minute I turn my back, you go pick a man like that, out of the blackberry patch. I bet a cow you wore your pink chambray, and carried grandmother's old blue bowl."

"Certainly," said Nancy Ellen, "and my pink sun-bonnet. I think maybe the bonnet started it."

Kate sat down limply on the first chair and studied the toes of her shoes. At last she roused and looked at Nancy Ellen, waiting in smiling complaisance as she returned the picture to her end of the bureau.

"Well, why don't you go ahead?" cried Kate in a thick, rasping voice. "Empty yourself! Who is he? Where did he come from? WHY was he IN our blackberry patch? Has he really been to see you, and is he courting you in earnest?—But of COURSE he is! There's the lilac bush, the lawn-mower, the house to be painted, and a humdinger dress. Is he a millionaire? For Heaven's sake tell me—"

"Give me some chance! I did meet him in the blackberry patch. He's a nephew of Henry Lang and his name is Robert Gray. He has just finished a medical course and he came here to rest and look at Hartley for a location, because Lang thinks it would be such a good one. And since we met he has decided to take an office in Hartley, and he has money to furnish it, and to buy and furnish a nice house."

"Great Jehoshaphat!" cried Kate. "And I bet he's got wings, too! I do have the rottenest luck!"

"You act for all the world as if it were a foregone conclusion that if you had been here, you'd have won him!"

Nancy Ellen glanced in the mirror and smiled, while Kate saw the smile. She picked up her comb and drew herself to full height.

"If anything ever was a 'foregone conclusion,'" she said, "it is a 'foregone conclusion' that if I

HAD been here, I'd have picked the blackberries, and so I'd have had the first chance at him, at least."

"Much good it would have done you!" cried Nancy Ellen. "Wait until he comes, and you see him!"

"You may do your mushing in private," said Kate. "I don't need a demonstration to convince me. He looks from the picture like a man who would be as soft as a frosted pawpaw."

Nancy Ellen's face flamed crimson. "You hateful spite-cat!" she cried.

Then she picked up the picture and laid it face down in her drawer, while two big tears ran down her cheeks. Kate saw those also. Instantly she relented.

"You big silly goose!" she said. "Can't you tell when any one is teasing? I think I never saw a finer face than the one in that picture. I'm jealous because I never left home a day before in all my life, and the minute I do, here you go and have such luck. Are you really sure of him, Nancy Ellen?"

"Well, he asked Father and Mother, and I've been to visit his folks, and he told them; and I've been with him to Hartley hunting a house; and I'm not to teach this winter, so I can have all my time to make my clothes and bedding. Father likes him finc, so hc is going to give me money to get all I need. He offered to, himself."

Kate finished her braid, pulled the combings from the comb and slowly wrapped the end of her hair as she digested these convincing facts. She swung the heavy braid around her head, placed a few pins, then crossed to her sister and laid a shaking hand on her shoulder. Her face was working strongly.

"Nancy Ellen, I didn't mean one ugly word I said. You gave me an awful surprise, and that was just my bald, ugly Bates way of taking it. I think you are one of the most beautiful women I ever have seen, alive or pictured. I have always thought you would make a fine marriage, and I am sure you will. I haven't a doubt that Robert Gray is all you think him, and I am as glad for you as I can be. You can keep house in Hartley for two with scarcely any work at all, and you can have all the pretty clothes you want, and time to wear them. Doctors always get rich if they are good ones, and he is sure to be a good one, once he gets a start. If only we weren't so beastly healthy there are enough Bates and Langs to support you for the first year. And I'll help you sew, and do all I can for you. Now wipe up and look your handsomest!"

Nancy Ellen arose and put her arms around Kate's neck, a stunningly unusual proceeding. "Thank you," she said. "That is big and fine of you. But I always have shirked and put my work on you; I guess now I'll quit, and do my sewing myself."

Then she slipped the pink dress over her head and stood slowly fastening it as Kate started to leave the room. Seeing her go: "I wish you would wait and meet Robert," she said. "I have told him about what a nice sister I have."

"I think I'll go on to Adam's now," said Kate. "I don't want to wait until they go some place, and I miss them. I'll do better to meet your man after I become more accustomed to bare facts, anyway. By the way, is he as tall as you?"

"Yes," said Nancy Ellen, laughing. "He is an inch and a half taller. Why?"

"Oh, I hate seeing a woman taller than her husband and I've always wondered where we'd find men to reach our shoulders. But if they can be picked at random from the berry patch—"

So Kate went on her way laughing, lifting her white skirts high from the late August dust. She took a short cut through the woods and at a small stream, with sure foot, crossed the log to within a few steps of the opposite bank. There she stopped, for a young man rounded the bushes and set a foot on the same log; then he and Kate looked straight into each other's eyes. Kate saw a clean-shaven, forceful young face, with strong lines and good colouring, clear gray eyes, sandy brown hair, even, hard, white teeth, and broad shoulders a little above her own. The man saw Kate, dressed in her best and looking her best. Slowly she extended her hand.

"I bet a picayune you are my new brother, Robert," she said.

The young man gripped her hand firmly, held it, and kept on looking in rather a stunned manner at Kate.

"Well, aren't you?" she asked, trying to withdraw the hand.

"I never, never would have believed it," he said.

"Believed what?" asked Kate, leaving the hand where it was.

"That there could be two in the same family," said he.

"But I'm as different from Nancy Ellen as night from day," said Kate, "besides, woe is me, I didn't wear a pink dress and pick you from the berry patch in a blue bowl."

Then the man released her hand and laughed. "You wouldn't have had the slightest trouble, if you had been there," he said.

"Except that I should have inverted my bowl," said Kate, calmly. "I am looking for a millionaire, riding a milk-white steed, and he must be much taller than you and have black hair and eyes. Good-bye, brother! I will see you this evening."

Then Kate went down the path to deliver the telescope, render her thanks, make her promise of speedy payment, and for the first time tell her good news about her school. She found that she was very happy as she went and quite convinced that her first flight would prove entirely successful.

CHAPTER IV

A QUESTION OF CONTRACTS

"HELLO, Folks!" cried Kate, waving her hand to the occupants of the veranda as she went up the walk. "Glad to find you at home."

"That is where you will always find me unless I am forced away on business," said her brother as they shook hands.

Agatha was pleased with this, and stiff as steel, she bent the length of her body toward Kate and gave her a tight-lipped little peck on the cheek.

"I came over, as soon as I could," said Kate as she took the chair her brother offered, "to thank you for the big thing you did for me, Agatha, when you lent me that money. If I had known where I was going, or the help it would be to me, I should have gone if I'd had to walk and work for my board. Why, I feel so sure of myself! I've learned so much that I'm like the girl fresh from boarding school: 'The only wonder is that one small head can contain it all.' Thank you over and over and I've got a good school, so I can pay you back the very first month, I think. If there are things I must have, I can pay part the first month and the remainder the second. I am eager for pay-day. I can't even picture the bliss of having that much money in my fingers, all my own, to do with as I please. Won't it be grand?"

In the same breath said Agatha: "Procure yourself some clothes!" Said Adam: "Start a bank account!"

Said Kate: "Right you are! I shall do both."

"Even our little Susan has a bank account," said Adam, Jr., proudly.

"Which is no reflection whatever on me," laughed Kate. "Susan did not have the same father and mother I had. I'd like to see a girl of my branch of the Bates family start a bank account at ten."

"No, I guess she wouldn't," admitted Adam, dryly.

"But have you heard that Nancy Ellen has started?" cried Kate. "Only think! A lawn-mower! The house and barn to be painted! All the dinge possible to remove scoured away, inside! She must have worn her fingers almost to the bone! And really, Agatha, have you seen the man? He's as big as Adam, and just fine looking. I'm simply consumed with envy."

"Miss Medira, Dora, Ann, cast her net, and catched a man!" recited Susan from the top step, at which they all laughed.

"No, I have not had the pleasure of casting my optics upon the individual of Nancy Ellen's choice," said Agatha primly, "but Miss Amelia Lang tells me he is a very distinguished person, of quite superior education in a medical way. I shall call him if I ever have the misfortune to fall ill again. I hope you will tell Nancy Ellen that we shall be very pleased to have her bring him to see us some evening, and if she will let me know a short time ahead I shall take great pleasure in compounding a cake and freezing custard."

"Of course I shall tell her, and she will feel a trifle more stuck up than she does now, if that is possible," laughed Kate in deep amusement.

She surely was feeling fine. Everything had come out so splendidly. That was what came of having a little spirit and standing up for your rights. Also she was bubbling inside while Agatha talked. Kate wondered how Adam survived it every day. She glanced at him to see if she could detect any marks of shattered nerves, then laughed outright.

Adam was the finest physical specimen of a man she knew. He was good looking also, and spoke as well as the average, better in fact, for from the day of their marriage, Agatha sat on his lap each night and said these words: "My beloved, to-day I noted an error in your speech. It would put a former teacher to much embarrassment to have this occur in public. In the future will you not try to remember that you should say, 'have gone,' instead of 'have went?'" As she talked Agatha rumpled Adam's hair, pulled off his string tie, upon which she insisted, even when he was plowing; laid her hard little face against his, and held him tight with her frail arms, so that Adam being part human as well as part Bates, held her closely also and said these words: "You bet your sweet life I will!" And what is more he did. He followed a furrow the next day, softly muttering over to himself: "Langs have gone to town. I have gone to work. The birds have gone to building nests." So Adam seldom said: "have went," or made any other error in speech that Agatha had once corrected.

As Kate watched him leaning back in his chair, vital, a study in well-being, the supremest kind of satisfaction on his face, she noted the flash that lighted his eye when Agatha offered to "freeze a custard." How like Agatha! Any other woman Kate knew would have said, "make ice cream." Agatha explained to them that when they beat up eggs, added milk, sugar, and corn-starch it was custard. When they used pure cream, sweetened and frozen, it was iced cream. Personally, she preferred the custard, but she did not propose to call it custard cream. It was not correct. Why persist in misstatements and inaccuracies when one knew better? So Agatha said iced cream when she meant it, and frozen custard, when custard it was, but every other woman in the neighbourhood, had she acted as she felt, would have slapped Agatha's face when she said it: this both Adam and Kate well knew, so it made Kate laugh despite the fact that she would not have offended Agatha purposely.

"I think—I think," said Agatha, "that Nancy Ellen has much upon which to congratulate herself. More education would not injure her, but she has enough that if she will allow her ambition to rule her and study in private and spend her spare time communing with the best writers, she can make an exceedingly fair intellectual showing, while she surely is a handsome woman. With a good home and such a fine young professional man as she has had the good fortune to attract, she should immediately put herself at the head of society in Hartley and become its leader to a much higher moral and intellectual plane than it now occupies."

"Bet she has a good time," said young Adam. "He's awful nice."

"Son," said Agatha, "'awful,' means full of awe. A cyclone, a cloudburst, a great conflagration are awful things. By no stretch of the imagination could they be called nice."

"But, Ma, if a cyclone blew away your worst enemy wouldn't it be nice?"

Adam, Jr., and Kate laughed. Not the trace of a smile crossed Agatha's pale face.

"The words do not belong in contiguity," she said. "They are diametrically opposite in meaning. Please do not allow my ears to be offended by hearing you place them in propinquity again."

"I'll try not to, Ma," said young Adam; then Agatha smiled on him approvingly. "When did you meet Mr. Gray, Katherine?" she asked.

"On the foot-log crossing the creek beside Lang's line fence. Near the spot Nancy Ellen first met him I imagine."

"How did you recognize him?"

"Nancy Ellen had just been showing me his picture and telling me about him. Great Day, but she's in love with him!"

"And so he is with her, if Lang's conclusions from his behaviour can be depended upon. They inform me that he can be induced to converse on no other subject. The whole arrangement appeals to me as distinctly admirable."

"And you should see the lilac bush and the cabbage roses," said Kate. "And the strangest thing is Father. He is peaceable as a lamb. She is not to teach, but to spend the winter sewing on her clothes and bedding, and Father told her he would give her the necessary money. She said so. And I suspect he will. He always favoured her because she was so pretty, and she can come closer to wheedling him than any of the rest of us excepting you, Agatha."

"It is an innovation, surely!"

"Mother is nearly as bad. Father furnishing money for clothes and painting the barn is no more remarkable than Mother letting her turn the house inside out. If it had been I, Father would have told me to teach my school this winter, buy my own clothes and linen with the money I had earned, and do my sewing next summer. But I am not jealous. It is because she is handsome, and the man fine-looking and with such good prospects."

"There you have it!" said Adam emphatically. "If it were you, marrying Jim Lang, to live on Lang's west forty, you WOULD pay your own way. But if it were you marrying a fine-looking young doctor, who will soon be a power in Hartley, no doubt, it would tickle Father's vanity until he would do the same for you."

"I doubt it!" said Kate. "I can't see the vanity in Father."

"You can't?" said Adam, Jr., bitterly. "Maybe not! You have not been with him in the Treasurer's office when he calls for 'the tax on those little parcels of land of mine.' He looks every inch of six feet six then, and swells like a toad. To hear him you would think sixteen hundred and fifty acres of the cream of this county could be tied in a bandanna and carried on a walking stick, he is so casual about it. And those men fly around like buttons on a barn door to wait on him and it's 'Mister Bates this' and 'Mister Bates that,' until it turns my stomach. Vanity! He rolls in it! He eats it! He risks losing our land for us that some of us have slaved over for twenty years, to feed that especial vein of his vanity. Where should we be if he let anything happen to those deeds?"

"How refreshing!" cried Kate. "I love to hear you grouching! I hear nothing else from the women of the Bates family, but I didn't even know the men had a grouch. Are Peter, and John, and Hiram, and the other boys sore, too?"

"I should say they are! But they are too diplomatic to say so. They are afraid to cheep. I just open my head and say right out loud in meeting that since I've turned in the taxes and insurance for all these years and improved my land more than fifty per cent., I'd like to own it, and pay my taxes myself, like a man."

"I'd like to have some land under any conditions," said Kate, "but probably I never shall. And I bet you never get a flipper on that deed until Father has crossed over Jordan, which with his health and strength won't be for twenty-five years yet at least. He's performing a miracle that will make the other girls rave, when he gives Nancy Ellen money to buy her outfit; but they won't dare let him hear a whisper of it. They'll take it all out on Mother, and she'll be afraid to tell him."

"Afraid? Mother afraid of him? Not on your life. She is hand in glove with him. She thinks as he does, and helps him in everything he undertakes."

"That's so, too. Come to think of it, she isn't a particle afraid of him. She agrees with him perfectly. It would be interesting to hear them having a private conversation. They never talk a word before us. But they always agree, and they heartily agree on Nancy Ellen's man, that is plainly to be seen."

"It will make a very difficult winter for you, Katherine," said Agatha. "When Nancy Ellen becomes interested in dresses and table linen and bedding she will want to sew all the time, and leave the cooking and dishes for you as well as your schoolwork."

Kate turned toward Agatha in surprise. "But I won't be there! I told you I had taken a school."

"You taken a school!" shouted Adam. "Why, didn't they tell you that Father has signed up for the home school for you?"

"Good Heavens!" said Kate. "What will be to pay now?"

"Did you contract for another school?" cried Adam.

"I surely did," said Kate slowly. "I signed an agreement to teach the village school in Walden. It's a brick building with a janitor to sweep and watch fires, only a few blocks to walk, and it pays twenty dollars a month more than the home school where you can wade snow three miles, build your own fires, and freeze all day in a little frame building at that. I teach the school I have taken."

"And throw our school out of a teacher? Father could be sued, and probably will be," said Adam. "And throw the housework Nancy Ellen expected you to do on her," said Agatha, at the same time.

"I see," said Kate. "Well, if he is sued, he will have to settle. He wouldn't help me a penny to go to school, I am of age, the debt is my own, and I don't owe it to him. He's had all my work has been worth all my life, and I've surely paid my way. I shall teach the school I have signed for."

"You will get into a pretty kettle of fish!" said Adam.

"Agatha, will you sell me your telescope for what you paid for it, and get yourself a new one the next time you go to Hartley? It is only a few days until time to go to my school, it opens sooner than in the country, and closes later. The term is four months longer, so I earn that much more. I haven't gotten a telescope yet. You can add it to my first payment."

"You may take it," said Agatha, "but hadn't you better reconsider, Katherine? Things are progressing so nicely, and this will upset everything for Nancy Ellen."

"That taking the home school will upset everything for me, doesn't seem to count. It is late, late to find teachers, and I can be held responsible if I break the contract I have made. Father can stand the racket better than I can. When he wouldn't consent to my going, he had no business to make plans for me. I had to make my own plans and go in spite of him; he might have known I'd do all in my power to get a school. Besides, I don't want the home school, or the home work piled on me. My hands look like a human being's for the first time in my life; then I need all my time outside of school to study and map out lessons. I am going to try for a room in the Hartley schools next year, or the next after that, surely. They sha'n't change my plans and boss me, I am going to be free to work, and study, and help myself, like other teachers."

"A grand row this will be," commented young Adam. "And as usual Kate will be right, while all of them will be trying to use her to their advantage. Ma has done her share. Now it is your turn, Pa. Ain't you going to go over and help her?"

"What could I do?" demanded his father. "The mischief is done now."

"Well, if you can't do anything to help, you can let me have the buggy to drive her to Walden, if they turn her out."

"'Forcibly invite her to proceed to her destination,' you mean, son," said Agatha.

"Yes, Ma, that is exactly what I mean," said young Adam. "Do I get the buggy?"

"Yes, you may take my private conveyance. But do nothing to publish the fact. There is no need to incur antagonism if it can be avoided."

"Kate, I'll be driving past the privet bush about nine in the morning. If you need me, hang a white rag on it, and I'll stop at the corner of the orchard."

"I shall probably be standing in the road waiting for you," said Kate.

"Oh, I hope not," said Agatha.

"Looks remarkably like it to me," said Kate.

Then she picked up the telescope, said good-bye to each of them, and in acute misery started back to her home. This time she followed the footpath beside the highway. She was so busy with her indignant thought that she forgot to protect her skirts from the dust of wayside weeds, while in her excitement she walked so fast her face was red and perspiring when she approached the church.

"Oh, dear, I don't know about it," said Kate to the small, silent building. "I am trying to follow your advice, but it seems to me that life is very difficult, any way you go at it. If it isn't one thing, it is another. An hour ago I was the happiest I have ever been in my life; only look at me now! Any one who wants 'the wings of morning' may have them for all of me. It seems definitely settled that I walk, carry a load, and fight for the chance to do even that."

A big tear rolled down either side of Kate's nose and her face twisted in self-pity for an instant. But when she came in sight of home her shoulders squared, the blue-gray of her eyes deepened to steel, and her lips set in a line that was an exact counterpart of her father's when he had made up his mind and was ready to drive his family, with their consent or without it. As she passed the vegetable garden—there was no time or room for flowers in a Bates garden—Kate, looking ahead, could see Nancy Ellen and Robert Gray beneath the cherry trees. She hoped Nancy Ellen would see that she was tired and dusty, and should have time to brush and make herself more presentable to meet a stranger, and so Nancy Ellen did; for which reason she immediately arose and came to the gate, followed by her suitor whom she at once introduced. Kate was in no mood for words; one glance at her proved to Robert Gray that she was tired and dusty, that there were tear marks dried on her face. They hastily shook hands, but neither mentioned the previous meeting. Excusing herself Kate went into the house saying she would soon return.

Nancy Ellen glanced at Robert, and saw the look of concern on his face.

"I believe she has been crying," she said. "And if she has, it's something new, for I never saw a tear on her face before in my life."

"Truly?" he questioned in amazement.

"Why, of course! The Bates family are not weepers."

"So I have heard," said the man, rather dryly.

Nancy Ellen resented his tone.

"Would you like us better if we were?"

"I couldn't like you better than I do, but because of what I have heard and seen, it naturally makes me wonder what could have happened that has made her cry."

"We are rather outspoken, and not at all secretive," said Nancy Ellen, carelessly, "you will soon know."

Kate followed the walk around the house and entered at the side door, finding her father and mother in the dining room reading the weekly papers. Her mother glanced up as she entered.

"What did you bring Agatha's telescope back with you for?" she instantly demanded.

For a second Kate hesitated. It had to come, she might as well get it over. Possibly it would be easier with them alone than if Nancy Ellen were present.

"It is mine," she said. "It represents my first purchase on my own hook and line."

"You are not very choicy to begin on second-hand stuff. Nancy Ellen would have had a new one."

"No doubt!" said Kate. "But this will do for me."

Her father lowered his paper and asked harshly: "What did you buy that thing for?"

Kate gripped the handle and braced herself.

"To pack my clothes in when I go to my school next week," she said simply.

"What?" he shouted. "What?" cried her mother.

"I don't know why you seem surprised," said Kate. "Surely you knew I went to Normal to prepare myself to teach. Did you think I couldn't find a school?"

"Now look here, young woman," shouted Adam Bates, "you are done taking the bit in your teeth. Nancy Ellen is not going to teach this winter. I have taken the home school for you; you will teach it. That is settled. I have signed the contract. It must be fulfilled."

"Then Nancy Ellen will have to fulfill it," said Kate. "I also have signed a contract that must be fulfilled. I am of age, and you had no authority from me to sign a contract for me."

For an instant Kate thought there was danger that the purple rush of blood to her father's head might kill him. He opened his mouth, but no distinct words came. Her face paled with fright, but she was of his blood, so she faced him quietly. Her mother was quicker of wit, and sharper of tongue.

"Where did you get a school? Why didn't you wait until you got home?" she demanded.

"I am going to teach the village school in Walden," said Kate. "It is a brick building, has a janitor, I can board reasonably, near my work, and I get twenty dollars more a month than our school pays, while the term is four months longer."

"Well, it is a pity about that; but it makes no difference," said her mother. "Our home school has got to be taught as Pa contracted, and Nancy Ellen has got to have her chance."

"What about my chance?" asked Kate evenly. "Not one of the girls, even Exceptional Ability, ever had as good a school or as high wages to start on. If I do well there this winter, I am sure I can get in the Hartley graded schools next fall."

"Don't you dare nickname your sister," cried Mrs. Bates, shrilly. "You stop your impudence and mind your father."

"Ma, you leave this to me," said Adam Bates, thickly. Then he glared at Kate as he arose, stretching himself to full height. "You've signed a contract for a school?" he demanded.

"I have," said Kate.

"Why didn't you wait until you got home and talked it over with us?" he questioned.

"I went to you to talk over the subject to going," said Kate. "You would not even allow me to speak. How was I to know that you would have the slightest interest in what school I took, or where."

"When did you sign this contract?" he continued.

"Yesterday afternoon, in Hartley," said Kate.

"Aha! Then I did miss a letter from my pocket. When did you get to be a thief?" he demanded.

"Oh, Father!" cried Kate. "It was my letter. I could see my name on the envelope. I ASKED you for it, before I took it."

"From behind my back, like the sneak-thief you are. You are not fit to teach in a school where half the scholars are the children of your brothers and sisters, and you are not fit to live with honest people. Pack your things and be off!"

"Now? This afternoon?" asked Kate.

"This minute!" he cried.

"All right. You will be surprised at how quickly I can go," said Kate.

She set down the telescope and gathered a straw sunshade and an apron from the hooks at the end of the room, opened the dish cupboard, and took out a mug decorated with the pinkest of wild roses and the reddest and fattest of robins, bearing the inscription in gold, "For a Good Girl" on a banner in its beak. Kate smiled at it grimly as she took the telescope and ran upstairs. It was the work of only a few minutes to gather her books and clothing and pack the big telescope, then she went down the front stairs and left the house by the front door carrying in her hand everything she possessed on earth. As she went down the walk Nancy Ellen sprang up and ran to her while Robert Gray followed.

"You'll have to talk to me on the road," said Kate. "I am forbidden the house which also means the grounds, I suppose."

She walked across the road, set the telescope on the grass under a big elm tree, and sat down beside it.

"I find I am rather tired," she said. "Will you share the sofa with me?"

Nancy Ellen lifted her pink skirt and sat beside Kate. Robert Gray stood looking down at them.

"What in the world is the matter?" asked Nancy Ellen.

"You know, of course, that Father signed a contract for me to teach the home school this winter," explained Kate. "Well, I am of age, and he had no authority from me, so his contract isn't legal. None of you would lift a finger to help me get away to Normal, how was I to know that you would take any interest in finding me a school while I was gone? I thought it was all up to me, so I applied for the school in Walden, got it, and signed the contract to teach it. It is a better school, at higher wages. I thought you would teach here—I can't break my contract. Father is furious and has ordered me out of the house. So there you are, or rather here I am."

"Well, it isn't much of a joke," said Nancy Ellen, thinking intently.

What she might have said had they been alone, Kate always wondered. What she did say while her betrothed looked at her with indignant eyes was possibly another matter. It proved to be merely: "Oh, Kate, I am so sorry!"

"So am I," said Kate. "If I had known what your plans were, of course I should gladly have helped you out. If only you had written me and told me."

"I wanted to surprise you," said Nancy Ellen.

"You have," said Kate. "Enough to last a lifetime. I don't see how you figured. You knew how late it was. You knew it would be nip and tuck if I got a school at all."

"Of course we did! We thought you couldn't possibly get one, this late, so we fixed up the scheme to let you have my school, and let me sew on my linen this winter. We thought you would be as pleased as we were."

"I am too sorry for words," said Kate. "If I had known your plan, I would have followed it, even though I gave up a better school at a higher salary. But I didn't know. I thought I had to paddle my own canoe, so I made my own plans. Now I must live up to them, because my contract is legal, while Father's is not. I would have taught the school for you, in the circumstances, but since I can't, so far as I am concerned, the arrangement I have made is much better. The thing that really hurts the worst, aside from disappointing you, is that Father says I was not honest in what I did."

"But what DID you do?" cried Nancy Ellen.

So Kate told them exactly what she had done.

"Of course you had a right to your own letter, when you could see the address on it, and it was where you could pick it up," said Robert Gray.

Kate lifted dull eyes to his face.

"Thank you for so much grace, at any rate," she said.

"I don't blame you a bit," said Nancy Ellen. "In the same place I'd have taken it myself."

"You wouldn't have had to," said Kate. "I'm too abrupt—too much like the gentleman himself. You would have asked him in a way that would have secured you the letter with no trouble."

Nancy Ellen highly appreciated these words of praise before her lover. She arose immediately.

"Maybe I could do something with him now," she said. "I'll go and see."

"You shall do nothing of the kind," said Kate. "I am as much Bates as he is. I won't be taunted afterward that he turned me out and that I sent you to him to plead for me."

"I'll tell him you didn't want me to come, that I came of my own accord," offered Nancy Ellen.

"And he won't believe you," said Kate.

"Would you consent for me to go?" asked Robert Gray.

"Certainly not! I can look out for myself."

"What shall you do?" asked Nancy Ellen anxiously.

"That is getting slightly ahead of me," said Kate. "If I had been diplomatic I could have evaded this until morning. Adam, 3d, is to be over then, prepared to take me anywhere I want to go. What I have to face now is a way to spend the night without letting the neighbours know that I am turned out. How can I manage that?"

Nancy Ellen and Robert each began making suggestions, but Kate preferred to solve her own problems.

"I think," she said, "that I shall hide the telescope under the privet bush, there isn't going to be rain to-night; and then I will go down to Hiram's and stay all night and watch for Adam when he passes in the morning. Hiram always grumbles because we don't come oftener."

"Then we will go with you," said Nancy Ellen. "It will be a pleasant evening walk, and we can keep you company and pacify my twin brother at the same time."

So they all walked to the adjoining farm on the south and when Nancy Ellen and Robert were ready to start back, Kate said she was tired and she believed she would stay until morning, which was agreeable to Hiram and his wife, a girlhood friend of Kate's. As Nancy Ellen and Robert walked back toward home: "How is this going to come out?" he asked, anxiously.

"It will come out all right," said Nancy Ellen, serenely. "Kate hasn't a particle of tact. She is Father himself, all over again. It will come out this way: he will tell me that Kate has gone back on him and I shall have to teach the school, and I will say that is the ONLY solution and the BEST thing to do. Then I shall talk all evening about how provoking it is, and how I hate to change my plans, and say I am afraid I shall lose you if I have to put off our wedding to teach the school, and things like that," Nancy Ellen turned a flushed sparkling face to Robert, smiling quizzically, "and to-morrow I shall go early to see Serena Woodruff, who is a fine scholar and a good teacher, but missed her school in the spring by being so sick she was afraid to contract for it. She is all right now, and she will be delighted to have the school, and when I know she will take it then I shall just happen to think of her in a day or two and I'll suggest her, after I've wailed a lot more; and Father will go to see her of his own accord, and it will all be settled as easy as falling off a chunk, only I shall not get on so fast with my sewing, because of having to help Mother; but I shall do my best, and everything will be all right."

The spot was secluded. Robert Gray stopped to tell Nancy Ellen what a wonderful girl she was. He said he was rather afraid of such diplomacy. He foresaw clearly that he was going to be a managed man. Nancy Ellen told him of course he was, all men were, the thing was not to let them know it. Then they laughed and listened to a wood robin singing out his little heart in an evening song that was almost as melodious as his spring performances had been.

CHAPTER V

THE PRODIGAL DAUGHTER

EARLY in the morning Kate set her young nephew on the gate-post to watch for his cousin, and he was to have a penny for calling at his approach. When his lusty shout came, Kate said good-bye to her sister-in-law, paid the penny, kissed the baby, and was standing in the road when Adam stopped. He looked at her inquiringly.

"Well, it happened," she said. "He turned me out instanter, with no remarks about when I might return, if ever, while Mother cordially seconded the motion. It's a good thing, Adam, that you offered to take care of me, because I see clearly that you are going to have it to do."

"Of course I will," said Adam promptly. "And of course I can. Do you want to go to Hartley for anything? Because if you don't, we can cut across from the next road and get to Walden in about fifteen miles, while it's seventeen by Hartley; but if you want to go we can, for I needn't hurry. I've got a box of lunch and a feed for my horse in the back of the buggy. Mother said I was to stay with you until I saw you settled in your room, if you had to go; and if you do, she is angry with Grandpa, and she is going to give him a portion of her mentality the very first time she comes in contact with him. She said so."

"Yes, I can almost hear her," said Kate, struggling to choke down a rising laugh. "She will never know how I appreciate what she has done for me, but I think talking to Father will not do any good. Home hasn't been so overly pleasant. It's been a small, dark, cramped house, dingy and hot, when it might have been big, airy, and comfortable, well furnished and pretty as Father's means would allow, and as all the neighbours always criticize him for not having it; it's meant hard work and plenty of it ever since I was set to scouring the tinware with rushes at the mature age of four, but it's been home, all the home I have had, and it hurts more than I can tell you to be ordered out of it as I was, but if I do well and make a big success, maybe he will let me come back for Christmas, or next summer's vacation."

"If he won't, Ma said you could come to our house," said Adam.

"That's kind of her, but I couldn't do it," said Kate.

"She SAID you could," persisted the boy.

"But if I did it, and Father got as mad as he was last night and tore up your father's deed, then where would I be?" asked Kate.

"You'd be a sixteenth of two hundred acres better off than you are now," said Adam.

"Possibly," laughed Kate, "but I wouldn't want to become a land shark that way. Look down the road."

"Who is it?" asked Adam.

"Nancy Ellen, with my telescope," answered Kate. "I am to go, all right."

"All right, then we will go," said the boy, angrily. "But it is a blame shame and there is no sense to it, as good a girl as you have been, and the way you have worked. Mother said at breakfast there was neither sense nor justice in the way Grandpa always has acted and she said she would wager all she was worth that he would live to regret it. She said it wasn't natural, and when people undertook to controvert—ain't that a peach? Bet there isn't a woman in ten miles using that word except Ma—nature they always hurt themselves worse than they hurt their victims. And I bet he does, too, and I, for one, don't care. I hope he does get a good jolt, just to pay him up for being so mean."

"Don't, Adam, don't!" cautioned Kate.

"I mean it!" cried the boy.

"I know you do. That's the awful thing about it," said Kate. "I am afraid every girl he has feels the same way, and from what your father said yesterday, even the sons he favours don't feel any too good toward him."

"You just bet they don't! They are every one as sore as boiled owls. Pa said so, and he knows, for they all talk it over every time they meet. He said they didn't feel like men, they felt like a lot of 'spanked school-boys.'"

"They needn't worry," said Kate. "Every deed is made out. Father reads them over whenever it rains. They'll all get their land when he dies. It is only his way."

"Yes, and THIS is only his way, too, and it's a dern poor way," said Adam. "Pa isn't going to do this way at all. Mother said he could go and live on his land, and she'd stay home with Susan and me, if he tried it. And when I am a man I am going to do just like Pa and Ma because they are the rightest people I know, only I am not going to save QUITE so close as Pa, and if I died for it, I never could converse or dance like Ma."

"I should hope not!" said Kate, and then added hastily, "it's all right for a lady, but it would seem rather sissy for a man, I believe."

"Yes, I guess it would, but it is language let me tell you, when Ma cuts loose," said Adam.

"Hello, Nancy Ellen," said Kate as Adam stopped the buggy. "Put my telescope in the back with the horse feed. Since you have it, I don't need ask whether I am the Prodigal Daughter or not. I see clearly I am."

Nancy Ellen was worried, until she was pale.

"Kate," she said, "I never have seen Father so angry in all my life. I thought last night that in a day or two I could switch the school over to Serena Woodruff, and go on with my plans, but Father said at breakfast if the Bates name was to stand for anything approaching honour, a Bates would teach that school this winter or he'd know the reason why. And you know how easy it is to change him. Oh, Kate, won't you see if that Walden trustee can't possibly find another teacher, and let you off? I know Robert will be disappointed, for he's rented his office and bought a house and he said last night to get ready as soon after Christmas as I could. Oh, Kate, won't you see if you can't possibly get that man to hire another teacher?"

"Why, Nancy Ellen—" said Kate.

Nancy Ellen, with a twitching face, looked at Kate.

"If Robert has to wait months, there in Hartley, handsome as he is, and he has to be nice to everybody to get practice, and you know how those Hartley girls are—"

"Yes, Nancy Ellen, I know," said Kate. "I'll see what I can do. Is it understood that if I give up the school and come back and take ours, Father will let me come home?"

"Yes, oh, yes!" cried Nancy Ellen.

"Well, nothing goes on guess-work. I'll hear him say it, myself," said Kate.

She climbed from the buggy. Nancy Ellen caught her arm.

"Don't go in there! Don't you go there," she cried. "He'll throw the first thing he can pick up at you. Mother says he hasn't been asleep all night."

"Pooh!" said Kate. "How childish! I want to hear him say that, and he'll scarcely kill me."

She walked swiftly to the side door.

"Father," she said, "Nancy Ellen is afraid she will lose Robert Gray if she has to put off her marriage for months—"

Kate stepped back quickly as a chair crashed against the door facing. She again came into view and continued—"so she asked me if I would get out of my school and come back if I could"—Kate dodged another chair; when she appeared again—"To save the furniture, of which we have none too much, I'll just step inside," she said. When her father started toward her, she started around the dining table, talking as fast as she could, he lunging after her like a furious bull. "She asked me to come back and teach the school—to keep her from putting off her wedding—because she is afraid to— If I can break my contract there—may I come back and help her out here?"

The pace was going more swiftly each round, it was punctuated at that instant by a heavy meat platter aimed at Kate's head. She saw it picked up and swayed so it missed.

"I guess that is answer enough for me," she panted, racing on. "A lovely father you are—no wonder your daughters are dishonest through fear of you—no wonder your wife has no mind of her own—no wonder your sons hate you and wish you would die—so they could have their deeds and be like men—instead of 'spanked school-boys' as they feel now—no wonder the whole posse of us hate you."

Directly opposite the door Kate caught the table and drew it with her to bar the opening. As it crashed against the casing half the dishes flew to the floor in a heap. When Adam Bates pulled it from his path he stepped in a dish of fried potatoes and fell heavily. Kate reached the road, climbed in the buggy, and said the Nancy Ellen: "You'd better hide! Cut a bundle of stuff and send it to me by Adam and I'll sew my fingers to the bone for you every night. Now drive like sin, Adam!"

As Adam Bates came lurching down the walk in fury the buggy dashed past and Kate had not even time to turn her head to see what happened.

"Take the first turn," she said to Adam. "I've done an awful thing."

"What did you do?" cried the boy.

"Asked him as nicely as I could; but he threw a chair at me. Something funny happened to me, and I wasn't afraid of him at all. I dodged it, and finished what I was saying, and another chair came, so the two Bates went at it."

"Oh, Kate, what did you do?" cried Adam.

"Went inside and ran around the dining table while I told him what all his sons and daughters think of him. 'Spanked school-boys' and all—"

"Did you tell him my father said that?" he demanded.

"No. I had more sense left than that," said Kate. "I only said all his boys FELT like that. Then I pulled the table after me to block the door, and smashed half the dishes and he slipped in the fried potatoes and went down with a crash—"

"Bloody Murder!" cried young Adam, aghast.

"Me, too!" said Kate. "I'll never step in that house again while he lives. I've spilled the beans, now."

"That you have," said Adam, slacking his horse to glance back. "He is standing in the middle of the road shaking his fist after you."

"Can you see Nancy Ellen?" asked Kate.

"No. She must have climbed the garden fence and hidden behind the privet bush."

"Well, she better make it a good long hide, until he has had plenty of time to cool off. He'd have killed me if he had caught me, after he fell—and wasted all those potatoes already cooked——"

Kate laughed a dry hysterical laugh, but the boy sat white-faced and awed.

"Never mind," said Kate, seeing how frightened he was. "When he has had plenty of time he'll cool off; but he'll never get over it. I hope he doesn't beat Mother, because I was born."

"Oh, drat such a man!" said young Adam. "I hope something worse that this happens to him. If ever I see Father begin to be the least bit like him as he grows older I shall——"

"Well, what shall you do?" asked Kate, as he paused.

"Tell Ma!" cried young Adam, emphatically.

Kate leaned her face in her hands and laughed. When she could speak she said: "Do you know, Adam, I think that would be the very best thing you could do."

"Why, of course!" said Adam.

They drove swiftly and reached Walden before ten o'clock. There they inquired their way to the home of the Trustee, but Kate said nothing about giving up the school. She merely made a few inquiries, asked for the key of the schoolhouse, and about boarding places. She was directed to four among which she might choose.

"Where would you advise me to go?" she asked the Trustee.

"Well, now, folks differ," said he. "All those folks is neighbours of mine and some might like one, and some might like another, best. I COULD say this: I think Means would be the cheapest, Knowls the dearest, but the last teacher was a good one, an' she seemed well satisfied with the Widder Holt."

"I see," said Kate, smiling.

Then she and young Adam investigated the schoolhouse and found it far better than any either of them had ever been inside. It promised every comfort and convenience, compared with schools to which they had been accustomed, so they returned the keys, inquired about the cleaning of the building, and started out to find a boarding place. First they went to the cheapest, but it could be seen at a glance that it was too cheap, so they eliminated that. Then they went to the most expensive, but it was obvious from the house and grounds that board there would be more than Kate would want to pay.

"I'd like to save my digestion, and have a place in which to study, where I won't freeze," said Kate, "but I want to board as cheaply as I can. This morning changes my plans materially. I shall want to go to school next summer part of the time, but the part I do not, I shall have to pay my way, so I mustn't spend money as I thought I would. Not one of you will dare be caught doing a thing for me. To make you safe I'll stay away, but it will cost me money that I'd hoped to have for clothes like other girls."

"It's too bad," said Adam, "but I'll stick to you, and so will Ma."

"Of course you will, you dear boy," said Kate. "Now let's try our third place; it is not far from here."

Soon they found the house, but Kate stopped short on sight of it.

"Adam, there has been little in life to make me particular," she said, "but I draw the line at that house. I would go crazy in a house painted bright red with brown and blue decoration. It should be prohibited by law. Let us hunt up the Widder Holt and see how her taste in colour runs."

"The joke is on you," said Adam, when they had found the house.

It was near the school, on a wide shady street across which big maples locked branches. There was a large lot filled with old fruit trees and long grass, with a garden at the back. The house was old and low, having a small porch in front, but if it ever had seen paint, it did not show it at that time. It was a warm linty gray, the shingles of the old roof almost moss-covered.

"The joke IS on me," said Kate. "I shall have no quarrel with the paint here, and will you look at that?"

Adam looked where Kate pointed across the street, and nodded.

"That ought to be put in a gold frame," he said.

"I think so, too," said Kate. "I shouldn't be a bit surprised if I stay where I can see it."

They were talking of a deep gully facing the house and running to a levee where the street crossed. A stream ran down it, dipped under a culvert, turned sharply, and ran away to a distant river, spanning which they could see the bridge. Tall old forest trees lined the banks, shrubs and bushes grew in a thicket. There were swaying, clambering vines and a babel of bird notes over the seed and berry bearing bushes.

"Let's go inside, and if we agree, then we will get some water and feed the horse and eat our lunch over there," said Kate.

"Just the thing!" said young Adam. "Come and we will proceed to the residence of Mrs. Holt and investigate her possibilities. How do you like that?"

"That is fine," said Kate gravely.

"It is," said Adam, promptly, "because it is Ma. And whatever is Ma, is right."

"Good for you!" cried Kate. "I am going to break a Bates record and kiss you good-bye, when you go. I probably shan't have another in years. Come on."

They walked up the grassy wooden walk, stepped on the tiny, vine-covered porch, and lifted and dropped a rusty old iron knocker. Almost at once the door opened, to reveal a woman of respectable appearance, a trifle past middle age. She made Kate think of dried sage because she had a dried-out look and her complexion, hair, and eyes were all that colour. She was neat and clean while the hall into which she invited them was clean and had a wholesome odour. Kate explained her errand. Mrs. Holt breathed a sigh of relief.

"Well, thank goodness I was before-handed," she said. "The teacher stayed here last year and she was satisfied, so I ast the Trustee to mention me to the new teacher. Nobody was expecting you until the last of the week, but I says to myself, 'always take time by the fetlock, Samantha, always be ready'; so last week I put in scouring my spare room to beat the nation, and it's all ready so's you can walk right in."

"Thank you," said Kate, rather resenting the assumption that she was to have no option in the matter. "I have four places on my list where they want the teacher, so I thought I would look at each of them and then decide."

"My, ain't we choicey!" said Mrs. Holt in sneering tones. Then she changed instantly, and in suave commendation went on: "That's exactly right. That's the very thing fer you to do. After you have seen what Walden has to offer, then a pretty young thing like you can make up your mind where you will have the most quiet fer your work, the best room, and be best fed. One of the greatest advantages here fer a teacher is that she can be quiet, an' not have her room rummaged. Every place else that takes boarders there's a lot of children; here there is only me and my son, and he is grown, and will be off to his medical work next week fer the year, so all your working time here, you'd be alone with me. This is the room."

"That surely would be a great advantage, because I have much studying to do," said Kate as they entered the room.

With one glance, she liked it. It was a large room with low ceiling, quaintly papered in very old creamy paper, scattered with delicately cut green leaves, but so carefully had the room been kept, that it was still clean. There were four large windows to let in light and air, freshly washed white curtains hanging over the deep green shades. The floor was carpeted with a freshly washed rag carpet stretched over straw, the bed was invitingly clean and looked comfortable, there was a wash stand with bowl and pitcher, soap and towels, a small table with a lamp, a straight-backed chair and a rocking chair. Mrs. Holt opened a large closet having hooks for dresses at one end and shelves at the other. On the top of these there were a comfort and a pair of heavy blankets.

"Your winter covers," said Mrs. Holt, indicating these, "and there is a good stove I take out in summer to make more room, and set up as soon as it gets cold, and that is a wood box."

She pointed out a shoe box covered with paper similar to that on the walls.

Kate examined the room carefully, the bed, the closet, and tried the chairs. Behind the girl, Mrs. Holt, with compressed lips, forgetting Adam's presence, watched in evident disapproval.

"I want to see the stove," said Kate.

"It is out in the woodhouse. It hasn't been cleaned up for the winter yet."

"Then it won't be far away. Let's look at it."

Almost wholly lacking experience, Kate was proceeding by instinct in exactly the same way her father would have taken through experience. Mrs. Holt hesitated, then turned: "Oh, very well," she said, leading the way down the hall, through the dining room, which was older in furnishing and much more worn, but still clean and wholesome, as were the small kitchen and back porch. From it there was only a step to the woodhouse, where on a little platform across one end sat two small stoves for burning wood, one so small as to be tiny. Kate walked to the larger, lifted the top, looked inside, tried the dampers and drafts and turning said: "That is very small. It will require more wood than a larger one."

Mrs. Holt indicated dry wood corded to the roof.

"We git all our wood from the thicket across the way. That little strip an' this lot is all we have left of father's farm. We kept this to live on, and sold the rest for town lots, all except that gully, which we couldn't give away. But I must say I like the trees and birds better than mebby I'd like people who might live there; we always git our wood from it, and the shade an' running water make it the coolest place in town."

"Yes, I suppose they do," said Kate.

She took one long look at everything as they returned to the hall.

"The Trustee told me your terms are four dollars and fifty cents a week, furnishing food and wood," she said, "and that you allowed the last teacher to do her own washing on Saturday, for nothing. Is that right?"

The thin lips drew more tightly. Mrs. Holt looked at Kate from head to foot in close scrutiny.

"I couldn't make enough to pay the extra work at that," she said. "I ought to have a dollar more, to really come out even. I'll have to say five-fifty this fall."

"If that is the case, good-bye," said Kate. "Thank you very much for showing me. Five-fifty is what I paid at Normal, it is more than I can afford in a village like this."

She turned away, followed by Adam. They crossed the street, watered the horse at the stream, placed his food conveniently for him, and taking their lunch box, seated themselves on a grassy place on the bank and began eating.

"Wasn't that a pretty nice room?" asked Adam. "Didn't you kind of hate to give it up?"

"I haven't the slightest intention of giving it up," answered Kate. "That woman is a skin-flint and I don't propose to let her beat me. No doubt she was glad to get four-fifty last fall. She's only trying to see if she can wring me for a dollar more. If I have to board all next summer, I shall have to watch every penny, or I'll not come out even, let alone saving anything. I'll wager you a nickel that before we leave, she comes over here and offers me the room at the same price she got last winter."

"I hope you are right," said Adam. "How do you like her?"

"Got a grouch, nasty temper, mean disposition; clean house, good room, good cook—maybe; lives just on the edge of comfort by daily skimping," summarized Kate.

"If she comes, are you going to try it?" asked Adam.

"Yes, I think I shall. It is nearest my purse and requirements and if the former teacher stayed there, it will seem all right for me; but she isn't going to put that little stove in my room. It wouldn't heat the closet. How did you like her?"

"Not much!" said Adam, promptly. "If glaring at your back could have killed you, you would have fallen dead when you examined the closet, and bedding, and stove. She honeyed up when she had to, but she was mad as hops. I nearly bursted right out when she talked about 'taking time by the fetlock.' I wanted to tell her she looked like she had, and almost got the life kicked out of her doing it, but I thought I'd better not."

Kate laughed. "Yes, I noticed," she said, "but I dared not look at you. I was afraid you'd laugh. Isn't this a fine lunch?"

"Bet your life it is," said Adam. "Ma never puts up any other kind."

"I wish someone admired me as much as you do your mother, Adam," said Kate.

"Well, you be as nice as Ma, and somebody is sure to," said he.

"But I never could," said Kate.

"Oh, yes, you could," said Adam, "if you would only set yourself to do it and try with all your might to be like her. Look, quick! That must be her 'Medical Course' man!"

Kate glanced across the way and saw a man she thought to be about thirty years of age. He did not resemble his mother in any particular, if he was the son of Mrs. Holt. He was above the average man in height, having broad, rather stooping shoulders, dark hair and eyes. He stopped at the gate and stood a few seconds looking at them, so they could not very well study him closely, then he went up the walk with loose, easy stride and entered the house.

"Yes, that is her son," said Kate. "That is exactly the way a man enters a house that belongs to him."

"That isn't the way I am going to enter my house," said Adam. "Now what shall we do?"

"Rest half an hour while they talk it over, and then get ready to go very deliberately. If she doesn't come across, literally and figuratively, we hunt another boarding place."

"I half believe she will come," said Adam. "She is watching us; I can see her pull back the blind of her room to peep."

"Keep looking ahead. Don't let her think you see her. Let's go up the creek and investigate this ravine. Isn't it a lovely place?"

"Yes. I'm glad you got it," said Adam, "that is, if she come across. I will think of you as having it to look at in summer; and this winter—my, what rabbit hunting there will be, and how pretty it will look!"

So they went wandering up the ravine, sometimes on one bank, sometimes crossing stepping-stones or logs to the other, looking, talking, until a full hour had passed when they returned to the buggy. Adam began changing the halter for the bridle while Kate shook out the lap robe.

"Nickel, please," whispered Kate.

Adam glanced across the street to see Mrs. Holt coming. She approached them and with no preliminaries said: "I have been telling my son about you an' he hates so bad to go away and leave me alone for the winter, that he says to take you at the same as the last teacher, even if I do lose money on it."

"Oh, you wouldn't do that, Mrs. Holt," said Kate, carelessly. "Of course it is for you to decide. I like the room, and if the board was right for the other teacher it will be for me. If you want me to stay, I'll bring my things over and take the room at once. If not, I'll look farther."

"Come right over," said Mrs. Holt, cordially. "I am anxious to git on the job of mothering such a sweet young lady. What will you have for your supper?"

"Whatever you are having," said Kate. "I am not accustomed to ordering my meals. Adam, come and help me unpack."

In half an hour Kate had her dresses on the hooks, her underclothing on the shelves, her books on the table, her pencils and pen in the robin cup, and was saying goodbye to Adam, and telling him what to tell his father, mother, and Nancy Ellen—if he could get a stolen interview with her on the way home. He also promised to write Kate what happened about the home school and everything in which she would be interested. Then she went back to her room, sat in the comfortable rocking chair, and with nothing in the world she was obliged to do immediately, she stared at the opposite wall and day by day reviewed the summer. She sat so long and stared at the wall so intently that gradually it dissolved and shaped into the deep green ravine across the way, which sank into soothing darkness and the slowly lightened until a peep of gold came over the tree tops; and then, a red sun crept up having a big wonderful widespread wing on each side of it. Kate's head fell with a jerk which awakened her, so she arose, removed her dress, washed and brushed her hair, put on a fresh dress and taking a book, she crossed the street and sat on the bank of the stream again, which she watched instead of reading, as she had intended.

CHAPTER VI

KATE'S PRIVATE PUPIL

AT FIRST Kate merely sat in a pleasant place and allowed her nerves to settle, after the short nap she had enjoyed in the rocking chair. It was such a novel experience for her to sit idle, that despite the attractions of growing things, running water, and singing birds, she soon veered to thoughts of what she would be doing if she were at home, and that brought her to the fact that she was forbidden her father's house; so if she might not go there, she was homeless. As she had known her father for nearly nineteen years, for she had a birth anniversary coming in a few days, she felt positive that he never would voluntarily see her again, while with his constitution, he would live for years. She might as well face the fact that she was homeless; and prepare to pay her way all the year round. She wondered why she felt so forlorn and what made the dull ache in her throat.

She remembered telling Nancy Ellen before going away to Normal that she wished her father would drive her from home. Now that was accomplished. She was away from home, in a place where there was not one familiar face, object, or plan of life, but she did not wish for it at all. She devoutly wished that she were back at home even if she were preparing supper, in order that Nancy Ellen might hem towels. She wondered what they were saying: her mind was crystal clear as to what they were doing. She wondered if Nancy Ellen would send Adam, 3d, with a parcel of cut-out sewing for her to work on. She resolved to sew quickly and with stitches of machine-like evenness, if it came. She wondered if Nancy Ellen would be compelled to put off her wedding and teach the home school in order that it might be taught by a Bates, as her father had demanded. She wondered if Nancy Ellen was forced to this uncongenial task, whether it would sour the wonderful sweetness developed by her courtship, and make her so provoked that she would not write or have anything to do with her. They were nearly the same age; they had shared rooms, and, until recently, beds, and whatever life brought them; now Kate lifted her head and ran her hand against her throat to ease the ache gathering there more intensely every minute. With eyes that did not see, she sat staring at the sheer walls of the ravine as it ran toward the east, where the water came tumbling and leaping down over stones and shale bed. When at last she arose she had learned one lesson, not in the History she carried. No matter what its disadvantages are, having a home of any kind is vastly preferable to having none. And the casualness of people so driven by the demands of living and money making that they do not take time even to be slightly courteous and kind, no matter how objectionable it may be, still that, even that, is better than their active displeasure. So she sat brooding and going over and over the summer, arguing her side of the case, honestly trying to see theirs, until she was mentally exhausted and still had accomplished nothing further than arriving at the conclusion that if Nancy Ellen was forced to postpone her wedding she would turn against her and influence Robert Gray in the same feeling.

Then Kate thought of Him. She capitalized him in her thought, for after nineteen years of Bates men Robert Gray would seem a deified creature to their women. She reviewed the scene at the crossing log, while her face flushed with pleasure. If she had remained at home and had gone after the blackberries, as it was sure as fate that she would have done, then she would have met him first, and he would have courted her instead of Nancy Ellen. Suddenly Kate shook herself savagely and sat straight. "Why, you big fool!" she said. "Nancy Ellen went to the berry patch in a pink dress, wearing a sunbonnet to match, and carrying a blue bowl. Think of the picture she made! But if I had gone, I'd have been in a ragged old dirt-coloured gingham, Father's boots, and his old straw hat jammed down to my ears; I'd have been hot and in a surly temper, rebelling because I had the berries to pick. He would have taken one look at me, jumped the fence, and run to Lang's for dear life. Better cut that idea right out!"

So Kate "cut that idea out" at once, but the operation was painful, because when one turns mental surgeon and operates on the ugly spots in one's disposition, there is no anaesthetic, nor is the work done with skilful hands, so the wounds are numerous and leave ugly scars; but Kate was ruthless. She resolved never to think of that brook scene again. In life, as she had lived it, she would not have profited by having been first at the berry patch. Yet she had a right to think of Robert Gray's face, grave in concern for her, his offers to help, the influence he would have in her favour with Nancy Ellen. Of course if he was forced to postpone his wedding he would not be pleased; but it was impossible that the fears which were tormenting Nancy Ellen would materialize into action on his part. No sane man loved a woman as beautiful as her sister and cast her aside because of a few months' enforced waiting, the cause of which he so very well knew; but it would make both of them unhappy and change their beautiful plans, after he even had found and purchased the house. Still Nancy Ellen said that her father was making it a point of honour that a Bates should teach the school, because he had signed the contract for Kate to take the place Nancy Ellen had intended to fill, and then changed her plans. He had sworn that a Bates should teach the school. Well, Hiram had taken the county examination, as all pupils of the past ten years had when they finished the country schools. It was a test required to prove whether they had done their work well. Hiram held a certificate for a year, given him by the County Superintendent, when he passed the examinations. He had never used it. He could teach; he was Nancy Ellen's twin. School did not begin until the first of November. He could hire help with his corn if he could not finish alone. He could arise earlier than usual and do his feeding and milking; he could clean the stables, haul wood on Saturday and Sunday, if he must, for the Bates family looked on Sunday more as a day of rest for the horses and physical man than as one of religious observances. They always worked if there was anything to be gained by it. Six months being the term, he would be free by the first of May; surely the money would be an attraction, while Nancy Ellen could coach him on any new methods she had learned at Normal. Kate sprang to her feet, ran across the street, and entering the hall, hurried to her room. She found Mrs. Holt there in the act of closing her closet door. Kate looked at her with astonished eyes.

"I was just telling my son," Mrs. Holt said rather breathlessly, "that I would take a peep and see if I had forgot to put your extra covers on the shelf."

Kate threw her book on the bed and walked to the table. She had experienced her share of battle for the day. "No children to rummage," passed through her brain. It was the final week of hot, dry August weather, while a point had been made of calling her attention to the extra cover when the room had been shown her. She might have said these things, but why say them? The shamed face of the woman convicted her of "rummaging," as she had termed it. Without a word Kate sat down beside the table, drew her writing material before her, and began addressing an envelope to her brother Hiram. Mrs. Holt left the room, disliking Kate more than if she had said what the woman knew she thought.

Kate wrote briefly, convincingly, covering every objection and every advantage she could conceive, and then she added the strongest plea she could make. What Hiram would do, she had no idea. As with all Bates men, land was his God, but it required money to improve it. He would feel timid about making a first attempt to teach after he was married and a father of a child, but Nancy Ellen's marriage would furnish plausible excuse; all of the family had done their school work as perfectly as all work they undertook; he could teach if he wanted to; would he want to? If he did, at least, she would be sure of the continued friendship of her sister and Robert Gray. Suddenly Kate understood what that meant to her as she had not realized before. She was making long strides toward understanding herself, which is the most important feature of any life.

She sent a line of pleading to her sister-in-law, a word of love to the baby, and finishing her letter, started to post it, as she remembered the office was only a few steps down the street. In the hall it occurred to her that she was the "Teacher" now, and so should be an example. Possibly the women of Walden did not run bareheaded down the street on errands. She laid the letter on a small shelf of an old hatrack, and stepped back to her room to put on her hat. Her return was so immediate that Mrs. Holt had the letter in her fingers when Kate came back, and was reading the address so intently, that with extended hand, the girl said in cold tones: "My letter, please!" before the woman realized she was there. Their eyes met in a level look. Mrs. Holt's mouth opened in ready excuse, but this time Kate's temper overcame her better judgment.

"Can you read it clearly, without your glasses?" she asked politely. "I wouldn't for the world have you make a mistake as to whom my letter is addressed. It goes to my brother Hiram Bates, youngest son of Adam Bates, Bates Corners, Hartley, Indiana."

"I was going to give it to my son, so that he could take it to the office," said Mrs. Holt.

"And I am going to take it myself, as I know your son is down town and I want it to go over on the evening hack, so it will be sure to go out early in the morning."

Surprise overcame Mrs. Holt's discomfiture.

"Land sakes!" she cried. "Bates is such a common name it didn't mean a thing to me. Be you a daughter of Adam Bates, the Land King, of Bates Corners?"

"I be," said Kate tersely.

"Well, I never! All them hundreds of acres of land an' money in the bank an' mortgages on half his neighbours. Whut the nation! An' no more of better clo's an' you got! An' teachin' school! I never heard of the like in all my days!"

"If you have Bates history down so fine, you should know that every girl of the entire Bates family has taught from the time she finished school until she married. Also we never buy more clothing than we need, or of the kind not suitable for our work. This may explain why we own some land and have a few cents in the Bank. My letter, please."

Kate turned and went down the street, a dull red tingeing her face. "I could hate that woman cordially without half trying," she said.

The house was filled with the odour of cooking food when she returned and soon she was called to supper. As she went to the chair indicated for her, a step was heard in the hall. Kate remained standing and when a young man entered the room Mrs. Holt at once introduced her son, George. He did not take the trouble to step around the table and shake hands, but muttered a gruff "howdy do?" and seating himself, at once picked up the nearest dish and began filling his plate.

His mother would have had matters otherwise. "Why, George," she chided. "What's your hurry? Why don't you brush up and wait on Miss Bates first?"

"Oh, if she is going to be one of the family," he said, "she will have to learn to get on without much polly-foxing. Grub is to eat. We can all reach at a table of this size."

Kate looked at George Holt with a searching glance. Surely he was almost thirty, of average height, appeared strong, and as if he might have a forceful brain; but he was loosely jointed and there was a trace of domineering selfishness on his face that was repulsive to her. "I could hate that MAN cordially, without half trying," she thought to herself, smiling faintly at the thought.

The sharp eyes of Mrs. Holt detected the smile. She probably would have noticed it, if Kate had merely thought of smiling.

"Why do you smile, my dear?" she asked in melting tone.

"Oh, I was feeling so at home," answered Kate, suavely. "Father and the boys hold exactly those opinions and practise them in precisely the same way; only if I were to think about it at all, I should think that a man within a year of finishing a medical course would begin exercising politeness with every woman he meets. I believe a doctor depends on women to be most of his patients, and women don't like a rude doctor."

"Rot!" said George Holt.

"Miss Bates is exactly right," said his mother. "Ain't I been tellin' you the whole endurin' time that you'd never get a call unless you practised manners as well as medicine? Ain't I, now?"

"Yes, you have," he said, angrily. "But if you think all of a sudden that manners are so essential, why didn't you hammer some into me when you had the whip hand and could do what you pleased? You didn't find any fault with my manners, then."

"How of all the world was I to know that you'd grow up and go in for doctorin'? I s'pos'd then you'd take the farm an' run it like your pa did, stead of forcin' me to sell it off by inches to live, an' then you wastin' half the money."

"Go it, Mother," said George Holt, rudely. "Tell all you know, and then piece out with anything you can think of that you don't."

Mrs. Holt's face flushed crimson. She looked at Kate and said vindictively: "If you want any comfort in life, never marry and bring a son inter the world. You kin humour him, and cook for him, an work your hands to the bone fur him, and sell your land, and spend all you can raise educatin' him for half a dozen things, an' him never stickin to none or payin' back a cent, but sass in your old age—"

"Go it, Mother, you're doing fine!" said George. "If you keep on Miss Bates will want to change her boarding place before morning."

"It will not be wholly your mother's fault, if I do," said Kate. "I would suggest that if we can't speak civilly, we eat our supper in silence. This is very good food; I could enjoy it, if I had a chance."

She helped herself to another soda biscuit and a second piece of fried chicken and calmly began eating them.

"That's a good idy!" said Mrs. Holt.

"Then why don't you practice it?" said her son.

Thereupon began a childish battle for the last word. Kate calmly arose, picked up her plate, walked from the room, down the hall, and entering her own room, closed the door quietly.

"You fool! You great big dunderheaded fool!" cried Mrs. Holt. "Now you have done it, for the thousandth time. She will start out in less than no time to find some place else to stay, an' who could blame her? Don't you know who she is? Ain't you sense in your head? If there was ever a girl you ort to go after, and go quick an' hard, there she is!"

"What? That big beef! What for?" asked George.

"You idjit! You idjit! Don't you sense that she's a daughter of Adam Bates? Him they call the Land King. Ain't you sense ner reason? Drive her from the house, will you? An' me relyin' on sendin' you half her board money to help you out? You fool!"

"Why under the Heavens didn't you tell me? How could I know? No danger but the bowl is upset, and it's all your fault. She should be worth ten thousand, maybe twenty!"

"I never knew till jist before supper. I got it frum a letter she wrote to her brother. I'd no chanct to tell you. Course I meant to, first chanct I had; but you go to work an upset everything before I get a chanct. You never did amount to anything, an' you never will."

"Oh, well, now stop that. I didn't know. I thought she was just common truck. I'll fix it up with her right after supper. Now shut up."

"You can't do it! It's gone too far. She'll leave the house inside fifteen minutes," said Mrs. Holt.

"Well, I'll just show you," he boasted.

George Holt pushed back his plate, wiped his mouth, brushed his teeth at the washing place on the back porch, and sauntered around the house to seat himself on the front porch steps. Kate saw him there and remained in her room. When he had waited an hour he arose and tapped on her door. Kate opened it.

"Miss Bates," he said. "I have been doing penance an hour. I am very sorry I was such a boor. I was in earnest when I said I didn't get the gad when I needed it. I had a big disappointment today, and I came in sore and cross. I am ashamed of myself, but you will never see me that way again. I know I will make a failure of my profession if I don't be more polite than Mother ever taught me to be. Won't you let me be your scholar, too? Please do come over to the ravine where it is cool and give me my first lesson. I need you dreadfully."

Kate was desperately in need of human companionship in that instant, herself, someone who could speak, and sin, and suffer, and repent. As she looked straight in the face of the man before her she saw, not him being rude and quarrelling pettily with his mother, but herself racing around the dining table pursued by her father raving like an insane man. Who was she to judge or to refuse help when it was asked? She went with him; and Mrs. Holt, listening and peering from the side of the window blind of her room across the hall, watched them cross the road and sit beside each other on the bank of the ravine in what seemed polite and amicable conversation. So she heaved a deep sigh of relief and went to wash the dishes and plan breakfast. "Better feed her up pretty well 'til she gits the habit of staying here and mebby the rest who take boarders will be full," she said to herself. "Time enough to go at skimpin' when she's settled, and busy, an' I get the whip hand."

But in planning to get the "whip hand" Mrs. Holt reckoned without Kate. She had been under the whip hand all her life. Her dash to freedom had not been accomplished without both mental and physical hurt. She was doing nothing but going over her past life minutely, and as she realized more fully with each review how barren and unlovely it had been, all the strength and fresh young pride in her arose in imperative demand for something better in the future. She listened with interest to what George Holt said to her. All her life she had been driven by a man of inflexible will, his very soul inoculated with greed for possessions which would give him power; his body endowed with unfailing strength to meet the demands he made on it, and his heart wholly lacking in sentiment; but she did not propose to start her new life by speaking of her family to strangers. George Holt's experiences had been those of a son spoiled by a weak woman, one day petted, the next bribed, the next nagged, again left to his own devices for days, with strong inherited tendencies to be fought, tendencies to what he did not say. Looking at his heavy jaw and swarthy face, Kate supplied "temper" and "not much inclination to work." He had asked her to teach him, she would begin by setting him an example in the dignity of self-control; then she would make him work. How she would make that big, strong man work! As she sat there on the bank of the ravine, with a background of delicately leafed bushes and the light of the setting sun on her face and her hair, George Holt studied her closely, mentally and physically, and would have given all he possessed if he had not been so hasty. He saw that she had a good brain and courage to follow her convictions, while on closer study he decided that she was moulded on the finest physical lines of any woman he ever had seen, also his study of medicine taught him to recognize glowing health, and to set a right estimate on it. Truly he was sorry, to the bottom of his soul, but he did not believe in being too humble. He said as much in apology as he felt forced, and then set himself the task of calling out and parading the level best he could think up concerning himself, or life in general. He had tried farming, teaching, merchandise, and law before he had decided his vocation was medicine.

On account of Robert Gray, Kate was much interested in this, but when she asked what college he was attending, he said he was going to a school in Chicago that was preparing to revolutionize the world of medicine. Then he started on a hobby that he had ridden for months, paying for the privilege, so Kate learned with surprise and no small dismay that in a few months a man could take a course in medicine that would enable him "to cure any ill to which the human flesh is heir," as he expressed it, without knowing anything of surgery, or drugs, or using either. Kate was amazed and said so at once. She disconcertingly inquired what he would do with patients who had sustained fractured skulls, developed cancers, or been exposed to smallpox. But the man before her proposed to deal with none of those disagreeable things, or their like. He was going to make fame and fortune in the world by treating mental and muscular troubles. He was going to be a Zonoletic Doctor. He turned teacher and spelled it for her, because she never had heard the word. Kate looked at George Holt long and with intense interest, while her mind was busy with new thoughts. On her pillow that night she decided that if she were a man, driven by a desire to heal the suffering of the world, she would be the man who took the long exhaustive course of training that enabled him to deal with accidents, contagions, and germ developments.

He looked at her with keen appreciation of her physical freshness and mental strength, and manoeuvred patiently toward the point where he would dare ask blankly how many there were in her family, and on exactly how many acres her father paid tax. He decided it would not do for at least a week yet; possibly he could raise the subject casually with someone down town who would know, so that he need never ask her at all. Whatever the answer might be, it was definitely settled in his own mind that Kate was the best chance he had ever had, or probably ever would have. He mapped out his campaign. This week, before he must go, he would be her pupil and her slave. The holiday week he would be her lover. In the spring he would propose, and in the fall he would marry her, and live on the income from her land ever afterward. It was a glowing prospect; so glowing that he seriously considered stopping school at once so that her could be at the courting part of his campaign three times a day and every evening. He was afraid to leave for fear people of the village would tell the truth about him. He again studied Kate carefully and decided that during the week that was coming, by deft and energetic work he could so win her approval that he could make her think that she knew him better than outsiders did. So the siege began.

Kate had decided to try making him work, to see if he would, or was accustomed to it. He was sufficiently accustomed to it that he could do whatever she suggested with facility that indicated practice, and there was no question of his willingness. He urged her to make suggestions as to what else he could do, after he had made all the needed repairs about the house and premises. Kate was enjoying herself immensely, before the week was over. She had another row of wood corded to the shed roof, in case the winter should be severe. She had the stove she thought would warm her room polished and set up while he was there to do it. She had the back porch mended and the loose board in the front walk replaced. She borrowed buckets and cloths and impressed George Holt for the cleaning of the school building which she superintended. Before the week was over she had every child of school age who came to the building to see what was going on, scouring out desks, blacking stoves, raking the yard, even cleaning the street before the building.

Across the street from his home George sawed the dead wood from the trees and then, with three days to spare, Kate turned her attention to the ravine. She thought that probably she could teach better there in the spring than in the school building. She and George talked it over. He raised all the objections he could think of that the townspeople would, while entirely agreeing with her himself, but it was of no use. She over-ruled the proxy objections he so kindly offered her, so he was obliged to drag his tired body up the trees on both banks for several hundred yards and drop the dead wood. Kate marshalled a corps of boys who would be her older pupils and they dragged out the dry branches, saved all that were suitable for firewood, and made bonfires from the remainder. They raked the tin cans and town refuse of years from the water and banks and induced the village delivery man to haul the stuff to the river bridge and dump it in the deepest place in the stream. They cleaned the creek bank to the water's edge and built rustic seats down the sides. They even rolled boulders to the bed and set them where the water would show their markings and beat itself to foam against them. Mrs. Holt looked on in breathless amazement and privately expressed to her son her opinion of him in terse and vigorous language. He answered laconically: "Has a fish got much to say about what happens to it after you get it out of the water?"

"No!" snapped Mrs. Holt, "and neither have you, if you kill yourself to get it."

"Do I look killed?" inquired her son.

"No. You look the most like a real man I ever saw you," she conceded.

"And Kate Bates won't need glasses for forty years yet," he said as he went back to his work in the ravine.

Kate was in the middle of the creek helping plant a big stone. He stood a second watching her as she told the boys surrounding her how best to help her, then he turned away, a dull red burning his cheek. "I'll have her if I die for it," he muttered, "but I hope to Heaven she doesn't think I am going to work like this for her every day of my life."

As the villagers sauntered past and watched the work of the new teacher, many of them thought of things at home they could do that would improve their premises greatly, and a few went home and began work of like nature. That made their neighbours' places look so unkempt that they were forced to trim, and rake, and mend in turn, so by the time the school began, the whole village was busy in a crusade that extended to streets and alleys, while the new teacher was the most popular person who had ever been there. Without having heard of such a thing, Kate had started Civic Improvement.

George Holt leaned against a tree trunk and looked down at her as he rested.

"Do you suppose there is such a thing as ever making anything out of this?" he asked.

"A perfectly lovely public park for the village, yes; money, selling it for anything, no! It's too narrow a strip, cut too deeply with the water, the banks too steep. Commercially, I can't see that it is worth ten cents."

"Cheering! It is the only thing on earth that truly and wholly belongs to me. The road divided the land. Father willed everything on the south side to Mother, so she would have the house, and the land on this side was mine. I sold off all I could to Jasper Linn to add to his farm, but he would only buy to within about twenty rods of the ravine. The land was too rocky and poor. So about half a mile of this comprises my earthly possessions."

"Do you keep up the taxes?" she asked.

"No. I've never paid them," he said carelessly.

"Then don't be too sure it is yours," she said. "Someone may have paid them and taken the land. You had better look it up."

"What for?" he demanded.

"It is beautiful. It is the shadiest, coolest place in town. Having it here doubles the value of your mother's house across the street. In some way, some day, it might turn out to be worth something."

"I can't see how," he said.

"Some of the trees may become valuable when lumber gets scarcer, as it will when the land grows older. Maybe a stone quarry could be opened up, if the stone runs back as far as you say. A lot of things might make it valuable. If I were you I would go to Hartley, quietly, to-morrow, and examine the records, and if there are back taxes I'd pay them."

"I'll look it up, anyway," he agreed. "You surely have made another place of it. It will be wonderful by spring."

"I can think of many uses for it," said Kate. "Here comes your mother to see how we are getting along."

Instead, she came to hand Kate a letter she had brought from the post office while doing her marketing. Kate took the letter, saw at a glance that it was from Nancy Ellen, and excusing herself, she went to one of the seats they had made, and turning her face so that it could not be seen, she read:

DEAR KATE: You can prepare yourself for the surprise of your life. Two Bates men have done something for one of their women. I hope you will survive the shock; it almost finished me and Mother is still speechless. I won't try to prepare you. I could not. Here it is. Father raged for three days and we got out of his way like scared rabbits. I saw I had to teach, so I said I would, but I had not told Robert, because I couldn't bear to. Then up came Hiram and offered to take the school for me. Father said no, I couldn't get out of it that way. Hiram said I had not seen him or sent him any word, and I could prove by mother I hadn't been away from the house, so Father believed him. He said he wanted the money to add two acres to his land from the Simms place; that would let his stock down to water on the far side of his land where it would be a great convenience and give him a better arrangement of fields so he could make more money. You know Father. He shut up like a clam and only said: "Do what you please. If a Bates teaches the school it makes my word good." So Hiram is going to teach for me. He is brushing up a little nights and I am helping him on "theory," and I am wild with joy, and so is Robert. I shall have plenty of time to do all my sewing and we shall be married at, or after, Christmas. Robert says to tell you to come to see him if you ever come to Hartley. He is there in his office now and it is lonesome, but I am busy and the time will soon pass. I might as well tell you that Father said right after you left that you should never enter his house again, and Mother and I should not speak your name before him. I do hope he gets over it before the wedding. Write me how you like your school, and where you board. Maybe Robert and I can slip off and drive over to see you some day. But that would make Father so mad if he found out that he would not give me the money he promised; so we had better not, but you come to see us as soon as we get in our home. Love from both, NANCY ELLEN.

Kate read the joyful letter slowly. It contained all she hoped for. She had not postponed Nancy Ellen's wedding. That was all she asked. She had known she would not be forgiven so soon, there was slight hope she ever would. Her only chance, thought Kate, lay in marrying a farmer having about a thousand acres of land. If she could do that, her father would let her come home again sometime. She read the letter slowly over, then tearing it in long strips she cross tore them and sifted the handful of small bits on the water, where they started a dashing journey toward the river. Mrs. Holt, narrowly watching her, turned with snaky gleaming eyes to her son and whispered: "A-ha! Miss Smart Alec has a secret!"

CHAPTER VII

HELPING NANCY ELLEN AND ROBERT TO ESTABLISH A HOME

THE remainder of the time before leaving, George Holt spent in the very strongest mental and physical effort to show Kate how much of a man he was. He succeeded in what he hoped he might do. He so influenced her in his favour that during the coming year whenever any one showed signs of criticising him, Kate stopped them by commendation, based upon what she supposed to be knowledge of him.

With the schoolhouse and grounds cleaned as they never had been before, the parents and pupils naturally expected new methods. During the week spent in becoming acquainted with the teacher, the parents heartily endorsed her, while the pupils liked her cordially. It could be seen at a glance that she could pick up the brawniest of them, and drop him from the window, if she chose. The days at the stream had taught them her physical strength, while at the same time they had glimpses of her mental processes. The boys learned many things: that they must not lie or take anything which did not belong to them; that they must be considerate and manly, if they were to be her friends; yet not one word had been said on any of these subjects. As she spoke to them, they answered her, and soon spoke in the same way to each other. She was very careful about each statement she made, often adducing convenient proof, so they saw that she was always right, and never exaggerated. The first hour of this made the boys think, the second they imitated, the third they instantly obeyed. She started in to interest and educate these children; she sent them home to investigate more subjects the first day than they had ever carried home in any previous month. Boys suddenly began asking their fathers about business; girls questioned their mothers about marketing and housekeeping.

The week of Christmas vacation was going to be the hardest; everyone expected the teacher to go home for the Holidays. Many of them knew that her sister was marrying the new doctor of Hartley. When Kate was wondering how she could possibly conceal the rupture with her family, Robert Gray drove into Walden and found her at the schoolhouse. She was so delighted to see him that she made no attempt to conceal her joy. He had driven her way for exercise and to pay her a call. When he realized from her greeting how she had felt the separation from her family, he had an idea that he at once propounded: "Kate, I have come to ask a favour of you," he said.

"Granted!" laughed Kate. "Whatever can it be?"

"Just this! I want you to pack a few clothes, drive to Hartley with me and do what you can to straighten out the house, so there won't be such confusion when Nancy Ellen gets there."

Kate stared at him in a happy daze. "Oh, you blessed Robert Gray! What a Heavenly idea!" she cried. "Of course it wouldn't be possible for me to fix Nancy Ellen's house the way she would, but I could put everything where it belonged, I could arrange well enough, and I could have a supper ready, so that you could come straight home."

"Then you will do it?" he asked.

"Do it?" cried Kate. "Do it! Why, I would be willing to pay you for the chance to do it. How do you think I'm to explain my not going home for the Holidays, and to my sister's wedding, and retain my self-respect before my patrons?"

"I didn't think of it in that way," he said.

"I'm crazy," said Kate. "Take me quickly! How far along are you?"

"House cleaned, blinds up, stoves all in, coal and wood, cellar stocked, carpets down, and furniture all there, but not unwrapped or in place. Dishes delivered but not washed; cooking utensils there, but not cleaned."

"Enough said," laughed Kate. "You go marry Nancy Ellen. I shall have the house warm, arranged so you can live in it, and the first meal ready when you come. Does Nancy Ellen know you are here?"

"No. I have enough country practice that I need a horse; I'm trying this one. I think of you often so I thought I'd drive out. How are you making it, Kate?"

"Just fine, so far as the school goes. I don't particularly like the woman I board with. Her son is some better, yes, he is much better. And Robert, what is a Zonoletic Doctor?"

"A poor fool, too lazy to be a real doctor, with no conscience about taking people's money for nothing," he said.

"As bad as THAT?" asked Kate.

"Worse! Why?" he said.

"Oh, I only wondered," said Kate. "Now I am ready, here; but I must run to the house where I board a minute. It's only a step. You watch where I go, and drive down."

She entered the house quietly and going back to the kitchen she said: "The folks have come for me, Mrs. Holt. I don't know exactly when I shall be back, but in plenty of time to start school. If George goes before I return, tell him 'Merry Christmas,' for me."

"He'll be most disappointed to death," said Mrs. Holt.

"I don't see why he should," said Kate, calmly. "You never have had the teacher here at Christmas."

"We never had a teacher that I wanted before," said Mrs. Holt; while Kate turned to avoid seeing the woman's face as she perjured herself. "You're like one of the family, George is crazy about you. He wrote me to be sure to keep you. Couldn't you possibly stay over Sunday?"

"No, I couldn't," said Kate.

"Who came after you?" asked Mrs. Holt.

"Dr. Gray," answered Kate.

"That new doctor at Hartley? Why, be you an' him friends?"

Mrs. Holt had followed down the hall, eagerly waiting in the doorway. Kate glanced at her and felt sudden pity. The woman was warped. Everything in her life had gone wrong. Possibly she could not avoid being the disagreeable person she was. Kate smiled at her.

"Worse than that," she said. "We be relations in a few days. He's going to marry my sister Nancy Ellen next Tuesday."

Kate understood the indistinct gurgle she heard to be approving, so she added: "He came after me early so I could go to Hartley and help get their new house ready for them to live in after the ceremony."

"Did your father give them the house?" asked Mrs. Holt eagerly.

"No. Dr. Gray bought his home," said Kate.

"How nice! What did your father give them?"

Kate's patience was exhausted. "You'll have to wait until I come back," she said. "I haven't the gift of telling about things before they have happened."

Then she picked up her telescope and saying "good-bye," left the house.

As they drove toward Hartley: "I'm anxious to see your house," said Kate. "Did you find one in a good neighbourhood?"

"The very best, I think," said the doctor. "That is all one could offer Nancy Ellen."

"I'm so glad for her! And I'm glad for you, too! She'll make you a beautiful wife in every way. She's a good cook, she knows how to economize, and she's too pretty for words, if she IS my sister."

"I heartily agree with you," said the doctor. "But I notice you put the cook first and the beauty last."

"You will, too, before you get through with it," answered Kate.

"Here we are!" said he, soon after they entered Hartley. "I'll drive around the block, so you can form an idea of the location." Kate admired every house in the block, the streets and trees, the one house Robert Gray had selected in every particular. They went inside and built fires, had lunch together at the hotel, and then Kate rolled up her sleeves and with a few yards of cheese-cloth for a duster, began unwrapping furniture and standing it in the room where it belonged. Robert moved the heavy pieces, then he left to call on a patient and spend the evening with Nancy Ellen.

So Kate spent several happy days setting Nancy Ellen's new home in order. From basement to garret she had it immaculate and shining. No Bates girl, not even Agatha, ever had gone into a home having so many comforts and conveniences.

Kate felt lonely the day she knew her home was overcrowded with all their big family; she sat very still thinking of them during the hour of the ceremony; she began preparing supper almost immediately, because Robert had promised her that he would not eat any more of the wedding feast than he could help, and he would bring Nancy Ellen as soon afterward as possible. Kate saw them drive to the gate and come up the walk together. As they entered the door Nancy Ellen was saying: "Why, how does the house come to be all lighted up? Seems to me I smell things to eat. Well, if the table isn't all set!"

There was a pause and then Nancy Ellen's clear voice called: "Kate! Kate! Where are you? Nobody else would be THIS nice to me. You dear girl, where are you?"

"I'll get to stay until I go back to school!" was Kate's mental comment as she ran to clasp Nancy Ellen in her arms, while they laughed and very nearly cried together, so that the doctor felt it incumbent upon him to hug both of them. Shortly afterward he said: "There is a fine show in town to-night, and I have three tickets. Let's all go."

"Let's eat before we go," said Nancy Ellen, "I haven't had time to eat a square meal for a week and things smell deliciously."

They finished their supper leisurely, stacked the dishes and went to the theatre, where they saw a fair performance of a good play, which was to both of the girls a great treat. When they returned home, Kate left Nancy Ellen and Robert to gloat over the carpets they had selected, as they appeared on their floors, to arrange the furniture and re-examine their wedding gifts; while she slipped into the kitchen and began washing the dishes and planning what she would have for breakfast. But soon they came to her and Nancy Ellen insisted on wiping the dishes, while Robert carried them to the cupboard. Afterward, they sat before their fireplace and talked over events since the sisters' separation.

Nancy Ellen told about getting ready for her wedding, life at home, the school, the news of the family; the Kate drew a perfect picture of the Walden school, her boarding place, Mrs. Holt, the ravine, the town and the people, with the exception of George Holt—him she never mentioned.

After Robert had gone to his office the following morning, Kate said to Nancy Ellen: "Now I wish you would be perfectly frank with me—"

"As if I could be anything else!" laughed the bride.

"All right, then," said Kate. "What I want is this: that these days shall always come back to you in memory as nearly perfect as possible. Now if my being here helps ever so little, I like to stay, and I'll be glad to cook and wash dishes, while you fix your house to suit you. But if you'd rather be alone, I'll go back to Walden and be satisfied and happy with the fine treat this has been. I can look everyone in the face now, talk about the wedding, and feel all right."

Nancy Ellen said slowly: "I shan't spare you until barely time to reach your school Monday morning. And I'm not keeping you to work for me, either! We'll do everything together, and then we'll plan how to make the house pretty, and go see Robert in his office, and go shopping. I'll never forgive you if you go."

"Why, Nancy Ellen—!" said Kate, then fled to the kitchen too happy to speak further.

None of them ever forgot that week. It was such a happy time that all of them dreaded its end; but when it came they parted cheerfully, and each went back to work, the better for the happy reunion. Kate did not return to Walden until Monday; then she found Mrs. Holt in an evil temper. Kate could not understand it. She had no means of knowing that for a week George had nagged his mother unceasingly because Kate was gone on his return, and would not be back until after time for him to go again. The only way for him to see her during the week he had planned to come out openly as her lover, was to try to find her at her home, or at her sister's. He did not feel that it would help him to go where he never had been asked. His only recourse was to miss a few days of school and do extra work to make it up; but he detested nothing in life as he detested work, so the world's happy week had been to them one of constant sparring and unhappiness, for which Mrs. Holt blamed Kate. Her son had returned expecting to court Kate Bates strenuously; his disappointment was not lightened by his mother's constant nagging. Monday forenoon she went to market, and came in gasping.

"Land sakes!" she cried as she panted down the hall. "I've got a good one on that impident huzzy now!"

"You better keep your mouth shut, and not gossip about her," he said. "Everyone likes her!"

"No, they don't, for I hate her worse 'n snakes! If it wa'n't for her money I'd fix her so's 'at she'd never marry you in kingdom come."

George Holt clenched his big fist.

"Just you try it!" he threatened. "Just you try that!"

"You'll live to see the day you'd thank me if I did. She ain't been home. Mind you, she ain't been HOME! She never seen her sister married at all! Tilly Nepple has a sister, living near the Bates, who worked in the kitchen. She's visitin' at Tilly's now. Miss High-and-Mighty never seen her sister married at all! An' it looked mighty queer, her comin' here a week ahead of time, in the fall. Looks like she'd done somepin she don't DARE go home. No wonder she tears every scrap of mail she gets to ribbons an' burns it. I told you she had a secret! If ever you'd listen to me."

"Why, you're crazy!" he exclaimed. "I did listen to you. What you told me was that I should go after her with all my might. So I did it. Now you come with this. Shut it up! Don't let her get wind of it for the world!"

"And Tilly Nepple's sister says old Land King Bates never give his daughter a cent, an' he never gives none of his girls a cent. It's up to the men they marry to take keer of them. The old skin-flint! What you want to do is to go long to your schoolin', if you reely are going to make somepin of yourself at last, an' let that big strap of a girl be, do—"

"Now, stop!" shouted George Holt. "Scenting another scandal, are you? Don't you dare mar Kate Bates' standing, or her reputation in this town, or we'll have a time like we never had before. If old Bates doesn't give his girls anything when they marry, they'll get more when he dies. And so far as money is concerned, this has gone PAST money with me. I'm going to marry Kate Bates, as soon as ever I can, and I've got to the place where I'd marry her if she hadn't a cent. If I can't take care of her, she can take care of me. I am crazy about her, an' I'm going to have her; so you keep still, an' do all you can to help me, or you'll regret it."

"It's you that will regret it!" she said.

"Stop your nagging, I tell you, or I'll come at you in a way you won't like," he cried.

"You do that every day you're here," said Mrs. Holt, starting to the kitchen to begin dinner.

Kate appeared in half an hour, fresh and rosy, also prepared; for one of her little pupils had said: "Tilly Nepple's sister say you wasn't at your sister's wedding at all. Did you cry 'cause you couldn't go?"

Instantly Kate comprehended what must be town gossip, so she gave the child a happy solution of the question bothering her, and went to her boarding house forewarned. She greeted both Mrs. Holt and her son cordially, then sat down to dinner, in the best of spirits. The instant her chance came, Mrs. Holt said: "Now tell us all about the lovely wedding."

"But I wasn't managing the wedding," said Kate cheerfully. "I was on the infare job. Mother and Nancy Ellen put the wedding through. You know our house isn't very large, and close relatives fill it to bursting. I've seen the same kind of wedding about every eighteen months all my life. I had a NEW job this time, and one I liked better."

She turned to George: "Of course your mother told you that Dr. Gray came after me. He came to ask me as an especial favour to go to his new house in Hartley, and do what I could to arrange it, and to have a supper ready. I was glad. I'd seen six weddings that I can remember, all exactly alike—there's nothing to them; but brushing those new carpets, unwrapping nice furniture and placing it, washing pretty new dishes, untying the loveliest gifts and arranging them—THAT was something new in a Bates wedding. Oh, but I had a splendid time!"

George Holt looked at his mother in too great disgust to conceal his feelings.

"ANOTHER gilt-edged scandal gone sky high," he said. Then he turned to Kate. "One of the women who worked in your mother's kitchen is visiting here, and she started a great hullabaloo because you were not at the wedding. You probably haven't got a leg left to stand on. I suspect the old cats of Walden have chewed them both off, and all the while you were happy, and doing the thing any girl would much rather have done. Lord, I hate this eternal picking! How did you come back, Kate?"

"Dr. Gray brought me."

"I should think it would have made talk, your staying there with him," commented Mrs. Holt.

"Fortunately, the people of Hartley seem reasonably busy attending their own affairs," said Kate. "Doctor Gray had been boarding at the hotel all fall, so he just went on living there until after the wedding."

George glared at his mother, but she avoided his eyes, and laughing in a silly, half-confused manner she said: "How much money did your father give the bride?"

"I can't tell you, in even dollars and cents," said Kate. "Nancy Ellen didn't say."

Kate saw the movement of George's foot under the table, and knew that he was trying to make his mother stop asking questions; so she began talking to him about his work. As soon as the meal was finished he walked with her to school, visiting until the session began. He remained three days, and before he left he told Kate he loved her, and asked her to be his wife. She looked at him in surprise and said: "Why, I never thought of such a thing! How long have you been thinking about it?"

"Since the first instant I saw you!" he declared with fervour.

"Hum! Matter of months," said Kate. "Well, when I have had that much time, I will tell you what I think about it."

CHAPTER VIII

THE HISTORY OF A LEGHORN HAT

Kate finished her school in the spring, then went for a visit with Nancy Ellen and Robert, before George Holt returned. She was thankful to leave Walden without having seen him, for she had decided, without giving the matter much thought, that he was not the man she wanted to marry. In her heart she regretted having previously contracted for the Walden school another winter because she felt certain that with the influence of Dr. Gray, she could now secure a position in Hartley that would enable her either to live with, or to be near, her sister. With this thought in mind, she tried to make the acquaintance of teachers in the school who lived in Hartley and she soon became rather intimate with one of them.

It was while visiting with this teacher that Kate spoke of attending Normal again in an effort to prepare herself still better for the work of the coming year. Her new friend advised against it. She said the course would be only the same thing over again, with so little change or advancement, that the trip was not worth the time and money it would cost. She proposed that Kate go to Lake Chautauqua and take the teachers' course, where all spare time could be put in attending lectures, and concerts, and studying the recently devised methods of education. Kate went from her to Nancy Ellen and Robert, determined at heart to go.

She was pleased when they strongly advised her to, and offered to help her get ready. Aside from having paid Agatha, and for her board, Kate had spent almost nothing on herself. She figured the probable expenses of the trip for a month, what it would cost her to live until school began again, if she were forced to go to Walden, and then spent all her remaining funds on the prettiest clothing she had ever owned. Each of the sisters knew how to buy carefully; then the added advantage of being able to cut and make their own clothes, made money go twice as far as where a dressmaker had to be employed. When everything they had planned was purchased, neatly made, and packed in a trunk, into which Nancy Ellen slipped some of her prettiest belongings, Kate made a trip to a milliner's shop to purchase her first real hat.

She had decided on a big, wide-brimmed Leghorn, far from cheap. While she was trying the effect of flowers and ribbon on it, the wily milliner slipped up and with the hat on Kate's golden crown, looped in front a bow of wide black velvet ribbon and drooped over the brim a long, exquisitely curling ostrich plume. Kate had one good view of herself, before she turned her back on the temptation.

"You look lovely in that," said the milliner. "Don't you like it?"

"I certainly do," said Kate. "I look the best in that hat, with the black velvet and the plume, I ever did, but there's no use to look twice, I can't afford it."

"Oh, but it is very reasonable! We haven't a finer hat in the store, nor a better plume," said the milliner.

She slowly waved it in all its glory before Kate's beauty-hungry eyes. Kate turned so she could not see it.

"Please excuse one question. Are you teaching in Walden this winter?" asked the milliner.

"Yes," said Kate. "I have signed the contract for that school."

"Then charge the hat and pay for it in September. I'd rather wait for my money than see you fail to spend the summer under that plume. It really is lovely against your gold hair."

"'Get thee behind me, Satan,'" quoted Kate. "No. I never had anything charged, and never expect to. Please have the black velvet put on and let me try it with the bows set and sewed."

"All right," said the milliner, "but I'm sorry."

She was so sorry that she carried the plume to the work room, and when she walked up behind Kate, who sat waiting before the mirror, and carefully set the hat on her head, at exactly the right angle, the long plume crept down one side and drooped across the girl's shoulder.

"I will reduce it a dollar more," she said, "and send the bill to you at Walden the last week of September."

Kate moved her head from side to side, lifted and dropped her chin. Then she turned to the milliner.

"You should be killed!" she said.

The woman reached for a hat box.

"No, I shouldn't!" she said. "Waiting that long, I'll not make much on the hat, but I'll make a good friend who will come again, and bring her friends. What is your name, please?"

Kate took one look at herself—smooth pink cheeks, gray eyes, gold hair, the sweeping wide brim, the trailing plume.

"Miss Katherine Eleanor Bates," she said. "Bates Corners, Hartley, Indiana. Please call my carriage?"

The milliner laughed heartily. "That's the spirit of '76," she commended. "I'd be willing to wager something worth while that this very hat brings you the carriage before fall, if you show yourself in it in the right place. It's a perfectly stunning hat. Shall I send it, or will you wear it?"

Kate looked in the mirror again. "You may put a fresh blue band on the sailor I was wearing, and send that to Dr. Gray's when it is finished," she said. "And put in a fancy bow, for my throat, of the same velvet as the hat, please. I'll surely pay you the last week of September. And if you can think up an equally becoming hat for winter——"

"You just bet I can, young lady," said the milliner to herself as Kate walked down the street.

From afar, Kate saw Nancy Ellen on the veranda, so she walked slowly to let the effect sink in, but it seemed to make no impression until she looked up at Nancy Ellen's very feet and said: "Well, how do you like it?"

"Good gracious!" cried Nancy Ellen. "I thought I was having a stylish caller. I didn't know you! Why, I never saw YOU walk that way before."

"You wouldn't expect me to plod along as if I were plowing, with a thing like this on my head, would you?"

"I wouldn't expect you to have a thing like that on your head; but since you have, I don't mind telling you that you are stunning in it," said Nancy Ellen.

"Better and better!" laughed Kate, sitting down on the step. "The milliner said it was a stunning HAT."

"The goose!" said Nancy Ellen. "You become that hat, Kate, quite as much as the hat becomes you."

The following day, dressed in a linen suit of natural colour, with the black bow at her throat, the new hat in a bandbox, and the renewed sailor on her head, Kate waved her farewells to Nancy Ellen and Robert on the platform, then walked straight to the dressing room of the car, and changed the hats. Nancy Ellen had told her this was NOT the thing to do. She should travel in a plain untrimmed hat, and when the dust and heat of her journey were past, she should bathe, put on fresh clothing, and wear such a fancy hat only with her best frocks, in the afternoon. Kate need not have been told that. Right instincts and Bates economy would have taught her the same thing, but she had a perverse streak in her nature. She had SEEN herself in the hat.

The milliner, who knew enough of the world and human nature to know how to sell Kate the hat, when she never intended to buy it, and knew she should not in the way she did, had said that before fall it would bring her a carriage, which put into bald terms meant a rich husband. Now Kate liked her school and she gave it her full attention; she had done, and still intended to keep on doing, first-class work in the future; but her school, or anything pertaining to it, was not worth mentioning beside Nancy Ellen's HOME, and the deep understanding and strong feeling that showed so plainly between her and Robert Gray. Kate expected to marry by the time she was twenty or soon after; all Bates girls had, most of them had married very well indeed. She frankly envied Nancy Ellen, while it never occurred to her that any one would criticise her for saying so. Only one thing could happen to her that would surpass what had come to her sister. If only she could have a man like Robert Gray, and have him on a piece of land of their own. Kate was a girl, but no man of the Bates tribe ever was more deeply bitten by the lust for land. She was the true daughter of her father, in more than one way. If that very expensive hat was going to produce the man why not let it begin to work from the very start? If her man was somewhere, only waiting to see her, and the hat would help him to speedy recognition, why miss a change?

She thought over the year, and while she deplored the estrangement from home, she knew that if she had to go back to one year ago, giving up the present and what it had brought and promised to bring, for a reconciliation with her father, she would not voluntarily return to the old driving, nagging, overwork, and skimping, missing every real comfort of life to buy land, in which she never would have any part.

"You get your knocks 'taking the wings of morning,'" thought Kate to herself, "but after all it is the only thing to do. Nancy Ellen says Sally Whistler is pleasing Mother very well, why should I miss my chance and ruin my temper to stay at home and do the work done by a woman who can do nothing else?"

Kate moved her head slightly to feel if the big, beautiful hat that sat her braids so lightly was still there. "Go to work, you beauty," thought Kate. "Do something better for me than George Holt. I'll have him to fall back on if I can't do better; but I think I can. Yes, I'm very sure I can! If you do your part, you lovely plume, I KNOW I can!"

Toward noon the train ran into a violent summer storm. The sky grew black, the lightning flashed, the wind raved, the rain fell in gusts. The storm was at its height when Kate quit watching it and arose, preoccupied with her first trip to a dining car, thinking about how little food she could order and yet avoid a hunger headache. The twisting whirlwind struck her face as she stepped from the day coach to go to the dining car. She threw back her head and sucked her lungs full of the pure, rain-chilled air. She was accustomed to being out in storms, she liked them. One second she paused to watch the gale sweeping the fields, the next a twitch at her hair caused her to throw up her hands and clutch wildly at nothing. She sprang to the step railing and leaned out in time to see her wonderful hat whirl against the corner of the car, hold there an instant with the pressure of the wind, then slide down, draw under, and drop across the rail, where passing wheels ground it to pulp.

Kate stood very still a second, then she reached up and tried to pat the disordered strands of hair into place. She turned and went back into the day coach, opened the bandbox, and put on the sailor. She resumed her old occupation of thinking things over. All the joy had vanished from the day and the trip. Looking forward, it had seemed all right to defy custom and Nancy Ellen's advice, and do as she pleased. Looking backward, she saw that she had made a fool of herself in the estimation of everyone in the car by not wearing the sailor, which was suitable for her journey, and would have made no such mark for a whirling wind.

She found travelling even easier than any one had told her. Each station was announced. When she alighted, there were conveyances to take her and her luggage to a hotel, patronized almost exclusively by teachers, near the schools and lecture halls. Large front suites and rooms were out of the question for Kate, but luckily a tiny corner room at the back of the building was empty and when Kate specified how long she would remain, she secured it at a less figure than she had expected to pay. She began by almost starving herself at supper in order to save enough money to replace her hat with whatever she could find that would serve passably, and be cheap enough. That far she proceeded stoically; but when night settled and she stood in her dressing jacket brushing her hair, something gave way. Kate dropped on her bed and cried into her pillow, as she never had cried before about anything. It was not ALL about the hat. While she was at it, she shed a few tears about every cruel thing that had happened to her since she could remember that she had borne tearlessly at the time. It was a deluge that left her breathless and exhausted. When she finally sat up, she found the room so close, she gently opened her door and peeped into the hall. There was a door opening on an outside veranda, running across the end of the building and the length of the front.

As she looked from her door and listened intently, she heard the sound of a woman's voice in choking, stifled sobs, in the room having a door directly across the narrow hall from hers.

"My Lord! THERE'S TWO OF US!" said Kate.

She leaned closer, listening again, but when she heard a short groan mingled with the sobs, she immediately tapped on the door. Instantly the sobs ceased and the room became still. Kate put her lips to the crack and said in her off-hand way: "It's only a school-marm, rooming next you. If you're ill, could I get anything for you?"

"Will you please come in?" asked a muffled voice.

Kate turned the knob, and stepping inside, closed the door after her. She could dimly see her way to the dresser, where she found matches and lighted the gas. On the bed lay in a tumbled heap a tiny, elderly, Dresden-china doll-woman. She was fully dressed, even to her wrap, bonnet, and gloves; one hand clutched her side, the other held a handkerchief to her lips. Kate stood an instant under the light, studying the situation. The dark eyes in the narrow face looked appealingly at her. The woman tried to speak, but gasped for breath. Kate saw that she had heart trouble.

"The remedy! Where is it?" she cried.

The woman pointed to a purse on the dresser. Kate opened it, took out a small bottle, and read the directions. In a second, she was holding a glass to the woman's lips; soon she was better. She looked at Kate eagerly.

"Oh, please don't leave me," she gasped.

"Of course not!" said Kate instantly. "I'll stay as long as you want me."

She bent over the bed and gently drew the gloves from the frail hands. She untied and slipped off the bonnet. She hunted keys in the purse, opened a travelling bag, and found what she required. Then slowly and carefully, she undressed the woman, helped her into a night robe, and stooping she lifted her into a chair until she opened the bed. After giving her time to rest, Kate pulled down the white wavy hair and brushed it for the night. As she worked, she said a word of encouragement now and again; when she had done all she could see to do, she asked if there was more. The woman suddenly clung to her hand and began to sob wildly. Kate knelt beside the bed, stroked the white hair, patted the shoulder she could reach, and talked very much as she would have to a little girl.

"Please don't cry," she begged. "It must be your heart; you'll surely make it worse."

"I'm trying," said the woman, "but I've been scared sick. I most certainly would have died if you hadn't come to me and found the medicine. Oh, that dreadful Susette! How could she?"

The clothing Kate had removed from the woman had been of finest cloth and silk. Her hands wore wonderful rings. A heavy purse was in her bag. Everything she had was the finest that money could buy, while she seemed as if a rough wind never had touched her. She appeared so frail that Kate feared to let her sleep without knowing where to locate her friends.

"She should be punished for leaving you alone among strangers," said Kate indignantly.

"If I only could learn to mind John," sighed the little woman. "He never liked Susette. But she was the very best maid I ever had. She was like a loving daughter, until all at once, on the train, among strangers, she flared out at me, and simply raved. Oh, it was dreadful!"

"And knowing you were subject to these attacks, she did the thing that would precipitate one, and then left you alone among strangers. How wicked! How cruel!" said Kate in tense indignation.

"John didn't want me to come. But I used to be a teacher, and I came here when this place was mostly woods, with my dear husband. Then after he died, through the long years of poverty and struggle, I would read of the place and the wonderful meetings, but I could never afford to come. Then when John began to work and made good so fast I was dizzy half the time with his successes, I didn't think about the place. But lately, since I've had everything else I could think of, something possessed me to come back here, and take a suite among the women and men who are teaching our young people so wonderfully; and to sail on the lake, and hear the lectures, and dream my youth over again. I think that was it most of all, to dream my youth over again, to try to relive the past."

"There now, you have told me all about it," said Kate, stroking the white forehead in an effort to produce drowsiness, "close your eyes and go to sleep."

"I haven't even BEGUN to tell you," said the woman perversely. "If I talked all night I couldn't tell you about John. How big he is, and how brave he is, and how smart he is, and how he is the equal of any business man in Chicago, and soon, if he keeps on, he will be worth as much as some of them—more than any one of his age, who has had a lot of help instead of having his way to make alone, and a sick old mother to support besides. No, I couldn't tell you in a week half about John, and he didn't want me to come. If I would come, then he wanted me to wait a few days until he finished a deal so he could bring me, but the minute I thought of it I was determined to come; you know how you get."

"I know how badly you want to do a thing you have set your heart on," admitted Kate.

"I had gone places with Susette in perfect comfort. I think the trouble was that she tried from the first to attract John. About the time we started, he let her see plainly that all he wanted of her was to take care of me; she was pretty and smart, so it made her furious. She was pampered in everything, as no maid I ever had before. John is young yet, and I think he is very handsome, and he wouldn't pay any attention to her. You see when other boys were going to school and getting acquainted with girls by association, even when he was a little bit of a fellow in knee breeches, I had to let him sell papers, and then he got into a shop, and he invented a little thing, and then a bigger, and bigger yet, and then he went into stocks and things, and he doesn't know anything about girls, only about sick old women like me. He never saw what Susette was up to. You do believe that I wasn't ugly to her, don't you?"

"You COULDN'T be ugly if you tried," said Kate.

The woman suddenly began to sob again, this time slowly, as if her forces were almost spent. She looked to Kate for the sympathy she craved and for the first time really saw her closely.

"Why, you dear girl," she cried. "Your face is all tear stained. You've been crying, yourself."

"Roaring in a pillow," admitted Kate.

"But my dear, forgive me! I was so upset with that dreadful woman. Forgive me for not having seen that you, too, are in trouble. Won't you please tell me?"

"Of course," said Kate. "I lost my new hat."

"But, my dear! Crying over a hat? When it is so easy to get another? How foolish!" said the woman.

"Yes, but you didn't see the hat," said Kate. "And it will be far from easy to get another, with this one not paid for yet. I'm only one season removed from sunbonnets, so I never should have bought it at all."

The woman moved in bed, and taking one of Kate's long, crinkly braids, she drew the wealth of gold through her fingers repeatedly.

"Tell me about your hat," she said.

So to humour this fragile woman, and to keep from thinking of her own trouble, Kate told the story of her Leghorn hat and ostrich plume, and many things besides, for she was not her usual terse self with her new friend who had to be soothed to forgetfulness.

Kate ended: "I was all wrong to buy such a hat in the first place. I couldn't afford it; it was foolish vanity. I'm not really good-looking; I shouldn't have flattered myself that I was. Losing it before it was paid for was just good for me. Never again will I be so foolish."

"Why, my dear, don't say such things or think them," chided the little woman. "You had as good a right to a becoming hat as any girl. Now let me ask you one question, and then I'll try to sleep. You said you were a teacher. Did you come here to attend the Summer School for Teachers?"

"Yes," said Kate.

"Would it make any great difference to you if you missed a few days?" she asked.

"Not the least," said Kate.

"Well, then, you won't be offended, will you, if I ask you to remain with me and take care of me until John comes? I could send him a message to-night that I am alone, and bring him by this time to-morrow; but I know he has business that will cause him to lose money should he leave, and I was so wilful about coming, I dread to prove him right so conclusively the very first day. That door opens into a room reserved for Susette, if only you'd take it, and leave the door unclosed to-night, and if only you would stay with me until John comes I could well afford to pay you enough to lengthen your stay as long as you'd like; and it makes me so happy to be with such a fresh young creature. Will you stay with me, my dear?"

"I certainly will," said Kate heartily. "If you'll only tell me what I should do; I'm not accustomed to rich ladies, you know."

"I'm not myself," said the little woman, "but I do seem to take to being waited upon with the most remarkable facility!"

CHAPTER IX

A SUNBONNET GIRL

WITH the first faint light of morning, Kate slipped to the door to find her charge still sleeping soundly. It was eight o'clock when she heard a movement in the adjoining room and went again to the door. This time the woman was awake and smilingly waved to Kate as she called: "Good morning! Come right in. I was wondering if you were regretting your hasty bargain."

"Not a bit of it!" laughed Kate. "I am here waiting to be told what to do first. I forgot to tell you my name last night. It is Kate Bates. I'm from Bates Corners, Hartley, Indiana."

The woman held out her hand. "I'm so very glad to meet you, Miss Bates," she said. "My name is Mariette Jardine. My home is in Chicago."

They shook hands, smiling at each other, and then Kate said: "Now, Mrs. Jardine, what shall I do for you first?"

"I will be dressed, I think, and then you may bring up the manager until I have an understanding with him, and give him a message I want sent, and an order for our breakfast. I wonder if it wouldn't be nice to have it served on the corner of the veranda in front of our rooms, under the shade of that big tree."

"I think that would be famous," said Kate.

They ate together under the spreading branches of a giant maple tree, where they could see into the nest of an oriole that brooded in a long purse of gray lint and white cotton cord. They could almost reach out and touch it. The breakfast was good, nicely served by a neat maid, evidently doing something so out of the ordinary that she was rather stunned; but she was a young person of some self-possession, for when she removed the tray, Mrs. Jardine thanked her and gave her a coin that brought a smiling: "Thank you very much. If you want your dinner served here and will ask for Jennie Weeks, I'd like to wait on you again."

"Thank you," said Mrs. Jardine, "I shall remember that. I don't like changing waiters each meal. It gives them no chance to learn what I want or how I want it."

Then she and Kate slowly walked the length of the veranda several times, while she pointed out parts of the grounds they could see that remained as she had known them formerly, and what were improvements.

When Mrs. Jardine was tired, they returned to the room and she lay on the bed while they talked of many things; talked of things with which Kate was familiar, and some concerning which she unhesitatingly asked questions until she felt informed. Mrs. Jardine was so dainty, so delicate, yet so full of life, so well informed, so keen mentally, that as she talked she kept Kate chuckling most of the time. She talked of her home life, her travels, her friends, her son. She talked of politics, religion, and education; then she talked of her son again. She talked of social conditions, Civic Improvement, and Woman's Rights, then she came back to her son, until Kate saw that he was the real interest in the world to her. The mental picture she drew of him was peculiar. One minute Mrs. Jardine spoke of him as a man among men, pushing, fighting, forcing matters to work to his will, so Kate imagined him tall, broad, and brawny, indefatigable in his undertakings; the next, his mother was telling of such thoughtfulness, such kindness, such loving care that Kate's mental picture shifted to a neat, exacting little man, purely effeminate as men ever can be; but whatever she thought, some right instinct prevented her from making a comment or asking a question.

Once she sat looking far across the beautiful lake with such an expression on her face that Mrs. Jardine said to her: "What are you thinking of, my dear?"

Kate said smilingly: "Oh, I was thinking of what a wonderful school I shall teach this winter."

"Tell me what you mean," said Mrs. Jardine.

"Why, with even a month of this, I shall have riches stored for every day of the year," said Kate. "None of my pupils ever saw a lake, that I know of. I shall tell them of this with its shining water, its rocky, shady, sandy shore lines; of the rowboats and steam-boats, and the people from all over the country. Before I go back, I can tell them of wonderful lectures, concerts, educational demonstrations here. I shall get much from the experiences of other teachers. I shall delight my pupils with just you."

"In what way?" asked Mrs. Jardine.

"Oh, I shall tell them of a dainty little woman who know everything. From you I shall teach my girls to be simple, wholesome, tender, and kind; to take the gifts of God thankfully, reverently, yet with self-respect. From you I can tell them what really fine fabrics are, and about laces, and linens. When the subjects arise, as they always do in teaching, I shall describe each ring you wear, each comb and pin, even the handkerchiefs you carry, and the bags you travel with. To teach means to educate, and it is a big task; but it is almost painfully interesting. Each girl of my school shall go into life a gentler, daintier woman, more careful of her person and speech because of my having met you. Isn't that a fine thought?"

"Why, you darling!" cried Mrs. Jardine. "Life is always having lovely things in store for me. Yesterday I thought Susette's leaving me as she did was the most cruel thing that ever happened to me. To-day I get from it this lovely experience. If you are straight from sunbonnets, as you told me last night, where did you get these advanced ideas?"

"If sunbonnets could speak, many of them would tell of surprising heads they have covered," laughed Kate. "Life deals with women much the same as with men. If we go back to where we start, history can prove to you that there are ten sunbonnets to one Leghorn hat, in the high places of the world."

"Not to entertain me, but because I am interested, my dear, will you tell me about your particular sunbonnet?" asked Mrs. Jardine.

Kate sat staring across the blue lake with wide eyes, a queer smile twisting her lips. At last she said slowly: "Well, then, my sunbonnet is in my trunk. I'm not so far away from it but that it still travels with me. It's blue chambray, made from pieces left from my first pretty dress. It is ruffled, and has white stitching. I made it myself. The head that it fits is another matter. I didn't make that, or its environment, or what was taught it, until it was of age, and had worked out its legal time of service to pay for having been a head at all. But my head is now free, in my own possession, ready to go as fast and far on the path of life as it develops the brains to carry it. You'd smile if I should tell you what I'd ask of life, if I could have what I want."

"I scarcely think so. Please tell me."

"You'll be shocked," warned Kate.

"Just so it isn't enough to set my heart rocking again," said Mrs. Jardine.

"We'll stop before that," laughed Kate. "Then if you will have it, I want of life by the time I am twenty a man of my stature, dark eyes and hair, because I am so light. I want him to be honest, forceful, hard working, with a few drops of the milk of human kindness in his heart, and the same ambitions I have."

"And what ARE your ambitions?" asked Mrs. Jardine.

"To own, and to cultivate, and to bring to the highest state of efficiency at least two hundred acres of land, with convenient and attractive buildings and pedigreed stock, and to mother at least twelve perfect physical and mental boys and girls."

"Oh, my soul!" cried Mrs. Jardine, falling back in her chair, her mouth agape. "My dear, you don't MEAN that? You only said that to shock me."

"But why should I wish to shock you? I sincerely mean it," persisted Kate.

"You amazing creature! I never heard a girl talk like that before," said Mrs. Jardine.

"But you can't look straight ahead of you any direction you turn without seeing a girl working for dear life to attract the man she wants; if she can't secure him, some other man; and in lieu of him, any man at all, in preference to none. Life shows us woman on the age-old quest every day, everywhere we go; why be so secretive about it? Why not say honestly what we want, and take it if we can get it? At any rate, that is the most important thing inside my sunbonnet. I knew you'd be shocked."

"But I am not shocked at what you say, I agree with you. What I am shocked at is your ideals. I thought you'd want to educate yourself to such superiority over common woman that you could take the platform, and backed by your splendid physique, work for suffrage or lecture to educate the masses."

"I think more could be accomplished with selected specimens, by being steadily on the job, than by giving an hour to masses. I'm not much interested in masses. They are too abstract for me; I prefer one stern reality. And as for Woman's Rights, if anybody gives this woman the right to do anything more than she already has the right to do, there'll surely be a scandal."

Mrs. Jardine lay back in her chair laughing.

"You are the most refreshing person I have met in all my travels. Then to put it baldly, you want of life a man, a farm, and a family."

"You comprehend me beautifully," said Kate. "All my life I've worked like a towhead to help earn two hundred acres of land for someone else. I think there's nothing I want so much as two hundred acres of land for myself. I'd undertake to do almost anything with it, if I had it. I know I could, if I had the shoulder-to-shoulder, real man. You notice it will take considerable of a man to touch shoulders with me; I'm a head taller than most of them."

Mrs. Jardine looked at her speculatively. "Ummm!" she murmured. Kate laughed.

"For eighteen years I have been under marching orders," said Kate. "Over a year ago I was advised by a minister to 'take the wings of morning' so I took wing. I started on one grand flight and fell ker-smash in short order. Life since has been a series of battering my wings until I have almost decided to buy some especially heavy boots, and walk the remainder of the way. As a concrete example, I started out yesterday morning wearing a hat that several very reliable parties assured me would so assist me to flight that I might at least have a carriage. Where, oh, where are my hat and my carriage now? The carriage, non est! The hat—I am humbly hoping some little country girl, who has lived a life as barren as mine, will find the remains and retrieve the velvet bow for a hair-ribbon. As for the man that Leghorn hat was supposed to symbolize, he won't even look my way when I appear in my bobby little sailor. He's as badly crushed out of existence as my beautiful hat."

"You never should have been wearing such a hat to travel in, my dear," murmured Mrs. Jardine.

"Certainly not!" said Kate. "I knew it. My sister told me that. Common sense told me that! But what has that got to do with the fact that I WAS wearing the hat? I guess I have you there!"

"Far from it!" said Mrs. Jardine. "If you're going to start out in life, calmly ignoring the advice of those who love you, and the dictates of common sense, the result will be that soon the wheels of life will be grinding you, instead of a train making bag-rags of your hat."

"Hummm!" said Kate. "There IS food for reflection there. But wasn't it plain logic, that if the hat was to bring the man, it should be worn where at any minute he might see it?"

"But my dear, my dear! If such a man as a woman like you should have, had seen you wearing that hat in the morning, on a railway train, he would merely have thought you prideful and extravagant. You would have been far more attractive to any man I know in your blue sunbonnet."

"I surely have learned that lesson," said Kate. "Hereafter, sailors or sunbonnets for me in the morning. Now what may I do to add to your comfort?"

"Leave me for an hour until I take a nap, and then we'll have lunch and go to a lecture. I can go to-day, perfectly well, after an hour's rest."

So Kate went for a very interesting walk around the grounds. When she returned Mrs. Jardine was still sleeping so she wrote Nancy Ellen, telling all about her adventure, but not a word about losing her hat. Then she had a talk with Jennie Weeks whom she found lingering in the hall near her door. When at last that nap was over, a new woman seemed to have developed. Mrs. Jardine was so refreshed and interested the remainder of the day that it was easier than before for Kate to see how shocked and ill she had been. As she helped dress her for lunch, Kate said to Mrs. Jardine: "I met the manager as I was going to post a letter to my sister, so I asked him always to send you the same waiter. He said he would, and I'd like you to pay particular attention to her appearance, and the way she does her work."

"Why?" asked Mrs. Jardine.

"I met her in the hall as I came back from posting my letter, so we 'visited' a little, as the country folks say. She has taught one winter of country school, a small school in an out county. She's here waiting table two hours three times a day, to pay for her room and board. In the meantime, she attends all the sessions and studies as much as she can; but she's very poor material for a teacher. I pity her pupils. She's a little thing, bright enough in her way, but she has not much initiative, not strong enough for the work, and she has not enough spunk. She'll never lead the minds of school children anywhere that will greatly benefit them."

"And your deduction is—"

"That she would make you a kind, careful, obedient maid, who is capable enough to be taught to wash your hair and manicure you with deftness, and who would serve you for respect as well as hire. I think it would be a fine arrangement for you and good for her."

"This surely is kind of you," said Mrs. Jardine. "I'll keep strict watch of Jennie Weeks. If I could find a really capable maid here and not have to wire John to bring one, I'd be so glad. It does so go against the grain to prove to a man that he has a right to be more conceited than he is naturally."

As they ate lunch Kate said to Mrs. Jardine: "I noticed one thing this morning that is going to be balm to my soul. I passed many teachers and summer resorters going to the lecture halls and coming from them, and half of them were bareheaded, so my state will not be remarkable, until I can get another hat."

"'God moves in a mysterious way, His wonders to perform,'" laughingly quoted Mrs. Jardine. "You thought losing that precious hat was a calamity; but if you hadn't lost it, you probably would have slept soundly while I died across the hall. My life is worth the price of a whole millinery shop to me; I think you value the friendship we are developing; I foresee I shall get a maid who will not disgrace my in public; you will have a full summer here; now truly, isn't all this worth many hats?"

"Of course! It's like a fairy tale," said Kate. "Still, you didn't see the hat!"

"But you described it in a truly graphic manner," said Mrs. Jardine.

"When I am the snowiest of great-grandmothers, I shall still be telling small people about the outcome of my first attempt at vanity," laughed Kate.

The third morning dawned in great beauty, a "misty, moisty morning," Mrs. Jardine called it. The sun tried to shine but could not quite pierce the intervening clouds, so on every side could be seen exquisite pictures painted in delicate pastel colours. Kate, fresh and rosy, wearing a blue chambray dress, was a picture well worth seeing. Mrs. Jardine kept watching her so closely that Kate asked at last: "Have you made up your mind, yet?"

"No, and I am afraid I never shall," answered Mrs. Jardine. "You are rather an astonishing creature. You're so big, so vital; you absorb knowledge like a sponge takes water—"

"And for the same purpose," laughed Kate. "That it may be used for the benefit of others. Tell me some more about me. I find me such an interesting subject."

"No doubt!" admitted Mrs. Jardine. "Not a doubt about that! We are all more interested in ourselves than in any one else in this world, until love comes; then we soon learn to a love man more than life, and when a child comes we learn another love, so clear, so high, so purifying, that we become of no moment at all, and live only for those we love."

"You speak for yourself, and a class of women like you," answered Kate gravely. "I'm very well acquainted with many women who have married and borne children, and who are possibly more selfish than before. The Great Experience never touched them at all."

There was a tap at the door. Kate opened it and delivered to Mrs. Jardine a box so big that it almost blocked the doorway.

Mrs. Jardine lifted from the box a big Leghorn hat of weave so white and fine it almost seemed like woven cloth instead of braid. There was a bow in front, but the bow was nested in and tied through a web of flowered gold lace. One velvet end was slightly long and concealed a wire which lifted one side of the brim a trifle, beneath which was fastened a smashing big, pale-pink velvet rose. There was an ostrich plume even longer than the other, broader, blacker, as wonderful a feather as ever dropped from the plumage of a lordly bird. Mrs. Jardine shook the hat in such a way as to set the feather lifting and waving after the confinement of the box. With slender, sure fingers she set the bow and lace as they should be, and touched the petals of the rose. She inspected the hat closely, shook it again, and held it toward Kate.

"A very small price to pay for the breath of life, which I was rapidly losing," she said. "Do me the favour to accept it as casually as I offer it. Did I understand your description anywhere near right? Is this your hat?"

"Thank you," said Kate. "It is just 'the speaking image' of my hat, but it's a glorified, sublimated, celestial image. What I described was merely a hat. This is what I think I have lately heard Nancy Ellen mention as a 'creation.' Wheuuuuuu!"

She went to the mirror, arranged her hair, set the hat on her head, and turned.

"Gracious Heaven!" said Mrs. Jardine. "My dear, I understand NOW why you wore that hat on your journey."

"I wore that hat," said Kate, "as an ascension stalk wears its crown of white lilies, as a bobolink wears its snowy courting crest, as a bride wears her veil; but please take this from me to-night, lest I sleep in it!"

That night Mrs. Jardine felt tired enough to propose resting in her room, with Jennie Weeks where she could be called; so for the first time Kate left her, and, donning her best white dress and the hat, attended a concert. At its close she walked back to the hotel with some of the other teachers stopping there, talked a few minutes in the hall, went to the office desk for mail, and slowly ascended the stairs, thinking intently. What she thought was: "If I am not mistaken, my hat did a small bit of execution to-night." She stepped to her room to lock the door and stopped a few minutes to arrange the clothing she had discarded when she dressed hurriedly before going to the concert, then, the letters in her hand, she opened Mrs. Jardine's door.

A few minutes before, there had been a tap on that same door.

"Come in," said Mrs. Jardine, expecting Kate or Jennie Weeks. She slowly lifted her eyes and faced a tall, slender man standing there.

"John Jardine, what in the world are you doing here?" she demanded after the manner of mothers, "and what in this world has happened to you?"

"Does it show on me like that?" he stammered.

"Was your train in a wreck? Are you in trouble?" she asked. "Something shows plainly enough, but I don't understand what it is."

"Are you all right, Mother?" He advanced a step, looking intently at her.

"Of course I'm all right! You can see that for yourself. The question is, what's the matter with you?"

"If you will have it, there is something the matter. Since I saw you last I have seen a woman I want to marry, that's all; unless I add that I want her so badly that I haven't much sense left. Now you have it!"

"No, I don't have it, and I won't have it! What designing creature has been trying to intrigue you now?" she demanded.

"Not any one. She didn't see me, even. I saw her. I've been following her for nearly two hours instead of coming straight to you, as I always have. So you see where I am. I expect you won't forgive me, but since I'm here, you must know that I could only come on the evening train."

He crossed the room, knelt beside the chair, and took it and its contents in his arms.

"Are you going to scold me?" he asked.

"I am," she said. "I am going to take you out and push you into the deepest part of the lake. I'm so disappointed. Why, John, for the first time in my life I've selected a girl for you, the very most suitable girl I ever saw, and I hoped and hoped for three days that when you came you'd like her. Of course I wasn't so rash as to say a word to her! But I've thought myself into a state where I'm going to be sick with disappointment."

"But wait, Mother, wait until I can manage to meet the girl I've seen. Wait until I have a chance to show her to you!" he begged.

"I suppose I shall be forced," she said. "I've always dreaded it, now here it comes. Oh, why couldn't it have been Kate? Why did she go to that silly concert? If only I'd kept her here, and we'd walked down to the station. I'd half a mind to!"

Then the door opened, and Kate stepped into the room. She stood still, looking at them. John Jardine stood up, looking at her. His mother sat staring at them in turn. Kate recovered first.

"Please excuse me," she said.

She laid the letters on a small table and turned to go. John caught his mother's hand closer, when he found himself holding it.

"If you know the young lady, Mother," he said, "why don't you introduce us?"

"Oh, I was so bewildered by your coming," she said. "Kate, dear, let me present my son."

Kate crossed the room, and looking straight into each other's eyes they shook hands and found chairs.

"How was your concert, my dear?" asked Mrs. Jardine.

"I don't think it was very good," said Kate. "Not at all up to my expectations. How did you like it, Mr. Jardine?"

"Was that a concert?" he asked.

"It was supposed to be," said Kate.

"Thank you for the information," he said. "I didn't see it, I didn't hear it, I don't know where I was."

"This is most astonishing," said Kate.

Mrs. Jardine looked at her son, her eyes two big imperative question marks. He nodded slightly.

"My soul!" she cried, then lay back in her chair half-laughing, half-crying, until Kate feared she might have another attack of heart trouble.

CHAPTER X

JOHN JARDINE'S COURTSHIP

THE following morning they breakfasted together under the branches of the big maple tree in a beautiful world. Mrs. Jardine was so happy she could only taste a bite now and then, when urged to. Kate was trying to keep her head level, and be natural. John Jardine wanted to think of everything, and succeeded fairly well. It seemed to Kate that he could invent more ways to spend money, and spend it with freer hand, than any man she ever had heard of, but she had to confess that the men she had heard about were concerned with keeping their money, not scattering it.

"Did you hear unusual sounds when John came to bid me good-night?" asked Mrs. Jardine of Kate.

"Yes," laughed Kate, "I did. And I'm sure I made a fairly accurate guess as to the cause."

"What did you think?" asked Mrs. Jardine.

"I thought Mr. Jardine had missed Susette, and you'd had to tell him," said Kate.

"You're quite right. It's a good thing she went on and lost herself in New York. I'm not at all sure that he doesn't contemplate starting out to find her yet."

"Let Susette go!" said Kate. "We're interested in forgetting her. There's a little country school-teacher here, who wants to take her place, and it will be the very thing for your mother and for her, too. She's the one serving us; notice her in particular."

"If she's a teacher, how does she come to be serving us?" he asked.

"I'm a teacher; how do I come to be dining with you?" said Kate. "This is such a queer world, when you go adventuring in it. Jennie had a small school in an out county, a widowed mother and a big family to help support; so she figured that the only way she could come here to try to prepare herself for a better school was to work for her room and board. She serves the table two hours, three times a day, and studies between times. She tells me that almost every waiter in the dining hall is a teacher. Please watch her movements and manner and see if you think her suitable. Goodness knows she isn't intended for a teacher."

"I like her very much," said John Jardine. "I'll engage her as soon as we finish."

Kate smiled, but when she saw the ease and dexterity with which he ended Jennie Weeks' work as a waiter and installed her as his mother's maid, making the least detail all right with his mother, with Jennie, with the manager, she realized that there had been nothing for her to smile about. Jennie was delighted, and began her new undertaking earnestly, with sincere desire to please. Kate helped her all she could, while Mrs. Jardine developed a fund of patience commensurate with the need of it. She would have endured more inconvenience than resulted from Jennie's inexperienced hands because of the realization that her son and the girl she had so quickly learned to admire were on the lake, rambling the woods, or hearing lectures together.

When she asked him how long he could remain, he said as long as she did. When she explained that she was enjoying herself thoroughly and had no idea how long she would want to stay, he said that was all right; he had only had one vacation in his life; it was time he was having another. When she marvelled at this he said: "Now, look here, Mother, let's get this business straight, right at the start. I told you when I came I'd seen the woman I wanted. If you want me to go back to business, the way to do it is to help me win her."

"But I don't want you 'to go back to business'; I want you to have a long vacation, and learn all you can from the educational advantages here."

"It's too late for me to learn more than I get every day by knocking around and meeting people. I've tried books two or three times, and I've given them up; I can't do it. I've waited too long, I've no way to get down to it, I can't remember to save my soul."

"But you can remember anything on earth about a business deal," she urged.

"Of course I can. I was born with a business head. It was remember, or starve, and see you starve. If I'd had the books at the time they would have helped; now it's too late, and I'll never try it again, that's settled. Much as I want to marry Miss Bates, she'll have to take me or leave me as I am. I can't make myself over for her or for you. I would if I could, but that's one of the things I can't do, and I admit it. If I'm not good enough for her as I am, she'll have the chance to tell me so the very first minute I think it's proper to ask her."

"John, you are good enough for the best woman on earth. There never was a better lad, it isn't that, and you know it. I am so anxious that I can scarcely wait; but you must wait. You must give her time and go slowly, and you must be careful, oh, so very careful! She's a teacher and a student; she came here to study."

"I'll fix that. I can rush things so that there'll be no time to study."

"You'll make a mistake if you try it. You'd far better let her go her own way and only appear when she has time for you," she advised.

"That's a fine idea!" he cried. "A lot of ice I'd cut, sitting back waiting for a signal to run after a girl, like a poodle. The way to do is the same as with any business deal. See what you want, overcome anything in your way, and get it. I'd go crazy hanging around like that. You've always told me I couldn't do the things in business I said I would; and I've always proved to you that I could, by doing them. Now watch me do this."

"You know I'll do anything to help you, John. You know how proud I am of you, how I love you! I realize now that I've talked volumes to Kate about you. I've told her everything from the time you were a little boy and I slaved for you, until now, when you slave for me."

"Including how many terms I'd gone to school?"

"Yes, I even told her that," she said.

"Well, what did she seem to think about it?" he asked.

"I don't know what she thought, she didn't say anything. There was nothing to say. It was a bare-handed fight with the wolf in those days. I'm sure I made her understand that," she said.

"Well, I'll undertake to make her understand this," he said. "Are you sure that Jennie Weeks is taking good care of you?"

"Jennie is well enough and is growing better each day, now be off to your courting, but if you love me, remember, and be careful," she said.

"Remember—one particular thing—you mean?" he asked.

She nodded, her lips closed.

"You bet I will!" he said. "All there is of me goes into this. Isn't she a wonder, Mother?"

Mrs. Jardine looked closely at the big man who was all the world to her, so like her in mentality, so like his father with his dark hair and eyes and big, well-rounded frame; looked at him with the eyes of love, then as he left her to seek the girl she had learned to love, she shut her eyes and frankly and earnestly asked the Lord to help her son to marry Kate Bates.

One morning as Kate helped Mrs. Jardine into her coat and gloves, preparing for one of their delightful morning drives, she said to her: "Mrs. Jardine, may I ask you a REAL question?"

"Of course you may," said Mrs. Jardine, "and I shall give you a 'real' answer if it lies in my power."

"You'll be shocked," warned Kate.

"Shock away," laughed Mrs. Jardine. "By now I flatter myself that I am so accustomed to you that you will have to try yourself to shock me."

"It's only this," said Kate: "If you were a perfect stranger, standing back and looking on, not acquainted with any of the parties, merely seeing things as they happen each day, would it be your honest opinion—would you say that I am being COURTED?"

Mrs. Jardine laughed until she was weak. When she could talk, she said: "Yes, my dear, under the conditions, and in the circumstances you mention, I would cheerfully go on oath and testify that you are being courted more openly, more vigorously, and as tenderly as I ever have seen woman courted in all my life. I always thought that John's father was a master hand at courting, but John has him beaten in many ways. Yes, my dear, you certainly are being courted assiduously."

"Now, then, on that basis," said Kate, "just one more question and we'll proceed with our drive. From the same standpoint: would you say from your observation and experience that the mother of the man had any insurmountable objection to the proceedings?"

Mrs. Jardine laughed again. Finally she said: "No, my dear. It's my firm conviction that the mother of the man in the case would be so delighted if you should love and marry her son that she would probably have a final attack of heart trouble and pass away from sheer joy."

"Thank you," said Kate. "I wasn't perfectly sure, having had no experience whatever, and I didn't want to make a mistake."

That drive was wonderful, over beautiful country roads, through dells, and across streams and hills. They stopped where they pleased, gathering flowers and early apples, visiting with people they met, lunching wherever they happened to be.

"If it weren't for wishing to hear John A. Logan to-night," said Kate, "I'd move that we drive on all day. I certainly am having the grandest time."

She sat with her sailor hat filled with Early Harvest apples, a big bunch of Canadian anemones in her belt, a little stream at her feet, July drowsy fullness all around her, congenial companions; taking the "wings of morning" paid, after all.

"Why do you want to hear him so much?" asked John.

Kate looked up at him in wonder.

"Don't you want to see and hear him?" she asked.

He hesitated, a thoughtful expression on his face. Finally he said: "I can't say that I do. Will you tell me why I should?"

"You should because he was one of the men who did much to preserve our Union, he may tell us interesting things about the war. Where were you when it was the proper time for you to be studying the speech of Logan's ancestor in McGuffey's Fourth?"

"That must have been the year I figured out the improved coupling pin in the C. N. W. shops, wouldn't you think, Mother?"

"Somewhere near, my dear," she said.

So they drove back as happily as they had set out, made themselves fresh, and while awaiting the lecture hour, Kate again wrote to Robert and Nancy Ellen, telling plainly and simply all that had occurred. She even wrote "John Jardine's mother is of the opinion that he is courting me. I am so lacking in experience myself that I scarcely dare venture an opinion, but it has at times appealed to me that if he isn't really, he certainly must be going through the motions."

Nancy Ellen wrote: I have read over what you say about John Jardine several times. Then I had Robert write Bradstreet's and look him up. He is rated so high that if he hasn't a million right now, he soon will have. You be careful, and do your level best. Are your clothes good enough? Shall I send more of my things? You know I'll do anything to help you. Oh, yes, that George Holt from your boarding place was here the other day hunting you. He seemed determined to know where you were and when you would be back, and asked for your address. I didn't think you had any time for him and I couldn't endure him or his foolish talk about a new medical theory; so I said you'd no time for writing and were going about so much I had no idea if you'd get a letter if he sent one, and I didn't give him what he wanted. He'll probably try general delivery, but you can drop it in the lake. I want you to be sure to change your boarding place this winter, if you teach; but I haven't an idea you will. Hadn't you better bring matters to a close if you can, and let the Director know? Love from us both, NANCY ELLEN.

Kate sat very still, holding this letter in her hand, when John Jardine came up and sat beside her. She looked at him closely. He was quite as good looking as his mother thought him, in a brawny masculine way; but Kate was not seeking the last word in mental or physical refinement. She was rather brawny herself, and perfectly aware of the fact. She wanted intensely to learn all she could, she disliked the idea that any woman should have more stored in her head than she, but she had no time to study minute social graces and customs. She wanted to be kind, to be polite, but she told Mrs. Jardine flatly the "she didn't give a flip about being overly nice," which was the exact truth. That required subtleties beyond Kate's depth, for she was at times alarmingly casual. So she held her letter and thought about John Jardine. As she thought, she decided that she did not know whether she was in love with him or not; she thought she was. She liked being with him, she liked all he did for her, she would miss him if he went away, she would be proud to be his wife, but she did wish that he were interested in land, instead of inventions and stocks and bonds. Stocks and bonds were almost as evanescent as rainbows to Kate. Land was something she could understand and handle. Maybe she could interest him in land; if she could, that would be ideal. What a place his wealth would buy and fit up. She wondered as she studied John Jardine, what was in his head; if he truly intended to ask her to be his wife, and since reading Nancy Ellen's letter, when? She should let the Trustee know if she were not going to teach the school again; but someway, she rather wanted to teach the school. When she started anything she did not know how to stop until she finished. She had so much she wanted to teach her pupils the coming winter.

Suddenly John asked: "Kate, if you could have anything you wanted, what would you have?"

"Two hundred acres of land," she said.

"How easy!" laughed John, rising to find a seat for his mother who was approaching them. "What do you think of that, Mother? A girl who wants two hundred acres of land more than anything else in the world."

"What is better?" asked Mrs. Jardine.

"I never heard you say anything about land before."

"Certainly not," said his mother, "and I'm not saying anything about it now, for myself; but I can see why it means so much to Kate, why it's her natural element."

"Well, I can't," he said. "I meet many men in business who started on land, and most of them were mighty glad to get away from it. What's the attraction?"

Kate waved her hand toward the distance.

"Oh, merely sky, and land, and water, and trees, and birds, and flowers, and fruit, and crops, and a few other things scarcely worth mentioning," she said, lightly. "I'm not in the mood to talk bushels, seed, and fertilization just now; but I understand them, they are in my blood. I think possibly the reason I want two hundred acres of land for myself is because I've been hard on the job of getting them for other people ever since I began to work, at about the age of four."

"But if you want land personally, why didn't you work to get it for yourself?" asked John Jardine.

"Because I happened to be the omega of my father's system," answered Kate.

Mrs. Jardine looked at her interestedly. She had never mentioned her home or parents before. The older woman did not intend to ask a word, but if Kate was going to talk, she did not want to miss one. Kate evidently was going to talk, for she continued: "You see my father is land mad, and son crazy. He thinks a BOY of all the importance in the world; a GIRL of none whatever. He has the biggest family of any one we know. From birth each girl is worked like a man, or a slave, from four in the morning until nine at night. Each boy is worked exactly the same way; the difference lies in the fact that the girls get plain food and plainer clothes out of it; the boys each get two hundred acres of land, buildings and stock, that the girls have been worked to the limit to help pay for; they get nothing personally, worth mentioning. I think I have two hundred acres of land on the brain, and I think this is the explanation of it. It's a pre-natal influence at our house; while we nurse, eat, sleep, and above all, WORK it, afterward."

She paused and looked toward John Jardine calmly: "I think," she said, "that there's not a task ever performed on a farm that I haven't had my share in. I have plowed, hoed, seeded, driven reapers and bound wheat, pitched hay and hauled manure, chopped wood and sheared sheep, and boiled sap; if you can mention anything else, go ahead, I bet a dollar I've done it."

"Well, what do you think of that?" he muttered, looking at her wonderingly.

"If you ask me, and want the answer in plain words, I think it's a shame!" said Kate. "If it were ONE HUNDRED acres of land, and the girls had as much, and were as willing to work it as the boys are, well and good. But to drive us like cattle, and turn all we earn into land for the boys, is another matter. I rebelled last summer, borrowed the money and went to Normal and taught last winter. I'm going to teach again this winter; but last summer and this are the first of my life that I haven't been in the harvest fields, at this time. Women in the harvest fields of Land King

Bates are common as men, and wagons, and horses, but not nearly so much considered. The women always walk on Sunday, to save the horses, and often on week days."

"Mother has it hammered into me that it isn't polite to ask questions," said John, "but I'd like to ask one."

"Go ahead," said Kate. "Ask fifty! What do I care?"

"How many boys are there in your family?"

"There are seven," said Kate, "and if you want to use them as a basis for a land estimate add two hundred and fifty for the home place. Sixteen hundred and fifty is what Father pays tax on, besides the numerous mortgages and investments. He's the richest man in the county we live in; at least he pays the most taxes."

Mother and son looked at each other in silence. They had been thinking her so poor that she would be bewildered by what they had to offer. But if two hundred acres of land were her desire, there was a possibility that she was a women who was not asking either ease or luxury of life, and would refuse it if it were proffered.

"I hope you will take me home with you, and let me see all that land, and how it is handled," said John Jardine. "I don't own an acre. I never even have thought of it, but there is no reason why I, or any member of my family shouldn't have all the land they want. Mother, do you feel a wild desire for two hundred acres of land? Same kind of a desire that took you to come here?"

"No, I don't," said Mrs. Jardine. "All I know about land is that I know it when I see it, and I know if I think it's pretty; but I can see why Kate feels that she would like that amount for herself, after having helped earn all those farms for her brothers. If it's land she wants, I hope she speedily gets all she desires in whatever location she wants it; and then I hope she lets me come to visit her and watch her do as she likes with it."

"Surely," said Kate, "you are invited right now; as soon as I ever get the land, I'll give you another invitation. And of course you may go home with me, Mr. Jardine, and I'll show you each of what Father calls 'those little parcels of land of mine.' But the one he lives on we shall have to gaze at from afar, because I'm a Prodigal Daughter. When I would leave home in spite of him for the gay and riotous life of a school-marm, he ordered me to take all my possessions with me, which I did in one small telescope. I was not to enter his house again while he lived. I was glad to go, he was glad to have me, while I don't think either of us has changed our mind since. Teaching school isn't exactly gay, but I'll fill my tummy with quite a lot of symbolical husks before he'll kill the fatted calf for me. They'll be glad to see you at my brother Adam's, and my sister, Nancy Ellen, would greatly enjoy meeting you. Surely you may go home with me, if you'd like."

"I can think of only one thing I'd like better," he said. "We've been such good friends here and had such a good time, it would be the thing I'd like best to take you home with us, and show you where and how we live. Mother, did you ever invite Kate to visit us?"

"I have, often, and she has said that she would," replied Mrs. Jardine. "I think it would be nice for her to go from here with us; and then you can take her home whenever she fails to find us interesting. How would that suit you for a plan, my dear?"

"I think that would be a perfect ending to a perfect summer," said Kate. "I can't see an objection in any way. Thank you very much."

"Then we'll call that settled," said John Jardine.

CHAPTER XI

A BUSINESS PROPOSITION

MID-AUGUST saw them on their way to Chicago. Kate had taken care of Mrs. Jardine a few days while Jennie Weeks went home to see her mother and arrange for her new work. She had no intention of going back to school teaching. She preferred to brush Mrs. Jardine's hair, button her shoes, write her letters, and read to her.

In a month, Jennie had grown so deft at her work and made herself so appreciated, that she was practically indispensable to the elderly woman, and therefore the greatest comfort to John. Immediately he saw that his mother was properly cared for, sympathetically and even lovingly, he made it his business to smooth Jennie's path in every way possible. In turn she studied him, and in many ways made herself useful to him. Often she looked at him with large and speculative eyes as he sat reading letters, or papers, or smoking.

The world was all right with Kate when they crossed the sand dunes as they neared the city. She was sorry about the situation in her home, but she smiled sardonically as she thought how soon her father would forget his anger when he heard about the city home and the kind of farm she could have, merely by consenting to take it. She was that sure of John Jardine; yet he had not asked her to marry him. He had seemed on the verge of it a dozen times, and then had paused as if better judgment told him it would be wise to wait a little longer. Now Kate had concluded that there was a definite thing he might be waiting for, since that talk about land.

She thought possibly she understood what it was. He was a business man; he knew nothing else; he said so frankly. He wanted to show her his home, his business, his city, his friends, and then he required—he had almost put it into words—that he be shown her home and her people. Kate not only acquiesced, she approved. She wanted to know as much of a man she married as Nancy Ellen had known, and Robert had taken her to his home and told his people she was his betrothed wife before he married her.

Kate's eyes were wide open and her brain busy, as they entered a finely appointed carriage and she heard John say: "Rather sultry. Home down the lake shore, George." She wished their driver had not been named "George," but after all it made no difference. There could not be a commoner name than John, and she knew of but one that she liked better. For the ensuing three days she lived in a Lake Shore home of wealth. She watched closely not to trip in the heavy rugs and carpets. She looked at wonderful paintings and long shelves of books. She never had touched such china, or tasted such food or seen so good service. She understood why John had opposed his mother's undertaking the trip without him, for everyone in the house seemed busy serving the little woman.

Jennie Weeks was frankly enchanted.

"My sakes!" she said to Kate. "If I'm not grateful to you for getting me into a place like this. I wouldn't give it up for all the school-teaching in the world. I'm going to snuggle right in here, and make myself so useful I won't have to leave until I die. I hope you won't turn me out when to come to take charge."

"Don't you think you're presuming?" said Kate.

Jennie drew back with a swift apology, but there was a flash in the little eyes and a spiteful look on the small face as she withdrew.

Then Kate was shown each of John's wonderful inventions. To her they seemed almost miracles, because they were so obvious, so simple, yet brought such astounding returns. She saw offices and heard the explanation of big business; but did not comprehend, farther than that when an invention was completed, the piling up of money began. Before the week's visit was over, Kate was trying to fit herself and her aims and objects of life into the surroundings, with no success whatever. She felt housed in, cribbed, confined, frustrated. When she realized that she was becoming plainly cross, she began keen self-analysis and soon admitted to herself that she did not belong there.

Kate watched with keen eyes. Repeatedly she tried to imagine herself in such surroundings for life, a life sentence, she expressed it, for soon she understood that it would be to her, a prison. The only way she could imagine herself enduring it at all was to think of the promised farm, and when she began to think of that on Jardine terms, she saw that it would mean to sit down and tell someone else what she wanted done. There would be no battle to fight. Her mind kept harking back to the day when she had said to John that she hoped there would be a lake on the land she owned, and he had answered casually: "If there isn't a lake, make one!" Kate thought that over repeatedly. "Make one!" Make a lake? It would have seemed no more magical to her if he had said, "Make a cloud," "Make a star," or "Make a rainbow." "What on earth would I do with myself, with my time, with my life?" pondered Kate.

She said "Good-bye" to Mrs. Jardine and Jennie Weeks, and started home with John, still pondering. When the train pulled into Hartley, Nancy Ellen and Robert were on the platform to meet them. From that time, Kate was on solid ground. She was reckoning in terms she could comprehend. All her former assurance and energy came back to her. She almost wished the visit were over, and that she were on the way to Walton to clean the school-house. She was eager to roll her sleeves and beat a tub of soapy clothes to foam, and boil them snowy white. She had a desire she could scarcely control to sweep, and dust, and cook. She had been out of the environment she thought she disliked and found when she returned to it after a wider change than she could have imagined, that she did not dislike it at all. It was her element, her work, what she knew. She could attempt it with sure foot, capable hand, and certain knowledge.

Sunday morning she said to Nancy Ellen as they washed the breakfast dishes, while the men smoked on the veranda: "Nancy Ellen, I don't believe I was ever cut out for a rich woman! If I have got a chance, I wish YOU had it, and I had THIS. This just suits my style to a T."

"Tell me about it," said Nancy Ellen.

Kate told all she could remember.

"You don't mean to say you didn't LIKE it?" cried Nancy Ellen.

"I didn't say anything," said Kate, "but if I were saying exactly what I feel, you'd know I despise it all."

"Why, Kate Barnes!" cried the horrified Nancy Ellen, "Whatever do you mean?"

"I haven't thought enough to put it to you clearly," said Kate, "but someway the city repels me. Facilities for manufacturing something start a city. It begins with the men who do the work, and the men who profit from that work, living in the same coop. It expands, and goes on, and grows, on that basis. It's the laborer, living on his hire, and the manufacturer living on the laborer's productions, coming in daily contact. The contrast is too great, the space is too small. Somebody is going to get the life crowded out of him at every turn, and it isn't always the work hand in the factory. The money kings eat each other for breakfast every day. As for work, we always thought we worked. You should take a peep into the shops and factories I've seen this week. Work? Why, we don't know what work is, and we waste enough food every day to keep a workman's family, and we're dressed liked queens, in comparison with them right now."

"Do you mean to say if he asks you—?" It was a small explosion.

"I mean to say if he asks me, 'buy me that two hundred acres of land where I want it, build me the house and barns I want, and guarantee that I may live there as I please, and I'll marry you to-morrow.' If it's Chicago—Never! I haven't stolen, murdered, or betrayed, who should I be imprisoned?"

"Why, you hopeless anarchist!" said Nancy Ellen, "I am going to tell John Jardine on you."

"Do!" urged Kate. "Sound him on the land question. It's our only hope of a common foundation. Have you send Agatha word that we will be out this afternoon?"

"I have," said Nancy Ellen. "And I don't doubt that now, even now, she is in the kitchen—how would she put it?"

"'Compounding a cake,'" said Kate, "while Adam is in the cellar 'freezing a custard.' Adam, 3d, will be raking the yard afresh and Susan will be sweeping the walks steadily from now until they sight us coming down the road. What you bet Agatha asked John his intentions? I almost wish she would," she added. "He has some, but there is a string to them in some way, and I can't just make out where, or why it is."

"Not even a guess?" asked Nancy Ellen.

"Not even a guess, with any sense to it. I've thought it was coming repeatedly; but I've got a stubborn Bates streak, and I won't lift a finger to help him. He'll speak up, loud and plain, or there will be no 'connubial bliss' for us, as Agatha says. I think he has ideas about other things than freight train gear. According to his programme we must have so much time to become acquainted, I must see his home and people, he must see mine. If there's more after that, I'm not informed. Like as not there is. It may come after we get back to-night, I can't say."

"Have you told him—?" asked Nancy Ellen.

"Not the details, but the essentials. He knows that I can't go home. It came up one day in talking about land. I guess they had thought before, that my people were poor as church mice. I happened to mention how much land I had helped earn for my brothers, and they seemed so interested I finished the job. Well, after they had heard about the Land King, it made a noticeable difference in their treatment of me. Not that they weren't always fine, but it made, I scarcely know how to put it, it was so intangible—but it was a difference, an added respect. You bet money is a power! I can see why Father hangs on to those deeds, when I get out in the world. They are his compensation for his years of hard work, the material evidence that he has succeeded in what he undertook. He'd show them to John Jardine with the same feeling John showed me improved car couplers, brakes, and air cushions. They stand for successes that win the deference of men. Out in the little bit of world I've seen, I notice that men fight, bleed, and die for even a tiny fraction of deference. Aren't they funny? What would I care—?"

"Well, I'D care a lot!" said Nancy Ellen.

Kate surveyed her slowly. "Yes, I guess you would."

They finished the dishes and went to church, because Robert was accustomed to going. They made a remarkable group. Then they went to the hotel for dinner, so that the girls would not have to prepare it, and then in a double carriage Robert had secured for the occasion, they drove to Bates Corners and as Kate said, "Viewed the landscape o'er." Those eight pieces of land, none under two hundred acres, some slightly over, all in the very highest state of cultivation, with modern houses, barns, outbuildings, and fine stock grazing in the pastures, made an impressive picture. It was probably the first time that any of the Bates girls had seen it all at once, and looked on it merely as a spectacle. They stopped at Adam's last, and while Robert was busy with the team and John had alighted to help him, Nancy Ellen, revealing tight lips and unnaturally red cheeks, leaned back to Kate.

"This is about as mean a trick, and as big a shame as I've ever seen," she said, hotly. "You know I was brought up with this, and I never looked at it with the eyes of a stranger before. If ever I get my fingers on those deeds, I'll make short work of them!"

"And a good job, too!" assented Kate, instantly. "Look out! There comes Adam."

"I'd just as soon tell him so as not!" whispered Nancy Ellen.

"Which would result in the deeds being recorded to-morrow and spoiling our trip to-day, and what good would it do you?" said Kate.

"None, of course! Nothing ever does a Bates girl any good, unless she gets out and does it for herself," retorted Nancy Ellen spitefully.

"There, there," said Robert as he came to help Nancy Ellen protect her skirts in alighting. "I was afraid this trip would breed discontent."

"What's the trouble?" asked John, as he performed the same service for Kate.

"Oh, the girls are grouching a little because they helped earn all this, and are to be left out of it," explained Robert in a low voice.

"Let's get each one of them a farm that will lay any of these completely in the shade," suggested John.

"All right for you, if you can do it," said Robert, laughing, "but I've gone my limit for the present. Besides, if you gave each of them two hundred acres of the Kingdom of Heaven, it wouldn't stop them from feeling that they had been defrauded of their birthright here."

"How would you feel if you was served the same way?" asked John, and even as she shook hands with Adam, and introduced John Jardine, Kate found herself wishing that he had said "were."

As the girls had predicted, the place was immaculate, the yard shady and cool from the shelter of many big trees, the house comfortable, convenient, the best of everything in sight. Agatha and Susan were in new white dresses, while Adam Jr. and 3d wore tan and white striped seersucker coats, and white duck trousers. It was not difficult to feel a glow of pride in the place and people. Adam made them cordially welcome.

"You undoubtedly are blessed with good fortune," said Agatha. "Won't you please enlighten us concerning your travels, Katherine?"

So Kate told them everything she could think of that she thought would interest and amuse them, even outlining for Agatha speeches she had heard made by Dr. Vincent, Chaplain McCabe, Jehu DeWitt Miller, a number of famous politicians, teachers, and ministers. Then all of them talked about everything. Adam took John and Robert to look over the farm, whereupon Kate handed over her hat for Agatha to finger and try on.

"And how long will it be, my dear," said Agatha to Kate, "before you enter connubial bliss?"

"My goodness! I'm glad you asked me that while the men are at the barn," said Kate. "Mr. Jardine hasn't said a word about it himself, so please be careful what you say before him."

Agatha looked at Kate in wonder.

"You amaze me," she said. "Why, he regards you as if he would devour you. He hasn't proposed for your hand, you say? Surely you're not giving him proper encouragement!"

"She isn't giving him any, further than allowing him to be around," said Nancy Ellen.

"Do enlighten me!" cried the surprised Agatha. "How astonishing! Why, Kate, my dear, there is a just and proper amount of encouragement that MUST be given any self-respecting youth, before he makes his declarations. You surely know that."

"No, I do not know it!" said Kate. "I thought it was a man's place to speak up loud and plain and say what he had to propose."

"Oh, dear!" wailed Agatha, wringing her thin hands, her face a mirror of distress. "Oh, dear, I very much fear you will lose him. Why, Katherine, after a man has been to see you a certain number of times, and evidenced enough interest in you, my dear, there are a thousand strictly womanly ways in which you can lend his enterprise a little, only a faint amount of encouragement, just enough to allow him to recognize that he is not—not—er—repulsive to you."

"But how many times must he come, and how much interest must he evince?" asked Kate.

"I can scarcely name an exact number," said Agatha. "That is personal. You must decide for yourself what is the psychological moment at which he is to be taken. Have you even signified to him that you—that you—that you could be induced, even to CONTEMPLATE marriage?"

"Oh, yes," said Kate, heartily. "I told his mother that it was the height of my ambition to marry by the time I'm twenty. I told her I wanted a man as tall as I am, two hundred acres of land, and at least twelve babies."

Agatha collapsed suddenly. She turned her shocked face toward Nancy Ellen.

"Great Day of Rest!" she cried. "No wonder the man doesn't propose!"

When the men returned from their stroll, Agatha and Susan served them with delicious frozen custard and Angel's food cake. Then they resumed their drive, passing Hiram's place last. At the corner Robert hesitated and turned to ask: "Shall we go ahead, Kate?"

"Certainly," said Kate. "I want Mr. Jardine to see where I was born and spent my time of legal servitude. I suppose we daren't stop. I doubt if Mother would want to see me, and I haven't the slightest doubt that Father would NOT; but he has no jurisdiction over the road. It's the shortest way—and besides, I want to see the lilac bush and the cabbage roses."

As they approached the place Nancy Ellen turned.

"Father's standing at the gate. What shall we do?"

"There's nothing you can do, but drive straight ahead and you and Robert speak to him," said Kate. "Go fast, Robert."

He touched the team and at fair speed they whirled past the white house, at the gate of which, stiffly erect, stood a brawny man of six feet six, his face ruddy and healthy in appearance. He was dressed as he prepared himself to take a trip to pay his taxes, or to go to Court. He stood squarely erect, with stern, forbidding face, looking directly at them. Robert spoke to him, and Nancy Ellen leaned forward and waved, calling "Father," that she might be sure he knew her, but he gave not the slightest sign of recognition. They carried away a distinct picture of him, at his best physically and in appearance; at his worst mentally.

"There you have it!" said Kate, bitterly. "I'd be safe in wagering a thousand dollars, if I had it, that Agatha or the children told, at Hiram's or to Mother's girl, that we were coming. They knew we would pass about this time. Mother was at the side door watching, and Father was in his Sunday best, waiting to show us what would happen if we stopped, and that he never changes his mind. It didn't happen by accident that he was standing there dressed that way. What do you think, Nancy Ellen?"

"That he was watching for us!" said Nancy Ellen.

"But why do you suppose that he did it?" asked Kate.

"He thought that if he were NOT standing guard there, we might stop in the road and at least call Mother out. He wanted to be seen, and seen at his best; but as always, in command, showing his authority."

"Don't mind," said John Jardine. "It's easy to understand the situation."

"Thank you," said Kate. "I hope you'll tell your mother that. I can't bear her to think that the trouble is wholly my fault."

"No danger of that," he said. "Mother thinks there's nobody in all the world like you, and so do I."

Nancy Ellen kicked Robert's shin, to let him know that she heard. Kate was very depressed for a time, but she soon recovered and they spent a final happy evening together. When John had parted from Robert and Nancy Ellen, with the arrangement that he was to come again the following Saturday evening and spend Sunday with them, he asked Kate to walk a short distance with him. He seemed to be debating some proposition in his mind, that he did not know how to approach. Finally he stopped abruptly and said: "Kate, Mother told me that she told you how I grew up. We have been together most of every day for six weeks. I have no idea how a man used to women goes at what I want, so I can only do what I think is right, and best, and above all honest, and fair. I'd be the happiest I've ever been, to do anything on earth I've got the money to do, for you. There's a question I'm going to ask you the next time I come. You can think over all you know of me, and of Mother, and of what we have, and are, and be ready to tell me how you feel about everything next Sunday. There's one question I want to ask you before I go. In case we can plan for a life together next Sunday, what about my mother?"

"Whatever pleases her best, of course," said Kate. "Any arrangement that you feel will make her happy, will be all right with me; in the event we agree on other things."

He laughed, shortly.

"This sounds cold-blooded and business-like," he said. "But Mother's been all the world to me, until I met you. I must be sure about her, and one other thing. I'll write you about that this week. If that is all right with you, you can get ready for a deluge. I've held in as long as I can. Kate, will you kiss me good-bye?"

"That's against the rules," said Kate. "That's getting the cart before the horse."

"I know it," he said. "But haven't I been an example for six weeks? Only one. Please?"

They were back at Dr. Gray's gate, standing in the deep shelter of a big maple. Kate said: "I'll make a bargain with you. I'll kiss you to-night, and if we come to an agreement next Sunday night, you shall kiss me. Is that all right?"

The reply was so indistinct Kate was not sure of it; but she took his face between her hands and gave him exactly the same kind of kiss she would have given Adam, 3d. She hesitated an instant, then gave him a second. "You may take that to your mother," she said, and fled up the walk.

CHAPTER XII

TWO LETTERS

NANCY ELLEN and Robert were sitting on the side porch, not seeming in the least sleepy, when Kate entered the house. As she stepped out to them, she found them laughing mysteriously.

"Take this chair, Kate," said Nancy Ellen. "Come on, Robert, let's go stand under the maple tree and let her see whether she can see us."

"If you're going to rehearse any momentous moment of your existence," said Kate, "I shouldn't think of even being on the porch. I shall keep discreetly in the house, even going at once to bed. Good-night! Pleasant dreams!"

"Now we've made her angry," said Robert.

"I think there WAS 'a little touch of asperity,' as Agatha would say, in that," said Nancy Ellen, "but Kate has a good heart. She'll get over it before morning."

"Would Agatha use such a common word as 'little'?" asked Robert.

"Indeed, no!" said Nancy Ellen. "She would say 'infinitesimal.' But all the same he kissed her."

"If she didn't step up and kiss him, never again shall I trust my eyes!" said the doctor.

"Hush!" cautioned Nancy Ellen. "She's provoked now; if she hears that, she'll never forgive us."

Kate did not need even a hint to start her talking in the morning. The day was fine, a snappy tinge of autumn in the air, her head and heart were full. Nancy Ellen would understand and sympathize; of course Kate told her all there was to tell.

"And even at that," said Nancy Ellen, "he hasn't just come out right square and said 'Kate, will you marry me?' as I understand it."

"Same here," laughed Kate. "He said he had to be sure about his mother, and there was 'one other thing' he'd write me about this week, and he'd come again next Sunday; then if things were all right with me—the deluge!"

"And what is 'the other thing?'" asked Nancy Ellen.

"There he has me guessing. We had six, long, lovely weeks of daily association at the lake, I've seen his home, and his inventions, and as much of his business as is visible to the eye of a woman who doesn't know a tinker about business. His mother has told me minutely of his life, every day since he was born, I think. She insists that he never paid the slightest attention to a girl before, and he says the same, so there can't be any hidden ugly feature to mar my joy. He is thoughtful, quick, kind, a self-made business man. He looks well enough, he acts like a gentleman, he seldom makes a mistake in speech—"

"He doesn't say enough to MAKE any mistakes. I haven't yet heard him talk freely, give an opinion, or discuss a question," said Nancy Ellen.

"Neither have I," said Kate. "He's very silent, thinking out more inventions, maybe. The worst thing about him is a kind of hard-headed self-assurance. He got it fighting for his mother from boyhood. He knew she would freeze and starve if he didn't take care of her; he HAD to do it. He soon found he could. It took money to do what he had to do. He got the money. Then he began performing miracles with it. He lifted his mother out of poverty, he dressed her 'in purple and fine linen,' he housed her in the same kind of home other rich men of the Lake Shore Drive live in, and gave her the same kind of service. As most men do, when things begin to come their way, he lived for making money alone. He was so keen on the chase he wouldn't stop to educate and culture himself; he drove headlong on, and on, piling up more, far more than any one man should be allowed to have; so you can see that it isn't strange that he thinks there's nothing on earth that money can't do. You can see THAT sticking out all over him. At the hotel, on boats, on the trains, anywhere we went, he pushed straight for the most conspicuous place, the most desirable thing, the most expensive. I almost prayed sometimes that in some way he would strike ONE SINGLE THING that he couldn't make come his way with money; but he never did. No. I haven't an idea what he has in his mind yet, but he's going to write me about it this week, and if I agree to whatever it is, he is coming Sunday; then he has threatened me with a 'deluge,' whatever he means by that."

"He means providing another teacher for Walden, taking you to Chicago shopping for a wonderful trousseau, marrying you in his Lake Shore palace, no doubt."

"Well, if that's what he means by a 'deluge,'" said Kate, "he'll find the flood coming his way. He'll strike the first thing he can't do with money. I shall teach my school this winter as I agreed to. I shall marry him in the clothes I buy with what I earn. I shall marry him quietly, here, or at Adam's, or before a Justice of the Peace, if neither of you wants me. He can't pick me up, and carry me away, and dress me, and marry me, as if I were a pauper."

"You're RIGHT about it," said Nancy Ellen. "I don't know how we came to be so different. I should do at once any way he suggested to get such a fine-looking man and that much money. That it would be a humiliation to me all my after life, I wouldn't think about until the humiliation began, and then I'd have no way to protect myself. You're right! But I'd get out of teaching this winter if I could. I'd love to have you here."

"But I must teach to the earn money for my outfit. I'll have to go back to school in the same old sailor."

"Don't you care," laughed Nancy Ellen. "We know a secret!"

"That we do!" agreed Kate.

Wednesday Kate noticed Nancy Ellen watching for the boy Robert had promised to send with the mail as soon as it was distributed, because she was, herself. Twice Thursday, Kate hoped in vain that the suspense would be over. It had to end Friday, if John were coming Saturday night. She began to resent the length of time he was waiting. It was like him to wait until the last minute, and then depend on money to carry him through.

"He is giving me a long time to think things over," Kate said to Nancy Ellen when there was no letter in the afternoon mail Thursday.

"It may have been lost or delayed," said Nancy Ellen. "It will come to-morrow, surely."

Both of them saw the boy turn in at the gate Friday morning. Each saw that he carried more than one letter. Nancy Ellen was on her feet and nearer to the door; she stepped to it, and took the letters, giving them a hasty glance as she handed them to Kate.

"Two," she said tersely. "One, with the address written in the clear, bold hand of a gentleman, and one, the straggle of a country clod-hopper."

Kate smiled as she took the letters: "I'll wager my hat, which is my most precious possession," she said, "that the one with the beautifully written address comes from the 'clod-hopper,' and the 'straggle' from the 'gentleman.'"

She glanced at the stamping and addresses and smiled again: "So it proves," she said. "While I'm about it, I'll see what the 'clod-hopper' has to say, and then I shall be free to give my whole attention to the 'gentleman.'"

"Oh, Kate, how can you!" cried Nancy Ellen.

"Way I'm made, I 'spect," said Kate. "Anyway, that's the way this is going to be done."

She dropped the big square letter in her lap and ran her finger under the flap of the long, thin, beautifully addressed envelope, and drew forth several quite as perfectly written sheets. She read them slowly and deliberately, sometimes turning back a page and going over a part of it again. When she finished, she glanced at Nancy Ellen while slowly folding the sheets. "Just for half a cent I'd ask you to read this," she said.

"I certainly shan't pay anything for the privilege, but I'll read it, if you want me to," offered Nancy Ellen.

"All right, go ahead," said Kate. "It might possibly teach you that you can't always judge a man by appearance, or hastily; though just why George Holt looks more like a 'clod-hopper' than Adam, or Hiram, or Andrew, it passes me to tell."

She handed Nancy Ellen the letter and slowly ripped open the flap of the heavy white envelope. She drew forth the sheet and sat an instant with it in her fingers, watching the expression of Nancy Ellen's face, while she read the most restrained yet impassioned plea that a man of George Holt's nature and opportunities could devise to make to a woman after having spent several months in the construction of it. It was a masterly letter, perfectly composed, spelled, and written; for among his other fields of endeavour, George Holt had taught several terms of country school, and taught them with much success; so that he might have become a fine instructor, had it been in his blood to stick to anything long enough to make it succeed. After a page as she turned the second sheet Nancy Ellen glanced at Kate, and saw that she had not opened the creased page in her hands. She flamed with sudden irritation.

"You do beat the band!" she cried. "You've watched for two days and been provoked because that letter didn't come. Now you've got it, there you sit like a mummy and let your mind be so filled with this idiotic drivel that you're not ever reading John Jardine's letter that is to tell you what both of us are crazy to know."

"If you were in any mood to be fair and honest, you'd admit that you never read a finer letter than THAT," said Kate. "As for THIS, I never was so AFRAID in all my life. Look at that!"

She threw the envelope in Nancy Ellen's lap.

"That is the very first line of John Jardine's writing I have ever seen," she said. "Do you see anything about it to ENCOURAGE me to go farther?"

"You Goose!" cried the exasperated Nancy Ellen. "I suppose he transacts so much business he scarcely ever puts pen to paper. What's the difference how he writes? Look at what he is and what he does! Go on and read his letter."

Kate arose and walked to the window, turning her back to Nancy Ellen, who sat staring at her, while she read John Jardine's letter. Once Nancy Ellen saw Kate throw up her head and twist her neck as if she were choking; then she heard a great gulping sob down in her throat; finally Kate turned and stared at her with dazed, incredulous eyes. Slowly she dropped the letter, deliberately set her foot on it, and leaving the room, climbed the stairs. Nancy Ellen threw George Holt's letter aside and snatched up John Jardine's. She read:

MY DEREST KATE: I am a day late with this becos as I told you I have no schooling and in writing a letter is where I prove it, so I never write them, but it was not fare to you for you not to know what kind of a letter I would write if I did write one, so here it is very bad no dout but the best I can possably do which has got nothing at all to do with my pashion for you and the aughful time I will have till I here from you. If you can stand for this telagraf me and I will come first train and we will forget this and I will never write another letter. With derest love from Mother, and from me all the love of my hart. Forever yours only, JOHN JARDINE.

The writing would have been a discredit to a ten-year-old schoolboy. Nancy Ellen threw the letter back on the floor; with a stiffly extended finger, she poked it into the position in which she thought she had found it, and slowly stepped back.

"Great God!" she said amazedly. "What does the man mean? Where does that dainty and wonderful little mother come in? She must be a regular parasite, to take such ease and comfort for herself out of him, and not see that he had time and chance to do better than THAT for himself. Kate will never endure it, never in the world! And by the luck of the very Devil, there comes that school-proof thing in the same mail, from that abominable George Holt, and Kate reads it FIRST. It's too bad! I can't believe it! What did his mother mean?"

Suddenly Nancy Ellen began to cry bitterly; between sobs she could hear Kate as she walked from closet and bureau to her trunk which she was packing. The lid slammed heavily and a few minutes later Kate entered the room dressed for the street.

"Why are you weeping?" she asked casually.

Her eyes were flaming, her cheeks scarlet, and her lips twitching. Nancy Ellen sat up and looked at her. She pointed to the letter: "I read that," she said.

"Well, what do I care?" said Kate. "If he has no more respect for me than to write me such an insult as that, why should I have the respect for him to protect him in it? Publish it in the paper if you want to."

"Kate, what are you going to do?" demanded Nancy Ellen.

"Three things," said Kate, slowly putting on her long silk gloves. "First, I'm going to telegraph John Jardine that I never shall see him again, if I can possibly avoid it. Second, I'm going to send a drayman to get my trunk and take it to Walden. Third, I'm going to start out and walk miles, I don't know or care where; but in the end, I'm going to Walden to clean the schoolhouse and get ready for my winter term of school."

"Oh, Kate, you are such a fine teacher! Teach him! Don't be so hurried! Take more time to think. You will break his heart," pleaded Nancy Ellen.

Kate threw out both hands, palms down.

"P-a-s-h, a-u-g-h, h-a-r-t, d-o-u-t, d-e-r-e," she slowly spelled out the letters. "What about my heart and my pride? Think I can respect that, or ask my children to respect it? But thank you and Robert, and come after me as often as you can, as a mercy to me. If John persists in coming, to try to buy me, as he thinks he can buy anything he wants, you needn't let him come to Walden; for probably I won't be there until I have to, and I won't see him, or his mother, so he needn't try to bring her in. Say good-bye to Robert for me."

She walked from the house, head erect, shoulders squared, and so down the street from sight. In half an hour a truckman came for her trunk, so Nancy Ellen made everything Kate had missed into a bundle to send with it. When she came to the letters, she hesitated.

"I guess she didn't want them," she said. "I'll just keep them awhile and if she doesn't ask about them, the next time she comes, I'll burn them. Robert must go after her every Friday evening, and we'll keep her until Monday, and do all we can to cheer her; and this very day he must find out all there is to know about that George Holt. That IS the finest letter I ever read; she does kind of stand up for him; and in the reaction, impulsive as she is and self-confident—of course she wouldn't, but you never can tell what kind of fool a girl will make of herself, in some cases."

Kate walked swiftly, finished two of the errands she set out to do, then her feet carried her three miles from Hartley on the Walden road, before she knew where she was, so she proceeded to the village.

Mrs. Holt was not at home, but the house was standing open. Kate found her room cleaned, shining, and filled with flowers. She paid the drayman, opened her trunk, and put away her dresses, laying out all the things which needed washing; then she bathed, put on heavy shoes, and old skirt and waist, and crossing the road sat in a secluded place in the ravine and looked stupidly at the water. She noticed that everything was as she had left it in the spring, with many fresher improvements, made, no doubt, to please her. She closed her eyes, leaned against a big tree, and slow, cold and hot shudders alternated in shaking her frame.

She did not open her eyes when she heard a step and her name called. She knew without taking the trouble to look that George had come home, found her luggage in her room, and was hunting for her. She heard him come closer and knew when he seated himself that he was watching her, but she did not care enough even to move. Finally she shifted her position to rest herself, opened her eyes, and looked at him without a word. He returned her gaze steadily, smiling gravely. She had never seen him looking so well. He had put in the summer grooming himself, he had kept up the house and garden, and spent all his spare time on the ravine, and farming on the shares with his mother's sister who lived three miles east of them. At last she roused herself and again looked at him.

"I had your letter this morning," she said.

"I was wondering about that," he replied.

"Yes, I got it just before I started," said Kate. "Are you surprised to see me?"

"No," he answered. "After last year, we figured you might come the last of this week or the first of next, so we got your room ready Monday."

"Thank you," said Kate. "It's very clean and nice."

"I hope soon to be able to offer you such a room and home as you should have," he said. "I haven't opened my office yet. It was late and hot when I got home in June and Mother was fussing about this winter—that she had no garden and didn't do her share at Aunt Ollie's, so I have farmed most of the summer, and lived on hope; but I'll start in and make things fly this fall, and by spring I'll be sailing around with a horse and carriage like the best of them. You bet I am going to make things hum, so I can offer you anything you want."

"You haven't opened an office yet?" she asked for the sake of saying something, and because a practical thing would naturally suggest itself to her.

"I haven't had a breath of time," he said in candid disclaimer.

"Why don't you ask me what's the matter?"

"Didn't figure that it was any of my business in the first place," he said, "and I have a pretty fair idea, in the second."

"But how could you have?" she asked in surprise.

"When your sister wouldn't give me your address, she hinted that you had all the masculine attention you cared for; then Tilly Nepple visited town again last week and she had been sick and called Dr. Gray. She asked him about you, and he told what I fine time you had at Chautauqua and Chicago, with the rich new friends you'd made. I was watching for you about this time, and I just happened to be at the station in Hartley last Saturday when you got off the train with your fine gentleman, so I stayed over with some friends of mine, and I saw you several times Sunday. I saw that I'd practically no chance with you at all; but I made up my mind I'd stick until I saw you marry him, so I wrote just as I would if I hadn't known there was another man in existence."

"That was a very fine letter," said Kate.

"It is a very fine, deep, sincere love that I am offering you," said George Holt. "Of course I could see prosperity sticking out all over that city chap, but it didn't bother me much, because I knew that you, of all women, would judge a man on his worth. A rising young professional man is not to be sneered at, at least until he makes his start and proves what he can do. I couldn't get an early start, because I've always had to work, just as you've seen me last summer and this, so I couldn't educate myself so fast, but I've gone as fast and far as I could."

Kate winced. This was getting on places that hurt and to matters she well understood, but she was the soul of candour. "You did very well to educate yourself as you have, with no help at all," she said.

"I've done my best in the past, I'm going to do marvels in the future, and whatever I do, it is all for you and yours for the taking," he said grandiosely.

"Thank you," said Kate. "But are you making that offer when you can't help seeing that I'm in deep trouble?"

"A thousand times over," he said. "All I want to know about your trouble is whether there is anything a man of my size and strength can do to help you."

"Not a thing," said Kate, "in the direction of slaying a gay deceiver, if that's what you mean. The extent of my familiarities with John Jardine consists in voluntarily kissing him twice last Sunday night for the first and last time, once for himself, and once for his mother, whom I have since ceased to respect."

George Holt was watching her with eyes lynx-sharp, but Kate never saw it. When she mentioned her farewell of Sunday night, a queer smile swept over his face and instantly disappeared.

"I should thing any girl might be permitted that much, in saying a final good-bye to a man who had shown her a fine time for weeks," he commented casually.

"But I didn't know I was saying good-bye," explained Kate. "I expected him back in a week, and that I would then arrange to marry him. That was the agreement we made then."

As she began to speak, George Holt's face flashed triumph at having led her on; at what she said it fell perceptibly, but he instantly controlled it and said casually: "In any event, it was your own business."

"It was," said Kate. "I had given no man the slightest encouragement, I was perfectly free. John Jardine was courting me openly in the presence of his mother and any one who happened to be around. I intended to marry him. I liked him as much as any man need be liked. I don't know whether it was the same feeling Nancy Ellen had for Robert Gray or not, but it was a whole lot of feeling of some kind. I was satisfied with it, and he would have been. I meant to be a good wife to him and a good daughter to his mother, and I could have done much good in the world and extracted untold pleasure from the money he would have put in my power to handle. All was going 'merry as a marriage bell,' and then this morning came my Waterloo, in the same post with your letter."

"Do you know what you are doing?" cried George Holt, roughly, losing self-control with hope. "YOU ARE PROVING TO ME, AND ADMITTING TO YOURSELF, THAT YOU NEVER LOVED THAT MAN AT ALL. You were flattered, and tempted with position and riches, but your heart was not his, or you would be mighty SURE of it, don't you forget that!"

"I am not interested in analyzing exactly what I felt for him," said Kate. "It made small difference then; it makes none at all now. I would have married him gladly, and I would have been to him all a good wife is to any man; then in a few seconds I turned squarely against him, and lost my respect for him. You couldn't marry me to him if he were the last and only man on earth; but it hurt terribly, let me tell you that!"

George Holt suddenly arose and went to Kate. He sat down close beside her and leaned toward her.

"There isn't the least danger of my trying to marry you to him," he said, "because I am going to marry you myself at the very first opportunity. Why not now? Why not have a simple ceremony somewhere at once, and go away until school begins, and forget him, having a good time by ourselves? Come on, Kate, let's do it! We can go stay with Aunt Ollie, and if he comes trying to force himself on you, he'll get what he deserves. He'll learn that there is something on earth he can't buy with his money."

"But I don't love you," said Kate.

"Neither did you love him," retorted George Holt. "I can prove it by what you say. Neither did you love him, but you were going to marry him, and use all his wonderful power of position and wealth, and trust to association to BRING love. You can try that with me. As for wealth, who cares? We are young and strong, and we have a fine chance in the world. You go on and teach this year, and I'll get such a start that by next year you can be riding around in your carriage, proud as Pompey."

"Of course we could make it all right, as to a living," said Kate. "Big and strong as we are, but—"

Then the torrent broke. At the first hint that she would consider his proposal George Holt drew her to him and talked volumes of impassioned love to her. He gave her no chance to say anything; he said all there was to say himself; he urged that Jardine would come, and she should not be there. He begged, he pleaded, he reasoned. Night found Kate sitting on the back porch at Aunt Ollie's with a confused memory of having stood beside the little stream with her hand in George Holt's while she assented to the questions of a Justice of the Peace, in the presence of the School Director and Mrs. Holt. She knew that immediately thereafter they had walked away along a hot, dusty country road; she had tried to eat something that tasted like salted ashes. She could hear George's ringing laugh of exultation breaking out afresh every few minutes; in sudden irritation at the latest guffaw she clearly remembered one thing: in her dazed and bewildered state she had forgotten to tell him that she was a Prodigal Daughter.

CHAPTER XIII

THE BRIDE

ONLY one memory in the ten days that followed before her school began ever stood out clearly and distinctly with Kate. That was the morning of the day after she married George Holt. She saw Nancy Ellen and Robert at the gate so she went out to speak with them. Nancy Ellen was driving, she held the lines and the whip in her hands. Kate in dull apathy wondered why they seemed so deeply agitated. Both of them stared at her as if she might be a maniac.

"Is this thing in the morning paper true?" cried Nancy Ellen in a high, shrill voice that made Kate start in wonder. She did not take the trouble to evade by asking "what thing?" she merely made assent with her head.

"You are married to that—that—" Nancy Ellen choked until she could not say what.

"It's TIME to stop, since I am married to him," said Kate, gravely.

"You rushed in and married him without giving Robert time to find out and tell you what everybody knows about him?" demanded Nancy Ellen.

"I married him for what I knew about him myself," said Kate. "We shall do very well."

"Do well!" cried Nancy. "Do well! You'll be hungry and in rags the rest of your life!"

"Don't, Nancy Ellen, don't!" plead Robert. "This is Kate's affair, wait until you hear what she has to say before you go further."

"I don't care what she has to say!" cried Nancy Ellen. "I'm saying my say right now. This is a disgrace to the whole Bates family. We may not be much, but there isn't a lazy, gambling, drunken loafer among us, and there won't be so far as I'm concerned."

She glared at Kate who gazed at her in wonder.

"You really married this lout?" she demanded.

"I told you I was married," said Kate, patiently, for she saw that Nancy Ellen was irresponsible with anger.

"You're going to live with him, you're going to stay in Walden to live?" she cried.

"That is my plan at present," said Kate.

"Well, see that YOU STAY THERE," said Nancy Ellen. "You can't bring that—that creature to my house, and if you're going to be his wife, you needn't come yourself. That's all I've got to say to you, you shameless, crazy—"

"Nancy Ellen, you shall not!" cried Robert Gray, deftly slipping the lines from her fingers, and starting the horse full speed. Kate saw Nancy Ellen's head fall forward, and her hands lifted to cover her face. She heard the deep, tearing sob that shook her, and then they were gone. She did not know what to do, so she stood still in the hot sunshine, trying to think; but her brain refused to act at her will. When the heat became oppressive, she turned back to the shade of a tree, sat down, and leaned against it. There she got two things clear after a time. She had married George Holt, there was nothing to do but make the best of it. But Nancy Ellen had said that if she lived with him she should not come to her home. Very well. She had to live with him, since she had consented to marry him, so she was cut off from Robert and Nancy Ellen. She was now a prodigal, indeed. And those things Nancy Ellen had said—she was wild with anger. She had been misinformed. Those things could not be true.

"Shouldn't you be in here helping Aunt Ollie?" asked George's voice from the front step where he seated himself with his pipe.

"Yes, in a minute," said Kate, rising. "Did you see who came?"

"No. I was out doing the morning work. Who was it?" he asked.

"Nancy Ellen and Robert," she answered.

He laughed hilariously: "Brought them in a hurry, didn't we? Why didn't they come in?"

"They came to tell me," said Kate, slowly, "that if I had married you yesterday, as I did, that they felt so disgraced that I wasn't to come to their home again."

"'Disgraced?'" he cried, his colour rising. "Well, what's the matter with me?"

"Not the things they said, I fervently hope."

"Well, they have some assurance to come out here and talk about me, and you've got as much to listen, and then come and tell me about it," he cried.

"It was over in a minute," said Kate. "I'd no idea what they were going to say. They said it, and went. Oh, I can't spare Nancy Ellen, she's all I had!"

Kate sank down on the step and covered her face. George took one long look at her, arose, and walked out of hearing. He went into the garden and watched from behind a honeysuckle bush until he saw her finally lift her head and wipe her eyes; then he sauntered back, and sat down on the step beside her.

"That's right," he said. "Cry it out, and get it over. It was pretty mean of them to come out here and insult you, and tell any lie they could think up, and then drive away and leave you; but don't mind, they'll soon get over it. Nobody ever keeps up a fuss over a wedding long."

"Nancy Ellen never told a lie in her life," said Kate. "She has too much self-respect. What she said she THOUGHT was true. My only chance is that somebody has told her a lie. You know best if they did."

"Of course they did," he broke in, glibly. "Haven't you lived in the same house with me long enough to know me better than any one else does?"

"You can live in the same house with people and know less about them than any one else, for that matter," said Kate, "but that's neither here nor there. We're in this together, we got to get on the job and pull, and make a success out of it that will make all of them proud to be our friends. That's the only thing left for me. As I know the Bates, once they make up their minds, they never change. With Nancy Ellen and Father both down on me, I'm a prodigal for sure."

"What?" he cried, loudly. "What? Is your father in this, too? Did he send you word you couldn't come home, either? This is a hell of a mess! Speak up!"

Kate closed her lips, looked at him with deep scorn, and walked around the corner of the house. For a second he looked after her threateningly, then he sprang to his feet, and ran to her, catching her in his arms.

"Forgive me, dearest," he cried. "That took the wind out of my sails until I was a brute. You'd no business to SAY a thing like that. Of course we can't have the old Land King down on us. We've got to have our share of that land and money to buy us a fine home in Hartley, and fix me up the kind of an office I should have. We'll borrow a rig and drive over to-morrow and fix things solid with the old folks. You bet I'm a star-spangled old persuader, look what I did with you—"

"You stop!" cried Kate, breaking from his hold. "You will drive me crazy! You're talking as if you married me expecting land and money from it. I haven't been home in a year, and my father would deliberately kill me if I went within his reach."

"Well, score one for little old scratchin', pickin', Mammy!" he cried. "She SAID you had a secret!"

Kate stood very still, looking at him so intently that a sense of shame must have stirred in his breast.

"Look here, Kate," he said, roughly. "Mother did say you had a secret, and she hinted at Christmas that the reason you didn't go home was because your folks were at outs with you, and you can ask her if I didn't tell her to shut up and leave you alone, that I was in love with you, and I'd marry you and we'd get along all right, even if you were barred from home, and didn't get a penny. I just dare you to ask her."

"It's no matter," said Kate, wearily. "I'd rather take your word."

"All right, you take it, for that's the truth," he said. "But what was the rumpus? How did you come to have a racket with your old man?"

"Over my wanting to teach," said Kate. Then she explained in detail.

"Pother! Don't you fret about that!" said George. "I'm taking care of you now, and I'll see that you soon get home and to Grays', too; that's all buncombe. As for your share of your father's estate, you watch me get it! You are his child, and there is law!"

"There's law that allows him to deed his land to his sons before he dies, and that is exactly what he has done," said Kate.

"The Devil, you say!" shouted George Holt, stepping back to stare at her. "You tell that at the Insane Asylum or the Feeble Minded Home! I've seen the records! I know to the acre how much land stands in your father's name. Don't try to work that on me, my lady."

"I am not trying to work anything on you," said Kate, dully, wondering to herself why she listened, why she went on with it. "I'm merely telling you. In Father's big chest at the head of his bed at home lies a deed for two hundred acres of land for each of his seven sons, all signed and ready to deliver. He keeps the land in his name on record to bring him distinction and feed his vanity. He makes the boys pay the taxes, and ko-tow, and help with his work; he keeps them under control; but the land is theirs; none of the girls get a penny's worth of it!"

George Holt cleared his face with an effort.

"Well, we are no worse off than the rest of them, then," he said, trying to speak naturally and cheerfully. "But don't you ever believe it! Little old Georgie will sleep with this in his night cap awhile, and it's a problem he will solve if he works himself to death on it."

"But that is Father's affair," said Kate. "You had best turn your efforts, and lie awake nights thinking how to make enough money to buy some land for us, yourself."

"Certainly! Certainly! I see myself doing it!" laughed George Holt. "And now, knowing how you feel, and feeling none to good myself, we are going to take a few days off and go upstream, fishing. I'll take a pack of comforts to sleep on, and the tackle and some food, and we will forget the whole bunch and go have a good time. There's a place, not so far away, where I have camped beside a spring since I was a little shaver, and it's quiet and cool. Go get what you can't possibly exist without, nothing more."

"But we must dig the potatoes," protested Kate.

"Let them wait until we get back; it's a trifle early, anyway," he said. "Stop objecting and get ready! I'll tell Aunt Ollie. We're chums. Whatever I do is always all right with her. Come on! This is our wedding trip. Not much like the one you had planned, no doubt, but one of some kind."

So they slipped beneath the tangle of vines and bushes, and, following the stream of the ravine, they walked until mid-afternoon, when they reached a spot that was very lovely, a clear, clean spring, grassy bank, a sheltered cave-in floored with clean sand, warm and golden. From the depths of the cave George brought an old frying pan and coffee pot. He spread a comfort on the sand of the cave for a bed, produced coffee, steak, bread, butter, and fruit from his load, and told Kate to make herself comfortable while he got dinner. They each tried to make allowances for, and to be as decent as possible with, the other, with the result that before they knew it, they were having a good time; at least, they were keeping the irritating things they thought to themselves, and saying only the pleasant ones.

After a week, which George enjoyed to the fullest extent, while Kate made the best of everything, they put away the coffee pot and frying pan, folded the comforts, and went back to Aunt Ollie's for dinner; then to Walden in the afternoon. Because Mrs. Holt knew they would be there that day she had the house clean and the best supper she could prepare ready for them. She was in a quandary as to how to begin with Kate. She heartily hated her. She had been sure the girl had a secret, now she knew it; for if she did not attend the wedding of her sister, if she had not been at home all summer, if her father and mother never mentioned her name or made any answer to any one who did, there was a reason, and a good reason. Of course a man as rich as Adam Bates could do no wrong; whatever the trouble was, Kate was at fault, she had done some terrible thing.

"Hidin' in the bushes!" spat Mrs. Holt. "Hidin' in the bushes! Marry a man who didn't know he was goin' to be married an hour before, unbeknownst to her folks, an' wouldn't even come in the house, an' have a few of the neighbours in. Nice doin's for the school-ma'am! Nice prospect for George."

Mrs. Holt hissed like a copperhead, which was a harmless little creature compared with her, as she scraped, and slashed, and dismembered the chicken she was preparing to fry. She had not been able, even by running into each store in the village, and the post office, to find one person who would say a word against Kate. The girl had laid her foundations too well. The one thing people could and did say was: "How could she marry George Holt?" The worst of them could not very well say it to his mother. They said it frequently to each other and then supplied the true answers. "Look how he spruced up after she came!" "Look how he worked!" "Look how he ran after and waited on her!" "Look how nice he has been all summer!" Plenty was being said in Walden, but not one word of it was for the itching ears of Mrs. Holt. They had told her how splendid Kate was, how they loved her, how glad they were that she was to have the school again, how fortunate her son was, how proud she should be, until she was almost bursting with repressed venom.

She met them at the gate, after their week's camping. They were feeling in splendid health, the best spirits possible in the circumstances, but appearing dirty and disreputable. They were both laughing as they approached the gate.

"Purty lookin' bride you be!" Mrs. Holt spat at Kate.

"Yes, aren't I?" laughed Kate. "But you just give me a tub of hot soapsuds and an hour, and you won't know me. How are you? Things look as if you were expecting us."

"Hump!" said Mrs. Holt.

Kate laughed and went into the house. George stepped in front of his mother.

"Now you look here," he said. "I know every nasty thing your mind has conjured up that you'd LIKE to say, and have other folks say, about Kate. And I know as well as if you were honest enough to tell me, that you haven't been able to root out one living soul who would say a single word against her. Swallow your secret! Swallow your suspicions! Swallow your venom, and forget all of them. Kate is as fine a woman as God ever made, and anybody who has common sense knows it. She can just MAKE me, if she wants to, and she will; she's coming on fine, much faster and better than I hoped for. Now you drop this! Stop it! Do you hear?"

He passed her and hurried up the walk. In an hour, both George and Kate had bathed and dressed in their very best. Kate put on her prettiest white dress and George his graduation suit. Then together they walked to the post office for their mail, which George had ordered held, before they left. Carrying the bundle, they entered several stores on trifling errands, and then went home. They stopped and spoke to everyone. Kate kissed all her little pupils she met, and told them to come to see her, and to be ready to help clean the schoolhouse in the morning. Word flew over town swiftly. The Teacher was back, wearing the loveliest dress, and nicer than ever, and she had invited folks to come to see her.

Kate and George had scarcely finished their supper, when the first pair of shy little girls came for their kisses and to bring "Teacher" a bunch of flowers and a pretty pocket handkerchief from each. They came in flocks, each with flowers, most with a towel or some small remembrance; then the elders began to come, merchants with comforts, blankets, and towels, hardware men with frying pans, flat irons, and tinware. By ten o'clock almost everyone in Walden had carried Kate some small gift, wished her joy all the more earnestly, because they felt the chances of her ever having it were so small, and had gone their way, leaving her feeling better than she had thought possible.

She slipped into her room alone and read two letters, one a few typewritten lines from John Jardine, saying he had been at Hartley, also at Walden, and having found her married and gone, there was nothing for him to do but wish that the man she married had it in his heart to guard her life and happiness as he would have done. He would never cease to love her, and if at any time in her life there was anything he could do for her, would she please let him know. Kate dropped the letter on her dresser, with a purpose, and let it lie there. The other was from Robert. He said he was very sorry, but he could do nothing with Nancy Ellen at present. He hoped she would change later. If there was ever anything he could do, to let him know. Kate locked that letter in her trunk. She wondered as she did so why both of them seemed to think she would need them in the future. She felt perfectly able to take care of herself.

Monday morning George carried Kate's books to school for her, saw that she was started on her work in good shape, then went home, put on his old clothes, and began the fall work at Aunt Ollie's. Kate, wearing her prettiest blue dress, forgot even the dull ache in her heart, as she threw herself into the business of educating those young people. She worked as she never had before. She seemed to have developed fresh patience, new perception, keener penetration; she made the dullest of them see her points, and interested the most inattentive. She went home to dinner feeling better. She decided to keep on teaching a few years until George was well started in his practice; if he ever got started. He was very slow in action it seemed to her, compared with his enthusiasm when he talked.

CHAPTER XIV

STARTING MARRIED LIFE

FOR two weeks Kate threw herself into the business of teaching with all her power. She succeeded in so interesting herself and her pupils that she was convinced she had done a wise thing. Marriage did not interfere with her teaching; she felt capable and independent so long as she had her salary. George was working and working diligently, to prepare for winter, whenever she was present or could see results. With her first month's salary she would buy herself a warm coat, a wool suit, an extra skirt for school, and some waists. If there was enough left, she would have another real hat. Then for the remainder of the year she would spend only for the barest necessities and save to help toward a home something like Nancy Ellen's. Whenever she thought of Nancy Ellen and Robert there was a choking sensation in her throat, a dull ache where she had been taught her heart was located.

For two weeks everything went as well as Kate hoped: then Mrs. Holt began to show the results of having been partially bottled up, for the first time in her life. She was careful to keep to generalities which she could claim meant nothing, if anything she said was taken up by either George or Kate. George was too lazy to quarrel unless he was personally angered; Kate thought best to ignore anything that did not come in the nature of a direct attack. So long as Mrs. Holt could not understand how some folks could see their way to live off of other folks, or why a girl who had a chance to marry a fortune would make herself a burden to a poor man, Kate made the mistake of ignoring her. Thus emboldened she soon became personal. It seemed as if she spent her spare time and mental force thinking up suggestive, sarcastic things to say, where Kate could not help hearing them. She paid no attention unless the attack was too mean and premeditated; but to her surprise she found that every ugly, malicious word the old woman said lodged in her brain and arose to confront her at the most inopportune times—in the middle of a recitation or when she roused enough to turn over in her bed at night. The more vigorously she threw herself into her school work, the more she realized a queer lassitude, creeping over her. She kept squaring her shoulders, lifting her chin, and brushing imaginary cobwebs from before her face.

The final Friday evening of the month, she stopped at the post office and carried away with her the bill for her Leghorn hat, mailed with nicely conceived estimate as to when her first check would be due. Kate visited the Trustee, and smiled grimly as she slipped the amount in an envelope and gave it to the hack driver to carry to Hartley on his trip the following day. She had intended all fall to go with him and select a winter headpiece that would be no discredit to her summer choice, but a sort of numbness was in her bones; so she decided to wait until the coming week before going. She declined George's pressing invitation to go along to Aunt Ollie's and help load and bring home a part of his share of their summer's crops, on the ground that she had some work to prepare for the coming week.

Then Kate went to her room feeling faint and heavy. She lay there most of the day, becoming sorrier for herself, and heavier every passing hour. By morning she was violently ill; when she tried to leave her bed, dizzy and faint. All day she could not stand. Toward evening, she appealed to George either to do something for her himself, or to send for the village doctor. He asked her a few questions and then, laughing coarsely, told her that a doctor would do her no good, and that it was very probable that she would feel far worse before she felt better. Kate stared at him in dumb wonder.

"But my school!" she cried. "My school! I must be able to go to school in the morning. Could that spring water have been infected with typhus? I've never been sick like this before."

"I should hope not!" said George. And then he told her bluntly what caused her trouble. Kate had been white to begin with, now she slowly turned greenish as she gazed at him with incredulous eyes. Then she sprang to her feet.

"But I can't be ill!" she cried. "I can't! There is my school! I've got to teach! Oh, what shall I do?"

George had a very clear conception of what she could do, but he did not intend to suggest it to her. She could think of it, and propose it herself. She could not think of anything at that minute, because she fainted, and fell half on the bed, half in his arms as he sprang to her. He laid her down, and stood a second smiling triumphantly at her unheeding face.

"Easy snap for you this winter, Georgie, my boy!" he muttered. "I don't see people falling over each other to get to you for professional services, and it's hard work anyway. Zonoletics are away above the head of these country ignoramuses; blue mass and quinine are about their limit."

He took his time to bathe Kate's face. Presently she sat up, then fell on the pillow again.

"Better not try that!" warned George. "You'll hurt yourself, and you can't make it. You're out of the game; you might as well get used to it."

"I won't be out of the game!" cried Kate. "I can't be! What will become of my school? Oh, George, could you possibly teach for me, only for a few days, until I get my stomach settled?"

"Why, I'd like to help you," he said, "but you see how it is with me. I've got my fall work finished up, and I'm getting ready to open my office next week. I'm going to rent that nice front room over the post office."

"But, George, you must," said Kate. "You've taught several terms. You've a license. You can take it until this passes. If you have waited from June to October to open your office, you can wait a few more days. Suppose you OPEN the office and patients don't come, or we haven't the school; what would we LIVE on? What would I buy things with, and pay doctor bills?"

"Why didn't you think of that before you got married? What was your rush, anyway? I can't figure it to save my soul," he said.

"George, the school can't go," she cried. "If what you say is true, and I suspect it is, I must have money to see me through."

"Then set your wits to work and fix things up with your father," he said casually.

Kate arose tall and straight, standing unwaveringly as she looked at him in blazing contempt.

"So?" she said. "This is the kind of man you are? I'm not so helpless as you think me. I have a refuge. I know where to find it. You'll teach my school until I'm able to take it myself, if the Trustee and patrons will allow you, or I'll sever my relations with you as quickly as I formed them. You have no practice; I have grave doubts if you can get any; this is our only chance for the money we must have this winter. Go ask the Trustee to come here until I can make arrangements with him."

Then she wavered and rolled on the bed again. George stood looking at her between narrowed eyelids.

"Tactics I use with Mother don't go with you, old girl," he said to himself. "Thing of fire and tow, stubborn as an ox; won't be pushed a hair's breadth; old Bates over again—alike as two peas. But I'll break you, damn you, I'll break you; only, I WANT that school. Lots easier than kneading somebody's old stiff muscles, while the money is sure. Oh, I go after the Trustee, all right!"

He revived Kate, and telling her to keep quiet, and not excite herself, he explained that it was a terrible sacrifice to him to put off opening his office any longer; she must forgive him for losing self-control when he thought of it; but for her dear sake he would teach until she was better—possibly she would be all right in a few days, and then she could take her work again. Because she so devoutly hoped it, Kate made that arrangement with the Trustee. Monday, she lay half starved, yet gagging and ill, while George went to teach her school. As she contemplated that, she grew sicker than she had been before. When she suddenly marshalled all the facts she knew of him, she stoutly refused to think of what Nancy Ellen had said; when she reviewed his character and disposition, and thought of him taking charge of the minds of her pupils, Kate suddenly felt she must not allow that to happen, she must not! Then came another thought, even more personal and terrible, a thought so disconcerting she mercifully lost consciousness again.

She sent for the village doctor, and found no consolation from her talk with him. She was out of the school; that was settled. No harpy ever went to its meat with one half the zest Mrs. Holt found in the situation. With Kate so ill she could not stand on her feet half the time, so ill she could not reply, with no spirit left to appeal to George, what more could be asked? Mrs. Holt could add to every grievance she formerly had, that of a sick woman in the house for her to wait on. She could even make vile insinuations to Kate, prostrate and helpless, that she would not have dared otherwise. She could prepare food that with a touch of salt or sugar where it was not supposed to be, would have sickened a well person. One day George came in from school and saw a bowl of broth sitting on a chair beside Kate's bed.

"Can't you drink it?" he asked. "Do, if you possibly can," he urged. "You'll get so weak you'll be helpless."

"I just can't," said Kate. "Things have such a sickening, sweetish taste, or they are bitter, or sour; not a thing is as it used to be. I simply can't!"

A curious look crept over George's face. He picked up the bowl and tasted the contents. Instantly his face went black; he started toward the kitchen. Kate heard part of what happened, but she never lifted her head. After a while he came back with more broth and a plate of delicate toast.

"Try this," he said. "I made it myself."

Kate ate ravenously.

"That's good!" she cried.

"I'll tell you what I'm going to do," he said. "I'm going to take you out to Aunt Ollie's for a week after school to-night. Want to go?"

"Yes! Oh, yes!" cried Kate.

"All right," he said. "I know where I can borrow a rig for an hour. Get ready if you are well enough, if you are not, I'll help you after school."

That week with Aunt Ollie remained a bright spot in Kate's memory. The October days were beginning to be crisp and cool. Food was different. She could sleep, she could eat many things Aunt Ollie knew to prepare especially; soon she could walk and be outdoors. She was so much better she wrote George a note, asking him to walk out and bring her sewing basket, and some goods she listed, and in the afternoons the two women cut and sewed quaint, enticing little garments. George found Kate so much better when he came that he proposed she remain another week. Then for the first time he talked to her about her theory of government and teaching, until she realized that the School Director had told him he was dissatisfied with him—so George was trying to learn her ways. Appalled at what might happen if he lost the school, Kate made notes, talked at length, begged him to do his best, and to come at once if anything went wrong. He did come, and brought the school books so she went over the lessons with him, and made marginal notes of things suggested to her mind by the text, for him to discuss and elucidate. The next time he came, he was in such good spirits she knew his work had been praised, so after that they went over the lessons together each evening. Thinking of what would help him also helped fill her day.

He took her home, greatly improved, in much better spirits, to her room, cleaned and ready for winter, with all of her things possible to use in place, so that it was much changed, prettier, and more convenient. As they drove in she said of him: "George, what about it? Did your mother purposely fix my food so I could not eat it?"

"Oh, I wouldn't say that," he said. "You know neither of you is violently attached to the other. She'll be more careful after this, I'm sure she will."

"Why, have you been sick?" asked Kate as soon as she saw Mrs. Holt.

She seemed so nervous and appeared so badly Kate was sorry for her; but she could not help noticing how she kept watch on her son. She seemed to keep the width of the room and a piece of furniture between them, while her cooking was so different that it was not in the least necessary for George to fix things for Kate himself, as he had suggested. Everything was so improved, Kate felt better. She began to sew, to read, to sit for long periods in profound thought, then to take walks that brought back her strength and colour. So through the winter and toward the approach of spring they lived in greater comfort. With Kate's help, George was doing so well with the school that he was frequently complimented by the parents. That he was trying to do good work and win the approval of both pupils and parents was evident to Kate. Once he said to her that he wondered if it would be a good thing for him to put in an application for the school the coming winter. Kate stared at him in surprise: "But your profession," she objected. "You should be in your office and having enough practice to support us by then."

"Yes, I should!" he said. "But this is a new thing, and you know how these clodhoppers are."

"If I came as near living in the country, and worked at farming as much as you do, that's the last thing I would call any human being," said Kate. "I certainly do know how they are, and what I know convinces me that you need not look to them for any patients."

"You seem to think I won't have any from any source," he said hotly.

"I confess myself dubious," said Kate. "You certainly are, or you wouldn't be talking of teaching."

"Well, I'll just show you!" he cried.

"I'm waiting," said Kate. "But as we must live in the meantime, and it will be so long before I can earn anything again, and so much expense, possibly it would be a good idea to have the school to fall back on, if you shouldn't have the patients you hope for this summer. I think you have done well with the school. Do your level best until the term closes, and you may have a chance."

Laughing scornfully, he repeated his old boast: "I'll just show you!"

"Go ahead," said Kate. "And while you are at it, be generous. Show me plenty. But in the meantime, save every penny you can, so you'll be ready to pay the doctor's bills and furnish your office."

"I love you advice; it's so Batesy," he said. "I have money saved for both contingencies you mention, but I'll tell you what I think, and about this I'm the one who knows. I've told you repeatedly winter is my best time. I've lost the winter trying to help you out; and I've little chance until winter comes again. It takes cold weather to make folks feel what ails their muscles, and my treatment is mostly muscular. To save so we can get a real start, wouldn't it be a good idea for you to put part of your things in my room, take what you must have, and fix Mother's bedroom for you, let her move her bed into her living room, and spare me all you can of your things to fix up your room for my office this summer. That would save rent, it's only a few steps from downtown, and when I wasn't busy with patients, I could be handy to the garden, and to help you."

"If your mother is willing, I'll do my share," said Kate, "although the room's cramped, and where I'll put the small party when he comes I don't know, but I'll manage someway. The big objection to it is that it will make it look to people as if it were a makeshift, instead of starting a real business."

"Real," was the wrong word. It was the red rag that started George raging, until to save her self-respect, Kate left the room. Later in the day he announced that his mother was willing, she would clean the living room and move in that day. How Kate hated the tiny room with its one exterior wall, only one small window, its scratched woodwork, and soiled paper, she could not say. She felt physically ill when she thought of it, and when she thought of the heat of the coming summer, she wondered what she would do; but all she could do was to acquiesce. She made a trip downtown and bought a quart of white paint and a few rolls of dainty, fresh paper. She made herself ill with turpentine odours in giving the woodwork three coats, and fell from a table almost killing herself while papering the ceiling. There was no room for her trunk; the closet would not hold half her clothes; her only easy chair was crowded out; she was sheared of personal comfort at a clip, just at a time when every comfort should have been hers. George ordered an operating table, on which to massage his patients, a few other necessities, and in high spirits, went about fixing up his office and finishing his school. He spent hours in the woodshed with the remainder of Kate's white paint, making a sign to hang in front of the house.

He was so pathetically anxious for a patient, after he had put his table in place, hung up his sign, and paid for an announcement in the county paper and the little Walden sheet, that Kate was sorry for him.

On a hot July morning Mrs. Holt was sweeping the front porch when a forlorn specimen of humanity came shuffling up the front walk and asked to see Dr. Holt. Mrs. Holt took him into the office and ran to the garden to tell George his first patient had come. His face had been flushed from pulling weeds, but it paled perceptibly as he started to the back porch to wash his hands.

"Do you know who it is, Mother?" he asked.

"It's that old Peter Mines," she said, "an' he looks fit to drop."

"Peter Mines!" said George. "He's had about fifty things the matter with him for about fifty years."

"Then you're a made man if you can even make him think he feels enough better so's he'll go round talking about it," said Mrs. Holt, shrewdly.

George stood with his hands dripping water an instant, thinking deeply.

"Well said for once, old lady," he agreed. "You are just exactly right."

He hurried to his room, and put on his coat.

"A patient that will be a big boom for me," he boasted to Kate as he went down the hall.

Mrs. Holt stood listening at the hall door. Kate walked around the dining room, trying to occupy herself. Presently cringing groans began to come from the room, mingling with George's deep voice explaining, and trying to encourage the man. Then came a wild shriek and then silence. Kate hurried out to the back walk and began pacing up and down in the sunshine. She did not know it, but she was praying.

A minute later George's pallid face appeared at the back door: "You come in here quick and help me," he demanded.

"What's the matter?" asked Kate.

"He's fainted. His heart, I think. He's got everything that ever ailed a man!" he said.

"Oh, George, you shouldn't have touched him," said Kate.

"Can't you see it will make me, if I can help him! Even Mother could see that," he cried.

"But if his heart is bad, the risk of massaging him is awful," said Kate as she hurried after George.

Kate looked at the man on the table, ran her hand over the heart region, and lifted terrified eyes to George.

"Do you think—?" he stammered.

"Sure of it!" she said, "but we can try. Bring your camphor bottle, and some water," she cried to Mrs. Holt.

For a few minutes, they worked frantically. Then Kate stepped back. "I'm scared, and I don't care who knows it," she said. "I'm going after Dr. James."

"No, you are not!" cried George. "You just hold yourself. I'll have him out in a minute. Begin at his feet and rub the blood up to his heart."

"They are swollen to a puff, he's got no circulation," said Kate. "Oh, George, how could you ever hope to do anything for a man in this shape, with MUSCULAR treatment?"

"You keep still and rub, for God's sake," he cried, frantically. "Can't you see that I am ruined if he dies on this table?"

"No, I can't," said Kate. "Everybody would know that he was practically dying when he came here. Nobody will blame you, only, you never should have touched him! George, I AM going after Dr. James."

"Well, go then," he said wildly.

Kate started. Mrs. Holt blocked the doorway.

"You just stop, Missy!" she cried. "You're away too smart, trying to get folks in here, and ruin my George's chances. You just stay where you are till I think what to do, to put the best face on this!"

"He may not be really gone! The doctor might save him!" cried Kate.

Mrs. Holt looked long at the man.

"He's deader 'an a doornail," she said. "You stay where you are!"

Kate picked her up by the shoulders, set her to one side, ran from the room and down the street as fast as possible. She found the doctor in his office with two patients. She had no time to think or temporize.

"Get your case and come to our house quick, doctor," she cried. "An old man they call Peter Mines came to see George, and his heart has failed. Please hurry!"

"Heart, eh?" said the doctor. "Well, wait a minute. No use to go about a bad heart without digitalis."

He got up and put on his hat, told the men he would be back soon, and went to the nearest drug store. Kate followed. The men who had been in the office came also.

"Doctor, hurry!" she panted. "I'm so frightened."

"You go to some of the neighbours, and stay away from there," he said.

"Hurry!" begged Kate. "Oh, do hurry!"

She was beside him as they sped down the street, and at his shoulder as they entered the room. With one glance she lurched against the casing and then she plunged down the hall, entered her room, closed the door behind her, and threw herself on the bed. She had only a glance, but in that glance she had seen Peter Mines sitting fully clothed, his hat on his head, his stick in his hands, in her easy chair; the operating table folded and standing against the wall; Mrs. Holt holding the camphor bottle to Peter's nose, while George had one hand over Peter's heart, the other steadying his head.

The doctor swung the table in place, and with George's help laid Peter on it, then began tearing open his clothes. As they worked the two men followed into the house to see if they could do anything and excited neighbours began to gather. George and his mother explained how Peter had exhausted himself walking two miles from the country that hot morning, how he had entered the office, tottering with fatigue, and had fallen in the chair in a fainting condition. Everything was plausible until a neighbour woman, eager to be the centre of attention for a second, cried: "Yes, we all see him come more'n an hour ago; and when he begin to let out the yells we says to each other, 'THERE! George has got his first patient, sure!' An' we all kind of waited to see if he'd come out better."

The doctor looked at her sharply: "More than an hour ago?" he said. "You heard cries?"

"Yes, more'n a good hour ago. Yes, we all heard him yell, jist once, good and loud!" she said.

The doctor turned to George. Before he could speak his mother intervened.

"That was our Kate done the yellin'," she said. "She was scart crazy from the start. He jest come in, and set in the chair and he's been there ever since."

"You didn't give him any treatment, Holt?" asked the doctor.

Again Mrs. Holt answered: "Never touched him! Hadn't even got time to get his table open. Wa'n't nothing he could 'a' done for him anyway. Peter was good as gone when he got here. His fool folks never ought 'a' let him out this hot day, sick as he was."

The doctor looked at George, at his mother, long at Peter. "He surely was too sick to walk that far in this heat," he said. "But to make sure, I'll look him over. George, you help me. Clear the room of all but these two men."

HE began minutely examining Peter's heart region. Then he rolled him over and started to compress his lungs. Long white streaks marked the puffy red of the swollen, dropsical flesh. The doctor examined the length of the body, and looked straight into George Holt's eyes.

"No use," he said. "Bill, go to the 'phone in my office, and tell Coroner Smith to get here from Hartley as soon as he can. All that's left to do here is to obey the law, and have a funeral. Better some of the rest of you go tell his folks. I've done all I can do. It's up to the Coroner now. The rest of you go home, and keep still till he comes."

When he and George were left alone he said tersely: "Of course you and your mother are lying. You had this man stripped, he did cry out, and he did die from the pain of the treatment you tried to give him, in his condition. By the way, where's your wife? This is a bad thing for her right now. Come, let's find her and see what state she is in."

Together they left the room and entered Kate's door. As soon as the doctor was busy with her, George slipped back into the closed room, rolled Peter on his back and covered him, in the hope that the blood would settle until it would efface the marks of his work before the Coroner arrived. By that time the doctor was too busy to care much what happened to Peter Mines; he was a poor old soul better off as he was. Across Kate's unconscious body he said to George Holt: "I'm going to let the Coroner make what he pleases out of this, solely for your wife's sake. But two things: take down that shingle. Take it down now, and never put it up again if you want me to keep still. I'll give you what you paid for that table. It's a good one. Get him out as soon as you can. Set him in another room. I've got to have Mrs. Holt where I can work. And send Sarah Nepple here to help me. Move fast! This is going to be a close call. And the other thing: I've heard you put in an application for our school this winter. Withdraw it! Now move!"

So they set Peter in the living room, cleaned Kate's room quickly, and moved in her bed. By the time the Coroner arrived, the doctor was too busy to care what happened. On oath he said a few words that he hoped would make life easier for Kate, and at the same time pass muster for truth; told the Coroner what witnesses to call; and gave an opinion as to Peter's condition. He also added that he was sure Peter's family would be very glad he was to suffer no more, and then he went back to Kate who was suffering entirely too much for safety. Then began a long vigil that ended at midnight with Kate barely alive and Sarah Nepple, the Walden mid-wife, trying to divide a scanty wardrobe between a pair of lusty twins.

CHAPTER XV

A NEW IDEA

KATE slowly came back to consciousness. She was conscious of her body, sore from head to foot, with plenty of pain in definite spots. Her first clear thought was that she was such a big woman; it seemed to her that she filled the room, when she was one bruised ache from head to heels. Then she became conscious of a moving bundle on the bed beside her, and laid her hand on it to reassure herself. The size and shape of the bundle were not reassuring.

"Oh, Lord!" groaned Kate. "Haven't You any mercy at all? It was Your advice I followed when I took wing and started out in life."

A big sob arose in her throat, while at the same time she began to laugh weakly. Dr. James heard her from the hall and entered hastily. At the sight of him, Kate's eyes filled with terrified remembrance. Her glance swept the room, and rested on her rocking chair. "Take that out of here!" she cried. "Take it out, split it into kindling wood, and burn it."

"All right," said Dr. James calmly. "I'll guarantee that you never see it again. Is there anything else you want?"

"You—you didn't—?"

The doctor shook his head. "Very sorry," he said, "but there wasn't a thing could be done."

"Where is he?" she asked in a whisper.

"His people took him home immediately after the Coroner's inquest, which found that he died from heart failure, brought on by his long walk in the heat."

Kate stared at him with a face pitiful to behold.

"You let him think THAT?" she whispered again.

"I did," said the old doctor. "I thought, and still think, that for the sake of you and yours," he waved toward the bundle, "it was the only course to pursue."

"Thank you," said Kate. "You're very kind. But don't you think that I and mine are going to take a lot of shielding? The next man may not be so kindly disposed. Besides, is it right? Is it honest?"

"It is for you," said the doctor. "You had nothing to do with it. If you had, things would not have gone as they did. As for me, I feel perfectly comfortable about it in my conscience, which is my best guide. All I had to do was to let them tell their story. I perjured myself only to the extent of testifying that you knew nothing about it. The Coroner could well believe that. George and his mother could easily manage the remainder."

Kate waved toward the bundle: "Am I supposed to welcome and love them?"

"A poet might expect you to," said the doctor. "In the circumstances, I do not. I shall feel that you have done your whole duty if you will try to nurse them when the time comes. You must have a long rest, and they must grow some before you'll discover what they mean to you. There's always as much chance that they'll resemble your people as that they will not. The boy will have dark hair and eyes I think, but he looks exactly like you. The girl is more Holt."

"Where is George?" she asked.

"He was completely upset," said the doctor. "I suggested that he go somewhere to rest up a few days, so he took his tackle and went fishing, and to the farm."

"Shouldn't he have stayed and faced it?" asked Kate.

"There was nothing for him to face, except himself, Kate," said the doctor.

Kate shook her head. She looked ghastly ill.

"Doctor," she said, "couldn't you have let me die?"

"And left your son and your little daughter to them?" he asked. "No, Kate, I couldn't have let you die; because you've your work in the world under your hand right now."

He said that because when he said "left your son and your little daughter to them," Kate had reached over and laid her hand possessively, defensively, on the little, squirming bundle, which was all Dr. James asked of her. Presently she looked the doctor straight in the face. "Exactly what do you know?" she asked.

"Everything," said the doctor. "And you?"

"Everything," said Kate.

There was a long silence. Then Kate spoke slowly: "That George didn't know that he shouldn't have touched that man, proves him completely incompetent," she said. "That he did, and didn't have the courage to face the results, proves him lacking in principle. He's not fit for either work to which he aspires."

"You are talking too much," said the doctor. "Nurse Nepple is in charge here, and Aunt Ollie. George's mother went to the farm to cook for him. You're in the hands of two fine women, who will make you comfortable. You have escaped lasting disgrace with your skirts clear, now rest and be thankful."

"I can't rest until I know one thing," said Kate. "You're not going to allow George to kill any one else?"

"No," said the doctor. "I regretted telling him very much; but I had to tell him THAT could not happen."

"And about the school?" she asked. "I half thought he might get it."

"He WON'T!" said the doctor. "I'm in a position to know that. Now try to take some rest."

Kate waved toward the babies: "Will you please take them away until they need me?" she asked.

"Of course," said the doctor. "But don't you want to see them, Kate? There isn't a mark or blemish on either of them. The boy weighs seven pounds and the girl six; they seem as perfect as children can be."

"You needn't worry about that," said Kate. "Twins are a Bates habit. My mother had three pairs, always a boy and a girl, always big and sound as any children; mine will be all right, too."

The doctor started to turn back the blanket. Kate turned her head away: "Don't you think I have had about enough at present?" she asked. "I'd stake my life that as a little further piece of my punishment, the girl looks exactly like Mrs. Holt."

"By Jove," said the doctor, "I couldn't just think who it was."

He carried the babies from the room, lowered the blinds, and Kate tried to sleep, and did sleep, because she was so exhausted she could not keep awake.

Later in the evening Aunt Ollie slipped in, and said George was in the woodhouse, almost crying himself to death, and begging to see her.

"You tell him I'm too sick to be seen for at least a week," said Kate.

"But, my dear, he's so broken up; he feels so badly," begged Aunt Ollie.

"So do I," said Kate. "I feel entirely too badly to be worried over seeing him. I must take the babies now."

"I do wish you would!" persisted Aunt Ollie.

"Well, I won't," said Kate. "I don't care if I never see him again. He knows WHY he is crying; ask him."

"I'll wager they ain't a word of truth in that tale they're telling," she said.

Kate looked straight at her: "Well, for their sakes and my sake, and the babies' sake, don't TALK about it."

"You poor thing!" said Aunt Ollie, "I'll do anything in the world to help you. If ever you need me, just call on me. I'll go start him back in a hurry."

He came every night, but Kate steadily refused, until she felt able to sit up in a chair, to see him, or his mother when she came to see the babies. She had recovered rapidly, was over the painful part of nursing the babies, and had a long talk with Aunt Ollie, before she consented to see George. At times she thought she never could see him again; at others, she realized her helplessness. She had her babies to nurse for a year; there was nothing she could think of she knew to do, that she could do, and take proper care of two children. She was tied "hand and foot," as Aunt Ollie said. And yet it was Aunt Ollie who solved her problem for her. Sitting beside the bed one day she said to Kate: "My dear, do you know that I'm having a mighty good time? I guess I was lonesomer than I thought out there all alone so much, and the work was nigh to breaking me during the long, cold winter. I got a big notion to propose somepin' to you that might be a comfort to all of us."

"Propose away," said Kate. "I'm at my wit's end."

"Well, what would you think of you and George taking the land, working it on the shares, and letting me have this room, an' live in Walden, awhile?"

Kate sat straight up in bed: "Oh, Aunt Ollie! Would you?" she cried. "Would you? That would be a mercy to me; it would give George every chance to go straight, if there is a straight impulse in him."

"Yes, I will," said Aunt Ollie, "and you needn't feel that I am getting the little end of the bargain, either. The only unpleasant thing about it will be my sister, and I'll undertake to manage her. I read a lot, an' I can always come to see you when mortal sperrits will bear her no more. She'll be no such trial to me, as she is to you."

"You're an angel," said Kate. "You've given me hope where I had not a glimmer. If I have George out there alone, away from his mother, I can bring out all the good there is in him, and we can get some results out of life, or I can assure myself that it is impossible, so that I can quit with a clear conscience. I do thank you."

"All right, then, I'll go out and begin packing my things, and see about moving this afternoon. I'll leave my stoves, and beds, and tables, and chairs for you; you can use your wedding things, and be downright comfortable. I'll like living in town a spell real well."

So once more Kate saw hope a beckoning star in the distance, and ruffled the wings of the spirit preparatory to another flight: only a short, humble flight this time, close earth; but still as full of promise as life seemed to hold in any direction for her. She greeted George casually, and as if nothing had happened, when she was ready to see him.

"You're at the place where words are not of the slightest use to me," she said. "I'm giving you one, and a final chance to ACT. This seems all that is open to us. Go to work like a man, and we will see what we can make of our last chance."

Kate was so glad when she sat in the carriage that was to take her from the house and the woman she abominated that she could scarcely behave properly. She clasped Adam tightly in her arms, and felt truly his mother. She reached over and tucked the blanket closer over Polly, but she did not carry her, because she resembled her grandmother, while Adam was a Bates.

George drove carefully. He was on behaviour too good to last, but fortunately both women with him knew him well enough not to expect that it would. When they came in sight of the house, Kate could see that the grass beside the road had been cut, the trees trimmed, and Oh, joy, the house freshly painted a soft, creamy white she liked, with a green roof. Aunt Ollie explained that she furnished the paint and George did the work. He had swung oblong clothes baskets from the ceiling of a big, cheery, old-fashioned bedroom for a cradle for each baby, and established himself in a small back room adjoining the kitchen. Kate said nothing about the arrangement, because she supposed it had been made to give her more room, and that George might sleep in peace, while she wrestled with two tiny babies.

There was no doubt about the wrestling. The babies seemed of nervous temperament, sleeping in short naps and lightly. Kate was on her feet from the time she reached her new home, working when she should not have worked; so that the result developed cross babies, each attacked with the colic, which raged every night from six o'clock until twelve and after, both frequently shrieking at the same time. George did his share by going to town for a bottle of soothing syrup, which Kate promptly threw in the creek. Once he took Adam and began walking the floor with him, extending his activities as far as the kitchen. In a few minutes he had the little fellow sound asleep and he did not waken until morning; then he seemed to droop and feel listless. When he took the baby the second time and made the same trip to the kitchen, Kate laid Polly on her bed and silently followed. She saw George lay the baby on the table, draw a flask from his pocket, pour a spoon partly full, filling it the remainder of the way from the teakettle. As he was putting the spoon to the baby's lips, Kate stepped beside him and taking it, she tasted the contents. Then she threw the spoon into the dishpan standing near and picked up the baby.

"I knew it!" she said. "Only I didn't know what. He acted like a drugged baby all last night and to-day. Since when did you begin carrying that stuff around with you, and feeding it to tiny babies?"

"It's a good thing. Dr. James recommended it. He said it was harmful to let them strain themselves crying, and very hard on you. You could save yourself a lot," he urged.

"I need saving all right," said Kate, "but I haven't a picture of myself saving myself by drugging a pair of tiny babies."

He slipped the bottle back in his pocket. Kate stood looking at him so long and so intently, he flushed and set the flask on a shelf in the pantry. "It may come in handy some day when some of us have a cold," he said.

Kate did her best, but she was so weakened by nursing both of the babies, by loss of sleep, and overwork in the house, that she was no help whatever to George in getting in the fall crops and preparing for spring. She had lost none of her ambition, but there was a limit to her capacity.

In the spring the babies were big and lusty, eating her up, and crying with hunger, until she was forced to resort to artificial feeding in part, which did not agree with either of them. As a saving of time and trouble she decided to nurse one and feed the other. It was without thought on her part, almost by chance, yet the chance was that she nursed Adam and fed Polly. Then the babies began teething, so that she was rushed to find time to prepare three regular meals a day, and as for the garden and poultry she had planned, George did what he pleased about them, which was little, if anything.

He would raise so much to keep from being hungry, he would grow so many roots, and so much cabbage for winter, he would tend enough corn for a team and to fatten pork; right there he stopped and went fishing, while the flask was in evidence on the pantry shelf only two days. Kate talked crop rotation, new seed, fertilization, until she was weary; George heartily agreed with her, but put nothing of it all into practice.

"As soon as the babies are old enough to be taken out," she said, "things will be better. I just can't do justice to them and my work, too. Three pairs! My poor mother! And she's alive yet! I marvel at it."

So they lived, and had enough to eat, and were clothed, but not one step did they advance toward Kate's ideals of progression, economy, accumulation. George always had a little money, more than she could see how he got from the farming. There were a few calves and pigs to sell occasionally; she thought possibly he saved his share from them.

For four years, Kate struggled valiantly to keep pace with what her mother always had done, and had required of her at home; but she learned long before she quit struggling that farming with George was hopeless. So at last she became so discouraged she began to drift into his way of doing merely what would sustain them, and then reading, fishing, or sleeping the remainder of the time. She began teaching her children while very small, and daily they had their lessons after dinner, while their father slept.

Kate thought often of what was happening to her; she hated it, she fought it; but with George Holt for a partner she could not escape it. She lay awake nights, planning ways to make a start toward prosperity; she propounded her ideas at breakfast. To save time in getting him early to work she began feeding the horses as soon as she was up, so that George could go to work immediately after breakfast; but she soon found she might as well save her strength. He would not start to harness until he had smoked, mostly three quarters of an hour. That his neighbours laughed at him and got ahead of him bothered him not at all. All they said and all Kate said, went, as he expressed it, "in at one ear, out at the other."

One day in going around the house Kate was suddenly confronted by a thing she might have seen for three years, but had not noticed. Leading from the path of bare, hard-beaten earth that ran around the house through the grass, was a small forking path not so wide and well defined, yet a path, leading to George's window. She stood staring at it a long time with a thoughtful expression on her face.

That night she did not go to bed when she went to her room. Instead she slipped out into the night and sitting under a sheltering bush she watched that window. It was only a short time until George crawled from it, went stealthily to the barn, and a few minutes later she saw him riding barebacked on one of the horses he had bridled, down the footpath beside the stream toward town. She got up and crossing the barnyard shut the gate after him, and closed the barn door. She went back to the house and closed his window and lighting a lamp set it on his dresser in front of his small clock. His door was open in the morning when she passed it on her way to the kitchen, so she got breakfast instead of feeding the horses. He came in slowly, furtively watching her. She worked as usual, saying no unpleasant word. At length he could endure it no longer.

"Kate," he said, "I broke a bolt in the plow yesterday, and I never thought of it until just as I was getting into bed, so to save time I rode in to Walden and got another last night. Ain't I a great old economist, though?"

"You are a great something," she said. "'Economist' would scarcely be my name for it. Really, George, can't you do better than that?"

"Better than what?" he demanded.

"Better than telling such palpable lies," she said. "Better than crawling out windows instead of using your doors like a man; better than being the most shiftless farmer of your neighbourhood in the daytime, because you have spend most of your nights, God and probably all Walden know how. The flask and ready money I never could understand give me an inkling."

"Anything else?" he asked, sneeringly.

"Nothing at present," said Kate placidly. "I probably could find plenty, if I spent even one night in Walden when you thought I was asleep."

"Go if you like," he said. "If you think I'm going to stay here, working like a dog all day, year in and year out, to support a daughter of the richest man in the county and her kids, you fool yourself. If you want more than you got, call on your rich folks for it. If you want to go to town, either night or day, go for all I care. Do what you damn please; that's what I am going to do in the future and I'm glad you know it. I'm tired climbing through windows and slinking like a dog. I'll come and go like other men after this."

"I don't know what other men you are referring to," said Kate. "You have a monopoly of your kind in this neighbourhood; there is none other like you. You crawl and slink as 'to the manner born.'"

"Don't you go too far," he menaced with an ugly leer.

"Keep that for your mother," laughed Kate. "You need never try a threat with me. I am stronger than you are, and you may depend upon it I shall see that my strength never fails me again. I know now that you are all Nancy Ellen said you were."

"Well, if you married me knowing it, what are you going to do about it?" he sneered.

"I didn't know it then. I thought I knew you. I thought she had been misinformed," said Kate, in self-defence.

"Well," he said insultingly, "if you hadn't been in such a big hurry, you could soon have found out all you wanted to know. I took advantage of it, but I never did understand your rush."

"You never will," said Kate.

Then she arose and went to see if the children had wakened. All day she was thinking so deeply she would stumble over the chairs in her preoccupation. George noticed it, and it frightened him. After supper he came and sat on the porch beside her.

"Kate," he said, "as usual you are 'making mountains out of mole hills.' It doesn't damn a fellow forever to ride or walk, I almost always walk, into town in the evening, to see the papers and have a little visit with the boys. Work all day in a field is mighty lonesome; a man has got the have a little change. I don't deny a glass of beer once in awhile, or a game of cards with the boys occasionally; but if you have lived with me over five years here, and never suspected it before, it can't be so desperately bad, can it? Come now, be fair!"

"It's no difference whether I am fair or unfair," Kate said, wearily. "It explains why you simply will not brace up, and be a real man, and do a man's work in the world, and achieve a man's success."

"Who can get anywhere, splitting everything in halves?" he demanded.

"The most successful men in this neighbourhood got their start exactly that way," she said.

"Ah, well, farming ain't my job, anyway," he said. "I always did hate it. I always will. If I could have a little capital to start with, I know a trick that would suit you, and make us independent in no time."

Kate said no word, and seeing she was not going to, he continued: "I've thought about this till I've got it all down fine, and it's a great scheme; you'll admit that, even angry as you are. It is this: get enough together to build a saw mill on my strip of ravine. A little damming would make a free water power worth a fortune. I could hire a good man to run the saw and do the work, and I could take a horse and ride, or drive around among the farmers I know, and buy up timber cheaper than most men could get it. I could just skin the eyes out of them."

"Did it ever occur to you that you could do better by being honest?" asked Kate, wearily.

"Aw, well, Smarty! you know I didn't mean that literally!" he scoffed. "You know I only meant

I could talk, and jolly, and buy at bed-rock prices; I know where to get the timber, and the two best mill men in the country; we are near the railroad; it's the dandiest scheme that ever struck Walden. What do you think about it?"

"I think if Adam had it he'd be rich from it in ten years," she said, quietly.

"Then you DO think it's a bully idea," he cried. "You WOULD try it if we had a chance?"

"I might," said Kate.

"You know," he cried, jumping up in excitement, "I've never mentioned this to a soul, but I've got it all thought out. Would you go to see your brother Adam, and see if you could get him to take an interest for young Adam? He could manage the money himself."

"I wouldn't go to a relative of mine for a cent, even if the children were starving," said Kate. "Get, and keep, THAT clear in your head."

"But you think there is something in it?" he persisted.

"I know there is," said Kate with finality. "In the hands of the right man, and with the capital to start."

"Kate, you can be the meanest," he said.

"I didn't intend to be, in this particular instance," she said. "But honestly, George, what have I ever seen of you in the way of financial success in the past that would give me hope for the future?"

"I know it," he said, "but I've never struck exactly the right thing. This is what I could make a success of, and I would make a good big one, you bet! Kate, I'll not go to town another night. I'll stop all that." He drew the flask from his pocket and smashed it against the closest tree. "And I'll stop all there ever was of that, even to a glass of beer on a hot day; if you say so, if you'll stand by me this once more, if I fail this time, I'll never ask you again; honest, I won't."

"If I had money, I'd try it, keeping the building in my own name and keeping the books myself; but I've none, and no way to get any, as you know," she said. "I can see what could be done, but I'm helpless."

"I'M NOT!" said George. "I've got it all worked out. You see I was doing something useful with my head, if I wasn't always plowing as fast as you thought I should. If you'll back me, if you'll keep books, if you'll handle the money until she is paid back, I know Aunt Ollie will sell enough of this land to build the mill and buy the machinery. She could keep the house, and orchard, and barn, and a big enough piece, say forty acres, to live on and keep all of us in grub. She and Mother could move out here—she said the other day she was tired of town and getting homesick—and we could go to town to put the children in school, and be on the job. I won't ever ask you and Mother to live together again. Kate, will you go in with me? Will you talk to Aunt Ollie? Will you let me show you, and explain, and prove to you?"

"I won't be a party to anything that would even remotely threaten to lose Aunt Ollie's money for her," she said.

"She's got nobody on earth but me. It's all mine in the end. Why not let me have this wonderful chance with it? Kate, will you?" he begged.

"I'll think about it," she conceded. "If I can study out a sure, honourable way. I'll promise to think. Now go out there, and hunt the last scrap of that glass; the children may cut their feet in the morning."

Then Kate went in to bed. If she had looked from her window, she might have seen George scratching matches and picking pieces of glass from the grass. When he came to the bottom of the bottle with upstanding, jagged edges, containing a few drops, he glanced at her room, saw that she was undressing in the dark, and lifting it, he poured the liquid on his tongue to the last drop that would fall.

CHAPTER XVI

THE WORK OF THE SUN

BEFORE Kate awakened the following morning George was out feeding the horses, cattle, and chickens, doing the milking, and working like the proverbial beaver. By the time breakfast was ready, he had convinced himself that he was a very exemplary man, while he expected Kate to be convinced also. He stood ready and willing to forgive her for every mean deceit and secret sin he ever had committed, or had it in his heart to commit in the future. All the world was rosy with him, he was flying with the wings of hope straight toward a wonderful achievement that would bring pleasure and riches, first to George Holt, then to his wife and children, then to the old aunt he really cared more for than any one else.

Incidentally, his mother might have some share, while he would bring such prosperity and activity to the village that all Walden would forget every bad thing it had ever thought or known of him, and delight to pay him honour. Kate might have guessed all this when she saw the pails full of milk on the table, and heard George whistling "Hail the Conquering Hero Comes," as he turned the cows into the pasture; but she had not slept well. Most of the night she had lain staring at the ceiling, her brain busy with calculations, computations, most of all with personal values.

She dared not be a party to anything that would lose Aunt Ollie her land; that was settled; but if she went into the venture herself, if she kept the deeds in Aunt Ollie's name, the bank account in hers, drew all the checks, kept the books, would it be safe? Could George buy timber as he thought; could she, herself, if he failed? The children were old enough to be in school now, she could have much of the day, she could soon train Polly and Adam to do even more than sweep and run errands; the scheme could be materialized in the Bates way, without a doubt; but could it be done in a Bates way, hampered and impeded by George Holt? Was the plan feasible, after all? She entered into the rosy cloud enveloping the kitchen without ever catching the faintest gleam of its hue. George came to her the instant he saw her and tried to put his arm around her. Kate drew back and looked at him intently.

"Aw, come on now, Kate," he said. "Leave out the heroics and be human. I'll do exactly as you say about everything if you will help me wheedle Aunt Ollie into letting me have the money."

Kate stepped back and put out her hands defensively: "A rare bargain," she said, "and one eminently worthy of you. You'll do what I say, if I'll do what you say, without the slightest reference as to whether it impoverishes a woman who has always helped and befriended you. You make me sick!"

"What's biting you now?" he demanded, sullenly.

Kate stood tall and straight before and above him

"If you have a good plan, if you can prove that it will work, what is the necessity for 'wheedling' anybody? Why not state what you propose in plain, unequivocal terms, and let the dear, old soul, who has done so much for us already, decide what she will do?"

"That's what I meant! That's all I meant!" he cried.

"In that case, 'wheedle' is a queer word to use."

"I believe you'd throw up the whole thing; I believe you'd let the chance to be a rich woman slip through your fingers, if it all depended on your saying only one word you thought wasn't quite straight," he cried, half in assertion, half in question.

"I honour you in that belief," said Kate. "I most certainly would."

"Then you turn the whole thing down? You won't have anything to do with it?" he cried, plunging into stoop-shouldered, mouth-sagging despair.

"Oh, I didn't SAY that!" said Kate. "Give me time! Let me think! I've got to know that there isn't a snare in it, from the title of the land to the grade of the creek bed. Have you investigated that? Is your ravine long enough and wide enough to dam it high enough at our outlet to get your power, and yet not back water on the road, and the farmers above you? Won't it freeze in winter? and can you get strong enough power from water to run a large saw? I doubt it!"

"Oh, gee! I never thought about that!" he cried.

"And if it would work, did you figure the cost of a dam into your estimate of the building and machinery?"

He snapped his fingers in impatience.

"By heck!" he cried, "I forgot THAT, too! But that wouldn't cost much. Look what we did in that ravine just for fun. Why, we could build that dam ourselves!"

"Yes, strong enough for conditions in September, but what about the January freshet?" she said.

"Croak! Croak! You blame old raven," cried George.

"And have you thought," continued Kate, "that there is no room on the bank toward town to set your mill, and it wouldn't be allowed there, if there were?"

"You bet I have!" he said defiantly. "I'm no such slouch as you think me. I've even stepped off the location!"

"Then," said Kate, "will you build a bridge across the ravine to reach it, or will you buy a strip from Linn and build a road?"

George collapsed with a groan.

"That's the trouble with you," said Kate. "You always build your castle with not even sand for a foundation. The most nebulous of rosy clouds serve you as perfectly as granite blocks. Before you go glimmering again, double your estimate to cover a dam and a bridge, and a lot of incidentals that no one ever seems able to include in a building contract. And whatever you do, keep a still head until we get these things figured, and have some sane idea of what the venture would cost."

"How long will it take?" he said sullenly.

"I haven't an idea. I'd have to go the Hartley and examine the records and be sure that there was no flaw in the deeds to the land; but the first thing is to get a surveyor and know for sure if you have a water-power that will work and not infringe on your neighbours. A thing like this can't be done in a few minutes' persuasive conversation. It will take weeks."

It really seemed as if it would take months. Kate went to Walden that afternoon, set the children playing in the ravine while she sketched it, made the best estimate she could of its fall, and approved the curve on the opposite bank which George thought could be cleared for a building site and lumber yard. Then she added a location for a dam and a bridge site, and went home to figure and think. The further she went in these processes the more hopeless the project seemed. She soon learned that there must be an engine with a boiler to run the saw. The dam could be used only to make a pond to furnish the water needed; but at that it would be cheaper than to dig a cistern or well. She would not even suggest to Aunt Ollie to sell any of the home forty. The sale of the remainder at the most hopeful price she dared estimate would not bring half the money needed, and it would come in long-time payments. Lumber, bricks, machinery, could not be had on time of any length, while wages were cash every Saturday night.

"It simply can't be done," said Kate, and stopped thinking about it, so far as George knew.

He was at once plunged into morose moping; he became sullen and indifferent about the work, ugly with Kate and the children, until she was driven almost frantic, and projects nearly as vague as some of George's began to float through her head.

One Saturday morning Kate had risen early and finished cleaning up her house, baking, and scrubbing porches. She had taken a bath to freshen and cool herself and was standing before her dresser, tucking the last pins in her hair, when she heard a heavy step on the porch and a loud knock on the screen door. She stood at an angle where she could peep; she looked as she reached for her dress. What she saw carried her to the door forgetful of the dress. Adam, Jr., stood there, white and shaken, steadying himself against the casing.

"Adam!" cried Kate. "Is Mother—?"

He shook his head.

"Father—?" she panted.

He nodded, seeming unable to speak. Kate's eyes darkened and widened. She gave Adam another glance and opened the door. "Come in," she said. "When did it happen? How did he get hurt?"

In that moment she recalled that she had left her father in perfect health, she had been gone more than seven years. In that time he could not fail to illness; how he had been hurt was her first thought. As she asked the question, she stepped into her room and snatched up her second best summer dress, waiting for Adam to speak as she slipped into it. But speaking seemed to be a very difficult thing for Adam. He was slow in starting and words dragged and came singly: "Yesterday—tired—big dinner—awful hot—sunstroke—"

"He's gone?" she cried.

Adam nodded in that queer way again.

"Why did you come? Does Mother want me?" the questions leaped from Kate's lips; her eyes implored him. Adam was too stricken to heed his sister's unspoken plea.

"Course," he said. "All there—your place—I want you. Only one in the family—not stark mad!"

Kate straightened tensely and looked at him again. "All right," she said. "I can throw a few things in my telescope, write the children a note to take to their father in the field, and we can stop in Walden and send Aunt Ollie out to cook for them; I can go as well as not, for as long as Mother wants me."

"Hurry!" said Adam.

In her room Kate stood still a second, her eyes narrow, her underlip sucked in, her heart almost stopped. Then she said aloud: "Father's sons have wished he would die too long for his death to strike even the most tolerant of them like that. Something dreadful has happened. I wonder to my soul—!"

She waited until they were past Hartley and then she asked suddenly: "Adam, what is the matter?"

Then Adam spoke: "I am one of a pack of seven poor fools, and every other girl in the family has gone raving mad, so I thought I'd come after you, and see if you had sense, or reason, or justice, left in you."

"What do you want of me?" she asked dazedly.

"I want you to be fair, to be honest, to do as you'd be done by. You came to me when you were in trouble," he reminded her.

Kate could not prevent the short laugh that sprang to her lips, nor what she said: "And you would not lift a finger; young Adam MADE his MOTHER help me. Why don't you go to George for what you want?"

Adam lost all self-control and swore sulphurously.

"I thought you'd be different," he said, "but I see you are going to be just like the rest of the—!"

"Stop that!" said Kate. "You're talking about my sisters—and yours. Stop this wild talk, and tell me exactly what is the matter."

"I'm telling nothing," said Adam. "You can find out what is the matter and go it with the rest of them, when you get there. Mother said this morning she wished you were there, because you'd be the only SANE one in the family, so I thought I'd bring you; but I wish now I hadn't done it, for it stands to reason that you will join the pack, and run as fast as the rest of the wolves."

"FROM a prairie fire, or TO a carcass?" asked Kate.

"I told you, you could find out when you got there. I'm not going to have them saying I influenced you, or bribed you," he said.

"Do you really think that they think you could, Adam?" asked Kate, wonderingly.

"I have said all I'm going to say," said Adam, and then he began driving his horse inhumanely fast, for the heat was deep, slow, and burning.

"Adam, is there any such hurry?" asked Kate. "You know you are abusing your horse dreadfully."

Adam immediately jerked the horse with all his might, and slashed the length of its body with two long stripes that rapidly raised in high welts, so Kate saw that he was past reasoning with and said no other word. She tried to think who would be at home, how they would treat her, the Prodigal, who had not been there in seven years; and suddenly it occurred to Kate that, if she had known all she now knew in her youth, and had the same decision to make again as when she knew nothing, she would have taken wing, just as she had. She had made failures, she had hurt herself, mind and body, but her honour, her self-respect were intact. Suddenly she sat straight. She was glad that she had taken a bath, worn a reasonably decent dress, and had a better one in the back of the buggy. She would cut the Gordian knot with a vengeance. She would not wait to see how they treated her, she would treat them! As for Adam's state, there was only one surmise she could make, and that seemed so incredible, she decided to wait until her mother told her all about whatever the trouble was.

As they came in sight of the house, queer feelings took possession of Kate. She struggled to think kindly of her father; she tried to feel pangs of grief over his passing. She was too forthright and had too good memory to succeed. Home had been so unbearable that she had taken desperate measures to escape it, but as the white house with its tree and shrub filled yard could be seen more plainly, Kate suddenly was filled with the strongest possessive feeling she ever had known. It was home. It was her home. Her place was there, even as Adam had said. She felt a sudden revulsion against herself that she had stayed away seven years; she should have taken her chances and at least gone to see her mother. She leaned from the buggy and watched for the first glimpse of the tall, gaunt, dark woman, who had brought their big brood into the world and stood squarely with her husband, against every one of them, in each thing he proposed.

Now he was gone. No doubt he had carried out his intentions. No doubt she was standing by him as always. Kate gathered her skirts, but Adam passed the house, driving furiously as ever, and he only slackened speed when he was forced to at the turn from the road to the lane. He stopped the buggy in the barnyard, got out, and began unharnessing the horse. Kate sat still and watched him until he led it away, then she stepped down and started across the barnyard, down the lane leading to the dooryard. As she closed the yard gate and rounded a widely spreading snowball bush, her heart was pounding wildly. What was coming? How would the other boys act, if Adam, the best balanced man of them all, was behaving as he was? How would her mother greet her? With the thought, Kate realized that she was so homesick for her mother that she would do or give anything in the world to see her. Then there was a dragging step, a short, sharp breath, and wheeling, Kate stood facing her mother. She had come from the potato patch back of the orchard, carrying a pail of potatoes in each hand. Her face was haggard, her eyes bloodshot, her hair falling in dark tags, her cheeks red with exertion. They stood facing each other. At the first glimpse Kate cried, "Oh, Mother," and sprang toward her. Then she stopped, while her heart again failed her, for from the astonishment on her mother's face, Kate saw instantly that she was surprised, and had neither sent for nor expected her. She was nauseatingly disappointed. Adam had said she was wanted, had been sent for. Kate's face was twitching, her lips quivering, but she did not hesitate more than an instant.

"I see you were not expecting me," she said. "I'm sorry. Adam came after me. I wouldn't have come if he hadn't said you sent for me."

Kate paused a minute hopefully. Her mother looked at her steadily.

"I'm sorry," Kate repeated. "I don't know why he said that."

By that time the pain in her heart was so fierce she caught her breath sharply, and pressed her hand hard against her side. Her mother stooped, set down the buckets, and taking off her sunbonnet, wiped the sweat from her lined face with the curtain.

"Well, I do," she said tersely.

"Why?" demanded Kate.

"To see if he could use you to serve his own interests, of course," answered her mother. "He lied good and hard when he said I sent for you; I didn't. I probably wouldn't a-had the sense to do it. But since you are here, I don't mind telling you that I never was so glad to see any one in all my born days."

Mrs. Bates drew herself full height, set her lips, stiffened her jaw, and again used the bonnet skirt on her face and neck. Kate picked up the potatoes, to hide the big tears that gushed from her eyes, and leading the way toward the house she said: "Come over here in the shade. Why should you be out digging potatoes?"

"Oh, they's enough here, and willing enough," said Mrs. Bates. "Slipped off to get away from them. It was the quietest and the peacefullest out there, Kate. I'd most liked to stay all day, but it's getting on to dinner time, and I'm short of potatoes."

"Never mind the potatoes," said Kate. "Let the folks serve themselves if they are hungry."

She went to the side of the smoke house, picked up a bench turned up there, and carrying it to the shady side of a widely spreading privet bush, she placed it where it would be best screened from both house and barn. Then setting the potatoes in the shade, she went to her mother, put her arm around her, and drew her to the seat. She took her handkerchief and wiped her face, smoothed back her straggled hair, and pulling out a pin, fastened the coil better.

"Now rest a bit," she said, "and then tell me why you are glad to see me, and exactly what you'd like me to do here. Mind, I've been away seven years, and Adam told me not a word, except that Father was gone."

"Humph! All missed the mark again," commented Mrs. Bates dryly. "They all said he'd gone to fill you up, and get you on his side."

"Mother, what is the trouble?" asked Kate. "Take your time and tell me what has happened, and what YOU want, not what Adam wants."

Mrs. Bates relaxed her body a trifle, but gripped her hands tightly together in her lap.

"Well, it was quick work," she said. "It all came yesterday afternoon just like being hit by lightning. Pa hadn't failed a particle that any one could see. Ate a big dinner of ham an' boiled dumplings, an' him an' Hiram was in the west field. It was scorchin' hot an' first Hiram saw, Pa was down. Sam Langley was passin' an' helped get him in, an' took our horse an' ran for Robert. He was in the country but Sam brought another doctor real quick, an' he seemed to fetch Pa out of it in good shape, so we thought he'd be all right, mebby by morning, though the doctor said he'd have to hole up a day or two. He went away, promisin' to send Robert back, and Hiram went home to feed. I set by Pa fanning him an' putting cloths on his head. All at once he began to chill.

"We thought it was only the way a-body was with sunstroke, and past pilin' on blankets, we didn't pay much attention. He SAID he was all right, so I went to milk. Before I left I gave him a drink, an' he asked me to feel in his pants pocket an' get the key an' hand him the deed box, till he'd see if everything was right. Said he guessed he'd had a close call. You know how he was. I got him the box and went to do the evening work. I hurried fast as I could. Coming back, clear acrost the yard I smelt burning wool, an' I dropped the milk an' ran. I dunno no more about just what happened 'an you do. The house was full of smoke. Pa was on the floor, most to the sitting-room door, his head and hair and hands awfully burned, his shirt burned off, laying face down, and clear gone. The minute I seen the way he laid, I knew he was gone. The bed was pourin' smoke and one little blaze about six inches high was shootin' up to the top. I got that out, and then I saw most of the fire was smothered between the blankets where he'd thrown them back to get out of the bed. I dunno why he fooled with the lamp. It always stood on the little table in his reach, but it was light enough to read fine print. All I can figure is that the light was going out of his EYES, an' he thought IT WAS GETTIN' DARK, so he tried to light the lamp to see the deeds. He was fingerin' them when I left, but he didn't say he couldn't see them. The lamp was just on the bare edge of the table, the wick way up an' blackened, the chimney smashed on the floor, the bed afire."

"Those deeds are burned?" gasped Kate. "All of them? Are they all gone?"

"Every last one," said Mrs. Bates.

"Well, if ONE is gone, thank God they all are," said Kate.

Her mother turned swiftly and caught her arm.

"Say that again!" she cried eagerly.

"Maybe I'm WRONG about it, but it's what I think," said Kate. "If the boys are crazy over all of them being gone, they'd do murder if part had theirs, and the others had not."

Mrs. Bates doubled over on Kate's shoulder suddenly and struggled with an inward spasm.

"You poor thing," said Kate. "This is dreadful. All of us know how you loved him, how you worked together. Can you think of anything I can do? Is there any special thing the matter?"

"I'm afraid!" whispered Mrs. Bates. "Oh, Katie, I'm so afraid. You know how SET he was, you know how he worked himself and all of us—he had to know what he was doing, when he fought the fire till the shirt burned off him"—her voice dropped to a harsh whisper—"what do you s'pose he's doing now?"

Any form of religious belief was a subject that never had been touched upon or talked of in the Bates family. Money was their God, work their religion; Kate looked at her mother curiously.

"You mean you believe in after life?" she asked.

"Why, I suppose there must be SOMETHING," she said.

"I think so myself," said Kate. "I always have. I think there is a God, and that Father is facing Him now, and finding out for the first time in his experience that he is very small potatoes, and what he planned and slaved for amounted to nothing, in the scheme of the universe. I can't imagine Father being subdued by anything on earth, but it appeals to me that he will cut a pathetic figure before the throne of an Almighty God."

A slow grin twisted Mrs. Bates' lips.

"Well, wherever he went," she said, "I guess he found out pretty quick that he was some place at last where he couldn't be boss."

"I'm very sure he has," said Kate, "and I am equally sure the discipline will be good for him. But his sons! His precious sons! What are they doing?"

"Taking it according to their bent," said Mrs. Bates. "Adam is insane, Hiram is crying."

"Have you had a lawyer?" asked Kate.

"What for? We all know the law on this subject better than we know our a, b, c's."

"Did your deed for this place go, too?" asked Kate.

"Yes," said Mrs. Bates, "but mine was recorded, none of the others were. I get a third, and the rest will be cut up and divided, share and share alike, among ALL OF YOU, equally. I think it's going to kill Adam and ruin Andrew."

"It won't do either. But this is awful. I can see how the boys feel, and really, Mother, this is no more fair to them than things always have been for the girls. By the way, what are they doing?"

"Same as the boys, acting out their natures. Mary is openly rejoicing. So is Nancy Ellen. Hannah and Bertha at least can see the boys' side. The others say one thing before the boys and another among themselves. In the end the girls will have their shares and nobody can blame them. I don't myself, but I think Pa will rise from his grave when those farms are torn up."

"Don't worry," said Kate. "He will have learned by now that graves are merely incidental, and that he has no option on real estate where he is. Leave him to his harp, and tell me what you want done."

"I want you to see that it was all accidental. I want you to take care of me. I want you should think out the FAIR thing for all of us to DO. I want you to keep sane and cool-headed and shame the others into behaving themselves. And I want you to smash down hard on their everlasting, 'why didn't you do this?' and 'why didn't you do that?' I reckon I've been told five hundred times a-ready that I shouldn't a-give him the deeds. Josie say it, an' then she sings it. NOT GIVE THEM TO HIM! How could I help giving them to him? He'd a-got up and got them himself if I hadn't—"

"You have cut out something of a job for me," said Kate, "but I'll do my best. Anyway, I can take care of you. Come on into the house now, and let me clean you up, and then I'll talk the rest of them into reason, if you stand back of me, and let them see I'm acting for you."

"You go ahead," said Mrs. Bates. "I'll back whatever you say. But keep them off of me! Keep them off of me!"

After Kate had bathed her mother, helped her into fresh clothes, and brushed her hair, she coaxed her to lie down, and by diplomatic talk and stroking her head, finally soothed her to sleep. Then she went down and announced the fact, asked them all to be quiet, and began making her way from group to group in an effort to restore mental balance and sanity. After Kate had invited all of them to go home and stay until time for the funeral Sunday morning, and all of them had emphatically declined, and eagerly had gone on straining the situation to the breaking point, Kate gave up and began setting the table. When any of them tried to talk or argue with her she said conclusively: "I shall not say one word about this until Monday. Then we will talk things over, and find where we stand, and what Mother wants. This would be much easier for all of us, if you'd all go home and calm down, and plan out what you think would be the fair and just thing to do."

Before evening Kate was back exactly where she left off, for when Mrs. Bates came downstairs, her nerves quieted by her long sleep, she asked Kate what would be best about each question that arose, while Kate answered as nearly for all of them as her judgment and common sense dictated; but she gave the answer in her own way, and she paved the way by making a short, sharp speech when the first person said in her hearing that "Mother never should have given him the deeds." Not one of them said that again, while at Kate's suggestion, mentally and on scraps of paper, every single one of them figured that one third of sixteen hundred and fifty was five hundred and fifty; subtracted from sixteen hundred and fifty this left one thousand one hundred, which, divided by sixteen, gave sixty-eight and three fourths. This result gave Josie the hysterics, strong and capable though she was; made Hiram violently ill, so that he resorted to garden palings for a support; while Agatha used her influence suddenly, and took Adam, Jr., home.

As she came to Kate to say that they were going, Agatha was white as possible, her thin lips compressed, a red spot burning on either cheek.

"Adam and I shall take our departure now, Katherine," she said, standing very stiffly, her head held higher than Kate ever had thought it could be lifted. Kate put her arm around her sister-in-law and gave her a hearty hug: "Tell Adam I'll do what I think is fair and just; and use all the influence I have to get the others to do the same," she said.

"Fruitless!" said Agatha. "Fruitless! Reason and justice have departed from this abode. I shall hasten my pace, and take Adam where my influence is paramount. The state of affairs here is deplorable, perfectly deplorable! I shall not be missed, and I shall leave my male offspring to take the place of his poor, defrauded father."

Adam, 3d, was now a tall, handsome young man of twenty-two, quite as fond of Kate as ever. He wiped the dishes, and when the evening work was finished, they talked with Mrs. Bates until they knew her every wish. The children had planned for a funeral from the church, because it was large enough to seat the family and friends in comfort; but when they mentioned this to Mrs. Bates, she delivered an ultimatum on the instant: "You'll do no such thing!" she cried. "Pa never went to that church living; I'll not sanction his being carried there feet first, when he's helpless. And we'll not scandalize the neighbours by fighting over money on Sunday, either. You'll all come Monday morning, if you want anything to say about this. If you don't, I'll put through the business in short order. I'm sick to my soul of the whole thing. I'll wash my hands of it as quick as possible."

So the families all went to their homes; Kate helped her mother to bed; and then she and Adam, 3d, tried to plan what would be best for the morrow; afterward they sat down and figured until almost dawn.

"There's no faintest possibility of pleasing everyone," said Kate. "The level best we can do is to devise some scheme whereby everyone will come as nearly being satisfied as possible."

"Can Aunt Josie and Aunt Mary keep from fighting across the grave?" asked Adam.

"Only Heaven knows," said Kate.

CHAPTER XVII

THE BANNER HAND

SUNDAY morning Kate arose early and had the house clean and everything ready when the first carriage load drove into the barnyard. As she helped her mother to dress, Mrs. Bates again evidenced a rebellious spirit. Nancy Ellen had slipped upstairs and sewed fine white ruching in the neck and sleeves of her mother's best dress, her only dress, in fact, aside from the calicoes she worked in. Kate combed her mother's hair and drew it in loose waves across her temples. As she produced the dress, Mrs. Bates drew back.

"What did you stick them gew-gaws onto my dress for?" she demanded.

"I didn't," said Kate.

"Oh, it was Nancy Ellen! Well, I don't see why she wanted to make a laughing stock of me," said Mrs. Bates.

"She didn't!" said Kate. "Everyone is wearing ruching now; she wanted her mother to have what the best of them have."

"Humph!" said Mrs. Bates. "Well, I reckon I can stand it until noon, but it's going to be a hot dose."

"Haven't you a thin black dress, Mother?" asked Kate.

"No," said Mrs. Bates, "I haven't; but you can make a pretty safe bet that I will have one before I start anywhere again in such weather as this."

"That's the proper spirit," said Kate. "There comes Andrew. Let me put your bonnet on."

She set the fine black bonnet Nancy Ellen had bought on Mrs. Bates' head at the proper angle and tied the long, wide silk ribbon beneath her chin. Mrs. Bates sat in martyr-like resignation. Kate was pleased with her mother's appearance.

"Look in the mirror," she said. "See what a handsome lady you are."

"I ain't seen in a looking-glass since I don't know when," said Mrs. Bates. "Why should I begin now? Chances are 'at you have rigged me up until I'll set the neighbours laughing, or else to saying that I didn't wait until the breath was out of Pa's body to begin primping."

"Nonsense, Mother," said Kate. "Nobody will say or think anything. Everyone will recognize Nancy Ellen's fine Spencerian hand in that bonnet and ruching. Now for your veil!"

Mrs. Bates arose from her chair, and stepped back.

"There, there, Katie!" she said. "You've gone far enough. I'll be sweat to a lather in this dress; I'll wear the head-riggin', because I've go to, or set the neighbours talkin' how mean Pa was not to let me have a bonnet; and between the two I'd rather they'd take it out on me than on him." She steadied herself by the chair back and looked Kate in the eyes. "Pa was always the banner hand to boss everything," she said. "He was so big and strong, and so all-fired sure he was right, I never contraried him in the start, so before I knowed it, I was waiting for him to say what to do, and then agreeing with him, even when I knowed he was WRONG. So goin' we got along FINE, but it give me an awful smothered feeling at times."

Kate stood looking at her mother intently, her brain racing, for she was thinking to herself: "Good Lord! She means that to preserve the appearance of self-respect she systematically agreed with him, whether she thought he was right or wrong; because she was not able to hold her own against him. Nearly fifty years of life like that!"

Kate tossed the heavy black crepe veil back on the bed. "Mother," she said, "here alone, and between us, if I promise never to tell a living soul, will you tell me the truth about that deed business?" Mrs. Bates seemed so agitated Kate added: "I mean how it started. If you thought it was right and a fair thing to do."

"Yes, I'll tell you that," said Mrs. Bates. "It was not fair, and I saw it; I saw it good and plenty. There was no use to fight him; that would only a-drove him to record them, but I was sick of it, an' I told him so."

Kate was pinning her hat.

"I have planned for you to walk with Adam," she said.

"Well, you can just change THAT plan, so far as I am concerned," said Mrs. Bates with finality. "I ain't a-goin' with Adam. Somebody had told him about the deeds before he got here. He came in ravin', and he talked to me something terrible. He was the first to say I shouldn't a-give Pa the box. NOT GIVE IT TO HIM! An' he went farther than that, till I just rose up an' called him down proper; but I ain't feelin' good at him, an' I ain't goin' with him. I am goin' with you. I want somebody with me that understands me, and feels a little for me, an' I want the neighbours to see that the minute I'm boss, such a fine girl as you has her rightful place in her home. I'll go with you, or I'll sit down on this chair, and sit here."

"But you didn't send for me," said Kate.

"No, I hadn't quite got round to it yet; but I was coming. I'd told all of them that you were the only one in the lot who had any sense; and I'd said I WISHED you were here, and as I see it, I'd a-sent for you yesterday afternoon about three o'clock. I was coming to it fast. I didn't feel just like standing up for myself; but I'd took about all fault-finding it was in me to bear. Just about three o'clock I'd a-sent for you, Katie, sure as God made little apples."

"All right then," said Kate, "but if you don't tell them, they'll always say I took the lead."

"Well, they got to say something," said Mrs. Bates. "Most of 'em would die if they had to keep their mouths shut awhile; but I'll tell them fast enough."

Then she led the way downstairs. There were enough members of the immediate family to pack the front rooms of the house, the neighbours filled the dining room and dooryard. The church choir sang a hymn in front of the house, the minister stood on the front steps and read a chapter, and told where Mr. Bates had been born, married, the size of his family and possessions, said he was a good father, an honest neighbour, and very sensibly left his future with his God. Then the choir sang again and all started to their conveyances. As the breaking up began outside, Mrs. Bates arose and stepped to the foot of the casket. She steadied herself by it and said: "Some time back, I promised Pa that if he went before I did, at this time in his funeral ceremony I would set his black tin box on the foot of his coffin and unlock before all of you, and in the order in which they lay, beginning with Adam, Jr., hand each of you boys the deed Pa had made you for the land you live on. You all know WHAT happened. None of you know just HOW. It wouldn't bring the deeds BACK if you did. They're gone. But I want you boys to follow your father to his grave with nothing in your hearts against HIM. He was all for the men. I don't ever want to hear any of you criticize him about this, or me, either. He did his best to make you upstanding men in your community, his one failing being that he liked being an upstanding man himself so well that he carried it too far; but his intentions was the best. As for me, I'd no idea how sick he was, and nobody else did. I minded him just like all the rest of you always did; the BOYS especially. From the church I want all of you to go home until to-morrow morning, and then I want my sons and daughters by BIRTH only, to come here, and we'll talk things over, quietly, QUIETLY, mind you; and decide what to do. Katie, will you come with me?"

It was not quite a tearless funeral. Some of the daughters-in-law wept from nervous excitement; and some of the little children cried with fear, but there were no tears from the wife of Adam Bates, or his sons and daughters. And when he was left to the mercies of time, all of them followed Mrs. Bates' orders, except Nancy Ellen and Robert, who stopped to help Kate with the dinner. Kate slipped into her second dress and went to work. Mrs. Bates untied her bonnet strings and unfastened her dress neck as they started home. She unbuttoned her waist going up the back walk and pulled it off at the door.

"Well, if I ever put that thing on in July again," she said, "you can use my head for a knock-maul. Nancy Ellen, can't you stop at a store as you come out in the morning and get the goods, and you girls run me up a dress that is nice enough to go out in, and not so hot it starts me burning before my time?"

"Of course I can," said Nancy Ellen. "About what do you want to pay, Mother?"

"Whatever it takes to get a decent and a cool dress; cool, mind you," said Mrs. Bates, "an' any colour but black."

"Why, Mother!" cried Nancy Ellen "it must be black!"

"No," said Mrs. Bates. "Pa kept me in black all my life on the supposition it showed the dirt the least. There's nothing in that. It shows dirt worse 'an white. I got my fill of black. You can get a nice cool gray, if you want me to wear it."

"Well, I never!" said Nancy Ellen. "What will the neighbours say?"

"What do I care?" asked Mrs. Bates. "They've talked about me all my life, I'd be kinda lonesome if they's to quit."

Dinner over, Kate proposed that her mother should lie down while they washed the dishes.

"I would like a little rest," said Mrs. Bates. "I guess I'll go upstairs."

"You'll do nothing of the kind," said Kate. "It's dreadfully hot up there. Go in the spare room, where it is cool; we'll keep quiet. I am going to stay Tuesday until I move you in there, anyway. It's smaller, but it's big enough for one, and you'll feel much better there."

"Oh, Katie, I'm so glad you thought of that," cried Mrs. Bates. "I been thinking and thinking about it, and it just seems as if I can't ever steel myself to go into that room to sleep again. I'll never enter that door that I don't see—"

"You'll never enter it again as your room," said Kate. "I'll fix you up before I go; and Sally Whistler told me last evening she would come and make her home with you if you wanted her. You like Sally, don't you?"

"Yes, I like her fine," said Mrs. Bates.

Quietly as possible the girls washed the dishes, pulled down the blinds, closed the front door, and slipped down in the orchard with Robert to talk things over. Nancy Ellen was stiffly reserved with Kate, but she WOULD speak when she was spoken to, which was so much better than silence that Kate was happy over it. Robert was himself. Kate thought she had never liked him so well. He seemed to grow even kinder and more considerate as the years passed. Nancy Ellen was prettier than Kate ever had seen her, but there was a line of discontent around her mouth, and she spoke pettishly on slight provocation, or none at all. Now she was openly, brazenly, brutally, frank in her rejoicing. She thought it was the best "JOKE" that ever happened to the boys; and she said so repeatedly. Kate found her lips closing more tightly and a slight feeling of revulsion growing in her heart. Surely in Nancy Ellen's lovely home, cared for and shielded in every way, she had no such need of money as Kate had herself. She was delighted when Nancy Ellen said she was sleepy, and was going to the living-room lounge for a nap. Then Kate produced her sheet of figures. She and Robert talked the situation over and carefully figured on how an adjustment, fair to all, could be made, until they were called to supper.

After supper Nancy Ellen and Robert went home, while Kate and her mother sat on the back porch and talked until Kate had a clear understanding and a definite plan in her mind, which was that much improvement over wearing herself out in bitter revilings, or selfish rejoicing over her brothers' misfortune. Her mother listened to all she had to say, asked a question occasionally, objected to some things, and suggested others. They arose when they had covered every contingency they could think of and went upstairs to bed, even though the downstairs was cooler.

As she undressed, Mrs. Bates said slowly: "Now in the morning, I'll speak my piece first; and I'll say it pretty plain. I got the whip-hand here for once in my life. They can't rave and fight here, and insult me again, as they did Friday night and Saturday till you got here an' shut 'em up. I won't stand it, that's flat! I'll tell 'em so, and that you speak for me, because you can figure faster and express yourself plainer; but insist that there be no fussing, an' I'll back you. I don't know just what life has been doing to you, Katie, but Lord! it has made a fine woman of you."

Kate set her lips in an even line and said nothing, but her heart was the gladdest it had been in years.

Her mother continued: "Seems like Nancy Ellen had all the chance. Most folks thought she was a lot the purtiest to start with, though I can't say that I ever saw so much difference. She's had leisure an' pettin', and her husband has made a mint o' money; she's gone all over the country with him, and the more chance she has, the narrower she grows, and the more discontenteder. One thing, she is awful disappointed about havin' no children. I pity her about that."

"Is it because she's a twin?" asked Kate.

"I'm afraid so," said Mrs. Bates. "You can't tell much about those things, they just seem to happen. Robert and Nancy Ellen feel awful bad about it. Still, she might do for others what she would for her own. The Lord knows there are enough mighty nice children in the world who need mothering. I want to see your children, Katie. Are they nice little folks, straight and good looking?"

"The boy is," said Kate. "The girl is good, with the exception of being the most stubborn child I've ever seen. She looks so much like a woman it almost sickens me to think of that I have to drive myself to do her justice."

"What a pity!" said Mrs. Bates, slowly.

"Oh, they are healthy, happy youngsters," said Kate. "They get as much as we ever did, and don't expect any more. I have yet to see a demonstrative Bates."

"Humph!" said Mrs. Bates. "Well, you ought to been here Friday night, and I thought Adam came precious near it Saturday."

"Demonstrating power, or anger, yes," said Kate. "I meant affection. And isn't it the queerest thing how people are made? Of all the boys, Adam is the one who has had the most softening influences, and who has made the most money, and yet he's acting the worst of all. It really seems as if failure and hardship make more of a human being of folks than success."

"You're right," said Mrs. Bates. "Look at Nancy Ellen and Adam. Sometimes I think Adam has been pretty much galled with Agatha and her money all these years; and it just drives him crazy to think of having still less than she has. Have you got your figures all set down, to back you up, Katie?"

"Yes," said Kate. "I've gone all over it with Robert, and he thinks it's the best and only thing that can be done. Now go to sleep."

Each knew that the other was awake most of the night, but very few words passed between them. They were up early, dressed, and waiting when the first carriage stopped at the gate. Kate told her mother to stay where she would not be worried until she was needed, and went down herself to meet her brothers and sisters in the big living room. When the last one arrived, she called her mother. Mrs. Bates came down looking hollow-eyed, haggard, and grim, as none of her children ever before had seen her. She walked directly to the little table at the end of the room, and while still standing she said: "Now I've got a few words to say, and then I'll turn this over to a younger head an' one better at figures than mine. I've said my say as to Pa, yesterday. Now I'll say THIS, for myself. I got my start, minding Pa, and agreeing with him, young; but you needn't any of you throw it in my teeth now, that I did. There is only ONE woman among you, and no MAN who ever disobeyed him. Katie stood up to him once, and got seven years from home to punish her and me. He wasn't RIGHT then, and I knew it, as I'd often known it before, and pretty often since; but no woman God ever made could have lived with Adam Bates as his wife and contraried him. I didn't mind him any quicker or any oftener than the rest of you; keep that pretty clear in your heads, and don't one of you dare open your mouth again to tell me, as you did Saturday, what I SHOULD a-done, and what I SHOULDN'T. I've had the law of this explained to me; you all know it for that matter. By the law, I get this place and one third of all the other land and money. I don't know just what money there is at the bank or in notes and mortgages, but a sixteenth of it after my third is taken out ain't going to make or break any of you. I've told Katie what I'm willing to do on my part and she will explain it, and then tell you about a plan she has fixed up. As for me, you can take it or leave it. If you take it, well and good; if you don't, the law will be set in motion to-day, and it will take its course to the end. It all depends on YOU.

"Now two things more. At the start, what Pa wanted to do seemed to me right, and I agreed with him and worked with him. But when my girls began to grow up and I saw how they felt, and how they struggled and worked, and how the women you boys married went ahead of my own girls, and had finer homes, an' carriages, and easier times, I got pretty sick of it, and I told Pa so more'n once. He just raved whenever I did, an' he always carried his keys in his pocket. I never touched his chest key in my life, till I handed him his deed box Friday afternoon. But I agree with my girls. It's fair and right, since things have come out as they have, that they should have their shares. I would, too.

"The other thing is just this: I'm tired to death of the whole business. I want peace and rest and I want it quick. Friday and Saturday I was so scared and so knocked out I s'pose I'd 'a' took it if one of the sucking babies had riz up and commenced to tell me what I should a-done, and what I shouldn't. I'm THROUGH with that. You will all keep civil tongues in your heads this morning, or I'll get up and go upstairs, an' lock myself in a room till you're gone, an' if I go, it will mean that the law takes its course; and if it does, there will be three hundred acres less land to divide. You've had Pa on your hands all your lives, now you will go civil, and you will go easy, or you will get a taste of Ma. I take no more talk from anybody. Katie, go ahead with your figures."

Kate spread her sheet on the table and glanced around the room:

"The Milton County records show sixteen hundred and fifty acres standing in Father's name," she said. "Of these, Mother is heir to five hundred and fifty acres, leaving one thousand one hundred acres to be divided among sixteen of us, which give sixty-eight and three-fourths acres to each. This land is the finest that proper fertilization and careful handling can make. Even the poorest is the cream of the country as compared with the surrounding farms. As a basis of estimate I have taken one hundred dollars an acre as a fair selling figure. Some is worth more, some less, but that is a good average. This would make the share of each of us in cash that could easily be realized, six thousand eight hundred and seventy-five dollars. Whatever else is in mortgages, notes, and money can be collected as it is due, deposited in some bank, and when it is all in, divided equally among us, after deducting Mother's third. Now this is the law, and those are the figures, but I shall venture to say that none of us feel RIGHT about it, or ever will."

An emphatic murmur of approval ran among the boys, Mary and Nancy Ellen stoutly declared that they did.

"Oh, no, you don't!" said Kate. "If God made any woman of you so that she feels right and clean in her conscience about this deal, he made her WRONG, and that is a thing that has not yet been proven of God. As I see it, here is the boys' side: from childhood they were told, bribed, and urged to miss holidays, work all week, and often on Sunday, to push and slave on the promise of this land at twenty-one. They all got the land and money to stock it and build homes. They were told it was theirs, required to pay the taxes on it, and also to labour at any time and without wages for Father. Not one of the boys but has done several hundred dollars' worth of work on Father's farm for nothing, to keep him satisfied and to insure getting his deed. All these years, each man has paid his taxes, put thousands in improvements, in rebuilding homes and barns, fertilizing, and developing his land. Each one of these farms is worth nearly twice what it was the day it was received. That the boys should lose all this is no cause for rejoicing on the part of any true woman; as a fact, no true woman would allow such a thing to happen—"

"Speak for yourself!" cried several of the girls at once.

"Now right here is where we come to a perfect understanding," said Kate. "I did say that for myself, but in the main what I say, I say for MOTHER. Now you will not one of you interrupt me again, or this meeting closes, and each of you stands to lose more than two thousand dollars, which is worth being civil for, for quite a while. No more of that! I say any woman should be ashamed to take advantage of her brother through an accident; and rob him of years of work and money he was perfectly justified in thinking was his. I, for one, refuse to do it, and I want and need money probably more than any of you. To tear up these farms, to take more than half from the boys, is too much. On the other hand, for the girls to help earn the land, to go with no inheritance at all, is even more unfair. Now in order to arrive at a compromise that will leave each boy his farm, and give each girl the nearest possible to a fair amount, figuring in what the boys have spent in taxes and work for Father, and what each girl has LOST by not having her money to handle all these years, it is necessary to split the difference between the time Adam, the eldest, has had his inheritance, and Hiram, the youngest, came into possession, which by taking from and adding to, gives a fair average of fifteen years. Now Mother proposes if we will enter into an agreement this morning with no words and no wrangling, to settle on this basis: she will relinquish her third of all other land, and keep only this home farm. She even will allow the fifty lying across the road to be sold and the money put into a general fund for the share of the girls. She will turn into this fund all money from notes and mortgages, and the sale of all stock, implements, etc., here, except what she wants to keep for her use, and the sum of three thousand dollars in cash, to provide against old age. This releases quite a sum of money, and three hundred and fifty acres of land, which she gives to the boys to start this fund as her recompense for their work and loss through a scheme in which she had a share in the start. She does this only on the understanding that the boys form a pool, and in some way take from what they have saved, sell timber or cattle, or borrow enough money to add to this sufficient to pay to each girl six thousand dollars in cash, in three months. Now get out your pencils and figure. Start with the original number of acres at fifty dollars an acre which is what it cost Father on an average. Balance against each other what the boys have lost in tax and work, and the girls have lost in not having their money to handle, and cross it off. Then figure, not on a basis of what the boys have made this land worth, but on what it cost Father's estate to buy, build on, and stock each farm. Strike the fifteen-year average on prices and profits. Figure that the girls get all their money practically immediately, to pay for the time they have been out of it; while each boy assumes an equal share of the indebtedness required to finish out the six thousand, after Mother has turned in what she is willing to, if this is settled HERE AND NOW."

"Then I understand," said Mary, "that if we take under the law, each of us is entitled to sixty-eight and three quarter acres; and if we take under Mother's proposition we are entitled to eighty-seven and a half acres."

"No, no, E. A.," said Kate, the old nickname for "Exceptional Ability" slipping out before she thought. "No, no! Not so! You take sixty-eight and three quarters under the law. Mother's proposition is made ONLY to the boys, and only on condition that they settle here and now; because she feels responsible to them for her share in rearing them and starting them out as she did. By accepting her proposition you lose eight hundred and seventy-five dollars, approximately. The boys lose on the same basis, figuring at fifty dollars and acre, six thousand five hundred and sixty-two dollars and fifty cents, plus their work and taxes, and minus what Mother will turn in, which will be about, let me see—It will take a pool of fifty-four thousand dollars to pay each of us six thousand. If Mother raises thirty-five thousand, plus sale money and notes, it will leave about nineteen thousand for the boys, which will divide up at nearly two thousand five hundred for them to lose, as against less than a thousand for us. That should be enough to square matters with any right-minded woman, even in our positions. It will give us that much cash in hand, it will leave the boys, some of the younger ones, in debt for years, if they hold their land. What more do you want?"

"I want the last cent that is coming to me," said Mary.

"I thought you would," said Kate. "Yet you have the best home, and the most money, of any of the girls living on farms. I settle under this proposition, because it is fair and just, and what Mother wants done. If she feels that this is defrauding the girls any, she can arrange to leave what she has to us at her death, which would more than square matters in our favour—"

"You hold on there, Katie," said Mrs. Bates. "You're going too fast! I'll get what's coming to me, and hang on to it awhile, before I decide which way the cat jumps. I reckon you'll all admit that in mothering the sixteen of you, doing my share indoors and out, and living with PA for all these years, I've earned it. I'll not tie myself up in any way. I'll do just what I please with mine. Figure in all I've told you to; for the rest—let be!"

"I beg your pardon," said Kate. "You're right, of course. I'll sign this, and I shall expect every sister I have to do the same, quickly and cheerfully, as the best way out of a bad business that has hurt all of us for years, and then I shall expect the boys to follow like men. It's the fairest, decentest thing we can do, let's get it over."

Kate picked up the pen, handed it to her mother, signed afterward herself, and then carried it to each of her sisters, leaving Nancy Ellen and Mary until last. All of them signed up to Nancy Ellen. She hesitated, and she whispered to Kate: "Did Robert—?" Kate nodded. Nancy Ellen thought deeply a minute and then said slowly: "I guess it is the quickest and best we can do." So she signed. Mary hesitated longer, but finally added her name. Kate passed on to the boys, beginning with Adam. Slowly he wrote his name, and as he handed back the paper he said: "Thank you, Kate, I believe it's the sanest thing we can do. I can make it easier than the younger boys."

"Then HELP them," said Kate tersely, passing on.

Each boy signed in turn, all of them pleased with the chance. It was so much better than they had hoped, that it was a great relief, which most of them admitted; so they followed Adam's example in thanking Kate, for all of them knew that in her brain had originated the scheme, which seemed to make the best of their troubles.

Then they sat closer and talked things over calmly and dispassionately. It was agreed that Adam and his mother should drive to Hartley the following afternoon and arrange for him to take out papers of administration for her, and start the adjustment of affairs. They all went home thinking more of each other, and Kate especially, than ever before. Mrs. Bates got dinner while Kate and Nancy Ellen went to work on the cool gray dress, so that it would be ready for the next afternoon. While her mother was away Kate cleaned the spare bedroom and moved her mother's possessions into it. She made it as convenient and comfortable and as pretty as she could, but the house was bare to austerity, so that her attempt at prettifying was rather a failure. Then she opened the closed room and cleaned it, after studying it most carefully as it stood. The longer she worked, the stronger became a conviction that was slowly working its way into her brain. When she could do no more she packed her telescope, installed Sally Whistler in her father's room, and rode to Hartley with a neighbour. From there she took the Wednesday hack for Walden.

CHAPTER XVIII

KATE TAKES THE BIT IN HER TEETH

THE hackman was obliging, for after delivering the mail and some parcels, he took Kate to her home. While she waited for him, she walked the ravine bank planning about the mill which was now so sure that she might almost begin work. Surely she might as soon as she finished figuring, for she had visited the Court House in Hartley and found that George's deeds were legal, and in proper shape. Her mind was filled with plans which this time must succeed.

As she approached the house she could see the children playing in the yard. It was the first time she ever had been away from them; she wondered if they had missed her. She was amazed to find that they were very decidedly disappointed to see her; but a few pertinent questions developed the reason. Their grandmother had come with her sister; she had spent her time teaching them that their mother was cold, and hard, and abused them, by not treating them as other children were treated. So far as Kate could see they had broken every rule she had ever laid down for them: eaten until their stomachs were out of order, and played in their better clothing, until it never would be nice again, while Polly shouted at her approach: "Give ME the oranges and candy. I want to divide them."

"Silly," said Kate. "This is too soon. I've no money yet, it will be a long time before I get any; but you shall each have an orange, some candy, and new clothing when I do. Now run see what big fish you can catch."

Satisfied, the children obeyed and ran to the creek. Aunt Ollie, worried and angered, told Adam to tell his father that Mother was home and for him to come and take her and grandmother to Walden at once. She had not been able to keep Mrs. Holt from one steady round of mischief; but she argued that her sister could do less, with her on guard, than alone, so she had stayed and done her best; but she knew how Kate would be annoyed, so she believed the best course was to leave as quickly as possible. Kate walked into the house, spoke to both women, and went to her room to change her clothing. Before she had finished, she heard George's voice in the house demanding: "Where's our millionaire lady? I want a look at her."

Kate was very tired, slowly relaxing from intense nerve strain, she was holding herself in check about the children. She took a tighter grip, and vowed she would not give Mrs. Holt the satisfaction of seeing her disturbed and provoked, if she killed herself in the effort at self-control. She stepped toward the door.

"Here," she called in a clear voice, the tone of which brought George swiftly.

"What was he worth, anyway?" he shouted.

"Oh, millions and millions," said Kate, sweetly, "at least I THINK so. It was scarcely a time to discuss finances, in the face of that horrible accident."

George laughed. "Oh, you're a good one!" he cried. "Think you can keep a thing like that still? The cats, and the dogs, and the chickens of the whole county know about the deeds the old Land King had made for his sons; and how he got left on it. Served him right, too! We could here Andrew swear, and see Adam beat his horse, clear over here! That's right! Go ahead! Put on airs! Tell us something we don't KNOW, will you? Maybe you think I wasn't hanging pretty close around that neighbourhood, myself!"

"Spying?" cried Kate.

"Looking for timber," he sneered. "And never in all my life have I seen anything to beat it. Sixteen hundred and fifty acres of the best land in the world. Your share of land and money together will be every cent of twelve thousand. Oh, I guess I know what you've got up your sleeve, my lady. Come on, shell out! Let's all go celebrate. What did you bring the children?"

Kate was rapidly losing patience in spite of her resolves.

"Myself," she said. "From their appearance and actions, goodness knows they needed me. I have been to my father's funeral, George; not to a circus."

"Humph!" said George. "And home for the first time in seven years. You needn't tell me it wasn't the biggest picnic you ever had! And say, about those deeds burning up—wasn't that too grand?"

"Even if my father burned with them?" she asked. "George, you make me completely disgusted."

"Big hypocrite!" he scoffed. "You know you're tickled silly. Why, you will get ten times as much as you would if those deeds hadn't burned. I know what that estate amounts to. I know what that land is worth. I'll see that you get your share to the last penny that can be wrung out of it. You bet I will! Things are coming our way at last. Now we can build the mill, and do everything we planned. I don't know as we will build a mill. With your fifteen thousand we could start a store in Hartley, and do bigger things."

"The thing for you to do right now is to hitch up and take Aunt Ollie and your mother home," said Kate. "I'll talk to you after supper and tell you all there is to know. I'm dusty and tired now."

"Well, you needn't try to fix up any shenanigan for me," he said. "I know to within five hundred dollars of what your share of that estate is worth, and I'll see that you get it."

"No one has even remotely suggested that I shouldn't have my share of that estate," said Kate.

While he was gone, Kate thought intently as she went about her work. She saw exactly what her position was, and what she had to do. Their talk would be disagreeable, but the matter had to gone into and gotten over. She let George talk as he would while she finished supper and they ate. When he went for his evening work, she helped the children scale their fish for breakfast and as they worked she talked to them, sanely, sensibly, explaining what she could, avoiding what she could not. She put them to bed, her heart almost sickened at what they had been taught and told. Kate was in no very propitious mood for her interview with George. As she sat on the front porch waiting for him, she was wishing with all her heart that she was back home with the children, to remain forever. That, of course, was out of the question, but she wished it. She had been so glad to be with her mother again, to be of service, to hear a word of approval now and then. She must be worthy of her mother's opinion, she thought, just as George stepped on the porch, sat on the top step, leaned against a pillar, and said: "Now go on, tell me all about it."

Kate thought intently a second. Instead of beginning with leaving Friday morning: "I was at the Court House in Hartley this morning," she said.

"You needn't have done that," he scoffed. "I spent most of the day there Monday. You bet folks shelled out the books when I told them who I was, and what I was after. I must say you folks have some little reason to be high and mighty. You sure have got the dough. No wonder the old man hung on to his deeds himself. He wasn't so FAR from a King, all right, all right."

"You mean you left your work Monday, and went to the Court House in Hartley and told who you were, and spent the day nosing into my father's affairs, before his SONS had done anything, or you had any idea WHAT was to be done?" she demanded.

"Oh, you needn't get so high and mighty," he said. "I propose to know just where I am, about this. I propose to have just what is coming to me—to you, to the last penny, and no Bates man will manage the affair, either."

Suddenly Kate leaned forward.

"I foresee that you've fixed yourself up for a big disappointment," she said. "My mother and her eldest son will settle my father's estate; and when it is settled I shall have exactly what the other girls have. Then if I still think it is wise, I shall at once go to work building the mill. Everything must be shaved to the last cent, must be done with the closest economy, I MUST come out of this with enough left to provide us a comfortable home."

"Do that from the first profits of the mill," he suggested.

"I'm no good at 'counting chickens before they're hatched,'" said Kate. "Besides, the first profits from the mill, as you very well know, if you would ever stop to think, must go to pay for logs to work on, and there must always be a good balance for that purpose. No. I reserve enough from my money to fix the home I want; but I shall wait to do it until the mill is working, so I can give all my attention to it, while you are out looking up timber."

"Of course I can do all of it perfectly well," he said. "And it's a MAN'S business. You'll make me look like fifty cents if you get out among men and go to doing a thing no woman in this part of the country ever did. Why, it will look like you didn't TRUST me!"

"I can't help how it will look," said Kate. "This is my last and only dollar; if I lose it, I am out for life; I shall take no risk. I've no confidence in your business ability, and you know it. It need not hurt your pride a particle to say that we are partners; that I'm going to build the mill, while you're going to bring in the timber. It's the only way I shall touch the proposition. I will give you two hundred dollars for the deed and abstract of the ravine. I'll give your mother eight hundred for the lot and house, which is two hundred more than it is worth. I'll lay away enough to rebuild and refurnish it, and with the remainder I'll build the dam, bridge, and mill, just as quickly as it can be done. As soon as I get my money, we'll buy timber for the mill and get it sawed and dried this winter. We can be all done and running by next June."

"Kate, how are you going to get all that land sold, and the money in hand to divide up that quickly? I don't think it ever can be done. Land is always sold on time, you know," he said.

Kate drew a deep breath. "THIS land isn't going to be sold," she said. "Most of the boys have owned their farms long enough to have enabled them to buy other land, and put money in the bank. They're going to form a pool, and put in enough money to pay the girls the share they have agreed to take; even if they have to borrow it, as some of the younger ones will; but the older ones will help them; so the girls are to have their money in cash, in three months. I was mighty glad of the arrangement for my part, because we can begin at once on our plans for the mill."

"And how much do the girls get?" he asked darkly.

"Can't say just yet," said Kate. "The notes and mortgages have to be gone over, and the thing figured out; it will take some time. Mother and Adam began yesterday; we shall know in a few weeks."

"Sounds to me like a cold-blooded Bates steal," he cried. "Who figured out what WAS a fair share for the girls; who planned that arrangement? Why didn't you insist on the thing going through court; the land belong sold, and equal divisions of all the proceeds?"

"Now if you'll agree not to say a word until I finish, I'll show you the figures," said Kate. "I'll tell you what the plan is, and why it was made, and I'll tell you further that it is already recorded, and in action. There are no minor heirs. We could make an agreement and record it. There was no will. Mother will administer. It's all settled. Wait until I get the figures."

Then slowly and clearly she went over the situation, explaining everything in detail. When she finished he sat staring at her with a snarling face.

"You signed that?" he demanded. "You signed that! YOU THREW AWAY AT LEAST HALF YOU MIGHT HAVE HAD! You let those lazy scoundrels of brothers of yours hoodwink you, and pull the wool over your eyes like that? Are you mad? Are you stark, staring mad?"

"No, I'm quite sane," said Kate. "It is you who are mad. You know my figures, don't you? Those were the only ones used yesterday. The whole scheme was mine, with help from Mother to the extent of her giving up everything except the home farm."

"You crazy fool!" he cried, springing up.

"Now stop," said Kate. "Stop right there! I've done what I think is right, and fair, and just, and I'm happy with the results. Act decently, I'll stay and build the mill. Say one, only one more of the nasty, insulting things in your head, and I'll go in there and wake up the children and we will leave now and on foot."

Confronted with Kate and her ultimatum, George arose and walked down to the road; he began pacing back and forth in the moonlight, struggling to regain command of himself. He had no money. He had no prospect of any until Aunt Ollie died and left him her farm. He was, as he expressed it, "up against it" there. Now he was "up against it" with Kate. What she decided upon and proposed to do was all he could do. She might shave prices, and cut, and skimp, and haggle to buy material, and put up her building at the least possible expense. She might sit over books and figure herself blind. He would be driving over the country, visiting with the farmers, booming himself for a fat county office maybe, eating big dinners, and being a jolly good fellow generally. Naturally as breathing, there came to him a scheme whereby he could buy at the very lowest figure he could extract; then he would raise the price to Kate enough to make him a comfortable income besides his share of the business. He had not walked the road long until his anger was all gone.

He began planning the kind of horse he would have to drive, the buggy he would want, and a box in it to carry a hatchet, a square, measures, an auger, other tools he would need, and by Jove! it would be a dandy idea to carry a bottle of the real thing. Many a farmer, for a good cigar and a few swallows of the right thing, would warm up and sign such a contract as could be got in no other manner; while he would need it on cold days himself. George stopped in the moonlight to slap his leg and laugh over the happy thought. "By George, Georgie, my boy," he said, "most days will be cold, won't they?"

He had no word to say to Kate of his change of feeling in the matter. He did not want to miss the chance of twitting her at every opportunity he could invent with having thrown away half her inheritance; but he was glad the whole thing was settled so quickly and easily. He was now busy planning how he would spend the money Kate agreed to pay him for the ravine; but that was another rosy cloud she soon changed in colour, for she told him if he was going to be a partner he could put in what money he had, as his time was no more valuable than she could make hers teaching school again—in other words, he could buy his horse and buggy with the price she paid for the location, so he was forced to agree. He was forced to do a great many things in the following months that he hated; but he had to do them or be left out of the proposition altogether.

Mrs. Bates and Adam administered the Bates estate promptly and efficiently. The girls had their money on time, the boys adjusted themselves as their circumstances admitted. Mrs. Bates had to make so many trips to town, before the last paper was signed, and the last transfer was made, that she felt she could not go any farther, so she did not. Nancy Ellen had reached the point where she would stop and talk a few minutes to Kate, if she met her on the streets of Hartley, as she frequently did now; but she would not ask her to come home with her, because she would not bring herself in contact with George Holt. The day Kate went to Hartley to receive and deposit her check, and start her bank account, her mother asked her if she had any plan as to what she would do with her money. Kate told her in detail. Mrs. Bates listened with grim face: "You better leave it in the bank," she said, "and use the interest to help you live, or put it in good farm mortgages, where you can easily get ten per cent."

Kate explained again and told how she was doing all the buying, how she would pay all bills, and keep the books. It was no use. Mrs. Bates sternly insisted that she should do no such thing. In some way she would be defrauded. In some way she would lose the money. What she was proposing was a man's work. Kate had most of her contracts signed and much material ordered, she could not stop. Sadly she saw her mother turn from her, declaring as she went that Kate would lose every cent she had, and when she did she need not come hanging around her. She had been warned. If she lost, she could take the consequences. For an instant Kate felt that she could not endure it then she sprang after her mother.

"Oh, but I won't lose!" she cried. "I'm keeping my money in my own hands. I'm spending it myself. Please, Mother, come and see the location, and let me show you everything."

"Too late now," said Mrs. Bates grimly, "the thing is done. The time to have told me was before you made any contracts. You're always taking the bit in your teeth and going ahead. Well, go! But remember, 'as you make your bed, so you can lie.'"

"All right," said Kate, trying to force a laugh. "Don't you worry. Next time you get into a tight place and want to borrow a few hundreds, come to me."

Mrs. Bates laughed derisively. Kate turned away with a faint sickness in her heart and when half an hour later she met Nancy Ellen, fresh from an interview with her mother, she felt no better—far worse, in fact—for Nancy Ellen certainly could say what was in her mind with free and forceful directness. With deft tongue and nimble brain, she embroidered all Mrs. Bates had said, and prophesied more evil luck in three minutes than her mother could have thought of in a year. Kate left them with no promise of seeing either of them again, except by accident, her heart and brain filled with misgivings. "Must I always have 'a fly in my ointment'?" she wailed to herself. "I thought this morning this would be the happiest day of my life. I felt as if I were flying. Ye Gods, but wings were never meant for me. Every time I take them, down I come kerflop, mostly in a 'gulf of dark despair,' as the hymn book says. Anyway, I'll keep my promise and give the youngsters a treat."

So she bought each of them an orange, some candy, and goods for a new Sunday outfit and comfortable school clothing. Then she took the hack for Walden, feeling in a degree as she had the day she married George Holt. As she passed the ravine and again studied the location her spirits arose. It WAS a good scheme. It would work. She would work it. She would sell from the yards to Walden and the surrounding country. She would see the dealers in Hartley and talk the business over, so she would know she was not being cheated in freight rates when she came to shipping. She stopped at Mrs. Holt's, laid a deed before her for her signature, and offered her a check for eight hundred for the Holt house and lot, which Mrs. Holt eagerly accepted. They arranged to move immediately, as the children were missing school. She had a deed with her for the ravine, which George signed in Walden, and both documents were acknowledged; but she would not give him the money until he had the horse and buggy he was to use, at the gate, in the spring.

He wanted to start out buying at once, but that was going too far in the future for Kate. While the stream was low, and the banks firm, Kate built her dam, so that it would be ready for spring, put in the abutments, and built the bridge. It was not a large dam, and not a big bridge, but both were solid, well constructed, and would serve every purpose. Then Kate set men hauling stone for the corner foundations. She hoped to work up such a trade and buy so much and so wisely in the summer that she could run all winter, so she was building a real mill in the Bates way, which way included letting the foundations freeze and settle over winter. That really was an interesting and a comfortable winter.

Kate and George both watched the children's studies at night, worked their plans finer in the daytime, and lived as cheaply and carefully as they could. Everything was going well. George was doing his best to promote the mill plan, to keep Kate satisfied at home, to steal out after she slept, and keep himself satisfied in appetite, and some ready money in his pockets, won at games of chance, at which he was an expert, and at cards, which he handled like a master.

CHAPTER XIX

"AS A MAN SOWETH"

AT THE earliest possible moment in the spring, the building of the mill began. It was scarcely well under way when the work was stopped by a week of heavy rains. The water filled the ravine to dangerous height and the roaring of the dam could be heard all over town. George talked of it incessantly. He said it was the sweetest music his ears had ever heard. Kate had to confess that she like the sound herself, but she was fearful over saying much on the subject because she was so very anxious about the stability of the dam. There was a day or two of fine weather; then the rains began again. Kate said she had all the music she desired; she proposed to be safe; so she went and opened the sluiceway to reduce the pressure on the dam. The result was almost immediate. The water gushed through, lowering the current and lessening the fall. George grumbled all day, threatening half a dozen times to shut the sluice; but Kate and the carpenter were against him, so he waited until he came slipping home after midnight, his brain in a muddle from drink, smoke, and cards. As he neared the dam, he decided that the reason he felt so badly was because he had missed hearing it all day, but he would have it to go to sleep by. So he crossed the bridge and shut the sluice gate. Even as he was doing it the thunder pealed; lightning flashed, and high Heaven gave him warning that he was doing a dangerous thing; but all his life he had done what he pleased; there was no probability that he would change then. He needed the roar of the dam to quiet his nerves.

The same roar that put him to sleep, awakened Kate. She lay wondering at it and fearing. She raised her window to listen. The rain was falling in torrents, while the roar was awful, so much worse than it had been when she fell asleep, that she had a suspicion of what might have caused it. She went to George's room and shook him awake.

"Listen to the dam!" she cried. "It will go, as sure as fate. George, did you, Oh, did you, close the sluice-gate when you came home?"

He was half asleep, and too defiant from drink to take his usual course.

"Sure!" he said. "Sweesish mushich ever hearsh. Push me shleep."

He fell back on the pillow and went on sleeping. Kate tried again to waken him, but he struck at her savagely. She ran to her room, hurried into a few clothes, and getting the lantern, started toward the bridge. At the gate she stepped into water. As far as she could see above the dam the street was covered. She waded to the bridge, which was under at each end but still bare in the middle, where it was slightly higher. Kate crossed it and started down the yard toward the dam. The earth was softer there, and she mired in places almost to her knees. At the dam, the water was tearing around each end in a mad race, carrying earth and everything before it. The mill side was lower than the street. The current was so broad and deep she could not see where the sluice was. She hesitated a second to try to locate it from the mill behind her; and in that instant there was a crack and a roar, a mighty rush that swept her from her feet and washed away the lantern. Nothing saved her but the trees on the bank. She struck one, clung to it, pulled herself higher, and in the blackness gripped the tree, while she heard the dam going gradually after the first break.

There was no use to scream, no one could have heard her. The storm raved on; Kate clung to her tree, with each flash of lightning trying to see the dam. At last she saw that it was not all gone. She was not much concerned about herself. She knew the tree would hold. Eagerly she strained her eyes toward the dam. She could feel the water dropping lower, while the roar subsided to a wild rush, and with flashes of lightning she could see what she thought was at least half of the dam holding firm. By that time Kate began to chill. She wrapped her arms around the tree, and pressing her cheek against the rough bark, she cried as hard as she could and did not care. God would not hear; the neighbours could not. She shook and cried until she was worn out. By that time the water was only a muddy flow around her ankles; if she had a light she could wade back to the bridge and reach home. But if she missed the bridge and went into the ravine, the current would be too strong for her. She held with one arm and tried to wipe her face with the other hand. "What a fool to cry!" she said. "As if there were any more water needed here!"

Then she saw a light in the house, and the figures of the children, carrying it from room to room, so she knew that one of them had awakened for a drink, or with the storm, and they had missed her. Then she could see them at the front door, Adam's sturdy feet planted widely apart, bracing him, as he held up the lamp which flickered in the wind. Then she could hear his voice shouting: "Mother!" Instantly Kate answered. Then she was sorry she had, for both of them began to scream wildly. There was a second of that, then even the children realized its futility.

"She is out there in the water, WE GOT TO GET HER," said Adam. "We got to do it!"

He started with the light held high. The wind blew it out. They had to go back to relight it. Kate knew they would burn their fingers, and she prayed they would not set the house on fire. When the light showed again, at the top of her lungs she screamed: "Adam, set the broom on fire and carry it to the end of the bridge; the water isn't deep enough to hurt you." She tried twice, then she saw him give Polly the lamp, and run down the hall. He came back in an instant with the broom. Polly held the lamp high, Adam went down the walk to the gate and started up the sidewalk. "He's using his head," said Kate to the tree. "He's going to wait until he reaches the bridge to start his light, so it will last longer. THAT is BATES, anyway. Thank God!"

Adam scratched several matches before he got the broom well ignited, then he held it high, and by its light found the end of the bridge. Kate called to him to stop and plunging and splashing through mud and water, she reached the bridge before the broom burned out. There she clung to the railing she had insisted upon, and felt her way across to the boy. His thin cotton night shirt was plastered to his sturdy little body. As she touched him Kate lifted him in her arms, and almost hugged the life from him.

"You big man!" she said. "You could help Mother! Good for you!"

"Is the dam gone?" he asked.

"Part of it," said Kate, sliding her feet before her, as she waded toward Polly in the doorway.

"Did Father shut the sluice-gate, to hear the roar?"

Kate hesitated. The shivering body in her arms felt so small to her.

"I 'spect he did," said Adam. "All day he was fussing after you stopped the roar." Then he added casually: "The old fool ought-a known better. I 'spect he was drunk again!"

"Oh, Adam!" cried Kate, setting him on the porch. "Oh, Adam! What makes you say that?"

"Oh, all of them at school say that," scoffed Adam. "Everybody knows it but you, don't they, Polly?"

"Sure!" said Polly. "Most every night; but don't you mind, Mother, Adam and I will take care of you."

Kate fell on her knees and gathered both of them in a crushing hug for an instant; then she helped them into to dry nightgowns and to bed. As she covered them she stooped and kissed each of them before she went to warm and put on dry clothes, and dry her hair. It was almost dawn when she walked to George Holt's door and looked in at him lying stretched in deep sleep.

"You may thank your God for your children," she said. "If it hadn't been for them, I know what I would have done to you."

Then she went to her room and lay down to rest until dawn. She was up at the usual time and had breakfast ready for the children. As they were starting to school George came into the room.

"Mother," said Polly, "there is a lot of folks over around the dam. What shall we tell them?"

Kate's heart stopped. She had heard that question before.

"Tell them the truth," said Adam scornfully, before Kate could answer. "Tell them that Mother opened the sluiceway to save the dam and Father shut it to hear it roar, and it busted!"

"Shall I, Mother?" asked Polly.

A slow whiteness spread over George's face; he stared down the hall to look.

"Tell them exactly what you please," said Kate, "only you watch yourself like a hawk. If you tell one word not the way it was, or in any way different from what happened, I'll punish you severely."

"May I tell them I held the lamp while Adam got you out of the water?" asked Polly. "That would be true, you know."

George turned to listen, his face still whiter.

"Yes, that would be true," said Kate, "but if you tell them that, the first thing they will ask will be 'where was your father?' What will you say then?"

"Why, we'll say that he was so drunk we couldn't wake him up," said Polly conclusively. "We pulled him, an' we shook him, an' we yelled at him. Didn't we, Adam?"

"I was not drunk!" shouted George.

"Oh, yes, you were," said Adam. "You smelled all sour, like it does at the saloon door!"

George made a rush at Adam. The boy spread his feet and put up his hands, but never flinched or moved. Kate looking on felt something in her heart that never had been there before. She caught George's arm, as he reached the child.

"You go on to school, little folks," she said. "And for Mother's sake try not to talk at all. If people question you, tell them to ask Mother. I'd be so proud of you, if you would do that."

"I WILL, if you'll hold me and kiss me again like you did last night when you got out of the water," said Polly.

"It is a bargain," said Kate. "How about you, Adam?"

"I will for THAT, too," said Adam, "but I'd like awful well to tell how fast the water went, and how it poured and roared, while I held the light, and you got across. Gee, if was awful, Mother! So black, and so crashy, and so deep. I'd LIKE to tell!"

"But you WON'T if I ask you not to?" queried Kate.

"I will not," said Adam.

Kate went down on her knees again, she held out her arms and both youngsters rushed to her. After they were gone, she and George Holt looked at each other an instant, then Kate turned to her work. He followed: "Kate—" he began.

"No use!" said Kate. "If you go out and look at the highest water mark, you can easily imagine what I had to face last night when I had to cross the bridge to open the sluice-gate, or the bridge would have gone, too. If the children had not wakened with the storm, and hunted me, I'd have had to stay over there until morning, if I could have clung to the tree that long. First they rescued me; and then they rescued YOU, if you only but knew it. By using part of the money I had saved for the house, I can rebuild the dam; but I am done with you. We're partners no longer. Not with business, money, or in any other way, will I ever trust you again. Sit down there and eat your breakfast, and then leave my sight."

Instead George put on his old clothing, crossed the bridge, and worked all day with all his might trying to gather building material out of the water, save debris from the dam, to clear the village street. At noon he came over and got a drink, and a piece of bread. At night he worked until he could see no longer, and then ate some food from the cupboard and went to bed. He was up and at work before daybreak in the morning, and for two weeks he kept this up, until he had done much to repair the work of the storm. The dam he almost rebuilt himself, as soon as the water lowered to normal again. Kate knew what he was trying to do, and knew also that in a month he had the village pitying him, and blaming her because he was working himself to death, and she was allowing it.

She doggedly went on with her work; the contracts were made; she was forced to. As the work neared completion, her faith in the enterprise grew. She studied by the hour everything she could find pertaining to the business. When the machinery began to arrive, George frequently spoke about having timber ready to begin work on, but he never really believed the thing which did happen, would happen, until the first load of logs slowly crossed the bridge and began unloading in the yards. A few questions elicited from the driver the reply that he had sold the timber to young Adam Bates of Bates Corners, who was out buying right and left and paying cash on condition the seller did his own delivering. George saw the scheme, and that it was good. Also the logs were good, while the price was less than he hoped to pay for such timber. His soul was filled with bitterness. The mill was his scheme. He had planned it all. Those thieving Bates had stolen his plan, and his location, and his home, and practically separated him from his wife and children. It was his mill, and all he was getting from it was to work with all his might, and not a decent word from morning until night. That day instead of working as before, he sat in the shade most of the time, and that night instead of going to bed he went down town.

When the mill was almost finished Kate employed two men who lived in Walden, but had been working in the Hartley mills for years. They were honest men of much experience. Kate made the better of them foreman, and consulted with him in every step of completing the mill, and setting up the machinery. She watched everything with sharp eyes, often making suggestions that were useful about the placing of different parts as a woman would arrange them. Some of these the men laughed at, some they were more than glad to accept. When the engine was set up, the big saw in place, George went to Kate.

"See here!" he said roughly. "I know I was wrong about the sluice-gate. I was a fool to shut it with the water that high, but I've learned my lesson; I'll never touch it again; I've worked like a dog for weeks to pay for it; now where do I come in? What's my job, how much is my share of the money, and when do I get it?"

"The trouble with you, George, is that you have to learn a new lesson about every thing you attempt. You can't carry a lesson about one thing in your mind, and apply it to the next thing that comes up. I know you have worked, and I know why. It is fair that you should have something, but I can't say what, just now. Having to rebuild the dam, and with a number of incidentals that have come up, in spite of the best figuring I could do, I have been forced to use my money saved for rebuilding the house; and even with that, I am coming out a hundred or two short. I'm strapped; and until money begins to come in I have none myself. The first must go toward paying the men's wages, the next for timber. If Jim Milton can find work for you, go to work at the mill, and when we get started I'll pay you what is fair and just, you may depend on that. If he hasn't work for you, you'll have to find a job at something else."

"Do you mean that?" he asked wonderingly.

"I mean it," said Kate.

"After stealing my plan, and getting my land for nothing, you'd throw me out entirely?" he demanded.

"You entreated me to put all I had into your plan, you told me repeatedly the ravine was worth nothing, you were not even keeping up the taxes on it until I came and urged you to, the dam is used merely for water, the engine furnishes the real power, and if you are thrown out, you have thrown yourself out. You have had every chance."

"You are going to keep your nephew on the buying job?" he asked

"I am," said Kate. "You can have no job that will give you a chance to involve me financially."

"Then give me Milton's place. It's so easy a baby could do it, and the wages you have promised him are scandalous," said George.

Kate laughed. "Oh, George," she said, "you can't mean that! Of all your hare-brained ideas, that you could operate that saw, is the wildest. Oh course you could start the engine, and set the saw running—I could myself; but to regulate its speed, to control it with judgment, you could no more do it than Polly. As for wages, Milton is working for less than he got in Hartley, because he can be at home, and save his hack fare, as you know."

George went over to Jim Milton, and after doing all he could see to do and ordering Milton to do several things he thought might be done, he said casually: "Of course I am BOSS around this shack, but this is new to me. You fellows will have to tell me what to do until I get my bearings. As soon as we get to running, I'll be yard-master, and manage the selling and shipping. I'm good at figures, and that would be the best place for me."

"You'll have to settle with Mrs. Holt about that," said Jim Milton.

"Of course," said George. "Isn't she a wonder? With my help, we'll soon wipe the Hartley mills off the map, and be selling till Grand Rapids will get her eye peeled. With you to run the machinery, me to manage the sales, and her to keep the books, we got a combination to beat the world."

"In the meantime," said Jim Milton dryly, "you might take that scoop shovel and clean the shavings and blocks off this floor. Leave me some before the engine to start the first fire, and shovel the rest into that bin there where it's handy. It isn't safe to start with so much loose, dry stuff lying around."

George went to work with the scoop shovel, but he watched every movement Jim Milton made about the engine and machinery. Often he dropped the shovel and stood studying things out for himself, and asking questions. Not being sure of his position, Jim Milton answered him patiently, and showed him all he wanted to know; but he constantly cautioned him not to touch anything, or try to start the machinery himself, as he might lose control of the gauge and break the saw, or let the power run away with him. George scoffed at the idea of danger and laughed at the simplicity of the engine and machinery. There was little for him to do. He hated to be seen cleaning up the debris; men who stopped in passing kept telling what a fine fellow young Bates was, what good timber he was sending in. Several of them told George frankly they thought that was to be his job. He was so ashamed of that, he began instant improvisation.

"That was the way we first planned things," he said boastfully, "but when it came to working out our plans, we found I would be needed here till I learned the business, and then I'm going on the road. I am going to be the salesman. To travel, dress well, eat well, flirt with the pretty girls, and take big lumber orders will just about suit little old Georgie."

"Wonder you remembered to put the orders in at all," said Jim Milton dryly.

George glared at him. "Well, just remember whom you take orders from," he said, pompously.

"I take them from Mrs. Holt, and nobody else," said Milton, with equal assurance. "And I've yet to hear her say the first word about this wonderful travelling proposition. She thinks she will do well to fill home orders and ship to a couple of factories she already has contracts with. Sure you didn't dream that travelling proposition, George?"

At that instant George wished he could slay Jim Milton. All day he brooded and grew sullen and ugly. By noon he quit working and went down town. By suppertime he went home to prove to his wife that he was all right. She happened to be coming across from the mill, where she had helped Milton lay the first fire under the boiler ready to touch off, and had seen the first log on the set carriage. It had been agreed that she was to come over at opening time in the morning and start the machinery. She was a proud and eager woman when she crossed the bridge and started down the street toward the gate. From the opposite direction came George, so unsteady that he was running into tree boxes, then lifting his hat and apologizing to them for his awkwardness. Kate saw at a glance that he might fall any instant. Her only thought was to help him from the street, to where children would not see him.

She went to him and taking his arm started down the walk with him. He took off his hat to her also, and walked with wavering dignity, setting his steps as if his legs were not long enough to reach the walk, so that each step ended with a decided thump. Kate could see the neighbours watching at their windows, and her own children playing on the roof of the woodshed. When the children saw their parents, they both stopped playing to stare at them. Then suddenly, shrill and high, arose Adam's childish voice:

"Father came home the other night,

Tried to blow out the 'lectric light,

Blew and blew with all his might,

And the blow almost killed Mother."

Polly joined him, and they sang and shrilled, and shrieked it; they jumped up and down and laughed and repeated it again and again. Kate guided George to his room and gave him a shove that landed him on his bed. Then to hush the children she called them to supper. They stopped suddenly, as soon as they entered the kitchen door, and sat, sorry and ashamed while she went around, her face white, her lips closed, preparing their food. George was asleep. The children ate alone, as she could take no food. Later she cleaned the kitchen, put the children to bed, and sat on the front porch looking at the mill, wondering, hoping, planning, praying unconsciously. When she went to bed at ten o'clock George was still asleep.

He awakened shortly after, burning with heat and thirst. He arose and slipped to the back porch for a drink. Water was such an aggravation, he crossed the yard, went out the back gate, and down the alley. When he came back up the street, he was pompously, maliciously, dangerously drunk. Either less or more would have been better. When he came in sight of the mill, standing new and shining in the moonlight, he was a lord of creation, ready to work creation to his will. He would go over and see if things were all right. But he did not cross the bridge, he went down the side street, and entered the yard at the back. The doors were closed and locked, but there was as yet no latch on the sliding windows above the work bench. He could push them open from the ground. He leaned a board against the side of the mill, set his foot on it, and pulled himself up, so that he could climb on the bench.

That much achieved, he looked around him. After a time his eyes grew accustomed to the darkness, so that he could see his way plainly. Muddled half-thoughts began to filter through his brain. He remembered he was abused. He was out of it. He remembered that he was not the buyer for the mill. He remembered how the men had laughed when he had said that he was to be the salesman. He remembered that Milton had said that he was not to touch the machinery. He at once slid from the bench and went to the boiler. He opened the door of the fire-box and saw the kindling laid ready to light, to get up steam. He looked at the big log on the set carriage. They had planned to start with a splurge in the morning. Kate was to open the throttle that started the machinery. He decided to show them that they were not so smart. He would give them a good surprise by sawing the log. That would be a joke on them to brag about the remainder of his life. He took matches from his pocket and started the fire. It seemed to his fevered imagination that it burned far too slowly. He shoved in more kindling, shavings, ends left from siding. This smothered his fire, so he made trip after trip to the tinder box, piling in armloads of dry, inflammable stuff.

Then suddenly the flames leaped up. He slammed shut the door and started toward the saw. He could not make it work. He jammed and pulled everything he could reach. Soon he realized the heat was becoming intense, and turned to the boiler to see that the fire-box was red hot almost all over, white hot in places.

"My God!" he muttered. "Too hot! Got to cool that down."

Then he saw the tank and the dangling hose, and remembered that he had not filled the boiler. Taking down the hose, he opened the watercock, stuck in the nozzle, and turned on the water full force. Windows were broken across the street. Parts of the fire-box, boiler, and fire flew everywhere. The walls blew out, the roof lifted and came down, the fire raged among the new, dry timbers of the mill.

When her windows blew in, Kate was thrown from her bed to the floor. She lay stunned a second, then dragged herself up to look across the street. There was nothing where the low white expanse of roof had spread an hour before, while a red glare was creeping everywhere over the ground. She ran to George's room and found it empty. She ran to the kitchen, calling him, and found the back door standing open. She rushed back to her room and began trying to put on her dress over her nightrobe. She could not control her shaking fingers, while at each step she cut her feet on broken glass. She reached the front door as the children came screaming with fright. In turning to warn them about the glass, she stumbled on the top step, pitched forward headlong, then lay still. The neighbours carried her back to her bed, called the doctor, and then saved all the logs in the yard they could. The following day, when the fire had burned itself out, the undertaker hunted assiduously, but nothing could be found to justify a funeral.

CHAPTER XX

"FOR A GOOD GIRL"

FOR a week, Kate lay so dazed she did not care whether she lived or died; then she slowly crept back to life, realizing that whether she cared or not, she must live. She was too young, too strong, to quit because she was soul sick; she had to go on. She had life to face for herself and her children. She wondered dully about her people, but as none of the neighbours who had taken care of her said anything concerning them, she realized that they had not been there. At first she was almost glad. They were forthright people. They would have had something to say; they would have said it tersely and to the point.

Adam, 3d, had wound up her affairs speedily by selling the logs he had bought for her to the Hartley mills, paying what she owed, and depositing the remainder in the Hartley Bank to her credit; but that remainder was less than one hundred dollars. That winter was a long, dreadful nightmare to Kate. Had it not been for Aunt Ollie, they would have been hungry some of the time; they were cold most of it. For weeks Kate thought of sending for her mother, or going to her; then as not even a line came from any of her family, she realized that they resented her losing that much Bates money so bitterly that they wished to have nothing to do with her. Often she sat for hours staring straight before her, trying to straighten out the tangle she had made of her life. As if she had not suffered enough in the reality of living, she now lived over in day and night dreams, hour by hour, her time with George Holt, and gained nothing thereby.

All winter Kate brooded, barely managing to keep alive, and the children in school. As spring opened, she shook herself, arose, and went to work. It was not planned, systematic, effective, Bates work. Piecemeal she did anything she saw needed the doing. The children helped to make garden and clean the yard. Then all of them went out to Aunt Ollie's and made a contract to plant and raise potatoes and vegetables on shares. They passed a neglected garden on the way, and learning that the woman of the house was ill, Kate stopped and offered to tend it for enough cords of windfall wood to pay her a fair price, this to be delivered in mid-summer.

With food and fire assured, Kate ripped up some of George's clothing, washed, pressed, turned, and made Adam warm clothes for school. She even achieved a dress for Polly by making a front and back from a pair of her father's trouser legs, and setting in side pieces, a yoke and sleeves from one of her old skirts. George's underclothing she cut down for both of the children; then drew another check for taxes and second-hand books. While she was in Hartley in the fall paying taxes, she stopped at a dry goods store for thread, and heard a customer asking for knitted mittens, which were not in stock. After he had gone, she arranged with the merchant for a supply of yarn which she carried home and began to knit into mittens such as had been called for. She used every minute of leisure during the day, she worked hours into the night, and soon small sums began coming her way. When she had a supply of teamster's heavy mittens, she began on fancy coloured ones for babies and children, sometimes crocheting, sometimes using needles. Soon she started both children on the rougher work with her. They were glad to help for they had a lively remembrance of one winter of cold and hunger, with no Christmas. That there were many things she might have done that would have made more money with less exertion Kate never seemed to realize. She did the obvious thing. Her brain power seemed to be on a level with that of Adam and Polly.

When the children began to carry home Christmas talk, Kate opened her mouth to say the things that had been said to her as a child; then tightly closed it. She began getting up earlier, sitting up later, knitting feverishly. Luckily the merchant could sell all she could furnish. As the time drew nearer, she gathered from the talk of the children what was the deepest desire of their hearts. One day a heavy wind driving ice-coated trees in the back yard broke quite a large limb from a cherry tree. Kate dragged it into the woodhouse to make firewood. She leaned it against the wall to wait until the ice melted, and as it stood there in its silvery coat, she thought how like a small tree the branch was shaped, and how pretty it looked. After the children had gone to school the next day she shaped it with the hatchet and saw, and fastened it in a small box. This she carried to her bedroom and locked the door. She had not much idea what she was going to do, but she kept thinking. Soon she found enough time to wrap every branch carefully with the red tissue paper her red knitting wool came in, and to cover the box smoothly. Then she thought of the country Christmas trees she had seen decorated with popcorn and cranberries. She popped the corn at night and the following day made a trip up the ravine, where she gathered all the bittersweet berries, swamp holly, and wild rose seed heads she could find. She strung the corn on fine cotton cord putting a rose seed pod between each grain, then used the bittersweet berries to terminate the blunt ends of the branches, and climb up the trunk. By the time she had finished this she was really interested. She achieved a gold star for the top from a box lid and a piece of gilt paper Polly had carried home from school. With yarn ends and mosquito netting, she whipped up a few little mittens, stockings, and bags. She cracked nuts from their fall store and melting a little sugar stirred in the kernels until they were covered with a sweet, white glaze. Then she made some hard candy, and some fancy cookies with a few sticks of striped candy cut in circles and dotted on the top. She polished red, yellow, and green apples and set them under the tree.

When she made her final trip to Hartley before Christmas the spirit of the day was in the air. She breathed so much of it that she paid a dollar and a half for a stout sled and ten cents for a dozen little red candles, five each for two oranges, and fifteen each for two pretty little books, then after long hesitation added a doll for Polly. She felt that she should not have done this, and said so, to herself; but knew if she had it to do over, she would do the same thing again. She shook her shoulders and took the first step toward regaining her old self-confidence.

"Pshaw! Big and strong as I am, and Adam getting such a great boy, we can make it," she said. Then she hurried to the hack and was driven home barely in time to rush her bundles into her room before school was out. She could scarcely wait until the children were in bed to open the parcels. The doll had to be dressed, but Kate was interested in Christmas by that time, and so contemplated the spider-waisted image with real affection. She never had owned a doll herself. She let the knitting go that night, and cut up an old waist to make white under-clothing with touches of lace, and a pretty dress. Then Kate went to her room, tied the doll in a safe place on the tree, put on the books, and set the candles with pins. As she worked she kept biting her lips, but when it was all finished she thought it was lovely, and so it was. As she set the sled in front of the tree she said: "There, little folks, I wonder what you will think of that! It's the best I can do. I've a nice chicken to roast; now if only, if only Mother or Nancy Ellen would come, or write a line, or merely send one word by Tilly Nepple."

Suddenly Kate lay down on the bed, buried her face in the pillow while her shoulders jerked and shook in dry sobs for a long time. At last she arose, went to the kitchen, bathed her face, and banked the fires. "I suppose it is the Bates way," she said, "but it's a cold, hard proposition. I know what's the matter with all of them. They are afraid to come near me, or show the slightest friendliness, for fear I'll ask them to help support us. They needn't worry, we can take care of ourselves."

She set her tree on the living room table, arranged everything to the best advantage, laid a fire in the stove, and went to sleep Christmas eve, feeling more like herself than she had since the explosion. Christmas morning she had the house warm and the tree ready to light while the children dressed. She slipped away their every-day clothing and laid out their best instead. She could hear them talking as they dressed, and knew the change of clothing had filled them with hope. She hastily lighted the tree, and was setting the table as they entered the dining room.

"Merry Christmas, little people," she cried in a voice they had not heard in a long time. They both rushed to her and Kate's heart stood still as they each hugged her tight, kissed her, and offered a tiny packet. From the size and feeling of these, she realized that they were giving her the candy they had received the day before at school. Surprises were coming thick and fast with Kate. That one shook her to her foundations. They loved candy. They had so little! They had nothing else to give. She held them an instant so tightly they were surprised at her, then she told them to lay the packages on the living room table until after breakfast. Polly opened the door, and screamed. Adam ran, and then both of them stood silently before the brave little tree, flaming red, touched with white, its gold star shining. They looked at it, and then at each other, while Kate, watching at an angle across the dining room, distinctly heard Polly say in an awed tone: "Adam, hadn't we better pray?"

Kate lifted herself full height, and drew a deep breath. "Well, I guess I manage a little Christmas after this," she said, "and maybe a Fourth of July, and a birthday, and a few other things. I needn't be such a coward. I believe I can make it."

From that hour she began trying to think of something she could do that would bring returns more nearly commensurate with the time and strength she was spending. She felt tied to Walden because she owned the house, and could rely on working on shares with Aunt Ollie for winter food; but there was nothing she could do there and take care of the children that would bring more than the most meagre living. Still they were living, each year more comfortably; the children were growing bigger and stronger; soon they could help at something, if only she could think what. The time flew, each day a repetition of yesterday's dogged, soul-tiring grind, until some days Kate was close to despair. Each day the house grew shabbier; things wore out and could not be replaced; poverty showed itself more plainly. So three more years of life in Walden passed, setting their indelible mark on Kate. Time and again she almost broke the spell that bound her, but she never quite reached the place where her thought cleared, her heart regained its courage, her soul dared take wing, and try another flight. When she thought of it, "I don't so much mind the falling," said Kate to herself; "but I do seem to select the hardest spots to light on."

Kate sat on the back steps, the sun shone, her nearest neighbour was spading an onion bed. She knew that presently she would get out the rake and spade and begin another year's work; but at that minute she felt too hopeless to move. Adam came and sat on the step beside her. She looked at him and was surprised at his size and apparent strength. Someway he gave her hope. He was a good boy, he had never done a mean, sneaking thing that she knew of. He was natural, normal, mischievous; but he had not an underhand inclination that she could discover. He would make a fine-looking, big man, quite as fine as any of the Bates men; even Adam, 3d, was no handsomer than the fourth Adam would be. Hope arose in her with the cool air of spring on her cheek and its wine in her nostrils. Then out of the clear sky she said it: "Adam, how long are we going to stay in the beggar class?"

Adam jumped, and turned surprised eyes toward her. Kate was forced to justify herself.

"Of course we give Aunt Ollie half we raise," she said, "but anybody would do that. We work hard, and we live little if any better than Jasons, who have the County Trustee in three times a winter. I'm big and strong, you're almost a man, why don't we DO something? Why don't we have some decent clothes, some money for out work and"—Kate spoke at random—"a horse and carriage?"

"A horse and carriage?" repeated Adam, staring at her.

"Why not?" said Kate, casually.

"But how?" cried the amazed boy.

"Why, earn the money, and buy it!" said Kate, impatiently. "I'm about fed up on earning cabbage, and potatoes, and skirmishing for wood. I'd prefer to have a dollar in my pocket, and BUY what we need. Can't you use your brain and help me figure out a way to earn some MONEY?"

"I meant to pretty soon now, but I thought I had to go to school a few years yet," he said.

"Of course you do," said Kate. "I must earn the money, but can't you help me think how?"

"Sure," said Adam, sitting straight and seeming thoughtful, "but give me a little time. What would you—could you, do?"

"I taught before I was married," said Kate; "but methods of teaching change so I'd have to have a Normal term to qualify for even this school. I could put you and Polly with Aunt Ollie this summer; but I wouldn't, not if we must freeze and starve together—"

"Because of Grandma?" asked the boy. Kate nodded.

"I borrowed money to go once, and I could again; but I have been away from teaching so long, and I don't know what to do with you children. The thing I would LIKE would be to find a piece of land somewhere, with a house, any kind of one on it, and take it to rent. Land is about all I really know. Working for money would be of some interest. I am so dead tired working for potatoes. Sometimes I see them flying around in the air at night."

"Do you know of any place you would like?" asked Adam.

"No, I don't," said Kate, "but I am going to begin asking and I'm going to keep my eyes open. I heard yesterday that Dr. James intends to build a new house. This house is nothing, but the lot is in the prettiest place in town. Let's sell it to him, and take the money, and buy us some new furniture and a cow, and a team, and wagon, and a buggy, and go on a piece of land, and live like other people. Seems to me I'll die if I have to work for potatoes any longer. I'm heart sick of them. Don't say a word to anybody, but Oh, Adam, THINK! Think HARD! Can't you just help me THINK?"

"You are sure you want land?" asked the boy.

"It is all I know," said Kate. "How do you feel about it?"

"I want horses, and cows, and pigs—lots of pigs—and sheep, and lots of white hens," said Adam, promptly.

"Get the spade and spade the onion bed until I think," said Kate. "And that reminds me, we didn't divide the sets last fall. Somebody will have to go after them."

"I'll go," said Adam, "but it's awful early. It'll snow again. Let me go after school Friday and stay over night. I'd like to go and stay over night with Aunt Ollie. Grandma can't say anything to me that I'll listen to. You keep Polly, and let me go alone. Sure I can."

"All right," said Kate. "Spade the bed, and let it warm a day. It will be good for it. But don't tell Polly you're going, or she'll want to go along."

Until Friday night, Kate and Adam went around in such a daze of deep thought that they stumbled, and ran against each other; then came back to their affairs suddenly, looking at each other and smiling understandingly. After one of these encounters Kate said to the boy: "You may not arrive at anything, Adam, but I certainly can't complain that you are not thinking."

Adam grinned: "I'm not so sure that I haven't got it," he said.

"Tell me quick and let me think, too" said Kate.

"But I can't tell you yet," said Adam. "I have to find out something first."

Friday evening he wanted to put off his trip until Saturday morning, so Kate agreed. She was surprised when he bathed and put on his clean shirt and trousers, but said not a word. She had made some study of child psychology, she thought making the trip alone was of so much importance to Adam that he was dressing for the occasion. She foresaw extra washing, yet she said nothing to stop the lad. She waved good-bye to him, thinking how sturdy and good looking he was, as he ran out of the front door. Kate was beginning to be worried when Adam had not returned toward dusk Sunday evening, and Polly was cross and fretful. Finally they saw him coming down the ravine bank, carrying his small bundle of sets. Kate felt a glow of relief; Polly ran to meet him. Kate watched as they met and saw Adam take Polly's hand.

"If only they looked as much alike as some twins do, I'd be thankful," said Kate.

Adam delivered the sets, said Aunt Ollie and Grandma were all right, that it was an awful long walk, and he was tired. Kate noticed that his feet were dust covered, but his clothes were so clean she said to him: "You didn't fish much."

"I didn't fish any," said Adam, "not like I always fish," he added.

"Had any time to THINK?" asked Kate.

"You just bet I did," said the boy. "I didn't waste a minute."

"Neither did I," said Kate. "I know exactly what the prettiest lot in town can be sold for."

"Good!" cried Adam. "Fine!"

Monday Kate wanted to get up early and stick the sets, but Adam insisted that Aunt Ollie said the sign would not be right until Wednesday. If they were stuck on Monday or Tuesday, they would all grow to top.

"My goodness! I knew that," said Kate. "I am thinking so hard I'm losing what little sense I had; but anyway, mere thinking is doing me a world of good. I am beginning to feel a kind of rising joy inside, and I can't imagine anything else that makes it."

Adam went to school, laughing. Kate did the washing and ironing, and worked in the garden getting beds ready. Tuesday she was at the same occupation, when about ten o'clock she dropped her spade and straightened, a flash of perfect amazement crossing her face. She stood immovable save for swaying forward in an attitude of tense listening.

"Hoo! hoo!"

Kate ran across the yard and as she turned the corner of the house she saw a one-horse spring wagon standing before the gate, while a stiff, gaunt figure sat bolt upright on the seat, holding the lines. Kate was at the wheel looking up with a face of delighted amazement.

"Why, Mother!" she cried. "Why, Mother!"

"Go fetch a chair and help me down," said Mrs. Bates, "this seat is getting tarnation hard."

Kate ran after a chair, and helped her mother to alight. Mrs. Bates promptly took the chair, on the sidewalk.

"Just drop the thills," she said. "Lead him back and slip on the halter. It's there with his feed."

Kate followed instructions, her heart beating wildly. Several times she ventured a quick glance at her mother. How she had aged! How lined and thin she was! But Oh, how blessed good it was to see her! Mrs. Bates arose and they walked into the house, where she looked keenly around, while her sharp eyes seemed to appraise everything as she sat down and removed her bonnet.

"Go fetch me a drink," she said, "and take the horse one and then I'll tell you why I came."

"I don't care why you came," said Kate, "but Oh, Mother, thank God you are here!"

"Now, now, don't get het up!" cautioned Mrs. Bates. "Water, I said."

Kate hurried to obey orders; then she sank on a chair and looked at her mother. Mrs. Bates wiped her face and settled in the chair comfortably.

"They's no use to waste words," she said. "Katie, you're the only one in the family that has any sense, and sometimes you ain't got enough so's you could notice it without a magnifyin' glass; but even so, you're ahead of the rest of them. Katie, I'm sick an' tired of the Neppleses and the Whistlers and being bossed by the whole endurin' Bates tribe; sick and tired of it, so I just came after you."

"Came after me?" repeated Kate stupidly.

"Yes, parrot, 'came after you,'" said Mrs. Bates. "I told you, you'd no great amount of sense. I'm speakin' plain, ain't I? I don't see much here to hold you. I want you should throw a few traps, whatever you are beholden to, in the wagon—that's why I brought it—and come on home and take care of me the rest of my time. It won't be so long; I won't interfere much, nor be much bother. I've kep' the place in order, but I'm about fashed. I won't admit it to the rest of them; but I don't seem to mind telling you, Katie, that I am almost winded. Will you come?"

"Of course I will," said Kate, a tide of effulgent joy surging up in her heart until it almost choked her. "Of course I will, Mother, but my children, won't they worry you?"

"Never having had a child about, I s'pect likely they may," said Mrs. Bates, dryly. "Why, you little fool! I think likely it's the children I am pinin' for most, though I couldn't a-stood it much longer without YOU. Will you get ready and come with me to-day?"

"Yes," said Kate, "if I can make it. There's very little here I care for; I can have the second-hand man give me what he will for the rest; and I can get a good price for the lot to-day, if I say so. Dr. James wants it to build on. I'll go and do the very best I can, and when you don't want me any longer, Adam will be bigger and we can look out for ourselves. Yes, I'll get ready at once if you want me to."

"Not much of a haggler, are you, Katie?" said Mrs. Bates. "Why don't you ask what rooms you're to have, and what I'll pay you, and how much work you'll have to do, and if you take charge of the farm, and how we share up?"

Kate laughed: "Mother," she said, "I have been going to school here, with the Master of Life for a teacher; and I've learned so many things that really count, that I know now NONE of the things you mention are essential. You may keep the answers to all those questions; I don't care a cent about any of them. If you want me, and want the children, all those things will settle themselves as we come to them. I didn't use to understand you; but we got well enough acquainted at Father's funeral, and I do, now. Whatever you do will be fair, just, and right. I'll obey you, as I shall expect Adam and Polly to."

"Well, for lands sakes, Katie," said Mrs. Bates. "Life must a-been weltin' it to you good and proper. I never expected to see you as meek as Moses. That Holt man wasn't big enough to beat you, was he?"

"The ways in which he 'beat' me no Bates would understand. I had eight years of them, and I don't understand them yet; but I am so cooked with them, that I shall be wild with joy if you truly mean for me to pack up and come home with you for awhile."

"Oh, Lordy, Katie!" said Mrs. Bates. "This whipped out, take-anything-anyway style ain't becomin' to a big, fine, upstanding woman like you. Hold up your head, child! Hold up your head, and say what you want, an' how you want it!"

"Honestly, Mother, I don't want a thing on earth but to go home with you and do as you say for the next ten years," said Kate.

"Stiffen up!" cried Mrs. Bates. "Stiffen up!" "Don't be no broken reed, Katie! I don't want you dependin' on ME; I came to see if you would let ME lean on YOU the rest of the way. I wa'n't figuring that there was anything on this earth that could get you down; so's I was calculatin' you'd be the very one to hold me up. Since you seem to be feeling unaccountably weak in the knees, let's see if we can brace them a little. Livin' with Pa so long must kind of given me a tendency toward nussin' a deed. I've got one here I had executed two years ago, and I was a coming with it along about now, when 'a little bird tole me' to come to-day, so here I am. Take that, Katie."

Mrs. Bates pulled a long sealed envelope from the front of her dress and tossed it in Kate's lap.

"Mother, what is this?" asked Kate in a hushed voice.

"Well, if you'd rather use your ears than your eyes, it's all the same to me," said Mrs. Bates. "The boys always had a mortal itchin' to get their fingers on the papers in the case. I can't say I don't like the difference; and I've give you every chance, too, an you WOULDN'T demand, you WOULDN'T specify. Well, I'll just specify myself. I'm dead tired of the neighbours taking care of me, and all of the children stoppin' every time they pass, each one orderin' or insinuatin' according to their lights, as to what I should do. I've always had a purty clear idea of what I wanted to do myself. Over forty years, I sided with Pa, to keep the peace; NOW I reckon I'm free to do as I like. That's my side. You can tell me yours, now."

Kate shook her head: "I have nothing to say."

"Jest as well," said Mrs. Bates. "Re-hashing don't do any good. Come back, and come to-day; but stiffen up. That paper you are holding is a warrantee deed to the home two hundred to you and your children after you. You take possession to-day. There's money in the bank to paper, an' paint, and make any little changes you'd like, such as cutting doors or windows different places, floorin' the kitchen new, or the like. Take it an' welcome. I got more 'an enough to last me all my days; all I ask of you is my room, my food, and your company. Take the farm, and do what you pretty please with it."

"But, Mother!" cried Kate. "The rest of them! They'd tear me limb for limb. I don't DARE take this."

"Oh, don't you?" asked Mrs. Bates. "Well, I still stand for quite a bit at Bates Corners, and I say you WILL take that farm, and run it as you like. It is mine, I give it to you. We all know it wasn't your fault you lost your money, though it was a dose it took some of us a good long time to swallow. You are the only one out of your share; you settled things fine for the rest of them; and they all know it, and feel it. You'll never know what you did for me the way you put me through Pa's funeral; now if you'll just shut up, and stick that deed somewhere it won't burn, and come home an' plant me as successfully as you did Pa, you'll have earned all you'll get, an' something coming. Now set us out a bite to eat, and let's be off."

Kate slowly arose and handed back the deed.

"I'll be flying around so lively I might lose that," she said, "you put it where you had it, till we get to Hartley, and then I'll get a place in the bank vault for it. I can't quite take this in, just yet, but you know I'll do my best for you, Mother!"

"Tain't likely I'd be here else," said Mrs. Bates, "and tea, Katie. A cup of good strong hot tea would fix me up about proper, right now."

Kate went to the kitchen and began setting everything she had to eat on the table. As she worked Polly came flying in the door crying: "Mother, who has come?" so Kate stepped toward the living room to show the child to her grandmother and as she advanced she saw a queer thing. Adam was sitting on his grandmother's lap. Her arms were tight around him, her face buried in his crisp hair, and he was patting her shoulder and telling her he would take care of her, while her voice said distinctly: "Of course you will, birdie!" Then the lad and the old woman laid their heads together and laughed almost hysterically.

"WELL, IF THAT ISN'T QUICK WORK!" said Kate to herself. Then she presented Polly, who followed Adam's lead in hugging the stranger first and looking at her afterward. God bless all little children. Then Adam ran to tell the second-hand man to come at one o'clock and Dr. James that he might have the keys at three. They ate hurriedly. Kate set out what she wished to save; the children carried things to the wagon; she packed while they ran after their books, and at three o'clock all of them climbed into the spring wagon, and started to Bates Corners.

Kate was the last one in. As she climbed on the seat beside her mother and took the lines, she handed Mrs. Bates a small china mug to hold for her. It was decorated with a very fat robin and on a banner floating from its beak was inscribed: "For a Good Girl."

CHAPTER XXI

LIFE'S BOOMERANG

AS THEY drove into Hartley, Mrs. Bates drew forth the deed.

"You are right about the bank being a safe place for this," she said. "I've had it round the house for two years, and it's a fair nervous thing to do. I wish I'd a-had sense to put it there and come after you the day I made it. But there's no use crying over spilt milk, nor fussin' with the grease spot it makes; salt it down safely now, and when you get it done, beings as this setting is fairly comfortable, take time to run into Harding's and pick up some Sunday-school clothes for the children that will tally up with the rest of their relations'; an' get yourself a cheap frock or two that will spruce you up a bit till you have time to decide what you really want."

Kate passed the lines to her mother, and climbed from the wagon. She returned with her confidence partly restored and a new look on her face. Her mother handed her two dimes.

"I can wait five minutes longer," she said. "Now get two nice oranges and a dime's worth of candy."

Kate took the money and obeyed orders. She handed the packages to her mother as she climbed into the wagon and again took the lines, heading the horse toward the old, familiar road. Her mother twisted around on the seat and gave each of the children an orange and a stick of candy.

"There!" she said. "Go on and spoil yourselves past redemption."

Kate laughed. "But, Mother," she said, "you never did that for us."

"Which ain't saying I never WANTED to," said Mrs. Bates, sourly. "You're a child only once in this world; it's a little too rough to strip childhood of everything. I ain't so certain Bates ways are right, that for the rest of my time I'm goin' to fly in the face of all creation to prove it. If God lets me live a few years more, I want the faces around me a little less discontenteder than those I've been used to. If God Almighty spares me long enough, I lay out to make sure that Adam and Polly will squeeze out a tear or two for Granny when she is laid away."

"I think you are right, Mother," said Kate. "It didn't cost anything, but we had a real pretty Christmas tree this year, and I believe we can do better next time. I want the children to love you, but don't BUY them."

"Well, I'd hardly call an orange and a stick of candy traffickin' in affection," said Mrs. Bates. "They'll survive it without underminin' their principles, I'll be bound, or yours either. Katie, let's make a beginning to-day. LET'S WORK WHAT IS RIGHT, AND HEALTHY, A FAIR PART OF THE DAY, AND THEN EACH DAY, AND SUNDAY ESPECIALLY, LET'S PLAY AND REST, JUST AS HARD AS WE WORK. IT'S BEEN ALL WORK AND NO PLAY TILL WE'VE BEEN MIGHTY 'DULL BOYS' AT OUR HOUSE; I'M FREE TO SAY THAT I HANKER FOR A CHANGE

BEFORE I DIE."

"Don't speak so often of dying," said Kate. "You're all right. You've been too much alone. You'll feel like yourself as soon as you get rested."

"I guess I been thinking about it too much," said Mrs. Bates. "I ain't been so well as I might, an' not being used to it, it worries me some. I got to buck up. The one thing I CAN'T do is to die; but I'm most tired enough to do it right now. I'll be glad when we get home."

Kate drove carefully, but as fast as she dared with her load. As they neared Bates Corners, the way became more familiar each mile. Kate forgot the children, forgot her mother, forgot ten years of disappointment and failure, and began a struggle to realize what was happening to her now. The lines slipped down, the horse walked slowly, the first thing she knew, big hot tears splashed on her hand. She gathered up the lines, drew a deep breath, and glanced at her mother, meeting her eye fairly. Kate tried to smile, but her lips were quivering.

"Glad, Katie?" asked Mrs. Bates.

Kate nodded.

"Me, too!" said Mrs. Bates.

They passed the orchard.

"There's the house, there, Polly!" cried Adam.

"Why, Adam, how did you know the place?" asked Kate, turning.

Adam hesitated a second. "Ain't you told us times a-plenty about the house and the lilac, and the snowball bush—" "Yes, and the cabbage roses," added Polly.

"So I have," said Kate. "Mostly last winter when we were knitting. Yes, this will be home for all the rest of our lives. Isn't it grand? How will we ever thank Grandmother? How will we ever be good enough to pay her?"

Both children thought this a hint, so with one accord they arose and fell on Mrs. Bates' back, and began to pay at once in coin of childhood.

"There, there," said Kate, drawing them away as she stopped the horse at the gate. "There, there, you will choke Grandmother."

Mrs. Bates pushed Kate's arm down.

"Mind your own business, will you?" she said. "I ain't so feeble that I can't speak for myself awhile yet."

In a daze Kate climbed down, and ran to bring a chair to help her mother. The children were boisterously half eating Mrs. Bates up; she had both of them in her arms, with every outward evidence of enjoying the performance immensely. That was a very busy evening, for the wagon was to be unpacked; all of them were hungry, while the stock was to be fed, and the milking done. Mrs. Bates and Polly attempted supper; Kate and Adam went to the barn; but they worked very hurriedly, for Kate could see how feeble her mother had grown.

When at last the children were bathed and in bed, Kate and her mother sat on the little front porch to smell spring a few minutes before going to rest. Kate reached over and took her mother's hand.

"There's no word I know in any language big enough to thank you for this, Mother," she said. "The best I can do is make each day as nearly a perfect expression of what I feel as possible."

Mrs. Bates drew away her hand and used it to wipe her eyes; but she said with her usual terse perversity: "My, Kate! You're most as wordy as Agatha. I'm no glibtonguer, but I bet you ten dollars it will hustle you some to be any gladder than I am."

Kate laughed and gave up the thanks question.

"To-morrow we must get some onions in," she said. "Have you made any plans about the farm work for this year yet?"

"No," said Mrs. Bates. "I was going to leave that till I decided whether I'd come after you this spring or wait until next. Since I decided to come now, I'll just leave your farm to you. Handle it as you please."

"Mother, what will the other children say?" implored Kate.

"Humph! You are about as well acquainted with them as I am. Take a shot at it yourself. If it will avoid a fuss, we might just say you had to come to stay with me, and run the farm for me, and let them get used to your being here, and bossing things by degrees; like the man that cut his dog's tail off an inch at a time, so it wouldn't hurt so bad."

"But by inches, or 'at one fell swoop,' it's going to hurt," said Kate.

"Sometimes it seems to me," said Mrs. Bates, "that the more we get HURT in this world the decenter it makes us. All the boys were hurt enough when Pa went, but every man of them has been a BIGGER, BETTER man since. Instead of competing as they always did, Adam and Andrew and the older, beforehandeder ones, took hold and helped the younger as you told them to, and it's done the whole family a world of good. One thing is funny. To hear Mary talk now, you'd think she engineered that plan herself. The boys are all thankful, and so are the girls. I leave it to you. Tell them or let them guess it by degrees, it's all one to me."

"Tell me about Nancy Ellen and Robert," said Kate.

"Robert stands head in Hartley. He gets bigger and broader every year. He is better looking than a man has any business to be; and I hear the Hartley ladies give him plenty of encouragement in being stuck on himself, but I think he is true to Nancy Ellen, and his heart is all in his work. No children. That's a burning shame! Both of them feel it. In a way, and strictly between you and me, Nancy Ellen is a disappointment to me, an' I doubt if she ain't been a mite of a one to him. He had a right to expect a good deal of Nancy Ellen. She had such a good brain, and good body, and purty face. I may miss my guess, but it always strikes me that she falls SHORT of what he expected of her. He's coined money, but she hasn't spent it in the ways he would. Likely I shouldn't say it, but he strikes me as being just a leetle mite too good for her."

"Oh, Mother!" said Kate.

"Now you lookey here," said Mrs. Bates. "Suppose you was a man of Robert's brains, and education, and professional ability, and you made heaps of money, and no children came, and you had to see all you earned, and stood for, and did in a community spent on the SELFISHNESS of one woman. How big would you feel? What end is that for the ambition and life work of a real man? How would you like it?"

"I never thought of such a thing," said Kate.

"Well, mark my word, you WILL think of it when you see their home, and her clothes, and see them together," said Mrs. Bates.

"She still loves pretty clothing so well?" asked Kate.

"She is the best-dressed woman in the county, and the best looking," said Mrs. Bates, "and that's all there is to her. I'm free to say with her chances, I'm ashamed of what she has, and hasn't made of herself. I'd rather stand in your shoes, than hers, this minute, Katie."

"Does she know I'm here?" asked Kate.

"Yes. I stopped and told her on my way out, this morning," said Mrs. Bates. "I asked them to come out for Sunday dinner, and they are coming."

"Did you deliver the invitation by force?" asked Kate.

"Now, none of your meddling," said Mrs. Bates. "I got what I went after, and that was all I wanted. I've told her an' told her to come to see you during the last three years, an' I know she WANTED to come; but she just had that stubborn Bates streak in her that wouldn't let her change, once her mind was made up. It did give us a purty severe jolt, Kate, havin' all that good Bates money burn up."

"I scarcely think it jolted any of you more than it did me," said Kate dryly.

"No, I reckon it didn't," said Mrs. Bates. "But they's no use hauling ourselves over the coals to go into that. It's past. You went out to face life bravely enough and it throwed you a boomerang that cut a circle and brought you back where you started from. Our arrangements for the future are all made. Now it's up to us to live so that we get the most out of life for us an' the children. Those are mighty nice children of yours, Kate. I take to that boy something amazin', and the girl is the nicest little old lady I've seen in many a day. I think we will like knittin' and sewin' together, to the top of our bent."

"My, but I'm glad you like them, Mother," said Kate. "They are all I've got to show for ten years of my life."

"Not by a long shot, Katie," said Mrs. Bates. "Life has made a real woman of you. I kept watchin' you to-day comin' over; an' I was prouder 'an Jehu of you. It's a debatable question whether you have thrown away your time and your money. I say you've got something to show for it that I wish to God the rest of my children had. I want you should brace your back, and stiffen your neck, and make things hum here. Get a carpenter first. Fix the house the way it will be most convenient and comfortable. Then paint and paper, and get what new things you like, in reason—of course, in reason—and then I want you should get all of us clothes so's there ain't a noticeable difference between us and the others when we come together here or elsewhere. Put in a telephone; they're mighty handy, and if you can scrape up a place—I washed in Nancy Ellen's tub a few weeks ago. I never was wet all over at once before in my life, and I'm just itching to try it again. I say, let's have it, if it knocks a fair-sized hole in a five-hundred-dollar bill. An' if we had the telephone right now, we could call up folks an' order what we want without ever budgin' out of our tracks. Go up ahead, Katie, I'll back you in anything you can think of. It won't hurt my feelings a mite if you can think of one or two things the rest of them haven't got yet. Can't you think of something that will lay the rest of them clear in the shade? I just wish you could. Now, I'm going to bed."

Kate went with her mother, opened her bed, pulled out the pins, and brushed her hair, drew the thin cover over her, and blew out the light. Then she went past the bed on her way to the door, and stooping, she kissed her mother for the first time since she could remember.

Then she lighted a lamp, hunted a big sheet of wrapping paper, and sitting down beside the living room table, she drew a rough sketch of the house. For hours she pored over it, and when at last she went to bed, on the reverse of the sheet she had a drawing that was quite a different affair; yet it was the same house with very few and easily made changes that a good contractor could accomplish in a short time. In the morning, she showed these ideas to her mother who approved all of them, but still showed disappointment visibly.

"That's nothing but all the rest of them have," she said. "I thought you could think up some frills that would be new, and different."

"Well," said Kate, "would you want to go to the expense of setting up a furnace in the cellar? It would make the whole house toasty warm; it would keep the bathroom from freezing in cold weather; and make a better way to heat the water."

"Now you're shouting!" cried Mrs. Bates. "That's it! But keep still. Don't you tell a soul about it, but go on and do it, Katie. Wade right in! What else can you think of?"

"A brain specialist for you," said Kate. "I think myself this is enough for a start; but if you insist on more, there's a gas line passing us out there on the road; we could hitch on for a very reasonable sum, and do away with lamps and cooking with wood."

"Goody for you! That's it!" cried Mrs. Bates. "That's the very thing! Now brush up your hair your prettiest, and put on your new blue dress, and take the buggy, and you and Adam go see how much of this can be started to-day. Me and Polly will keep house."

In a month all of these changes had been made, and were in running order; the painting was finished, new furniture in place, a fair start made on the garden, while a strong, young, hired man was not far behind Hiram with his plowing. Kate was so tired she almost staggered; but she was so happy she arose each morning refreshed, and accomplished work enough for three average women before the day was over. She suggested to her mother that she use her money from the sale of the Walden home to pay for what furniture she had bought, and then none of the others could feel that they were entitled to any share in it, at any time. Mrs. Bates thought that a good idea, so much ill will was saved among the children.

They all stopped in passing; some of them had sharp words to say, which Kate instantly answered in such a way that this was seldom tried twice. In two months the place was fresh, clean, convenient, and in good taste. All of them had sufficient suitable clothing, while the farm work had not been neglected enough to hurt the value of the crops.

In the division of labour, Adam and the hired man took the barn and field work, Mrs. Bates and Polly the house, while Kate threw all her splendid strength wherever it was most needed. If a horse was sick, she went to the barn and doctored it. If the hay was going to get wet, she pitched hay. If the men had not time for the garden she attended it, and hoed the potatoes. For a change, everything went right. Mrs. Bates was happier than she ever had been before, taking the greatest interest in the children. They had lived for three years in such a manner that they would never forget it. They were old enough to appreciate what changes had come to them, and to be very keen about their new home and life. Kate threw herself into the dream of her heart with all the zest of her being. Always she had loved and wanted land. Now she had it. She knew how to handle it. She could make it pay as well as any Bates man, for she had man strength, and all her life she had heard men discuss, and helped men apply man methods.

There was a strong strain of her father's spirit of driving in Kate's blood; but her mother was so tired of it that whenever Kate had gone just so far the older woman had merely to caution: "Now, now, Katie!" to make Kate realized what she was doing and take a slower pace. All of them were well, happy, and working hard; but they also played at proper times, and in convenient places. Kate and her mother went with the children when they fished in the meadow brook, or hunted wild flowers in the woods for Polly's bed in the shade of the pear tree beside the garden. There were flowers in the garden now, as well as vegetables. There was no work done on Sunday. The children always went to Sunday-school and the full term of the District School at Bates Corners. They were respected, they were prosperous, they were finding a joy in life they never before had known, while life had taught them how to appreciate its good things as they achieved them.

The first Christmas Mrs. Bates and Kate made a Christmas tree from a small savine in the dooryard that stood where Kate wanted to set a flowering shrub she had found in the woods. Guided by the former year, and with a few dollars they decided to spend, these women made a real Christmas tree, with gifts and ornaments, over which Mrs. Bates was much more excited than the children. Indeed, such is the perversity of children that Kate's eyes widened and her mouth sagged when she heard Adam say in a half-whisper to Polly: "This is mighty pretty, but gee, Polly, there'll never be another tree as pretty as ours last year!"

While Polly answered: "I was just thinking about it, Adam. Wasn't it the grandest thing?"

The next Christmas Mrs. Bates advanced to a tree that reached the ceiling, with many candles, real ornaments, and an orange, a stocking of candy and nuts, and a doll for each girl, and a knife for each boy of her grandchildren, all of whom she invited for dinner. Adam, 3d, sat at the head of the table, Mrs. Bates at the foot. The tiniest tots that could be trusted without their parents ranged on the Dictionary and the Bible, of which the Bates family possessed a fat edition for birth records; no one had ever used it for any other purpose, until it served to lift Hiram's baby, Milly, on a level with her roast turkey and cranberry jelly. For a year before her party Mrs. Bates planned for it. The tree was beautiful, the gifts amazing, the dinner, as Kate cooked and served it, a revelation, with its big centre basket of red, yellow, and green apples, oranges, bananas, grapes, and flowers. None of them ever had seen a table like that. Then when dinner was over, Kate sat before the fire and in her clear voice, with fine inflections, she read from the Big Book the story of the guiding star and the little child in the manger. Then she told stories, and they played games until four o'clock; and then Adam rolled all of the children into the big wagon bed mounted on the sled runners, and took them home. Then he came back and finished the day. Mrs. Bates could scarcely be persuaded to go to bed. When at last Kate went to put out her mother's light, and see that her feet were warm and her covers tucked, she found her crying.

"Why, Mother!" exclaimed Kate in frank dismay. "Wasn't everything all right?"

"I'm just so endurin' mad," sobbed Mrs. Bates, "that I could a-most scream and throw things. Here I am, closer the end of my string than anybody knows. Likely I'll not see another Christmas. I've lived the most of my life, and never knowed there was a time like that on earth to be had. There wasn't expense to it we couldn't easy have stood, always. Now, at the end of my tether, I go and do this for my grandchildren. 'Tween their little shining faces and me, there kept coming all day the little, sad, disappointed faces of you and Nancy Ellen, and Mary, and Hannah, and Adam, and Andrew, and Hiram and all the others. Ever since he went I've thought the one thing I COULDN'T DO WAS TO DIE AND FACE ADAM BATES, but to-day I ain't felt so scared of him. Seems to me HE has got about as much to account for as I have."

Kate stood breathlessly still, looking at her mother. Mrs. Bates wiped her eyes. "I ain't so mortal certain," she said, "that I don't open up on him and take the first word. I think likely I been defrauded out of more that really counts in this world, than he has. Ain't that little roly-poly of Hannah's too sweet? Seems like I'll hardly quit feeling her little sticky hands and her little hot mouth on my face when I die; and as she went out she whispered in my ear: 'Do it again, Grandma, Oh, please do it again!' an it's more'n likely I'll not get the chance, no matter how willing I am. Kate, I am going to leave you what of my money is left—I haven't spent so much—and while you live here, I wish each year you would have this same kind of a party and pay for it out of that money, and call it 'Grandmother's Party.' Will you?"

"I surely will," said Kate. "And hadn't I better have ALL of them, and put some little thing from you on the tree for them? You know how Hiram always was wild for cuff buttons, and Mary could talk by the hour about a handkerchief with lace on it, and Andrew never yet has got that copy of 'Aesop's Fables,' he always wanted. Shall I?"

"Yes," said Mrs. Bates. "Oh, yes, and when you do it, Katie, if they don't chain me pretty close in on the other side, I think likely I'll be sticking around as near as I can get to you."

Kate slipped a hot brick rolled in flannel to the cold old feet, and turning out the light she sat beside the bed and stroked the tired head until easy breathing told her that her mother was sound asleep. Then she went back to the fireplace and sitting in the red glow she told Adam, 3d, PART of what her mother had said. Long after he was gone, she sat gazing into the slowly graying coals, her mind busy with what she had NOT told.

That spring was difficult for Kate. Day after day she saw her mother growing older, feebler, and frailer. And as the body failed, up flamed the wings of the spirit, carrying her on and on, each day keeping her alive, when Kate did not see how it could be done. With all the force she could gather, each day Mrs. Bates struggled to keep going, denied that she felt badly, drove herself to try to help about the house and garden. Kate warned the remainder of the family what they might expect at any hour; but when they began coming in oftener, bringing little gifts and being unusually kind, Mrs. Bates endured a few of the visits in silence, then she turned to Kate and said after her latest callers: "I wonder what in the name of all possessed ails the folks? Are they just itching to start my funeral? Can't they stay away until you send them word that the breath's out of my body?"

"Mother, you shock me," said Kate. "They come because they LOVE you. They try to tell you so with the little things they bring. Most people would think they were neglected, if their children did NOT come to see them when they were not so well."

"Not so well!" cried Mrs. Bates. "Folly! I am as well as I ever was. They needn't come snooping around, trying to make me think I'm not. If they'd a-done it all their lives, well and good; it's no time for them to begin being cotton-mouthed now."

"Mother," said Kate gently, "haven't YOU changed, yourself, about things like Christmas, for example? Maybe your children are changing, too. Maybe they feel that they have missed something they'd like to have from you, and give back to you, before it's too late. Just maybe," said Kate.

Mrs. Bates sat bolt upright still, but her flashing eyes softened.

"I hadn't just thought of that," she said. "I think it's more than likely. Well, if it's THAT way, I s'pose I've got to button up my lip and stand it; but it's about more than I can go, when I know that the first time I lose my grip I'll land smash up against Adam Bates and my settlement with him."

"Mother," said Kate still more gently, "I thought we had it settled at the time Father went that each of you would be accountable to GOD, not to each other. I am a wanderer in darkness myself, when it come to talking about God, but this I know, He is SOMEWHERE and He is REDEEMING love. If Father has been in the light of His love all these years, he must have changed more, far more than you have. He'll understand now how wrong he was to force ways on you he knew you didn't think right; he'll have more to account to you for than you ever will to him; and remember this only, neither of you is accountable, save to your God."

Mrs. Bates arose and walked to the door, drawn to full height, her head very erect. The world was at bloom-time. The evening air was heavily sweet with lilacs, and the widely branching, old apple trees of the dooryard with loaded with flowers. She stepped outside. Kate followed. Her mother went down the steps and down the walk to the gate. Kate kept beside her, in reach, yet not touching her. At the gate she gripped the pickets to steady herself as she stared long and unflinchingly at the red setting sun dropping behind a white wall of bloom. Then she slowly turned, life's greatest tragedy lining her face, her breath coming in short gasps. She spread her hands at each side, as if to balance herself, her passing soul in her eyes, and looked at Kate.

"Katherine Eleanor," she said slowly and distinctly, "I'm going now. I can't fight it off any longer. I confess myself. I burned those deeds. Every one of them. Pa got himself afire, but he'd thrown THEM out of it. It was my chance. I took it. Are you going to tell them?"

Kate was standing as tall and straight as her mother, her hands extended the same, but not touching her.

"No," she said. "You were an instrument in the hands of God to right a great wrong. No! I shall never tell a soul while I live. In a minute God himself will tell you that you did what He willed you should."

"Well, we will see about that right now," said Mrs. Bates, lifting her face to the sky. "Into thy hands, O Lord, into thy hands!"

Then she closed her eyes and ceased to breathe. Kate took her into her arms and carried her to her bed.

CHAPTER XXII

SOMEWHAT OF POLLY

IF THE spirit of Mrs. Bates hovered among the bloom-whitened apple trees as her mortal remains were carried past the lilacs and cabbage rose bushes, through a rain of drifting petals, she must have been convinced that time had wrought one great change in the hearts of her children. They had all learned to weep; while if the tears they shed were a criterion of their feelings for her, surely her soul must have been satisfied. They laid her away with simple ceremony and then all of them went to their homes, except Nancy Ellen and Robert, who stopped in passing to learn if there was anything they could do for Kate. She was grieving too deeply for many words; none of them would ever understand the deep bond of sympathy and companionship that had grown to exist between her and her mother. She stopped at the front porch and sat down, feeling unable to enter the house with Nancy Ellen, who was deeply concerned over the lack of taste displayed in Agatha's new spring hat. When Kate could endure it no longer she interrupted: "Why didn't all of them come?"

"What for?" asked Nancy Ellen.

"They had a right to know what Mother had done," said Kate in a low voice.

"But what was the use?" asked Nancy Ellen. "Adam had been managing the administrator business for Mother and paying her taxes with his, of course when she made a deed to you, and had it recorded, they told him. All of us knew it for two years before she went after you. And the new furniture was bought with your money, so it's yours; what was there to have a meeting about?"

"Mother didn't understand that you children knew," said Kate.

"Sometimes I thought there were a lot of things Mother didn't understand," said Nancy Ellen, "and sometimes I thought she understood so much more than any of the rest of us, that all of us would have had a big surprise if we could have seen her brain."

"Yes, I believe we would," said Kate. "Do you mind telling me how the boys and girls feel about this?"

Nancy Ellen laughed shortly. "Well, the boys feel that you negotiated such a fine settlement of Father's affairs for them, that they owe this to you. The girls were pretty sore at first, and some of them are nursing their wrath yet; but there wasn't a thing on earth they could do. All of them were perfectly willing that you should have something—after the fire—of course, most of them thought Mother went too far."

"I think so myself," said Kate. "But she never came near me, or wrote me, or sent me even one word, until the day she came after me. I had nothing to do with it—"

"All of us know that, Kate," said Nancy Ellen. "You needn't worry. We're all used to it, and we're all at the place where we have nothing to say."

To escape grieving for her mother, Kate worked that summer as never before. Adam was growing big enough and strong enough to be a real help. He was interested in all they did, always after the reason, and trying to think of a better way. Kate secured the best agricultural paper for him and they read it nights together. They kept an account book, and set down all they spent, and balanced against it all they earned, putting the difference, which was often more than they hoped for, in the bank.

So the years ran. As the children grew older, Polly discovered that the nicest boy in school lived across the road half a mile north of them; while Adam, after a real struggle in his loyal twin soul, aided by the fact that Henry Peters usually had divided his apples with Polly before Adam reached her, discovered that Milly York, across the road, half a mile south, liked his apples best, and was as nice a girl as Polly ever dared to be. In a dazed way, Kate learned these things from their after-school and Sunday talk, saw that they nearly reached her shoulder, and realized that they were sixteen. So quickly the time goes, when people are busy, happy, and working together. At least Kate and Adam were happy, for they were always working together. By tacit agreement, they left Polly the easy housework, and went themselves to the fields to wrestle with the rugged work of a farm. They thought they were shielding Polly, teaching her a woman's real work, and being kind to her.

Polly thought they were together because they liked to be; doing the farm work because it suited them better; while she had known from babyhood that for some reason her mother did not care for her as she did for Adam. She thought at first that it was because Adam was a boy. Later, when she noticed her mother watching her every time she started to speak, and interrupting with the never-failing caution: "Now be careful! THINK before you speak! Are you SURE?" she wondered why this should happen to her always, to Adam never. She asked Adam about it, but Adam did not know. It never occurred to Polly to ask her mother, while Kate was so uneasy it never occurred to her that the child would notice or what she would think. The first time Polly deviated slightly from the truth, she and Kate had a very terrible time. Kate felt fully justified; the child astonished and abused.

Polly arrived at the solution of her problem slowly. As she grew older, she saw that her mother, who always was charitable to everyone else, was repelled by her grandmother, while she loved Aunt Ollie. Older still, Polly realized that SHE was a reproduction of her grandmother. She had only to look at her to see this; her mother did not like her grandmother, maybe Mother did not like her as well as Adam, because she resembled her grandmother. By the time she was sixteen, Polly had arrived at a solution that satisfied her as to why her mother liked Adam better, and always left her alone in the house to endless cooking, dishwashing, sweeping, dusting, washing, and ironing, while she hoed potatoes, pitched hay, or sheared sheep. Polly thought the nicer way would have been to do the housework together and then go to the fields together; but she was a good soul, so she worked alone and brooded in silence, and watched up the road for a glimpse of Henry Peters, who liked to hear her talk, and to whom it mattered not a mite that her hair was lustreless, her eyes steel coloured, and her nose like that of a woman he never had seen. In her way, Polly admired her mother, loved her, and worked until she was almost dropping for Kate's scant, infrequent words of praise.

So Polly had to be content in the kitchen. One day, having finished her work two hours before dinnertime, she sauntered to the front gate. How strange that Henry Peters should be at the end of the field joining their land. When he waved, she waved back. When he climbed the fence she opened the gate. They met halfway, under the bloomful shade of a red haw. Henry wondered who two men he had seen leaving the Holt gate were, and what they wanted, but he was too polite to ask. He merely hoped they did not annoy her. Oh, no, they were only some men to see Mother about some business, but it was most kind of him to let her know he was looking out for her. She got so lonely; Mother never would let her go to the field with her. Of course not! The field was no place for such a pretty girl; there was enough work in the house for her. His sister should not work in the field, if he had a sister, and Polly should not work there, if she belonged to him; No-sir-ee! Polly looked at Henry with shining, young girl eyes, and when he said she was pretty, her blue-gray eyes softened, her cheeks pinked up, the sun put light in her hair nature had failed to, and lo and behold, the marvel was wrought—plain little Polly became a thing of beauty. She knew it instantly, because she saw herself in Henry Peters' eyes. And Henry was so amazed when this wonderful transformation took place in little Polly, right there under the red haw tree, that his own eyes grew big and tender, his cheeks flooded with red blood, his heart shook him, and he drew to full height, and became possessed of an overwhelming desire to dance before Polly, and sing to her. He grew so splendid, Polly caught her breath, and then she smiled on him a very wondering smile, over the great discovery; and Henry grew so bewildered he forgot either to dance or sing as a preliminary. He merely, just merely, reached out and gathered Polly in his arms, and held her against him, and stared down at her wonderful beauty opening right out under his eyes.

"Little Beautiful!" said Henry Peters in a hushed, choking voice, "Little Beautiful!"

Polly looked up at him. She was every bit as beautiful as he thought her, while he was so beautiful to Polly that she gasped for breath. How did he happen to look as he did, right under the red haw, in broad daylight? He had been hers, of course, ever since, shy and fearful, she had first entered Bates Corners school, and found courage in his broad, encouraging smile. Now she smiled on him, the smile of possession that was in her heart. Henry instantly knew she always had belonged to him, so he grasped her closer, and bent his head.

When Henry went back to the plow, and Polly ran down the road, with the joy of the world surging in her heart and brain, she knew that she was going to have to account to her tired, busy mother for being half an hour late with dinner; and he knew he was going to have to explain to an equally tired father why he was four furrows short of where he should be.

He came to book first, and told the truth. He had seen some men go to the Holts'. Polly was his little chum; and she was always alone all summer, so he just walked that way to be sure she was safe. His father looked at him quizzically.

"So THAT'S the way the wind blows!" he said. "Well, I don't know where you could find a nicer little girl or a better worker. I'd always hoped you'd take to Milly York; but Polly is better; she can work three of Milly down. Awful plain, though!"

This sacrilege came while Henry's lips were tingling with their first kiss, and his heart was drunken with the red wine of innocent young love.

"Why, Dad, you're crazy!" he cried. "There isn't another girl in the whole world as pretty and sweet as Polly. Milly York? She can't hold a candle to Polly! Besides, she's been Adam's as long as Polly has been mine!"

"God bless my soul!" cried Mr. Peters. "How these youngsters to run away with us. And are you the most beautiful young man at Bates Corners, Henry?"

"I'm beautiful enough that Polly will put her arms around my neck and kiss me, anyway," blurted Henry. "So you and Ma can get ready for a wedding as soon as Polly says the word. I'm ready, right now."

"So am I," said Mr. Peters, "and from the way Ma complains about the work I and you boys make her, I don't think she will object to a little help. Polly is a good, steady worker."

Polly ran, but she simply could not light the fire, set the table, and get things cooked on time, while everything she touched seemed to spill or slip. She could not think what, or how, to do the usual for the very good reason that Henry Peters was a Prince, and a Knight, and a Lover, and a Sweetheart, and her Man; she had just agreed to all this with her soul, less than an hour ago under the red haw. No wonder she was late, no wonder she spilled and smeared; and red of face she blundered and bungled, for the first time in her life. Then in came Kate. She must lose no time, the corn must be finished before it rained. She must hurry—for the first time dinner was late, while Polly was messing like a perfect little fool.

Kate stepped in and began to right things with practised hand. Disaster came when she saw Polly, at the well, take an instant from bringing in the water, to wave in the direction of the Peters farm. As she entered the door, Kate swept her with a glance.

"Have to upset the bowl, as usual?" she said, scathingly. "Just as I think you're going to make something of yourself, and be of some use, you begin mooning in the direction of that big, gangling Hank Peters. Don't you ever let me see you do it again. You are too young to start that kind of foolishness. I bet a cow he was hanging around here, and made you late with dinner."

"He was not! He didn't either!" cried Polly, then stopped in dismay, her cheeks burning. She gulped and went on bravely: "That is, he wasn't here, and he didn't make ME late, any more than I kept HIM from his work. He always watches when there are tramps and peddlers on the road, because he knows I'm alone. I knew he would be watching two men who stopped to see you, so I just went as far as the haw tree to tell him I was all right, and we got to talking—"

If only Kate had been looking at Polly then! But she was putting the apple butter and cream on the table. As she did so, she thought possibly it was a good idea to have Henry Peters seeing that tramps did not frighten Polly, so she missed dawn on the face of her child, and instead of what might have been, she said: "Well, I must say THAT is neighbourly of him; but don't you dare let him get any foolish notions in his head. I think Aunt Nancy Ellen will let you stay at her house after this, and go to the Hartley High School in winter, so you can come out of that much better prepared to teach than I ever was. I had a surprise planned for you to-night, but now I don't know whether you deserve it or not. I'll have to think."

Kate did not think at all. After the manner of parents, she SAID that, but her head was full of something she thought vastly more important just then; of course Polly should have her share in it. Left alone to wash the dishes and cook supper while her mother went to town, it was Polly, who did the thinking. She thought entirely too much, thought bitterly, thought disappointedly, and finally thought resentfully, and then alas, Polly thought deceitfully. Her mother had said: "Never let me see you." Very well, she would be extremely careful that she was NOT seen; but before she slept she rather thought she would find a way to let Henry know how she was being abused, and about that plan to send her away all the long winter to school. She rather thought Henry would have something to say about how his "Little Beautiful" was being treated. Here Polly looked long and searchingly in the mirror to see if by any chance Henry was mistaken, and she discovered he was. She stared in amazement at the pink-cheeked, shining eyed girl she saw mirrored. She pulled her hair looser around the temples, and drew her lips over her teeth. Surely Henry was mistaken. "Little Beautiful" was too moderate. She would see that he said "perfectly lovely," the next time, and he did.

CHAPTER XXIII

KATE'S HEAVENLY TIME

ONE evening Kate and Polly went to the front porch to rest until bedtime and found a shining big new trunk sitting there, with Kate's initials on the end, her name on the check tag, and a key in the lock. They unbuckled the straps, turned the key, and lifted the lid. That trunk contained underclothing, hose, shoes, two hats, a travelling dress with half a dozen extra waists, and an afternoon and an evening dress, all selected with especial reference to Kate's colouring, and made one size larger than Nancy Ellen wore, which fitted Kate perfectly. There were gloves, a parasol, and a note which read:

DEAR KATE: Here are some clothes. I am going to go North a week after harvest. You can be spared then as well as not. Come on! Let's run away and have one good time all by ourselves. It is my treat from start to finish. The children can manage the farm perfectly well. Any one of her cousins will stay with Polly, if she will be lonely. Cut loose and come on, Kate. I am going. Of course Robert couldn't be pried away from his precious patients; we will have to go alone; but we do not care. We like it. Shall we start about the tenth, on the night train, which will be cooler? NANCY ELLEN.

"We shall!" said Kate emphatically, when she finished the note. "I haven't cut loose and had a good time since I was married; not for eighteen years. If the children are not big enough to take care of themselves, they never will be. I can go as well as not."

She handed the note to Polly, while she shook out dresses and gloated over the contents of the trunk.

"Of course you shall go!" shouted Polly as she finished the note, but even as she said it she glanced obliquely up the road and waved a hand behind her mother's back.

"Sure you shall go!" cried Adam, when he finished the note, and sat beside the trunk seeing all the pretty things over again. "You just bet you shall go. Polly and I can keep house, fine! We don't need any cousins hanging around. I'll help Polly with her work, and then we'll lock the house and she can come out with me. Sure you go! We'll do all right." Then he glanced obliquely down the road, where a slim little figure in white moved under the cherry trees of the York front yard, aimlessly knocking croquet balls here and there.

It was two weeks until time to go, but Kate began taking care of herself at once, solely because she did not want Nancy Ellen to be ashamed of her. She rolled her sleeves down to meet her gloves and used a sunbonnet instead of a sunshade. She washed and brushed her hair with care she had not used in years. By the time the tenth of July came, she was in very presentable condition, while the contents of the trunk did the remainder. As she was getting ready to go, she said to Polly: "Now do your best while I'm away, and I am sure I can arrange with Nancy Ellen about school this winter. When I get back, the very first thing I shall do will be to go to Hartley and buy some stuff to begin on your clothes. You shall have as nice dresses as the other girls, too. Nancy Ellen will know exactly what to get you."

But she never caught a glimpse of Polly's flushed, dissatisfied face or the tightening of her lips that would have suggested to her, had she seen them, that Miss Polly felt perfectly capable of selecting the clothing she was to wear herself. Adam took his mother's trunk to the station in the afternoon. In the evening she held Polly on her knee, while they drove to Dr. Gray's. Kate thought the children would want to wait and see them take the train, but Adam said that would make them very late getting home, they had better leave that to Uncle Robert and go back soon; so very soon they were duly kissed and unduly cautioned; then started back down a side street that would not even take them through the heart of the town. Kate looked after them approvingly: "Pretty good youngsters," she said. "I told them to go and get some ice cream; but you see they are saving the money and heading straight home." She turned to Robert. "Can anything happen to them?" she asked, in evident anxiety.

"Rest in peace, Kate," laughed the doctor. "You surely know that those youngsters are going to be eighteen in a few weeks. You've reared them carefully. Nothing can, or will, happen to them, that would not happen right under your nose if you were at home. They will go from now on according to their inclinations."

Kate looked at him sharply: "What do you mean by that?" she demanded.

He laughed: "Nothing serious," he said. "Polly is half Bates, so she will marry in a year or two, while Adam is all Bates, so he will remain steady as the Rock of Ages, and strictly on the job. Go have your good time, and if I possibly can, I'll come after you."

"You'll do nothing of the kind," said Nancy Ellen, with finality. "You wouldn't leave your patients, and you couldn't leave dear Mrs. Southey."

"If you feel that way about it, why do you leave me?" he asked.

"To show the little fool I'm not afraid of her, for one thing," said Nancy Ellen with her head high. She was very beautiful in her smart travelling dress, while her eyes flashed as she spoke. The doctor looked at her approvingly.

"Good!" he cried. "I like a plucky woman! Go to have a good time, Nancy Ellen; but don't go for that. I do wish you would believe that there isn't a thing the matter with the little woman, she's—"

"I can go even farther than that," said Nancy Ellen, dryly. "I KNOW 'there isn't a thing the matter with the little woman,' except that she wants you to look as if you were running after her. I'd be safe in wagering a thousand dollars that when she hears I'm gone, she will send for you before to-morrow evening."

"You may also wager this," he said. "If she does, I shall be very sorry, but I'm on my way to the country on an emergency call. Nancy Ellen, I wish you wouldn't!"

"Wouldn't go North, or wouldn't see what every other living soul in Hartley sees?" she asked curtly. Then she stepped inside to put on her hat and gloves.

Kate looked at the doctor in dismay. "Oh, Robert!" she said.

"I give you my word of honour, Kate," he said. "If Nancy Ellen only would be reasonable, the woman would see shortly that my wife is all the world to me. I never have been, and never shall be, untrue to her. Does that satisfy you?"

"Of course," said Kate. "I'll do all in my power to talk Nancy Ellen out of that, on this trip. Oh, if she only had children to occupy her time!"

"That's the whole trouble in a nutshell," said the doctor; "but you know there isn't a scarcity of children in the world. Never a day passes but I see half a dozen who need me, sorely. But with Nancy Ellen, NO CHILD will do unless she mothers it, and unfortunately, none comes to her."

"Too bad!" said Kate. "I'm so sorry!"

"Cheer her up, if you can," said the doctor.

An hour later they were speeding north, Nancy Ellen moody and distraught, Kate as frankly delighted as any child. The spring work was over; the crops were fine; Adam would surely have the premium wheat to take to the County Fair in September; he would work unceasingly for his chance with corn; he and Polly would be all right; she could see Polly waiting in the stable yard while Adam unharnessed and turned out the horse.

Kate kept watching Nancy Ellen's discontented face. At last she said: "Cheer up, child! There isn't a word of truth in it!"

"I know it," said Nancy Ellen.

"Then why take the way of all the world to start, and KEEP people talking?" asked Kate.

"I'm not doing a thing on earth but attending strictly to my own business," said Nancy Ellen.

"That's exactly the trouble," said Kate. "You're not. You let the little heifer have things all her own way. If it were my man, and I loved him as you do Robert Gray, you can stake your life I should be doing something, several things, in fact."

"This is interesting," said Nancy Ellen. "For example—?"

Kate had not given such a matter a thought. She looked from the window a minute, her lips firmly compressed. Then she spoke slowly: "Well, for one thing, I should become that woman's bosom companion. About seven times a week I should uncover her most aggravating weakness all unintentionally before the man in the case, at the same time keeping myself, strictly myself. I should keep steadily on doing and being what he first fell in love with. Lastly, since eighteen years have brought you no fulfillment of the desire of your heart, I should give it up, and content myself and delight him by taking into my heart and home a couple of the most attractive tiny babies I could find. Two are scarcely more trouble than one; you can have all the help you will accept; the children would never know the difference, if you took them as babies, and soon you wouldn't either; while Robert would be delighted. If I were you, I'd give myself something to work for besides myself, and I'd give him so much to think about at home, that charming young grass widows could go to grass!"

"I believe you would," said Nancy Ellen, wonderingly. "I believe you would!"

"You're might right, I would," said Kate. "If I were married to a man like Robert Gray, I'd fight tooth and nail before I'd let him fall below his high ideals. It's as much your job to keep him up, as it is his to keep himself. If God didn't make him a father, I would, and I'd keep him BUSY on the job, if I had to adopt sixteen."

Nancy Ellen laughed, as they went to their berths. The next morning they awakened in cool Michigan country and went speeding north among evergreen forests and clear lakes mirroring the pointed forest tops and blue sky, past slashing, splashing streams, in which they could almost see the speckled trout darting over the beds of white sand. By late afternoon they had reached their destination and were in their rooms, bathed, dressed, and ready for the dinner hour. In the evening they went walking, coming back to the hotel tired and happy. After several days they began talking to people and making friends, going out in fishing and boating parties in the morning, driving or boating in the afternoon, and attending concerts or dances at night. Kate did not dance, but she loved to see Nancy Ellen when she had a sufficiently tall, graceful partner; while, as she watched the young people and thought how innocent and happy they seemed, she asked her sister if they could not possibly arrange for Adam and Polly to go to Hartley a night or two a week that winter, and join the dancing class. Nancy Ellen was frankly delighted, so Kate cautiously skirted the school question in such a manner that she soon had Nancy Ellen asking if it could not be arranged. When that was decided, Nancy Ellen went to dance, while Kate stood on the veranda watching her. The lights from the window fell strongly on Kate. She was wearing her evening dress of smoky gray, soft fabric, over shining silk, with knots of dull blue velvet and gold lace here and there. She had dressed her hair carefully; she appeared what she was, a splendid specimen of healthy, vigorous, clean womanhood.

"Pardon me, Mrs. Holt," said a voice at her elbow, "but there's only one head in this world like yours, so this, of course, must be you."

Kate's heart leaped and stood still. She turned slowly, then held out her hand, smiling at John Jardine, but saying not a word. He took her hand, and as he gripped it tightly he studied her frankly.

"Thank God for this!" he said, fervently. "For years I've dreamed of you and hungered for the sight of your face; but you cut me off squarely, so I dared not intrude on you—only the Lord knows how delighted I am to see you here, looking like this."

Kate smiled again.

"Come away," he begged. "Come out of this. Come walk a little way with me, and tell me WHO you are, and HOW you are, and all the things I think of every day of my life, and now I must know. It's brigandage! Come, or I shall carry you!"

"Pooh! You couldn't!" laughed Kate. "Of course I'll come! And I don't own a secret. Ask anything you want to know. How good it is to see you! Your mother—?"

"At rest, years ago," he said. "She never forgave me for what I did, in the way I did it. She said it would bring disaster, and she was right. I thought it was not fair and honest not to let you know the worst. I thought I was too old, and too busy, and too flourishing, to repair neglected years at that date, but believe me, Kate, you waked me up. Try the hardest one you know, and if I can't spell it, I'll pay a thousand to your pet charity."

Kate laughed spontaneously. "Are you in earnest?" she asked.

"I am incomprehensibly, immeasurably in earnest," he said, guiding her down a narrow path to a shrub-enclosed, railed-in platform, built on the steep side of a high hill, where they faced the moon-whitened waves, rolling softly in a dancing procession across the face of the great inland sea. Here he found a seat.

"I've nothing to tell," he said. "I lost Mother, so I went on without her. I learned to spell, and a great many other things, and I'm still making money. I never forget you for a day; I never have loved and never shall love any other woman. That's all about me, in a nutshell; now go on and tell me a volume, tell me all night, about you. Heavens, woman, I wish you could see yourself, in that dress with the moon on your hair. Kate, you are the superbest thing! I always shall be mad about you. Oh, if only you could have had a little patience with me. I thought I COULDN'T learn, but of course I COULD. But, proceed! I mustn't let myself go."

Kate leaned back and looked a long time at the shining white waves and the deep blue sky, then she turned to John Jardine, and began to talk. She told him simply a few of the most presentable details of her life: how she had lost her money, then had been given her mother's farm, about the children, and how she now lived. He listened with deep interest, often interrupting to ask a question, and when she ceased talking he said half under his breath: "And you're now free! Oh, the wonder of it! You're now, free!"

Kate had that night to think about the remainder of her life. She always sincerely hoped that the moonlight did not bewitch her into leading the man beside her into saying things he seemed to take delight in saying.

She had no idea what time it was; in fact, she did not care even what Nancy Ellen thought or whether she would worry. The night was wonderful; John Jardine had now made a man of himself worthy of all consideration; being made love to by him was enchanting. She had been occupied with the stern business of daily bread for so long that to be again clothed as other women and frankly adored by such a man as John Jardine was soul satisfying. What did she care who worried or what time it was?

"But I'm keeping you here until you will be wet with these mists," John Jardine cried at last. "Forgive me, Kate, I never did have any sense where you were concerned! I'll take you back now, but you must promise me to meet me here in the morning, say at ten o'clock. I'll take you back now, if you'll agree to that."

"There's no reason why I shouldn't," said Kate.

"And you're free, free!" he repeated.

The veranda, halls, and ballroom were deserted when they returned to the hotel. As Kate entered her room, Nancy Ellen sat up in bed and stared at her sleepily, but she was laughing in high good humour. She drew her watch from under her pillow and looked at it.

"Goodness gracious, Miss!" she cried. "Do you know it's almost three o'clock?"

"I don't care in the least," said Kate, "if it's four or five. I've had a perfectly heavenly time. Don't talk to me. I'll put out the light and be quiet as soon as I get my dress off. I think likely I've ruined it."

"What's the difference?" demanded Nancy Ellen, largely. "You can ruin half a dozen a day now, if you want to."

"What do you mean?" asked Kate.

"'Mean?'" laughed Nancy Ellen. "I mean that I saw John Jardine or his ghost come up to you on the veranda, looking as if he'd eat you alive, and carry you away about nine o'clock, and you've been gone six hours and come back having had a 'perfectly heavenly time.' What should I mean! Go up head, Kate! You have earned your right to a good time. It isn't everybody who gets a second chance in this world. Tell me one thing, and I'll go to sleep in peace and leave you to moon the remainder of the night, if you like. Did he say he still loved you?"

"Still and yet," laughed Kate. "As I remember, his exact words were that he 'never had loved and never would love any other woman.' Now are you satisfied?"

Nancy Ellen sprang from the bed and ran to Kate, gathering her in her strong arms. She hugged and kissed her ecstatically. "Good! Good! Oh, you darling!" she cried. "There'll be nothing in the world you can't have! I just know he had gone on making money; he was crazy about you. Oh, Kate, this is too good! How did I ever think of coming here, and why didn't I think of it seven years ago? Kate, you must promise me you'll marry him, before I let you go."

"I'll promise to THINK about it," said Kate, trying to free herself, for despite the circumstances and the hour, her mind flew back to a thousand times when only one kind word from Nancy Ellen would have saved her endless pain. It was endless, for it was burning in her heart that instant. At the prospect of wealth, position, and power, Nancy Ellen could smother her with caresses; but poverty, pain, and disgrace she had endured alone.

"I shan't let you go till you promise," threatened Nancy Ellen. "When are you to see him again?"

"Ten, this morning," said Kate. "You better let me get to bed, or I'll look a sight."

"Then promise," said Nancy Ellen.

Kate laid firm hands on the encircling arms. "Now, look here," she said, shortly, "it's about time to stop this nonsense. There's nothing I can promise you. I must have time to think. I've got not only myself, but the children to think for. And I've only got till ten o'clock, so I better get at it."

Kate's tone made Nancy Ellen step back.

"Kate, you haven't still got that letter in your mind, have you?" she demanded.

"No!" laughed Kate, "I haven't! He offered me a thousand dollars if I could pronounce him a word he couldn't spell; and it's perfectly evident he's studied until he is exactly like anybody else. No, it's not that!"

"Then what is it? Simpleton, there WAS nothing else!" cried Nancy Ellen.

"Not so much at that time; but this is nearly twenty years later, and I have the fate of my children in my hands. I wish you'd go to bed and let me think!" said Kate.

"Yes, and the longer you think the crazier you will act," cried Nancy Ellen. "I know you! You better promise me now, and stick to it."

For answer Kate turned off the light; but she did not go to bed. She sat beside the window and she was still sitting there when dawn crept across the lake and began to lighten the room. Then she stretched herself beside Nancy Ellen, who roused and looked at her.

"You just coming to bed?" she cried in wonder.

"At least you can't complain that I didn't think," said Kate, but Nancy Ellen found no comfort in what she said, or the way she said it. In fact, she arose when Kate did, feeling distinctly sulky. As they returned to their room from breakfast, Kate laid out her hat and gloves and began to get ready to keep her appointment. Nancy Ellen could endure the suspense no longer.

"Kate," she said in her gentlest tones, "if you have no mercy on yourself, have some on your children. You've no right, positively no right, to take such a chance away from them."

"Chance for what?" asked Kate tersely.

"Education, travel, leisure, every opportunity in the world," enumerated Nancy Ellen.

Kate was handling her gloves, her forehead wrinkled, her eyes narrowed in concentration.

"That is one side of it," she said. "The other is that neither my children nor I have in our blood, breeding, or mental cosmos, the background that it takes to make one happy with money in unlimited quantities. So far as I'm concerned personally, I'm happier this minute as I am, than John Jardine's money ever could make me. I had a fierce struggle with that question long ago; since I have had nearly eight years of life I love, that is good for my soul, the struggle to leave it would be greater now. Polly would be happier and get more from life as the wife of big gangling Henry Peters, than she would as a millionaire's daughter. She'd be very suitable in a farmhouse parlour; she'd be a ridiculous little figure at a ball. As for Adam, he'd turn this down quick and hard."

"Just you try him!" cried Nancy Ellen.

"For one thing, he won't be here at ten o'clock," said Kate, "and for another, since it involves my becoming the wife of John Jardine, it isn't for Adam to decide. This decision is strictly my own. I merely mention the children, because if I married him, it would have an inevitable influence on their lives, an influence that I don't in the least covet either for them or for myself. Nancy Ellen, can't you remotely conceive of such a thing as one human being in the world who is SATISFIED THAT HE HAS HIS SHARE, and who believes to the depths of his soul that no man should be allowed to amass, and to use for his personal indulgence, the amount of money that John Jardine does?"

"Yes, I can," cried Nancy Ellen, "when I see you, and the way you act! You have chance after chance, but you seem to think that life requires of you a steady job of holding your nose to the grindstone. It was rather stubby to begin with, go on and grind it clear off your face, if you like."

"All right," said Kate. "Then I'll tell you definitely that I have no particular desire to marry anybody; I like my life immensely as I'm living it. I'm free, independent, and my children are in the element to which they were born, and where they can live naturally, and spend their lives helping in the great work of feeding, clothing, and housing their fellow men. I've no desire to leave my job or take them from theirs, to start a lazy, shiftless life of self-indulgence. I don't meddle much with the Bible, but I have a profound BELIEF in it, and a large RESPECT for it, as the greatest book in the world, and it says: 'By the sweat of his brow shall man earn his bread,' or words to that effect. I was born a sweater, I shall just go on sweating until I die; I refuse to begin perspiring at my time of life."

"You big fool!" cried Nancy Ellen.

"Look out! You're 'in danger of Hell fire,' when you call me that!" warned Kate.

"Fire away!" cried Nancy Ellen, with tears in her eyes and voice. "When I think what you've gone through—"

Kate stared at her fixedly. "What do you know about what I've gone though?" she demanded in a cold, even voice. "Personally, I think you're not qualified to MENTION that subject; you better let it rest. Whatever it has been, it's been of such a nature that I have come out of it knowing when I have my share and when I'm well off, for me. If John Jardine wants to marry me, and will sell all he has, and come and work on the farm with me, I'll consider marrying him. To leave my life and what I love to go to Chicago with him, I do not feel called on, or inclined to do. No, I'll not marry him, and in about fifteen minutes I'll tell him so."

"And go on making a mess of your life such as you did for years," said Nancy Ellen, drying her red eyes.

"At least it was my life," said Kate. "I didn't mess things for any one else."

"Except your children," said Nancy Ellen.

"As you will," said Kate, rising. "I'll not marry John Jardine; and the sooner I tell him so and get it over, the better. Good-bye. I'll be back in half an hour."

Kate walked slowly to the observation platform, where she had been the previous evening with John Jardine; and leaning on the railing, she stood looking out over the water, and down the steep declivity, thinking how best she could word what she had to say. She was so absorbed she did not hear steps behind her or turn until a sharp voice said: "You needn't wait any longer. He's not coming!"

Kate turned and glanced at the speaker, and then around to make sure she was the person being addressed. She could see no one else. The woman was small, light haired, her face enamelled, dressed beyond all reason, and in a manner wholly out of place for morning at a summer resort in Michigan.

"If you are speaking to me, will you kindly tell me to whom you refer, and give me the message you bring?" said Kate.

"I refer to Mr. John Jardine, Mrs. Holt," said the little woman and then Kate saw that she was shaking, and gripping her hands for self-control.

"Very well," said Kate. "It will save me an unpleasant task if he doesn't come. Thank you," and she turned back to the water.

"You certainly didn't find anything unpleasant about being with him half last night," said the little woman.

Kate turned again, and looked narrowly at the speaker. Then she laughed heartily. "Well done, Jennie!" she cried. "Why, you are such a fashionable lady, such a Dolly Varden, I never saw who you were. How do you do? Won't you sit down and have a chat? It's just dawning on me that very possibly, from your dress and manner, I SHOULD have called you Mrs. Jardine."

"Didn't he tell you?" cried Jennie.

"He did not," said Kate. "Your name was not mentioned. He said no word about being married."

"We have been married since a few weeks after Mrs. Jardine died. I taught him the things you turned him down for not knowing; I have studied him, and waited on him, and borne his children, and THIS is my reward. What are you going to do?"

"Go back to the hotel, when I finish with this view," said Kate. "I find it almost as attractive by day as it was by night."

"Brazen!" cried Mrs. Jardine.

"Choose your words carefully," said Kate. "I was here first; since you have delivered your message, suppose you go and leave me to my view."

"Not till I get ready," said Mrs. Jardine. "Perhaps it will help you to know that I was not twenty feet from you at any time last night; and that I stood where I could have touched you, while my husband made love to you for hours."

"So?" said Kate. "I'm not at all surprised. That's exactly what I should have expected of you. But doesn't it clarify the situation any, at least for me, when I tell you that Mr. Jardine gave me no faintest hint that he was married? If you heard all we said, you surely remember that you were not mentioned?"

Mrs. Jardine sat down suddenly and gripped her little hands. Kate studied her intently. She wondered what she would look like when her hair was being washed; at this thought she smiled broadly. That made the other woman frantic.

"You can well LAUGH at me," she said. "I made the banner fool of the ages of myself when I schemed to marry him. I knew he loved you. He told me so. He told me, just as he told you last night, that he never had loved any other woman and he never would. I thought he didn't know himself as I knew him. He was so grand to his mother, I thought if I taught him, and helped him back to self-respect, and gave him children, he must, and would love me. Well, I was mistaken. He does not, and never will. Every day he thinks of you; not a night but he speaks your name. He thinks all things can be done with money—"

"So do you, Jennie," interrupted Kate. "Well, I'll show you that this CAN'T!"

"Didn't you hear him exulting because you are now free?" cried Jennie. "He thinks he will give me a home, the children, a big income; then secure his freedom and marry you."

"Oh, don't talk such rot!" cried Kate. "John Jardine thinks no such thing. He wouldn't insult me by thinking I thought such a thing. That thought belongs where it sprang from, right in your little cramped, blonde brain, Jennie."

"You wouldn't? Are you sure you wouldn't?" cried Jennie, leaning forward with hands clutched closely.

"I should say not!" said Kate. "The last thing on earth I want is some other woman's husband. Now look here, Jennie, I'll tell you the plain truth. I thought last night that John Jardine was as free as I was; or I shouldn't have been here with him. I thought he was asking me again to marry him, and I was not asleep last night, thinking it over. I came here to tell him that I would not. Does that satisfy you?"

"Satisfy?" cried Jennie. "I hope no other woman lives in the kind of Hell I do."

"It's always the way," said Kate, "when people will insist on getting out of their class. You would have gotten ten times more from life as the wife of a village merchant, or a farmer, than you have as the wife of a rich man. Since you're married to him, and there are children, there's nothing for you to do but finish your job as best you can. Rest your head easy about me. I wouldn't touch John Jardine married to you; I wouldn't touch him with a ten-foot pole, divorced from you. Get that clear in your head, and do please go!"

Kate turned again to the water, but when she was sure Jennie was far away she sat down suddenly and asked of the lake: "Well, wouldn't that freeze you?"

CHAPTER XXIV

POLLY TRIES HER WINGS

FINALLY Kate wandered back to the hotel and went to their room to learn if Nancy Ellen was there. She was and seemed very much perturbed. The first thing she did was to hand Kate a big white envelope, which she opened and found to be a few lines from John Jardine, explaining that he had been unexpectedly called away on some very important business. He reiterated his delight in having seen her, and hoped for the same pleasure at no very distant date. Kate read it and tossed it on the dresser. As she did so, she saw a telegram, lying opened among Nancy Ellen's toilet articles, and thought with pleasure that Robert was coming. She glanced at her sister for confirmation, and saw that she was staring from the window as if she were in doubt about something. Kate thought probably she was still upset about John Jardine, and that might as well be gotten over, so she said: "That note was not delivered promptly. It is from John Jardine. I should have had it before I left. He was called away on important business and wrote to let me know he would not be able to keep his appointment; but without his knowledge, he had a representative on the spot."

Nancy Ellen seemed interested so Kate proceeded: "You couldn't guess in a thousand years. I'll have to tell you spang! It was his wife."

"His wife!" cried Nancy Ellen. "But you said—"

"So I did," said Kate. "And so he did. Since the wife loomed on the horizon, I remembered that he said no word to me of marriage; he merely said he always had loved me and always would—"

"Merely?" scoffed Nancy Ellen. "Merely!"

"Just 'merely,'" said Kate. "He didn't lay a finger on me; he didn't ask me to marry him; he just merely met me after a long separation, and told me that he still loved me."

"The brute!" said Nancy Ellen. "He should be killed."

"I can't see it," said Kate. "He did nothing ungentlemanly. If we jumped to wrong conclusions that was not his fault. I doubt if he remembered or thought at all of his marriage. It wouldn't be much to forget. I am fresh from an interview with his wife. She's an old acquaintance of mine. I once secured her for his mother's maid. You've heard me speak of her."

"Impossible! John Jardine would not do that!" cried Nancy Ellen.

"There's a family to prove it," said Kate. "Jennie admits that she studied him, taught him, made herself indispensable to him, and a few weeks after his mother's passing, married him, after he had told her he did not love her and never could. I feel sorry for him."

"Sure! Poor defrauded creature!" said Nancy Ellen. "What about her?"

"Nothing, so far as I can see," said Kate. "By her own account she was responsible. She should have kept in her own class."

"All right. That settles Jennie!" said Nancy Ellen. "I saw you notice the telegram from Robert—now go on and settle me!"

"Is he coming?" asked Kate.

"No, he's not coming," said Nancy Ellen.

"Has he eloped with the widder?" asked Kate flippantly.

"He merely telegraphs that he thinks it would be wise for us to come home on the first train," said Nancy Ellen. "For all I can make of that, the elopement might quite as well be in your family as mine."

Kate held out her hand, Nancy Ellen laid the message in it. Kate studied it carefully; then she raised steady eyes to her sister's face.

"Do you know what I should do about this?" she asked.

"Catch the first train, of course," she said.

"Far be it from me," said Kate. "I should at once telegraph him that his message was not clear, to kindly particularize. We've only got settled. We're having a fine time; especially right now. Why should we pack up and go home? I can't think of any possibility that could arise that would make it necessary for him to send for us. Can you?"

"I can think of two things," said Nancy Ellen. "I can think of a very pretty, confiding, little cat of a woman, who is desperately infatuated with my husband; and I can think of two children fathered by George Holt, who might possibly, just possibly, have enough of his blood in their veins to be like him, given opportunity. Alone for a week, there is barely a FAINT possibility that YOU might be needed. Alone for the same week, there is the faintest possibility that ROBERT is in a situation where I could help him."

Kate drew a deep breath.

"Isn't life the most amusing thing?" she asked. "I had almost forgotten my wings. I guess we'd better take them, and fly straight home."

She arose and called the office to learn about trains, and then began packing her trunk. As she folded her dresses and stuffed them in rather carelessly she said: "I don't know why I got it into my head that I could go away and have a few days of a good time without something happening at home."

"But you are not sure anything has happened at home. This call may be for me," said Nancy Ellen.

"It MAY, but this is July," said Kate. "I've been thinking hard and fast. It's probable I can put my finger on the spot."

Nancy Ellen paused and standing erect she looked questioningly at Kate.

"The weak link in my chain at the present minute is Polly," said Kate. "I didn't pay much attention at the time, because there wasn't enough of it really to attract attention; but since I think, I can recall signs of growing discontent in Polly, lately. She fussed about the work, and resented being left in the house while I went to the fields, and she had begun looking up the road to Peters' so much that her head was slightly turned toward the north most of the time. With me away—"

"What do you think?" demanded Nancy Ellen.

"Think very likely she has decided that she'll sacrifice her chance for more schooling and to teach, for the sake of marrying a big, green country boy named Hank Peters," said Kate.

"Thereby keeping in her own class," suggested Nancy Ellen.

Kate laughed shortly. "Exactly!" she said. "I didn't aspire to anything different for her from what she has had; but I wanted her to have more education, and wait until she was older. Marriage is too hard work for a girl to begin at less than eighteen. If it is Polly, and she has gone away with Hank Peters, they've no place to go but his home; and if ever she thought I worked her too hard, she'll find out she has played most of her life, when she begins taking orders from Mrs. Amanda Peters. You know her! She never can keep a girl more than a week, and she's always wanting one. If Polly has tackled THAT job, God help her."

"Cheer up! We're in that delightful state of uncertainty where Polly may be blacking the cook stove, like a dutiful daughter; while Robert has decided that he'd like a divorce," said Nancy Ellen.

"Nancy Ellen, there's nothing in that, so far as Robert is concerned. He told me so the evening we came away," said Kate.

Nancy Ellen banged down a trunk lid and said: "Well, I am getting to the place where I don't much care whether there is or there is not."

"What a whopper!" laughed Kate. "But cheer up. This is my trouble. I feel it in my bones. Wish I knew for sure. If she's eloped, and it's all over with, we might as well stay and finish our visit. If she's married, I can't unmarry her, and I wouldn't if I could."

"How are you going to apply your philosophy to yourself?" asked Nancy Ellen.

"By letting time and Polly take their course," said Kate. "This is a place where parents are of no account whatever. They stand back until it's time to clean up the wreck, and then they get theirs—usually theirs, and several of someone's else, in the bargain."

As the train stopped at Hartley, Kate sat where she could see Robert on the platform. It was only a fleeting glance, but she thought she had never seen him look so wholesome, so vital, so much a man to be desired.

"No wonder a woman lacking in fine scruples would covet him," thought Kate. To Nancy Ellen she said hastily: "The trouble's mine. Robert's on the platform."

"Where?" demanded Nancy Ellen, peering from the window.

Kate smiled as she walked from the car and confronted Robert.

"Get it over quickly," she said. "It's Polly?"

He nodded.

"Did she remember to call on the Squire?" she asked.

"Oh, yes," said Robert. "It was at Peters', and they had the whole neighbourhood in."

Kate swayed slightly, then lifted her head, her eyes blazing. She had come, feeling not altogether guiltless, and quite prepared to overlook a youthful elopement. The insult of having her only daughter given a wedding at the home of the groom, about which the whole neighbourhood would be laughing at her, was a different matter. Slowly the high colour faded from Kate's face, as she stepped back. "Excuse me, Nancy Ellen," she said. "I didn't mean to deprive you of the chance of even speaking to Robert. I KNEW this was for me; I was over-anxious to learn what choice morsel life had in store for me now. It's one that will be bitter on my tongue to the day of my death."

"Oh, Kate, I as so sorry that if this had to happen, it happened in just that way," said Nancy Ellen, "but don't mind. They're only foolish kids!"

"Who? Mr. and Mrs. Peters, and the neighbours, who attended the wedding! Foolish kids? Oh, no!" said Kate. "Where's Adam?"

"I told him I'd bring you out," said Robert.

"Why didn't he send for you, or do something?" demanded Kate.

"I'm afraid the facts are that Polly lied to him," said Robert. "She told him that Peters were having a party, and Mrs. Peters wanted her to come early and help her with the supper. They had the Magistrate out from town and had the ceremony an hour before Adam got there. When he arrived, and found out what had happened, he told Polly and the Peters family exactly his opinion of them; and then he went home and turned on all the lights, and sat where he could be seen on the porch all evening, as a protest in evidence of his disapproval, I take it."

Slowly the colour began to creep back into Kate's face. "The good boy!" she said, in commendation.

"He called me at once, and we talked it over and I sent you the telegram; but as he said, it was done; there was no use trying to undo it. One thing will be a comfort to you. All of your family, and almost all of your friends, left as soon as Adam spoke his piece, and they found it was a wedding and not a party to which they'd been invited. It was a shabby trick of Peters."

Kate assented. "It was because I felt instinctively that Mrs. Peters had it in her to do tricks like that, that I never would have anything to do with her," said Kate, "more than to be passing civil. This is how she gets her revenge, and her hired girl, for no wages, I'll be bound! It's a shabby trick. I'm glad Adam saved me the trouble of telling her so."

Robert took Nancy Ellen home, and then drove to Bates Corners with Kate.

"In a few days now I hope we can see each other oftener," he said, on the way. "I got a car yesterday, and it doesn't seem so complicated. Any intelligent person can learn to drive in a short time. I like it so much, and I knew I'd have such constant use for it that—now this is a secret—I ordered another for Nancy Ellen, so she can drive about town, and run out here as she chooses. Will she be pleased?"

"She'll be overjoyed! That was dear of you, Robert. Only one thing in world would please her more," said Kate.

"What's that?" asked Robert.

Kate looked him in the eye, and smiled.

"Oh," he said. "But there is nothing in it!"

"Except TALK, that worries and humiliates Nancy Ellen," said Kate.

"Kate," he said suddenly, "if you were in my shoes, what would you do?"

"The next time I got a phone call, or a note from Mrs. Southey, and she was having one of those terrible headaches, I should say: 'I'm dreadfully sorry, Mrs. Southey, but a breath of talk that might be unpleasant for you, and for my wife, has come to my ear, so I know you'll think it wiser to call Dr. Mills, who can serve you better than I. In a great rush this afternoon. Good-bye!' THAT is what I should do, Robert, and I should do it quickly, and emphatically. Then I should interest Nancy Ellen in her car for a time, and then I should keep my eyes open, and the first time I found in my practice a sound baby with a clean bill of health, and no encumbrances, I should have it dressed attractively, and bestow it on Nancy Ellen as casually as I did the car. And in the meantime, love her plenty, Robert. You can never know how she FEELS about this; and it's in no way her fault. She couldn't possibly have known; while you would have married her just the same if you had known. Isn't that so?"

"It's quite so. Kate, I think your head is level, and I'll follow your advice to the letter. Now you have 'healed my lame leg,' as the dog said in McGuffey's Third, what can I do for THIS poor dog?"

"Nothing," said Kate. "I've got to hold still, and take it. Life will do the doing. I don't want to croak, but remember my word, it will do plenty."

"We'll come often," he said as he turned to go back.

Kate slowly walked up the path, dreading to meet Adam. He evidently had been watching for her, for he came around the corner of the house, took her arm, and they walked up the steps and into the living room together. She looked at him; he looked at her. At last he said: "I'm afraid that a good deal of this is my fault, Mother."

"How so?" asked Kate, tersely.

"I guess I betrayed your trust in me," said Adam, heavily. "Of course I did all my work and attended to things; but in the evening after work was over, the very first evening on the way home we stopped to talk to Henry at the gate, and he got in and came on down. We could see Milly at their gate, and I wanted her, I wanted her so much, Mother; and it was going to be lonesome, so all of us went on there, and she came up here and we sat on the porch, and then I took her home and that left Henry and Polly together. The next night Henry took us to town for a treat, and we were all together, and the next night Milly asked us all there, and so it went. It was all as open and innocent as it could be; only Henry and Polly were in awful earnest and she was bound she wouldn't be sent to town to school—"

"Why didn't she tell me so? She never objected a word, to me," said Kate.

"Well, Mother, you are so big, and Polly was so little, and she was used to minding—"

"Yes, this looks like it," said Kate. "Well, go on!"

"That's all," said Adam. "It was only that instead of staying at home and attending to our own affairs we were somewhere every night, or Milly and Henry were here. That is where I was to blame. I'm afraid you'll never forgive me, Mother; but I didn't take good care of Sister. I left her to Henry Peters, while I tried to see how nice I could be to Milly. I didn't know what Polly and Henry were planning; honest, I didn't, Mother. I would have told Uncle Robert and sent for you if I had. I thought when I went there it was to be our little crowd like it was at York's. I was furious when I found they were married. I told Mr. and Mrs. Peters what they were, right before the company, and then I came straight home and all the family, and York's, and most of the others, came straight away. Only a few stayed to the supper. I was so angry with Polly I just pushed her away, and didn't even say good-night to her. The little silly fool! Mother, if she had told you, you would have let her stay at home this winter and got her clothing, and let her be married here, when she was old enough, wouldn't you?"

"Certainly!" said Kate. "All the world knows that. Bates all marry; and they all marry young. Don't blame yourself, Adam. If Polly had it in her system to do this, and she did, or she wouldn't have done it, the thing would have happened when I was here, and right under my nose. It was a scheme all planned and ready before I left. I know that now. Let it go! There's nothing we can do, until things begin to go WRONG, as they always do in this kind of wedding; then we shall get our call. In the meantime, you mustn't push your sister away. She may need you sooner than you'd think; and will you just please have enough confidence in my common sense and love for you, to come to me, FIRST, when you feel that there's a girl who is indispensable to your future, Adam?"

"Yes, I will," said Adam. "And it won't be long, and the girl will be Milly York."

"All right," said Kate, gravely, "whenever the time comes, let me know about it. Now see if you can find me something to eat till I lay off my hat and wash. It was a long, hot ride, and I'm tired. Since there's nothing I can do, I wish I had stayed where I was. No, I don't, either! I see joy coming over the hill for Nancy Ellen."

"Why is joy coming to Nancy Ellen?" asked the boy, pausing an instant before he started to the kitchen.

"Oh, because she's had such a very tough, uncomfortable time with life," said Kate, "that in the very nature of things joy SHOULD come her way."

The boy stood mystified until the expression on his face so amused Kate that she began laughing, then he understood.

"That's WHY it's coming," said Kate; "and, here's HOW it's coming. She is going to get rid of a bothersome worry that's troubling her head—and she's going to have a very splendid gift, but it's a deep secret."

"Then you'll have to whisper it," said Adam, going to her and holding a convenient ear. Kate rested her hands on his shoulder a minute, as she leaned on him, her face buried in his crisp black hair. Then she whispered the secret.

"Crickey, isn't that grand!" cried the boy, backing away to stare at her.

"Yes, it is so grand I'm going to try it ourselves," said Kate. "We've a pretty snug balance in the bank, and I think it would be great fun evenings or when we want to go to town in a hurry and the horses are tired."

Adam was slowly moving toward the kitchen, his face more of a study than before.

"Mother," he said as he reached the door, "I be hanged if I know how to take you! I thought you'd just raise Cain over what Polly has done; but you act so sane and sensible; someway it doesn't seem so bad as it did, and I feel more sorry for Polly than like going back on her. And are you truly in earnest about a car?"

"I'm going to think very seriously about it this winter, and I feel almost sure it will come true by early spring," said Kate. "But who said anything about 'going back on Polly?'"

"Oh, Mrs. York and all the neighbours said that you'd never forgive her, and that she'd never darken your door again, and things like that until I was almost crazy," answered Adam.

Kate smiled grimly. "Adam," she said, "I had seven years of that 'darken you door' business, myself. It's a mighty cold, hard proposition. It's a wonder the neighbours didn't remember that. Maybe they did, and thought I was so much of a Bates leopard that I couldn't change my spots.

If they are watching me, they will find that I am not spotted; I'm sorry and humiliated over what Polly has done; but I'm not going to gnash my teeth, and tear my hair, and wail in public, or in private. I'm trying to keep my real mean spot so deep it can't be seen. If ever I get my chance, Adam, you watch me pay back Mrs. Peters. THAT is the size and location of my spot; but it's far deeper than my skin. Now go on and find me food, man, food!"

Adam sat close while Kate ate her supper, then he helped her unpack her trunk and hang away her dresses, and then they sat on the porch talking for a long time.

When at last they arose to go to bed Kate said: "Adam, about Polly: first time you see her, if she asks, tell her she left home of her own free will and accord, and in her own way, which, by the way, happens to be a Holt way; but you needn't mention that. I think by this time she has learned or soon she will learn that; and whenever she wants to come back and face me, to come right ahead. I can stand it if she can. Can you get that straight?"

Adam said he could. He got that straight and so much else that by the time he finished, Polly realized that both he and her mother had left her in the house to try to SHIELD her; that if she had told what she wanted in a straightforward manner she might have had a wedding outfit prepared and been married from her home at a proper time and in a proper way, and without putting her mother to shame before the community. Polly was very much ashamed of herself by the time Adam finished. She could not find it in her heart to blame Henry; she knew he was no more to blame than she was; but she did store up a grievance against Mr. and Mrs. Peters. They were older and had had experience with the world; they might have told Polly what she should do instead of having done everything in their power to make her do what she had done, bribing, coaxing, urging, all in the direction of her inclinations.

At heart Polly was big enough to admit that she had followed her inclinations without thinking at all what the result would be. Adam never would have done what she had. Adam would have thought of his mother and his name and his honour. Poor little Polly had to admit that honour with her had always been a matter of, "Now remember," "Be careful," and like caution on the lips of her mother.

The more Polly thought, the worse she felt. The worse she felt, the more the whole Peters family tried to comfort her. She was violently homesick in a few days; but Adam had said she was to come when she "could face her mother," and Polly suddenly found that she would rather undertake to run ten miles than to face her mother, so she began a process of hiding from her. If she sat on the porch, and saw her mother coming, she ran in the house. She would go to no public place where she might meet her. For a few weeks she lived a life of working for Mrs. Peters from dawn to dark, under the stimulus of what a sweet girl she was, how splendidly she did things, how fortunate Henry was, interspersed with continual kissing, patting, and petting, all very new and unusual to Polly. By that time she was so very ill, she could not lift her head from the pillow half the day, but it was to the credit of the badly disappointed Peters family that they kept up the petting. When Polly grew better, she had no desire to go anywhere; she worked to make up for the trouble she had been during her illness, to sew every spare moment, and to do her full share of the day's work in the house of an excessively nice woman, whose work never was done, and most hopeless thing of all, never would be. Mrs. Peters' head was full of things that she meant to do three years in the future. Every night found Polly so tired she staggered to bed early as possible; every morning found her confronting the same round, which from the nature of her condition every morning was more difficult for her.

Kate and Adam followed their usual routine with only the alterations required by the absence of Polly. Kate now prepared breakfast while Adam did the feeding and milking; washed the dishes and made the beds while he hitched up; then went to the field with him. On rainy days he swept and she dusted; always they talked over and planned everything they did, in the house or afield; always they schemed, contrived, economized, and worked to attain the shortest, easiest end to any result they strove for. They were growing in physical force, they were efficient, they attended their own affairs strictly. Their work was always done on time, their place in order, their deposits at the bank frequent. As the cold days came they missed Polly, but scarcely ever mentioned her. They had more books and read and studied together, while every few evenings Adam picked up his hat and disappeared, but soon he and Milly came in together. Then they all read, popped corn, made taffy, knitted, often Kate was called away by some sewing or upstairs work she wanted to do, so that the youngsters had plenty of time alone to revel in the wonder of life's greatest secret.

To Kate's ears came the word that Polly would be a mother in the spring, that the Peters family were delighted and anxious for the child to be a girl, as they found six males sufficient for one family. Polly was looking well, feeling fine, was a famous little worker, and seldom sat on a chair because some member of the Peters family usually held her.

"I should think she would get sick of all that mushing," said Adam when he repeated these things.

"She's not like us," said Kate. "She'll take all she can get, and call for more. She's a long time coming; but I'm glad she's well and happy."

"Buncombe!" said Adam. "She isn't so very well. She's white as putty, and there are great big, dark hollows under her eyes, and she's always panting for breath like she had been running. Nearly every time I pass there I see her out scrubbing the porches, or feeding the chickens, or washing windows, or something. You bet Mrs. Peters has got a fine hired girl now, and she's smiling all over about it."

"She really has something to smile about," said Kate.

To Polly's ears went the word that Adam and her mother were having a fine time together, always together; and that they had Milly York up three times a week to spend the evening; and that Milly said that it passed her to see why Polly ran away from Mrs. Holt. She was the grandest woman alive, and if she had any running to do in her neighbourhood, she would run TO her, and not FROM her. Whereupon Polly closed her lips firmly and looked black, but not before she had said: "Well, if Mother had done just one night a week of that entertaining for Henry and me, we wouldn't have run from her, either."

Polly said nothing until April, then Kate answered the telephone one day and a few seconds later was ringing for Adam as if she would pull down the bell. He came running and soon was on his way to Peters' with the single buggy, with instructions to drive slowly and carefully and on no account to let Polly slip getting out. The Peters family had all gone to bury an aunt in the neighbourhood, leaving Polly alone for the day; and Polly at once called up her mother, and said she was dying to see her, and if she couldn't come home for the day, she would die soon, and be glad of it. Kate knew the visit should not have been made at that time and in that way; but she knew that Polly was under a dangerous nervous strain; she herself would not go to Peters' in Mrs. Peters' absence; she did not know what else to do. As she waited for Polly she thought of many things she would say; when she saw her, she took her in her arms and almost carried her into the house, and she said nothing at all, save how glad she was to see her, and she did nothing at all, except to try with all her might to comfort and please her, for to Kate, Polly did not seem like a strong, healthy girl approaching maternity. She appeared like a very sick woman, who sorely needed attention, while a few questions made her so sure of it that she at once called Robert. He gave both of them all the comfort he could, but what he told Nancy Ellen was: "Polly has had no attention whatever. She wants me, and I'll have to go; but it's a case I'd like to side-step. I'll do all I can, but the time is short."

"Oh, Lord!" said Nancy Ellen. "Is it one more for Kate?"

"Yes," said Robert, "I am very much afraid it's 'one more for Kate.'"

CHAPTER XXV

ONE MORE FOR KATE

POLLY and Kate had a long day together, while Adam was about the house much of the time. Both of them said and did everything they could think of to cheer and comfort Polly, whose spirits seemed most variable. One minute she would be laughing and planning for the summer gaily, the next she would be gloomy and depressed, and declaring she never would live through the birth of her baby. If she had appeared well, this would not have worried Kate; but she looked even sicker than she seemed to feel. She was thin while her hands were hot and tremulous. As the afternoon went on and time to go came nearer, she grew more and more despondent, until Kate proposed watching when the Peters family came home, calling them up, and telling them that Polly was there, would remain all night, and that Henry should come down.

Polly flatly vetoed the proposition, but she seemed to feel much better after it had been made. She was like herself again for a short time, and then she turned to Kate and said suddenly: "Mother, if I don't get over this, will you take my baby?"

Kate looked at Polly intently. What she saw stopped the ready answer that was on her lips. She stood thinking deeply. At last she said gently: "Why, Polly, would you want to trust a tiny baby with a woman you ran away from yourself?"

"Mother, I haven't asked you to forgive me for the light I put you in before the neighbours," said Polly, "because I knew you couldn't honestly do it, and wouldn't lie to say you did. I don't know WHAT made me do that. I was TIRED staying alone at the house so much, I was WILD about Henry, I was BOUND I wouldn't leave him and go away to school. I just thought it would settle everything easily and quickly. I never once thought of how it would make you look and feel. Honestly I didn't, Mother. You believe me, don't you?"

"Yes, I believe you," said Kate.

"It was an awful thing for me to do," said Polly. "I was foolish and crazy, and I suppose I shouldn't say it, but I certainly did have a lot of encouragement from the Peters family. They all seemed to think it would be a great joke, that it wouldn't make any difference, and all that, so I just did it. I knew I shouldn't have done it; but, Mother, you'll never know the fight I've had all my life to keep from telling stories and sneaking. I hated your everlasting: 'Now be careful,' but when I hated it most, I needed it worst; and I knew it, when I grew older. If only you had been here to say, 'Now be careful,' just once, I never would have done it; but of course I couldn't have you to keep me straight all my life. All I can say is that I'd give my life and never whimper, if I could be back home as I was this time last year, and have a chance to do things your way. But that is past, and I can't change it. What I came for to-day, and what I want to know now is, if I go, will you take my baby?"

"Polly, you KNOW the Peters family wouldn't let me have it," said Kate.

"If it's a boy, they wouldn't WANT it," said Polly. "Neither would you, for that matter. If it's a girl, they'll fight for it; but it won't do them any good. All I want to know is, WILL YOU TAKE IT?"

"Of course I would, Polly," said Kate.

"Since I have your word, I'll feel better," said Polly. "And Mother, you needn't be AFRAID of it. It will be all right. I have thought about it so much I have it all figured out. It's going to be a girl, and it's going to be exactly like you, and its name is going to be Katherine Eleanor. I have thought about you every hour I was awake since I have been gone; so the baby will have to be exactly like you. There won't be the taint of Grandmother in it that there is in me. You needn't be afraid. I quit sneaking forever when Adam told me what I had done to you. I have gone straight as a dart, Mother, every single minute since, Mother; truly I have!"

Kate sat down suddenly, an awful sickness in her heart.

"Why, you poor child you!" she said.

"Oh, I've been all right," said Polly. "I've been almost petted and loved to death; but Mother, there never should be the amount of work attached to living that there is in that house. It's never ending, it's intolerable. Mrs. Peters just goes until she drops, and then instead of sleeping, she lies awake planning some hard, foolish, unnecessary thing to do next. Maybe she can stand it herself, but I'm tired out. I'm going to sit down, and not budge to do another stroke until after the baby comes, and then I am going to coax Henry to rent a piece of land, and move to ourselves."

Kate took heart. "That will be fine!" she cried. "That will be the very thing. I'll ask the boys to keep their eyes open for any chance for you."

"You needn't take any bother about it," said Polly, "because that isn't what is going to happen. All I want to be sure of now is that you and Adam will take my baby. I'll see to the rest."

"How will you see to it, Polly?" asked Kate, gently.

"Well, it's already seen to, for matter of that," said Polly conclusively. "I've known for quite a while that I was sick; but I couldn't make them do anything but kiss me, and laugh at me, until I am so ill that I know better how I feel than anybody else. I got tired being laughed at, and put off about everything, so one day in Hartley, while Mother Peters was shopping, I just went in to the lawyer Grandmother always went to, and told him all about what I wanted. He has the papers made out all right and proper; so when I send for Uncle Robert, I am going to send for him, too, and soon as the baby comes I'll put in its name and sign it, and make Henry, and then if I have to go, you won't have a bit of trouble."

Kate gazed at Polly in dumb amazement. She was speechless for a time, then to break the strain she said: "My soul! Did you really, Polly? I guess there is more Bates in you than I had thought!"

"Oh, there's SOME Bates in me," said Polly. "There's enough to make me live until I sign that paper, and make Henry Peters sign it, and send Mr. Thomlins to you with it and the baby. I can do that, because I'm going to!"

Ten days later she did exactly what she had said she would. Then she turned her face to the wall and went into a convulsion out of which she never came. While the Peters family refused Kate's plea to lay Polly beside her grandmother, and laid her in their family lot, Kate, moaning dumbly, sat clasping a tiny red girl in her arms. Adam drove to Hartley to deposit one more paper, the most precious of all, in the safety deposit box.

Kate and Adam mourned too deeply to talk about it. They went about their daily rounds silently, each busy with regrets and self investigations. They watched each other carefully, were kinder than they ever had been to everyone they came in contact with; the baby they frankly adored. Kate had reared her own children with small misgivings, quite casually, in fact; but her heart was torn to the depths about this baby. Life never would be even what it had been before Polly left them, for into her going there entered an element of self-reproach and continual self-condemnation. Adam felt that if he had been less occupied with Milly York and had taken proper care of his sister, he would not have lost her. Kate had less time for recrimination, because she had the baby.

"Look for a good man to help you this summer, Adam," she said. "The baby is full of poison which can be eliminated only slowly. If I don't get it out before teething, I'll lose her, and then we never shall hear the last from the Peters family." Adam consigned the Peters family to a location he thought suitable for them on the instant. He spoke with unusual bitterness, because he had heard that the Peters family were telling that Polly had grieved herself to death, while his mother had engineered a scheme whereby she had stolen the baby. Occasionally a word drifted to Kate here and there, until she realized much of what they were saying. At first she grieved too deeply to pay any attention, but as the summer went on and the baby flourished and grew fine and strong, and she had time in the garden, she began to feel better; grief began to wear away, as it always does.

By midsummer the baby was in short clothes, sitting in a high chair, which if Miss Baby only had known it, was a throne before which knelt her two adoring subjects. Polly had said the baby would be like Kate. Its hair and colouring were like hers, but it had the brown eyes of its father, and enough of his facial lines to tone down the too generous Bates features. When the baby was five months old it was too pretty for adequate description. One baby has no business with perfect features, a mop of curly, yellow silk hair, and big brown eyes. One of the questions Kate and Adam discussed most frequently was where they would send her to college, while one they did not discuss was how sick her stomach teeth would make her. They merely lived in mortal dread of that. "Convulsion," was a word that held a terror for Kate above any other in the medical books.

The baby had a good, formal name, but no one ever used it. Adam, on first lifting the blanket, had fancied the child resembled its mother and had called her "Little Poll." The name clung to her. Kate could not call such a tiny morsel either Kate or Katherine; she liked "Little Poll," better. The baby had three regular visitors. One was her father. He was not fond of Kate; Little Poll suited him. He expressed his feeling by bringing gifts of toys, candy, and unsuitable clothes. Kate kept these things in evidence when she saw him coming and swept them from sight when he went; for she had the good sense not to antagonize him. Nancy Ellen came almost every day, proudly driving her new car, and with the light of a new joy on her face. She never said anything to Kate, but Kate knew what had happened. Nancy Ellen came to see the baby. She brought it lovely and delicate little shoes, embroidered dresses and hoods, cloaks and blankets. One day as she sat holding it she said to Kate: "Isn't the baby a dreadful bother to you? You're not getting half your usual work done."

"No, I'm doing UNUSUAL work," said Kate, lightly. "Adam is hiring a man who does my work very well in the fields; there isn't money that would hire me to let any one else take my job indoors, right now."

A slow red crept into Nancy Ellen's cheeks. She had meant to be diplomatic, but diplomacy never worked well with Kate. As Nancy Ellen often said, Kate understood a sledge-hammer better. Nancy Ellen used the hammer. Her face flushed, her arms closed tightly. "Give me this baby," she demanded.

Kate looked at her in helpless amazement.

"Give it to me," repeated Nancy Ellen.

"She's a gift to me," said Kate, slowly. "One the Peters family are searching heaven and earth to find an excuse to take from me. I hear they've been to a lawyer twice, already. I wouldn't give her up to save my soul alive, for myself; for you, if I would let you have her, they would not leave you in possession a day."

"Are they really trying to get her?" asked Nancy Ellen, slowly loosening her grip.

"They are," said Kate. "They sent a lawyer to get a copy of the papers, to see if they could pick a flaw in them."

"Can they?" cried Nancy Ellen.

"God knows!" said Kate, slowly. "I HOPE not. Mr. Thomlins is the best lawyer in Hartley; he says not. He says Henry put his neck in the noose when he signed the papers. The only chance I can see for him would be to plead undue influence. When you look at her, you can't blame him for wanting her. I've two hopes. One that his mother will not want the extra work; the other that the next girl he selects will not want the baby. If I can keep them going a few months more with a teething scare, I hope they will get over wanting her."

"If they do, then may we have her?" asked Nancy Ellen.

Kate threw out her hands. "Take my eyes, or my hands, or my feet," she said; "but leave me my heart."

Nancy Ellen went soon after, and did not come again for several days. Then she began coming as usual, so that the baby soon knew her and laughed in high glee when she appeared. Dr. Gray often stopped in passing to see her; if he was in great haste, he hallooed at the gate to ask if she was all right. Kate was thankful for this, more than thankful for the telephone and car that would bring him in fifteen minutes day or night, if he were needed. But he was not needed. Little Poll throve and grew fat and rosy; for she ate measured food, slept by the clock, in a sanitary bed, and was a bathed, splendidly cared for baby. When Kate's family and friends laughed, she paid not the slightest heed.

"Laugh away," she said. "I've got something to fight with this baby; I don't propose for the battle to come and find the chances against me, because I'm unprepared."

With scrupulous care Kate watched over the child, always putting her first, the house and land afterward. One day she looked up the road and saw Henry Peters coming. She had been expecting Nancy Ellen. She had finished bathing the baby and making her especially attractive in a dainty lace ruffled dress with blue ribbons and blue shoes that her sister had brought on her latest trip. Little Poll was a wonderful picture, for her eyes were always growing bigger, her cheeks pinker, her skin fairer, her hair longer and more softly curling. At first thought Kate had been inclined to snatch off the dress and change to one of the cheap, ready-made ginghams Henry brought, but the baby was so lovely as she was, she had not the heart to spoil the picture, while Nancy Ellen might come any minute. So she began putting things in place while Little Poll sat crowing and trying to pick up a sunbeam that fell across her tray. Her father came to the door and stood looking at her. Suddenly he dropped in a chair, covered his face with his hands and began to cry, in deep, shuddering sobs. Kate stood still in wonderment. As last she seated herself before him and said gently: "Won't you tell me about it, Henry?"

Henry struggled for self-control. He looked at the baby longingly. Finally he said: "It's pretty tough to give up a baby like that, Mrs. Holt. She's my little girl. I wish God had struck my right hand with palsy, when I went to sign those papers."

"Oh, no, you don't, Henry," said Kate, suavely. "You wouldn't like to live the rest of your life a cripple. And is it any worse for me to have your girl in spite of the real desires and dictates of your heart, than it was for you to have mine? And you didn't take the intelligent care of my girl that I'm taking of yours, either. A doctor and a little right treatment at the proper time would have saved Polly to rear her own baby; but there's no use to go into that. I was waiting for Polly to come home of her own accord, as she left it; and while I waited, a poison crept into her system that took her. I never shall feel right about it; neither shall you—"

"No, I should say I won't!" said Henry emphatically. "I never thought of anything being the matter with Polly that wouldn't be all over when the baby came—"

"I know you didn't, Henry," said Kate. "I know how much you would have done, and how gladly, if you had known. There is no use going into that, we are both very much to blame; we must take our punishment. Now what is this I hear about your having been to see lawyers and trying to find a way to set aside the adoption papers you signed? Let's have a talk, and see what we can arrive at. Tell me all about it."

So Henry told Kate how he had loved Polly, how he felt guilty of her death, how he longed for and wanted her baby, how he had signed the paper which Polly put before him so unexpectedly, to humour her, because she was very ill; but he had not dreamed that she could die; how he did not feel that he should be bound by that signature now. Kate listened with the deepest sympathy, assenting to most he said until he was silent. Then she sat thinking a long time. At last she said: "Henry, if you and Polly had waited until I came home, and told me what you wanted and how you felt, I should have gotten her ready, and given you a customary wedding, and helped you to start a life that I think would have saved her to you, and to me. That is past, but the fact remains. You are hurt over giving up the baby as you have; I'm hurt over losing my daughter as I did; we are about even on the past, don't you think?"

"I suppose we are," he said, heavily.

"That being agreed," said Kate, "let us look to the future. You want the baby now, I can guess how much, by how much I want her, myself. I know YOUR point of view; there are two others, one is mine, and the other is the baby's. I feel that it is only right and just that I should have this little girl to replace the one you took from me, in a way far from complimentary to me. I feel that she is mine, because Polly told me the day she came to see me how sick she had been, how she had begged for a doctor, and been kissed and told there was nothing the matter with her, when she knew she was very ill. She gave the baby to me, and at that time she had been to see a lawyer, and had her papers all made out except the signatures and dates. Mr. Thomlins can tell you that; and you know that up to that time I had not seen Polly, or had any communication with her. She simply was unnerved at the thought of trusting her baby to the care she had had."

Kate was hitting hard and straight from the shoulder. The baby, busy with her sunbeam, jabbered unnoticed.

"When Polly died as she did," continued Kate, "I knew that her baby would be full of the same poison that killed her; and that it must be eliminated before it came time to cut her worst teeth, so I undertook the work, and sleeping or waking, I have been at it ever since. Now, Henry, is there any one at your house who would have figured this out, and taken the time, pains, and done work that I have? Is there?"

"Mother raised six of us." he said defensively.

"But she didn't die of diathesis giving birth to the first of you," said Kate. "You were all big, strong boys with a perfectly sound birthright. And your mother is now a much older, wearier woman than she was then, and her hands are far too full every day, as it is. If she knew how to handle the baby as I have, and was willing to add the work to her daily round, would you be willing to have her? I have three times her strength, while I consider that I've the first right. Then there is the baby's side of the question. I have had her through the worst, hardest part of babyhood; she is accustomed to a fixed routine that you surely will concede agrees with her; she would miss me, and she would not thrive as she does with me, for her food and her hours would not be regular, while you, and your father, and the boys would tire her to death handling her. That is the start. The finish would be that she would grow up, if she survived, to take the place Polly took at your house, while you would marry some other girl, as you WILL before a year from now. I'm dreadfully sorry to say these things to you, Henry, but you know they are the truth. If you're going to try to take the baby, I'm going to fight you to the last dollar I can raise, and the last foot of land I own. That's all. Look at the baby; think it over; and let me know what you'll do as soon as you can. I'm not asking mercy at your hands, but I do feel that I have suffered about my share."

"You needn't suffer any longer," said Henry, drying his eyes. "All you say is true; just as what I said was true; but I might as well tell you, and let one of us be happy. I saw my third lawyer yesterday, and he said the papers were unbreakable unless I could prove that the child was neglected, and not growing right, or not having proper care. Look at her! I might do some things! I did do a thing as mean as to persuade a girl to marry me without her mother's knowledge, and ruined her life thereby, but God knows I couldn't go on the witness stand and swear that that baby is not properly cared for! Mother's job is big enough; and while it doesn't seem possible now, very likely I shall marry again, as other men do; and in that event, Little Poll WOULD be happier with you. I give her up. I think I came this morning to say that I was defeated; and to tell you that I'd give up if I saw that you would fight. Keep the baby, and be as happy as you can. You shan't be worried any more about her. Polly shall have this thing as she desired and planned it. Good-bye."

When he had gone Kate knelt on the floor, laid her head on the chair tray, and putting her arms around the baby she laughed and cried at the same time, while Miss Baby pulled her hair, patted her face, and plastered it with wet, uncertain kisses. Then Kate tied a little bonnet on the baby's head and taking her in her arms, she went to the field to tell Adam. It seemed to Kate that she could see responsibility slipping from his shoulders, could see him grow taller as he listened. The breath of relief he drew was long and deep.

"Fine!" he cried. "Fine! I haven't told you HALF I knew. I've been worried until I couldn't sleep."

Kate went back to the house so glad she did not realize she was touching earth at all. She fed the baby and laid her down for her morning nap, and then went out in the garden; but she was too restless to work. She walked bareheaded in the sun and was glad as she never before in her life had known how to be glad. The first thing Kate knew she was standing at the gate looking up at the noonday sky and from the depths of her heart she was crying aloud: "Praise ye the Lord, Oh my soul. Let all that is within me praise His holy name!"

For the remainder of the day Kate was unblushingly insane. She started to do a hundred things and abandoned all of them to go out and look up at the sky and to cry repeatedly: "Praise the Lord!"

If she had been asked to explain why she did this, Kate could have answered, and would have answered: "Because I FEEL like it!" She had been taught no religion as a child, she had practised no formal mode of worship as a woman. She had been straight, honest, and virtuous. She had faced life and done with small question the work that she thought fell to her hand. She had accepted joy, sorrow, shame, all in the same stoic way. Always she had felt that there was a mighty force in the universe that could as well be called God as any other name; it mattered not about the name; it was a real force, and it was there.

That day Kate exulted. She carried the baby down to the brook in the afternoon and almost shouted; she sang until she could have been heard a mile. She kept straight on praising the Lord, because expression was imperative, and that was the form of expression that seemed to come naturally to her. Without giving a thought as to how, or why, she followed her impulses and praised the Lord. The happier she grew, the more clearly she saw how uneasy and frightened she had been.

When Nancy Ellen came, she took only one glance at Kate's glorified face and asked: "What in this world has happened to you?"

Kate answered in all seriousness: "My Lord has 'shut the lions' mouths,' and they are not going to harm me."

Nancy Ellen regarded her closely. "I hope you aren't running a temperature," she said. "I'll take a shot at random. You have found out that the Peters family can't take Little Poll."

Kate laughed joyously. "Better than that, sister mine!" she cried. "I have convinced Henry that he doesn't want her himself as much as he wants me to have her, and he can speedily convert his family. He will do nothing more! He will leave me in peace with her."

"Thank God!" said Nancy Ellen.

"There you go, too!" cried Kate. "That's the very first thought that came to me, only I said, 'Praise the Lord,' which is exactly the same thing; and Nancy Ellen, since Robert has been trying to praise the Lord for twenty years, and both of us do praise Him when our time comes, wouldn't it be a good idea to open up our heads and say so, not only to ourselves and to the Lord, but to the neighbours? I'm afraid she won't understand much of it, but I think I shall find the place and read to Little Poll about Abraham and Isaac to-night, and probably about Hagar and Ishmael to-morrow night, and it wouldn't surprise me a mite to hear myself saying 'Praise the Lord,' right out loud, any time, any place. Let's gather a great big bouquet of our loveliest flowers, and go tell Mother and Polly about it."

Without a word Nancy Ellen turned toward the garden. They gathered the flowers and getting in Nancy Ellen's car drove the short distance to the church where Nancy Ellen played with the baby in the shade of a big tree while Kate arranged her flowers. Then she sat down and they talked over their lives from childhood.

"Nancy Ellen, won't you stay to supper with us?" asked Kate.

"Yes," said Nancy Ellen, rising, "I haven't had such a good time in years. I'm as glad for you as I'd be if I had such a child assured me, myself."

"You can't bring yourself—?" began Kate.

"Yes, I think so," said Nancy Ellen. "Getting things for Little Poll has broken me up so, I told Robert how I felt, and he's watching in his practice, and he's written several letters of inquiry to friends in Chicago. Any day now I may have my work cut out for me."

"Praise the Lord again!" cried Kate. "I see where you will be happier than you ever have been. Real life is just beginning for you."

Then they went home and prepared a good supper and had such a fine time they were exalted in heart and spirit. When Nancy Ellen started home, Kate took the baby and climbed in the car with her, explaining that they would go a short way and walk back. She went only as far as the Peters gate; then she bravely walked up to the porch, where Mr. Peters and some of the boys sat, and said casually: "I just thought I'd bring Little Poll up to get acquainted with her folks. Isn't she a dear?"

An hour later, as she walked back in the moonlight, Henry beside her carrying the baby, he said to her: "This is a mighty big thing, and a kind thing for you to do, Mrs. Holt. Mother has been saying scandalous things about you."

"I know," said Kate. "But never mind! She won't any more."

The remainder of the week she passed in the same uplifted mental state. She carried the baby in her arms and walked all over the farm, going often to the cemetery with fresh flowers. Sunday morning, when the work was all done, the baby dressed her prettiest, Kate slipped into one of her fresh white dresses and gathering a big bunch of flowers started again to whisper above the graves of her mother and Polly the story of her gladness, and to freshen the flowers, so that the people coming from church would see that her family were remembered. When she had finished she arose, took up the baby, and started to return across the cemetery, going behind the church, taking the path she had travelled the day she followed the minister's admonition to "take the wings of morning." She thought of that. She stood very still, thinking deeply.

"I took them," she said. "I've tried flight after flight; and I've fallen, and risen, and fallen, and got up and tried again, but never until now have I felt that I could really 'fly to the uttermost parts of the earth.' There is a rising power in me that should benefit more than myself. I guess I'll just join in."

She walked into the church as the last word of the song the congregation were singing was finished, and the minister was opening his lips to say: "Let us pray." Straight down the aisle came Kate, her bare, gold head crowned with a flash of light at each window she passed. She paused at the altar, directly facing the minister.

"Baby and I would like the privilege of praising the Lord with you," she said simply, "and we would like to do our share in keeping up this church and congregation to His honour and glory. There's some water. Can't you baptize us now?"

The minister turned to the pitcher, which always stood on his desk, filled his palm, and asked: "What is the baby's name?"

"Katherine Eleanor Peters," said Kate.

"Katherine Eleanor, I baptize thee," said the minister, and he laid his hand on the soft curls of the baby. She scattered the flowers she was holding over the altar as she reached to spat her hands in the water on her head and laughed aloud.

"What is your name?" asked the minister.

"Katherine Eleanor Holt," said Kate.

Again the minister repeated the formula, and then he raised both hands and said: "Let us pray."

CHAPTER XXVI

THE WINGED VICTORY

KATE turned and placing the baby on the front seat, she knelt and put her arms around the little thing, but her lips only repeated the words: "Praise the Lord for this precious baby!" Her heart was filled with high resolve. She would rear the baby with such care. She would be more careful with Adam. She would make heroic effort to help him to clean, unashamed manhood. She would be a better sister to all her family. She would be friendlier, and have more patience with the neighbours. She would join in whatever effort the church was making to hold and increase its membership among the young people, and to raise funds to keep up the organization. All the time her mind was busy thinking out these fine resolves, her lips were thanking the Lord for Little Poll. Kate arose with the benediction, picked up the baby, and started down the aisle among the people she had known all her life. On every side strong hands stretched out to greet and welcome her. A daughter of Adam Bates was something new as a church member. They all knew how she could work, and what she could give if she chose; while that she had stood at the altar and been baptized, meant that something not customary with the Bates family was taking place in her heart. So they welcomed her, and praised the beauty and sweetness of the baby until Kate went out into the sunshine, her face glowing.

Slowly she walked home and as she reached the veranda, Adam took the baby.

"Been to the cemetery?" he asked.

Kate nodded and dropped into a chair.

"That's too far to walk and carry this great big woman," he said, snuggling his face in the baby's neck, while she patted his cheeks and pulled his hair. "Why didn't you tell me you wanted to go, and let me get out the car?"

Kate looked at him speculatively.

"Adam," she said, "when I started out, I meant only to take some flowers to Mother and Polly. As I came around the corner of the church to take the footpath, they were singing 'Rejoice in the Lord!' I went inside and joined. I'm going to church as often as I can after this, and I'm going to help with the work of running it."

"Well, I like that!" cried Adam, indignantly. "Why didn't you let me go with you?"

Kate sat staring down the road. She was shocked speechless. Again she had followed an impulse, without thinking of any one besides herself. Usually she could talk, but in that instant she had nothing to say. Then a carriage drew into the line of her vision, stopped at York's gate, and Mr. York alighted and swung to the ground a slim girlish figure and then helped his wife. Kate had a sudden inspiration. "But you would want to wait a little and join with Milly, wouldn't you?" she asked. "Uncle Robert always has been a church member. I think it's a fine stand for a man to take."

"Maybe that would be better," he said. "I didn't think of Milly. I only thought I'd like to have been with you and Little Poll."

"I'm sure Milly will be joining very soon, and that she'll want you with her," said Kate.

She was a very substantial woman, but for the remainder of that day she felt that she was moving with winged feet. She sang, she laughed, she was unspeakably happy. She kept saying over and over: "And a little child shall lead them." Then she would catch Little Poll, almost crushing her in her strong arms. It never occurred to Kate that she had done an unprecedented thing. She had done as her heart dictated. She did not know that she put the minister into a most uncomfortable position, when he followed her request to baptize her and the child. She had never thought of probations, and examinations, and catechisms. She had read the Bible, as was the custom, every morning before her school. In that book, when a man wanted to follow Jesus, he followed; Jesus accepted him; and that was all there was to it, with Kate.

The middle of the week Nancy Ellen came flying up the walk on winged feet, herself. She carried photographs of several small children, one of them a girl so like Little Poll that she might have been the original of the picture.

"They just came," said Nancy Ellen rather breathlessly. "I was wild for that little darling at once. I had Robert telegraph them to hold her until we could get there. We're going to start on the evening train and if her blood seems good, and her ancestors respectable, and she looks like that picture, we're going to bring her back with us. Oh, Kate, I can scarcely wait to get my fingers on her. I'm hungry for a baby all of my own."

Kate studied the picture.

"She's charming!" she said. "Oh, Nancy Ellen, this world is getting entirely too good to be true."

Nancy Ellen looked at Kate and smiled peculiarly.

"I knew you were crazy," she said, "but I never dreamed of you going such lengths. Mrs. Whistler told Robert, when she called him in about her side, Tuesday. I can't imagine a Bates joining church."

"If that is joining church, it's the easiest thing in the world," said Kate. "We just loved doing it, didn't we, Little Poll? Adam and Milly are going to come in soon, I'm almost sure. At least he is willing. I don't know what it is that I am to do, but I suppose they will give me my work soon."

"You bet they'll give you work soon, and enough," said Nancy Ellen, laughing. "But you won't mind. You'll just put it through, as you do things out here. Kate, you are making this place look fine. I used to say I'd rather die than come back here to live, but lately it has been growing so attractive, I've been here about half my time, and wished I were the other half."

Kate slipped her arm around Nancy Ellen as they walked to the gate.

"You know," said Nancy Ellen, "the MORE I study you, the LESS I know about you. Usually it's sickness, and sorrow, and losing their friends that bring people to the consolations of the church. You bore those things like a stoic. When they are all over, and you are comfortable and happy, just the joy of being sure of Little Poll has transformed you. Kate, you make me think of the 'Winged Victory,' this afternoon. If I get this darling little girl, will she make me big, and splendid, and fine, like you?"

Kate suddenly drew Nancy Ellen to her and kissed her a long, hard kiss on the lips.

"Nancy Ellen," she said, "you ARE 'big, and splendid, and fine,' or you never would be going to Chicago after this little motherless child. You haven't said a word, but I know from the joy of you and Robert during the past months that Mrs. Southey isn't troubling you any more; and I'm sure enough to put it into words that when you get your little child, she will lead you straight where mine as led me. Good-bye and good luck to you, and remember me to Robert."

Nancy Ellen stood intently studying the picture she held in her hand. Then she looked at Kate, smiling with misty eyes: "I think, Kate, I'm very close, if I am not really where you are this minute," she said. Then she started her car; but she looked back, waving and smiling until the car swerved so that Kate called after her: "Do drive carefully, Nancy Ellen!"

Kate went slowly up the walk. She stopped several times to examine the shrubs and bushes closely, to wish for rain for the flowers. She sat on the porch a few minutes talking to Little Poll, then she went inside to answer the phone.

"Kate?" cried a sharp voice.

"Yes," said Kate, recognizing a neighbour, living a few miles down the road.

"Did Nancy Ellen just leave your house?" came a breathless query.

"Yes," said Kate again.

"I just saw a car that looked like hers slip in the fresh sand at the river levee, and it went down, and two or three times over."

"O God!" said Kate. Then after an instant: "Ring the dinner bell for your men to get her out. I'll phone Robert, and come as soon as I can get there."

Kate called Dr. Gray's office. She said to the girl: "Tell the doctor that Mrs. Howe thinks she saw Nancy Ellen's car go down the river levee, and two or three times over. Have him bring what he might need to Howe's, and hurry. Rush him!"

Then she ran to her bell and rang so frantically that Adam came running. Kate was at the little garage they had built, and had the door open. She told him what she had heard, ran to get the baby, and met him at the gate. On the way she said, "You take the baby when we get there, and if I'm needed, take her back and get Milly and her mother to come stay with you. You know where her things are, and how to feed her. Don't you dare let them change any way I do. Baby knows Milly; she will be good for her and for you. You'll be careful?"

"Of course, Mother," said Adam.

He called her attention to the road.

"Look at those tracks," he said. "Was she sick? She might have been drunk, from them."

"No," said Kate, "she wasn't sick. She WAS drunk, drunken with joy. She had a picture of the most beautiful little baby girl. They were to start to Chicago after her to-night. I suspect she was driving with the picture in one hand. Oh, my God, have mercy!"

They had come to deep grooves in loose gravel, then the cut in the embankment, then they could see the wrecked car standing on the engine and lying against a big tree, near the water, while two men and a woman were carrying a limp form across the meadow toward the house. As their car stopped, Kate kissed the baby mechanically, handed her to Adam, and ran into the house where she dragged a couch to the middle of the first room she entered, found a pillow, and brought a bucket of water and a towel from the kitchen. They carried Nancy Ellen in and laid her down. Kate began unfastening clothing and trying to get the broken body in shape for the doctor to work upon; but she spread the towel over what had been a face of unusual beauty. Robert came in a few minutes, then all of them worked under his directions until he suddenly sank to the floor, burying his face in Nancy Ellen's breast; then they knew. Kate gathered her sister's feet in her arms and hid her face beside them. The neighbours silently began taking away things that had been used, while Mrs. Howe chose her whitest sheet, and laid it on a chair near Robert.

Two days later they laid Nancy Ellen beside her mother. Then they began trying to face the problem of life without her. Robert said nothing. He seemed too stunned to think. Kate wanted to tell him of her final visit with Nancy Ellen, but she could not at that time. Robert's aged mother came to him, and said she could remain as long as he wanted her, so that was a comfort to Kate, who took time to pity him, even in her blackest hour. She had some very black ones. She could have wailed, and lamented, and relinquished all she had gained, but she did not. She merely went on with life, as she always had lived it, to the best of her ability when she was so numbed with grief she scarcely knew what she was doing. She kept herself driven about the house, and when she could find no more to do, took Little Poll in her arms and went out in the fields to Adam, where she found the baby a safe place, and then cut and husked corn as usual. Every Sabbath, and often during the week, her feet carried her to the cemetery, where she sat in the deep grass and looked at those three long mounds and tried to understand life; deeper still, to fathom death.

She and her mother had agreed that there was "something." Now Kate tried as never before to understand what, and where, and why, that "something" was. Many days she would sit for an hour at a time, thinking, and at last she arrived at fixed convictions that settled matters forever with her. One day after she had arranged the fall roses she had grown, and some roadside asters she had gathered in passing, she sat in deep thought, when a car stopped on the road. Kate looked up to see Robert coming across the churchyard with his arms full of greenhouse roses. He carried a big bunch of deep red for her mother, white for Polly, and a large sheaf of warm pink for Nancy Ellen. Kate knelt up and taking her flowers, she moved them lower, and silently helped Robert place those he had brought. Then she sat where she had been, and looked at him.

Finally he asked: "Still hunting the 'why,' Kate?"

"'Why' doesn't so much matter," said Kate, "as 'where.' I'm enough of a fatalist to believe that Mother is here because she was old and worn out. Polly had a clear case of uric poison, while I'd stake my life Nancy Ellen was gloating over the picture she carried when she ran into that loose sand. In each of their cases I am satisfied as to 'why,' as well as about Father. The thing that holds me, and fascinates me, and that I have such a time being sure of, is 'where.'"

Robert glanced upward and asked: "Isn't there room enough up there, Kate?"

"Too much!" said Kate. "And what IS the soul, and HOW can it bridge the vortex lying between us and other worlds, that man never can, because of the lack of air to breathe, and support him?"

"I don't know," said Robert; "and in spite of the fact that I do know what a man CANNOT do, I still believe in the immortality of the soul."

"Oh, yes," said Kate. "If there is any such thing in science as a self-evident fact, that is one. THAT is provable."

Robert looked at her eager face. "How would you go about proving it, Kate?" he asked.

"Why, this way," said Kate, leaning to straighten and arrange the delicate velvet petalled roses with her sure, work-abused fingers. "Take the history of the world from as near dawn as we have any record, and trace it from the igloo of the northernmost Esquimo, around the globe, and down to the ice of the southern pole again, and in blackest Africa, farthest, wildest Borneo, you will never discover one single tribe of creatures, upright and belonging to the race of man, who did not come into the world with four primal instincts. They all reproduce themselves, they all make something intended for music, they all express a feeling in their hearts by the exercise we call dance, they all believe in the after life of the soul. This belief is as much a PART of any man, ever born in any location, as his hands and his feet. Whether he believes his soul enters a cat and works back to man again after long transmigration, or goes to a Happy Hunting Ground as our Indians, makes no difference with the fact that he enters this world with belief in after life of some kind. We see material evidence in increase that man is not defeated in his desire to reproduce himself; we have advanced to something better than tom-toms and pow-wows for music and dance; these desires are fulfilled before us, now tell me why the very strongest of all, the most deeply rooted, the belief in after life, should come to nothing. Why should the others be real, and that a dream?"

"I don't think it is," said Robert.

"It's my biggest self-evident fact," said Kate, conclusively. "I never heard any one else say these things, but I think them, and they are provable. I always believed there was something; but since I saw Mother go, I know there is. She stood in full evening light, I looked straight in her face, and Robert, you know I'm no creature of fancies and delusions, I tell you I SAW HER SOUL PASS. I saw the life go from her and go on, and on. I saw her body stand erect, long enough for me to reach her, and pick her up, after its passing. That I know."

"I shouldn't think of questioning it, Kate," said Robert. "But don't you think you are rather limiting man, when you narrow him to four primal instincts?"

"Oh, I don't know," said Kate. "Air to breathe and food to sustain are presupposed. Man LEARNS to fight in self-defense, and to acquire what he covets. He learns to covet by seeing stronger men, in better locations, surpass his achievements, so if he is strong enough he goes and robs them by force. He learns the desire for the chase in food hunting; I think four are plenty to start with."

"Probably you are right," said the doctor, rising. "I must go now. Shall I take you home?"

Kate glanced at the sun and shook her head. "I can stay half an hour longer. I don't mind the walk. I need exercise to keep me in condition. Good-bye!"

As he started his car he glanced back. She was leaning over the flowers absorbed in their beauty. Kate sat looking straight before her until time to help with the evening work, and prepare supper, then she arose. She stood looking down a long time; finally she picked up a fine specimen of each of the roses and slowly dropped them on her father's grave.

"There! You may have that many," she said. "You look a little too lonely, lying here beside the others with not a single one, but if you could speak, I wonder whether you would say, 'Thank you!' or 'Take the damn weeds off me!'"

CHAPTER XXVII

BLUE RIBBON CORN

NEVER in her life had Kate worked harder than she did that fall; but she retained her splendid health. Everything was sheltered and housed, their implements under cover, their stock in good condition, their store-room filled, and their fruits and vegetables buried in hills and long rows in the garden. Adam had a first wheat premium at the County Fair and a second on corn, concerning which he felt abused. He thought his corn scored the highest number of points, but that the award was given another man because of Adam's having had first on wheat. In her heart Kate agreed with him; but she tried to satisfy him with the blue ribbon on wheat and keep him interested sufficiently to try for the first on corn the coming year. She began making suggestions for the possible improvement of his corn. Adam was not easily propitiated.

"Mother," he said, "you know as well as you know you're alive, that if I had failed on wheat, or had second, I would have been given FIRST on my corn; my corn was the best in every way, but they thought I would swell up and burst if I had two blue ribbons. That was what ailed the judges. What encouragement is that to try again? I might grow even finer corn in the coming year than I did this, and be given no award at all, because I had two this year. It would amount to exactly the same thing."

"We'll get some more books, and see if we can study up any new wrinkles, this winter," said Kate. "Now cheer up, and go tell Milly about it. Maybe she can console you, if I can't."

"Nothing but justice will console me," said Adam. "I'm not complaining about losing the prize; I'm fighting mad because my corn, my beautiful corn, that grew and grew, and held its head so high, and waved its banners of triumph to me with every breeze, didn't get its fair show. What encouragement is there for it to try better the coming year? The crows might as well have had it, or the cutworms; while all my work is for nothing."

"You're making a big mistake," said Kate. "If your corn was the finest, it was, and the judges knew it, and you know it, and very likely the man who has the first prize, knows it. You have a clean conscience, and you know what you know. They surely can't feel right about it, or enjoy what they know. You have had the experience, you have the corn for seed; with these things to back you, clear a small strip of new land beside the woods this winter, and try what that will do for you."

Adam looked at her with wide eyes. "By jing, Mother, you are a dandy!" he said. "You just bet I'll try that next year, but don't you tell a soul; there are more than you who will let a strip be cleared, in an effort to grow blue ribbon corn. How did you come to think of it?"

"Your saying all your work had been for nothing, made me think of it," she answered. "Let them give another man the prize, when they know your corn is the best. It's their way of keeping a larger number of people interested and avoiding the appearance of partiality; this contest was too close; next year, you grow such corn, that the CORN will force the decision in spite of the judges. Do you see?"

"I see," said Adam. "I'll try again."

After that life went on as usual. The annual Christmas party was the loveliest of all, because Kate gave it loving thought, and because all of their hearts were especially touched. As spring came on again, Kate and Adam studied over their work, planning many changes for the better, but each time they talked, when everything else was arranged, they came back to corn. More than once, each of them dreamed corn that winter while asleep, they frankly talked of it many times a day. Location, soil, fertilizers, seed, cultivation—they even studied the almanacs for a general forecast of the weather. These things brought them very close together. Also it was admitted between them, that Little Poll "grappled them with hooks of steel." They never lacked subjects for conversation. Poll always came first, corn next, and during the winter there began to be discussion of plans for Adam and Milly. Should Milly come with them, or should they build a small house on the end of the farm nearest her mother? Adam did not care, so he married Milly speedily. Kate could not make up her mind. Milly had the inclination of a bird for a personal and private nest of her own. So spring came to them.

August brought the anniversary of Nancy Ellen's death, which again saddened all of them. Then came cooler September weather, and the usual rush of preparation for winter. Kate was everywhere and enjoying her work immensely. On sturdy, tumbly legs Little Poll trotted after her or rode in state on her shoulder, when distances were too far. If Kate took her to the fields, as she did every day, she carried along the half of an old pink and white quilt, which she spread in a shaded place and filled the baby's lap with acorns, wild flowers, small brightly coloured stones, shells, and whatever she could pick up for playthings. Poll amused herself with these until the heat and air made her sleepy, then she laid herself down and slept for an hour or two. Once she had trouble with stomach teeth that brought Dr. Gray racing, and left Kate white and limp with fear. Everything else had gone finely and among helping Adam, working in her home, caring for the baby, doing whatever she could see that she thought would be of benefit to the community, and what was assigned her by church committees, Kate had a busy life. She had earned, in a degree, the leadership she exercised in her first days in Walden. Everyone liked her; but no one ever ventured to ask her for an opinion unless they truly wanted it.

Adam came from a run to Hartley for groceries one evening in late September, with a look of concern that Kate noticed on his face. He was very silent during supper and when they were on the porch as usual, he still sat as if thinking deeply. Kate knew that he would tell her what he was thinking about when he was ready but she was not in the least prepared for what he said.

"Mother, how do you feel about Uncle Robert marrying again?" he asked suddenly.

Kate was too surprised to answer. She looked at him in amazement. Instead of answering, she asked him a question: "What makes you ask that?"

"You know how that Mrs. Southey pursued him one summer. Well, she's back in Hartley, staying at the hotel right across from his office; she's dressed to beat the band, she's pretty as a picture; her car stands out in front all day, and to get to ride in it, and take meals with her, all the women are running after her. I hear she has even had Robert's old mother out for a drive. What do you think of that?"

"Think she's in love with him, of course, and trying to marry him, and that she will very probably succeed. If she has located where she is right under his eye, and lets him know that she wants him very much, he'll, no doubt, marry her."

"But what do you THINK about it?" asked Adam.

"I've had no TIME to think," said Kate. "At first blush, I'd say that I shall hate it, as badly as I could possibly hate anything that was none of my immediate business. Nancy Ellen loved him so. I never shall forget that day she first told me about him, and how loving him brought out her beauty, and made her shine and glow as if from an inner light. I was always with her most, and I loved her more than all the other girls put together. I know that Southey woman tried to take him from her one summer not long ago, and that he gave her to understand that she could not, so she went away. If she's back, it means only one thing, and I think probably she'll succeed; but you can be sure it will make me squirm properly."

"I THOUGHT you wouldn't like it," he said emphatically.

"Now understand me, Adam," said Kate. "I'm no fool. I didn't expect Robert to be more than human. He has no children, and he'd like a child above anything else on earth. I've known that for years, ever since it became apparent that none was coming to Nancy Ellen. I hadn't given the matter a thought, but if I had been thinking, I would have thought that as soon as was proper, he would select a strong, healthy young woman, and make her his wife. I know his mother is homesick, and wants to go back to her daughters and their children, which is natural. I haven't an objection in the world to him marrying a PROPER woman, at a proper time and place; but Oh, dear Lord, I do dread and despise to see that little Southey cat come back and catch him, because she knows how."

"Did you ever see her, Mother?"

"No, I never," said Kate, "and I hope I never shall. I know what Nancy Ellen felt, because she told me all about it that time we were up North. I'm trying with all my might to have a Christian spirit. I swallowed Mrs. Peters, and never blinked, that anybody saw; but I don't, I truly don't know from where I could muster grace to treat a woman decently, who tried to do to my sister, what I KNOW Mrs. Southey tried to do to Nancy Ellen. She planned to break up my sister's home; that I know. Now that Nancy Ellen is gone, I feel to-night as if I just couldn't endure to see Mrs. Southey marry Robert."

"Bet she does it!" said Adam.

"Did you see her?" asked Kate.

"See her!" cried Adam. "I saw her half a dozen times in an hour. She's in the heart of the town, nothing to do but dress and motor. Never saw such a peach of a car. I couldn't help looking at it. Gee, I wish I could get you one like that!"

"What did you think of her looks?" asked Kate.

"Might pretty!" said Adam, promptly. "Small, but not tiny; plump, but not fat; pink, light curls, big baby blue eyes and a sort of hesitating way about her, as if she were anxious to do the right thing, but feared she might not, and wished somebody would take care of her."

Kate threw out her hands with a rough exclamation. "I get the picture!" she said. "It's a dead centre shot. THAT gets a man, every time. No man cares a picayune about a woman who can take care of herself, and help him with his job if he has a ghost of a chance at a little pink and white clinger, who will suck the life and talent out of him, like the parasite she is, while she makes him believe he is on the job, taking care of her. You can rest assured it will be settled before Christmas."

Kate had been right in her theories concerning the growing of blue ribbon corn. At the County Fair in late September Adam exhibited such heavy ears of evenly grained white and yellow corn that the blue ribbon he carried home was not an award of the judges; it was a concession to the just demands of the exhibit.

Then they began husking their annual crop. It had been one of the country's best years for corn. The long, even, golden ears they were stripping the husks from and stacking in heaps over the field might profitably have been used for seed by any farmer. They had divided the field in halves and Adam was husking one side, Kate the other. She had a big shock open and kneeling beside it she was busy stripping open the husks, and heaping up the yellow ears. Behind her the shocks stood like rows of stationed sentinels; above, the crisp October sunshine warmed the air to a delightful degree; around the field, the fence rows were filled with purple and rose coloured asters, and everywhere goldenrod, yellower than the corn, was hanging in heavy heads of pollen-spraying bloom.

On her old pink quilt Little Poll, sound asleep, was lifted from the shade of one shock to another, while Kate worked across her share of the field. As she worked she kept looking at the child. She frankly adored her, but she kept her reason and held to rigid rules in feeding, bathing, and dressing. Poll minded even a gesture or a nod.

Above, the flocking larks pierced the air with silver notes, on the fence-rows the gathering robins called to each other; high in the air the old black vulture that homed in a hollow log in Kate's woods, looked down on the spots of colour made by the pink quilt, the gold corn, the blue of Kate's dress, and her yellow head. An artist would have paused long, over the rich colour, the grouping and perspective of that picture, while the hazy fall atmosphere softened and blended the whole. Kate, herself, never had appeared or felt better. She worked rapidly, often glancing across the field to see if she was even with, or slightly in advance of Adam. She said it would never do to let the boy get "heady," so she made a point of keeping even with him, and caring for

Little Poll, "for good measure."

She was smiling as she watched him working like a machine as he ripped open husks, gave the ear a twist, tossed it aside, and reached for the next. Kate was doing the same thing, quite as automatically. She was beginning to find the afternoon sun almost hot on her bare head, so she turned until it fell on her back. Her face was flushed to coral pink, and framed in a loose border of her beautiful hair. She was smiling at the thought of how Adam was working to get ahead of her, smiling because Little Poll looked such a picture of healthy loveliness, smiling because she was so well, she felt super-abundant health rising like a stimulating tide in her body, smiling because the corn was the finest she ever had seen in a commonly cultivated field, smiling because she and Adam were of one accord about everything, smiling because the day was very beautiful, because her heart was at peace, her conscience clear.

She heard a car stop at her gate, saw a man alight and start across the yard toward the field, and knew that her visitor had seen her, and was coming to her. Kate went on husking corn and when the man swung over the fence of the field she saw that he was Robert, and instantly thought of Mrs. Southey, so she ceased to smile. "I've got a big notion to tell him what I think of him," she said to herself, even as she looked up to greet him. Instantly she saw that he had come for something.

"What is it?" she asked.

"Agatha," he said. "She's been having some severe heart attacks lately, and she just gave me a real scare."

Instantly Kate forgot everything, except Agatha, whom she cordially liked, and Robert, who appeared older, more tired, and worried than she ever had seen him. She thought Agatha had "given him a real scare," and she decided that it scarcely would have been bad enough to put lines in his face she never had noticed before, dark circles under his eyes, a look of weariness in his bearing. She doubted as she looked at him if he were really courting Mrs. Southey. Even as she thought of these things she was asking: "She's better now?"

"Yes, easier, but she suffered terribly. Adam was upset completely. Adam, 3d, and Susan and their families are away from home and won't be back for a few days unless I send for them. They went to Ohio to visit some friends. I stopped to ask if it would be possible for you to go down this evening and sleep there, so that if there did happen to be a recurrence, Adam wouldn't be alone."

"Of course," said Kate, glancing at the baby. "I'll go right away!"

"No need for that," he said, "if you'll arrange to stay with Adam to-night, as a precaution. You needn't go till bed-time. I'm going back after supper to put them in shape for the night. I'm almost sure she'll be all right now; but you know how frightened we can get about those we love."

"Yes, I know," said Kate, quietly, going straight on ripping open ear after ear of corn. Presently she wondered why he did not go. She looked up at him and met his eyes. He was studying her intently. Kate was vividly conscious in an instant of her bare wind-teased head, her husking gloves; she was not at all sure that her face was clean. She smiled at him, and picking up the sunbonnet lying beside her, she wiped her face with the skirt.

"If this sun hits too long on the same spot, it grows warm," she told him.

"Kate, I do wish you wouldn't!" he exclaimed abruptly.

Kate was too forthright for sparring.

"Why not?" she asked.

"For one thing, you are doing a man's work," he said. "For another, I hate to see you burn the loveliest hair I ever saw on the head of a woman, and coarsen your fine skin."

Kate looked down at the ear of corn she held in her hands, and considered an instant.

"There hasn't any man been around asking to relieve me of this work," she said. "I got my start in life doing a man's work, and I'm frank to say that I'd far rather do it any day, than what is usually considered a woman's. As for my looks, I never set a price on them or let them interfere with business, Robert."

"No, I know you don't," he said. "But it's a pity to spoil you."

"I don't know what's the matter with you," said Kate, patiently. She bent her head toward him. "Feel," she said, "and see if my hair isn't soft and fine. I always cover it in really burning sun; this autumn haze is good for it. My complexion is exactly as smooth and even now, as it was the day I first met you on the footlog over twenty years ago. There's one good thing about the Bates women. They wear well. None of us yet have ever faded, and frazzled out. Have you got many Hartley women, doing what you call women's work, to compare with me physically, Robert?"

"You know the answer to that," he said.

"So I do!" said Kate. "I see some of them occasionally, when business calls me that way. Now, Robert, I'm so well, I feel like running a footrace the first thing when I wake up every morning. I'm making money, I'm starting my boy in a safe, useful life; have you many year and a half babies in your practice that can beat Little Poll? I'm as happy as it's humanly possible for me to be without Mother, and Polly, and Nancy Ellen. Mother used always to say that when death struck a family it seldom stopped until it took three. That was my experience, and saving Adam and Little Poll, it took my three dearest; but the separation isn't going to be so very long. If I were you I wouldn't worry about me, Robert. There are many women in the world willing to pay for your consideration; save it for them."

"Kate, I'm sorry I said anything," he said hastily. "I wouldn't offend you purposely, you know."

Kate looked at him in surprise. "But I'm not offended," she said, snapping an ear and reaching for another. "I am merely telling you! Don't give me a thought! I'm all right! If you'll save me an hour the next time Little Poll has a tooth coming through, you'll have completely earned my gratitude. Tell Agatha I'll come as soon as I finish my evening work."

That was clearly a dismissal, for Kate glancing across the field toward Adam, saw that he had advanced to a new shock, so she began husking faster than before.

CHAPTER XXVIII

THE ELEVENTH HOUR

ROBERT said good-bye and started back toward his car. Kate looked after him as he reached the fence. A surge of pity for him swept up in her heart. He seemed far from happy, and he surely was very tired. Impulsive as always, she lifted her clear voice and called: "Robert!"

He paused with his foot on a rail of the fence, and turned toward her.

"Have you had any dinner?" she asked.

He seemed to be considering. "Come to think of it, I don't believe I have," he said.

"I thought you looked neglected," said Kate. "Sonny across the field is starting a shock ahead of me; I can't come, but go to the kitchen—the door is unlocked—you'll find fried chicken and some preserves and pickles in the pantry; the bread box is right there, and the milk and butter are in the spring house."

He gave Kate one long look. "Thank you," he said and leaped the fence. He stopped on the front walk and stood a minute, then he turned and went around the house. She laughed aloud. She was sending him to chicken perfectly cooked, barely cold, melon preserves, pickled cucumbers, and bread like that which had for years taken a County Fair prize each fall; butter yellow as the goldenrod lining the fences, and cream stiff enough to stand alone. Also, he would find neither germ nor mould in her pantry and spring house, while it would be a new experience for him to let him wait on himself. Kate husked away in high good humour, but she quit an hour early to be on time to go to Agatha. She explained this to Adam, when she told him that he would have to milk alone, while she bathed and dressed herself and got supper.

When she began to dress, Kate examined her hair minutely, and combed it with unusual care. If Robert was at Agatha's when she got there, she would let him see that her hair was not sunburned and ruined. To match the hair dressing, she reached back in her closet and took down her second best white dress. She was hoping that Agatha would be well enough to have a short visit. Kate worked so steadily that she seldom saw any of her brothers and sisters during the summer. In winter she spent a day with each of them, if she could possibly manage. Anyway, Agatha would like to see her appearing well, so she put on the plain snowy linen, and carefully pinning a big apron over it, she went to the kitchen. They always had a full dinner at noon and worked until dusk. Her bath had made her later than she intended to be. Dusk was deepening, evening chill was beginning to creep into the air. She closed the door, fed Little Poll and rolled her into bed; set the potatoes boiling, and began mixing the biscuit. She had them just ready to roll when steam lifted the lid of the potato pot; with the soft dough in her hand she took a step to right it. While it was in her fingers, she peered into the pot.

She did not look up on the instant the door opened, because she thought it would be Adam. When she glanced toward the door, she saw Robert standing looking at her. He had stepped inside, closed the door, and with his hand on the knob was waiting for her to see him.

"Oh! Hello!" said Kate. "I thought it was Adam. Have you been to Agatha's yet?"

"Yes. She is very much better," he said. "I only stopped to tell you that her mother happened to come out for the night, and they'll not need you."

"I'm surely glad she is better," said Kate, "but I'm rather disappointed. I've been swimming, and I'm all ready to go."

She set the pot lid in place accurately and gave her left hand a deft turn to save the dough from dripping. She glanced from it to Robert, expecting to see him open the door and disappear. Instead he stood looking at her intently. Suddenly he said: "Kate, will you marry me?"

Kate mechanically saved the dough again, as she looked at the pot an instant, then she said casually: "Sure! It would be splendid to have a doctor right in the house when Little Poll cuts her double teeth."

"Thank you!" said Robert, tersely. "No doubt that WOULD be a privilege, but I decline to marry you in order to see Little Poll safely through teething. Good-night!"

He stepped outside and closed the door very completely, and somewhat pronouncedly.

Kate stood straight an instant, then realized biscuit dough was slowly creeping down her wrist. With a quick fling, she shot the mass into the scrap bucket and sinking on the chair she sat on to peel vegetables, she lifted her apron, laid her head on her knees, and gave a big gulping sob or two. Then she began to cry silently. A minute later the door opened again. That time it had to be Adam, but Kate did not care what he saw or what he thought. She cried on in perfect abandon.

Then steps crossed the room, someone knelt beside her, put an arm around her and said: "Kate, why are you crying?"

Kate lifted her head suddenly, and applied her apron skirt. "None of your business," she said to Robert's face, six inches from hers.

"Are you so anxious as all this about Little Poll's teeth?" he asked.

"Oh, DRAT Little Poll's teeth!" cried Kate, the tears rolling uninterruptedly.

"Then WHY did you say that to me?" he demanded.

"Well, you said you 'only stopped to tell me that I needn't go to Agatha's,'" she explained. "I had to say something, to get even with you!"

"Oh," said Robert, and took possession. Kate put her arms around his neck, drew his head against hers, and knew a minute of complete joy.

When Adam entered the house his mother was very busy. She was mixing more biscuit dough, she was laughing like a girl of sixteen, she snatched out one of their finest tablecloths, and put on many extra dishes for supper, while Uncle Robert, looking like a different man, was helping her. He was actually stirring the gravy, and getting the water, and setting up chairs. And he was under high tension, too. He was saying things of no moment, as if they were profound wisdom, and laughing hilariously at things that were scarcely worth a smile. Adam looked on, and marvelled and all the while his irritation grew. At last he saw a glance of understanding pass between them. He could endure it no longer.

"Oh, you might as well SAY what you think," he burst forth. "You forgot to pull down the blinds."

Both the brazen creatures laughed as if that were a fine joke. They immediately threw off all reserve. By the time the meal was finished, Adam was struggling to keep from saying the meanest things he could think of. Also, he had to go to Milly, with nothing very definite to tell. But when he came back, his mother was waiting for him. She said at once: "Adam, I'm very sorry the blind was up to-night. I wanted to talk to you, and tell you myself, that the first real love for a man that I have ever known, is in my heart to-night."

"Why, Mother!" said Adam.

"It's true," said Kate, quietly. "You see Adam, the first time I ever saw Robert Gray, I knew, and he knew, that he had made a mistake in engaging himself to Nancy Ellen; but the thing was done, she was happy, we simply realized that we would have done better together, and let it go at that. But all these years I have known that I could have made him a wife who would have come closer to his ideals than my sister, and SHE should have had the man who wanted to marry me. They would have had a wonderful time together."

"And where did my father come in?" asked Adam, quietly.

"He took advantage of my blackest hour," said Kate. "I married him when I positively didn't care what happened to me. The man I could have LOVED was married to my sister, the man I could have married and lived with in comfort to both of us was out of the question; it was in the Bates blood to marry about the time I did; I had seen only the very best of your father, and he was an attractive lover, not bad looking, not embarrassed with one single scruple—it's the way of the world. I took it. I paid for it. Only God knows how dearly I paid; but Adam, if you love me, stand by me now. Let me have this eleventh hour happiness, with no alloy. Anything I feel for your Uncle Robert has nothing in the world to do with my being your mother; with you being my son. Kiss me, and tell me you're glad, Adam."

Adam rose up and put his arms around his mother. All his resentment was gone. He was happy as he could be for his mother, and happier than he ever before had been for himself.

The following afternoon, Kate took the car and went to see Agatha instead of husking corn. She dressed with care and arrived about three o'clock, leading Poll in whitest white, with cheeks still rosy from her afternoon nap. Agatha was sitting up and delighted to see them. She said they were the first of the family who had come to visit her, and she thought they had come because she was thinking of them. Then she told Kate about her illness. She said it dated from father Bates stroke, and the dreadful days immediately following, when Adam had completely lost self-control, and she had not been able to influence him. "I think it broke my heart," she said simply. Then they talked the family over, and at last Agatha said: "Kate, what is this I hear about Robert? Have you been informed that Mrs. Southey is back in Hartley, and that she is working every possible chance and using multifarious blandishments on him?"

Kate laughed heartily and suddenly. She never had heard "blandishments" used in common conversation. As she struggled to regain self-possession Agatha spoke again.

"It's no laughing matter," she said. "The report has every ear-mark of verisimilitude. The Bates family has a way of feeling deeply. We all loved Nancy Ellen. We all suffered severely and lost something that never could be replaced when she went. Of course all of us realized that Robert would enter the bonds of matrimony again; none of us would have objected, even if he remarried soon; but all of us do object to his marrying a woman who would have broken Nancy Ellen's heart if she could; and yesterday I took advantage of my illness, and TOLD him so. Then I asked him why a man of his standing and ability in this community didn't frustrate that unprincipled creature's vermiculations toward him, by marrying you, at once."

Slowly Kate sank down in her chair. Her face whitened and then grew greenish. She breathed with difficulty.

"Oh, Agatha!" was all she could say.

"I do not regret it," said Agatha. "If he is going to ruin himself, he is not going to do it without knowing that the Bates family highly disapprove of his course."

"But why drag me in?" said Kate, almost too shocked to speak at all. "Maybe he LOVES Mrs. Southey. She has let him see how she feels about him; possibly he feels the same about her."

"He does, if he weds her," said Agatha, conclusively. "Anything any one could say or do would have no effect, if he had centred his affections upon her, of that you may be very sure."

"May I?" asked Kate, dully.

"Indeed, you may!" said Agatha. "The male of the species, when he is a man of Robert's attainments and calibre, can be swerved from pursuit of the female he covets, by nothing save extinction."

"You mean," said Kate with an effort, "that if Robert asked a woman to marry him, it would mean that he loved her."

"Indubitably!" cried Agatha.

Kate laughed until she felt a little better, but she went home in a mood far different from that in which she started. Then she had been very happy, and she had intended to tell Agatha about her happiness, the very first of all. Now she was far from happy. Possibly—a thousand things, the most possible, that Robert had responded to Agatha's suggestion, and stopped and asked her that abrupt question, from an impulse as sudden and inexplicable as had possessed her when she married George Holt. Kate fervently wished she had gone to the cornfield as usual that afternoon.

"That's the way it goes," she said angrily, as she threw off her better dress and put on her every-day gingham to prepare supper. "That's the way it goes! Stay in your element, and go on with your work, and you're all right. Leave your job and go trapesing over the country, wasting your time, and you get a heartache to pay you. I might as well give up the idea that I'm ever to be happy, like anybody else. Every time I think happiness is coming my way, along comes something that knocks it higher than Gilderoy's kite. Hang the luck!"

She saw Robert pass while she was washing the dishes, and knew he was going to Agatha's, and would stop when he came back. She finished her work, put Little Poll to bed, and made herself as attractive as she knew how in her prettiest blue dress. All the time she debated whether she would say anything to him about what Agatha had said or not. She decided she would wait awhile, and watch how he acted. She thought she could soon tell. So when Robert came, she was as nearly herself as possible, but when he began to talk about being married soon, the most she would say was that she would begin to think about it at Christmas, and tell him by spring. Robert was bitterly disappointed. He was very lonely; he needed better housekeeping than his aged mother was capable of, to keep him up to a high mark in his work. Neither of them was young any longer; he could see no reason why they should not be married at once. Of the reason in Kate's mind, he had not a glimmering. But Kate had her way. She would not even talk of a time, or express an opinion as to whether she would remain on the farm, or live in Nancy Ellen's house, or sell it and build whatever she wanted for herself. Robert went away baffled, and disappointed over some intangible thing he could not understand.

For six weeks Kate tortured herself, and kept Robert from being happy. Then one morning Agatha stopped to visit with her, while Adam drove on to town. After they had exhausted farming, Little Poll's charms, and the neighbours, Agatha looked at Kate and said: "Katherine, what is this I hear about Robert coming here every day, now? It appeals to me that he must have followed my advice."

"Of course he never would have thought of coming, if you hadn't told him so," said Kate dryly.

"Now THERE you are in error," said the literal Agatha, as she smoothed down Little Poll's skirts and twisted her ringlets into formal corkscrews. "Right THERE, you are in error, my dear. The reason I told Robert to marry you was because he said to me, when he suggested going after you to stay the night with me, that he had seen you in the field when he passed, and that you were the most glorious specimen of womanhood that he ever had seen. He said you were the one to stay with me, in case there should be any trouble, because your head was always level, and your heart was big as a barrel."

"Yes, that's the reason I can't always have it with me," said Kate, looking glorified instead of glorious. "Agatha, it just happens to mean very much to me. Will you just kindly begin at the beginning, and tell me every single word Robert said to you, and you said to him, that day?"

"Why, I have informed you explicitly," said Agatha, using her handkerchief on the toe of Poll's blue shoe. "He mentioned going after you, and said what I told you, and I told him to go. He praised you so highly that when I spoke to him about the Southey woman I remembered it, so I suggested to him, as he seemed to think so well of you. It just that minute flashed into my mind; but HE made me think of it, calling you 'glorious,' and 'level headed,' and 'big hearted.' Heavens! Katherine Eleanor, what more could you ask?"

"I guess that should be enough," said Kate.

"One certainly would presume so," said Agatha.

Then Adam came, and handed Kate her mail as she stood beside his car talking to him a minute, while Agatha settled herself. As Kate closed the gate behind her, she saw a big, square white envelope among the newspapers, advertisements, and letters. She slipped it out and looked at it intently. Then she ran her finger under the flap and read the contents. She stood studying the few lines it contained, frowning deeply. "Doesn't it beat the band?" she asked of the surrounding atmosphere. She went up the walk, entered the living room, slipped the letter under the lid of the big family Bible, and walking to the telephone she called Dr. Gray's office. He answered the call in person.

"Robert, this is Kate," she said. "Would you have any deeply rooted objections to marrying me at six o'clock this evening?"

"Well, I should say not!" boomed Robert's voice, the "not" coming so forcibly Kate dodged.

"Have you got the information necessary for a license?" she asked.

"Yes," he answered.

"Then bring one, and your minister, and come at six," she said. "And Oh, yes, Robert, will it be all right with you if I stay here and keep house for Adam until he and Milly can be married and move in? Then I'll come to your house just as it is. I don't mind coming to Nancy Ellen's home, as I would another woman's."

"Surely!" he cried. "Any arrangement you make will satisfy me."

"All right, I'll expect you with the document and the minister at six, then," said Kate, and hung up the receiver.

Then she took it down again and calling Milly, asked her to bring her best white dress, and come up right away, and help her get ready to entertain a few people that evening. Then she called her sister Hannah, and asked her if she thought that in the event she, Kate, wished that evening at six o'clock to marry a very fine man, and had no preparations whatever made, her family would help her out to the extent of providing the supper. She wanted all of them, and all the children, but the arrangement had come up suddenly, and she could not possibly prepare a supper herself, for such a big family, in the length of time she had. Hannah said she was perfectly sure everyone of them would drop everything, and be tickled to pieces to bring the supper, and to come, and they would have a grand time. What did Kate want? Oh, she wanted bread, and chicken for meat, maybe some potato chips, and Angel's Food cake, and a big freezer or two of Agatha's best ice cream, and she thought possibly more butter, and coffee, than she had on hand. She had plenty of sugar, and cream, and pickles and jelly. She would have the tables all set as she did for Christmas. Then Kate rang for Adam and put a broom in his hand as he entered the back door. She met Milly with a pail of hot water and cloths to wash the glass. She went to her room and got out her best afternoon dress of dull blue with gold lace and a pink velvet rose. She shook it out and studied it. She had worn it twice on the trip North. None of them save Adam ever had seen it. She put it on, and looked at it critically. Then she called Milly and they changed the neck and sleeves a little, took a yard of width from the skirt, and behold! it became a "creation," in the very height of style. Then Kate opened her trunk, and got out the petticoat, hose, and low shoes to match it, and laid them on her bed.

Then they set the table, laid a fire ready to strike in the cook stove, saw that the gas was all right, set out the big coffee boiler, and skimmed a crock full of cream. By four o'clock, they could think of nothing else to do. Then Kate bathed and went to her room to dress. Adam and Milly were busy making themselves fine. Little Poll sat in her prettiest dress, watching her beloved "Tate," until Adam came and took her. He had been instructed to send Robert and the minister to his mother's room as soon as they came. Kate was trying to look her best, yet making haste, so that she would be ready on time. She had made no arrangements except to spread a white goatskin where she and Robert would stand at the end of the big living room near her door. Before she was fully dressed she began to hear young voices and knew that her people were coming. When she was ready Kate looked at herself and muttered: "I'll give Robert and all of them a good surprise. This is a real dress, thanks to Nancy Ellen. The poor girl! It's scarcely fair to her to marry her man in a dress she gave me; but I'd stake my life she'd rather I'd have him than any other woman."

It was an evening of surprises. At six, Adam lighted a big log, festooned with leaves and berries so that the flames roared and crackled up the chimney. The early arrivals were the young people who had hung the mantel, gas fixtures, curtain poles and draped the doors with long sprays of bittersweet, northern holly, and great branches of red spice berries, dogwood with its red leaves and berries, and scarlet and yellow oak leaves. The elders followed and piled the table with heaps of food, then trailed red vines between dishes. In a quandary as to what to wear, without knowing what was expected of him further than saying "I will," at the proper moment, Robert ended by slipping into Kate's room, dressed in white flannel. The ceremony was over at ten minutes after six. Kate was lovely, Robert was handsome, everyone was happy, the supper was a banquet. The Bates family went home, Adam disappeared with Milly, while Little Poll went to sleep.

Left to themselves, Robert took Kate in his arms and tried to tell her how much he loved her, but felt he expressed himself poorly. As she stood before him, he said: "And now, dear, tell me what changed you, and why we are married to-night instead of at Christmas, or in the spring."

"Oh, yes," said Kate, "I almost forgot! Why, I wanted you to answer a letter for me."

"Lucid!" said Robert. He seated himself beside the table. "Bring on the ink and stationary, and let me get it over."

Kate obeyed, and with the writing material, laid down the letter she had that morning received from John Jardine, telling her that his wife had died suddenly, and that as soon as he had laid her away, he was coming to exact a definite promise from her as to the future; and that he would move Heaven and earth before he would again be disappointed. Robert read the letter and laid it down, his face slowing flushing scarlet.

"You called me out here, and married me expressly to answer this?" he demanded.

"Of course!" said Kate. "I thought if you could tell him that his letter came the day I married you, it would stop his coming, and not be such a disappointment to him."

Robert pushed the letter from him violently, and arose "By——!" he checked himself and stared at her. "Kate, you don't MEAN that!" he cried. "Tell me, you don't MEAN that!"

"Why, SURE I do," said Kate. "It gave me a fine excuse. I was so homesick for you, and tired waiting to begin life with you. Agatha told me about her telling you the day she was ill, to marry me; and the reason I wouldn't was because I thought maybe you asked me so offhandlike, because she TOLD you to, and you didn't really love me. Then this morning she was here, and we were talking, and she got round it again, and then she told me ALL you said, and I saw you did love me, and that you would have asked me if she hadn't said anything, and I wanted you so badly. Robert, ever since that day we met on the footlog, I've know that you were the only man I'd every really WANT to marry. Robert, I've never come anywhere near loving anybody else. The minute Agatha told me this morning, I began to think how I could take back what I'd been saying, how I could change, and right then Adam handed me that letter, and it gave me a fine way out, and so I called you. Sure, I married you to answer that, Robert; now go and do it."

"All right," he said. "In a minute."

Then he walked to her and took her in his arms again, but Kate could not understand why he was laughing until he shook when he kissed her.

THE END

BOOK TWO

A GIRL OF THE LIMBERLOST

To All Girls Of The Limberlost In General
And One Jeanette Helen Porter In Particular

CHARACTERS:

ELNORA, who collects moths to pay for her education, and lives the Golden Rule.

PHILIP AMMON, who assists in moth hunting, and gains a new conception of love.

MRS. COMSTOCK, who lost a delusion and found a treasure.

WESLEY SINTON, who always did his best.

MARGARET SINTON, who "mothers" Elnora.

BILLY, a boy from real life.

EDITH CARR, who discovers herself.

HART HENDERSON, to whom love means all things.

POLLY AMMON, who pays an old score.

TOM LEVERING, engaged to Polly.

TERENCE O'MORE, Freckles grown tall.

MRS. O'MORE, who remained the Angel.

TERENCE, ALICE and LITTLE BROTHER, the O'MORE children.

CHAPTER I. WHEREIN ELNORA GOES TO HIGH SCHOOL AND LEARNS MANY LESSONS NOT FOUND IN HER BOOKS

"Elnora Comstock, have you lost your senses?" demanded the angry voice of Katharine Comstock while she glared at her daughter.

"Why mother!" faltered the girl.

"Don't you 'why mother' me!" cried Mrs. Comstock. "You know very well what I mean. You've given me no peace until you've had your way about this going to school business; I've fixed you good enough, and you're ready to start. But no child of mine walks the streets of Onabasha looking like a play-actress woman. You wet your hair and comb it down modest and decent and then be off, or you'll have no time to find where you belong."

Elnora gave one despairing glance at the white face, framed in a most becoming riot of reddish-brown hair, which she saw in the little kitchen mirror. Then she untied the narrow black ribbon, wet the comb and plastered the waving curls close to her head, bound them fast, pinned on the skimpy black hat and opened the back door.

"You've gone so plumb daffy you are forgetting your dinner," jeered her mother.

"I don't want anything to eat," replied Elnora.

"You'll take your dinner or you'll not go one step. Are you crazy? Walk almost three miles and no food from six in the morning until six at night. A pretty figure you'd cut if you had your way! And after I've gone and bought you this nice new pail and filled it especial to start on!"

Elnora came back with a face still whiter and picked up the lunch. "Thank you, mother! Good-bye!" she said. Mrs. Comstock did not reply. She watched the girl follow the long walk to the gate and go from sight on the road, in the bright sunshine of the first Monday of September.

"I bet a dollar she gets enough of it by night!" commented Mrs. Comstock.

Elnora walked by instinct, for her eyes were blinded with tears. She left the road where it turned south, at the corner of the Limberlost, climbed a snake fence and entered a path worn by her own feet. Dodging under willow and scrub oak branches she came at last to the faint outline of an old trail made in the days when the precious timber of the swamp was guarded by armed men. This path she followed until she reached a thick clump of bushes. From the debris in the end of a hollow log she took a key that unlocked the padlock of a large weatherbeaten old box, inside of which lay several books, a butterfly apparatus, and a small cracked mirror. The walls were lined thickly with gaudy butterflies, dragonflies, and moths. She set up the mirror and once more pulling the ribbon from her hair, she shook the bright mass over her shoulders, tossing it dry in the sunshine. Then she straightened it, bound it loosely, and replaced her hat. She tugged vainly at the low brown calico collar and gazed despairingly at the generous length of the narrow skirt. She lifted it as she would have cut it if possible. That disclosed the heavy high leather shoes, at sight of which she seemed positively ill, and hastily dropped the skirt. She opened the pail, removed the lunch, wrapped it in the napkin, and placed it in a small pasteboard box. Locking the case again she hid the key and hurried down the trail.

She followed it around the north end of the swamp and then entered a footpath crossing a farm leading in the direction of the spires of the city to the northeast. Again she climbed a fence and was on the open road. For an instant she leaned against the fence staring before her, then turned and looked back. Behind her lay the land on which she had been born to drudgery and a mother who made no pretence of loving her; before her lay the city through whose schools she hoped to find means of escape and the way to reach the things for which she cared. When she thought of how she appeared she leaned more heavily against the fence and groaned; when she thought of turning back and wearing such clothing in ignorance all the days of her life she set her teeth firmly and went hastily toward Onabasha.

On the bridge crossing a deep culvert at the suburbs she glanced around, and then kneeling she thrust the lunch box between the foundation and the flooring. This left her empty-handed as she approached the big stone high school building. She entered bravely and inquired her way to the office of the superintendent. There she learned that she should have come the previous week and arranged about her classes. There were many things incident to the opening of school, and one man unable to cope with all of them.

"Where have you been attending school?" he asked, while he advised the teacher of Domestic Science not to telephone for groceries until she knew how many she would have in her classes; wrote an order for chemicals for the students of science; and advised the leader of the orchestra to hire a professional to take the place of the bass violist, reported suddenly ill.

"I finished last spring at Brushwood school, district number nine," said Elnora. "I have been studying all summer. I am quite sure I can do the first year work, if I have a few days to get started."

"Of course, of course," assented the superintendent. "Almost invariably country pupils do good work. You may enter first year, and if it is too difficult, we will find it out speedily. Your teachers will tell you the list of books you must have, and if you will come with me I will show you the way to the auditorium. It is now time for opening exercises. Take any seat you find vacant."

Elnora stood before the entrance and stared into the largest room she ever had seen. The floor sloped to a yawning stage on which a band of musicians, grouped around a grand piano, were tuning their instruments. She had two fleeting impressions. That it was all a mistake; this was no school, but a grand display of enormous ribbon bows; and the second, that she was sinking, and had forgotten how to walk. Then a burst from the orchestra nerved her while a bevy of daintily clad, sweet-smelling things that might have been birds, or flowers, or possibly gaily dressed, happy young girls, pushed her forward. She found herself plodding across the back of the auditorium, praying for guidance, to an empty seat.

As the girls passed her, vacancies seemed to open to meet them. Their friends were moving over, beckoning and whispering invitations. Every one else was seated, but no one paid any attention to the white-faced girl stumbling half-blindly down the aisle next the farthest wall. So she went on to the very end facing the stage. No one moved, and she could not summon courage to crowd past others to several empty seats she saw. At the end of the aisle she paused in desperation, while she stared back at the whole forest of faces most of which were now turned upon her.

In a flash came the full realization of her scanty dress, her pitiful little hat and ribbon, her big, heavy shoes, her ignorance of where to go or what to do; and from a sickening wave which crept over her, she felt she was going to become very ill. Then out of the mass she saw a pair of big, brown boy eyes, three seats from her, and there was a message in them. Without moving his body he reached forward and with a pencil touched the back of the seat before him. Instantly Elnora took another step which brought her to a row of vacant front seats.

She heard laughter behind her; the knowledge that she wore the only hat in the room burned her; every matter of moment, and some of none at all, cut and stung. She had no books. Where should she go when this was over? What would she give to be on the trail going home! She was shaking with a nervous chill when the music ceased, and the superintendent arose, and coming down to the front of the flower-decked platform, opened a Bible and began to read. Elnora did not know what he was reading, and she felt that she did not care. Wildly she was racking her brain to decide whether she should sit still when the others left the room or follow, and ask some one where the Freshmen went first.

In the midst of the struggle one sentence fell on her ear. "Hide me under the shadow of Thy wings."

Elnora began to pray frantically. "Hide me, O God, hide me, under the shadow of Thy wings."

Again and again she implored that prayer, and before she realized what was coming, every one had arisen and the room was emptying rapidly. Elnora hurried after the nearest girl and in the press at the door touched her sleeve timidly.

"Will you please tell me where the Freshmen go?" she asked huskily.

The girl gave her one surprised glance, and drew away.

"Same place as the fresh women," she answered, and those nearest her laughed.

Elnora stopped praying suddenly and the colour crept into her face. "I'll wager you are the first person I meet when I find it," she said and stopped short. "Not that! Oh, I must not do that!" she thought in dismay. "Make an enemy the first thing I do. Oh, not that!"

She followed with her eyes as the young people separated in the hall, some climbing stairs, some disappearing down side halls, some entering adjoining doors. She saw the girl overtake the brown-eyed boy and speak to him. He glanced back at Elnora with a scowl on his face. Then she stood alone in the hall.

Presently a door opened and a young woman came out and entered another room. Elnora waited until she returned, and hurried to her. "Would you tell me where the Freshmen are?" she panted.

"Straight down the hall, three doors to your left," was the answer, as the girl passed.

"One minute please, oh please," begged Elnora: "Should I knock or just open the door?"

"Go in and take a seat," replied the teacher.

"What if there aren't any seats?" gasped Elnora.

"Classrooms are never half-filled, there will be plenty," was the answer.

Elnora removed her hat. There was no place to put it, so she carried it in her hand. She looked infinitely better without it. After several efforts she at last opened the door and stepping inside faced a smaller and more concentrated battery of eyes.

"The superintendent sent me. He thinks I belong here," she said to the professor in charge of the class, but she never before heard the voice with which she spoke. As she stood waiting, the girl of the hall passed on her way to the blackboard, and suppressed laughter told Elnora that her thrust had been repeated.

"Be seated," said the professor, and then because he saw Elnora was desperately embarrassed he proceeded to lend her a book and to ask her if she had studied algebra. She said she had a little, but not the same book they were using. He asked her if she felt that she could do the work they were beginning, and she said she did.

That was how it happened, that three minutes after entering the room she was told to take her place beside the girl who had gone last to the board, and whose flushed face and angry eyes avoided meeting Elnora's. Being compelled to concentrate on her proposition she forgot herself. When the professor asked that all pupils sign their work she firmly wrote "Elnora Comstock" under her demonstration. Then she took her seat and waited with white lips and trembling limbs, as one after another professor called the names on the board, while their owners arose and explained their propositions, or "flunked" if they had not found a correct solution. She was so eager to catch their forms of expression and prepare herself for her recitation, that she never looked from the work on the board, until clearly and distinctly, "Elnora Cornstock," called the professor.

The dazed girl stared at the board. One tiny curl added to the top of the first curve of the m in her name, had transformed it from a good old English patronymic that any girl might bear proudly, to Cornstock. Elnora sat speechless. When and how did it happen? She could feel the wave of smothered laughter in the air around her. A rush of anger turned her face scarlet and her soul sick. The voice of the professor addressed her directly.

"This proposition seems to be beautifully demonstrated, Miss Cornstalk," he said. "Surely, you can tell us how you did it."

That word of praise saved her. She could do good work. They might wear their pretty clothes, have their friends and make life a greater misery than it ever before had been for her, but not one of them should do better work or be more womanly. That lay with her. She was tall, straight, and handsome as she arose.

"Of course I can explain my work," she said in natural tones. "What I can't explain is how I happened to be so stupid as to make a mistake in writing my own name. I must have been a little nervous. Please excuse me."

She went to the board, swept off the signature with one stroke, then rewrote it plainly. "My name is Comstock," she said distinctly. She returned to her seat and following the formula used by the others made her first high school recitation.

As Elnora resumed her seat Professor Henley looked at her steadily. "It puzzles me," he said deliberately, "how you can write as beautiful a demonstration, and explain it as clearly as ever has been done in any of my classes and still be so disturbed as to make a mistake in your own name. Are you very sure you did that yourself, Miss Comstock?"

"It is impossible that any one else should have done it," answered Elnora.

"I am very glad you think so," said the professor. "Being Freshmen, all of you are strangers to me. I should dislike to begin the year with you feeling there was one among you small enough to do a trick like that. The next proposition, please."

When the hour had gone the class filed back to the study room and Elnora followed in desperation, because she did not know where else to go. She could not study as she had no books, and when the class again left the room to go to another professor for the next recitation, she went also. At least they could put her out if she did not belong there. Noon came at last, and she kept with the others until they dispersed on the sidewalk. She was so abnormally self-conscious she fancied all the hundreds of that laughing, throng saw and jested at her. When she passed the brown-eyed boy walking with the girl of her encounter, she knew, for she heard him say: "Did you really let that gawky piece of calico get ahead of you?" The answer was indistinct.

Elnora hurried from the city. She intended to get her lunch, eat it in the shade of the first tree, and then decide whether she would go back or go home. She knelt on the bridge and reached for her box, but it was so very light that she was prepared for the fact that it was empty, before opening it. There was one thing for which to be thankful. The boy or tramp who had seen her hide it, had left the napkin. She would not have to face her mother and account for its loss. She put it in her pocket, and threw the box into the ditch. Then she sat on the bridge and tried to think, but her brain was confused.

"Perhaps the worst is over," she said at last. "I will go back. What would mother say to me if I came home now?"

So she returned to the high school, followed some other pupils to the coat room, hung her hat, and found her way to the study where she had been in the morning. Twice that afternoon, with aching head and empty stomach, she faced strange professors, in different branches. Once she escaped notice; the second time the worst happened. She was asked a question she could not answer.

"Have you not decided on your course, and secured your books?" inquired the professor.

"I have decided on my course," replied Elnora, "I do not know where to ask for my books."

"Ask?" the professor was bewildered.

"I understood the books were furnished," faltered Elnora.

"Only to those bringing an order from the township trustee," replied the Professor.

"No! Oh no!" cried Elnora. "I will have them to-morrow," and gripped her desk for support for she knew that was not true. Four books, ranging perhaps at a dollar and a half apiece; would her mother buy them? Of course she would not—could not.

Did not Elnora know the story of old. There was enough land, but no one to do clearing and farm. Tax on all those acres, recently the new gravel road tax added, the expense of living and only the work of two women to meet all of it. She was insane to think she could come to the city to school. Her mother had been right. The girl decided that if only she lived to reach home, she would stay there and lead any sort of life to avoid more of this torture. Bad as what she wished to escape had been, it was nothing like this. She never could live down the movement that went through the class when she inadvertently revealed the fact that she had expected books to be furnished. Her mother would not secure them; that settled the question.

But the end of misery is never in a hurry to come; before the day was over the superintendent entered the room and explained that pupils from the country were charged a tuition of twenty dollars a year. That really was the end. Previously Elnora had canvassed a dozen methods for securing the money for books, ranging all the way from offering to wash the superintendent's dishes to breaking into the bank. This additional expense made her plans so wildly impossible, there was nothing to do but hold up her head until she was from sight.

Down the long corridor alone among hundreds, down the long street alone among thousands, out into the country she came at last. Across the fence and field, along the old trail once trodden by a boy's bitter agony, now stumbled a white-faced girl, sick at heart. She sat on a log and began to sob in spite of her efforts at self-control. At first it was physical breakdown, later, thought came crowding.

Oh the shame, the mortification! Why had she not known of the tuition? How did she happen to think that in the city books were furnished? Perhaps it was because she had read they were in several states. But why did she not know? Why did not her mother go with her? Other mothers—but when had her mother ever been or done anything at all like other mothers? Because she never had been it was useless to blame her now. Elnora realized she should have gone to town the week before, called on some one and learned all these things herself. She should have remembered how her clothing would look, before she wore it in public places. Now she knew, and her dreams were over. She must go home to feed chickens, calves, and pigs, wear calico and coarse shoes, and with averted head, pass a library all her life. She sobbed again.

"For pity's sake, honey, what's the matter?" asked the voice of the nearest neighbour, Wesley Sinton, as he seated himself beside Elnora. "There, there," he continued, smearing tears all over her face in an effort to dry them. "Was it as bad as that, now? Maggie has been just wild over you all day. She's got nervouser every minute. She said we were foolish to let you go. She said your clothes were not right, you ought not to carry that tin pail, and that they would laugh at you. By gum, I see they did!"

"Oh, Uncle Wesley," sobbed the girl, "why didn't she tell me?"

"Well, you see, Elnora, she didn't like to. You got such a way of holding up your head, and going through with things. She thought some way that you'd make it, till you got started, and then she begun to see a hundred things we should have done. I reckon you hadn't reached that building before she remembered that your skirt should have been pleated instead of gathered, your shoes been low, and lighter for hot September weather, and a new hat. Were your clothes right, Elnora?"

The girl broke into hysterical laughter. "Right!" she cried. "Right! Uncle Wesley, you should have seen me among them! I was a picture! They'll never forget me. No, they won't get the chance, for they'll see me again to-morrow!

"Now that is what I call spunk, Elnora! Downright grit," said Wesley Sinton. "Don't you let them laugh you out. You've helped Margaret and me for years at harvest and busy times, what you've earned must amount to quite a sum. You can get yourself a good many clothes with it."

"Don't mention clothes, Uncle Wesley," sobbed Elnora, "I don't care now how I look. If I don't go back all of them will know it's because I am so poor I can't buy my books."

"Oh, I don't know as you are so dratted poor," said Sinton meditatively. "There are three hundred acres of good land, with fine timber as ever grew on it."

"It takes all we can earn to pay the tax, and mother wouldn't cut a tree for her life."

"Well then, maybe, I'll be compelled to cut one for her," suggested Sinton. "Anyway, stop tearing yourself to pieces and tell me. If it isn't clothes, what is it?"

"It's books and tuition. Over twenty dollars in all."

"Humph! First time I ever knew you to be stumped by twenty dollars, Elnora," said Sinton, patting her hand.

"It's the first time you ever knew me to want money," answered Elnora. "This is different from anything that ever happened to me. Oh, how can I get it, Uncle Wesley?"

"Drive to town with me in the morning and I'll draw it from the bank for you. I owe you every cent of it."

"You know you don't owe me a penny, and I wouldn't touch one from you, unless I really could earn it. For anything that's past I owe you and Aunt Margaret for all the home life and love I've ever known. I know how you work, and I'll not take your money."

"Just a loan, Elnora, just a loan for a little while until you can earn it. You can be proud with all the rest of the world, but there are no secrets between us, are there, Elnora?"

"No," said Elnora, "there are none. You and Aunt Margaret have given me all the love there has been in my life. That is the one reason above all others why you shall not give me charity. Hand me money because you find me crying for it! This isn't the first time this old trail has known tears and heartache. All of us know that story. Freckles stuck to what he undertook and won out. I stick, too. When Duncan moved away he gave me all Freckles left in the swamp, and as I have inherited his property maybe his luck will come with it. I won't touch your money, but I'll win some way. First, I'm going home and try mother. It's just possible I could find second-hand books, and perhaps all the tuition need not be paid at once. Maybe they would accept it quarterly. But oh, Uncle Wesley, you and Aunt Margaret keep on loving me! I'm so lonely, and no one else cares!"

Wesley Sinton's jaws met with a click. He swallowed hard on bitter words and changed what he would have liked to say three times before it became articulate.

"Elnora," he said at last, "if it hadn't been for one thing I'd have tried to take legal steps to make you ours when you were three years old. Maggie said then it wasn't any use, but I've always held on. You see, I was the first man there, honey, and there are things you see, that you can't ever make anybody else understand. She loved him Elnora, she just made an idol of him. There was that oozy green hole, with the thick scum broke, and two or three big bubbles slowly rising that were the breath of his body. There she was in spasms of agony, and beside her the great heavy log she'd tried to throw him. I can't ever forgive her for turning against you, and spoiling your childhood as she has, but I couldn't forgive anybody else for abusing her. Maggie has got no mercy on her, but Maggie didn't see what I did, and I've never tried to make it very clear to her. It's been a little too plain for me ever since. Whenever I look at your mother's face, I see what she saw, so I hold my tongue and say, in my heart, 'Give her a mite more time.' Some day it will come. She does love you, Elnora. Everybody does, honey. It's just that she's feeling so much, she can't express herself. You be a patient girl and wait a little longer. After all, she's your mother, and you're all she's got, but a memory, and it might do her good to let her know that she was fooled in that."

"It would kill her!" cried the girl swiftly. "Uncle Wesley, it would kill her! What do you mean?"

"Nothing," said Wesley Sinton soothingly. "Nothing, honey. That was just one of them fool things a man says, when he is trying his best to be wise. You see, she loved him mightily, and they'd been married only a year, and what she was loving was what she thought he was. She hadn't really got acquainted with the man yet. If it had been even one more year, she could have borne it, and you'd have got justice. Having been a teacher she was better educated and smarter than the rest of us, and so she was more sensitive like. She can't understand she was loving a dream. So I say it might do her good if somebody that knew, could tell her, but I swear to gracious, I never could. I've heard her out at the edge of that quagmire calling in them wild spells of hers off and on for the last sixteen years, and imploring the swamp to give him back to her, and I've got out of bed when I was pretty tired, and come down to see she didn't go in herself, or harm you. What she feels is too deep for me. I've got to respectin' her grief, and I can't get over it. Go home and tell your ma, honey, and ask her nice and kind to help you. If she won't, then you got to swallow that little lump of pride in your neck, and come to Aunt Maggie, like you been a-coming all your life."

"I'll ask mother, but I can't take your money, Uncle Wesley, indeed I can't. I'll wait a year, and earn some, and enter next year."

"There's one thing you don't consider, Elnora," said the man earnestly. "And that's what you are to Maggie. She's a little like your ma. She hasn't given up to it, and she's struggling on brave, but when we buried our second little girl the light went out of Maggie's eyes, and it's not come back. The only time I ever see a hint of it is when she thinks she's done something that makes you happy, Elnora. Now, you go easy about refusing her anything she wants to do for you. There's times in this world when it's our bounden duty to forget ourselves, and think what will help other people. Young woman, you owe me and Maggie all the comfort we can get out of you. There's the two of our own we can't ever do anything for. Don't you get the idea into your head that a fool thing you call pride is going to cut us out of all the pleasure we have in life beside ourselves."

"Uncle Wesley, you are a dear," said Elnora. "Just a dear! If I can't possibly get that money any way else on earth, I'll come and borrow it of you, and then I'll pay it back if I must dig ferns from the swamp and sell them from door to door in the city. I'll even plant them, so that they will be sure to come up in the spring. I have been sort of panic stricken all day and couldn't think. I can gather nuts and sell them. Freckles sold moths and butterflies, and I've a lot collected. Of course, I am going back to-morrow! I can find a way to get the books. Don't you worry about me. I am all right!

"Now, what do you think of that?" inquired Wesley Sinton of the swamp in general. "Here's our Elnora come back to stay. Head high and right as a trivet! You've named three ways in three minutes that you could earn ten dollars, which I figure would be enough, to start you. Let's go to supper and stop worrying!"

Elnora unlocked the case, took out the pail, put the napkin in it, pulled the ribbon from her hair, binding it down tightly again and followed to the road. From afar she could see her mother in the doorway. She blinked her eyes, and tried to smile as she answered Wesley Sinton, and indeed she did feel better. She knew now what she had to expect, where to go, and what to do. Get the books she must; when she had them, she would show those city girls and boys how to prepare and recite lessons, how to walk with a brave heart; and they could show her how to wear pretty clothes and have good times.

As she neared the door her mother reached for the pail. "I forgot to tell you to bring home your scraps for the chickens," she said.

Elnora entered. "There weren't any scraps, and I'm hungry again as I ever was in my life."

"I thought likely you would be," said Mrs. Comstock, "and so I got supper ready. We can eat first, and do the work afterward. What kept you so? I expected you an hour ago."

Elnora looked into her mother's face and smiled. It was a queer sort of a little smile, and would have reached the depths with any normal mother.

"I see you've been bawling," said Mrs. Comstock. "I thought you'd get your fill in a hurry. That's why I wouldn't go to any expense. If we keep out of the poor-house we have to cut the corners close. It's likely this Brushwood road tax will eat up all we've saved in years. Where the land tax is to come from I don't know. It gets bigger every year. If they are going to dredge the swamp ditch again they'll just have to take the land to pay for it. I can't, that's all! We'll get up early in the morning and gather and hull the beans for winter, and put in the rest of the day hoeing the turnips."

Elnora again smiled that pitiful smile.

"Do you think I didn't know that I was funny and would be laughed at?" she asked.

"Funny?" cried Mrs. Comstock hotly.

"Yes, funny! A regular caricature," answered Elnora. "No one else wore calico, not even one other. No one else wore high heavy shoes, not even one. No one else had such a funny little old hat; my hair was not right, my ribbon invisible compared with the others, I did not know where to go, or what to do, and I had no books. What a spectacle I made for them!" Elnora laughed nervously at her own picture. "But there are always two sides! The professor said in the algebra class that he never had a better solution and explanation than mine of the proposition he gave me, which scored one for me in spite of my clothes."

"Well, I wouldn't brag on myself!"

"That was poor taste," admitted Elnora. "But, you see, it is a case of whistling to keep up my courage. I honestly could see that I would have looked just as well as the rest of them if I had been dressed as they were. We can't afford that, so I have to find something else to brace me. It was rather bad, mother!"

"Well, I'm glad you got enough of it!"

"Oh, but I haven't," hurried in Elnora. "I just got a start. The hardest is over. To-morrow they won't be surprised. They will know what to expect. I am sorry to hear about the dredge. Is it really going through?"

"Yes. I got my notification today. The tax will be something enormous. I don't know as I can spare you, even if you are willing to be a laughing-stock for the town."

With every bite Elnora's courage returned, for she was a healthy young thing.

"You've heard about doing evil that good might come from it," she said. "Well, mother mine, it's something like that with me. I'm willing to bear the hard part to pay for what I'll learn. Already I have selected the ward building in which I shall teach in about four years. I am going to ask for a room with a south exposure so that the flowers and moths I take in from the swamp to show the children will do well."

"You little idiot!" said Mrs. Comstock. "How are you going to pay your expenses?"

"Now that is just what I was going to ask you!" said Elnora. "You see, I have had two startling pieces of news to-day. I did not know I would need any money. I thought the city furnished the books, and there is an out-of-town tuition, also. I need ten dollars in the morning. Will you please let me have it?"

"Ten dollars!" cried Mrs. Comstock. "Ten dollars! Why don't you say a hundred and be done with it! I could get one as easy as the other. I told you! I told you I couldn't raise a cent. Every year expenses grow bigger and bigger. I told you not to ask for money!"

"I never meant to," replied Elnora. "I thought clothes were all I needed and I could bear them. I never knew about buying books and tuition."

"Well, I did!" said Mrs. Comstock. "I knew what you would run into! But you are so bull-dog stubborn, and so set in your way, I thought I would just let you try the world a little and see how you liked it!"

Elnora pushed back her chair and looked at her mother.

"Do you mean to say," she demanded, "that you knew, when you let me go into a city classroom and reveal the fact before all of them that I expected to have my books handed out to me; do you mean to say that you knew I had to pay for them?"

Mrs. Comstock evaded the direct question.

"Anybody but an idiot mooning over a book or wasting time prowling the woods would have known you had to pay. Everybody has to pay for everything. Life is made up of pay, pay, pay! It's always and forever pay! If you don't pay one way you do another! Of course, I knew you had to pay. Of course, I knew you would come home blubbering! But you don't get a penny! I haven't one cent, and can't get one! Have your way if you are determined, but I think you will find the road somewhat rocky."

"Swampy, you mean, mother," corrected Elnora. She arose white and trembling. "Perhaps some day God will teach me how to understand you. He knows I do not now. You can't possibly realize just what you let me go through to-day, or how you let me go, but I'll tell you this: You understand enough that if you had the money, and would offer it to me, I wouldn't touch it now. And I'll tell you this much more. I'll get it myself. I'll raise it, and do it some honest way. I am going back to-morrow, the next day, and the next. You need not come out, I'll do the night work, and hoe the turnips."

It was ten o'clock when the chickens, pigs, and cattle were fed, the turnips hoed, and a heap of bean vines was stacked beside the back door.

CHAPTER II. WHEREIN WESLEY AND MARGARET GO SHOPPING, AND ELNORA'S WARDROBE IS REPLENISHED

Wesley Sinton walked down the road half a mile and turned at the lane leading to his home. His heart was hot and filled with indignation. He had told Elnora he did not blame her mother, but he did. His wife met him at the door.

"Did you see anything of Elnora?" she questioned.

"Most too much, Maggie," he answered. "What do you say to going to town? There's a few things has to be got right away."

"Where did you see her, Wesley?"

"Along the old Limberlost trail, my girl, torn to pieces sobbing. Her courage always has been fine, but the thing she met to-day was too much for her. We ought to have known better than to let her go that way. It wasn't only clothes; there were books, and entrance fees for out-of-town people, that she didn't know about; while there must have been jeers, whispers, and laughing. Maggie, I feel as if I'd been a traitor to those girls of ours. I ought to have gone in and seen about this school business. Don't cry, Maggie. Get me some supper, and I'll hitch up and see what we can do now."

"What can we do, Wesley?

"I don't just know. But we've got to do something. Kate Comstock will be a handful, while Elnora will be two, but between us we must see that the girl is not too hard pressed about money, and that she is dressed so she is not ridiculous. She's saved us the wages of a woman many a day, can't you make her some decent dresses?"

"Well, I'm not just what you call expert, but I could beat Kate Comstock all to pieces. I know that skirts should be pleated to the band instead of gathered, and full enough to sit in, and short enough to walk in. I could try. There are patterns for sale. Let's go right away, Wesley."

"Set me a bit of supper, while I hitch up."

Margaret built a fire, made coffee, and fried ham and eggs. She set out pie and cake and had enough for a hungry man by the time the carriage was at the door, but she had no appetite. She dressed while Wesley ate, put away the food while he dressed, and then they drove toward the city through the beautiful September evening, and as they went they planned for Elnora. The trouble was, not whether they were generous enough to buy what she needed, but whether she would accept their purchases, and what her mother would say.

They went to a drygoods store and when a clerk asked what they wanted to see neither of them knew, so they stepped aside and held a whispered consultation.

"What had we better get, Wesley?"

"Dresses," said Wesley promptly,

"But how many dresses, and what kind?"

"Blest if I know!" exclaimed Wesley. "I thought you would manage that. I know about some things I'm going to get."

At that instant several high school girls came into the store and approached them.

"There!" exclaimed Wesley breathlessly. "There, Maggie! Like them! That's what she needs! Buy like they have!"

Margaret stared. What did they wear? They were rapidly passing; they seemed to have so much, and she could not decide so quickly. Before she knew it she was among them.

"I beg your pardon, but won't you wait one minute?" she asked.

The girls stopped with wondering faces.

"It's your clothes," explained Mrs. Sinton. "You look just beautiful to me. You look exactly as I should have wanted to see my girls. They both died of diphtheria when they were little, but they had yellow hair, dark eyes and pink cheeks, and everybody thought they were lovely. If they had lived, they'd been near your age now, and I'd want them to look like you."

There was sympathy on every girl face.

"Why thank you!" said one of them. "We are very sorry for you."

"Of course you are," said Margaret. "Everybody always has been. And because I can't ever have the joy of a mother in thinking for my girls and buying pretty things for them, there is nothing left for me, but to do what I can for some one who has no mother to care for her. I know a girl, who would be just as pretty as any of you, if she had the clothes, but her mother does not think about her, so I mother her some myself."

"She must be a lucky girl," said another.

"Oh, she loves me," said Margaret, "and I love her. I want her to look just like you do. Please tell me about your clothes. Are these the dresses and hats you wear to school? What kind of goods are they, and where do you buy them?"

The girls began to laugh and cluster around Margaret. Wesley strode down the store with his head high through pride in her, but his heart was sore over the memory of two little faces under Brushwood sod. He inquired his way to the shoe department.

"Why, every one of us have on gingham or linen dresses," they said, "and they are our school clothes."

For a few moments there was a babel of laughing voices explaining to the delighted Margaret that school dresses should be bright and pretty, but simple and plain, and until cold weather they should wash.

"I'll tell you," said Ellen Brownlee, "my father owns this store, I know all the clerks. I'll take you to Miss Hartley. You tell her just how much you want to spend, and what you want to buy, and she will know how to get the most for your money. I've heard papa say she was the best clerk in the store for people who didn't know precisely what they wanted."

"That's the very thing," agreed Margaret. "But before you go, tell me about your hair. Elnora's hair is bright and wavy, but yours is silky as hackled flax. How do you do it?"

"Elnora?" asked four girls in concert.

"Yes, Elnora is the name of the girl I want these things for."

"Did she come to the high school to-day?" questioned one of them.

"Was she in your classes?" demanded Margaret without reply.

Four girls stood silent and thought fast. Had there been a strange girl among them, and had she been overlooked and passed by with indifference, because she was so very shabby? If she had appeared as much better than they, as she had looked worse, would her reception have been the same?

"There was a strange girl from the country in the Freshman class to-day," said Ellen Brownlee, "and her name was Elnora."

"That was the girl," said Margaret.

"Are her people so very poor?" questioned Ellen.

"No, not poor at all, come to think of it," answered Margaret. "It's a peculiar case. Mrs. Comstock had a great trouble and she let it change her whole life and make a different woman of her. She used to be lovely; now she is forever saving and scared to death for fear they will go to the poorhouse; but there is a big farm, covered with lots of good timber. The taxes are high for women who can't manage to clear and work the land. There ought to be enough to keep two of them in good shape all their lives, if they only knew how to do it. But no one ever told Kate Comstock anything, and never will, for she won't listen. All she does is droop all day, and walk the edge of the swamp half the night, and neglect Elnora. If you girls would make life just a little easier for her it would be the finest thing you ever did."

All of them promised they would.

"Now tell me about your hair," persisted Margaret Sinton.

So they took her to a toilet counter, and she bought the proper hair soap, also a nail file, and cold cream, for use after windy days. Then they left her with the experienced clerk, and when at last Wesley found her she was loaded with bundles and the light of other days was in her beautiful eyes. Wesley also carried some packages.

"Did you get any stockings?" he whispered.

"No, I didn't," she said. "I was so interested in dresses and hair ribbons and a—a hat——" she hesitated and glanced at Wesley. "Of course, a hat!" prompted Wesley. "That I forgot all about those horrible shoes. She's got to have decent shoes, Wesley."

"Sure!" said Wesley. "She's got decent shoes. But the man said some brown stockings ought to go with them. Take a peep, will you!"

Wesley opened a box and displayed a pair of thick-soled, beautifully shaped brown walking shoes of low cut. Margaret cried out with pleasure.

"But do you suppose they are the right size, Wesley? What did you get?"

"I just said for a girl of sixteen with a slender foot."

"Well, that's about as near as I could come. If they don't fit when she tries them, we will drive straight in and change them. Come on now, let's get home."

All the way they discussed how they should give Elnora their purchases and what Mrs. Comstock would say.

"I am afraid she will be awful mad," said Margaret.

"She'll just rip!" replied Wesley graphically. "But if she wants to leave the raising of her girl to the neighbours, she needn't get fractious if they take some pride in doing a good job. From now on I calculate Elnora shall go to school; and she shall have all the clothes and books she needs, if I go around on the back of Kate Comstock's land and cut a tree, or drive off a calf to pay for them. Why I know one tree she owns that would put Elnora in heaven for a year. Just think of it, Margaret! It's not fair. One-third of what is there belongs to Elnora by law, and if Kate Comstock raises a row I'll tell her so, and see that the girl gets it. You go to see Kate in the morning, and I'll go with you. Tell her you want Elnora's pattern, that you are going to make her a dress, for helping us. And sort of hint at a few more things. If Kate balks, I'll take a hand and settle her. I'll go to law for Elnora's share of that land and sell enough to educate her."

"Why, Wesley Sinton, you're perfectly wild."

"I'm not! Did you ever stop to think that such cases are so frequent there have been laws made to provide for them? I can bring it up in court and force Kate to educate Elnora, and board and clothe her till she's of age, and then she can take her share."

"Wesley, Kate would go crazy!"

"She's crazy now. The idea of any mother living with as sweet a girl as Elnora and letting her suffer till I find her crying like a funeral. It makes me fighting mad. All uncalled for. Not a grain of sense in it. I've offered and offered to oversee clearing her land and working her fields. Let her sell a good tree, or a few acres. Something is going to be done, right now. Elnora's been fairly happy up to this, but to spoil the school life she's planned, is to ruin all her life. I won't have it! If Elnora won't take these things, so help me, I'll tell her what she is worth, and loan her the money and she can pay me back when she comes of age. I am going to have it out with Kate Comstock in the morning. Here we are! You open up what you got while I put away the horses, and then I'll show you."

When Wesley came from the barn Margaret had four pieces of crisp gingham, a pale blue, a pink, a gray with green stripes and a rich brown and blue plaid. On each of them lay a yard and a half of wide ribbon to match. There were handkerchiefs and a brown leather belt. In her hands she held a wide-brimmed tan straw hat, having a high crown banded with velvet strips each of which fastened with a tiny gold buckle.

"It looks kind of bare now," she explained. "It had three quills on it here."

"Did you have them taken off?" asked Wesley.

"Yes, I did. The price was two and a half for the hat, and those things were a dollar and a half apiece. I couldn't pay that."

"It does seem considerable," admitted Wesley, "but will it look right without them?"

"No, it won't!" said Margaret. "It's going to have quills on it. Do you remember those beautiful peacock wing feathers that Phoebe Simms gave me? Three of them go on just where those came off, and nobody will ever know the difference. They match the hat to a moral, and they are just a little longer and richer than the ones that I had taken off. I was wondering whether I better sew them on to-night while I remember how they set, or wait till morning."

"Don't risk it!" exclaimed Wesley anxiously. "Don't you risk it! Sew them on right now!"

"Open your bundles, while I get the thread," said Margaret.

Wesley unwrapped the shoes. Margaret took them up and pinched the leather and stroked them.

"My, but they are fine!" she cried.

Wesley picked up one and slowly turned it in his big hands. He glanced at his foot and back to the shoe.

"It's a little bit of a thing, Margaret," he said softly. "Like as not I'll have to take it back. It seems as if it couldn't fit."

"It seems as if it didn't dare do anything else," said Margaret. "That's a happy little shoe to get the chance to carry as fine a girl as Elnora to high school. Now what's in the other box?"

Wesley looked at Margaret doubtfully.

"Why," he said, "you know there's going to be rainy days, and those things she has now ain't fit for anything but to drive up the cows——"

"Wesley, did you get high shoes, too?"

"Well, she ought to have them! The man said he would make them cheaper if I took both pairs at once."

Margaret laughed aloud. "Those will do her past Christmas," she exulted. "What else did you buy?"

"Well sir," said Wesley, "I saw something to-day. You told me about Kate getting that tin pail for Elnora to carry to high school and you said you told her it was a shame. I guess Elnora was ashamed all right, for to-night she stopped at the old case Duncan gave her, and took out that pail, where it had been all day, and put a napkin inside it. Coming home she confessed she was half starved because she hid her dinner under a culvert, and a tramp took it. She hadn't had a bite to eat the whole day. But she never complained at all, she was pleased that she hadn't lost the napkin. So I just inquired around till I found this, and I think it's about the ticket."

Wesley opened the package and laid a brown leather lunch box on the table. "Might be a couple of books, or drawing tools or most anything that's neat and genteel. You see, it opens this way."

It did open, and inside was a space for sandwiches, a little porcelain box for cold meat or fried chicken, another for salad, a glass with a lid which screwed on, held by a ring in a corner, for custard or jelly, a flask for tea or milk, a beautiful little knife, fork, and spoon fastened in holders, and a place for a napkin.

Margaret was almost crying over it.

"How I'd love to fill it!" she exclaimed.

"Do it the first time, just to show Kate Comstock what love is!" said Wesley. "Get up early in the morning and make one of those dresses to-morrow. Can't you make a plain gingham dress in a day? I'll pick a chicken, and you fry it and fix a little custard for the cup, and do it up brown. Go on, Maggie, you do it!"

"I never can," said Margaret. "I am slow as the itch about sewing, and these are not going to be plain dresses when it comes to making them. There are going to be edgings of plain green, pink, and brown to the bias strips, and tucks and pleats around the hips, fancy belts and collars, and all of it takes time."

"Then Kate Comstock's got to help," said Wesley. "Can the two of you make one, and get that lunch to-morrow?"

"Easy, but she'll never do it!"

"You see if she doesn't!" said Wesley. "You get up and cut it out, and soon as Elnora is gone I'll go after Kate myself. She'll take what I'll say better alone. But she'll come, and she'll help make the dress. These other things are our Christmas gifts to Elnora. She'll no doubt need them more now than she will then, and we can give them just as well. That's yours, and this is mine, or whichever way you choose."

Wesley untied a good brown umbrella and shook out the folds of a long, brown raincoat. Margaret dropped the hat, arose and took the coat. She tried it on, felt it, cooed over it and matched it with the umbrella.

"Did it look anything like rain to-night?" she inquired so anxiously that Wesley laughed.

"And this last bundle?" she said, dropping back in her chair, the coat still over her shoulders.

"I couldn't buy this much stuff for any other woman and nothing for my own," said Wesley. "It's Christmas for you, too, Margaret!" He shook out fold after fold of soft gray satiny goods that would look lovely against Margaret's pink cheeks and whitening hair.

"Oh, you old darling!" she exclaimed, and fled sobbing into his arms.

But she soon dried her eyes, raked together the coals in the cooking stove and boiled one of the dress patterns in salt water for half an hour. Wesley held the lamp while she hung the goods on the line to dry. Then she set the irons on the stove so they would be hot the first thing in the morning.

CHAPTER III. WHEREIN ELNORA VISITS THE BIRD WOMAN, AND OPENS A BANK ACCOUNT

Four o'clock the following morning Elnora was shelling beans. At six she fed the chickens and pigs, swept two of the rooms of the cabin, built a fire, and put on the kettle for breakfast. Then she climbed the narrow stairs to the attic she had occupied since a very small child, and dressed in the hated shoes and brown calico, plastered down her crisp curls, ate what breakfast she could, and pinning on her hat started for town.

"There is no sense in your going for an hour yet," said her mother.

"I must try to discover some way to earn those books," replied Elnora. "I am perfectly positive I shall not find them lying beside the road wrapped in tissue paper, and tagged with my name."

She went toward the city as on yesterday. Her perplexity as to where tuition and books were to come from was worse but she did not feel quite so badly. She never again would have to face all of it for the first time. There had been times yesterday when she had prayed to be hidden, or to drop dead, and neither had happened. "I believe the best way to get an answer to prayer is to work for it," muttered Elnora grimly.

Again she followed the trail to the swamp, rearranged her hair and left the tin pail. This time she folded a couple of sandwiches in the napkin, and tied them in a neat light paper parcel which she carried in her hand. Then she hurried along the road to Onabasha and found a book-store. There she asked the prices of the list of books that she needed, and learned that six dollars would not quite supply them. She anxiously inquired for second-hand books, but was told that the only way to secure them was from the last year's Freshmen. Just then Elnora felt that she positively could not approach any of those she supposed to be Sophomores and ask to buy their old books. The only balm the girl could see for the humiliation of yesterday was to appear that day with a set of new books.

"Do you wish these?" asked the clerk hurriedly, for the store was rapidly filling with school children wanting anything from a dictionary to a pen.

"Yes," gasped Elnora, "Oh, yes! But I cannot pay for them just now. Please let me take them, and I will pay for them on Friday, or return them as perfect as they are. Please trust me for them a few days."

"I'll ask the proprietor," he said. When he came back Elnora knew the answer before he spoke.

"I'm sorry," he said, "but Mr. Hann doesn't recognize your name. You are not a customer of ours, and he feels that he can't take the risk."

Elnora clumped out of the store, the thump of her heavy, shoes beating as a hammer on her brain. She tried two other dealers with the same result, and then in sick despair came into the street. What could she do? She was too frightened to think. Should she stay from school that day and canvass the homes appearing to belong to the wealthy, and try to sell beds of wild ferns, as she had suggested to Wesley Sinton? What would she dare ask for bringing in and planting a clump of ferns? How could she carry them? Would people buy them? She slowly moved past the hotel and then glanced around to see if there were a clock anywhere, for she felt sure the young people passing her constantly were on their way to school.

There it stood in a bank window in big black letters staring straight at her:

WANTED: CATERPILLARS, COCOONS, CHRYSALIDES, PUPAE CASES, BUTTERFLIES, MOTHS, INDIAN RELICS OF ALL KINDS. HIGHEST SCALE OF PRICES PAID IN CASH

Elnora caught the wicket at the cashier's desk with both hands to brace herself against disappointment.

"Who is it wants to buy cocoons, butterflies, and moths?" she panted.

"The Bird Woman," answered the cashier. "Have you some for sale?"

"I have some, I do not know if they are what she would want."

"Well, you had better see her," said the cashier. "Do you know where she lives?"

"Yes," said Elnora. "Would you tell me the time?"

"Twenty-one after eight," was the answer.

She had nine minutes to reach the auditorium or be late. Should she go to school, or to the Bird Woman? Several girls passed her walking swiftly and she remembered their faces. They were hurrying to school. Elnora caught the infection. She would see the Bird Woman at noon. Algebra came first, and that professor was kind. Perhaps she could slip to the superintendent and ask him for a book for the next lesson, and at noon—"Oh, dear Lord make it come true," prayed Elnora, at noon possibly she could sell some of those wonderful shining-winged things she had been collecting all her life around the outskirts of the Limberlost.

As she went down the long hall she noticed the professor of mathematics standing in the door of his recitation room. When she passed him he smiled and spoke to her.

"I have been watching for you," he said, and Elnora stopped bewildered.

"For me?" she questioned.

"Yes," said Professor Henley. "Step inside."

Elnora followed him into the room and closed the door behind them.

"At teachers' meeting last evening, one of the professors mentioned that a pupil had betrayed in class that she had expected her books to be furnished by the city. I thought possibly it was you. Was it?"

"Yes," breathed Elnora.

"That being the case," said Professor Henley, "it just occurred to me as you had expected that, you might require a little time to secure them, and you are too fine a mathematician to fall behind for want of supplies. So I telephoned one of our Sophomores to bring her last year's books this morning. I am sorry to say they are somewhat abused, but the text is all here. You can have them for two dollars, and pay when you are ready. Would you care to take them?"

Elnora sat suddenly, because she could not stand another instant. She reached both hands for the books, and said never a word. The professor was silent also. At last Eleanor arose, hugging those books to her heart as a mother clasps a baby.

"One thing more," said the professor. "You may pay your tuition quarterly. You need not bother about the first instalment this month. Any time in October will do."

It seemed as if Elnora's gasp of relief must have reached the soles of her brogans.

"Did any one ever tell you how beautiful you are!" she cried.

As the professor was lank, tow-haired and so near-sighted, that he peered at his pupils through spectacles, no one ever had.

"No," said Professor Henley, "I've waited some time for that; for which reason I shall appreciate it all the more. Come now, or we shall be late for opening exercises."

So Elnora entered the auditorium a second time. Her face was like the brightest dawn that ever broke over the Limberlost. No matter about the lumbering shoes and skimpy dress. No matter about anything, she had the books. She could take them home. In her garret she could commit them to memory, if need be. She could prove that clothes were not all. If the Bird Woman did not want any of the many different kinds of specimens she had collected, she was quite sure now she could sell ferns, nuts, and a great many things. Then, too, a girl made a place for her that morning, and several smiled and bowed. Elnora forgot everything save her books, and that she was where she could use them intelligently—everything except one little thing away back in her head. Her mother had known about the books and the tuition, and had not told her when she agreed to her coming.

At noon Elnora took her little parcel of lunch and started to the home of the Bird Woman. She must know about the specimens first and then she would walk to the suburbs somewhere and eat a few bites. She dropped the heavy iron knocker on the door of a big red log cabin, and her heart thumped at the resounding stroke.

"Is the Bird Woman at home?" she asked of the maid.

"She is at lunch," was the answer.

"Please ask her if she will see a girl from the Limberlost about some moths?" inquired Elnora.

"I never need ask, if it's moths," laughed the girl. "Orders are to bring any one with specimens right in. Come this way."

Elnora followed down the hall and entered a long room with high panelled wainscoting, old English fireplace with an overmantel and closets of peculiar china filling the corners. At a bare table of oak, yellow as gold, sat a woman Elnora often had watched and followed covertly around the Limberlost. The Bird Woman was holding out a hand of welcome.

"I heard!" she laughed. "A little pasteboard box, or just the mere word 'specimen,' passes you at my door. If it is moths I hope you have hundreds. I've been very busy all summer and unable to collect, and I need so many. Sit down and lunch with me, while we talk it over. From the Limberlost, did you say?"

"I live near the swamp," replied Elnora. "Since it's so cleared I dare go around the edge in daytime, though we are all afraid at night."

"What have you collected?" asked the Bird Woman, as she helped Elnora to sandwiches unlike any she ever before had tasted, salad that seemed to be made of many familiar things, and a cup of hot chocolate that would have delighted any hungry schoolgirl.

"I am afraid I am bothering you for nothing, and imposing on you," she said. "That 'collected' frightens me. I've only gathered. I always loved everything outdoors, so I made friends and playmates of them. When I learned that the moths die so soon, I saved them especially, because there seemed no wickedness in it."

"I have thought the same thing," said the Bird Woman encouragingly. Then because the girl could not eat until she learned about the moths, the Bird Woman asked Elnora if she knew what kinds she had.

"Not all of them," answered Elnora. "Before Mr. Duncan moved away he often saw me near the edge of the swamp and he showed me the box he had fixed for Freckles, and gave me the key. There were some books and things, so from that time on I studied and tried to take moths right, but I am afraid they are not what you want."

"Are they the big ones that fly mostly in June nights?" asked the Bird Woman.

"Yes," said Elnora. "Big gray ones with reddish markings, pale blue-green, yellow with lavender, and red and yellow."

"What do you mean by 'red and yellow?'" asked the Bird Woman so quickly that the girl almost jumped.

"Not exactly red," explained Elnora, with tremulous voice. "A reddish, yellowish brown, with canary-coloured spots and gray lines on their wings."

"How many of them?" It was the same quick question.

"I had over two hundred eggs," said Elnora, "but some of them didn't hatch, and some of the caterpillars died, but there must be at least a hundred perfect ones."

"Perfect! How perfect?" cried the Bird Woman.

"I mean whole wings, no down gone, and all their legs and antennae," faltered Elnora.

"Young woman, that's the rarest moth in America," said the Bird Woman solemnly. "If you have a hundred of them, they are worth a hundred dollars according to my list. I can use all that are not damaged."

"What if they are not pinned right," quavered Elnora.

"If they are perfect, that does not make the slightest difference. I know how to soften them so that I can put them into any shape I choose. Where are they? When may I see them?"

"They are in Freckles's old case in the Limberlost," said Elnora. "I couldn't carry many for fear of breaking them, but I could bring a few after school."

"You come here at four," said the Bird Woman, "and we will drive out with some specimen boxes, and a price list, and see what you have to sell. Are they your very own? Are you free to part with them?"

"They are mine," said Elnora. "No one but God knows I have them. Mr. Duncan gave me the books and the box. He told Freckles about me, and Freckles told him to give me all he left. He said for me to stick to the swamp and be brave, and my hour would come, and it has! I know most of them are all right, and oh, I do need the money!"

"Could you tell me?" asked the Bird Woman softly.

"You see the swamp and all the fields around it are so full," explained Elnora. "Every day I felt smaller and smaller, and I wanted to know more and more, and pretty soon I grew desperate, just as Freckles did. But I am better off than he was, for I have his books, and I have a mother; even if she doesn't care for me as other girls' mothers do for them, it's better than no one."

The Bird Woman's glance fell, for the girl was not conscious of how much she was revealing. Her eyes were fixed on a black pitcher filled with goldenrod in the centre of the table and she was saying what she thought.

"As long as I could go to the Brushwood school I was happy, but I couldn't go further just when things were the most interesting, so I was determined I'd come to high school and mother wouldn't consent. You see there's plenty of land, but father was drowned when I was a baby, and mother and I can't make money as men do. The taxes are higher every year, and she said it was too expensive. I wouldn't give her any rest, until at last she bought me this dress, and these shoes and I came. It was awful!"

"Do you live in that beautiful cabin at the northwest end of the swamp?" asked the Bird Woman.

"Yes," said Elnora.

"I remember the place and a story about it, now. You entered the high school yesterday?"

"Yes."

"It was rather bad?"

"Rather bad!" echoed Elnora.

The Bird Woman laughed.

"You can't tell me anything about that," she said. "I once entered a city school straight from the country. My dress was brown calico, and my shoes were heavy."

The tears began to roll down Elnora's cheeks.

"Did they——?" she faltered.

"They did!" said the Bird Woman. "All of it. I am sure they did not miss one least little thing."

Then she wiped away some tears that began coursing her cheeks, and laughed at the same time.

"Where are they now?" asked Elnora suddenly.

"They are widely scattered, but none of them have attained heights out of range. Some of the rich are poor, and some of the poor are rich. Some of the brightest died insane, and some of the dullest worked out high positions; some of the very worst to bear have gone out, and I frequently hear from others. Now I am here, able to remember it, and mingle laughter with what used to be all tears; for every day I have my beautiful work, and almost every day God sends some one like you to help me. What is your name, my girl?"

"Elnora Comstock," answered Elnora. "Yesterday on the board it changed to Cornstock, and for a minute I thought I'd die, but I can laugh over that already."

The Bird Woman arose and kissed her. "Finish your lunch," she said, "and I will bring my price lists, and make a memorandum of what you think you have, so I will know how many boxes to prepare. And remember this: What you are lies with you. If you are lazy, and accept your lot, you may live in it. If you are willing to work, you can write your name anywhere you choose, among the only ones who live beyond the grave in this world, the people who write books that help, make exquisite music, carve statues, paint pictures, and work for others. Never mind the calico dress, and the coarse shoes. Work at your books, and before long you will hear yesterday's tormentors boasting that they were once classmates of yours. 'I could a tale unfold'——!"

She laughingly left the room and Elnora sat thinking, until she remembered how hungry she was, so she ate the food, drank the hot chocolate and began to feel better.

Then the Bird Woman came back and showed Elnora a long printed slip giving a list of graduated prices for moths, butterflies, and dragonflies.

"Oh, do you want them!" exulted Elnora. "I have a few and I can get more by the thousand, with every colour in the world on their wings."

"Yes," said the Bird Woman, "I will buy them, also the big moth caterpillars that are creeping everywhere now, and the cocoons that they will spin just about this time. I have a sneaking impression that the mystery, wonder, and the urge of their pure beauty, are going to force me to picture and paint our moths and put them into a book for all the world to see and know. We Limberlost people must not be selfish with the wonders God has given to us. We must share with those poor cooped-up city people the best we can. To send them a beautiful book, that is the way, is it not, little new friend of mine?"

"Yes, oh yes!" cried Elnora. "And please God they find a way to earn the money to buy the books, as I have those I need so badly."

"I will pay good prices for all the moths you can find," said the Bird Woman, "because you see I exchange them with foreign collectors. I want a complete series of the moths of America to trade with a German scientist, another with a man in India, and another in Brazil. Others I can exchange with home collectors for those of California and Canada, so you see I can use all you can raise, or find. The banker will buy stone axes, arrow points, and Indian pipes. There was a teacher from the city grade schools here to-day for specimens. There is a fund to supply the ward buildings. I'll help you get in touch with that. They want leaves of different trees, flowers, grasses, moths, insects, birds' nests and anything about birds."

Elnora's eyes were blazing. "Had I better go back to school or open a bank account and begin being a millionaire? Uncle Wesley and I have a bushel of arrow points gathered, a stack of axes, pipes, skin-dressing tools, tubes and mortars. I don't know how I ever shall wait three hours."

"You must go, or you will be late," said the Bird Woman. "I will be ready at four."

After school closed Elnora, seated beside the Bird Woman, drove to Freckles's room in the Limberlost. One at a time the beautiful big moths were taken from the interior of the old black case. Not a fourth of them could be moved that night and it was almost dark when the last box was closed, the list figured, and into Elnora's trembling fingers were paid fifty-nine dollars and sixteen cents. Elnora clasped the money closely.

"Oh you beautiful stuff!" she cried. "You are going to buy the books, pay the tuition, and take me to high school."

Then because she was a woman, she sat on a log and looked at her shoes. Long after the Bird Woman drove away Elnora remained. She had her problem, and it was a big one. If she told her mother, would she take the money to pay the taxes? If she did not tell her, how could she account for the books, and things for which she would spend it. At last she counted out what she needed for the next day, placed the remainder in the farthest corner of the case, and locked the door. She then filled the front of her skirt from a heap of arrow points beneath the case and started home.

CHAPTER IV. WHEREIN THE SINTONS ARE DISAPPOINTED, AND MRS. COMSTOCK LEARNS THAT SHE CAN LAUGH

With the first streak of red above the Limberlost Margaret Sinton was busy with the gingham and the intricate paper pattern she had purchased. Wesley cooked the breakfast and worked until he thought Elnora would be gone, then he started to bring her mother.

"Now you be mighty careful," cautioned Margaret. "I don't know how she will take it."

"I don't either," said Wesley philosophically, "but she's got to take it some way. That dress has to be finished by school time in the morning."

Wesley had not slept well that night. He had been so busy framing diplomatic speeches to make to Mrs. Comstock that sleep had little chance with him. Every step nearer to her he approached his position seemed less enviable. By the time he reached the front gate and started down the walk between the rows of asters and lady slippers he was perspiring, and every plausible and convincing speech had fled his brain. Mrs. Comstock helped him. She met him at the door.

"Good morning," she said. "Did Margaret send you for something?"

"Yes," said Wesley. "She's got a job that's too big for her, and she wants you to help."

"Of course I will," said Mrs. Comstock. It was no one's affair how lonely the previous day had been, or how the endless hours of the present would drag. "What is she doing in such a rush?"

Now was his chance.

"She's making a dress for Elnora," answered, Wesley. He saw Mrs. Comstock's form straighten, and her face harden, so he continued hastily. "You see Elnora has been helping us at harvest time, butchering, and with unexpected visitors for years. We've made out that she's saved us a considerable sum, and as she wouldn't ever touch any pay for anything, we just went to town and got a few clothes we thought would fix her up a little for the high school. We want to get a dress done to-day mighty bad, but Margaret is slow about sewing, and she never can finish alone, so I came after you."

"And it's such a simple little matter, so dead easy; and all so between old friends like, that you can't look above your boots while you explain it," sneered Mrs. Comstock. "Wesley Sinton, what put the idea into your head that Elnora would take things bought with money, when she wouldn't take the money?"

Then Sinton's eyes came up straightly.

"Finding her on the trail last night sobbing as hard as I ever saw any one at a funeral. She wasn't complaining at all, but she's come to me all her life with her little hurts, and she couldn't hide how she'd been laughed at, twitted, and run face to face against the fact that there were books and tuition, unexpected, and nothing will ever make me believe you didn't know that, Kate Comstock."

"If any doubts are troubling you on that subject, sure I knew it! She was so anxious to try the world, I thought I'd just let her take a few knocks and see how she liked them."

"As if she'd ever taken anything but knocks all her life!" cried Wesley Sinton. "Kate Comstock, you are a heartless, selfish woman. You've never shown Elnora any real love in her life. If ever she finds out that thing you'll lose her, and it will serve you right."

"She knows it now," said Mrs. Comstock icily, "and she'll be home to-night just as usual."

"Well, you are a brave woman if you dared put a girl of Elnora's make through what she suffered yesterday, and will suffer again to-day, and let her know you did it on purpose. I admire your nerve. But I've watched this since Elnora was born, and I got enough. Things have come to a pass where they go better for her, or I interfere."

"As if you'd ever done anything but interfere all her life! Think I haven't watched you? Think I, with my heart raw in my breast, and too numb to resent it openly, haven't seen you and Mag Sinton trying to turn Elnora against me day after day? When did you ever tell her what her father meant to me? When did you ever try to make her see the wreck of my life, and what I've suffered? No indeed! Always it's been poor little abused Elnora, and cakes, kissing, extra clothes, and encouraging her to run to you with a pitiful mouth every time I tried to make a woman of her."

"Kate Comstock, that's unjust," cried Sinton. "Only last night I tried to show her the picture I saw the day she was born. I begged her to come to you and tell you pleasant what she needed, and ask you for what I happen to know you can well afford to give her."

"I can't!" cried Mrs. Comstock. "You know I can't!"

"Then get so you can!" said Wesley Sinton. "Any day you say the word you can sell six thousand worth of rare timber off this place easy. I'll see to clearing and working the fields cheap as dirt, for Elnora's sake. I'll buy you more cattle to fatten. All you've got to do is sign a lease, to pull thousands from the ground in oil, as the rest of us are doing all around you!"

"Cut down Robert's trees!" shrieked Mrs. Comstock. "Tear up his land! Cover everything with horrid, greasy oil! I'll die first."

"You mean you'll let Elnora go like a beggar, and hurt and mortify her past bearing. I've got to the place where I tell you plain what I am going to do. Maggie and I went to town last night, and we bought what things Elnora needs most urgent to make her look a little like the rest of the high school girls. Now here it is in plain English. You can help get these things ready, and let us give them to her as we want——"

"She won't touch them!" cried Mrs. Comstock.

"Then you can pay us, and she can take them as her right——"

"I won't!"

"Then I will tell Elnora just what you are worth, what you can afford, and how much of this she owns. I'll loan her the money to buy books and decent clothes, and when she is of age she can sell her share and pay me."

Mrs. Comstock gripped a chair-back and opened her lips, but no words came.

"And," Sinton continued, "if she is so much like you that she won't do that, I'll go to the county seat and lay complaint against you as her guardian before the judge. I'll swear to what you are worth, and how you are raising her, and have you discharged, or have the judge appoint some man who will see that she is comfortable, educated, and decent looking!"

"You—you wouldn't!" gasped Kate Comstock.

"I won't need to, Kate!" said Sinton, his heart softening the instant the hard words were said. "You won't show it, but you do love Elnora! You can't help it! You must see how she needs things; come help us fix them, and be friends. Maggie and I couldn't live without her, and you couldn't either. You've got to love such a fine girl as she is; let it show a little!"

"You can hardly expect me to love her," said Mrs. Comstock coldly. "But for her a man would stand back of me now, who would beat the breath out of your sneaking body for the cowardly thing with which you threaten me. After all I've suffered you'd drag me to court and compel me to tear up Robert's property. If I ever go they carry me. If they touch one tree, or put down one greasy old oil well, it will be over all I can shoot, before they begin. Now, see how quick you can clear out of here!"

"You won't come and help Maggie with the dress?"

For answer Mrs. Comstock looked around swiftly for some object on which to lay her hands. Knowing her temper, Wesley Sinton left with all the haste consistent with dignity. But he did not go home. He crossed a field, and in an hour brought another neighbour who was skilful with her needle. With sinking heart Margaret saw them coming.

"Kate is too busy to help to-day, she can't sew before to-morrow," said Wesley cheerfully as they entered.

That quieted Margaret's apprehension a little, though she had some doubts. Wesley prepared the lunch, and by four o'clock the dress was finished as far as it possibly could be until it was fitted on Elnora. If that did not entail too much work, it could be completed in two hours.

Then Margaret packed their purchases into the big market basket. Wesley took the hat, umbrella, and raincoat, and they went to Mrs. Comstock's. As they reached the step, Margaret spoke pleasantly to Mrs. Comstock, who sat reading just inside the door, but she did not answer and deliberately turned a leaf without looking up.

Wesley Sinton opened the door and went in followed by Margaret.

"Kate," he said, "you needn't take out your mad over our little racket on Maggie. I ain't told her a word I said to you, or you said to me. She's not so very strong, and she's sewed since four o'clock this morning to get this dress ready for to-morrow. It's done and we came down to try it on Elnora."

"Is that the truth, Mag Sinton?" demanded Mrs. Comstock.

"You heard Wesley say so," proudly affirmed Mrs. Sinton.

"I want to make you a proposition," said Wesley. "Wait till Elnora comes. Then we'll show her the things and see what she says."

"How would it do to see what she says without bribing her," sneered Mrs. Comstock.

"If she can stand what she did yesterday, and will to-day, she can bear 'most anything," said Wesley. "Put away the clothes if you want to, till we tell her."

"Well, you don't take this waist I'm working on," said Margaret, "for I have to baste in the sleeves and set the collar. Put the rest out of sight if you like."

Mrs. Comstock picked up the basket and bundles, placed them inside her room and closed the door.

Margaret threaded her needle and began to sew. Mrs. Comstock returned to her book, while Wesley fidgeted and raged inwardly. He could see that Margaret was nervous and almost in tears, but the lines in Mrs. Comstock's impassive face were set and cold. So they sat while the clock ticked off the time—one hour, two, dusk, and no Elnora. Just when Margaret and Wesley were discussing whether he had not better go to town to meet Elnora, they heard her coming up the walk. Wesley dropped his tilted chair and squared himself. Margaret gripped her sewing, and turned pleading eyes toward the door. Mrs. Comstock closed her book and grimly smiled.

"Mother, please open the door," called Elnora.

Mrs. Comstock arose, and swung back the screen. Elnora stepped in beside her, bent half double, the whole front of her dress gathered into a sort of bag filled with a heavy load, and one arm stacked high with books. In the dim light she did not see the Sintons.

"Please hand me the empty bucket in the kitchen, mother," she said. "I just had to bring these arrow points home, but I'm scared for fear I've spoiled my dress and will have to wash it. I'm to clean them, and take them to the banker in the morning, and oh, mother, I've sold enough stuff to pay for my books, my tuition, and maybe a dress and some lighter shoes besides. Oh, mother I'm so happy! Take the books and bring the bucket!"

Then she saw Margaret and Wesley. "Oh, glory!" she exulted. "I was just wondering how I'd ever wait to tell you, and here you are! It's too perfectly splendid to be true!"

"Tell us, Elnora," said Sinton.

"Well sir," said Elnora, doubling down on the floor and spreading out her skirt, "set the bucket here, mother. These points are brittle, and should be put in one at a time. If they are chipped I can't sell them. Well sir! I've had a time! You know I just had to have books. I tried three stores, and they wouldn't trust me, not even three days, I didn't know what in this world I could do quickly enough. Just when I was almost frantic I saw a sign in a bank window asking for caterpillars, cocoons, butterflies, arrow points, and everything. I went in, and it was this Bird Woman who wants the insects, and the banker wants the stones. I had to go to school then, but, if you'll believe it"—Elnora beamed on all of them in turn as she talked and slipped the arrow points from her dress to the pail—"if you'll believe it—but you won't, hardly, until you look at the books—there was the mathematics teacher, waiting at his door, and he had a set of books for me that he had telephoned a Sophomore to bring."

"How did he happen to do that, Elnora?" interrupted Sinton.

Elnora blushed.

"It was a fool mistake I made yesterday in thinking books were just handed out to one. There was a teachers' meeting last night and the history teacher told about that. Professor Henley thought of me. You know I told you what he said about my algebra, mother. Ain't I glad I studied out some of it myself this summer! So he telephoned and a girl brought the books. Because they are marked and abused some I get the whole outfit for two dollars. I can erase most of the marks, paste down the covers, and fix them so they look better. But I must hurry to the joy part. I didn't stop to eat, at noon, I just ran to the Bird Woman's, and I had lunch with her. It was salad, hot chocolate, and lovely things, and she wants to buy most every old scrap I ever gathered. She wants dragonflies, moths, butterflies, and he—the banker, I mean—wants everything Indian. This very night she came to the swamp with me and took away enough stuff to pay for the books and tuition, and to-morrow she is going to buy some more."

Elnora laid the last arrow point in the pail and arose, shaking leaves and bits of baked earth from her dress. She reached into her pocket, produced her money and waved it before their wondering eyes.

"And that's the joy part!" she exulted. "Put it up in the clock till morning, mother. That pays for the books and tuition and—" Elnora hesitated, for she saw the nervous grasp with which her mother's fingers closed on the bills. Then she continued, but more slowly and thinking before she spoke.

"What I get to-morrow pays for more books and tuition, and maybe a few, just a few, things to wear. These shoes are so dreadfully heavy and hot, and they make such a noise on the floor. There isn't another calico dress in the whole building, not among hundreds of us. Why, what is that? Aunt Margaret, what are you hiding in your lap?"

She snatched the waist and shook it out, and her face was beaming. "Have you taken to waists all fancy and buttoned in the back? I bet you this is mine!"

"I bet you so too," said Margaret Sinton. "You undress right away and try it on, and if it fits, it will be done for morning. There are some low shoes, too!"

Elnora began to dance. "Oh, you dear people!" she cried. "I can pay for them to-morrow night! Isn't it too splendid! I was just thinking on the way home that I certainly would be compelled to have cooler shoes until later, and I was wondering what I'd do when the fall rains begin."

"I meant to get you some heavy dress skirts and a coat then," said Mrs. Comstock.

"I know you said so!" cried Elnora. "But you needn't, now! I can buy every single stitch I need myself. Next summer I can gather up a lot more stuff, and all winter on the way to school. I am sure I can sell ferns, I know I can nuts, and the Bird Woman says the grade rooms want leaves, grasses, birds' nests, and cocoons. Oh, isn't this world lovely! I'll be helping with the tax, next, mother!"

Elnora waved the waist and started for the bedroom. When she opened the door she gave a little cry.

"What have you people been doing?" she demanded. "I never saw so many interesting bundles in all my life. I'm 'skeered' to death for fear I can't pay for them, and will have to give up something."

"Wouldn't you take them, if you could not pay for them, Elnora?" asked her mother instantly.

"Why, not unless you did," answered Elnora. "People have no right to wear things they can't afford, have they?"

"But from such old friends as Maggie and Wesley!" Mrs. Comstock's voice was oily with triumph.

"From them least of all," cried Elnora stoutly. "From a stranger sooner than from them, to whom I owe so much more than I ever can pay now."

"Well, you don't have to," said Mrs. Comstock. "Maggie just selected these things, because she is more in touch with the world, and has got such good taste. You can pay as long as your money holds out, and if there's more necessary, maybe I can sell the butcher a calf, or if things are too costly for us, of course, they can take them back. Put on the waist now, and then you can look over the rest and see if they are suitable, and what you want."

Elnora stepped into the adjoining room and closed the door. Mrs. Comstock picked up the bucket and started for the well with it. At the bedroom she paused.

"Elnora, were you going to wash these arrow points?"

"Yes. The Bird Woman says they sell better if they are clean, so it can be seen that there are no defects in them."

"Of course," said Mrs. Comstock. "Some of them seem quite baked. Shall I put them to soak? Do you want to take them in the morning?"

"Yes, I do," answered Elnora. "If you would just fill the pail with water."

Mrs. Comstock left the room. Wesley Sinton sat with his back to the window in the west end of the cabin which overlooked the well. A suppressed sound behind him caused him to turn quickly. Then he arose and leaned over Margaret.

"She's out there laughing like a blamed monkey!" he whispered indignantly.

"Well, she can't help it!" exclaimed Margaret.

"I'm going home!" said Wesley.

"Oh no, you are not!" retorted Margaret. "You are missing the point. The point is not how you look, or feel. It is to get these things in Elnora's possession past dispute. You go now, and to-morrow Elnora will wear calico, and Kate Comstock will return these goods. Right here I stay until everything we bought is Elnora's."

"What are you going to do?" asked Wesley.

"I don't know yet, myself," said Margaret.

Then she arose and peered from the window. At the well curb stood Katharine Comstock. The strain of the day was finding reaction. Her chin was in the air, she was heaving, shaking and strangling to suppress any sound. The word that slipped between Margaret Sinton's lips shocked Wesley until he dropped on his chair, and recalled her to her senses. She was fairly composed as she turned to Elnora, and began the fitting. When she had pinched, pulled, and patted she called, "Come see if you think this fits, Kate."

Mrs. Comstock had gone around to the back door and answered from the kitchen. "You know more about it than I do. Go ahead! I'm getting supper. Don't forget to allow for what it will shrink in washing!"

"I set the colours and washed the goods last night; it can be made to fit right now," answered Margaret.

When she could find nothing more to alter she told Elnora to heat some water. After she had done that the girl began opening packages.

The hat came first.

"Mother!" cried Elnora. "Mother, of course, you have seen this, but you haven't seen it on me. I must try it on."

"Don't you dare put that on your head until your hair is washed and properly combed," said Margaret.

"Oh!" cried Elnora. "Is that water to wash my hair? I thought it was to set the colour in another dress."

"Well, you thought wrong," said Margaret simply. "Your hair is going to be washed and brushed until it shines like copper. While it dries you can eat your supper, and this dress will be finished. Then you can put on your new ribbon, and your hat. You can try your shoes now, and if they don't fit, you and Wesley can drive to town and change them. That little round bundle on the top of the basket is your stockings."

Margaret sat down and began sewing swiftly, and a little later opened the machine, and ran several long scams.

Elnora returned in a few minutes holding up her skirts and stepping daintily in the new shoes.

"Don't soil them, honey, else you're sure they fit," cautioned Wesley.

"They seem just a trifle large, maybe," said Elnora dubiously, and Wesley knelt to feel. He and Margaret thought them a fit, and then Elnora appealed to her mother. Mrs. Comstock appeared wiping her hands on her apron. She examined the shoes critically.

"They seem to fit," she said, "but they are away too fine to walk country roads."

"I think so, too," said Elnora instantly. "We had better take these back and get a cheaper pair."

"Oh, let them go for this time," said Mrs. Comstock. "They are so pretty, I hate to part with them. You can get cheaper ones after this."

Wesley and Margaret scarcely breathed for a long time.

When Wesley went to do the feeding. Elnora set the table. When the water was hot, Margaret pinned a big towel around Elnora's shoulders and washed and dried the lovely hair according to the instructions she had been given the previous night. As the hair began to dry it billowed out in a sparkling sheen that caught the light and gleamed and flashed.

"Now, the idea is to let it stand naturally, just as the curl will make it. Don't you do any of that nasty, untidy snarling, Elnora," cautioned Margaret. "Wash it this way every two weeks while you are in school, shake it out, and dry it. Then part it in the middle and turn a front quarter on each side from your face. You tie the back at your neck with a string—so, and the ribbon goes in a big, loose bow. I'll show you." One after another Margaret Sinton tied the ribbons, creasing each of them so they could not be returned, as she explained that she was trying to find the colour most becoming. Then she produced the raincoat which carried Elnora into transports.

Mrs. Comstock objected. "That won't be warm enough for cold weather, and you can't afford it and a coat, too."

"I'll tell you what I thought," said Elnora. "I was planning on the way home. These coats are fine because they keep you dry. I thought I would get one, and a warm sweater to wear under it cold days. Then I always would be dry, and warm. The sweater only costs three dollars, so I could get it and the raincoat both for half the price of a heavy cloth coat."

"You are right about that," said Mrs. Comstock. "You can change more with the weather, too.

Keep the raincoat, Elnora."

"Wear it until you try the hat," said Margaret. "It will have to do until the dress is finished."

Elnora picked up the hat dubiously. "Mother, may I wear my hair as it is now?" she asked.

"Let me take a good look," said Katharine Comstock.

Heaven only knows what she saw. To Wesley and to Margaret the bright young face of Elnora, with its pink tints, its heavy dark brows, its bright blue-gray eyes, and its frame of curling reddish-brown hair was the sweetest sight on earth, and at that instant Elnora was radiant.

"So long as it's your own hair, and combed back as plain as it will go, I don't suppose it cuts much ice whether it's tied a little tighter or looser," conceded Mrs. Comstock. "If you stop right there, you may let it go at that."

Elnora set the hat on her head. It was only a wide tan straw with three exquisite peacock quills at one side. Margaret Sinton cried out, Wesley slapped his knee and sighed deeply while Mrs. Comstock stood speechless for a second.

"I wish you had asked the price before you put that on," she said impatiently. "We never can afford it."

"It's not so much as you think," said Margaret. "Don't you see what I did? I had them take off the quills, and put on some of those Phoebe Simms gave me from her peacocks. The hat will only cost you a dollar and a half."

She avoided Wesley's eyes, and looked straight at Mrs. Comstock. Elnora removed the hat to examine it.

"Why, they are those reddish-tan quills of yours!" she cried. "Mother, look how beautifully they are set on! I'd much rather have them than those from the store."

"So would I," said Mrs. Comstock. "If Margaret wants to spare them, that will make you a beautiful hat; dirt cheap, too! You must go past Mrs. Simms and show her. She would be pleased to see them."

Elnora sank into a chair and contemplated her toe. "Landy, ain't I a queen?" she murmured. "What else have I got?"

"Just a belt, some handkerchiefs, and a pair of top shoes for rainy days and colder weather," said Margaret.

"About those high shoes, that was my idea," said Wesley. "Soon as it rains, low shoes won't do, and by taking two pairs at once I could get them some cheaper. The low ones are two and the high ones two fifty, together three seventy-five. Ain't that cheap?"

"That's a real bargain," said Mrs. Comstock, "if they are good shoes, and they look it."

"This," said Wesley, producing the last package, "is your Christmas present from your Aunt Maggie. I got mine, too, but it's at the house. I'll bring it up in the morning."

He handed Margaret the umbrella, and she passed it over to Elnora who opened it and sat laughing under its shelter. Then she kissed both of them. She brought a pencil and a slip of paper to set down the prices they gave her of everything they had brought except the umbrella, added the sum, and said laughingly: "Will you please wait till to-morrow for the money? I will have it then, sure."

"Elnora," said Wesley Sinton. "Wouldn't you——"

"Elnora, hustle here a minute!" called Mrs. Comstock from the kitchen. "I need you!"

"One second, mother," answered Elnora, throwing off the coat and hat, and closing the umbrella as she ran. There were several errands to do in a hurry, and then supper. Elnora chattered incessantly, Wesley and Margaret talked all they could, while Mrs. Comstock said a word now and then, which was all she ever did. But Wesley Sinton was watching her, and time and again he saw a peculiar little twist around her mouth. He knew that for the first time in sixteen years she really was laughing over something. She had all she could do to preserve her usually sober face. Wesley knew what she was thinking.

After supper the dress was finished, the pattern for the next one discussed, and then the Sintons went home. Elnora gathered her treasures. When she started upstairs she stopped. "May I kiss you good-night, mother?" she asked lightly.

"Never mind any slobbering," said Mrs. Comstock. "I should think you'd lived with me long enough to know that I don't care for it."

"Well, I'd love to show you in some way how happy I am, and how I thank you."

"I wonder what for?" said Mrs. Comstock. "Mag Sinton chose that stuff and brought it here and you pay for it."

"Yes, but you seemed willing for me to have it, and you said you would help me if I couldn't pay all."

"Maybe I did," said Mrs. Comstock. "Maybe I did. I meant to get you some heavy dress skirts about Thanksgiving, and I still can get them. Go to bed, and for any sake don't begin mooning before a mirror, and make a dunce of yourself."

Mrs. Comstock picked up several papers and blew out the kitchen light. She stood in the middle of the sitting-room floor for a time and then went into her room and closed the door. Sitting on the edge of the bed she thought for a few minutes and then suddenly buried her face in the pillow and again heaved with laughter.

Down the road plodded Margaret and Wesley Sinton. Neither of them had words to utter their united thought.

"Done!" hissed Wesley at last. "Done brown! Did you ever feel like a bloomin', confounded donkey? How did the woman do it?"

"She didn't do it!" gulped Margaret through her tears. "She didn't do anything. She trusted to Elnora's great big soul to bring her out right, and really she was right, and so it had to bring her. She's a darling, Wesley! But she's got a time before her. Did you see Kate Comstock grab that money? Before six months she'll be out combing the Limberlost for bugs and arrow points to help pay the tax. I know her."

"Well, I don't!" exclaimed Sinton, "she's too many for me. But there is a laugh left in her yet! I didn't s'pose there was. Bet you a dollar, if we could see her this minute, she'd be chuckling over the way we got left."

Both of them stopped in the road and looked back.

"There's Elnora's light in her room," said Margaret. "The poor child will feel those clothes, and pore over her books till morning, but she'll look decent to go to school, anyway. Nothing is too big a price to pay for that."

"Yes, if Kate lets her wear them. Ten to one, she makes her finish the week with that old stuff!"

"No, she won't," said Margaret. "She'll hardly dare. Kate made some concessions, all right; big ones for her—if she did get her way in the main. She bent some, and if Elnora proves that she can walk out barehanded in the morning and come back with that much money in her pocket, an armful of books, and buy a turnout like that, she proves that she is of some consideration, and Kate's smart enough. She'll think twice before she'll do that. Elnora won't wear a calico dress to high school again. You watch and see if she does. She may have the best clothes she'll get for a time, for the least money, but she won't know it until she tries to buy goods herself at the same rates. Wesley, what about those prices? Didn't they shrink considerable?"

"You began it," said Wesley. "Those prices were all right. We didn't say what the goods cost us, we said what they would cost her. Surely, she's mistaken about being able to pay all that. Can she pick up stuff of that value around the Limberlost? Didn't the Bird Woman see her trouble, and just give her the money?"

"I don't think so," said Margaret. "Seems to me I've heard of her paying, or offering to pay those who would take the money, for bugs and butterflies, and I've known people who sold that banker Indian stuff. Once I heard that his pipe collection beat that of the Government at the Philadelphia Centennial. Those things have come to have a value."

"Well, there's about a bushel of that kind of valuables piled up in the woodshed, that belongs to Elnora. At least, I picked them up because she said she wanted them. Ain't it queer that she'd take to stones, bugs, and butterflies, and save them. Now they are going to bring her the very thing she wants the worst. Lord, but this is a funny world when you get to studying! Looks like things didn't all come by accident. Looks as if there was a plan back of it, and somebody driving that knows the road, and how to handle the lines. Anyhow, Elnora's in the wagon, and when I get out in the night and the dark closes around me, and I see the stars, I don't feel so cheap. Maggie, how the nation did Kate Comstock do that?"

"You will keep on harping, Wesley. I told you she didn't do it. Elnora did it! She walked in and took things right out of our hands. All Kate had to do was to enjoy having it go her way, and she was cute enough to put in a few questions that sort of guided Elnora. But I don't know, Wesley. This thing makes me think, too. S'pose we'd taken Elnora when she was a baby, and we'd heaped on her all the love we can't on our own, and we'd coddled, petted, and shielded her, would she have made the woman that living alone, learning to think for herself, and taking all the knocks Kate Comstock could give, have made of her?"

"You bet your life!" cried Wesley, warmly. "Loving anybody don't hurt them. We wouldn't have done anything but love her. You can't hurt a child loving it. She'd have learned to work, to study, and grown into a woman with us, without suffering like a poor homeless dog."

"But you don't see the point, Wesley. She would have grown into a fine woman with us; but as we would have raised her, would her heart ever have known the world as it does now? Where's the anguish, Wesley, that child can't comprehend? Seeing what she's seen of her mother hasn't hardened her. She can understand any mother's sorrow. Living life from the rough side has only broadened her. Where's the girl or boy burning with shame, or struggling to find a way, that will cross Elnora's path and not get a lift from her? She's had the knocks, but there'll never be any of the thing you call 'false pride' in her. I guess we better keep out. Maybe Kate Comstock knows what she's doing. Sure as you live, Elnora has grown bigger on knocks than she would on love."

"I don't s'pose there ever was a very fine point to anything but I missed it," said Wesley, "because I am blunt, rough, and have no book learning to speak of. Since you put it into words I see what you mean, but it's dinged hard on Elnora, just the same. And I don't keep out. I keep watching closer than ever. I got my slap in the face, but if I don't miss my guess, Kate Comstock learned her lesson, same as I did. She learned that I was in earnest, that I would haul her to court if she didn't loosen up a bit, and she'll loosen. You see if she doesn't. It may come hard, and the hinges creak, but she'll fix Elnora decent after this, if Elnora doesn't prove that she can fix herself. As for me, I found out that what I was doing was as much for myself as for Elnora. I wanted her to take those things from us, and love us for giving them. It didn't work, and but for you, I'd messed the whole thing and stuck like a pig in crossing a bridge. But you helped me out; Elnora's got the clothes, and by morning, maybe I won't grudge Kate the only laugh she's had in sixteen years. You been showing me the way quite a spell now, ain't you, Maggie?"

In her attic Elnora lighted two candles, set them on her little table, stacked the books, and put away the precious clothes. How lovingly she hung the hat and umbrella, folded the raincoat, and spread the new dress over a chair. She fingered the ribbons, and tried to smooth the creases from them. She put away the hose neatly folded, touched the handkerchiefs, and tried the belt. Then she slipped into her white nightdress, shook down her hair that it might become thoroughly dry, set a chair before the table, and reverently opened one of the books. A stiff draught swept the attic, for it stretched the length of the cabin, and had a window in each end. Elnora arose and going to the east window closed it. She stood for a minute looking at the stars, the sky, and the dark outline of the straggling trees of the rapidly dismantling Limberlost. In the region of her case a tiny point of light flashed and disappeared. Elnora straightened and wondered. Was it wise to leave her precious money there? The light flashed once more, wavered a few seconds, and died out. The girl waited. She did not see it again, so she turned to her books.

In the Limberlost the hulking figure of a man sneaked down the trail.

"The Bird Woman was at Freckles's room this evening," he muttered. "Wonder what for?"

He left the trail, entered the enclosure still distinctly outlined, and approached the case. The first point of light flashed from the tiny electric lamp on his vest. He took a duplicate key from his pocket, felt for the padlock and opened it. The door swung wide. The light flashed the second time. Swiftly his glance swept the interior.

"'Bout a fourth of her moths gone. Elnora must have been with the Bird Woman and given them to her." Then he stood tense. His keen eyes discovered the roll of bills hastily thrust back in the bottom of the case. He snatched them up, shut off the light, relocked the case by touch, and swiftly went down the trail. Every few seconds he paused and listened intently. Just as he reached the road, a second figure approached him.

"Is it you, Pete?" came the whispered question.

"Yes," said the first man.

"I was coming down to take a peep, when I saw your flash," he said. "I heard the Bird Woman had been at the case to-day. Anything doing?"

"Not a thing," said Pete. "She just took away about a fourth of the moths. Probably had the Comstock girl getting them for her. Heard they were together. Likely she'll get the rest to-morrow. Ain't picking gettin' bare these days?"

"Well, I should say so," said the second man, turning back in disgust. "Coming home, now?"

"No, I am going down this way," answered Pete, for his eyes caught the gleam from the window of the Comstock cabin, and he had a desire to learn why Elnora's attic was lighted at that hour.

He slouched down the road, occasionally feeling the size of the roll he had not taken time to count.

The attic was too long, the light too near the other end, and the cabin stood much too far back from the road. He could see nothing although he climbed the fence and walked back opposite the window. He knew Mrs. Comstock was probably awake, and that she sometimes went to the swamp behind her home at night. At times a cry went up from that locality that paralyzed any one near, or sent them fleeing as if for life. He did not care to cross behind the cabin. He returned to the road, passed, and again climbed the fence. Opposite the west window he could see Elnora. She sat before a small table reading from a book between two candles. Her hair fell in a bright sheen around her, and with one hand she lightly shook, and tossed it as she studied. The man stood out in the night and watched.

For a long time a leaf turned at intervals and the hair-drying went on. The man drew nearer. The picture grew more beautiful as he approached. He could not see so well as he desired, for the screen was of white mosquito netting, and it angered him. He cautiously crept closer. The elevation shut off his view. Then he remembered the large willow tree shading the well and branching across the window fit the west end of the cabin. From childhood Elnora had stepped from the sill to a limb and slid down the slanting trunk of the tree. He reached it and noiselessly swung himself up. Three steps out on the big limb the man shuddered. He was within a few feet of the girl.

He could see the throb of her breast under its thin covering and smell the fragrance of the tossing hair. He could see the narrow bed with its pieced calico cover, the whitewashed walls with gay lithographs, and every crevice stuck full of twigs with dangling cocoons. There were pegs for the few clothes, the old chest, the little table, the two chairs, the uneven floor covered with rag rugs and braided corn husk. But nothing was worth a glance except the perfect face and form within reach by one spring through the rotten mosquito bar. He gripped the limb above that on which he stood, licked his lips, and breathed through his throat to be sure he was making no sound. Elnora closed the book and laid it aside. She picked up a towel, and turning the gathered ends of her hair rubbed them across it, and dropping the towel on her lap, tossed the hair again. Then she sat in deep thought. By and by words began to come softly. Near as he was the man could not hear at first. He bent closer and listened intently.

"—ever could be so happy," murmured the soft voice. "The dress is so pretty, such shoes, the coat, and everything. I won't have to be ashamed again, not ever again, for the Limberlost is full of precious moths, and I always can collect them. The Bird Woman will buy more to-morrow, and the next day, and the next. When they are all gone, I can spend every minute gathering cocoons, and hunting other things I can sell. Oh, thank God, for my precious, precious money. Why, I didn't pray in vain after all! I thought when I asked the Lord to hide me, there in that big hall, that He wasn't doing it, because I wasn't covered from sight that instant. But I'm hidden now, I feel that." Elnora lifted her eyes to the beams above her. "I don't know much about praying properly," she muttered, "but I do thank you, Lord, for hiding me in your own time and way."

Her face was so bright that it shone with a white radiance. Two big tears welled from her eyes, and rolled down her smiling cheeks. "Oh, I do feel that you have hidden me," she breathed. Then she blew out the lights, and the little wooden bed creaked under her weight.

Pete Corson dropped from the limb and found his way to the road. He stood still a long time, then started back to the Limberlost. A tiny point of light flashed in the region of the case. He stopped with an oath.

"Another hound trying to steal from a girl," he exclaimed. "But it's likely he thinks if he gets anything it will be from a woman who can afford it, as I did."

He went on, but beside the fences, and very cautiously.

"Swamp seems to be alive to-night," he muttered. "That's three of us out."

He entered a deep place at the northwest corner, sat on the ground and taking a pencil from his pocket, he tore a leaf from a little notebook, and laboriously wrote a few lines by the light he carried. Then he went back to the region of the case and waited. Before his eyes swept the vision of the slender white creature with tossing hair. He smiled, and worshipped it, until a distant rooster faintly announced dawn.

Then he unlocked the case again, and replaced the money, laid the note upon it, and went back to concealment, where he remained until Elnora came down the trail in the morning, appearing very lovely in her new dress and hat.

CHAPTER V. WHEREIN ELNORA RECEIVES A WARNING, AND BILLY APPEARS ON THE SCENE

It would be difficult to describe how happy Elnora was that morning as she hurried through her work, bathed and put on the neat, dainty gingham dress, and the tan shoes. She had a struggle with her hair. It crinkled, billowed, and shone, and she could not avoid seeing the becoming frame it made around her face. But in deference to her mother's feelings the girl set her teeth, and bound her hair closely to her head with a shoe-string. "Not to be changed at the case," she told herself.

That her mother was watching she was unaware. Just as she picked up the beautiful brown ribbon Mrs. Comstock spoke.

"You had better let me tie that. You can't reach behind yourself and do it right."

Elnora gave a little gasp. Her mother never before had proposed to do anything for the girl that by any possibility she could do herself. Her heart quaked at the thought of how her mother would arrange that bow, but Elnora dared not refuse. The offer was too precious. It might never be made again.

"Oh thank you!" said the girl, and sitting down she held out the ribbon.

Her mother stood back and looked at her critically.

"You haven't got that like Mag Sinton had it last night," she announced. "You little idiot! You've tried to plaster it down to suit me, and you missed it. I liked it away better as Mag fixed it, after I saw it. You didn't look so peeled."

"Oh mother, mother!" laughed Elnora, with a half sob in her voice.

"Hold still, will you?" cried Mrs. Comstock. "You'll be late, and I haven't packed your dinner yet."

She untied the string and shook out the hair. It rose with electricity and clung to her fingers and hands. Mrs. Comstock jumped back as if bitten. She knew that touch. Her face grew white, and her eyes angry.

"Tie it yourself," she said shortly, "and then I'll put on the ribbon. But roll it back loose like Mag did. It looked so pretty that way."

Almost fainting Elnora stood before the glass, divided off the front parts of her hair, and rolled them as Mrs. Sinton had done; tied it at the nape of her neck, then sat while her mother arranged the ribbon.

"If I pull it down till it comes tight in these creases where she had it, it will be just right, won't it?" queried Mrs. Comstock, and the amazed Elnora stammered,

"Yes."

When she looked in the glass the bow was perfectly tied, and how the gold tone of the brown did match the lustre of the shining hair! "That's pretty," commented Mrs. Comstock's soul, but her stiff lips had said all that could be forced from them for once. Just then Wesley Sinton came to the door.

"Good morning," he cried heartily. "Elnora, you look a picture! My, but you're sweet! If any of the city boys get sassy you tell your Uncle Wesley, and he'll horsewhip them. Here's your Christmas present from me." He handed Elnora the leather lunch box, with her name carved across the strap in artistic lettering.

"Oh Uncle Wesley!" was all Elnora could say.

"Your Aunt Maggie filled it for me for a starter," he said. "Now, if you are ready, I'm going to drive past your way and you can ride almost to Onabasha with me, and save the new shoes that much."

Elnora was staring at the box. "Oh I hope it isn't impolite to open it before you," she said. "I just feel as if I must see inside."

"Don't you stand on formality with the neighbours," laughed Sinton. "Look in your box if you want to!"

Elnora slipped the strap and turned back the lid.

This disclosed the knife, fork, napkin, and spoon, the milk flask, and the interior packed with dainty sandwiches wrapped in tissue paper, and the little compartments for meat, salad, and the custard cup.

"Oh mother!" cried Elnora. "Oh mother, isn't it fine? What made you think of it, Uncle Wesley? How will I ever thank you? No one will have a finer lunch box than I. Oh I do thank you! That's the nicest gift I ever had. How I love Christmas in September!"

"It's a mighty handy thing," assented Mrs. Comstock, taking in every detail with sharp eyes. "I guess you are glad now you went and helped Mag and Wesley when you could, Elnora?"

"Deedy, yes," laughed Elnora, "and I'm going again first time they have a big day if I stay from school to do it."

"You'll do no such thing!" said the delighted Sinton. "Come now, if you're going!"

"If I ride, can you spare me time to run into the swamp to my box a minute?" asked Elnora.

The light she had seen the previous night troubled her.

"Sure," said Wesley largely. So they drove away and left a white-faced woman watching them from the door, her heart a little sorer than usual.

"I'd give a pretty to hear what he'll say to her!" she commented bitterly. "Always sticking in, always doing things I can't ever afford. Where on earth did he get that thing and what did it cost?"

Then she entered the cabin and began the day's work, but mingled with the brooding bitterness of her soul was the vision of a sweet young face, glad with a gladness never before seen on it, and over and over she repeated: "I wonder what he'll say to her!"

What he said was that she looked as fresh and sweet as a posy, and to be careful not to step in the mud or scratch her shoes when she went to the case.

Elnora found her key and opened the door. Not where she had placed it, but conspicuously in front lay her little heap of bills, and a crude scrawl of writing beside it. Elnora picked up the note in astonishment.

DERE ELNORY,

the lord amighty is hiding you all right done you ever dout it this money of yourn was took for some time las nite but it is returned with intres for god sake done ever come to the swamp at nite or late evnin or mornin or far in any time sompin worse an you know could git you

A FREND.

Elnora began to tremble. She hastily glanced around. The damp earth before the case had been trodden by large, roughly shod feet. She caught up the money and the note, thrust them into her guimpe, locked the case, and ran to the road.

She was so breathless and her face so white Sinton noticed it.

"What in the world's the matter, Elnora?" he asked.

"I am half afraid!" she panted.

"Tut, tut, child!" said Wesley Sinton. "Nothing in the world to be afraid of. What happened?"

"Uncle Wesley," said Elnora, "I had more money than I brought home last night, and I put it in my case. Some one has been there. The ground is all trampled, and they left this note."

"And took your money, I'll wager," said Sinton angrily.

"No," answered Elnora. "Read the note, and oh Uncle Wesley, tell me what it means!"

Sinton's face was a study. "I don't know what it means," he said. "Only one thing is clear. It means some beast who doesn't really want to harm you has got his eye on you, and he is telling you plain as he can, not to give him a chance. You got to keep along the roads, in the open, and not let the biggest moth that ever flew toll you out of hearing of us, or your mother. It means that, plain and distinct."

"Just when I can sell them! Just when everything is so lovely on account of them! I can't! I can't stay away from the swamp. The Limberlost is going to buy the books, the clothes, pay the tuition, and even start a college fund. I just can't!"

"You've got to," said Sinton. "This is plain enough. You go far in the swamp at your own risk, even in daytime."

"Uncle Wesley," said the girl, "last night before I went to bed, I was so happy I tried to pray, and I thanked God for hiding me 'under the shadow of His wing.' But how in the world could any one know it?"

Wesley Sinton's heart leaped in his breast. His face was whiter than the girl's now.

"Were you praying out loud, honey?" he almost whispered.

"I might have said words," answered Elnora. "I know I do sometimes. I've never had any one to talk with, and I've played with and talked to myself all my life. You've caught me at it often, but it always makes mother angry when she does. She says it's silly. I forget and do it, when I'm alone. But Uncle Wesley, if I said anything last night, you know it was the merest whisper, because I'd have been so afraid of waking mother. Don't you see? I sat up late, and studied two lessons."

Sinton was steadying himself "I'll stop and examine the case as I come back," he said. "Maybe I can find some clue. That other—that was just accidental. It's a common expression. All the preachers use it. If I tried to pray, that would be the very first thing I'd say."

The colour returned to Elnora's face.

"Did you tell your mother about this money, Elnora?" he asked.

"No, I didn't," said Elnora. "It's dreadful not to, but I was afraid. You see they are clearing the swamp so fast. Every year it grows more difficult to find things, and Indian stuff becomes scarcer. I want to graduate, and that's four years unless I can double on the course. That means twenty dollars tuition each year, and new books, and clothes. There won't ever be so much at one time again, that I know. I just got to hang to my money. I was afraid to tell her, for fear she would want it for taxes, and she really must sell a tree or some cattle for that, mustn't she, Uncle Wesley?"

"On your life, she must!" said Wesley. "You put your little wad in the bank all safe, and never mention it to a living soul. It doesn't seem right, but your case is peculiar. Every word you say is a true word. Each year you will find less in the swamp, and things everywhere will be scarcer. If you ever get a few dollars ahead, that can start your college fund. You know you are going to college, Elnora!"

"Of course I am," said Elnora. "I settled that as soon as I knew what a college was. I will put all my money in the bank, except what I owe you. I'll pay that now."

"If your arrows are heavy," said Wesley, "I'll drive on to Onabasha with you."

"But they are not. Half of them were nicked, and this little box held all the good ones. It's so surprising how many are spoiled when you wash them."

"What does he pay?"

"Ten cents for any common perfect one, fifty for revolvers, a dollar for obsidian, and whatever is right for enormous big ones."

"Well, that sounds fair," said Sinton. "You can come down Saturday and wash the stuff at our house, and I'll take it in when we go marketing in the afternoon."

Elnora jumped from the carriage. She soon found that with her books, her lunch box, and the points she had a heavy load. She had almost reached the bridge crossing the culvert when she heard distressed screams of a child. Across an orchard of the suburbs came a small boy, after him a big dog, urged by a man in the background. Elnora's heart was with the small fleeing figure in any event whatever. She dropped her load on the bridge, and with practised hand flung a stone at the dog. The beast curled double with a howl. The boy reached the fence, and Elnora was there to help him over. As he touched the top she swung him to the ground, but he clung to her, clasping her tightly, sobbing with fear. Elnora helped him to the bridge, and sat with him in her arms. For a time his replies to her questions were indistinct, but at last he became quieter and she could understand.

He was a mite of a boy, nothing but skin-covered bones, his burned, freckled face in a mortar of tears and dust, his clothing unspeakably dirty, one great toe in a festering mass from a broken nail, and sores all over the visible portions of the small body.

"You won't let the mean old thing make his dog get me!" he wailed.

"Indeed no," said Elnora, holding him closely.

"You wouldn't set a dog on a boy for just taking a few old apples when you fed 'em to pigs with a shovel every day, would you?"

"No, I would not," said Elnora hotly.

"You'd give a boy all the apples he wanted, if he hadn't any breakfast, and was so hungry he was all twisty inside, wouldn't you?"

"Yes, I would," said Elnora.

"If you had anything to eat you would give me something right now, wouldn't you?"

"Yes," said Elnora. "There's nothing but just stones in the package. But my dinner is in that case. I'll gladly divide."

She opened the box. The famished child gave a little cry and reached both hands. Elnora caught them back.

"Did you have any supper?"

"No."

"Any dinner yesterday?"

"An apple and some grapes I stole."

"Whose boy are you?"

"Old Tom Billings's."

"Why doesn't your father get you something to eat?"

"He does most days, but he's drunk now."

"Hush, you must not!" said Elnora. "He's your father!"

"He's spent all the money to get drunk, too," said the boy, "and Jimmy and Belle are both crying for breakfast. I'd a got out all right with an apple for myself, but I tried to get some for them and the dog got too close. Say, you can throw, can't you?"

"Yes," admitted Elnora. She poured half the milk into the cup. "Drink this," she said, holding it to him.

The boy gulped the milk and swore joyously, gripping the cup with shaking fingers.

"Hush!" cried Elnora. "That's dreadful!"

"What's dreadful?"

"To say such awful words."

"Huh! pa says worser 'an that every breath he draws."

Elnora saw that the child was older than she had thought. He might have been forty judging by his hard, unchildish expression.

"Do you want to be like your father?"

"No, I want to be like you. Couldn't a angel be prettier 'an you. Can I have more milk?"

Elnora emptied the flask. The boy drained the cup. He drew a breath of satisfaction as he gazed into her face.

"You wouldn't go off and leave your little boy, would you?" he asked.

"Did some one go away and leave you?"

"Yes, my mother went off and left me, and left Jimmy and Belle, too," said the boy. "You wouldn't leave your little boy, would you?"

"No."

The boy looked eagerly at the box. Elnora lifted a sandwich and uncovered the fried chicken. The boy gasped with delight.

"Say, I could eat the stuff in the glass and the other box and carry the bread and the chicken to Jimmy and Belle," he offered.

Elnora silently uncovered the custard with preserved cherries on top and handed it and the spoon to the child. Never did food disappear faster. The salad went next, and a sandwich and half a chicken breast followed.

"I better leave the rest for Jimmy and Belle," he said, "they're 'ist fightin' hungry."

Elnora gave him the remainder of the carefully prepared lunch. The boy clutched it and ran with a sidewise hop like a wild thing. She covered the dishes and cup, polished the spoon, replaced it, and closed the case. She caught her breath in a tremulous laugh.

"If Aunt Margaret knew that, she'd never forgive me," she said. "It seems as if secrecy is literally forced upon me, and I hate it. What shall I do for lunch? I'll have to sell my arrows and keep enough money for a restaurant sandwich."

So she walked hurriedly into town, sold her points at a good price, deposited her funds, and went away with a neat little bank book and the note from the Limberlost carefully folded inside. Elnora passed down the hall that morning, and no one paid the slightest attention to her. The truth was she looked so like every one else that she was perfectly inconspicuous. But in the coat room there were members of her class. Surely no one intended it, but the whisper was too loud.

"Look at the girl from the Limberlost in the clothes that woman gave her!"

Elnora turned on them. "I beg your pardon," she said unsteadily, "I couldn't help hearing that! No one gave me these clothes. I paid for them myself."

Some one muttered, "Pardon me," but incredulous faces greeted her.

Elnora felt driven. "Aunt Margaret selected them, and she meant to give them to me," she explained, "but I wouldn't take them. I paid for them myself." There was silence.

"Don't you believe me?" panted Elnora.

"Really, it is none of our affair," said another girl. "Come on, let's go."

Elnora stepped before the girl who had spoken. "You have made this your affair," she said, "because you told a thing which was not true. No one gave me what I am wearing. I paid for my clothes myself with money I earned selling moths to the Bird Woman. I just came from the bank where I deposited what I did not use. Here is my credit." Elnora drew out and offered the little red book. "Surely you will believe that," she said.

"Why of course," said the girl who first had spoken. "We met such a lovely woman in Brownlee's store, and she said she wanted our help to buy some things for a girl, and that's how we came to know."

"Dear Aunt Margaret," said Elnora, "it was like her to ask you. Isn't she splendid?"

"She is indeed," chorused the girls. Elnora set down her lunch box and books, unpinned her hat, hanging it beside the others, and taking up the books she reached to set the box in its place and dropped it. With a little cry she snatched at it and caught the strap on top. That pulled from the fastening, the cover unrolled, the box fell away as far as it could, two porcelain lids rattled on the floor, and the one sandwich rolled like a cartwheel across the room. Elnora lifted a ghastly face. For once no one laughed. She stood an instant staring.

"It seems to be my luck to be crucified at every point of the compass," she said at last. "First two days you thought I was a pauper, now you will think I'm a fraud. All of you will believe I bought an expensive box, and then was too poor to put anything but a restaurant sandwich in it. You must stop till I prove to you that I'm not."

Elnora gathered up the lids, and kicked the sandwich into a corner.

"I had milk in that bottle, see! And custard in the cup. There was salad in the little box, fried chicken in the large one, and nut sandwiches in the tray. You can see the crumbs of all of them. A man set a dog on a child who was so starved he was stealing apples. I talked with him, and I thought I could bear hunger better, he was such a little boy, so I gave him my lunch, and got the sandwich at the restaurant."

Elnora held out the box. The girls were laughing by that time. "You goose," said one, "why didn't you give him the money, and save your lunch?"

"He was such a little fellow, and he really was hungry," said Elnora. "I often go without anything to eat at noon in the fields and woods, and never think of it."

She closed the box and set it beside the lunches of other country pupils. While her back was turned, into the room came the girl of her encounter on the first day, walked to the rack, and with an exclamation of approval took down Elnora's hat.

"Just the thing I have been wanting!" she said. "I never saw such beautiful quills in all my life. They match my new broadcloth to perfection. I've got to have that kind of quills for my hat. I never saw the like! Whose is it, and where did it come from?"

No one said a word, for Elnora's question, the reply, and her answer, had been repeated. Every one knew that the Limberlost girl had come out ahead and Sadie Reed had not been amiable, when the little flourish had been added to Elnora's name in the algebra class. Elnora's swift glance was pathetic, but no one helped her. Sadie Reed glanced from the hat to the faces around her and wondered.

"Why, this is the Freshman section, whose hat is it?" she asked again, this time impatiently.

"That's the tassel of the cornstock," said Elnora with a forced laugh.

The response was genuine. Every one shouted. Sadie Reed blushed, but she laughed also.

"Well, it's beautiful," she said, "especially the quills. They are exactly what I want. I know I don't deserve any kindness from you, but I do wish you would tell me at whose store you found those quills."

"Gladly!" said Elnora. "You can't buy quills like those at a store. They are from a living bird. Phoebe Simms gathers them in her orchard as her peacocks shed them. They are wing quills from the males."

Then there was perfect silence. How was Elnora to know that not a girl there would have told that?

"I haven't a doubt but I can get you some," she offered. "She gave Aunt Margaret a large bunch, and those are part of them. I am quite sure she has more, and would spare some."

Sadie Reed laughed shortly. "You needn't trouble," she said, "I was fooled. I thought they were expensive quills. I wanted them for a twenty-dollar velvet toque to match my new suit. If they are gathered from the ground, really, I couldn't use them."

"Only in spots!" said Elnora. "They don't just cover the earth. Phoebe Simms's peacocks are the only ones within miles of Onabasha, and they moult but once a year. If your hat cost only twenty dollars, it's scarcely good enough for those quills. You see, the Almighty made and coloured those Himself; and He puts the same kind on Phoebe Simms's peacocks that He put on the head of the family in the forests of Ceylon, away back in the beginning. Any old manufactured quill from New York or Chicago will do for your little twenty-dollar hat. You should have something infinitely better than that to be worthy of quills that are made by the Creator."

How those girls did laugh! One of them walked with Elnora to the auditorium, sat beside her during exercises, and tried to talk whenever she dared, to keep Elnora from seeing the curious and admiring looks bent upon her.

For the brown-eyed boy whistled, and there was pantomime of all sorts going on behind Elnora's back that day. Happy with her books, no one knew how much she saw, and from her absorption in her studies it was evident she cared too little to notice.

After school she went again to the home of the Bird Woman, and together they visited the swamp and carried away more specimens. This time Elnora asked the Bird Woman to keep the money until noon of the next day, when she would call for it and have it added to her bank account. She slowly walked home, for the visit to the swamp had brought back full force the experience of the morning. Again and again she examined the crude little note, for she did not know what it meant, yet it bred vague fear. The only thing of which Elnora knew herself afraid was her mother; when with wild eyes and ears deaf to childish pleading, she sometimes lost control of herself in the night and visited the pool where her husband had sunk before her, calling his name in unearthly tones and begging of the swamp to give back its dead.

CHAPTER VI. WHEREIN MRS. COMSTOCK INDULGES IN "FRILLS," AND BILLY REAPPEARS

It was Wesley Sinton who really wrestled with Elnora's problem while he drove about his business. He was not forced to ask himself what it meant; he knew. The old Corson gang was still holding together. Elder members who had escaped the law had been joined by a younger brother of Jack's, and they met in the thickest of the few remaining fast places of the swamp to drink, gamble, and loaf. Then suddenly, there would be a robbery in some country house where a farmer that day had sold his wheat or corn and not paid a visit to the bank; or in some neighbouring village.

The home of Mrs. Comstock and Elnora adjoined the swamp. Sinton's land lay next, and not another residence or man easy to reach in case of trouble. Whoever wrote that note had some human kindness in his breast, but the fact stood revealed that he feared his strength if Elnora were delivered into his hands. Where had he been the previous night when he heard that prayer? Was that the first time he had been in such proximity? Sinton drove fast, for he wished to reach the swamp before Elnora and the Bird Woman would go there.

At almost four he came to the case, and dropping on his knees studied the ground, every sense alert. He found two or three little heel prints. Those were made by Elnora or the Bird Woman. What Sinton wanted to learn was whether all the remainder were the footprints of one man. It was easily seen, they were not. There were deep, even tracks made by fairly new shoes, and others where a well-worn heel cut deeper on the inside of the print than at the outer edge. Undoubtedly some of Corson's old gang were watching the case, and the visits of the women to it. There was no danger that any one would attack the Bird Woman. She never went to the swamp at night, and on her trips in the daytime, every one knew that she carried a revolver, understood how to use it, and pursued her work in a fearless manner.

Elnora, prowling around the swamp and lured into the interior by the flight of moths and butterflies; Elnora, without father, money, or friends save himself, to defend her—Elnora was a different proposition. For this to happen just when the Limberlost was bringing the very desire of her heart to the girl, it was too bad.

Sinton was afraid for her, yet he did not want to add the burden of fear to Katharine Comstock's trouble, or to disturb the joy of Elnora in her work. He stopped at the cabin and slowly went up the walk. Mrs. Comstock was sitting on the front steps with some sewing. The work seemed to Sinton as if she might be engaged in putting a tuck in a petticoat. He thought of how Margaret had shortened Elnora's dress to the accepted length for girls of her age, and made a mental note of Mrs. Comstock's occupation.

She dropped her work on her lap, laid her hands on it and looked into his face with a sneer.

"You didn't let any grass grow under your feet," she said.

Sinton saw her white, drawn face and comprehended.

"I went to pay a debt and see about this opening of the ditch, Kate."

"You said you were going to prosecute me."

"Good gracious, Kate!" cried Sinton. "Is that what you have been thinking all day? I told you before I left yesterday that I would not need do that. And I won't! We can't afford to quarrel over Elnora. She's all we've got. Now that she has proved that if you don't do just what I think you ought by way of clothes and schooling, she can take care of herself, I put that out of my head. What I came to see you about is a kind of scare I've had to-day. I want to ask you if you ever see anything about the swamp that makes you think the old Corson gang is still at work?"

"Can't say that I do," said Mrs. Comstock. "There's kind of dancing lights there sometimes, but I supposed it was just people passing along the road with lanterns. Folks hereabout are none too fond of the swamp. I hate it like death. I've never stayed here a night in my life without Robert's revolver, clean and loaded, under my pillow, and the shotgun, same condition, by the bed. I can't say that I'm afraid here at home. I'm not. I can take care of myself. But none of the swamp for me!"

"Well, I'm glad you are not afraid, Kate, because I must tell you something. Elnora stopped at the case this morning, and somebody had been into it in the night."

"Broke the lock?"

"No. Used a duplicate key. To-day I heard there was a man here last night. I want to nose around a little."

Sinton went to the east end of the cabin and looked up at the window. There was no way any one could have reached it without a ladder, for the logs were hewed and mortar filled the cracks even. Then he went to the west end, the willow faced him as he turned the corner. He examined the trunk carefully. There was no mistake about small particles of black swamp muck adhering to the sides of the tree. He reached the low branches and climbed the willow. There was earth on the large limb crossing Elnora's window. He stood on it, holding the branch as had been done the night before, and looked into the room. He could see very little, but he knew that if it had been dark outside and sufficiently light for Elnora to study inside he could have seen vividly. He brought his face close to the netting, and he could see the bed with its head to the east, at its foot the table with the candles and the chair before it, and then he knew where the man had been who had heard Elnora's prayer.

Mrs. Comstock had followed around the corner and stood watching him. "Do you think some slinking hulk was up there peekin' in at Elnora?" she demanded indignantly.

"There is muck on the trunk, and plenty on the limb," said Sinton. "Hadn't you better get a saw and let me take this branch off?"

"No, I hadn't," said Mrs. Comstock. "First place, Elnora's climbed from that window on that limb all her life, and it's hers. Second place, no one gets ahead of me after I've had warning. Any crow that perches on that roost again will get its feathers somewhat scattered. Look along the fence, there, and see if you can find where he came in."

The place was easy to find as was a trail leading for some distance west of the cabin.

"You just go home, and don't fret yourself," said Mrs. Comstock. "I'll take care of this. If you should hear the dinner bell at any time in the night you come down. But I wouldn't say anything to Elnora. She better keep her mind on her studies, if she's going to school."

When the work was finished that night Elnora took her books and went to her room to prepare some lessons, but every few minutes she looked toward the swamp to see if there were lights near the case. Mrs. Comstock raked together the coals in the cooking stove, got out the lunch box, and sitting down she studied it grimly. At last she arose.

"Wonder how it would do to show Mag Sinton a frill or two," she murmured.

She went to her room, knelt before a big black-walnut chest and hunted through its contents until she found an old-fashioned cook book. She tended the fire as she read and presently was in action. She first sawed an end from a fragrant, juicy, sugar-cured ham and put it to cook. Then she set a couple of eggs boiling, and after long hesitation began creaming butter and sugar in a crock. An hour later the odour of the ham, mingled with some of the richest spices of "happy Araby," in a combination that could mean nothing save spice cake, crept up to Elnora so strongly that she lifted her head and sniffed amazedly. She would have given all her precious money to have gone down and thrown her arms around her mother's neck, but she did not dare move.

Mrs. Comstock was up early, and without a word handed Elnora the case as she left the next morning.

"Thank you, mother," said Elnora, and went on her way.

She walked down the road looking straight ahead until she came to the corner, where she usually entered the swamp. She paused, glanced that way and smiled. Then she turned and looked back. There was no one coming in any direction. She followed the road until well around the corner, then she stopped and sat on a grassy spot, laid her books beside her and opened the lunch box. Last night's odours had in a measure prepared her for what she would see, but not quite. She scarcely could believe her senses. Half the bread compartment was filled with dainty sandwiches of bread and butter sprinkled with the yolk of egg and the remainder with three large slices of the most fragrant spice cake imaginable. The meat dish contained shaved cold ham, of which she knew the quality, the salad was tomatoes and celery, and the cup held preserved pear, clear as amber. There was milk in the bottle, two tissue-wrapped cucumber pickles in the folding drinking-cup, and a fresh napkin in the ring. No lunch was ever daintier or more palatable; of that Elnora was perfectly sure. And her mother had prepared it for her! "She does love me!" cried the happy girl. "Sure as you're born she loves me; only she hasn't found it out yet!"

She touched the papers daintily, and smiled at the box as if it were a living thing. As she began closing it a breath of air swept by, lifting the covering of the cake. It was like an invitation, and breakfast was several hours away. Elnora picked up a piece and ate it. That cake tasted even better than it looked. Then she tried a sandwich. How did her mother come to think of making them that way. They never had any at home. She slipped out the fork, sampled the salad, and one-quarter of pear. Then she closed the box and started down the road nibbling one of the pickles and trying to decide exactly how happy she was, but she could find no standard high enough for a measure.

She was to go to the Bird Woman's after school for the last load from the case. Saturday she would take the arrow points and specimens to the bank. That would exhaust her present supplies and give her enough money ahead to pay for books, tuition, and clothes for at least two years. She would work early and late gathering nuts. In October she would sell all the ferns she could find. She must collect specimens of all tree leaves before they fell, gather nests and cocoons later, and keep her eyes wide open for anything the grades could use. She would see the superintendent that night about selling specimens to the ward buildings. She must be ahead of any one else if she wanted to furnish these things. So she approached the bridge.

That it was occupied could be seen from a distance. As she came up she found the small boy of yesterday awaiting her with a confident smile.

"We brought you something!" he announced without greeting. "This is Jimmy and Belle—and we brought you a present."

He offered a parcel wrapped in brown paper.

"Why, how lovely of you!" said Elnora. "I supposed you had forgotten me when you ran away so fast yesterday."

"Naw, I didn't forget you," said the boy. "I wouldn't forget you, not ever! Why, I was ist a-hurrying to take them things to Jimmy and Belle. My they was glad!"

Elnora glanced at the children. They sat on the edge of the bridge, obviously clad in a garment each, very dirty and unkept, a little boy and a girl of about seven and nine. Elnora's heart began to ache.

"Say," said the boy. "Ain't you going to look what we have gave you?"

"I thought it wasn't polite to look before people," answered Elnora. "Of course, I will, if you would like to have me."

Elnora opened the package. She had been presented with a quarter of a stale loaf of baker's bread, and a big piece of ancient bologna.

"But don't you want this yourselves?" she asked in surprise.

"Gosh, no! I mean ist no," said the boy. "We always have it. We got stacks this morning. Pa's come out of it now, and he's so sorry he got more 'an ever we can eat. Have you had any before?"

"No," said Elnora, "I never did!"

The boy's eyes brightened and the girl moved restlessly.

"We thought maybe you hadn't," said the boy. "First you ever have, you like it real well; but when you don't have anything else for a long time, years an' years, you git so tired." He hitched at the string which held his trousers and watched Elnora speculatively.

"I don't s'pose you'd trade what you got in that box for ist old bread and bologna now, would you? Mebby you'd like it! And I know, I ist know, what you got would taste like heaven to Jimmy and Belle. They never had nothing like that! Not even Belle, and she's most ten! No, sir-ee, they never tasted things like you got!"

It was in Elnora's heart to be thankful for even a taste in time, as she knelt on the bridge, opened the box and divided her lunch into three equal parts, the smaller boy getting most of the milk. Then she told them it was school time and she must go.

"Why don't you put your bread and bologna in the nice box?" asked the boy.

"Of course," said Elnora. "I didn't think."

When the box was arranged to the children's satisfaction all of them accompanied Elnora to the corner where she turned toward the high school.

"Billy," said Elnora, "I would like you much better if you were cleaner. Surely, you have water! Can't you children get some soap and wash yourselves? Gentlemen are never dirty. You want to be a gentleman, don't you?"

"Is being clean all you have to do to be a gentleman?"

"No," said Elnora. "You must not say bad words, and you must be kind and polite to your sister."

"Must Belle be kind and polite to me, else she ain't a lady?"

"Yes."

"Then Belle's no lady!" said Billy succinctly.

Elnora could say nothing more just then, and she bade them good-bye and started them home.

"The poor little souls!" she mused. "I think the Almighty put them in my way to show me real trouble. I won't be likely to spend much time pitying myself while I can see them." She glanced at the lunchbox. "What on earth do I carry this for? I never had anything that was so strictly ornamental! One sure thing! I can't take this stuff to the high school. You never seem to know exactly what is going to happen to you while you are there."

As if to provide a way out of her difficulty a big dog arose from a lawn, and came toward the gate wagging his tail. "If those children ate the stuff, it can't possibly kill him!" thought Elnora, so she offered the bologna. The dog accepted it graciously, and being a beast of pedigree he trotted around to a side porch and laid the bologna before his mistress. The woman snatched it, screaming: "Come, quick! Some one is trying to poison Pedro!" Her daughter came running from the house. "Go see who is on the street. Hurry!" cried the excited mother.

Ellen Brownlee ran and looked. Elnora was half a block away, and no one nearer. Ellen called loudly, and Elnora stopped. Ellen came running toward her.

"Did you see any one give our dog something?" she cried as she approached.

Elnora saw no escape.

"I gave it a piece of bologna myself," she said. "It was fit to eat. It wouldn't hurt the dog."

Ellen stood and looked at her. "Of course, I didn't know it was your dog," explained Elnora. "I had something I wanted to throw to some dog, and that one looked big enough to manage it."

Ellen had arrived at her conclusions. "Pass over that lunch box," she demanded.

"I will not!" said Elnora.

"Then I will have you arrested for trying to poison our dog," laughed the girl as she took the box.

"One chunk of stale bread, one half mile of antique bologna contributed for dog feed; the remains of cake, salad and preserves in an otherwise empty lunch box. One ham sandwich yesterday. I think it's lovely you have the box. Who ate your lunch to-day?"

"Same," confessed Elnora, "but there were three of them this time."

"Wait, until I run back and tell mother about the dog, and get my books."

Elnora waited. That morning she walked down the hall and into the auditorium beside one of the very nicest girls in Onabasha, and it was the fourth day. But the surprise came at noon when Ellen insisted upon Elnora lunching at the Brownlee home, and convulsed her parents and family, and overwhelmed Elnora with a greatly magnified, but moderately accurate history of her lunch box.

"Gee! but it's a box, daddy!" cried the laughing girl. "It's carved leather and fastens with a strap that has her name on it. Inside are trays for things all complete, and it bears evidence of having enclosed delicious food, but Elnora never gets any. She's carried it two days now, and both times it has been empty before she reached school. Isn't that killing?"

"It is, Ellen, in more ways than one. No girl is going to eat breakfast at six o'clock, walk three miles, and do good work without her lunch. You can't tell me anything about that box. I sold it last Monday night to Wesley Sinton, one of my good country customers. He told me it was a present for a girl who was worthy of it, and I see he was right."

"He's so good to me," said Elnora. "Sometimes I look at him and wonder if a neighbour can be so kind to one, what a real father would be like. I envy a girl with a father unspeakably."

"You have cause," said Ellen Brownlee. "A father is the very dearest person in the whole round world, except a mother, who is just a dear." The girl, starting to pay tribute to her father, saw that she must include her mother, and said the thing before she remembered what Mrs. Sinton had told the girls in the store. She stopped in dismay. Elnora's face paled a trifle, but she smiled bravely.

"Then I'm fortunate in having a mother," she said.

Mr. Brownlee lingered at the table after the girls had excused themselves and returned to school.

"There's a girl Ellen can't see too much of, in my opinion," he said. "She is every inch a lady, and not a foolish notion or action about her. I can't understand just what combination of circumstances produced her in this day."

"It has been an unusual case of repression, for one thing. She waits on her elders and thinks before she speaks," said Mrs. Brownlee.

"She's mighty pretty. She looks so sound and wholesome, and she's neatly dressed."

"Ellen says she was a fright the first two days. Long brown calico dress almost touching the floor, and big, lumbering shoes. Those Sinton people bought her clothes. Ellen was in the store, and the woman stopped her crowd and asked them about their dresses. She said the girl was not poor, but her mother was selfish and didn't care for her. But Elnora showed a bank book the next day, and declared that she paid for the things herself, so the Sinton people must just have selected them. There's something peculiar about it, but nothing wrong I am sure. I'll encourage Ellen to ask her again."

"I should say so, especially if she is going to keep on giving away her lunch."

"She lunched with the Bird Woman one day this week."

"She did!"

"Yes, she lives out by the Limberlost. You know the Bird Woman works there a great deal, and probably knows her that way. I think the girl gathers specimens for her. Ellen says she knows more than the teachers about any nature question that comes up, and she is going to lead all of them in mathematics, and make them work in any branch."

When Elnora entered the coat room after having had luncheon with Ellen Brownlee there was such a difference in the atmosphere that she could feel it.

"I am almost sorry I have these clothes," she said to Ellen.

"In the name of sense, why?" cried the astonished girl.

"Every one is so nice to me in them, it sets me to wondering if in time I could have made them be equally friendly in the others."

Ellen looked at her introspectively. "I believe you could," she announced at last. "But it would have taken time and heartache, and your mind would have been less free to work on your studies. No one is happy without friends, and I just simply can't study when I am unhappy."

That night the Bird Woman made the last trip to the swamp. Every specimen she possibly could use had been purchased at a fair price, and three additions had been made to the bank book, carrying the total a little past two hundred dollars. There remained the Indian relics to sell on Saturday, and Elnora had secured the order to furnish material for nature work for the grades. Life suddenly grew very full. There was the most excitingly interesting work for every hour, and that work was to pay high school expenses and start the college fund. There was one little rift in her joy. All of it would have been so much better if she could have told her mother, and given the money into her keeping; but the struggle to get a start had been so terrible, Elnora was afraid to take the risk. When she reached home, she only told her mother that the last of the things had been sold that evening.

"I think," said Mrs. Comstock, "that we will ask Wesley to move that box over here back of the garden for you. There you are apt to get tolled farther into the swamp than you intend to go, and you might mire or something. There ought to be just the same things in our woods, and along our swampy places, as there are in the Limberlost. Can't you hunt your stuff here?"

"I can try," said Elnora. "I don't know what I can find until I do. Our woods are undisturbed, and there is a possibility they might be even better hunting than the swamp. But I wouldn't have Freckles's case moved for the world. He might come back some day, and not like it. I've tried to keep his room the best I could, and taking out the box would make a big hole in one side of it. Store boxes don't cost much. I will have Uncle Wesley buy me one, and set it up wherever hunting looks the best, early in the spring. I would feel safer at home."

"Shall we do the work or have supper first?"

"Let's do the work," said Elnora. "I can't say that I'm hungry now. Doesn't seem as if I ever could be hungry again with such a lunch. I am quite sure no one carried more delicious things to eat than I."

Mrs. Comstock was pleased. "I put in a pretty good hunk of cake. Did you divide it with any one?"

"Why, yes, I did," admitted Elnora.

"Who?"

This was becoming uncomfortable. "I ate the biggest piece myself," said Elnora, "and gave the rest to a couple of boys named Jimmy and Billy and a girl named Belle. They said it was the very best cake they ever tasted in all their lives."

Mrs. Comstock sat straight. "I used to be a master hand at spice cake," she boasted. "But I'm a little out of practice. I must get to work again. With the very weeds growing higher than our heads, we should raise plenty of good stuff to eat on this land, if we can't afford anything else but taxes."

Elnora laughed and hurried up stairs to change her dress. Margaret Sinton came that night bringing a beautiful blue one in its place, and carried away the other to launder.

"Do you mean to say those dresses are to be washed every two days?" questioned Mrs. Comstock.

"They have to be, to look fresh," replied Margaret. "We want our girl sweet as a rose."

"Well, of all things!" cried Mrs. Comstock. "Every two days! Any girl who can't keep a dress clean longer than that is a dirty girl. You'll wear the goods out and fade the colours with so much washing."

"We'll have a clean girl, anyway."

"Well, if you like the job you can have it," said Mrs. Comstock. "I don't mind the washing, but I'm so inconvenient with an iron."

Elnora sat late that night working over her lessons. The next morning she put on her blue dress and ribbon and in those she was a picture. Mrs. Comstock caught her breath with a queer stirring around her heart, and looked twice to be sure of what she saw. As Elnora gathered her books her mother silently gave her the lunch box.

"Feels heavy," said Elnora gaily. "And smelly! Like as not I'll be called upon to divide again."

"Then you divide!" said Mrs. Comstock. "Eating is the one thing we don't have to economize on, Elnora. Spite of all I can do food goes to waste in this soil every day. If you can give some of those city children a taste of the real thing, why, don't be selfish."

Elnora went down the road thinking of the city children with whom she probably would divide. Of course, the bridge would be occupied again. So she stopped and opened the box.

"I don't want to be selfish," murmured Elnora, "but it really seems as if I can't give away this lunch. If mother did not put love into it, she's substituted something that's likely to fool me."

She almost felt her steps lagging as she approached the bridge. A very hungry dog had been added to the trio of children. Elnora loved all dogs, and as usual, this one came to her in friendliness. The children said "Good morning!" with alacrity, and another paper parcel lay conspicuous.

"How are you this morning?" inquired Elnora.

"All right!" cried the three, while the dog sniffed ravenously at the lunch box, and beat a perfect tattoo with his tail.

"How did you like the bologna?" questioned Billy eagerly.

"One of the girls took me to lunch at her home yesterday," answered Elnora.

Dawn broke beautifully over Billy's streaked face. He caught the package and thrust it toward Elnora.

"Then maybe you'd like to try the bologna to-day!"

The dog leaped in glad apprehension of something, and Belle scrambled to her feet and took a step forward. The look of famished greed in her eyes was more than Elnora could endure. It was not that she cared for the food so much. Good things to eat had been in abundance all her life. She wanted with this lunch to try to absorb what she felt must be an expression of some sort from her mother, and if it were not a manifestation of love, she did not know what to think it. But it was her mother who had said "be generous." She knelt on the bridge. "Keep back the dog!" she warned the elder boy.

She opened the box and divided the milk between Billy and the girl. She gave each a piece of cake leaving one and a sandwich. Billy pressed forward eagerly, bitter disappointment on his face, and the elder boy forgot his charge.

"Aw, I thought they'd be meat!" lamented Billy.

Elnora could not endure that.

"There is!" she said gladly. "There is a little pigeon bird. I want a teeny piece of the breast, for a sort of keepsake, just one bite, and you can have the rest among you."

Elnora drew the knife from its holder and cut off the wishbone. Then she held the bird toward the girl.

"You can divide it," she said. The dog made a bound and seizing the squab sprang from the bridge and ran for life. The girl and boy hurried after him. With awful eyes Billy stared and swore tempestuously. Elnora caught him and clapped her hand over the little mouth. A delivery wagon came tearing down the street, the horse running full speed, passed the fleeing dog with the girl and boy in pursuit, and stopped at the bridge. High school girls began to roll from all sides of it.

"A rescue! A rescue!" they shouted.

It was Ellen Brownlee and her crowd, and every girl of them carried a big parcel. They took in the scene as they approached. The fleeing dog with something in its mouth, the half-naked girl and boy chasing it told the story. Those girls screamed with laughter as they watched the pursuit.

"Thank goodness, I saved the wishbone!" said Elnora. "As usual, I can prove that there was a bird." She turned toward the box. Billy had improved the time. He had the last piece of cake in one hand, and the last bite of salad disappeared in one great gulp. Then the girls shouted again.

"Let's have a sample ourselves," suggested one. She caught up the box and handed out the remaining sandwich. Another girl divided it into bites each little over an inch square, and then she lifted the cup lid and deposited a preserved strawberry on each bite. "One, two, three, altogether now!" she cried.

"You old mean things!" screamed Billy.

In an instant he was down in the road and handfuls of dust began to fly among them. The girls scattered before him.

"Billy!" cried Elnora. "Billy! I'll never give you another bite, if you throw dust on any one!"

Then Billy dropped the dust, bored both fists into his eyes, and fled sobbing into Elnora's new blue skirt. She stooped to meet him and consolation began. Those girls laughed on. They screamed and shouted until the little bridge shook.

"To-morrow might as well be a clear day," said Ellen, passing around and feeding the remaining berries to the girls as they could compose themselves enough to take them. "Billy, I admire your taste more than your temper."

Elnora looked up. "The little soul is nothing but skin and bones," she said. "I never was really hungry myself; were any of you?"

"Well, I should say so," cried a plump, rosy girl. "I'm famished right now. Let's have breakfast immediate!"

"We got to refill this box first!" said Ellen Brownlee. "Who's got the butter?" A girl advanced with a wooden tray.

"Put it in the preserve cup, a little strawberry flavour won't hurt it. Next!" called Ellen.

A loaf of bread was produced and Ellen cut off a piece which filled the sandwich box.

"Next!" A bottle of olives was unwrapped. The grocer's boy who was waiting opened that, and Ellen filled the salad dish.

"Next!"

A bag of macaroons was produced and the cake compartment filled.

"Next!"

"I don't suppose this will make quite as good dog feed as a bird," laughed a girl holding open a bag of sliced ham while Ellen filled the meat dish.

"Next!"

A box of candy was handed her and she stuffed every corner of the lunch box with chocolates and nougat. Then it was closed and formally presented to Elnora. The girls each helped themselves to candy and olives, and gave Billy the remainder of the food. Billy took one bite of ham, and approved. Belle and Jimmy had given up chasing the dog, and angry and ashamed, stood waiting half a block away.

"Come back!" cried Billy. "You great big dunces, come back! They's a new kind of meat, and cake and candy."

The boy delayed, but the girl joined Billy. Ellen wiped her fingers, stepped to the cement abutment and began reciting "Horatio at the Bridge!" substituting Elnora wherever the hero appeared in the lines.

Elnora gathered up the sacks, and gave them to Belle, telling her to take the food home, cut and spread the bread, set things on the table, and eat nicely.

Then Elnora was taken into the wagon with the girls, and driven on the run to the high school. They sang a song beginning—

"Elnora, please give me a sandwich.
I'm ashamed to ask for cake!"

as they went. Elnora did not know it, but that was her initiation. She belonged to "the crowd." She only knew that she was happy, and vaguely wondered what her mother and Aunt Margaret would have said about the proceedings.

CHAPTER VII. WHEREIN MRS. COMSTOCK MANIPULATES MARGARET AND BILLY ACQUIRES A RESIDENCE

Saturday morning Elnora helped her mother with the work. When she had finished Mrs. Comstock told her to go to Sintons' and wash her Indian relics, so that she would be ready to accompany Wesley to town in the afternoon. Elnora hurried down the road and was soon at the cistern with a tub busily washing arrow points, stone axes, tubes, pipes, and skin-cleaning implements.

Then she went home, dressed and was waiting when the carriage reached the gate. She stopped at the bank with the box, and Sinton went to do his marketing and some shopping for his wife.

At the dry goods store Mr. Brownlee called to him, "Hello, Sinton! How do you like the fate of your lunch box?" Then he began to laugh—

"I always hate to see a man laughing alone," said Sinton. "It looks so selfish! Tell me the fun, and let me help you."

Mr. Brownlee wiped his eyes.

"I supposed you knew, but I see she hasn't told."

Then the three days' history of the lunch box was repeated with particulars which included the dog.

"Now laugh!" concluded Mr. Brownlee.

"Blest if I see anything funny!" replied Wesley Sinton. "And if you had bought that box and furnished one of those lunches yourself, you wouldn't either. I call such a work a shame! I'll have it stopped."

"Some one must see to that, all right. They are little leeches. Their father earns enough to support them, but they have no mother, and they run wild. I suppose they are crazy for cooked food. But it is funny, and when you think it over you will see it, if you don't now."

"About where would a body find that father?" inquired Wesley Sinton grimly. Mr. Brownlee told him and he started, locating the house with little difficulty. House was the proper word, for of home there was no sign. Just a small empty house with three unkept little children racing through and around it. The girl and the elder boy hung back, but dirty little Billy greeted Sinton with: "What you want here?"

"I want to see your father," said Sinton.

"Well, he's asleep," said Billy.

"Where?" asked Sinton.

"In the house," answered Billy, "and you can't wake him."

"Well, I'll try," said Wesley.

Billy led the way. "There he is!" he said. "He is drunk again."

On a dirty mattress in a corner lay a man who appeared to be strong and well. Billy was right. You could not awake him. He had gone the limit, and a little beyond.

He was now facing eternity. Sinton went out and closed the door.

"Your father is sick and needs help," he said. "You stay here, and I will send a man to see him."

"If you just let him 'lone, he'll sleep it off," volunteered Billy. "He's that way all the time, but he wakes up and gets us something to eat after awhile. Only waitin' twists you up inside pretty bad."

The boy wore no air of complaint. He was merely stating facts.

Wesley Sinton looked intently at Billy. "Are you twisted up inside now?" he asked.

Billy laid a grimy hand on the region of his stomach and the filthy little waist sank close to the backbone. "Bet yer life, boss," he said cheerfully.

"How long have you been twisted?" asked Sinton.

Billy appealed to the others. "When was it we had the stuff on the bridge?"

"Yesterday morning," said the girl.

"Is that all gone?" asked Sinton.

"She went and told us to take it home," said Billy ruefully, "and 'cos she said to, we took it. Pa had come back, he was drinking some more, and he ate a lot of it—almost the whole thing, and it made him sick as a dog, and he went and wasted all of it. Then he got drunk some more, and now he's asleep again. We didn't get hardly none."

"You children sit on the steps until the man comes," said Sinton. "I'll send you some things to eat with him. What's your name, sonny?"

"Billy," said the boy.

"Well, Billy, I guess you better come with me. I'll take care of him," Sinton promised the others. He reached a hand to Billy.

"I ain't no baby, I'm a boy!" said Billy, as he shuffled along beside Sinton, taking a kick at every movable object without regard to his battered toes.

Once they passed a Great Dane dog lolling after its master, and Billy ascended Sinton as if he were a tree, and clung to him with trembling hot hands.

"I ain't afraid of that dog," scoffed Billy, as he was again placed on the walk, "but onc't he took me for a rat or somepin' and his teeth cut into my back. If I'd a done right, I'd a took the law on him."

Sinton looked down into the indignant little face. The child was bright enough, he had a good head, but oh, such a body!

"I 'bout got enough of dogs," said Billy. "I used to like 'em, but I'm getting pretty tired. You ought to seen the lickin' Jimmy and Belle and me give our dog when we caught him, for taking a little bird she gave us. We waited 'till he was asleep 'nen laid a board on him and all of us jumped on it to onc't. You could a heard him yell a mile. Belle said mebbe we could squeeze the bird out of him. But, squeeze nothing! He was holler as us, and that bird was lost long 'fore it got to his stummick. It was ist a little one, anyway. Belle said it wouldn't 'a' made a bite apiece for three of us nohow, and the dog got one good swaller. We didn't get much of the meat, either. Pa took most of that. Seems like pas and dogs gets everything."

Billy laughed dolefully. Involuntarily Wesley Sinton reached his hand. They were coming into the business part of Onabasha and the streets were crowded. Billy understood it to mean that he might lose his companion and took a grip. That little hot hand clinging tight to his, the sore feet recklessly scouring the walk, the hungry child panting for breath as he tried to keep even, the brave soul jesting in the face of hard luck, caught Sinton in a tender, empty spot.

"Say, son," he said. "How would you like to be washed clean, and have all the supper your skin could hold, and sleep in a good bed?"

"Aw, gee!" said Billy. "I ain't dead yet! Them things is in heaven! Poor folks can't have them. Pa said so."

"Well, you can have them if you want to go with me and get them," promised Sinton.

"Honest?"

"Yes, honest."

"Crost yer heart?"

"Yes," said Sinton.

"Kin I take some to Jimmy and Belle?"

"If you'll come with me and be my boy, I'll see that they have plenty."

"What will pa say?"

"Your pa is in that kind of sleep now where he won't wake up, Billy," said Sinton. "I am pretty sure the law will give you to me, if you want to come."

"When people don't ever wake up they're dead," announced Billy. "Is my pa dead?"

"Yes, he is," answered Sinton.

"And you'll take care of Jimmy and Belle, too?"

"I can't adopt all three of you," said Sinton. "I'll take you, and see that they are well provided for. Will you come?"

"Yep, I'll come," said Billy. "Let's eat, first thing we do."

"All right," agreed Sinton. "Come into this restaurant." He lifted Billy to the lunch counter and ordered the clerk to give him as many glasses of milk as he wanted, and a biscuit. "I think there's going to be fried chicken when we get home, Billy," he said, "so you just take the edge off now, and fill up later."

While Billy lunched Sinton called up the different departments and notified the proper authorities ending with the Women's Relief Association. He sent a basket of food to Belle and Jimmy, bought Billy a pair of trousers, and a shirt, and went to bring Elnora.

"Why, Uncle Wesley!" cried the girl. "Where did you find Billy?"

"I've adopted him for the time being, if not longer," replied Wesley Sinton.

"Where did you get him?"

"Well, young woman," said Wesley Sinton, "Mr. Brownlee told me the history of your lunch box. It didn't seem so funny to me as it does to the rest of them; so I went to look up the father of Billy's family, and make him take care of them, or allow the law to do it for him. It will have to be the law."

"He's deader than anything!" broke in Billy. "He can't ever take all the meat any more."

"Billy!" gasped Elnora.

"Never you mind!" said Sinton. "A child doesn't say such things about a father who loved and raised him right. When it happens, the father alone is to blame. You won't hear Billy talk like that about me when I cross over."

"You don't mean you are going to take him to keep!"

"I'll soon need help," said Wesley. "Billy will come in just about right ten years from now, and if I raise him I'll have him the way I want him."

"But Aunt Margaret doesn't like boys," objected Elnora.

"Well, she likes me, and I used to be a boy. Anyway, as I remember she has had her way about everything at our house ever since we were married. I am going to please myself about Billy. Hasn't she always done just as she chose so far as you know? Honest, Elnora!"

"Honest!" replied Elnora. "You are beautiful to all of us, Uncle Wesley; but Aunt Margaret won't like Billy. She won't want him in her home."

"In our home," corrected Wesley.

"What makes you want him?" marvelled Elnora.

"God only knows," said Sinton. "Billy ain't so beautiful, and he ain't so smart, I guess it's because he's so human. My heart goes out to him."

"So did mine," said Elnora. "I love him. I'd rather see him eat my lunch than have it myself any time."

"What makes you like him?" asked Wesley.

"Why, I don't know," pondered Elnora. "He's so little, he needs so much, he's got such splendid grit, and he's perfectly unselfish with his brother and sister. But we must wash him before Aunt Margaret sees him. I wonder if mother——"

"You needn't bother. I'm going to take him home the way he is," said Sinton. "I want Maggie to see the worst of it."

"I'm afraid——" began Elnora.

"So am I," said Wesley, "but I won't give him up. He's taken a sort of grip on my heart. I've always been crazy for a boy. Don't let him hear us."

"Don't let him be killed!" cried Elnora. During their talk Billy had wandered to the edge of the walk and barely escaped the wheels of a passing automobile in an effort to catch a stray kitten that seemed in danger.

Wesley drew Billy back to the walk, and held his hand closely. "Are you ready, Elnora?"

"Yes; you were gone a long time," she said.

Wesley glanced at a package she carried. "Have to have another book?" he asked.

"No, I bought this for mother. I've had such splendid luck selling my specimens, I didn't feel right about keeping all the money for myself, so I saved enough from the Indian relics to get a few things I wanted. I would have liked to have gotten her a dress, but I didn't dare, so I compromised on a book."

"What did you select, Elnora?" asked Wesley wonderingly.

"Well," said she, "I have noticed mother always seemed interested in anything Mark Twain wrote in the newspapers, and I thought it would cheer her up a little, so I just got his 'Innocents Abroad.' I haven't read it myself, but I've seen mention made of it all my life, and the critics say it's genuine fun."

"Good!" cried Sinton. "Good! You've made a splendid choice. It will take her mind off herself a lot. But she will scold you."

"Of course," assented Elnora. "But, possibly she will read it, and feel better. I'm going to serve her a trick. I am going to hide it until Monday, and set it on her little shelf of books the last thing before I go away. She must have all of them by heart. When, she sees a new one she can't help being glad, for she loves to read, and if she has all day to become interested, maybe she'll like it so she won't scold so much."

"We are both in for it, but I guess we are prepared. I don't know what Margaret will say, but I'm going to take Billy home and see. Maybe he can win with her, as he did with us."

Elnora had doubts, but she did not say anything more. When they started home Billy sat on the front seat. He drove with the hitching strap tied to the railing of the dash-board, flourished the whip, and yelled with delight. At first Sinton laughed with him, but by the time he left Elnora with several packages at her gate, he was looking serious enough.

Margaret was at the door as they drove up the lane. Wesley left Billy in the carriage, hitched the horses and went to explain to her. He had not reached her before she cried, "Look, Wesley, that child! You'll have a runaway!"

Wesley looked and ran. Billy was standing in the carriage slashing the mettlesome horses with the whip.

"See me make 'em go!" he shouted as the whip fell a second time.

He did make them go. They took the hitching post and a few fence palings, which scraped the paint from a wheel. Sinton missed the lines at the first effort, but the dragging post impeded the horses, and he soon caught them. He led them to the barn, and ordered Billy to remain in the carriage while he unhitched. Then leading Billy and carrying his packages he entered the yard.

"You run play a few minutes, Billy," he said. "I want to talk to the nice lady."

The nice lady was looking rather stupefied as Wesley approached her.

"Where in the name of sense did you get that awful child?" she demanded.

"He is a young gentleman who has been stopping Elnora and eating her lunch every day, part of the time with the assistance of his brother and sister, while our girl went hungry. Brownlee told me about it at the store. It's happened three days running. The first time she went without anything, the second time Brownlee's girl took her to lunch, and the third a crowd of high school girls bought a lot of stuff and met them at the bridge. The youngsters seemed to think they could rob her every day, so I went to see their father about having it stopped."

"Well, I should think so!" cried Margaret.

"There were three of them, Margaret," said Wesley, "that little fellow——"

"Hyena, you mean," interpolated Margaret.

"Hyena," corrected Wesley gravely, "and another boy and a girl, all equally dirty and hungry. The man was dead. They thought he was in a drunken sleep, but he was stone dead. I brought the little boy with me, and sent the officers and other help to the house. He's half starved. I want to wash him, and put clean clothes on him, and give him some supper."

"Have you got anything to put on him?"

"Yes."

"Where did you get it?"

"Bought it. It ain't much. All I got didn't cost a dollar."

"A dollar is a good deal when you work and save for it the way we do."

"Well, I don't know a better place to put it. Have you got any hot water? I'll use this tub at the cistern. Please give me some soap and towels."

Instead Margaret pushed by him with a shriek. Billy had played by producing a cord from his pocket, and having tied the tails of Margaret's white kittens together, he had climbed on a box and hung them across the clothes line. Wild with fright the kittens were clawing each other to death, and the air was white with fur. The string had twisted and the frightened creatures could not recognize friends. Margaret stepped back with bleeding hands. Sinton cut the cord with his knife and the poor little cats raced under the house bleeding and disfigured. Margaret white with wrath faced Wesley.

"If you don't hitch up and take that animal back to town," she said, "I will."

Billy threw himself on the grass and began to scream.

"You said I could have fried chicken for supper," he wailed. "You said she was a nice lady!"

Wesley lifted him and something in his manner of handling the child infuriated Margaret. His touch was so gentle. She reached for Billy and gripped his shirt collar in the back. Wesley's hand closed over hers.

"Gently, girl!" he said. "This little body is covered with sores."

"Sores!" she ejaculated. "Sores? What kind of sores?"

"Oh, they might be from bruises made by fists or boot toes, or they might be bad blood, from wrong eating, or they might be pure filth. Will you hand me some towels?"

"No, I won't!" said Margaret.

"Well, give me some rags, then."

Margaret compromised on pieces of old tablecloth. Wesley led Billy to the cistern, pumped cold water into the tub, poured in a kettle of hot, and beginning at the head scoured him. The boy shut his little teeth, and said never a word though he twisted occasionally when the soap struck a raw spot. Margaret watched the process from the window in amazed and ever-increasing anger. Where did Wesley learn it? How could his big hands be so gentle? He came to the door.

"Have you got any peroxide?" he asked.

"A little," she answered stiffly.

"Well, I need about a pint, but I'll begin on what you have."

Margaret handed him the bottle. Wesley took a cup, weakened the drug and said to Billy: "Man, these sores on you must be healed. Then you must eat the kind of food that's fit for little men. I am going to put some medicine on you, and it is going to sting like fire. If it just runs off, I won't use any more. If it boils, there is poison in these places, and they must be tied up, dosed every day, and you must be washed, and kept mighty clean. Now, hold still, because I am going to put it on."

"I think the one on my leg is the worst," said the undaunted Billy, holding out a raw place. Sinton poured on the drug. Billy's body twisted and writhed, but he did not run.

"Gee, look at it boil!" he cried. "I guess they's poison. You'll have to do it to all of them."

Wesley's teeth were set, as he watched the boy's face. He poured the drug, strong enough to do effective work, on a dozen places over that little body and bandaged all he could. Billy's lips quivered at times, and his chin jumped, but he did not shed a tear or utter a sound other than to take a deep interest in the boiling. As Wesley put the small shirt on the boy, and fastened the trousers, he was ready to reset the hitching post and mend the fence without a word.

"Now am I clean?" asked Billy.

"Yes, you are clean outside," said Wesley. "There is some dirty blood in your body, and some bad words in your mouth, that we have to get out, but that takes time. If we put right things to eat into your stomach that will do away with the sores, and if you know that I don't like bad words you won't say them any oftener than you can help, will you Billy?"

Billy leaned against Wesley in apparent indifference.

"I want to see me!" he demanded.

Wesley led the boy into the house, and lifted him to a mirror.

"My, I'm purty good-looking, ain't I?" bragged Billy. Then as Wesley stooped to set him on the floor Billy's lips passed close to the big man's ear and hastily whispered a vehement "No!" as he ran for the door.

"How long until supper, Margaret?" asked Wesley as he followed.

"You are going to keep him for supper?" she asked

"Sure!" said Wesley. "That's what I brought him for. It's likely he never had a good square meal of decent food in his life. He's starved to the bone."

Margaret arose deliberately, removed the white cloth from the supper table and substituted an old red one she used to wrap the bread. She put away the pretty dishes they commonly used and set the table with old plates for pies and kitchen utensils. But she fried the chicken, and was generous with milk and honey, snowy bread, gravy, potatoes, and fruit.

Wesley repainted the scratched wheel. He mended the fence, with Billy holding the nails and handing the pickets. Then he filled the old hole, digged a new one and set the hitching post.

Billy hopped on one foot at his task of holding the post steady as the earth was packed around it. There was not the shadow of a trouble on his little freckled face.

Sinton threw in stones and pounded the earth solid around the post. The sound of a gulping sob attracted him to Billy. The tears were rolling down his cheeks. "If I'd a knowed you'd have to get down in a hole, and work so hard I wouldn't 'a' hit the horses," he said.

"Never you mind, Billy," said Wesley. "You will know next time, so you can think over it, and make up your mind whether you really want to before you strike."

Wesley went to the barn to put away the tools. He thought Billy was at his heels, but the boy lagged on the way. A big snowy turkey gobbler resented the small intruder in his especial preserves, and with spread tail and dragging wings came toward him threateningly. If that turkey gobbler had known the sort of things with which Billy was accustomed to holding his own, he never would have issued the challenge. Billy accepted instantly. He danced around with stiff arms at his sides and imitated the gobbler. Then came his opportunity, and he jumped on the big turkey's back. Wesley heard Margaret's scream in time to see the flying leap and admire its dexterity. The turkey tucked its tail and scampered. Billy slid from its back and as he fell he clutched wildly, caught the folded tail, and instinctively clung to it. The turkey gave one scream and relaxed its muscles. Then it fled in disfigured defeat to the haystack. Billy scrambled to his feet holding the tail, while his eyes were bulging.

"Why, the blasted old thing came off!" he said to Wesley, holding out the tail in amazed wonder.

The man, caught suddenly, forgot everything and roared. Seeing which, Billy thought a turkey tail of no account and flung that one high above him shouting in wild childish laughter, when the feathers scattered and fell.

Margaret, watching, began to cry. Wesley had gone mad. For the first time in her married life she wanted to tell her mother. When Wesley had waited until he was so hungry he could wait no longer he invaded the kitchen to find a cooked supper baking on the back of the stove, while Margaret with red eyes nursed a pair of demoralized white kittens.

"Is supper ready?" he asked.

"It has been for an hour," answered Margaret.

"Why didn't you call us?"

That "us" had too much comradeship in it. It irritated Margaret.

"I supposed it would take you even longer than this to fix things decent again. As for my turkey, and my poor little kittens, they don't matter."

"I am mighty sorry about them, Margaret, you know that. Billy is very bright, and he will soon learn——"

"Soon learn!" cried Margaret. "Wesley Sinton, you don't mean to say that you think of keeping that creature here for some time?"

"No, I think of keeping a well-behaved little boy."

Margaret set the supper on the table. Seeing the old red cloth Wesley stared in amazement. Then he understood. Billy capered around in delight.

"Ain't that pretty?" he exulted. "I wish Jimmy and Belle could see. We, why we ist eat out of our hands or off a old dry goods box, and when we fix up a lot, we have newspaper. We ain't ever had a nice red cloth like this."

Wesley looked straight at Margaret, so intently that she turned away, her face flushing. He stacked the dictionary and the geography of the world on a chair, and lifted Billy beside him. He heaped a plate generously, cut the food, put a fork into Billy's little fist, and made him eat slowly and properly. Billy did his best. Occasionally greed overcame him, and he used his left hand to pop a bite into his mouth with his fingers. These lapses Wesley patiently overlooked, and went on with his general instructions. Luckily Billy did not spill anything on his clothing or the cloth. After supper Wesley took him to the barn while he finished the night work. Then he went and sat beside Margaret on the front porch. Billy appropriated the hammock, and swung by pulling a rope tied around a tree. The very energy with which he went at the work of swinging himself appealed to Wesley.

"Mercy, but he's an active little body," he said. "There isn't a lazy bone in him. See how he works to pay for his fun."

"There goes his foot through it!" cried Margaret. "Wesley, he shall not ruin my hammock."

"Of course he shan't!" said Wesley. "Wait, Billy, let me show you."

Thereupon he explained to Billy that ladies wearing beautiful white dresses sat in hammocks, so little boys must not put their dusty feet in them. Billy immediately sat, and allowed his feet to swing.

"Margaret," said Wesley after a long silence on the porch, "isn't it true that if Billy had been a half-starved sore cat, dog, or animal of any sort, that you would have pitied, and helped care for it, and been glad to see me get any pleasure out of it I could?"

"Yes," said Margaret coldly.

"But because I brought a child with an immortal soul, there is no welcome."

"That isn't a child, it's an animal."

"You just said you would have welcomed an animal."

"Not a wild one. I meant a tame beast."

"Billy is not a beast!" said Wesley hotly. "He is a very dear little boy. Margaret, you've always done the church-going and Bible reading for this family. How do you reconcile that 'Suffer little children to come unto Me' with the way you are treating Billy?"

Margaret arose. "I haven't treated that child. I have only let him alone. I can barely hold myself. He needs the hide tanned about off him!"

"If you'd cared to look at his body, you'd know that you couldn't find a place to strike without cutting into a raw spot," said Wesley. "Besides, Billy has not done a thing for which a child should be punished. He is only full of life, no training, and with a boy's love of mischief. He did abuse your kittens, but an hour before I saw him risk his life to save one from being run over. He minds what you tell him, and doesn't do anything he is told not to. He thinks of his brother and sister right away when anything pleases him. He took that stinging medicine with the grit of a bulldog. He is just a bully little chap, and I love him."

"Oh good heavens!" cried Margaret, going into the house as she spoke.

Sinton sat still. At last Billy tired of the swing, came to him and leaned his slight body against the big knee.

"Am I going to sleep here?" he asked.

"Sure you are!" said Sinton.

Billy swung his feet as he laid across Wesley's knee. "Come on," said Wesley, "I must clean you up for bed."

"You have to be just awful clean here," announced Billy. "I like to be clean, you feel so good, after the hurt is over."

Sinton registered that remark, and worked with especial tenderness as he redressed the ailing places and washed the dust from Billy's feet and hands.

"Where can he sleep?" he asked Margaret.

"I'm sure I don't know," she answered.

"Oh, I can sleep ist any place," said Billy. "On the floor or anywhere. Home, I sleep on pa's coat on a store-box, and Jimmy and Belle they sleep on the storebox, too. I sleep between them, so's I don't roll off and crack my head. Ain't you got a storebox and a old coat?"

Wesley arose and opened a folding lounge. Then he brought an armload of clean horse blankets from a closet.

"These don't look like the nice white bed a little boy should have, Billy," he said, "but we'll make them do. This will beat a storebox all hollow."

Billy took a long leap for the lounge. When he found it bounced, he proceeded to bounce, until he was tired. By that time the blankets had to be refolded. Wesley had Billy take one end and help, while both of them seemed to enjoy the job. Then Billy lay down and curled up in his clothes like a small dog. But sleep would not come.

Finally he sat up. He stared around restlessly. Then he arose, went to Wesley, and leaned against his knee. He picked up the boy and folded his arms around him. Billy sighed in rapturous content.

"That bed feels so lost like," he said. "Jimmy always jabbed me on one side, and Belle on the other, and so I knew I was there. Do you know where they are?"

"They are with kind people who gave them a fine supper, a clean bed, and will always take good care of them."

"I wisht I was—" Billy hesitated and looked earnestly at Wesley. "I mean I wish they was here."

"You are about all I can manage, Billy," said Wesley.

Billy sat up. "Can't she manage anything?" he asked, waving toward Margaret.

"Indeed, yes," said Wesley. "She has managed me for twenty years."

"My, but she made you nice!" said Billy. "I just love you. I wisht she'd take Jimmy and Belle and make them nice as you."

"She isn't strong enough to do that, Billy. They will grow into a good boy and girl where they are."

Billy slid from Wesley's arms and walked toward Margaret until he reached the middle of the room. Then he stopped, and at last sat on the floor. Finally he lay down and closed his eyes. "This feels more like my bed; if only Jimmy and Belle was here to crowd up a little, so it wasn't so alone like."

"Won't I do, Billy?" asked Wesley in a husky voice.

Billy moved restlessly. "Seems like—seems like toward night as if a body got kind o' lonesome for a woman person—like her."

Billy indicated Margaret and then closed his eyes so tight his small face wrinkled.

Soon he was up again. "Wisht I had Snap," he said. "Oh, I ist wisht I had Snap!"

"I thought you laid a board on Snap and jumped on it," said Wesley.

"We did!" cried Billy—"oh, you ought to heard him squeal!" Billy laughed loudly, then his face clouded.

"But I want Snap to lay beside me so bad now—that if he was here I'd give him a piece of my chicken, 'for, I ate any. Do you like dogs?"

"Yes, I do," said Wesley.

Billy was up instantly. "Would you like Snap?"

"I am sure I would," said Wesley.

"Would she?" Billy indicated Margaret. And then he answered his own question. "But of course, she wouldn't, cos she likes cats, and dogs chases cats. Oh, dear, I thought for a minute maybe Snap could come here." Billy lay down and closed his eyes resolutely.

Suddenly they flew open. "Does it hurt to be dead?" he demanded.

"Nothing hurts you after you are dead, Billy," said Wesley.

"Yes, but I mean does it hurt getting to be dead?"

"Sometimes it does. It did not hurt your father, Billy. It came softly while he was asleep."

"It ist came softly?"

"Yes."

"I kind o' wisht he wasn't dead!" said Billy. "'Course I like to stay with you, and the fried chicken, and the nice soft bed, and—and everything, and I like to be clean, but he took us to the show, and he got us gum, and he never hurt us when he wasn't drunk."

Billy drew a deep breath, and tightly closed his eyes. But very soon they opened. Then he sat up. He looked at Wesley pitifully, and then he glanced at Margaret. "You don't like boys, do you?" he questioned.

"I like good boys," said Margaret.

Billy was at her knee instantly. "Well say, I'm a good boy!" he announced joyously.

"I do not think boys who hurt helpless kittens and pull out turkeys' tails are good boys."

"Yes, but I didn't hurt the kittens," explained Billy. "They got mad 'bout ist a little fun and scratched each other. I didn't s'pose they'd act like that. And I didn't pull the turkey's tail. I ist held on to the first thing I grabbed, and the turkey pulled. Honest, it was the turkey pulled." He turned to Wesley. "You tell her! Didn't the turkey pull? I didn't know its tail was loose, did I?"

"I don't think you did, Billy," said Wesley.

Billy stared into Margaret's cold face. "Sometimes at night, Belle sits on the floor, and I lay my head in her lap. I could pull up a chair and lay my head in your lap. Like this, I mean." Billy pulled up a chair, climbed on it and laid his head on Margaret's lap. Then he shut his eyes again. Margaret could have looked little more repulsed if he had been a snake. Billy was soon up.

"My, but your lap is hard," he said. "And you are a good deal fatter 'an Belle, too!" He slid from the chair and came back to the middle of the room.

"Oh but I wisht he wasn't dead!" he cried. The flood broke and Billy screamed in desperation.

Out of the night a soft, warm young figure flashed through the door and with a swoop caught him in her arms. She dropped into a chair, nestled him closely, drooped her fragrant brown head over his little bullet-eyed red one, and rocked softly while she crooned over him—

"Billy, boy, where have you been?
Oh, I have been to seek a wife,
She's the joy of my life,
But then she's a young thing and she can't leave her mammy!"

Billy clung to her frantically. Elnora wiped his eyes, kissed his face, swayed and sang.

"Why aren't you asleep?" she asked at last.

"I don't know," said Billy. "I tried. I tried awful hard cos I thought he wanted me to, but it ist wouldn't come. Please tell her I tried." He appealed to Margaret.

"He did try to go to sleep," admitted Margaret.

"Maybe he can't sleep in his clothes," suggested Elnora. "Haven't you an old dressing sacque? I could roll the sleeves."

Margaret got an old sacque, and Elnora put it on Billy. Then she brought a basin of water and bathed his face and head. She gathered him up and began to rock again.

"Have you got a pa?" asked Billy.

"No," said Elnora.

"Is he dead like mine?"

"Yes."

"Did it hurt him to die?"

"I don't know."

Billy was wide awake again. "It didn't hurt my pa," he boasted; "he ist died while he was asleep. He didn't even know it was coming."

"I am glad of that," said Elnora, pressing the small head against her breast again.

Billy escaped her hand and sat up. "I guess I won't go to sleep," he said. "It might 'come softly' and get me."

"It won't get you, Billy," said Elnora, rocking and singing between sentences. "It doesn't get little boys. It just takes big people who are sick."

"Was my pa sick?"

"Yes," said Elnora. "He had a dreadful sickness inside him that burned, and made him drink things. That was why he would forget his little boys and girl. If he had been well, he would have gotten you good things to eat, clean clothes, and had the most fun with you."

Billy leaned against her and closed his eyes, and Elnora rocked hopefully.

"If I was dead would you cry?" he was up again.

"Yes, I would," said Elnora, gripping him closer until Billy almost squealed with the embrace.

"Do you love me tight as that?" he questioned blissfully.

"Yes, bushels and bushels," said Elnora. "Better than any little boy in the whole world."

Billy looked at Margaret. "She don't!" he said. "She'd be glad if it would get me 'softly,' right now. She don't want me here 't all."

Elnora smothered his face against her breast and rocked.

"You love me, don't you?"

"I will, if you will go to sleep."

"Every single day you will give me your dinner for the bologna, won't you," said Billy.

"Yes, I will," replied Elnora. "But you will have as good lunch as I do after this. You will have milk, eggs, chicken, all kinds of good things, little pies, and cakes, maybe."

Billy shook his head. "I am going back home soon as it is light," he said, "she don't want me. She thinks I'm a bad boy. She's going to whip me—if he lets her. She said so. I heard her. Oh, I wish he hadn't died! I want to go home." Billy shrieked again.

Mrs. Comstock had started to walk slowly to meet Elnora. The girl had been so late that her mother reached the Sinton gate and followed the path until the picture inside became visible. Elnora had told her about Wesley taking Billy home. Mrs. Comstock had some curiosity to see how Margaret bore the unexpected addition to her family. Billy's voice, raised with excitement, was plainly audible. She could see Elnora holding him, and hear his excited wail. Wesley's face was drawn and haggard, and Margaret's set and defiant. A very imp of perversity entered the breast of Mrs. Comstock.

"Hoity, toity!" she said as she suddenly appeared in the door. "Blest if I ever heard a man making sounds like that before!"

Billy ceased suddenly. Mrs. Comstock was tall, angular, and her hair was prematurely white. She was only thirty-six, although she appeared fifty. But there was an expression on her usually cold face that was attractive just then, and Billy was in search of attractions.

"Have I stayed too late, mother?" asked Elnora anxiously. "I truly intended to come straight back, but I thought I could rock Billy to sleep first. Everything is strange, and he's so nervous."

"Is that your ma?" demanded Billy.

"Yes."

"Does she love you?"

"Of course!"

"My mother didn't love me," said Billy. "She went away and left me, and never came back. She don't care what happens to me. You wouldn't go away and leave your little girl, would you?"

questioned Billy.

"No," said Katharine Comstock, "and I wouldn't leave a little boy, either."

Billy began sliding from Elnora's knees.

"Do you like boys?" he questioned.

"If there is anything I love it is a boy," said Mrs. Comstock assuringly. Billy was on the floor.

"Do you like dogs?"

"Yes. Almost as well as boys. I am going to buy a dog as soon as I can find a good one."

Billy swept toward her with a whoop.

"Do you want a boy?" he shouted.

Katharine Comstock stretched out her arms, and gathered him in.

"Of course, I want a boy!" she rejoiced.

"Maybe you'd like to have me?" offered Billy.

"Sure I would," triumphed Mrs. Comstock. "Any one would like to have you. You are just a real boy, Billy."

"Will you take Snap?"

"I'd like to have Snap almost as well as you."

"Mother!" breathed Elnora imploringly. "Don't! Oh, don't! He thinks you mean it!"

"And so I do mean it," said Mrs. Comstock. "I'll take him in a jiffy. I throw away enough to feed a little tyke like him every day. His chatter would be great company while you are gone. Blood soon can be purified with right food and baths, and as for Snap, I meant to buy a bulldog, but possibly Snap will serve just as well. All I ask of a dog is to bark at the right time. I'll do the rest. Would you like to come and be my boy, Billy?"

Billy leaned against Mrs. Comstock, reached his arms around her neck and gripped her with all his puny might. "You can whip me all you want to," he said. "I won't make a sound."

Mrs. Comstock held him closely and her hard face was softening; of that there could be no doubt.

"Now, why would any one whip a nice little boy like you?" she asked wonderingly.

"She"—Billy from his refuge waved toward Margaret—"she was going to whip me 'cause her cats fought, when I tied their tails together and hung them over the line to dry. How did I know her old cats would fight?"

Mrs. Comstock began to laugh suddenly, and try as she would she could not stop so soon as she desired. Billy studied her.

"Have you got turkeys?" he demanded.

"Yes, flocks of them," said Mrs. Comstock, vainly struggling to suppress her mirth, and settle her face in its accustomed lines.

"Are their tails fast?" demanded Billy.

"Why, I think so," marvelled Mrs. Comstock.

"Hers ain't!" said Billy with the wave toward Margaret that was becoming familiar. "Her turkey pulled, and its tail comed right off. She's going to whip me if he lets her. I didn't know the turkey would pull. I didn't know its tail would come off. I won't ever touch one again, will I?"

"Of course, you won't," said Mrs. Comstock. "And what's more, I don't care if you do! I'd rather have a fine little man like you than all the turkeys in the country. Let them lose their old tails if they want to, and let the cats fight. Cats and turkeys don't compare with boys, who are going to be fine big men some of these days."

Then Billy and Mrs. Comstock hugged each other rapturously, while their audience stared in silent amazement.

"You like boys!" exulted Billy, and his head dropped against Mrs. Comstock in unspeakable content.

"Yes, and if I don't have to carry you the whole way home, we must start right now," said Mrs. Comstock. "You are going to be asleep before you know it."

Billy opened his eyes and braced himself. "I can walk," he said proudly.

"All right, we must start. Come, Elnora! Good-night, folks!" Mrs. Comstock set Billy on the floor, and arose gripping his hand. "You take the other side, Elnora, and we will help him as much as we can," she said.

Elnora stared piteously at Margaret, then at Wesley, and arose in white-faced bewilderment.

"Billy, are you going to leave without even saying good-bye to me?" asked Wesley, with a gulp.

Billy held tight to Mrs. Comstock and Elnora.

"Good-bye!" he said casually. "I'll come and see you some time."

Wesley Sinton gave a smothered sob, and strode from the room.

Mrs. Comstock started toward the door, dragging at Billy while Elnora pulled back, but Mrs. Sinton was before them, her eyes flashing.

"Kate Comstock, you think you are mighty smart, don't you?" she cried.

"I ain't in the lunatic asylum, where you belong, anyway," said Mrs. Comstock. "I am smart enough to tell a dandy boy when I see him, and I'm good and glad to get him. I'll love to have him!"

"Well, you won't have him!" exclaimed Margaret Sinton. "That boy is Wesley's! He found him, and brought him here. You can't come in and take him like that! Let go of him!"

"Not much, I won't!" cried Mrs. Comstock. "Leave the poor sick little soul here for you to beat, because he didn't know just how to handle things! Of course, he'll make mistakes. He must have a lot of teaching, but not the kind he'll get from you! Clear out of my way!"

"You let go of our boy," ordered Margaret.

"Why? Do you want to whip him, before he can go to sleep?" jeered Mrs. Comstock.

"No, I don't!" said Margaret. "He's Wesley's, and nobody shall touch him. Wesley!"

Wesley Sinton appeared behind Margaret in the doorway, and she turned to him. "Make Kate Comstock let go of our boy!" she demanded.

"Billy, she wants you now," said Wesley Sinton. "She won't whip you, and she won't let any one else. You can have stacks of good things to eat, ride in the carriage, and have a great time. Won't you stay with us?"

Billy drew away from Mrs. Comstock and Elnora.

He faced Margaret, his eyes shrewd with unchildish wisdom. Necessity had taught him to strike the hot iron, to drive the hard bargain.

"Can I have Snap to live here always?" he demanded.

"Yes, you can have all the dogs you want," said Margaret Sinton.

"Can I sleep close enough so's I can touch you?"

"Yes, you can move your lounge up so that you can hold my hand," said Margaret.

"Do you love me now?" questioned Billy.

"I'll try to love you, if you are a good boy," said Margaret.

"Then I guess I'll stay," said Billy, walking over to her.

Out in the night Elnora and her mother went down the road in the moonlight; every few rods Mrs. Comstock laughed aloud.

"Mother, I don't understand you," sobbed Elnora.

"Well, maybe when you have gone to high school longer you will," said Mrs. Comstock. "Anyway, you saw me bring Mag Sinton to her senses, didn't you?"

"Yes, I did," answered Elnora, "but I thought you were in earnest. So did Billy, and Uncle Wesley, and Aunt Margaret."

"Well, wasn't I?" inquired Mrs. Comstock.

"But you just said you brought Aunt Margaret to!"

"Well, didn't I?"

"I don't understand you."

"That's the reason I am recommending more schooling!"

Elnora took her candle and went to bed. Mrs. Comstock was feeling too good to sleep. Twice of late she really had enjoyed herself for the first in sixteen years, and greediness for more of the same feeling crept into her blood like intoxication. As she sat brooding alone she knew the truth. She would have loved to have taken Billy. She would not have minded his mischief, his chatter, or his dog. He would have meant a distraction from herself that she greatly needed; she was even sincere about the dog. She had intended to tell Wesley to buy her one at the very first opportunity. Her last thought was of Billy. She chuckled softly, for she was not saintly, and now she knew how she could even a long score with Margaret and Wesley in a manner that would fill her soul with grim satisfaction.

CHAPTER VIII. WHEREIN THE LIMBERLOST TEMPTS ELNORA, AND BILLY BURIES HIS FATHER

Immediately after dinner on Sunday Wesley Sinton stopped at the Comstock gate to ask if Elnora wanted to go to town with them. Billy sat beside him and he did not appear as if he were on his way to a funeral. Elnora said she had to study and could not go, but she suggested that her mother take her place. Mrs. Comstock put on her hat and went at once, which surprised Elnora. She did not know that her mother was anxious for an opportunity to speak with Sinton alone. Elnora knew why she was repeatedly cautioned not to leave their land, if she went specimen hunting.

She studied two hours and was several lessons ahead of her classes. There was no use to go further. She would take a walk and see if she could gather any caterpillars or find any freshly spun cocoons. She searched the bushes and low trees behind the garden and all around the edge of the woods on their land, and having little success, at last came to the road. Almost the first thorn bush she examined yielded a Polyphemus cocoon. Elnora lifted her head with the instinct of a hunter on the chase, and began work. She reached the swamp before she knew it, carrying five fine cocoons of different species as her reward. She pushed back her hair and gazed around longingly. A few rods inside she thought she saw cocoons on a bush, to which she went, and found several. Sense of caution was rapidly vanishing; she was in a fair way to forget everything and plunge into the swamp when she thought she heard footsteps coming down the trail. She went back, and came out almost facing Pete Corson.

That ended her difficulty. She had known him since childhood. When she sat on the front bench of the Brushwood schoolhouse, Pete had been one of the big boys at the back of the room. He had been rough and wild, but she never had been afraid of him, and often he had given her pretty things from the swamp.

"What luck!" she cried. "I promised mother I would not go inside the swamp alone, and will you look at the cocoons I've found! There are more just screaming for me to come get them, because the leaves will fall with the first frost, and then the jays and crows will begin to tear them open. I haven't much time, since I'm going to school. You will go with me, Pete! Please say yes! Just a little way!"

"What are those things?" asked the man, his keen black eyes staring at her.

"They are the cases these big caterpillars spin for winter, and in the spring they come out great night moths, and I can sell them. Oh, Pete, I can sell them for enough to take me through high school and dress me so like the others that I don't look different, and if I have very good luck I can save some for college. Pete, please go with me?"

"Why don't you go like you always have?"

"Well, the truth is, I had a little scare," said Elnora. "I never did mean to go alone; sometimes I sort of wandered inside farther than I intended, chasing things. You know Duncan gave me Freckles's books, and I have been gathering moths like he did. Lately I found I could sell them. If I can make a complete collection, I can get three hundred dollars for it. Three such collections would take me almost through college, and I've four years in the high school yet. That's a long time. I might collect them."

"Can every kind there is be found here?"

"No, not all of them, but when I get more than I need of one kind, I can trade them with collectors farther north and west, so I can complete sets. It's the only way I see to earn the money. Look what I have already. Big gray Cecropias come from this kind; brown Polyphemus from that, and green Lunas from these. You aren't working on Sunday. Go with me only an hour, Pete!"

The man looked at her narrowly. She was young, wholesome, and beautiful. She was innocent, intensely in earnest, and she needed the money, he knew that.

"You didn't tell me what scared you," he said.

"Oh, I thought I did! Why you know I had Freckles's box packed full of moths and specimens, and one evening I sold some to the Bird Woman. Next morning I found a note telling me it wasn't safe to go inside the swamp. That sort of scared me. I think I'll go alone, rather than miss the chance, but I'd be so happy if you would take care of me. Then I could go anywhere I chose, because if I mired you could pull me out. You will take care of me, Pete?"

"Yes, I'll take care of you," promised Pete Corson.

"Goody!" said Elnora. "Let's start quick! And Pete, you look at these closely, and when you are hunting or going along the road, if one dangles under your nose, you cut off the little twig and save it for me, will you?"

"Yes, I'll save you all I see," promised Pete. He pushed back his hat and followed Elnora. She plunged fearlessly among bushes, over underbrush, and across dead logs. One minute she was crying wildly, that here was a big one, the next she was reaching for a limb above her head or on her knees overturning dead leaves under a hickory or oak tree, or working aside black muck with her bare hands as she searched for buried pupae cases. For the first hour Pete bent back bushes and followed, carrying what Elnora discovered. Then he found one.

"Is this the kind of thing you are looking for?" he asked bashfully, as he presented a wild cherry twig.

"Oh Pete, that's a Promethea! I didn't even hope to find one."

"What's the bird like?" asked Pete.

"Almost black wings," said Elnora, "with clay-coloured edges, and the most wonderful wine-coloured flush over the under side if it's a male, and stronger wine above and below if it's a female. Oh, aren't I happy!"

"How would it do to make what you have into a bunch that we could leave here, and come back for them?"

"That would be all right."

Relieved of his load Pete began work. First, he narrowly examined the cocoons Elnora had found. He questioned her as to what other kinds would be like. He began to use the eyes of a trained woodman and hunter in her behalf. He saw several so easily, and moved through the forest so softly, that Elnora forgot the moths in watching him. Presently she was carrying the specimens, and he was making the trips of investigation to see which was a cocoon and which a curled leaf, or he was on his knees digging around stumps. As he worked he kept asking questions. What kind of logs were best to look beside, what trees were pupae cases most likely to be under; on what bushes did caterpillars spin most frequently? Time passed, as it always does when one's occupation is absorbing.

When the Sintons took Mrs. Comstock home, they stopped to see Elnora. She was not there. Mrs. Comstock called at the edge of her woods and received no reply. Then Wesley turned and drove back to the Limberlost. He left Margaret and Mrs. Comstock holding the team and entertaining Billy, while he entered the swamp.

Elnora and Pete had made a wide trail behind them. Before Sinton had thought of calling, he heard voices and approached with some caution. Soon he saw Elnora, her flushed face beaming as she bent with an armload of twigs and branches and talked to a kneeling man.

"Now go cautiously!" she was saying. "I am just sure we will find an Imperialis here. It's their very kind of a place. There! What did I tell you! Isn't that splendid? Oh, I am so glad you came with me!"

Wesley stood staring in speechless astonishment, for the man had arisen, brushed the dirt from his hands, and held out to Elnora a small shining dark pupa case. As his face came into view Sinton almost cried out, for he was the one man of all others Wesley knew with whom he most feared for Elnora's safety. She had him on his knees digging pupae cases for her from the swamp.

"Elnora!" called Sinton. "Elnora!"

"Oh, Uncle Wesley!" cried the girl. "See what luck we've had! I know we have a dozen and a half cocoons and we have three pupae cases. It's much harder to get the cases because you have to dig for them, and you can't see where to look. But Pete is fine at it! He's found three, and he says he will keep watch beside the roads, and through the woods while he hunts. Isn't that splendid of him? Uncle Wesley, there is a college over there on the western edge of the swamp. Look closely, and you can see the great dome up among the clouds."

"I should say you have had luck," said Wesley, striving to make his voice natural. "But I thought you were not coming to the swamp?"

"Well, I wasn't," said Elnora, "but I couldn't find many anywhere else, honest, I couldn't, and just as soon as I came to the edge I began to see them here. I kept my promise. I didn't come in alone. Pete came with me. He's so strong, he isn't afraid of anything, and he's perfectly splendid to locate cocoons! He's found half of these. Come on, Pete, it's getting dark now, and we must go."

They started toward the trail, Pete carrying the cocoons. He left them at the case, while Elnora and Wesley went on to the carriage together.

"Elnora Comstock, what does this mean?" demanded her mother.

"It's all right, one of the neighbours was with her, and she got several dollars' worth of stuff," interposed Wesley.

"You oughter seen my pa," shouted Billy. "He was ist all whited out, and he laid as still as anything. They put him away deep in the ground."

"Billy!" breathed Margaret in a prolonged groan.

"Jimmy and Belle are going to be together in a nice place. They are coming to see me, and Snap is right down here by the wheel. Here, Snap! My, but he'll be tickled to get something to eat! He's 'most twisted as me. They get new clothes, and all they want to eat, too, but they'll miss me. They couldn't have got along without me. I took care of them. I had a lot of things give to me 'cause I was the littlest, and I always divided with them. But they won't need me now."

When she left the carriage Mrs. Comstock gravely shook hands with Billy. "Remember," she said to him, "I love boys, and I love dogs. Whenever you don't have a good time up there, take your dog and come right down and be my little boy. We will just have loads of fun. You should hear the whistles I can make. If you aren't treated right you come straight to me."

Billy wagged his head sagely. "You ist bet I will!" he said.

"Mother, how could you?" asked Elnora as they walked up the path.

"How could I, missy? You better ask how couldn't I? I just couldn't! Not for enough to pay, my road tax! Not for enough to pay the road tax, and the dredge tax, too!"

"Aunt Margaret always has been lovely to me, and I don't think it's fair to worry her."

"I choose to be lovely to Billy, and let her sweat out her own worries just as she has me, these sixteen years. There is nothing in all this world so good for people as taking a dose of their own medicine. The difference is that I am honest. I just say in plain English, 'if they don't treat you right, come to me.' They have only said it in actions and inferences. I want to teach Mag Sinton how her own doses taste, but she begins to sputter before I fairly get the spoon to her lips. Just you wait!"

"When I think what I owe her——" began Elnora.

"Well, thank goodness, I don't owe her anything, and so I'm perfectly free to do what I choose. Come on, and help me get supper. I'm hungry as Billy!"

Margaret Sinton rocked slowly back and forth in her chair. On her breast lay Billy's red head, one hand clutched her dress front with spasmodic grip, even after he was unconscious.

"You mustn't begin that, Margaret," said Sinton. "He's too heavy. And it's bad for him. He's better off to lie down and go to sleep alone."

"He's very light, Wesley. He jumps and quivers so. He has to be stronger than he is now, before he will sleep soundly."

CHAPTER IX. WHEREIN ELNORA DISCOVERS A VIOLIN, AND BILLY DISCIPLINES MARGARET

Elnora missed the little figure at the bridge the following morning. She slowly walked up the street and turned in at the wide entrance to the school grounds. She scarcely could comprehend that only a week ago she had gone there friendless, alone, and so sick at heart that she was physically ill. To-day she had decent clothing, books, friends, and her mind was at ease to work on her studies.

As she approached home that night the girl paused in amazement. Her mother had company, and she was laughing. Elnora entered the kitchen softly and peeped into the sitting-room. Mrs. Comstock sat in her chair holding a book and every few seconds a soft chuckle broke into a real laugh. Mark Twain was doing his work; while Mrs. Comstock was not lacking in a sense of humour. Elnora entered the room before her mother saw her. Mrs. Comstock looked up with flushed face.

"Where did you get this?" she demanded.

"I bought it," said Elnora.

"Bought it! With all the taxes due!"

"I paid for it out of my Indian money, mother," said Elnora. "I couldn't bear to spend so much on myself and nothing at all on you. I was afraid to buy the dress I should have liked to, and I thought the book would be company, while I was gone. I haven't read it, but I do hope it's good."

"Good! It's the biggest piece of foolishness I have read in all my life. I've laughed all day, ever since I found it. I had a notion to go out and read some of it to the cows and see if they wouldn't laugh."

"If it made you laugh, it's a wise book," said Elnora.

"Wise!" cried Mrs. Comstock. "You can stake your life it's a wise book. It takes the smartest man there is to do this kind of fooling," and she began laughing again.

Elnora, highly satisfied with her purchase, went to her room and put on her working clothes. Thereafter she made a point of bringing a book that she thought would interest her mother, from the library every week, and leaving it on the sitting-room table. Each night she carried home at least two school books and studied until she had mastered the points of her lessons. She did her share of the work faithfully, and every available minute she was in the fields searching for cocoons, for the moths promised to become her largest source of income.

She gathered baskets of nests, flowers, mosses, insects, and all sorts of natural history specimens and sold them to the grade teachers. At first she tried to tell these instructors what to teach their pupils about the specimens; but recognizing how much more she knew than they, one after another begged her to study at home, and use her spare hours in school to exhibit and explain nature subjects to their pupils. Elnora loved the work, and she needed the money, for every few days some matter of expense arose that she had not expected.

From the first week she had been received and invited with the crowd of girls in her class, and it was their custom in passing through the business part of the city to stop at the confectioners' and take turns in treating to expensive candies, ice cream sodas, hot chocolate, or whatever they fancied. When first Elnora was asked she accepted without understanding. The second time she went because she seldom had tasted these things, and they were so delicious she could not resist. After that she went because she knew all about it, and had decided to go.

She had spent half an hour on the log beside the trail in deep thought and had arrived at her conclusions. She worked harder than usual for the next week, but she seemed to thrive on work. It was October and the red leaves were falling when her first time came to treat. As the crowd flocked down the broad walk that night Elnora called, "Girls, it's my treat to-night! Come on!"

She led the way through the city to the grocery they patronized when they had a small spread, and entering came out with a basket, which she carried to the bridge on her home road. There she arranged the girls in two rows on the cement abutments and opening her basket she gravely offered each girl an exquisite little basket of bark, lined with red leaves, in one end of which nestled a juicy big red apple and in the other a spicy doughnut not an hour from Margaret

Sinton's frying basket.

Another time she offered big balls of popped corn stuck together with maple sugar, and liberally sprinkled with beechnut kernels. Again it was hickory-nut kernels glazed with sugar, another time maple candy, and once a basket of warm pumpkin pies. She never made any apology, or offered any excuse. She simply gave what she could afford, and the change was as welcome to those city girls accustomed to sodas and French candy, as were these same things to Elnora surfeited on popcorn and pie. In her room was a little slip containing a record of the number of weeks in the school year, the times it would be her turn to treat and the dates on which such occasions would fall, with a number of suggestions beside each. Once the girls almost fought over a basket lined with yellow leaves, and filled with fat, very ripe red haws. In late October there was a riot over one which was lined with red leaves and contained big fragrant pawpaws frost-bitten to a perfect degree. Then hazel nuts were ripe, and once they served. One day Elnora at her wits' end, explained to her mother that the girls had given her things and she wanted to treat them. Mrs. Comstock, with characteristic stubbornness, had said she would leave a basket at the grocery for her, but firmly declined to say what would be in it. All day Elnora struggled to keep her mind on her books. For hours she wavered in tense uncertainty. What would her mother do? Should she take the girls to the confectioner's that night or risk the basket? Mrs. Comstock could make delicious things to eat, but would she?

As they left the building Elnora made a final rapid mental calculation. She could not see her way clear to a decent treat for ten people for less than two dollars and if the basket proved to be nice, then the money would be wasted. She decided to risk it. As they went to the bridge the girls were betting on what the treat would be, and crowding near Elnora like spoiled small children. Elnora set down the basket.

"Girls," she said, "I don't know what this is myself, so all of us are going to be surprised. Here goes!"

She lifted the cover and perfumes from the land of spices rolled up. In one end of the basket lay ten enormous sugar cakes the tops of which had been liberally dotted with circles cut from stick candy. The candy had melted in baking and made small transparent wells of waxy sweetness and in the centre of each cake was a fat turtle made from a raisin with cloves for head and feet. The remainder of the basket was filled with big spiced pears that could be held by their stems while they were eaten. The girls shrieked and attacked the cookies, and of all the treats Elnora offered perhaps none was quite so long remembered as that.

When Elnora took her basket, placed her books in it, and started home, all the girls went with her as far as the fence where she crossed the field to the swamp. At parting they kissed her good-bye. Elnora was a happy girl as she hurried home to thank her mother. She was happy over her books that night, and happy all the way to school the following morning.

When the music swelled from the orchestra her heart almost broke with throbbing joy. For music always had affected her strangely, and since she had been comfortable enough in her surroundings to notice things, she had listened to every note to find what it was that literally hurt her heart, and at last she knew. It was the talking of the violins. They were human voices, and they spoke a language Elnora understood. It seemed to her that she must climb up on the stage, take the instruments from the fingers of the players and make them speak what was in her heart.

That night she said to her mother, "I am perfectly crazy for a violin. I am sure I could play one, sure as I live. Did any one——" Elnora never completed that sentence.

"Hush!" thundered Mrs. Comstock. "Be quiet! Never mention those things before me again—never as long as you live! I loathe them! They are a snare of the very devil himself! They were made to lure men and women from their homes and their honour. If ever I see you with one in your fingers I will smash it in pieces."

Naturally Elnora hushed, but she thought of nothing else after she had finished her lessons. At last there came a day when for some reason the leader of the orchestra left his violin on the grand piano. That morning Elnora made her first mistake in algebra. At noon, as soon as the building was empty, she slipped into the auditorium, found the side door which led to the stage, and going through the musicians' entrance she took the violin. She carried it back into the little side room where the orchestra assembled, closed all the doors, opened the case and lifted out the instrument.

She laid it on her breast, dropped her chin on it and drew the bow softly across the strings. One after another she tested the open notes. Gradually her stroke ceased to tremble and she drew the bow firmly. Then her fingers began to fall and softly, slowly she searched up and down those strings for sounds she knew. Standing in the middle of the floor, she tried over and over. It seemed scarcely a minute before the hall was filled with the sound of hurrying feet, and she was forced to put away the violin and go to her classes. The next day she prayed that the violin would be left again, but her petition was not answered. That night when she returned from the school she made an excuse to go down to see Billy. He was engaged in hulling walnuts by driving them through holes in a board. His hands were protected by a pair of Margaret's old gloves, but he had speckled his face generously. He appeared well, and greeted Elnora hilariously.

"Me an' the squirrels are laying up our winter stores," he shouted. "Cos the cold is coming, an' the snow an' if we have any nuts we have to fix 'em now. But I'm ahead, cos Uncle Wesley made me this board, and I can hull a big pile while the old squirrel does only ist one with his teeth."

Elnora picked him up and kissed him. "Billy, are you happy?" she asked.

"Yes, and so's Snap," answered Billy. "You ought to see him make the dirt fly when he gets after a chipmunk. I bet you he could dig up pa, if anybody wanted him to."

"Billy!" gasped Margaret as she came out to them.

"Well, me and Snap don't want him up, and I bet you Jimmy and Belle don't, either. I ain't been twisty inside once since I been here, and I don't want to go away, and Snap don't, either. He told me so."

"Billy! That is not true. Dogs can't talk," cautioned Margaret.

"Then what makes you open the door when he asks you to?" demanded Billy.

"Scratching and whining isn't talking."

"Anyway, it's the best Snap can talk, and you get up and do things he wants done. Chipmunks can talk too. You ought to hear them damn things holler when Snap gets them!"

"Billy! When you want a cooky for supper and I don't give it to you it is because you said a wrong word."

"Well, for——" Billy clapped his hand over his mouth and stained his face in swipes. "Well, for—anything! Did I go an' forget again! The cookies will get all hard, won't they? I bet you ten dollars I don't say that any more."

He espied Wesley and ran to show him a walnut too big to go through the holes, and Elnora and Margaret entered the house.

They talked of many things for a time and then Elnora said suddenly: "Aunt Margaret, I like music."

"I've noticed that in you all your life," answered Margaret.

"If dogs can't talk, I can make a violin talk," announced Elnora, and then in amazement watched the face of Margaret Sinton grow pale.

"A violin!" she wavered. "Where did you get a violin?"

"They fairly seemed to speak to me in the orchestra. One day the conductor left his in the auditorium, and I took it, and Aunt Margaret, I can make it do the wind in the swamp, the birds, and the animals. I can make any sound I ever heard on it. If I had a chance to practise a little, I could make it do the orchestra music, too. I don't know how I know, but I do."

"Did—did you ever mention it to your mother?" faltered Margaret.

"Yes, and she seems prejudiced against them. But oh, Aunt Margaret, I never felt so about anything, not even going to school. I just feel as if I'd die if I didn't have one. I could keep it at school, and practise at noon a whole hour. Soon they'd ask me to play in the orchestra. I could keep it in the case and practise in the woods in summer. You'd let me play over here Sunday. Oh, Aunt Margaret, what does one cost? Would it be wicked for me to take of my money, and buy a very cheap one? I could play on the least expensive one made."

"Oh, no you couldn't! A cheap machine makes cheap music. You got to have a fine fiddle to make it sing. But there's no sense in your buying one. There isn't a decent reason on earth why you shouldn't have your fa——"

"My father's!" cried Elnora. She caught Margaret Sinton by the arm. "My father had a violin! He played it. That's why I can! Where is it! Is it in our house? Is it in mother's room?"

"Elnora!" panted Margaret. "Your mother will kill me! She always hated it."

"Mother dearly loves music," said Elnora.

"Not when it took the man she loved away from her to make it!"

"Where is my father's violin?"

"Elnora!"

"I've never seen a picture of my father. I've never heard his name mentioned. I've never had a scrap that belonged to him. Was he my father, or am I a charity child like Billy, and so she hates me?"

"She has good pictures of him. Seems she just can't bear to hear him talked about. Of course, he was your father. They lived right there when you were born. She doesn't dislike you; she merely tries to make herself think she does. There's no sense in the world in you not having his violin. I've a great notion——"

"Has mother got it?"

"No. I've never heard her mention it. It was not at home when he—when he died."

"Do you know where it is?"

"Yes. I'm the only person on earth who does, except the one who has it."

"Who is that?"

"I can't tell you, but I will see if they have it yet, and get it if I can. But if your mother finds it out she will never forgive me."

"I can't help it," said Elnora. "I want that violin."

"I'll go to-morrow, and see if it has been destroyed."

"Destroyed! Oh, Aunt Margaret! Would any one dare?"

"I hardly think so. It was a good instrument. He played it like a master."

"Tell me!" breathed Elnora.

"His hair was red and curled more than yours, and his eyes were blue. He was tall, slim, and the very imp of mischief. He joked and teased all day until he picked up that violin. Then his head bent over it, and his eyes got big and earnest. He seemed to listen as if he first heard the notes, and then copied them. Sometimes he drew the bow trembly, like he wasn't sure it was right, and he might have to try again. He could almost drive you crazy when he wanted to, and no man that ever lived could make you dance as he could. He made it all up as he went. He seemed to listen for his dancing music, too. It appeared to come to him; he'd begin to play and you had to keep time. You couldn't be still; he loved to sweep a crowd around with that bow of his. I think it was the thing you call inspiration. I can see him now, his handsome head bent, his cheeks red, his eyes snapping, and that bow going across the strings, and driving us like sheep. He always kept his body swinging, and he loved to play. He often slighted his work shamefully, and sometimes her a little; that is why she hated it—Elnora, what are you making me do?"

The tears were rolling down Elnora's cheeks. "Oh, Aunt Margaret," she sobbed. "Why haven't you told me about him sooner? I feel as if you had given my father to me living, so that I could touch him. I can see him, too! Why didn't you ever tell me before? Go on! Go on!"

"I can't, Elnora! I'm scared silly. I never meant to say anything. If I hadn't promised her not to talk of him to you she wouldn't have let you come here. She made me swear it."

"But why? Why? Was he a shame? Was he disgraced?"

"Maybe it was that unjust feeling that took possession of her when she couldn't help him from the swamp. She had to blame some one, or go crazy, so she took it out on you. At times, those first ten years, if I had talked to you, and you had repeated anything to her, she might have struck you too hard. She was not master of herself. You must be patient with her, Elnora. God only knows what she has gone through, but I think she is a little better, lately."

"So do I," said Elnora. "She seems more interested in my clothes, and she fixes me such delicious lunches that the girls bring fine candies and cake and beg to trade. I gave half my lunch for a box of candy one day, brought it home to her, and told her. Since, she has wanted me to carry a market basket and treat the crowd every day, she was so pleased. Life has been too monotonous for her. I think she enjoys even the little change made by my going and coming. She sits up half the night to read the library books I bring, but she is so stubborn she won't even admit that she touches them. Tell me more about my father."

"Wait until I see if I can find the violin."

So Elnora went home in suspense, and that night she added to her prayers: "Dear Lord, be merciful to my father, and oh, do help Aunt Margaret to get his violin."

Wesley and Billy came in to supper tired and hungry. Billy ate heartily, but his eyes often rested on a plate of tempting cookies, and when Wesley offered them to the boy he reached for one. Margaret was compelled to explain that cookies were forbidden that night.

"What!" said Wesley. "Wrong words been coming again. Oh Billy, I do wish you could remember! I can't sit and eat cookies before a little boy who has none. I'll have to put mine back, too." Billy's face twisted in despair.

"Aw go on!" he said gruffly, but his chin was jumping, for Wesley was his idol.

"Can't do it," said Wesley. "It would choke me."

Billy turned to Margaret. "You make him," he appealed.

"He can't, Billy," said Margaret. "I know how he feels. You see, I can't myself."

Then Billy slid from his chair, ran to the couch, buried his face in the pillow and cried heartbrokenly. Wesley hurried to the barn, and Margaret to the kitchen. When the dishes were washed Billy slipped from the back door.

Wesley piling hay into the mangers heard a sound behind him and inquired, "That you, Billy?"

"Yes," answered Billy, "and it's all so dark you can't see me now, isn't it?"

"Well, mighty near," answered Wesley.

"Then you stoop down and open your mouth."

Sinton had shared bites of apple and nuts for weeks, for Billy had not learned how to eat anything without dividing with Jimmy and Belle. Since he had been separated from them, he shared with Wesley and Margaret. So he bent over the boy and received an instalment of cooky that almost choked him.

"Now you can eat it!" shouted Billy in delight. "It's all dark! I can't see what you're doing at all!"

Wesley picked up the small figure and set the boy on the back of a horse to bring his face level so that they could talk as men. He never towered from his height above Billy, but always lifted the little soul when important matters were to be discussed.

"Now what a dandy scheme," he commented. "Did you and Aunt Margaret fix it up?"

"No. She ain't had hers yet. But I got one for her. Ist as soon as you eat yours, I am going to take hers, and feed her first time I find her in the dark."

"But Billy, where did you get the cookies? You know Aunt Margaret said you were not to have any."

"I ist took them," said Billy, "I didn't take them for me. I ist took them for you and her."

Wesley thought fast. In the warm darkness of the barn the horses crunched their corn, a rat gnawed at a corner of the granary, and among the rafters the white pigeon cooed a soft sleepy note to his dusky mate.

"Did—did—I steal?" wavered Billy.

Wesley's big hands closed until he almost hurt the boy.

"No!" he said vehemently. "That is too big a word. You made a mistake. You were trying to be a fine little man, but you went at it the wrong way. You only made a mistake. All of us do that, Billy. The world grows that way. When we make mistakes we can see them; that teaches us to be more careful the next time, and so we learn."

"How wouldn't it be a mistake?"

"If you had told Aunt Margaret what you wanted to do, and asked her for the cookies she would have given them to you."

"But I was 'fraid she wouldn't, and you ist had to have it."

"Not if it was wrong for me to have it, Billy. I don't want it that much."

"Must I take it back?"

"You think hard, and decide yourself."

"Lift me down," said Billy, after a silence, "I got to put this in the jar, and tell her."

Wesley set the boy on the floor, but as he did so he paused one second and strained him close to his breast.

Margaret sat in her chair sewing; Billy slipped in and crept beside her. The little face was lined with tragedy.

"Why Billy, whatever is the matter?" she cried as she dropped her sewing and held out her arms. Billy stood back. He gripped his little fists tight and squared his shoulders. "I got to be shut up in the closet," he said.

"Oh Billy! What an unlucky day! What have you done now?"

"I stold!" gulped Billy. "He said it was ist a mistake, but it was worser 'an that. I took something you told me I wasn't to have."

"Stole!" Margaret was in despair. "What, Billy?"

"Cookies!" answered Billy in equal trouble.

"Billy!" wailed Margaret. "How could you?"

"It was for him and you," sobbed Billy. "He said he couldn't eat it 'fore me, but out in the barn it's all dark and I couldn't see. I thought maybe he could there. Then we might put out the light and you could have yours. He said I only made it worse, cos I mustn't take things, so I got to go in the closet. Will you hold me tight a little bit first? He did."

Margaret opened her arms and Billy rushed in and clung to her a few seconds, with all the force of his being, then he slipped to the floor and marched to the closet. Margaret opened the door. Billy gave one glance at the light, clinched his fists and, walking inside, climbed on a box. Margaret closed the door.

Then she sat and listened. Was the air pure enough? Possibly he might smother. She had read something once. Was it very dark? What if there should be a mouse in the closet and it should run across his foot and frighten him into spasms. Somewhere she had heard—Margaret leaned forward with tense face and listened. Something dreadful might happen. She could bear it no longer. She arose hurriedly and opened the door. Billy was drawn up on the box in a little heap, and he lifted a disapproving face to her.

"Shut that door!" he said. "I ain't been in here near long enough yet!"

CHAPTER X. WHEREIN ELNORA HAS MORE FINANCIAL TROUBLES, AND MRS. COMSTOCK AGAIN HEARS THE SONG OF THE LIMBERLOST

The following night Elnora hurried to Sintons'. She threw open the back door and with anxious eyes searched Margaret's face.

"You got it!" panted Elnora. "You got it! I can see by your face that you did. Oh, give it to me!"

"Yes, I got it, honey, I got it all right, but don't be so fast. It had been kept in such a damp place it needed glueing, it had to have strings, and a key was gone. I knew how much you wanted it, so I sent Wesley right to town with it. They said they could fix it good as new, but it should be varnished, and that it would take several days for the glue to set. You can have it Saturday."

"You found it where you thought it was? You know it's his?"

"Yes, it was just where I thought, and it's the same violin I've seen him play hundreds of times. It's all right, only laying so long it needs fixing."

"Oh Aunt Margaret! Can I ever wait?"

"It does seem a long time, but how could I help it? You couldn't do anything with it as it was. You see, it had been hidden away in a garret, and it needed cleaning and drying to make it fit to play again. You can have it Saturday sure. But Elnora, you've got to promise me that you will leave it here, or in town, and not let your mother get a hint of it. I don't know what she'd do."

"Uncle Wesley can bring it here until Monday. Then I will take it to school so that I can practise at noon. Oh, I don't know how to thank you. And there's more than the violin for which to be thankful. You've given me my father. Last night I saw him plainly as life."

"Elnora you were dreaming!"

"I know I was dreaming, but I saw him. I saw him so closely that a tiny white scar at the corner of his eyebrow showed. I was just reaching out to touch him when he disappeared."

"Who told you there was a scar on his forehead?"

"No one ever did in all my life. I saw it last night as he went down. And oh, Aunt Margaret! I saw what she did, and I heard his cries! No matter what she does, I don't believe I ever can be angry with her again. Her heart is broken, and she can't help it. Oh, it was terrible, but I am glad I saw it. Now, I will always understand."

"I don't know what to make of that," said Margaret. "I don't believe in such stuff at all, but you couldn't make it up, for you didn't know."

"I only know that I played the violin last night, as he played it, and while I played he came through the woods from the direction of Carneys'. It was summer and all the flowers were in bloom. He wore gray trousers and a blue shirt, his head was bare, and his face was beautiful. I could almost touch him when he sank."

Margaret stood perplexed. "I don't know what to think of that!" she ejaculated. "I was next to the last person who saw him before he was drowned. It was late on a June afternoon, and he was dressed as you describe. He was bareheaded because he had found a quail's nest before the bird began to brood, and he gathered the eggs in his hat and left it in a fence corner to get on his way home; they found it afterward."

"Was he coming from Carneys'?"

"He was on that side of the quagmire. Why he ever skirted it so close as to get caught is a mystery you will have to dream out. I never could understand it."

"Was he doing something he didn't want my mother to know?"

"Why?"

"Because if he had been, he might have cut close the swamp so he couldn't be seen from the garden. You know, the whole path straight to the pool where he sank can be seen from our back door. It's firm on our side. The danger is on the north and east. If he didn't want mother to know, he might have tried to pass on either of those sides and gone too close. Was he in a hurry?"

"Yes, he was," said Margaret. "He had been away longer than he expected, and he almost ran when he started home."

"And he'd left his violin somewhere that you knew, and you went and got it. I'll wager he was going to play, and didn't want mother to find it out!"

"It wouldn't make any difference to you if you knew every little thing, so quit thinking about it, and just be glad you are to have what he loved best of anything."

"That's true. Now I must hurry home. I am dreadfully late."

Elnora sprang up and ran down the road, but when she approached the cabin she climbed the fence, crossed the open woods pasture diagonally and entered at the back garden gate. As she often came that way when she had been looking for cocoons her mother asked no questions.

Elnora lived by the minute until Saturday, when, contrary to his usual custom, Wesley went to town in the forenoon, taking her along to buy some groceries. Wesley drove straight to the music store, and asked for the violin he had left to be mended.

In its new coat of varnish, with new keys and strings, it seemed much like any other violin to Sinton, but to Elnora it was the most beautiful instrument ever made, and a priceless treasure. She held it in her arms, touched the strings softly and then she drew the bow across them in whispering measure. She had no time to think what a remarkably good bow it was for sixteen years' disuse. The tan leather case might have impressed her as being in fine condition also, had she been in a state to question anything. She did remember to ask for the bill and she was gravely presented with a slip calling for four strings, one key, and a coat of varnish, total, one dollar fifty. It seemed to Elnora she never could put the precious instrument in the case and start home.

Wesley left her in the music store where the proprietor showed her all he could about tuning, and gave her several beginners' sheets of notes and scales. She carried the violin in her arms as far as the crossroads at the corner of their land, then reluctantly put it under the carriage seat.

As soon as her work was done she ran down to Sintons' and began to play, and on Monday the violin went to school with her. She made arrangements with the superintendent to leave it in his office and scarcely took time for her food at noon, she was so eager to practise. Often one of the girls asked her to stay in town all night for some lecture or entertainment. She could take the violin with her, practise, and secure help. Her skill was so great that the leader of the orchestra offered to give her lessons if she would play to pay for them, so her progress was rapid in technical work. But from the first day the instrument became hers, with perfect faith that she could play as her father did, she spent half her practice time in imitating the sounds of all outdoors and improvising the songs her happy heart sang in those days.

So the first year went, and the second and third were a repetition; but the fourth was different, for that was the close of the course, ending with graduation and all its attendant ceremonies and expenses. To Elnora these appeared mountain high. She had hoarded every cent, thinking twice before she parted with a penny, but teaching natural history in the grades had taken time from her studies in school which must be made up outside. She was a conscientious student, ranking first in most of her classes, and standing high in all branches. Her interest in her violin had grown with the years. She went to school early and practised half an hour in the little room adjoining the stage, while the orchestra gathered. She put in a full hour at noon, and remained another half hour at night. She carried the violin to Sintons' on Saturday and practised all the time she could there, while Margaret watched the road to see that Mrs. Comstock was not coming. She had become so skilful that it was a delight to hear her play music of any composer, but when she played her own, that was joy inexpressible, for then the wind blew, the water rippled, the Limberlost sang her songs of sunshine, shadow, black storm, and white night.

Since her dream Elnora had regarded her mother with peculiar tenderness. The girl realized, in a measure, what had happened. She avoided anything that possibly could stir bitter memories or draw deeper a line on the hard, white face. This cost many sacrifices, much work, and sometimes delayed progress, but the horror of that awful dream remained with Elnora. She worked her way cheerfully, doing all she could to interest her mother in things that happened in school, in the city, and by carrying books that were entertaining from the public library.

Three years had changed Elnora from the girl of sixteen to the very verge of womanhood. She had grown tall, round, and her face had the loveliness of perfect complexion, beautiful eyes and hair and an added touch from within that might have been called comprehension. It was a compound of self-reliance, hard knocks, heart hunger, unceasing work, and generosity. There was no form of suffering with which the girl could not sympathize, no work she was afraid to attempt, no subject she had investigated she did not understand. These things combined to produce a breadth and depth of character altogether unusual. She was so absorbed in her classes and her music that she had not been able to gather many specimens. When she realized this and hunted assiduously, she soon found that changing natural conditions had affected such work. Men all around were clearing available land. The trees fell wherever corn would grow. The swamp was broken by several gravel roads, dotted in places around the edge with little frame houses, and the machinery of oil wells; one especially low place around the region of Freckles's room was nearly all that remained of the original. Wherever the trees fell the moisture dried, the creeks ceased to flow, the river ran low, and at times the bed was dry. With unbroken sweep the winds of the west came, gathering force with every mile and howled and raved; threatening to tear the shingles from the roof, blowing the surface from the soil in clouds of fine dust and rapidly changing everything. From coming in with two or three dozen rare moths in a day, in three years' time Elnora had grown to be delighted with finding two or three. Big pursy caterpillars could not be picked from their favourite bushes, when there were no bushes. Dragonflies would not hover over dry places, and butterflies became scarce in proportion to the flowers, while no land yields over three crops of Indian relics.

All the time the expense of books, clothing and incidentals had continued. Elnora added to her bank account whenever she could, and drew out when she was compelled, but she omitted the important feature of calling for a balance. So, one early spring morning in the last quarter of the fourth year, she almost fainted when she learned that her funds were gone. Commencement with its extra expense was coming, she had no money, and very few cocoons to open in June, which would be too late. She had one collection for the Bird Woman complete to a pair of Imperialis moths, and that was her only asset. On the day she added these big Yellow Emperors she had been promised a check for three hundred dollars, but she would not get it until these specimens were secured. She remembered that she never had found an Emperor before June.

Moreover, that sum was for her first year in college. Then she would be of age, and she meant to sell enough of her share of her father's land to finish. She knew her mother would oppose her bitterly in that, for Mrs. Comstock had clung to every acre and tree that belonged to her husband. Her land was almost complete forest where her neighbours owned cleared farms, dotted with wells that every hour sucked oil from beneath her holdings, but she was too absorbed in the grief she nursed to know or care. The Brushwood road and the redredging of the big Limberlost ditch had been more than she could pay from her income, and she had trembled before the wicket as she asked the banker if she had funds to pay it, and wondered why he laughed when he assured her she had. For Mrs. Comstock had spent no time on compounding interest, and never added the sums she had been depositing through nearly twenty years. Now she thought her funds were almost gone, and every day she worried over expenses. She could see no reason in going through the forms of graduation when pupils had all in their heads that was required to graduate. Elnora knew she had to have her diploma in order to enter the college she wanted to attend, but she did not dare utter the word, until high school was finished, for, instead of softening as she hoped her mother had begun to do, she seemed to remain very much the same.

When the girl reached the swamp she sat on a log and thought over the expense she was compelled to meet. Every member of her particular set was having a large photograph taken to exchange with the others. Elnora loved these girls and boys, and to say she could not have their pictures to keep was more than she could endure. Each one would give to all the others a handsome graduation present. She knew they would prepare gifts for her whether she could make a present in return or not. Then it was the custom for each graduating class to give a great entertainment and use the funds to present the school with a statue for the entrance hall. Elnora had been cast for and was practising a part in that performance. She was expected to furnish her dress and personal necessities. She had been told that she must have a green gauze dress, and where was it to come from?

Every girl of the class would have three beautiful new frocks for Commencement: one for the baccalaureate sermon, another, which could be plain, for graduation exercises, and a handsome one for the banquet and ball. Elnora faced the past three years and wondered how she could have spent so much money and not kept account of it. She did not realize where it had gone. She did not know what she could do now. She thought over the photographs, and at last settled that question to her satisfaction. She studied longer over the gifts, ten handsome ones there must be, and at last decided she could arrange for them. The green dress came first. The lights would be dim in the scene, and the setting deep woods. She could manage that. She simply could not have three dresses. She would have to get a very simple one for the sermon and do the best she could for graduation. Whatever she got for that must be made with a guimpe that could be taken out to make it a little more festive for the ball. But where could she get even two pretty dresses?

The only hope she could see was to break into the collection of the man from India, sell some moths, and try to replace them in June. But in her soul she knew that never would do. No June ever brought just the things she hoped it would. If she spent the college money she knew she could not replace it. If she did not, the only way was to secure a room in the grades and teach a year. Her work there had been so appreciated that Elnora felt with the recommendation she knew she could get from the superintendent and teachers she could secure a position. She was sure she could pass the examinations easily. She had once gone on Saturday, taken them and secured a license for a year before she left the Brushwood school.

She wanted to start to college when the other girls were going. If she could make the first year alone, she could manage the remainder. But make that first year herself, she must. Instead of selling any of her collection, she must hunt as she never before had hunted and find a Yellow Emperor. She had to have it, that was all. Also, she had to have those dresses. She thought of Wesley and dismissed it. She thought of the Bird Woman, and knew she could not tell her. She thought of every way in which she ever had hoped to earn money and realized that with the play, committee meetings, practising, and final examinations she scarcely had time to live, much less to do more than the work required for her pictures and gifts. Again Elnora was in trouble, and this time it seemed the worst of all.

It was dark when she arose and went home.

"Mother," she said, "I have a piece of news that is decidedly not cheerful."

"Then keep it to yourself!" said Mrs. Comstock. "I think I have enough to bear without a great girl like you piling trouble on me."

"My money is all gone!" said Elnora.

"Well, did you think it would last forever? It's been a marvel to me that it's held out as well as it has, the way you've dressed and gone."

"I don't think I've spent any that I was not compelled to," said Elnora. "I've dressed on just as little as I possibly could to keep going. I am heartsick. I thought I had over fifty dollars to put me through Commencement, but they tell me it is all gone."

"Fifty dollars! To put you through Commencement! What on earth are you proposing to do?"

"The same as the rest of them, in the very cheapest way possible."

"And what might that be?"

Elnora omitted the photographs, the gifts and the play. She told only of the sermon, graduation exercises, and the ball.

"Well, I wouldn't trouble myself over that," sniffed Mrs. Comstock. "If you want to go to a sermon, put on the dress you always use for meeting. If you need white for the exercises wear the new dress you got last spring. As for the ball, the best thing for you to do is to stay a mile away from such folly. In my opinion you'd best bring home your books, and quit right now. You can't be fixed like the rest of them, don't be so foolish as to run into it. Just stay here and let these last few days go. You can't learn enough more to be of any account."

"But, mother," gasped Elnora. "You don't understand!"

"Oh, yes, I do!" said Mrs. Comstock. "I understand perfectly. So long as the money lasted, you held up your head, and went sailing without even explaining how you got it from the stuff you gathered. Goodness knows I couldn't see. But now it's gone, you come whining to me. What have I got? Have you forgot that the ditch and the road completely strapped me? I haven't any money. There's nothing for you to do but get out of it."

"I can't!" said Elnora desperately. "I've gone on too long. It would make a break in everything. They wouldn't let me have my diploma!"

"What's the difference? You've got the stuff in your head. I wouldn't give a rap for a scrap of paper. That don't mean anything!"

"But I've worked four years for it, and I can't enter—I ought to have it to help me get a school, when I want to teach. If I don't have my grades to show, people will think I quit because I couldn't pass my examinations. I must have my diploma!"

"Then get it!" said Mrs. Comstock.

"The only way is to graduate with the others."

"Well, graduate if you are bound to!"

"But I can't, unless I have things enough like the class, that I don't look as I did that first day."

"Well, please remember I didn't get you into this, and I can't get you out. You are set on having your own way. Go on, and have it, and see how you like it!"

Elnora went upstairs and did not come down again that night, which her mother called pouting.

"I've thought all night," said the girl at breakfast, "and I can't see any way but to borrow the money of Uncle Wesley and pay it back from some that the Bird Woman will owe me, when I get one more specimen. But that means that I can't go to—that I will have to teach this winter, if I can get a city grade or a country school."

"Just you dare go dinging after Wesley Sinton for money," cried Mrs. Comstock. "You won't do any such a thing!"

"I can't see any other way. I've got to have the money!"

"Quit, I tell you!"

"I can't quit!—I've gone too far!"

"Well then, let me get your clothes, and you can pay me back."

"But you said you had no money!"

"Maybe I can borrow some at the bank. Then you can return it when the Bird Woman pays you."

"All right," said Elnora. "I don't need expensive things. Just some kind of a pretty cheap white dress for the sermon, and a white one a little better than I had last summer, for Commencement and the ball. I can use the white gloves and shoes I got myself for last year, and you can get my dress made at the same place you did that one. They have my measurements, and do perfect work. Don't get expensive things. It will be warm so I can go bareheaded."

Then she started to school, but was so tired and discouraged she scarcely could walk. Four years' plans going in one day! For she felt that if she did not start to college that fall she never would. Instead of feeling relieved at her mother's offer, she was almost too ill to go on. For the thousandth time she groaned: "Oh, why didn't I keep account of my money?"

After that the days passed so swiftly she scarcely had time to think, but several trips her mother made to town, and the assurance that everything was all right, satisfied Elnora. She worked very hard to pass good final examinations and perfect herself for the play. For two days she had remained in town with the Bird Woman in order to spend more time practising and at her work.

Often Margaret had asked about her dresses for graduation, and Elnora had replied that they were with a woman in the city who had made her a white dress for last year's Commencement when she was a junior usher, and they would be all right. So Margaret, Wesley, and Billy concerned themselves over what they would give her for a present. Margaret suggested a beautiful dress. Wesley said that would look to every one as if she needed dresses. The thing was to get a handsome gift like all the others would have. Billy wanted to present her a five-dollar gold piece to buy music for her violin. He was positive Elnora would like that best of anything.

It was toward the close of the term when they drove to town one evening to try to settle this important question. They knew Mrs. Comstock had been alone several days, so they asked her to accompany them. She had been more lonely than she would admit, filled with unusual unrest besides, and so she was glad to go. But before they had driven a mile Billy had told that they were going to buy Elnora a graduation present, and Mrs. Comstock devoutly wished that she had remained at home. She was prepared when Billy asked: "Aunt Kate, what are you going to give Elnora when she graduates?"

"Plenty to eat, a good bed to sleep in, and do all the work while she trollops," answered Mrs. Comstock dryly.

Billy reflected. "I guess all of them have that," he said. "I mean a present you buy at the store, like Christmas?"

"It is only rich folks who buy presents at stores," replied Mrs. Comstock. "I can't afford it."

"Well, we ain't rich," he said, "but we are going to buy Elnora something as fine as the rest of them have if we sell a corner of the farm. Uncle Wesley said so."

"A fool and his land are soon parted," said Mrs. Comstock tersely. Wesley and Billy laughed, but Margaret did not enjoy the remark.

While they were searching the stores for something on which all of them could decide, and Margaret was holding Billy to keep him from saying anything before Mrs. Comstock about the music on which he was determined, Mr. Brownlee met Wesley and stopped to shake hands.

"I see your boy came out finely," he said.

"I don't allow any boy anywhere to be finer than Billy," said Wesley.

"I guess you don't allow any girl to surpass Elnora," said Mr. Brownlee. "She comes home with Ellen often, and my wife and I love her. Ellen says she is great in her part to-night. Best thing in the whole play! Of course, you are in to see it! If you haven't reserved seats, you'd better start pretty soon, for the high school auditorium only seats a thousand. It's always jammed at these home-talent plays. All of us want to see how our children perform."

"Why yes, of course," said the bewildered Wesley. Then he hurried to Margaret. "Say," he said, "there is going to be a play at the high school to-night; and Elnora is in it. Why hasn't she told us?"

"I don't know," said Margaret, "but I'm going."

"So am I," said Billy.

"Me too!" said Wesley, "unless you think for some reason she doesn't want us. Looks like she would have told us if she had. I'm going to ask her mother."

"Yes, that's what's she's been staying in town for," said Mrs. Comstock. "It's some sort of a swindle to raise money for her class to buy some silly thing to stick up in the school house hall to remember them by. I don't know whether it's now or next week, but there's something of the kind to be done."

"Well, it's to-night," said Wesley, "and we are going. It's my treat, and we've got to hurry or we won't get in. There are reserved seats, and we have none, so it's the gallery for us, but I don't care so I get to take one good peep at Elnora."

"S'pose she plays?" whispered Margaret in his ear.

"Aw, tush! She couldn't!" said Wesley.

"Well, she's been doing it three years in the orchestra, and working like a slave at it."

"Oh, well that's different. She's in the play to-night. Brownlee told me so. Come on, quick! We'll drive and hitch closest place we can find to the building."

Margaret went in the excitement of the moment, but she was troubled.

When they reached the building Wesley tied the team to a railing and Billy sprang out to help Margaret. Mrs. Comstock sat still.

"Come on, Kate," said Wesley, reaching his hand.

"I'm not going anywhere," said Mrs. Comstock, settling comfortably back against the cushions.

All of them begged and pleaded, but it was no use. Not an inch would Mrs. Comstock budge. The night was warm and the carriage comfortable, the horses were securely hitched. She did not care to see what idiotic thing a pack of school children were doing, she would wait until the Sintons returned. Wesley told her it might be two hours, and she said she did not care if it were four, so they left her.

"Did you ever see such——?"

"Cookies!" cried Billy.

"Such blamed stubbornness in all your life?" demanded Wesley. "Won't come to see as fine a girl as Elnora in a stage performance. Why, I wouldn't miss it for fifty dollars!

"I think it's a blessing she didn't," said Margaret placidly. "I begged unusually hard so she wouldn't. I'm scared of my life for fear Elnora will play."

They found seats near the door where they could see fairly well. Billy stood at the back of the hall and had a good view. By and by, a great volume of sound welled from the orchestra, but Elnora was not playing.

"Told you so!" said Sinton. "Got a notion to go out and see if Kate won't come now. She can take my seat, and I'll stand with Billy."

"You sit still!" said Margaret emphatically. "This is not over yet."

So Wesley remained in his seat. The play opened and progressed very much as all high school plays have gone for the past fifty years. But Elnora did not appear in any of the scenes.

Out in the warm summer night a sour, grim woman nursed an aching heart and tried to justify herself. The effort irritated her intensely. She felt that she could not afford the things that were being done. The old fear of losing the land that she and Robert Comstock had purchased and started clearing was strong upon her. She was thinking of him, how she needed him, when the orchestra music poured from the open windows near her. Mrs. Comstock endured it as long as she could, and then slipped from the carriage and fled down the street.

She did not know how far she went or how long she stayed, but everything was still, save an occasional raised voice when she wandered back. She stood looking at the building. Slowly she entered the wide gates and followed up the walk. Elnora had been coming here for almost four years. When Mrs. Comstock reached the door she looked inside. The wide hall was lighted with electricity, and the statuary and the decorations of the walls did not seem like pieces of foolishness. The marble appeared pure, white, and the big pictures most interesting. She walked the length of the hall and slowly read the titles of the statues and the names of the pupils who had donated them. She speculated on where the piece Elnora's class would buy could be placed to advantage.

Then she wondered if they were having a large enough audience to buy marble. She liked it better than the bronze, but it looked as if it cost more. How white the broad stairway was! Elnora had been climbing those stairs for years and never told her they were marble. Of course, she thought they were wood. Probably the upper hall was even grander than this. She went over to the fountain, took a drink, climbed to the first landing and looked around her, and then without thought to the second. There she came opposite the wide-open doors and the entrance to the auditorium packed with people and a crowd standing outside. When they noticed a tall woman with white face and hair and black dress, one by one they stepped a little aside, so that Mrs. Comstock could see the stage. It was covered with curtains, and no one was doing anything. Just as she turned to go a sound so faint that every one leaned forward and listened, drifted down the auditorium. It was difficult to tell just what it was; after one instant half the audience looked toward the windows, for it seemed only a breath of wind rustling freshly opened leaves; merely a hint of stirring air.

Then the curtains were swept aside swiftly. The stage had been transformed into a lovely little corner of creation, where trees and flowers grew and moss carpeted the earth. A soft wind blew and it was the gray of dawn. Suddenly a robin began to sing, then a song sparrow joined him, and then several orioles began talking at once. The light grew stronger, the dew drops trembled, flower perfume began to creep out to the audience; the air moved the branches gently and a rooster crowed. Then all the scene was shaken with a babel of bird notes in which you could hear a cardinal whistling, and a blue finch piping. Back somewhere among the high branches a dove cooed and then a horse neighed shrilly. That set a blackbird crying, "T'check," and a whole flock answered it. The crows began to caw and a lamb bleated. Then the grosbeaks, chats, and vireos had something to say, and the sun rose higher, the light grew stronger and the breeze rustled the treetops loudly; a cow bawled and the whole barnyard answered. The guineas were clucking, the turkey gobbler strutting, the hens calling, the chickens cheeping, the light streamed down straight overhead and the bees began to hum. The air stirred strongly, and away in an unseen field a reaper clacked and rattled through ripening wheat while the driver whistled. An uneasy mare whickered to her colt, the colt answered, and the light began to decline. Miles away a rooster crowed for twilight, and dusk was coming down. Then a catbird and a brown thrush sang against a grosbeak and a hermit thrush. The air was tremulous with heavenly notes, the lights went out in the hall, dusk swept across the stage, a cricket sang and a katydid answered, and a wood pewee wrung the heart with its lonesome cry. Then a night hawk screamed, a whip-poor-will complained, a belated killdeer swept the sky, and the night wind sang a louder song. A little screech owl tuned up in the distance, a barn owl replied, and a great horned owl drowned both their voices. The moon shone and the scene was warm with mellow light. The bird voices died and soft exquisite melody began to swell and roll. In the centre of the stage, piece by piece the grasses, mosses and leaves dropped from an embankment, the foliage softly blew away, while plainer and plainer came the outlines of a lovely girl figure draped in soft clinging green. In her shower of bright hair a few green leaves and white blossoms clung, and they fell over her robe down to her feet. Her white throat and arms were bare, she leaned forward a little and swayed with the melody, her eyes fast on the clouds above her, her lips parted, a pink tinge of exercise in her cheeks as she drew her bow. She played as only a peculiar chain of circumstances puts it in the power of a very few to play. All nature had grown still, the violin sobbed, sang, danced and quavered on alone, no voice in particular; the soul of the melody of all nature combined in one great outpouring.

At the doorway, a white-faced woman endured it as long as she could and then fell senseless. The men nearest carried her down the hall to the fountain, revived her, and then placed her in the carriage to which she directed them. The girl played on and never knew. When she finished, the uproar of applause sounded a block down the street, but the half-senseless woman scarcely realized what it meant. Then the girl came to the front of the stage, bowed, and lifting the violin she played her conception of an invitation to dance. Every living soul within sound of her notes strained their nerves to sit still and let only their hearts dance with her. When that began the woman ran toward the country. She never stopped until the carriage overtook her half-way to her cabin. She said she had grown tired of sitting, and walked on ahead. That night she asked Billy to remain with her and sleep on Elnora's bed. Then she pitched headlong upon her own, and suffered agony of soul such as she never before had known. The swamp had sent back the soul of her loved dead and put it into the body of the daughter she resented, and it was almost more than she could endure and live.

CHAPTER XI. WHEREIN ELNORA GRADUATES, AND FRECKLES AND THE ANGEL SEND GIFTS

That was Friday night. Elnora came home Saturday morning and began work. Mrs. Comstock asked no questions, and the girl only told her that the audience had been large enough to more than pay for the piece of statuary the class had selected for the hall. Then she inquired about her dresses and was told they would be ready for her. She had been invited to go to the Bird Woman's to prepare for both the sermon and Commencement exercises. Since there was so much practising to do, it had been arranged that she should remain there from the night of the sermon until after she was graduated. If Mrs. Comstock decided to attend she was to drive in with the Sintons. When Elnora begged her to come she said she cared nothing about such silliness.

It was almost time for Wesley to come to take Elnora to the city, when fresh from her bath, and dressed to her outer garment, she stood with expectant face before her mother and cried: "Now my dress, mother!"

Mrs. Comstock was pale as she replied: "It's on my bed. Help yourself."

Elnora opened the door and stepped into her mother's room with never a misgiving. Since the night Margaret and Wesley had brought her clothing, when she first started to school, her mother had selected all of her dresses, with Mrs. Sinton's help made most of them, and Elnora had paid the bills. The white dress of the previous spring was the first made at a dressmaker's. She had worn that as junior usher at Commencement; but her mother had selected the material, had it made, and it had fitted perfectly and had been suitable in every way. So with her heart at rest on that point, Elnora hurried to the bed to find only her last summer's white dress, freshly washed and ironed. For an instant she stared at it, then she picked up the garment, looked at the bed beneath it, and her gaze slowly swept the room.

It was unfamiliar. Perhaps this was the third time she had been in it since she was a very small child. Her eyes ranged over the beautiful walnut dresser, the tall bureau, the big chest, inside which she never had seen, and the row of masculine attire hanging above it. Somewhere a dainty lawn or mull dress simply must be hanging: but it was not. Elnora dropped on the chest because she felt too weak to stand. In less than two hours she must be in the church, at Onabasha. She could not wear a last year's washed dress. She had nothing else. She leaned against the wall and her father's overcoat brushed her face. She caught the folds and clung to it with all her might.

"Oh father! Father!" she moaned. "I need you! I don't believe you would have done this!" At last she opened the door.

"I can't find my dress," she said.

"Well, as it's the only one there I shouldn't think it would be much trouble."

"You mean for me to wear an old washed dress to-night?"

"It's a good dress. There isn't a hole in it! There's no reason on earth why you shouldn't wear it."

"Except that I will not," said Elnora. "Didn't you provide any dress for Commencement, either?"

"If you soil that to-night, I've plenty of time to wash it again."

Wesley's voice called from the gate.

"In a minute," answered Elnora.

She ran upstairs and in an incredibly short time came down wearing one of her gingham school dresses. Her face cold and hard, she passed her mother and went into the night. Half an hour later Margaret and Billy stopped for Mrs. Comstock with the carriage. She had determined fully that she would not go before they called. With the sound of their voices a sort of horror of being left seized her, so she put on her hat, locked the door and went out to them.

"How did Elnora look?" inquired Margaret anxiously.

"Like she always does," answered Mrs. Comstock curtly.

"I do hope her dresses are as pretty as the others," said Margaret. "None of them will have prettier faces or nicer ways."

Wesley was waiting before the big church to take care of the team. As they stood watching the people enter the building, Mrs. Comstock felt herself growing ill. When they went inside among the lights, saw the flower-decked stage, and the masses of finely dressed people, she grew no better. She could hear Margaret and Billy softly commenting on what was being done.

"That first chair in the very front row is Elnora's," exulted Billy, "cos she's got the highest grades, and so she gets to lead the procession to the platform."

"The first chair!" "Lead the procession!" Mrs. Comstock was dumbfounded. The notes of the pipe organ began to fill the building in a slow rolling march. Would Elnora lead the procession in a gingham dress? Or would she be absent and her chair vacant on this great occasion? For now, Mrs. Comstock could see that it was a great occasion. Every one would remember how Elnora had played a few nights before, and they would miss her and pity her. Pity? Because she had no one to care for her. Because she was worse off than if she had no mother. For the first time in her life, Mrs. Comstock began to study herself as she would appear to others. Every time a junior girl came fluttering down the aisle, leading some one to a seat, and Mrs. Comstock saw a beautiful white dress pass, a wave of positive illness swept over her. What had she done? What would become of Elnora?

As Elnora rode to the city, she answered Wesley's questions in monosyllables so that he thought she was nervous or rehearsing her speech and did not care to talk. Several times the girl tried to tell him and realized that if she said the first word it would bring uncontrollable tears. The Bird Woman opened the screen and stared unbelievingly.

"Why, I thought you would be ready; you are so late!" she said. "If you have waited to dress here, we must hurry."

"I have nothing to put on," said Elnora.

In bewilderment the Bird Woman drew her inside.

"Did—did—" she faltered. "Did you think you would wear that?"

"No. I thought I would telephone Ellen that there had been an accident and I could not come. I don't know yet how to explain. I'm too sick to think. Oh, do you suppose I can get something made by Tuesday, so that I can graduate?"

"Yes; and you'll get something on you to-night, so that you can lead your class, as you have done for four years. Go to my room and take off that gingham, quickly. Anna, drop everything, and come help me."

The Bird Woman ran to the telephone and called Ellen Brownlee.

"Elnora has had an accident. She will be a little late," she said. "You have got to make them wait. Have them play extra music before the march."

Then she turned to the maid. "Tell Benson to have the carriage at the gate, just as soon as he can get it there. Then come to my room. Bring the thread box from the sewing-room, that roll of wide white ribbon on the cutting table, and gather all the white pins from every dresser in the house. But first come with me a minute."

"I want that trunk with the Swamp Angel's stuff in it, from the cedar closet," she panted as they reached the top of the stairs.

They hurried down the hall together and dragged the big trunk to the Bird Woman's room. She opened it and began tossing out white stuff.

"How lucky that she left these things!" she cried. "Here are white shoes, gloves, stockings, fans, everything!"

"I am all ready but a dress," said Elnora.

The Bird Woman began opening closets and pulling out drawers and boxes.

"I think I can make it this way," she said.

She snatched up a creamy lace yoke with long sleeves that recently had been made for her and held it out. Elnora slipped into it, and the Bird Woman began smoothing out wrinkles and sewing in pins. It fitted very well with a little lapping in the back. Next, from among the Angel's clothing she caught up a white silk waist with low neck and elbow sleeves, and Elnora put it on. It was large enough, but distressingly short in the waist, for the Angel had worn it at a party when she was sixteen. The Bird Woman loosened the sleeves and pushed them to a puff on the shoulders, catching them in places with pins. She began on the wide draping of the yoke, fastening it front, back and at each shoulder. She pulled down the waist and pinned it. Next came a soft white dress skirt of her own. By pinning her waist band quite four inches above Elnora's, the Bird Woman could secure a perfect Empire sweep, with the clinging silk. Then she began with the wide white ribbon that was to trim a new frock for herself, bound it three times around the high waist effect she had managed, tied the ends in a knot and let them fall to the floor in a beautiful sash.

"I want four white roses, each with two or three leaves," she cried.

Anna ran to bring them, while the Bird Woman added pins.

"Elnora," she said, "forgive me, but tell me truly. Is your mother so poor as to make this necessary?"

"No," answered Elnora. "Next year I am heir to my share of over three hundred acres of land covered with almost as valuable timber as was in the Limberlost. We adjoin it. There could be thirty oil wells drilled that would yield to us the thousands our neighbours are draining from under us, and the bare land is worth over one hundred dollars an acre for farming. She is not poor, she is—I don't know what she is. A great trouble soured and warped her. It made her peculiar. She does not in the least understand, but it is because she doesn't care to, instead of ignorance. She does not——"

Elnora stopped.

"She is—is different," finished the girl.

Anna came with the roses. The Bird Woman set one on the front of the draped yoke, one on each shoulder and the last among the bright masses of brown hair. Then she turned the girl facing the tall mirror.

"Oh!" panted Elnora. "You are a genius! Why, I will look as well as any of them."

"Thank goodness for that!" cried the Bird Woman. "If it wouldn't do, I should have been ill. You are lovely; altogether lovely! Ordinarily I shouldn't say that; but when I think of how you are carpentered, I'm admiring the result."

The organ began rolling out the march as they came in sight. Elnora took her place at the head of the procession, while every one wondered. Secretly they had hoped that she would be dressed well enough, that she would not appear poor and neglected. What this radiant young creature, gowned in the most recent style, her smooth skin flushed with excitement, and a rose-set coronet of red gold on her head, had to do with the girl they knew was difficult to decide. The signal was given and Elnora began the slow march across the vestry and down the aisle. The music welled softly, and Margaret began to sob without knowing why.

Mrs. Comstock gripped her hands together and shut her eyes. It seemed an eternity to the suffering woman before Margaret caught her arm and whispered, "Oh, Kate! For any sake look at her! Here! The aisle across!"

Mrs. Comstock opened her eyes and directing them where she was told, gazed intently, and slid down in her seat close to collapse. She was saved by Margaret's tense clasp and her command: "Here! Idiot! Stop that!"

In the blaze of light Elnora climbed the steps to the palm-embowered platform, crossed it and took her place. Sixty young men and women, each of them dressed the best possible, followed her. There were manly, fine-looking men in that class which Elnora led. There were girls of beauty and grace, but not one of them was handsomer or clothed in better taste than she.

Billy thought the time never would come when Elnora would see him, but at last she met his eye, then Margaret and Wesley had faint signs of recognition in turn, but there was no softening of the girl's face and no hint of a smile when she saw her mother.

Heartsick, Katharine Comstock tried to prove to herself that she was justified in what she had done, but she could not. She tried to blame Elnora for not saying that she was to lead a procession and sit on a platform in the sight of hundreds of people; but that was impossible, for she realized that she would have scoffed and not understood if she had been told. Her heart pained until she suffered with every breath.

When at last the exercises were over she climbed into the carriage and rode home without a word. She did not hear what Margaret and Billy were saying. She scarcely heard Wesley, who drove behind, when he told her that Elnora would not be home until Wednesday. Early the next morning Mrs. Comstock was on her way to Onabasha. She was waiting when the Brownlee store opened. She examined ready-made white dresses, but they had only one of the right size, and it was marked forty dollars. Mrs. Comstock did not hesitate over the price, but whether the dress would be suitable. She would have to ask Elnora. She inquired her way to the home of the Bird Woman and knocked.

"Is Elnora Comstock here?" she asked the maid.

"Yes, but she is still in bed. I was told to let her sleep as long as she would."

"Maybe I could sit here and wait," said Mrs. Comstock. "I want to see about getting her a dress for to-morrow. I am her mother."

"Then you don't need wait or worry," said the girl cheerfully. "There are two women up in the sewing-room at work on a dress for her right now. It will be done in time, and it will be a beauty."

Mrs. Comstock turned and trudged back to the Limberlost. The bitterness in her soul became a physical actuality, which water would not wash from her lips. She was too late! She was not needed. Another woman was mothering her girl. Another woman would prepare a beautiful dress such as Elnora had worn the previous night. The girl's love and gratitude would go to her. Mrs. Comstock tried the old process of blaming some one else, but she felt no better. She nursed her grief as closely as ever in the long days of the girl's absence. She brooded over Elnora's possession of the forbidden violin and her ability to play it until the performance could not have been told from her father's. She tried every refuge her mind could conjure, to quiet her heart and remove the fear that the girl never would come home again, but it persisted. Mrs. Comstock could neither eat nor sleep. She wandered around the cabin and garden. She kept far from the pool where Robert Comstock had sunk from sight for she felt that it would entomb her also if Elnora did not come home Wednesday morning. The mother told herself that she would wait, but the waiting was as bitter as anything she ever had known.

When Elnora awoke Monday another dress was in the hands of a seamstress and was soon fitted. It had belonged to the Angel, and was a soft white thing that with a little alteration would serve admirably for Commencement and the ball. All that day Elnora worked, helping prepare the auditorium for the exercises, rehearsing the march and the speech she was to make in behalf of the class. The following day was even busier. But her mind was at rest, for the dress was a soft delicate lace easy to change, and the marks of alteration impossible to detect.

The Bird Woman had telephoned to Grand Rapids, explained the situation and asked the Angel if she might use it. The reply had been to give the girl the contents of the chest. When the Bird Woman told Elnora, tears filled her eyes.

"I will write at once and thank her," she said. "With all her beautiful gowns she does not need them, and I do. They will serve for me often, and be much finer than anything I could afford. It is lovely of her to give me the dress and of you to have it altered for me, as I never could."

The Bird Woman laughed. "I feel religious to-day," she said. "You know the first and greatest rock of my salvation is 'Do unto others.' I'm only doing to you what there was no one to do for me when I was a girl very like you. Anna tells me your mother was here early this morning and that she came to see about getting you a dress."

"She is too late!" said Elnora coldly. "She had over a month to prepare my dresses, and I was to pay for them, so there is no excuse."

"Nevertheless, she is your mother," said the Bird Woman, softly. "I think almost any kind of a mother must be better than none at all, and you say she has had great trouble."

"She loved my father and he died," said Elnora. "The same thing, in quite as tragic a manner, has happened to thousands of other women, and they have gone on with calm faces and found happiness in life by loving others. There was something else I am afraid I never shall forget; this I know I shall not, but talking does not help. I must deliver my presents and photographs to the crowd. I have a picture and I made a present for you, too, if you would care for them."

"I shall love anything you give me," said the Bird Woman. "I know you well enough to know that whatever you do will be beautiful."

Elnora was pleased over that, and as she tried on her dress for the last fitting she was really happy. She was lovely in the dainty gown: it would serve finely for the ball and many other like occasions, and it was her very own.

The Bird Woman's driver took Elnora in the carriage and she called on all the girls with whom she was especially intimate, and left her picture and the package containing her gift to them. By the time she returned parcels for her were arriving. Friends seemed to spring from everywhere. Almost every one she knew had some gift for her, while because they so loved her the members of her crowd had made her beautiful presents. There were books, vases, silver pieces, handkerchiefs, fans, boxes of flowers and candy. One big package settled the trouble at Sinton's, for it contained a dainty dress from Margaret, a five-dollar gold piece, conspicuously labelled, "I earned this myself," from Billy, with which to buy music; and a gorgeous cut-glass perfume bottle, it would have cost five dollars to fill with even a moderate-priced scent, from Wesley.

In an expressed crate was a fine curly-maple dressing table, sent by Freckles. The drawers were filled with wonderful toilet articles from the Angel. The Bird Woman added an embroidered linen cover and a small silver vase for a few flowers, so no girl of the class had finer gifts. Elnora laid her head on the table sobbing happily, and the Bird Woman was almost crying herself. Professor Henley sent a butterfly book, the grade rooms in which Elnora had taught gave her a set of volumes covering every phase of life afield, in the woods, and water. Elnora had no time to read so she carried one of these books around with her hugging it as she went. After she had gone to dress a queer-looking package was brought by a small boy who hopped on one foot as he handed it in and said: "Tell Elnora that is from her ma."

"Who are you?" asked the Bird Woman as she took the bundle.

"I'm Billy!" announced the boy. "I gave her the five dollars. I earned it myself dropping corn, sticking onions, and pulling weeds. My, but you got to drop, and stick, and pull a lot before it's five dollars' worth."

"Would you like to come in and see Elnora's gifts?"

"Yes, ma'am!" said Billy, trying to stand quietly.

"Gee-mentley!" he gasped. "Does Elnora get all this?"

"Yes."

"I bet you a thousand dollars I be first in my class when I graduate. Say, have the others got a lot more than Elnora?"

"I think not."

"Well, Uncle Wesley said to find out if I could, and if she didn't have as much as the rest, he'd buy till she did, if it took a hundred dollars. Say, you ought to know him! He's just scrumptious! There ain't anybody any where finer 'an he is. My, he's grand!"

"I'm very sure of it!" said the Bird Woman. "I've often heard Elnora say so."

"I bet you nobody can beat this!" he boasted. Then he stopped, thinking deeply. "I don't know, though," he began reflectively. "Some of them are awful rich; they got big families to give them things and wagon loads of friends, and I haven't seen what they have. Now, maybe Elnora is getting left, after all!"

"Don't worry, Billy," she said. "I will watch, and if I find Elnora is 'getting left' I'll buy her some more things myself. But I'm sure she is not. She has more beautiful gifts now than she will know what to do with, and others will come. Tell your Uncle Wesley his girl is bountifully remembered, very happy, and she sends her dearest love to all of you. Now you must go, so I can help her dress. You will be there to-night of course?"

"Yes, sir-ee! She got me a seat, third row from the front, middle section, so I can see, and she's going to wink at me, after she gets her speech off her mind. She kissed me, too! She's a perfect lady, Elnora is. I'm going to marry her when I am big enough."

"Why isn't that splendid!" laughed the Bird Woman as she hurried upstairs.

"Dear!" she called. "Here is another gift for you."

Elnora was half disrobed as she took the package and, sitting on a couch, opened it. The Bird Woman bent over her and tested the fabric with her fingers.

"Why, bless my soul!" she cried. "Hand-woven, hand-embroidered linen, fine as silk. It's priceless' I haven't seen such things in years. My mother had garments like those when I was a child, but my sisters had them cut up for collars, belts, and fancy waists while I was small. Look at the exquisite work!"

"Where could it have come from?" cried Elnora.

She shook out a petticoat, with a hand-wrought ruffle a foot deep, then an old-fashioned chemise the neck and sleeve work of which was elaborate and perfectly wrought. On the breast was pinned a note that she hastily opened.

"I was married in these," it read, "and I had intended to be buried in them, but perhaps it would be more sensible for you to graduate and get married in them yourself, if you like. Your mother."

"From my mother!" Wide-eyed, Elnora looked at the Bird Woman. "I never in my life saw the like. Mother does things I think I never can forgive, and when I feel hardest, she turns around and does something that makes me think she just must love me a little bit, after all. Any of the girls would give almost anything to graduate in hand-embroidered linen like that. Money can't buy such things. And they came when I was thinking she didn't care what became of me. Do you suppose she can be insane?"

"Yes," said the Bird Woman. "Wildly insane, if she does not love you and care what becomes of you."

Elnora arose and held the petticoat to her. "Will you look at it?" she cried. "Only imagine her not getting my dress ready, and then sending me such a petticoat as this! Ellen would pay fifty dollars for it and never blink. I suppose mother has had it all my life, and I never saw it before."

"Go take your bath and put on those things," said the Bird Woman. "Forget everything and be happy. She is not insane. She is embittered. She did not understand how things would be. When she saw, she came at once to provide you a dress. This is her way of saying she is sorry she did not get the other. You notice she has not spent any money, so perhaps she is quite honest in saying she has none."

"Oh, she is honest!" said Elnora. "She wouldn't care enough to tell an untruth. She'd say just how things were, no matter what happened."

Soon Elnora was ready for her dress. She never had looked so well as when she again headed the processional across the flower and palm decked stage of the high school auditorium. As she sat there she could have reached over and dropped a rose she carried into the seat she had occupied that September morning when she entered the high school. She spoke the few words she had to say in behalf of the class beautifully, had the tiny wink ready for Billy, and the smile and nod of recognition for Wesley and Margaret. When at last she looked into the eyes of a white-faced woman next them, she slipped a hand to her side and raised her skirt the fraction of an inch, just enough to let the embroidered edge of a petticoat show a trifle. When she saw the look of relief which flooded her mother's face, Elnora knew that forgiveness was in her heart, and that she would go home in the morning.

It was late afternoon before she arrived, and a dray followed with a load of packages. Mrs. Comstock was overwhelmed. She sat half dazed and made Elnora show her each costly and beautiful or simple and useful gift, tell her carefully what it was and from where it came. She studied the faces of Elnora's particular friends. The gifts from them had to be set in a group. Several times she started to speak and then stopped. At last, between her dry lips, came a harsh whisper.

"Elnora, what did you give back for these things?"

"I'll show you," said Elnora cheerfully. "I made the same gifts for the Bird Woman, Aunt Margaret and you if you care for it. But I have to run upstairs to get it."

When she returned she handed her mother an oblong frame, hand carved, enclosing Elnora's picture, taken by a schoolmate's camera. She wore her storm-coat and carried a dripping umbrella. From under it looked her bright face; her books and lunchbox were on her arm, and across the bottom of the frame was carved, "Your Country Classmate."

Then she offered another frame.

"I am strong on frames," she said. "They seemed to be the best I could do without money. I located the maple and the black walnut myself, in a little corner that had been overlooked between the river and the ditch. They didn't seem to belong to any one so I just took them. Uncle Wesley said it was all right, and he cut and hauled them for me. I gave the mill half of each tree for sawing and curing the remainder. Then I gave the wood-carver half of that for making my frames. A photographer gave me a lot of spoiled plates, and I boiled off the emulsion, and took the specimens I framed from my stuff. The man said the white frames were worth three and a half, and the black ones five. I exchanged those little framed pictures for the photographs of the others. For presents, I gave each one of my crowd one like this, only a different moth. The Bird Woman gave me the birch bark. She got it up north last summer."

Elnora handed her mother a handsome black-walnut frame a foot and a half wide by two long. It finished a small, shallow glass-covered box of birch bark, to the bottom of which clung a big night moth with delicate pale green wings and long exquisite trailers.

"So you see I did not have to be ashamed of my gifts," said Elnora. "I made them myself and raised and mounted the moths."

"Moth, you call it," said Mrs. Comstock. "I've seen a few of the things before."

"They are numerous around us every June night, or at least they used to be," said Elnora. "I've sold hundreds of them, with butterflies, dragonflies, and other specimens. Now, I must put away these and get to work, for it is almost June and there are a few more I want dreadfully. If I find them I will be paid some money for which I have been working."

She was afraid to say college at that time. She thought it would be better to wait a few days and see if an opportunity would not come when it would work in more naturally. Besides, unless she could secure the Yellow Emperor she needed to complete her collection, she could not talk college until she was of age, for she would have no money.

CHAPTER XII. WHEREIN MARGARET SINTON REVEALS A SECRET, AND MRS. COMSTOCK POSSESSES THE LIMBERLOST

"Elnora, bring me the towel, quick!" cried Mrs Comstock.

"In a minute, mother," mumbled Elnora.

She was standing before the kitchen mirror, tying the back part of her hair, while the front turned over her face.

"Hurry! There's a varmint of some kind!"

Elnora ran into the sitting-room and thrust the heavy kitchen towel into her mother's hand. Mrs. Comstock swung open the screen door and struck at some object, Elnora tossed the hair from her face so that she could see past her mother. The girl screamed wildly.

"Don't! Mother, don't!"

Mrs. Comstock struck again. Elnora caught her arm. "It's the one I want! It's worth a lot of money! Don't! Oh, you shall not!"

"Shan't, missy?" blazed Mrs. Comstock. "When did you get to bossing me?"

The hand that held the screen swept a half-circle and stopped at Elnora's cheek. She staggered with the blow, and across her face, paled with excitement, a red mark arose rapidly. The screen slammed shut, throwing the creature on the floor before them. Instantly Mrs. Comstock crushed it with her foot. Elnora stepped back. Excepting the red mark, her face was very white.

"That was the last moth I needed," she said, "to complete a collection worth three hundred dollars. You've ruined it before my eyes!"

"Moth!" cried Mrs. Comstock. "You say that because you are mad. Moths have big wings. I know a moth!"

"I've kept things from you," said Elnora, "because I didn't dare confide in you. You had no sympathy with me. But you know I never told you untruths in all my life."

"It's no moth!" reiterated Mrs. Comstock.

"It is!" cried Elnora. "It's from a case in the ground. Its wings take two or three hours to expand and harden."

"If I had known it was a moth——" Mrs. Comstock wavered.

"You did know! I told you! I begged you to stop! It meant just three hundred dollars to me."

"Bah! Three hundred fiddlesticks!"

"They are what have paid for books, tuition, and clothes for the past four years. They are what I could have started on to college. You've ruined the very one I needed. You never made any pretence of loving me. At last I'll be equally frank with you. I hate you! You are a selfish, wicked woman! I hate you!"

Elnora turned, went through the kitchen and from the back door. She followed the garden path to the gate and walked toward the swamp a short distance when reaction overtook her. She dropped on the ground and leaned against a big log. When a little child, desperate as now, she had tried to die by holding her breath. She had thought in that way to make her mother sorry, but she had learned that life was a thing thrust upon her and she could not leave it at her wish.

She was so stunned over the loss of that moth, which she had childishly named the Yellow Emperor, that she scarcely remembered the blow. She had thought no luck in all the world would be so rare as to complete her collection; now she had been forced to see a splendid Imperialis destroyed before her. There was a possibility that she could find another, but she was facing the certainty that the one she might have had and with which she undoubtedly could have attracted others, was spoiled by her mother. How long she sat there Elnora did not know or care. She simply suffered in dumb, abject misery, an occasional dry sob shaking her. Aunt Margaret was right. Elnora felt that morning that her mother never would be any different. The girl had reached the place where she realized that she could endure it no longer.

As Elnora left the room, Mrs. Comstock took one step after her.

"You little huzzy!" she gasped.

But Elnora was gone. Her mother stood staring.

"She never did lie to me," she muttered. "I guess it was a moth. And the only one she needed to get three hundred dollars, she said. I wish I hadn't been so fast! I never saw anything like it. I thought it was some deadly, stinging, biting thing. A body does have to be mighty careful here. But likely I've spilt the milk now. Pshaw! She can find another! There's no use to be foolish. Maybe moths are like snakes, where there's one, there are two."

Mrs. Comstock took the broom and swept the moth out of the door. Then she got down on her knees and carefully examined the steps, logs and the earth of the flower beds at each side. She found the place where the creature had emerged from the ground, and the hard, dark-brown case which had enclosed it, still wet inside. Then she knew Elnora had been right. It was a moth. Its wings had been damp and not expanded. Mrs. Comstock never before had seen one in that state, and she did not know how they originated. She had thought all of them came from cases spun on trees or against walls or boards. She had seen only enough to know that there were such things; as a flash of white told her that an ermine was on her premises, or a sharp "buzzzzz" warned her of a rattler.

So it was from creatures like that Elnora had secured her school money. In one sickening sweep there rushed into the heart of the woman a full realization of the width of the gulf that separated her from her child. Lately many things had pointed toward it, none more plainly than when Elnora, like a reincarnation of her father, had stood fearlessly before a large city audience and played with even greater skill than he, on what Mrs. Comstock felt very certain was his violin. But that little crawling creature of earth, crushed by her before its splendid yellow and lavender wings could spread and carry it into the mystery of night, had performed a miracle.

"We are nearer strangers to each other than we are with any of the neighbours," she muttered.

So one of the Almighty's most delicate and beautiful creations was sacrificed without fulfilling the law, yet none of its species ever served so glorious a cause, for at last Mrs. Comstock's inner vision had cleared. She went through the cabin mechanically. Every few minutes she glanced toward the back walk to see if Elnora were coming. She knew arrangements had been made with Margaret to go to the city some time that day, so she grew more nervous and uneasy every moment. She was haunted by the fear that the blow might discolour Elnora's cheek; that she would tell Margaret. She went down the back walk, looking intently in all directions, left the garden and followed the swamp path. Her step was noiseless on the soft, black earth, and soon she came close enough to see Elnora. Mrs. Comstock stood looking at the girl in troubled uncertainty. Not knowing what to say, at last she turned and went back to the cabin.

Noon came and she prepared dinner, calling, as she always did, when Elnora was in the garden, but she got no response, and the girl did not come. A little after one o'clock Margaret stopped at the gate.

"Elnora has changed her mind. She is not going," called Mrs. Comstock.

She felt that she hated Margaret as she hitched her horse and came up the walk instead of driving on.

"You must be mistaken," said Margaret. "I was going on purpose for her. She asked me to take her. I had no errand. Where is she?"

"I will call her," said Mrs. Comstock.

She followed the path again, and this time found Elnora sitting on the log. Her face was swollen and discoloured, and her eyes red with crying. She paid no attention to her mother.

"Mag Sinton is here," said Mrs. Comstock harshly. "I told her you had changed your mind, but she said you asked her to go with you, and she had nothing to go for herself."

Elnora arose, recklessly waded through the deep swamp grasses and so reached the path ahead of her mother. Mrs. Comstock followed as far as the garden, but she could not enter the cabin. She busied herself among the vegetables, barely looking up when the back-door screen slammed noisily. Margaret Sinton approached colourless, her eyes so angry that Mrs. Comstock shrank back.

"What's the matter with Elnora's face?" demanded Margaret.

Mrs. Comstock made no reply.

"You struck her, did you?"

"I thought you wasn't blind!"

"I have been, for twenty long years now, Kate Comstock," said Margaret Sinton, "but my eyes are open at last. What I see is that I've done you no good and Elnora a big wrong. I had an idea that it would kill you to know, but I guess you are tough enough to stand anything. Kill or cure, you get it now!"

"What are you frothing about?" coolly asked Mrs. Comstock.

"You!" cried Margaret. "You! The woman who doesn't pretend to love her only child. Who lets her grow to a woman, as you have let Elnora, and can't be satisfied with every sort of neglect, but must add abuse yet; and all for a fool idea about a man who wasn't worth his salt!"

Mrs. Comstock picked up a hoe.

"Go right on!" she said. "Empty yourself. It's the last thing you'll ever do!"

"Then I'll make a tidy job of it," said Margaret. "You'll not touch me. You'll stand there and hear the truth at last, and because I dare face you and tell it, you will know in your soul it is truth. When Robert Comstock shaved that quagmire out there so close he went in, he wanted to keep you from knowing where he was coming from. He'd been to see Elvira Carney. They had plans to go to a dance that night——"

"Close your lips!" said Mrs. Comstock in a voice of deadly quiet.

"You know I wouldn't dare open them if I wasn't telling you the truth. I can prove what I say. I was coming from Reeds. It was hot in the woods and I stopped at Carney's as I passed for a drink. Elvira's bedridden old mother heard me, and she was so crazy for some one to talk with, I stepped in a minute. I saw Robert come down the path. Elvira saw him, too, so she ran out of the house to head him off. It looked funny, and I just deliberately moved where I could see and hear. He brought her his violin, and told her to get ready and meet him in the woods with it that night, and they would go to a dance. She took it and hid it in the loft to the well-house and promised she'd go."

"Are you done?" demanded Mrs. Comstock.

"No. I am going to tell you the whole story. You don't spare Elnora anything. I shan't spare you. I hadn't been here that day, but I can tell you just how he was dressed, which way he went and every word they said, though they thought I was busy with her mother and wouldn't notice them. Put down your hoe, Kate. I went to Elvira, told her what I knew and made her give me Comstock's violin for Elnora over three years ago. She's been playing it ever since. I won't see her slighted and abused another day on account of a man who would have broken your heart if he had lived. Six months more would have showed you what everybody else knew. He was one of those men who couldn't trust himself, and so no woman was safe with him. Now, will you drop grieving over him, and do Elnora justice?"

Mrs. Comstock grasped the hoe tighter and turning she went down the walk, and started across the woods to the home of Elvira Carney. With averted head she passed the pool, steadily pursuing her way. Elvira Carney, hanging towels across the back fence, saw her coming and went toward the gate to meet her. Twenty years she had dreaded that visit. Since Margaret Sinton had compelled her to produce the violin she had hidden so long, because she was afraid to destroy it, she had come closer expectation than dread. The wages of sin are the hardest debts on earth to pay, and they are always collected at inconvenient times and unexpected places. Mrs. Comstock's face and hair were so white, that her dark eyes seemed burned into their setting. Silently she stared at the woman before her a long time.

"I might have saved myself the trouble of coming," she said at last, "I see you are guilty as sin!"

"What has Mag Sinton been telling you?" panted the miserable woman, gripping the fence.

"The truth!" answered Mrs. Comstock succinctly. "Guilt is in every line of your face, in your eyes, all over your wretched body. If I'd taken a good look at you any time in all these past years, no doubt I could have seen it just as plain as I can now. No woman or man can do what you've done, and not get a mark set on them for every one to read."

"Mercy!" gasped weak little Elvira Carney. "Have mercy!"

"Mercy?" scoffed Mrs. Comstock. "Mercy! That's a nice word from you! How much mercy did you have on me? Where's the mercy that sent Comstock to the slime of the bottomless quagmire, and left me to see it, and then struggle on in agony all these years? How about the mercy of letting me neglect my baby all the days of her life? Mercy! Do you really dare use the word to me?"

"If you knew what I've suffered!"

"Suffered?" jeered Mrs. Comstock. "That's interesting. And pray, what have you suffered?"

"All the neighbours have suspected and been down on me. I ain't had a friend. I've always felt guilty of his death! I've seen him go down a thousand times, plain as ever you did. Many's the night I've stood on the other bank of that pool and listened to you, and I tried to throw myself in to keep from hearing you, but I didn't dare. I knew God would send me to burn forever, but I'd better done it; for now, He has set the burning on my body, and every hour it is slowly eating the life out of me. The doctor says it's a cancer——"

Mrs. Comstock exhaled a long breath. Her grip on the hoe relaxed and her stature lifted to towering height.

"I didn't know, or care, when I came here, just what I did," she said. "But my way is beginning to clear. If the guilt of your soul has come to a head, in a cancer on your body, it looks as if the Almighty didn't need any of my help in meting out His punishments. I really couldn't fix up anything to come anywhere near that. If you are going to burn until your life goes out with that sort of fire, you don't owe me anything!"

"Oh, Katharine Comstock!" groaned Elvira Carney, clinging to the fence for support.

"Looks as if the Bible is right when it says, 'The wages of sin is death,' doesn't it?" asked Mrs. Comstock. "Instead of doing a woman's work in life, you chose the smile of invitation, and the dress of unearned cloth. Now you tell me you are marked to burn to death with the unquenchable fire. And him! It was shorter with him, but let me tell you he got his share! He left me with an untruth on his lips, for he told me he was going to take his violin to Onabasha for a new key, when he carried it to you. Every vow of love and constancy he ever made me was a lie, after he touched your lips, so when he tried the wrong side of the quagmire, to hide from me the direction in which he was coming, it reached out for him, and it got him. It didn't hurry, either! It sucked him down, slow and deliberate."

"Mercy!" groaned Elvira Carney. "Mercy!"

"I don't know the word," said Mrs. Comstock. "You took all that out of me long ago. The past twenty years haven't been of the sort that taught mercy. I've never had any on myself and none on my child. Why in the name of justice, should I have mercy on you, or on him? You were both older than I, both strong, sane people, you deliberately chose your course when you lured him, and he, when he was unfaithful to me. When a Loose Man and a Light Woman face the end the Almighty ordained for them, why should they shout at me for mercy? What did I have to do with it?"

Elvira Carney sobbed in panting gasps.

"You've got tears, have you?" marvelled Mrs. Comstock. "Mine all dried long ago. I've none left to shed over my wasted life, my disfigured face and hair, my years of struggle with a man's work, my wreck of land among the tilled fields of my neighbours, or the final knowledge that the man I so gladly would have died to save, wasn't worth the sacrifice of a rattlesnake. If anything yet could wring a tear from me, it would be the thought of the awful injustice I always have done my girl. If I'd lay hand on you for anything, it would be for that."

"Kill me if you want to," sobbed Elvira Carney. "I know that I deserve it, and I don't care."

"You are getting your killing fast enough to suit me," said Mrs. Comstock. "I wouldn't touch you, any more than I would him, if I could. Once is all any man or woman deceives me about the holiest things of life. I wouldn't touch you any more than I would the black plague. I am going back to my girl."

Mrs. Comstock turned and started swiftly through the woods, but she had gone only a few rods when she stopped, and leaning on the hoe, she stood thinking deeply. Then she turned back. Elvira still clung to the fence, sobbing bitterly.

"I don't know," said Mrs. Comstock, "but I left a wrong impression with you. I don't want you to think that I believe the Almighty set a cancer to burning you as a punishment for your sins. I don't! I think a lot more of the Almighty. With a whole sky-full of worlds on His hands to manage, I'm not believing that He has time to look down on ours, and pick you out of all the millions of us sinners, and set a special kind of torture to eating you. It wouldn't be a gentlemanly thing to do, and first of all, the Almighty is bound to be a gentleman. I think likely a bruise and bad blood is what caused your trouble. Anyway, I've got to tell you that the cleanest housekeeper I ever knew, and one of the noblest Christian women, was slowly eaten up by a cancer. She got hers from the careless work of a poor doctor. The Almighty is to forgive sin and heal disease, not to invent and spread it."

She had gone only a few steps when she again turned back.

"If you will gather a lot of red clover bloom, make a tea strong as lye of it, and drink quarts, I think likely it will help you, if you are not too far gone. Anyway, it will cool your blood and make the burning easier to bear."

Then she swiftly went home. Enter the lonely cabin she could not, neither could she sit outside and think. She attacked a bed of beets and hoed until the perspiration ran from her face and body, then she began on the potatoes. When she was too tired to take another stroke she bathed and put on dry clothing. In securing her dress she noticed her husband's carefully preserved clothing lining one wall. She gathered it in an armload and carried it to the swamp. Piece by piece she pitched into the green maw of the quagmire all those articles she had dusted carefully and fought moths from for years, and stood watching as it slowly sucked them down. She went back to her room and gathered every scrap that had in any way belonged to Robert Comstock, excepting his gun and revolver, and threw it into the swamp. Then for the first time she set her door wide open.

She was too weary now to do more, but an urging unrest drove her. She wanted Elnora. It seemed to her she never could wait until the girl came and delivered her judgment. At last in an effort to get nearer to her, Mrs. Comstock climbed the stairs and stood looking around Elnora's room. It was very unfamiliar. The pictures were strange to her. Commencement had filled it with packages and bundles. The walls were covered with cocoons; moths and dragonflies were pinned everywhere. Under the bed she could see half a dozen large white boxes. She pulled out one and lifted the lid. The bottom was covered with a sheet of thin cork, and on long pins sticking in it were large, velvet-winged moths. Each one was labelled, always there were two of a kind, in many cases four, showing under and upper wings of both male and female. They were of every colour and shape.

Mrs. Comstock caught her breath sharply. When and where had Elnora found them? They were the most exquisite sight the woman ever had seen, so she opened all the boxes to feast on their beautiful contents. As she did so there came more fully a sense of the distance between her and her child. She could not understand how Elnora had gone to school, and performed so much work secretly. When it was finished, to the last moth, she, the mother who should have been the first confidant and helper, had been the one to bring disappointment. Small wonder Elnora had come to hate her.

Mrs. Comstock carefully closed and replaced the boxes; and again stood looking around the room. This time her eyes rested on some books she did not remember having seen before, so she picked up one and found that it was a moth book. She glanced over the first pages and was soon eagerly reading. When the text reached the classification of species, she laid it down, took up another and read the introductory chapters. By that time her brain was in a confused jumble of ideas about capturing moths with differing baits and bright lights.

She went down stairs thinking deeply. Being unable to sit still and having nothing else to do she glanced at the clock and began preparing supper. The work dragged. A chicken was snatched up and dressed hurriedly. A spice cake sprang into being. Strawberries that had been intended for preserves went into shortcake. Delicious odours crept from the cabin. She put many extra touches on the table and then commenced watching the road. Everything was ready, but Elnora did not come. Then began the anxious process of trying to keep cooked food warm and not spoil it. The birds went to bed and dusk came. Mrs. Comstock gave up the fire and set the supper on the table. Then she went out and sat on the front-door step watching night creep around her. She started eagerly as the gate creaked, but it was only Wesley Sinton coming.

"Katharine, Margaret and Elnora passed where I was working this afternoon, and Margaret got out of the carriage and called me to the fence. She told me what she had done. I've come to say to you that I am sorry. She has heard me threaten to do it a good many times, but I never would have got it done. I'd give a good deal if I could undo it, but I can't, so I've come to tell you how sorry I am."

"You've got something to be sorry for," said Mrs. Comstock, "but likely we ain't thinking of the same thing. It hurts me less to know the truth, than to live in ignorance. If Mag had the sense of a pewee, she'd told me long ago. That's what hurts me, to think that both of you knew Robert was not worth an hour of honest grief, yet you'd let me mourn him all these years and neglect Elnora while I did it. If I have anything to forgive you, that is what it is."

Wesley removed his hat and sat on a bench.

"Katharine," he said solemnly, "nobody ever knows how to take you."

"Would it be asking too much to take me for having a few grains of plain common sense?" she inquired. "You've known all this time that Comstock got what he deserved, when he undertook to sneak in an unused way across a swamp, with which he was none too familiar. Now I should have thought that you'd figure that knowing the same thing would be the best method to cure me of pining for him, and slighting my child."

"Heaven only knows we have thought of that, and talked of it often, but we were both too big cowards. We didn't dare tell you."

"So you have gone on year after year, watching me show indifference to Elnora, and yet a little horse-sense would have pointed out to you that she was my salvation. Why look at it! Not married quite a year. All his vows of love and fidelity made to me before the Almighty forgotten in a few months, and a dance and a Light Woman so alluring he had to lie and sneak for them. What kind of a prospect is that for a life? I know men and women. An honourable man is an honourable man, and a liar is a liar; both are born and not made. One cannot change to the other any more than that same old leopard can change its spots. After a man tells a woman the first untruth of that sort, the others come piling thick, fast, and mountain high. The desolation they bring in their wake overshadows anything I have suffered completely. If he had lived six months more I should have known him for what he was born to be. It was in the blood of him. His father and grandfather before him were fiddling, dancing people; but I was certain of him. I thought we could leave Ohio and come out here alone, and I could so love him and interest him in his work, that he would be a man. Of all the fool, fruitless jobs, making anything of a creature that begins by deceiving her, is the foolest a sane woman ever undertook. I am more than sorry you and Margaret didn't see your way clear to tell me long ago. I'd have found it out in a few more months if he had lived, and I wouldn't have borne it a day. The man who breaks his vows to me once, doesn't get the second chance. I give truth and honour. I have a right to ask it in return. I am glad I understand at last. Now, if Elnora will forgive me, we will take a new start and see what we can make out of what is left of life. If she won't, then it will be my time to learn what suffering really means."

"But she will," said Wesley. "She must! She can't help it when things are explained."

"I notice she isn't hurrying any about coming home. Do you know where she is or what she is doing?"

"I do not. But likely she will be along soon. I must go help Billy with the night work. Good-bye, Katharine. Thank the Lord you have come to yourself at last!"

They shook hands and Wesley went down the road while Mrs. Comstock entered the cabin. She could not swallow food. She stood in the back door watching the sky for moths, but they did not seem to be very numerous. Her spirits sank and she breathed unevenly. Then she heard the front screen. She reached the middle door as Elnora touched the foot of the stairs.

"Hurry, and get ready, Elnora," she said. "Your supper is almost spoiled now."

Elnora closed the stair door behind her, and for the first time in her life, threw the heavy lever which barred out anyone from down stairs. Mrs. Comstock heard the thud, and knew what it meant. She reeled slightly and caught the doorpost for support. For a few minutes she clung there, then sank to the nearest chair. After a long time she arose and stumbling half blindly, she put the food in the cupboard and covered the table. She took the lamp in one hand, the butter in the other, and started to the spring house. Something brushed close by her face, and she looked just in time to see a winged creature rise above the cabin and sail away.

"That was a night bird," she muttered. As she stopped to set the butter in the water, came another thought. "Perhaps it was a moth!" Mrs. Comstock dropped the butter and hurried out with the lamp; she held it high above her head and waited until her arms ached. Small insects of night gathered, and at last a little dusty miller, but nothing came of any size.

"I must go where they are, if I get them," muttered Mrs. Comstock.

She went to the barn after the stout pair of high boots she used in feeding stock in deep snow. Throwing these beside the back door she climbed to the loft over the spring house, and hunted an old lard oil lantern and one of first manufacture for oil. Both these she cleaned and filled. She listened until everything up stairs had been still for over half an hour. By that time it was past eleven o'clock. Then she took the lantern from the kitchen, the two old ones, a handful of matches, a ball of twine, and went from the cabin, softly closing the door.

Sitting on the back steps, she put on the boots, and then stood gazing into the perfumed June night, first in the direction of the woods on her land, then toward the Limberlost. Its outline was so dark and forbidding she shuddered and went down the garden, following the path toward the woods, but as she neared the pool her knees wavered and her courage fled. The knowledge that in her soul she was now glad Robert Comstock was at the bottom of it made a coward of her, who fearlessly had mourned him there, nights untold. She could not go on. She skirted the back of the garden, crossed a field, and came out on the road. Soon she reached the Limberlost. She hunted until she found the old trail, then followed it stumbling over logs and through clinging vines and grasses. The heavy boots clumped on her feet, overhanging branches whipped her face and pulled her hair. But her eyes were on the sky as she went straining into the night, hoping to find signs of a living creature on wing.

By and by she began to see the wavering flight of something she thought near the right size. She had no idea where she was, but she stopped, lighted a lantern and hung it as high as she could reach. A little distance away she placed the second and then the third. The objects came nearer and sick with disappointment she saw that they were bats. Crouching in the damp swamp grasses, without a thought of snakes or venomous insects, she waited, her eyes roving from lantern to lantern. Once she thought a creature of high flight dropped near the lard oil light, so she arose breathlessly waiting, but either it passed or it was an illusion. She glanced at the old lantern, then at the new, and was on her feet in an instant creeping close. Something large as a small bird was fluttering around. Mrs. Comstock began to perspire, while her hand shook wildly. Closer she crept and just as she reached for it, something similar swept past and both flew away together.

Mrs. Comstock set her teeth and stood shivering. For a long time the locusts rasped, the whip-poor-wills cried and a steady hum of night life throbbed in her ears. Away in the sky she saw something coming when it was no larger than a falling leaf. Straight toward the light it flew. Mrs. Comstock began to pray aloud.

"This way, O Lord! Make it come this way! Please! O Lord, send it lower!"

The moth hesitated at the first light, then slowly, easily it came toward the second, as if following a path of air. It touched a leaf near the lantern and settled. As Mrs. Comstock reached for it a thin yellow spray wet her hand and the surrounding leaves. When its wings raised above its back, her fingers came together. She held the moth to the light. It was nearer brown than yellow, and she remembered having seen some like it in the boxes that afternoon. It was not the one needed to complete the collection, but Elnora might want it, so Mrs. Comstock held on. Then the Almighty was kind, or nature was sufficient, as you look at it, for following the law of its being when disturbed, the moth again threw the spray by which some suppose it attracts its kind, and liberally sprinkled Mrs. Comstock's dress front and arms. From that instant, she became the best moth bait ever invented. Every Polyphemus in range hastened to her, and other fluttering creatures of night followed. The influx came her way. She snatched wildly here and there until she had one in each hand and no place to put them. She could see more coming, and her aching heart, swollen with the strain of long excitement, hurt pitifully. She prayed in broken exclamations that did not always sound reverent, but never was human soul in more intense earnest.

Moths were coming. She had one in each hand. They were not yellow, and she did not know what to do. She glanced around to try to discover some way to keep what she had, and her throbbing heart stopped and every muscle stiffened. There was the dim outline of a crouching figure not two yards away, and a pair of eyes their owner thought hidden, caught the light in a cold stream. Her first impulse was to scream and fly for life. Before her lips could open a big moth alighted on her breast while she felt another walking over her hair. All sense of caution deserted her. She did not care to live if she could not replace the yellow moth she had killed. She turned her eyes to those among the leaves.

"Here, you!" she cried hoarsely. "I need you! Get yourself out here, and help me. These critters are going to get away from me. Hustle!"

Pete Corson parted the bushes and stepped into the light.

"Oh, it's you!" said Mrs. Comstock. "I might have known! But you gave me a start. Here, hold these until I make some sort of bag for them. Go easy! If you break them I don't guarantee what will happen to you!"

"Pretty fierce, ain't you!" laughed Pete, but he advanced and held out his hands. "For Elnora, I s'pose?"

"Yes," said Mrs. Comstock. "In a mad fit, I trampled one this morning, and by the luck of the old boy himself it was the last moth she needed to complete a collection. I got to get another one or die."

"Then I guess it's your funeral," said Pete. "There ain't a chance in a dozen the right one will come. What colour was it?"

"Yellow, and big as a bird."

"The Emperor, likely," said Pete. "You dig for that kind, and they are not numerous, so's 'at you can smash 'em for fun."

"Well, I can try to get one, anyway," said Mrs. Comstock. "I forgot all about bringing anything to put them in. You take a pinch on their wings until I make a poke."

Mrs. Comstock removed her apron, tearing off the strings. She unfastened and stepped from the skirt of her calico dress. With one apron string she tied shut the band and placket. She pulled a wire pin from her hair, stuck it through the other string, and using it as a bodkin ran it around the hem of her skirt, so shortly she had a large bag. She put several branches inside to which the moths could cling, closed the mouth partially and held it toward Pete.

"Put your hand well down and let the things go!" she ordered. "But be careful, man! Don't run into the twigs! Easy! That's one. Now the other. Is the one on my head gone? There was one on my dress, but I guess it flew. Here comes a kind of a gray-looking one."

Pete slipped several more moths into the bag.

"Now, that's five, Mrs. Comstock," he said. "I'm sorry, but you'll have to make that do. You must get out of here lively. Your lights will be taken for hurry calls, and inside the next hour a couple of men will ride here like fury. They won't be nice Sunday-school men, and they won't hold bags and catch moths for you. You must go quick!"

Mrs. Comstock laid down the bag and pulled one of the lanterns lower.

"I won't budge a step," she said. "This land doesn't belong to you. You have no right to order me off it. Here I stay until I get a Yellow Emperor, and no little petering thieves of this neighbourhood can scare me away."

"You don't understand," said Pete. "I'm willing to help Elnora, and I'd take care of you, if I could, but there will be too many for me, and they will be mad at being called out for nothing."

"Well, who's calling them out?" demanded Mrs. Comstock. "I'm catching moths. If a lot of good-for-nothings get fooled into losing some sleep, why let them, they can't hurt me, or stop my work."

"They can, and they'll do both."

"Well, I'll see them do it!" said Mrs. Comstock. "I've got Robert's revolver in my dress, and I can shoot as straight as any man, if I'm mad enough. Any one who interferes with me to-night will find me mad a-plenty. There goes another!"

She stepped into the light and waited until a big brown moth settled on her and was easily taken. Then in light, airy flight came a delicate pale green thing, and Mrs. Comstock started in pursuit. But the scent was not right. The moth fluttered high, then dropped lower, still lower, and sailed away. With outstretched hands Mrs. Comstock pursued it. She hurried one way and another, then ran over an object which tripped her and she fell. She regained her feet in an instant, but she had lost sight of the moth. With livid face she turned to the crouching man.

"You nasty, sneaking son of Satan!" she cried. "Why are you hiding there? You made me lose the one I wanted most of any I've had a chance at yet. Get out of here! Go this minute, or I'll fill your worthless carcass so full of holes you'll do to sift cornmeal. Go, I say! I'm using the Limberlost to-night, and I won't be stopped by the devil himself! Cut like fury, and tell the rest of them they can just go home. Pete is going to help me, and he is all of you I need. Now go!"

The man turned and went. Pete leaned against a tree, held his mouth shut and shook inwardly. Mrs. Comstock came back panting.

"The old scoundrel made me lose that!" she said. "If any one else comes snooping around here I'll just blow them up to start with. I haven't time to talk. Suppose that had been yellow! I'd have killed that man, sure! The Limberlost isn't safe to-night, and the sooner those whelps find it out, the better it will be for them."

Pete stopped laughing to look at her. He saw that she was speaking the truth. She was quite past reason, sense, or fear. The soft night air stirred the wet hair around her temples, the flickering lanterns made her face a ghastly green. She would stop at nothing, that was evident. Pete suddenly began catching moths with exemplary industry. In putting one into the bag, another escaped.

"We must not try that again," said Mrs. Comstock. "Now, what will we do?"

"We are close to the old case," said Pete. "I think I can get into it. Maybe we could slip the rest in there."

"That's a fine idea!" said Mrs. Comstock. "They'll have so much room there they won't be likely to hurt themselves, and the books say they don't fly in daytime unless they are disturbed, so they will settle when it's light, and I can come with Elnora to get them."

They captured two more, and then Pete carried them to the case.

"Here comes a big one!" he cried as he returned.

Mrs. Comstock looked up and stepped out with a prayer on her lips. She could not tell the colour at that distance, but the moth appeared different from the others. On it came, dropping lower and darting from light to light. As it swept near her, "O Heavenly Father!" exulted Mrs. Comstock, "it's yellow! Careful Pete! Your hat, maybe!"

Pete made a long sweep. The moth wavered above the hat and sailed away. Mrs. Comstock leaned against a tree and covered her face with her shaking hands.

"That is my punishment!" she cried. "Oh, Lord, if you will give a moth like that into my possession, I'll always be a better woman!"

The Emperor again came in sight. Pete stood tense and ready. Mrs. Comstock stepped into the light and watched the moth's course. Then a second appeared in pursuit of the first. The larger one wavered into the radius of light once more. The perspiration rolled down the man's face. He half lifted the hat.

"Pray, woman! Pray now!" he panted.

"I guess I best get over by that lard oil light and go to work," breathed Mrs. Comstock. "The Lord knows this is all in prayer, but it's no time for words just now. Ready, Pete! You are going to get a chance first!"

Pete made another long, steady sweep, but the moth darted beneath the hat. In its flight it came straight toward Mrs. Comstock. She snatched off the remnant of apron she had tucked into her petticoat band and held the calico before her. The moth struck full against it and clung to the goods. Pete crept up stealthily. The second moth followed the first, and the spray showered the apron.

"Wait!" gasped Mrs. Comstock. "I think they have settled. The books say they won't leave now."

The big pale yellow creature clung firmly, lowering and raising its wings. The other came nearer. Mrs. Comstock held the cloth with rigid hands, while Pete could hear her breathing in short gusts.

"Shall I try now?" he implored.

"Wait!" whispered the woman. "Something seems to say wait!"

The night breeze stiffened and gently waved the apron. Locusts rasped, mosquitoes hummed and frogs sang uninterruptedly. A musky odour slowly filled the air.

"Now shall I?" questioned Pete.

"No. Leave them alone. They are safe now. They are mine. They are my salvation. God and the Limberlost gave them to me! They won't move for hours. The books all say so. O Heavenly Father, I am thankful to You, and you, too, Pete Corson! You are a good man to help me. Now, I can go home and face my girl."

Instead, Mrs. Comstock dropped suddenly. She spread the apron across her knees. The moths remained undisturbed. Then her tired white head dropped, the tears she had thought forever dried gushed forth, and she sobbed for pure joy.

"Oh, I wouldn't do that now, you know!" comforted Pete. "Think of getting two! That's more than you ever could have expected. A body would think you would cry, if you hadn't got any. Come on, now. It's almost morning. Let me help you home."

Pete took the bag and the two old lanterns. Mrs. Comstock carried her moths and the best lantern and went ahead to light the way.

Elnora had sat beside her window far into the night. At last she undressed and went to bed, but sleep would not come. She had gone to the city to talk with members of the School Board about a room in the grades. There was a possibility that she might secure the moth, and so be able to start to college that fall, but if she did not, then she wanted the school. She had been given some encouragement, but she was so unhappy that nothing mattered. She could not see the way open to anything in life, save a long series of disappointments, while she remained with her mother. Yet Margaret Sinton had advised her to go home and try once more. Margaret had seemed so sure there would be a change for the better, that Elnora had consented, although she had no hope herself. So strong is the bond of blood, she could not make up her mind to seek a home elsewhere, even after the day that had passed. Unable to sleep she arose at last, and the room being warm, she sat on the floor close the window. The lights in the swamp caught her eye. She was very uneasy, for quite a hundred of her best moths were in the case. However, there was no money, and no one ever had touched a book or any of her apparatus. Watching the lights set her thinking, and before she realized it, she was in a panic of fear.

She hurried down the stairway softly calling her mother. There was no answer. She lightly stepped across the sitting-room and looked in at the open door. There was no one, and the bed had not been used. Her first thought was that her mother had gone to the pool; and the Limberlost was alive with signals. Pity and fear mingled in the heart of the girl. She opened the kitchen door, crossed the garden and ran back to the swamp. As she neared it she listened, but she could hear only the usual voices of night.

"Mother!" she called softly. Then louder, "Mother!"

There was not a sound. Chilled with fright she hurried back to the cabin. She did not know what to do. She understood what the lights in the Limberlost meant. Where was her mother? She was afraid to enter, while she was growing very cold and still more fearful about remaining outside. At last she went to her mother's room, picked up the gun, carried it into the kitchen, and crowding in a little corner behind the stove, she waited in trembling anxiety. The time was dreadfully long before she heard her mother's voice. Then she decided some one had been ill and sent for her, so she took courage, and stepping swiftly across the kitchen she unbarred the door and drew back from sight beside the table.

Mrs. Comstock entered dragging her heavy feet. Her dress skirt was gone, her petticoat wet and drabbled, and the waist of her dress was almost torn from her body. Her hair hung in damp strings; her eyes were red with crying. In one hand she held the lantern, and in the other stiffly extended before her, on a wad of calico reposed a magnificent pair of Yellow Emperors. Elnora stared, her lips parted.

"Shall I put these others in the kitchen?" inquired a man's voice.

The girl shrank back to the shadows.

"Yes, anywhere inside the door," replied Mrs. Comstock as she moved a few steps to make way for him. Pete's head appeared. He set down the moths and was gone.

"Thank you, Pete, more than ever woman thanked you before!" said Mrs. Comstock.

She placed the lantern on the table and barred the door. As she turned Elnora came into view. Mrs. Comstock leaned toward her, and held out the moths. In a voice vibrant with tones never before heard she said: "Elnora, my girl, mother's found you another moth!"

CHAPTER XIII. WHEREIN MOTHER LOVE IS BESTOWED ON ELNORA, AND SHE FINDS AN ASSISTANT IN MOTH HUNTING

Elnora awoke at dawn and lay gazing around the unfamiliar room. She noticed that every vestige of masculine attire and belongings was gone, and knew, without any explanation, what that meant. For some reason every tangible evidence of her father was banished, and she was at last to be allowed to take his place. She turned to look at her mother. Mrs. Comstock's face was white and haggard, but on it rested an expression of profound peace Elnora never before had seen. As she studied the features on the pillow beside her, the heart of the girl throbbed in tenderness. She realized as fully as any one else could what her mother had suffered. Thoughts of the night brought shuddering fear. She softly slipped from the bed, went to her room, dressed and entered the kitchen to attend the Emperors and prepare breakfast. The pair had been left clinging to the piece of calico. The calico was there and a few pieces of beautiful wing. A mouse had eaten the moths!

"Well, of all the horrible luck!" gasped Elnora.

With the first thought of her mother, she caught up the remnants of the moths, burying them in the ashes of the stove. She took the bag to her room, hurriedly releasing its contents, but there was not another yellow one. Her mother had said some had been confined in the case in the Limberlost. There was still a hope that an Emperor might be among them. She peeped at her mother, who still slept soundly.

Elnora took a large piece of mosquito netting, and ran to the swamp. Throwing it over the top of the case, she unlocked the door. She reeled, faint with distress. The living moths that had been confined there in their fluttering to escape to night and the mates they sought not only had wrecked the other specimens of the case, but torn themselves to fringes on the pins. A third of the rarest moths of the collection for the man of India were antennaless, legless, wingless, and often headless. Elnora sobbed aloud.

"This is overwhelming," she said at last. "It is making a fatalist of me. I am beginning to think things happen as they are ordained from the beginning, this plainly indicating that there is to be no college, at least, this year, for me. My life is all mountain-top or canon. I wish some one would lead me into a few days of 'green pastures.' Last night I went to sleep on mother's arm, the moths all secured, love and college, certainties. This morning I wake to find all my hopes wrecked. I simply don't dare let mother know that instead of helping me, she has ruined my collection. Everything is gone—unless the love lasts. That actually seemed true. I believe I will go see."

The love remained. Indeed, in the overflow of the long-hardened, pent-up heart, the girl was almost suffocated with tempestuous caresses and generous offerings. Before the day was over, Elnora realized that she never had known her mother. The woman who now busily went through the cabin, her eyes bright, eager, alert, constantly planning, was a stranger. Her very face was different, while it did not seem possible that during one night the acid of twenty years could disappear from a voice and leave it sweet and pleasant.

For the next few days Elnora worked at mounting the moths her mother had taken. She had to go to the Bird Woman and tell about the disaster, but Mrs. Comstock was allowed to think that Elnora delivered the moths when she made the trip. If she had told her what actually happened, the chances were that Mrs. Comstock again would have taken possession of the Limberlost, hunting there until she replaced all the moths that had been destroyed. But Elnora knew from experience what it meant to collect such a list in pairs. It would require steady work for at least two summers to replace the lost moths. When she left the Bird Woman she went to the president of the Onabasha schools and asked him to do all in his power to secure her a room in one of the ward buildings.

The next morning the last moth was mounted, and the housework finished. Elnora said to her mother, "If you don't mind, I believe I will go into the woods pasture beside Sleepy Snake Creek and see if I can catch some dragonflies or moths."

"Wait until I get a knife and a pail and I will go along," answered Mrs. Comstock. "The dandelions are plenty tender for greens among the deep grasses, and I might just happen to see something myself. My eyes are pretty sharp."

"I wish you could realize how young you are," said Elnora. "I know women in Onabasha who are ten years older than you, yet they look twenty years younger. So could you, if you would dress your hair becomingly, and wear appropriate clothes."

"I think my hair puts me in the old woman class permanently," said Mrs. Comstock.

"Well, it doesn't!" cried Elnora. "There is a woman of twenty-eight who has hair as white as yours from sick headaches, but her face is young and beautiful. If your face would grow a little fuller and those lines would go away, you'd be lovely!"

"You little pig!" laughed Mrs. Comstock. "Any one would think you would be satisfied with having a splinter new mother, without setting up a kick on her looks, first thing. Greedy!"

"That is a good word," said Elnora. "I admit the charge. I am greedy over every wasted year. I want you young, lovely, suitably dressed and enjoying life like the other girls' mothers."

Mrs. Comstock laughed softly as she pushed back her sunbonnet so that shrubs and bushes beside the way could be scanned closely. Elnora walked ahead with a case over her shoulder, a net in her hand. Her head was bare, the rolling collar of her lavender gingham dress was cut in a V at the throat, the sleeves only reached the elbows. Every few steps she paused and examined the shrubbery carefully, while Mrs. Comstock was watching until her eyes ached, but there were no dandelions in the pail she carried.

Early June was rioting in fresh grasses, bright flowers, bird songs, and gay-winged creatures of air. Down the footpath the two went through the perfect morning, the love of God and all nature in their hearts. At last they reached the creek, following it toward the bridge. Here Mrs. Comstock found a large bed of tender dandelions and stopped to fill her pail. Then she sat on the bank, picking over the greens, while she listened to the creek softly singing its June song.

Elnora remained within calling distance, and was having good success. At last she crossed the creek, following it up to a bridge. There she began a careful examination of the under sides of the sleepers and flooring for cocoons. Mrs. Comstock could see her and the creek for several rods above. The mother sat beating the long green leaves across her hand, carefully picking out the white buds, because Elnora liked them, when a splash up the creek attracted her attention.

Around the bend came a man. He was bareheaded, dressed in a white sweater, and waders which reached his waist. He walked on the bank, only entering the water when forced. He had a queer basket strapped on his hip, and with a small rod he sent a long line spinning before him down the creek, deftly manipulating with it a little floating object. He was closer Elnora than her mother, but Mrs. Comstock thought possibly by hurrying she could remain unseen and yet warn the girl that a stranger was coming. As she approached the bridge, she caught a sapling and leaned over the water to call Elnora. With her lips parted to speak she hesitated a second to watch a sort of insect that flashed past on the water, when a splash from the man attracted the girl.

She was under the bridge, one knee planted in the embankment and a foot braced to support her. Her hair was tousled by wind and bushes, her face flushed, and she lifted her arms above her head, working to loosen a cocoon she had found. The call Mrs. Comstock had intended to utter never found voice, for as Elnora looked down at the sound, "Possibly I could get that for you," suggested the man.

Mrs. Comstock drew back. He was a young man with a wonderfully attractive face, although it was too white for robust health, broad shoulders, and slender, upright frame.

"Oh, I do hope you can!" answered Elnora. "It's quite a find! It's one of those lovely pale red cocoons described in the books. I suspect it comes from having been in a dark place and screened from the weather."

"Is that so?" cried the man. "Wait a minute. I've never seen one. I suppose it's a Cecropia, from the location."

"Of course," said Elnora. "It's so cool here the moth hasn't emerged. The cocoon is a big, baggy one, and it is as red as fox tail."

"What luck!" he cried. "Are you making a collection?"

He reeled in his line, laid his rod across a bush and climbed the embankment to Elnora's side, produced a knife and began the work of whittling a deep groove around the cocoon.

"Yes. I paid my way through the high school in Onabasha with them. Now I am starting a collection which means college."

"Onabasha!" said the man. "That is where I am visiting. Possibly you know my people—Dr. Ammon's? The doctor is my uncle. My home is in Chicago. I've been having typhoid fever, something fierce. In the hospital six weeks. Didn't gain strength right, so Uncle Doc sent for me. I am to live out of doors all summer, and exercise until I get in condition again. Do you know my uncle?"

"Yes. He is Aunt Margaret's doctor, and he would be ours, only we are never ill."

"Well, you look it!" said the man, appraising Elnora at a glance.

"Strangers always mention it," sighed Elnora. "I wonder how it would seem to be a pale, languid lady and ride in a carriage."

"Ask me!" laughed the man. "It feels like the—dickens! I'm so proud of my feet. It's quite a trick to stand on them now. I have to keep out of the water all I can and stop to baby every half-mile. But with interesting outdoor work I'll be myself in a week."

"Do you call that work?" Elnora indicated the creek.

"I do, indeed! Nearly three miles, banks too soft to brag on and never a strike. Wouldn't you call that hard labour?"

"Yes," laughed Elnora. "Work at which you might kill yourself and never get a fish. Did any one tell you there were trout in Sleepy Snake Creek?"

"Uncle said I could try."

"Oh, you can," said Elnora. "You can try no end, but you'll never get a trout. This is too far south and too warm for them. If you sit on the bank and use worms you might catch some perch or catfish."

"But that isn't exercise."

"Well, if you only want exercise, go right on fishing. You will have a creel full of invisible results every night."

"I object," said the man emphatically. He stopped work again and studied Elnora. Even the watching mother could not blame him. In the shade of the bridge Elnora's bright head and her lavender dress made a picture worthy of much contemplation.

"I object!" repeated the man. "When I work I want to see results. I'd rather exercise sawing wood, making one pile grow little and the other big than to cast all day and catch nothing because there is not a fish to take. Work for work's sake doesn't appeal to me."

He digged the groove around the cocoon with skilled hand. "Now there is some fun in this!" he said. "It's going to be a fair job to cut it out, but when it comes, it is not only beautiful, but worth a price; it will help you on your way. I think I'll put up my rod and hunt moths. That would be something like! Don't you want help?"

Elnora parried the question. "Have you ever hunted moths, Mr. Ammon?"

"Enough to know the ropes in taking them and to distinguish the commonest ones. I go wild on Catocalae. There's too many of them, all too much alike for Philip, but I know all these fellows. One flew into my room when I was about ten years old, and we thought it a miracle. None of us ever had seen one so we took it over to the museum to Dr. Dorsey. He said they were common enough, but we didn't see them because they flew at night. He showed me the museum collection, and I was so interested I took mine back home and started to hunt them. Every year after that we went to our cottage a month earlier, so I could find them, and all my family helped. I stuck to it until I went to college. Then, keeping the little moths out of the big ones was too much for the mater, so father advised that I donate mine to the museum. He bought a fine case for them with my name on it, which constitutes my sole contribution to science. I know enough to help you all right."

"Aren't you going north this year?"

"All depends on how this fever leaves me. Uncle says the nights are too cold and the days too hot there for me. He thinks I had better stay in an even temperature until I am strong again. I am going to stick pretty close to him until I know I am. I wouldn't admit it to any one at home, but I was almost gone. I don't believe anything can eat up nerve much faster than the burning of a slow fever. No, thanks, I have enough. I stay with Uncle Doc, so if I feel it coming again he can do something quickly."

"I don't blame you," said Elnora. "I never have been sick, but it must be dreadful. I am afraid you are tiring yourself over that. Let me take the knife awhile."

"Oh, it isn't so bad as that! I wouldn't be wading creeks if it were. I only need a few more days to get steady on my feet again. I'll soon have this out."

"It is kind of you to get it," said Elnora. "I should have had to peel it, which would spoil the cocoon for a' specimen and ruin the moth."

"You haven't said yet whether I may help you while I am here."

Elnora hesitated.

"You better say 'yes,'" he persisted. "It would be a real kindness. It would keep me outdoors all day and give an incentive to work. I'm good at it. I'll show you if I am not in a week or so. I can 'sugar,' manipulate lights, and mirrors, and all the expert methods. I'll wager, moths are numerous in the old swamp over there."

"They are," said Elnora. "Most I have I took there. A few nights ago my mother caught a number, but we don't dare go alone."

"All the more reason why you need me. Where do you live? I can't get an answer from you, I'll go tell your mother who I am and ask her if I may help you. I warn you, young lady, I have a very effective way with mothers. They almost never turn me down."

"Then it's probable you will have a new experience when you meet mine," said Elnora. "She never was known to do what any one expected she surely would."

The cocoon came loose. Philip Ammon stepped down the embankment turning to offer his hand to Elnora. She ran down as she would have done alone, and taking the cocoon turned it end for end to learn if the imago it contained were alive. Then Ammon took back the cocoon to smooth the edges. Mrs. Comstock gave them one long look as they stood there, and returned to her dandelions. While she worked she paused occasionally, listening intently. Presently they came down the creek, the man carrying the cocoon as if it were a jewel, while Elnora made her way along the bank, taking a lesson in casting. Her face was flushed with excitement, her eyes shining, the bushes taking liberties with her hair. For a picture of perfect loveliness she scarcely could have been surpassed, and the eyes of Philip Ammon seemed to be in working order.

"Moth-er!" called Elnora.

There was an undulant, caressing sweetness in the girl's voice, as she sung out the call in perfect confidence that it would bring a loving answer, that struck deep in Mrs. Comstock's heart. She never had heard that word so pronounced before and a lump arose in her throat.

"Here!" she answered, still cleaning dandelions.

"Mother, this is Mr. Philip Ammon, of Chicago," said Elnora. "He has been ill and he is staying with Dr. Ammon in Onabasha. He came down the creek fishing and cut this cocoon from under the bridge for me. He feels that it would be better to hunt moths than to fish, until he is well. What do you think about it?"

Philip Ammon extended his hand. "I am glad to know you," he said.

"You may take the hand-shaking for granted," replied Mrs. Comstock. "Dandelions have a way of making fingers sticky, and I like to know a man before I take his hand, anyway. That introduction seems mighty comprehensive on your part, but it still leaves me unclassified. My name is Comstock."

Philip Ammon bowed.

"I am sorry to hear you have been sick," said Mrs. Comstock. "But if people will live where they have such vile water as they do in Chicago, I don't see what else they are to expect."

Philip studied her intently.

"I am sure I didn't have a fever on purpose," he said.

"You do seem a little wobbly on your legs," she observed. "Maybe you had better sit and rest while I finish these greens. It's late for the genuine article, but in the shade, among long grass they are still tender."

"May I have a leaf?" he asked, reaching for one as he sat on the bank, looking from the little creek at his feet, away through the dim cool spaces of the June forest on the opposite side. He drew a deep breath. "Glory, but this is good after almost two months inside hospital walls!"

He stretched on the grass and lay gazing up at the leaves, occasionally asking the interpretation of a bird note or the origin of an unfamiliar forest voice. Elnora began helping with the dandelions.

"Another, please," said the young man, holding out his hand.

"Do you suppose this is the kind of grass Nebuchadnezzar ate?" Elnora asked, giving the leaf.

"He knew a good thing if it is."

"Oh, you should taste dandelions boiled with bacon and served with mother's cornbread."

"Don't! My appetite is twice my size now. While it is—how far is it to Onabasha, shortest cut?"

"Three miles."

The man lay in perfect content, nibbling leaves.

"This surely is a treat," he said. "No wonder you find good hunting here. There seems to be foliage for almost every kind of caterpillar. But I suppose you have to exchange for northern species and Pacific Coast kinds?"

"Yes. And every one wants Regalis in trade. I never saw the like. They consider a Cecropia or a Polyphemus an insult, and a Luna is barely acceptable."

"What authorities have you?"

Elnora began to name text-books which started a discussion. Mrs. Comstock listened. She cleaned dandelions with greater deliberation than they ever before were examined. In reality she was taking stock of the young man's long, well-proportioned frame, his strong hands, his smooth, fine-textured skin, his thick shock of dark hair, and making mental notes of his simple manly speech and the fact that he evidently did know much about moths. It pleased her to think that if he had been a neighbour boy who had lain beside her every day of his life while she worked, he could have been no more at home. She liked the things he said, but she was proud that Elnora had a ready answer which always seemed appropriate.

At last Mrs. Comstock finished the greens.

"You are three miles from the city and less than a mile from where we live," she said. "If you will tell me what you dare eat, I suspect you had best go home with us and rest until the cool of the day before you start back. Probably some one that you can ride in with will be passing before evening."

"That is mighty kind of you," said Philip. "I think I will. It doesn't matter so much what I eat, the point is that I must be moderate. I am hungry all the time."

"Then we will go," said Mrs. Comstock, "and we will not allow you to make yourself sick with us."

Philip Ammon arose: picking up the pail of greens and his fishing rod, he stood waiting. Elnora led the way. Mrs. Comstock motioned Philip to follow and she walked in the rear. The girl carried the cocoon and the box of moths she had taken, searching every step for more. The young man frequently set down his load to join in the pursuit of a dragonfly or moth, while Mrs. Comstock watched the proceedings with sharp eyes. Every time Philip picked up the pail of greens she struggled to suppress a smile.

Elnora proceeded slowly, chattering about everything beside the trail. Philip was interested in all the objects she pointed out, noticing several things which escaped her. He carried the greens as casually when they took a short cut down the roadway as on the trail. When Elnora turned toward the gate of her home Philip Ammon stopped, took a long look at the big hewed log cabin, the vines which clambered over it, the flower garden ablaze with beds of bright bloom interspersed with strawberries and tomatoes, the trees of the forest rising north and west like a green wall and exclaimed: "How beautiful!"

Mrs. Comstock was pleased. "If you think that," she said, "perhaps you will understand how, in all this present-day rush to be modern, I have preferred to remain as I began. My husband and I took up this land, and enough trees to build the cabin, stable, and outbuildings are nearly all we ever cut. Of course, if he had lived, I suppose we should have kept up with our neighbours. I hear considerable about the value of the land, the trees which are on it, and the oil which is supposed to be under it, but as yet I haven't brought myself to change anything. So we stand for one of the few remaining homes of first settlers in this region. Come in. You are very welcome to what we have."

Mrs. Comstock stepped forward and took the lead. She had a bowl of soft water and a pair of boots to offer for the heavy waders, for outer comfort, a glass of cold buttermilk and a bench on which to rest, in the circular arbour until dinner was ready. Philip Ammon splashed in the water. He followed to the stable and exchanged boots there. He was ravenous for the buttermilk, and when he stretched on the bench in the arbour the flickering patches of sunlight so tantalized his tired eyes, while the bees made such splendid music, he was soon sound asleep. When Elnora and her mother came out with a table they stood a short time looking at him. It is probable Mrs. Comstock voiced a united thought when she said: "What a refined, decent looking young man! How proud his mother must be of him! We must be careful what we let him eat."

Then they returned to the kitchen where Mrs. Comstock proceeded to be careful. She broiled ham of her own sugar-curing, creamed potatoes, served asparagus on toast, and made a delicious strawberry shortcake. As she cooked dandelions with bacon, she feared to serve them to him, so she made an excuse that it took too long to prepare them, blanched some and made a salad. When everything was ready she touched Philip's sleeve.

"Best have something to eat, lad, before you get too hungry," she said.

"Please hurry!" he begged laughingly as he held a plate toward her to be filled. "I thought I had enough self-restraint to start out alone, but I see I was mistaken. If you would allow me, just now, I am afraid I should start a fever again. I never did smell food so good as this. It's mighty kind of you to take me in. I hope I will be man enough in a few days to do something worth while in return."

Spots of sunshine fell on the white cloth and blue china, the bees and an occasional stray butterfly came searching for food. A rose-breasted grosbeak, released from a three hours' siege of brooding, while his independent mate took her bath and recreation, mounted the top branch of a maple in the west woods from which he serenaded the dinner party with a joyful chorus in celebration of his freedom. Philip's eyes strayed to the beautiful cabin, to the mixture of flowers and vegetables stretching down to the road, and to the singing bird with his red-splotched breast of white and he said: "I can't realize now that I ever lay in ice packs in a hospital. How I wish all the sick folks could come here to grow strong!"

The grosbeak sang on, a big Turnus butterfly sailed through the arbour and poised over the table. Elnora held up a lump of sugar and the butterfly, clinging to her fingers, tasted daintily. With eager eyes and parted lips, the girl held steadily. When at last it wavered away, "That made a picture!" said Philip. "Ask me some other time how I lost my illusions concerning butterflies. I always thought of them in connection with sunshine, flower pollen, and fruit nectar, until one sad day."

"I know!" laughed Elnora. "I've seen that, too, but it didn't destroy any illusion for me. I think quite as much of the butterflies as ever."

Then they talked of flowers, moths, dragonflies, Indian relics, and all the natural wonders the swamp afforded, straying from those subjects to books and school work. When they cleared the table Philip assisted, carrying several tray loads to the kitchen. He and Elnora mounted specimens while Mrs Comstock washed the dishes. Then she came out with a ruffle she was embroidering.

"I wonder if I did not see a picture of you in Onabasha last night," Philip said to Elnora. "Aunt Anna took me to call on Miss Brownlee. She was showing me her crowd—of course, it was you! But it didn't half do you justice, although it was the nearest human of any of them. Miss Brownlee is very fond of you. She said the finest things."

Then they talked of Commencement, and at last Philip said he must go or his friends would become anxious about him.

Mrs. Comstock brought him a blue bowl of creamy milk and a plate of bread. She stopped a passing team and secured a ride to the city for him, as his exercise of the morning had been too violent, and he was forced to admit he was tired.

"May I come to-morrow afternoon and hunt moths awhile?" he asked Mrs. Comstock as he arose. "We will 'sugar' a tree and put a light beside it, if I can get stuff to make the preparation. Possibly we can take some that way. I always enjoy moth hunting, I'd like to help Miss Elnora, and it would be a charity to me. I've got to remain outdoors some place, and I'm quite sure I'd get well faster here than anywhere else. Please say I may come."

"I have no objections, if Elnora really would like help," said Mrs. Comstock.

In her heart she wished he would not come. She wanted her newly found treasure all to herself, for a time, at least. But Elnora's were eager, shining eyes. She thought it would be splendid to have help, and great fun to try book methods for taking moths, so it was arranged. As Philip rode away, Mrs. Comstock's eyes followed him. "What a nice young man!" she said.

"He seems fine," agreed Elnora.

"He comes of a good family, too. I've often heard of his father. He is a great lawyer."

"I am glad he likes it here. I need help. Possibly——"

"Possibly what?"

"We can find many moths."

"What did he mean about the butterflies?"

"That he always had connected them with sunshine, flowers, and fruits, and thought of them as the most exquisite of creations; then one day he found some clustering thickly over carrion."

"Come to think of it, I have seen butterflies——"

"So had he," laughed Elnora. "And that is what he meant."

CHAPTER XIV. WHEREIN A NEW POSITION IS TENDERED ELNORA, AND PHILIP AMMON IS SHOWN LIMBERLOST VIOLETS

The next morning Mrs. Comstock called to Elnora, "The mail carrier stopped at our box."

Elnora ran down the walk and came back carrying an official letter. She tore it open and read:

MY DEAR MISS COMSTOCK:

At the weekly meeting of the Onabasha School Board last night, it was decided to add the position of Lecturer on Natural History to our corps of city teachers. It will be the duty of this person to spend two hours a week in each of the grade schools exhibiting and explaining specimens of the most prominent objects in nature: animals, birds, insects, flowers, vines, shrubs, bushes, and trees. These specimens and lectures should be appropriate to the seasons and the comprehension of the grades. This position was unanimously voted to you. I think you will find the work delightful and much easier than the routine grind of the other teachers. It is my advice that you accept and begin to prepare yourself at once. Your salary will be $750 a year, and you will be allowed $200 for expenses in procuring specimens and books. Let us know at once if you want the position, as it is going to be difficult to fill satisfactorily if you do not.

Very truly yours,

DAVID THOMPSON, President, Onabasha Schools.

"I hardly understand," marvelled Mrs. Comstock.

"It is a new position. They never have had anything like it before. I suspect it arose from the help I've been giving the grade teachers in their nature work. They are trying to teach the children something, and half the instructors don't know a blue jay from a king-fisher, a beech leaf from an elm, or a wasp from a hornet."

"Well, do you?" anxiously inquired Mrs. Comstock.

"Indeed, I do!" laughed Elnora, "and several other things beside. When Freckles bequeathed me the swamp, he gave me a bigger inheritance than he knew. While you have thought I was wandering aimlessly, I have been following a definite plan, studying hard, and storing up the stuff that will earn these seven hundred and fifty dollars. Mother dear, I am going to accept this, of course. The work will be a delight. I'd love it most of anything in teaching. You must help me. We must find nests, eggs, leaves, queer formations in plants and rare flowers. I must have flower boxes made for each of the rooms and filled with wild things. I should begin to gather specimens this very day."

Elnora's face was flushed and her eyes bright.

"Oh, what great work that will be!" she cried. "You must go with me so you can see the little faces when I tell them how the goldfinch builds its nest, and how the bees make honey."

So Elnora and her mother went into the woods behind the cabin to study nature.

"I think," said Elnora, "the idea is to begin with fall things in the fall, keeping to the seasons throughout the year."

"What are fall things?" inquired Mrs. Comstock.

"Oh, fringed gentians, asters, ironwort, every fall flower, leaves from every tree and vine, what makes them change colour, abandoned bird nests, winter quarters of caterpillars and insects, what becomes of the butterflies and grasshoppers—myriads of stuff. I shall have to be very wise to select the things it will be most beneficial for the children to learn."

"Can I really help you?" Mrs. Comstock's strong face was pathetic.

"Indeed, yes!" cried Elnora. "I never can get through it alone. There will be an immense amount of work connected with securing and preparing specimens."

Mrs. Comstock lifted her head proudly and began doing business at once. Her sharp eyes ranged from earth to heaven. She investigated everything, asking innumerable questions. At noon Mrs. Comstock took the specimens they had collected, and went to prepare dinner, while Elnora followed the woods down to the Sintons' to show her letter.

She had to explain what became of her moths, and why college would have to be abandoned for that year, but Margaret and Wesley vowed not to tell. Wesley waved the letter excitedly, explaining it to Margaret as if it were a personal possession. Margaret was deeply impressed, while Billy volunteered first aid in gathering material.

"Now anything you want in the ground, Snap can dig it out," he said. "Uncle Wesley and I found a hole three times as big as Snap, that he dug at the roots of a tree."

"We will train him to hunt pupae cases," said Elnora.

"Are you going to the woods this afternoon?" asked Billy.

"Yes," answered Elnora. "Dr. Ammon's nephew from Chicago is visiting in Onabasha. He is going to show me how men put some sort of compound on a tree, hang a light beside it, and take moths that way. It will be interesting to watch and learn."

"May I come?" asked Billy.

"Of course you may come!" answered Elnora.

"Is this nephew of Dr. Ammon a young man?" inquired Margaret.

"About twenty-six, I should think," said Elnora. "He said he had been out of college and at work in his father's law office three years."

"Does he seem nice?" asked Margaret, and Wesley smiled.

"Finest kind of a person," said Elnora. "He can teach me so much. It is very interesting to hear him talk. He knows considerable about moths that will be a help to me. He had a fever and he has to stay outdoors until he grows strong again."

"Billy, I guess you better help me this afternoon," said Margaret. "Maybe Elnora had rather not bother with you."

"There's no reason on earth why Billy should not come!" cried Elnora, and Wesley smiled again.

"I must hurry home or I won't be ready," she added.

Hastening down the road she entered the cabin, her face glowing.

"I thought you never would come," said Mrs. Comstock. "If you don't hurry Mr. Ammon will be here before you are dressed."

"I forgot about him until just now," said Elnora. "I am not going to dress. He's not coming to visit. We are only going to the woods for more specimens. I can't wear anything that requires care. The limbs take the most dreadful liberties with hair and clothing."

Mrs. Comstock opened her lips, looked at Elnora and closed them. In her heart she was pleased that the girl was so interested in her work that she had forgotten Philip Ammon's coming. But it did seem to her that such a pleasant young man should have been greeted by a girl in a fresh dress. "If she isn't disposed to primp at the coming of a man, heaven forbid that I should be the one to start her," thought Mrs. Comstock.

Philip came whistling down the walk between the cinnamon pinks, pansies, and strawberries. He carried several packages, while his face flushed with more colour than on the previous day.

"Only see what has happened to me!" cried Elnora, offering her letter.

"I'll wager I know!" answered Philip. "Isn't it great! Every one in Onabasha is talking about it. At last there is something new under the sun. All of them are pleased. They think you'll make a big success. This will give an incentive to work. In a few days more I'll be myself again, and we'll overturn the fields and woods around here."

He went on to congratulate Mrs. Comstock.

"Aren't you proud of her, though?" he asked. "You should hear what folks are saying! They say she created the necessity for the position, and every one seems to feel that it is a necessity. Now, if she succeeds, and she will, all of the other city schools will have such departments, and first thing you know she will have made the whole world a little better. Let me rest a few seconds; my feet are acting up again. Then we will cook the moth compound and put it to cool."

He laughed as he sat breathing shortly.

"It doesn't seem possible that a fellow could lose his strength like this. My knees are actually trembling, but I'll be all right in a minute. Uncle Doc said I could come. I told him how you took care of me, and he said I would be safe here."

Then he began unwrapping packages and explaining to Mrs. Comstock how to cook the compound to attract the moths. He followed her into the kitchen, kindled the fire, and stirred the preparation as he talked. While the mixture cooled, he and Elnora walked through the vegetable garden behind the cabin and strayed from there into the woods.

"What about college?" he asked. "Miss Brownlee said you were going."

"I had hoped to," replied Elnora, "but I had a streak of dreadful luck, so I'll have to wait until next year. If you won't speak of it, I'll tell you."

Philip promised, so Elnora recited the history of the Yellow Emperor. She was so interested in doing the Emperor justice she did not notice how many personalities went into the story. A few pertinent questions told him the remainder. He looked at the girl in wonder. In face and form she was as lovely as any one of her age and type he ever had seen. Her school work far surpassed that of most girls of her age he knew. She differed in other ways. This vast store of learning she had gathered from field and forest was a wealth of attraction no other girl possessed. Her frank, matter-of-fact manner was an inheritance from her mother, but there was something more. Once, as they talked he thought "sympathy" was the word to describe it and again "comprehension." She seemed to possess a large sense of brotherhood for all human and animate creatures. She spoke to him as if she had known him all her life. She talked to the grosbeak in exactly the same manner, as she laid strawberries and potato bugs on the fence for his family. She did not swerve an inch from her way when a snake slid past her, while the squirrels came down from the trees and took corn from her fingers. She might as well have been a boy, so lacking was she in any touch of feminine coquetry toward him. He studied her wonderingly. As they went along the path they reached a large slime-covered pool surrounded by decaying stumps and logs thickly covered with water hyacinths and blue flags. Philip stopped.

"Is that the place?" he asked.

Elnora assented. "The doctor told you?"

"Yes. It was tragic. Is that pool really bottomless?"

"So far as we ever have been able to discover."

Philip stood looking at the water, while the long, sweet grasses, thickly sprinkled with blue flag bloom, over which wild bees clambered, swayed around his feet. Then he turned to the girl. She had worked hard. The same lavender dress she had worn the previous day clung to her in limp condition. But she was as evenly coloured and of as fine grain as a wild rose petal, her hair was really brown, but never was such hair touched with a redder glory, while her heavy arching brows added a look of strength to her big gray-blue eyes.

"And you were born here?"

He had not intended to voice that thought.

"Yes," she said, looking into his eyes. "Just in time to prevent my mother from saving the life of my father. She came near never forgiving me."

"Ah, cruel!" cried Philip.

"I find much in life that is cruel, from our standpoints," said Elnora. "It takes the large wisdom of the Unfathomable, the philosophy of the Almighty, to endure some of it. But there is always right somewhere, and at last it seems to come."

"Will it come to you?" asked Philip, who found himself deeply affected.

"It has come," said the girl serenely. "It came a week ago. It came in fullest measure when my mother ceased to regret that I had been born. Now, work that I love has come—that should constitute happiness. A little farther along is my violet bed. I want you to see it."

As Philip Ammon followed he definitely settled upon the name of the unusual feature of Elnora's face. It should be called "experience." She had known bitter experiences early in life. Suffering had been her familiar more than joy. He watched her earnestly, his heart deeply moved. She led him into a swampy half-open space in the woods, stopped and stepped aside. He uttered a cry of surprised delight.

A few decaying logs were scattered around, the grass grew in tufts long and fine. Blue flags waved, clusters of cowslips nodded gold heads, but the whole earth was purple with a thick blanket of violets nodding from stems a foot in length. Elnora knelt and slipping her fingers between the leaves and grasses to the roots, gathered a few violets and gave them to Philip.

"Can your city greenhouses surpass them?" she asked.

He sat on a log to examine the blooms.

"They are superb!" he said. "I never saw such length of stem or such rank leaves, while the flowers are the deepest blue, the truest violet I ever saw growing wild. They are coloured exactly like the eyes of the girl I am going to marry."

Elnora handed him several others to add to those he held. "She must have wonderful eyes," she commented.

"No other blue eyes are quite so beautiful," he said. "In fact, she is altogether lovely."

"Is it customary for a man to think the girl he is going to marry lovely? I wonder if I should find her so."

"You would," said Philip. "No one ever fails to. She is tall as you, very slender, but perfectly rounded; you know about her eyes; her hair is black and wavy—while her complexion is clear and flushed with red."

"Why, she must be the most beautiful girl in the whole world!" she cried.

"No, indeed!" he said. "She is not a particle better looking in her way than you are in yours. She is a type of dark beauty, but you are equally as perfect. She is unusual in her combination of black hair and violet eyes, although every one thinks them black at a little distance. You are quite as unusual with your fair face, black brows, and brown hair; indeed, I know many people who would prefer your bright head to her dark one. It's all a question of taste—and being engaged to the girl," he added.

"That would be likely to prejudice one," laughed Elnora.

"Edith has a birthday soon; if these last will you let me have a box of them to send her?"

"I will help gather and pack them for you, so they will carry nicely. Does she hunt moths with you?"

Back went Philip Ammon's head in a gale of laughter.

"No!" he cried. "She says they are 'creepy.' She would go into a spasm if she were compelled to touch those caterpillars I saw you handling yesterday."

"Why would she?" marvelled Elnora. "Haven't you told her that they are perfectly clean, helpless, and harmless as so much animate velvet?"

"No, I have not told her. She wouldn't care enough about caterpillars to listen."

"In what is she interested?"

"What interests Edith Carr? Let me think! First, I believe she takes pride in being a little handsomer and better dressed than any girl of her set. She is interested in having a beautiful home, fine appointments, in being petted, praised, and the acknowledged leader of society.

"She likes to find new things which amuse her, and to always and in all circumstances have her own way about everything."

"Good gracious!" cried Elnora, staring at him. "But what does she do? How does she spend her time?"

"Spend her time!" repeated Philip. "Well, she would call that a joke. Her days are never long enough. There is endless shopping, to find the pretty things; regular visits to the dressmakers, calls, parties, theatres, entertainments. She is always rushed. I never am able to be with her half as much as I would like."

"But I mean work," persisted Elnora. "In what is she interested that is useful to the world?"

"Me!" cried Philip promptly.

"I can understand that," laughed Elnora. "What I can't understand is how you can be in—— " She stopped in confusion, but she saw that he had finished the sentence as she had intended. "I beg your pardon!" she cried. "I didn't intend to say that. But I cannot understand these people I hear about who live only for their own amusement. Perhaps it is very great; I'll never have a chance to know. To me, it seems the only pleasure in this world worth having is the joy we derive from living for those we love, and those we can help. I hope you are not angry with me."

Philip sat silently looking far away, with deep thought in his eyes.

"You are angry," faltered Elnora.

His look came back to her as she knelt before him among the flowers and he gazed at her steadily.

"No doubt I should be," he said, "but the fact is I am not. I cannot understand a life purely for personal pleasure myself. But she is only a girl, and this is her playtime. When she is a woman in her own home, then she will be different, will she not?"

Elnora never resembled her mother so closely as when she answered that question.

"I would have to be well acquainted with her to know, but I should hope so. To make a real home for a tired business man is a very different kind of work from that required to be a leader of society. It demands different talent and education. Of course, she means to change, or she would not have promised to make a home for you. I suspect our dope is cool now, let's go try for some butterflies."

As they went along the path together Elnora talked of many things but Philip answered absently. Evidently he was thinking of something else. But the moth bait recalled him and he was ready for work as they made their way back to the woods. He wanted to try the Limberlost, but Elnora was firm about remaining on home ground. She did not tell him that lights hung in the swamp would be a signal to call up a band of men whose presence she dreaded. So they started, Ammon carrying the dope, Elnora the net, Billy and Mrs. Comstock following with cyanide boxes and lanterns.

First they tried for butterflies and captured several fine ones without trouble. They also called swarms of ants, bees, beetles, and flies. When it grew dusk, Mrs. Comstock and Philip went to prepare supper. Elnora and Billy remained until the butterflies disappeared. Then they lighted the lanterns, repainted the trees and followed the home trail.

"Do you 'spec you'll get just a lot of moths?" asked Billy, as he walked beside Elnora.

"I am sure I hardly know," said the girl. "This is a new way for me. Perhaps they will come to the lights, but few moths eat; and I have some doubt about those which the lights attract settling on the right trees. Maybe the smell of that dope will draw them. Between us, Billy, I think I like my old way best. If I can find a hidden moth, slip up and catch it unawares, or take it in full flight, it's my captive, and I can keep it until it dies naturally. But this way you seem to get it under false pretences, it has no chance, and it will probably ruin its wings struggling for freedom before morning."

"Well, any moth ought to be proud to be taken anyway, by you," said Billy. "Just look what you do! You can make everybody love them. People even quit hating caterpillars when they see you handle them and hear you tell all about them. You must have some to show people how they are. It's not like killing things to see if you can, or because you want to eat them, the way most men kill birds. I think it is right for you to take enough for collections, to show city people, and to illustrate the Bird Woman's books. You go on and take them! The moths don't care. They're glad to have you. They like it!"

"Billy, I see your future," said Elnora. "We will educate you and send you up to Mr. Ammon to make a great lawyer. You'd beat the world as a special pleader. You actually make me feel that I am doing the moths a kindness to take them."

"And so you are!" cried Billy. "Why, just from what you have taught them Uncle Wesley and Aunt Margaret never think of killing a caterpillar until they look whether it's the beautiful June moth kind, or the horrid tent ones. That's what you can do. You go straight ahead!"

"Billy, you are a jewel!" cried Elnora, throwing her arm across his shoulders as they came down the path.

"My, I was scared!" said Billy with a deep breath.

"Scared?" questioned Elnora.

"Yes sir-ee! Aunt Margaret scared me. May I ask you a question?"

"Of course, you may!"

"Is that man going to be your beau?"

"Billy! No! What made you think such a thing?"

"Aunt Margaret said likely he would fall in love with you, and you wouldn't want me around any more. Oh, but I was scared! It isn't so, is it?"

"Indeed, no!"

"I am your beau, ain't I?"

"Surely you are!" said Elnora, tightening her arm.

"I do hope Aunt Kate has ginger cookies," said Billy with a little skip of delight.

CHAPTER XV. WHEREIN MRS. COMSTOCK FACES THE ALMIGHTY, AND PHILIP AMMON WRITES A LETTER

Mrs. Comstock and Elnora were finishing breakfast the following morning when they heard a cheery whistle down the road. Elnora with surprised eyes looked at her mother.

"Could that be Mr. Ammon?" she questioned.

"I did not expect him so soon," commented Mrs. Comstock.

It was sunrise, but the musician was Philip Ammon. He appeared stronger than on yesterday.

"I hope I am not too early," he said. "I am consumed with anxiety to learn if we have made a catch. If we have, we should beat the birds to it. I promised Uncle Doc to put on my waders and keep dry for a few days yet, when I go to the woods. Let's hurry! I am afraid of crows. There might be a rare moth."

The sun was topping the Limberlost when they started. As they neared the place Philip stopped.

"Now we must use great caution," he said. "The lights and the odours always attract numbers that don't settle on the baited trees. Every bush, shrub, and limb may hide a specimen we want."

So they approached with much care.

"There is something, anyway!" cried Philip.

"There are moths! I can see them!" exulted Elnora.

"Those you see are fast enough. It's the ones for which you must search that will escape. The grasses are dripping, and I have boots, so you look beside the path while I take the outside," suggested Ammon.

Mrs. Comstock wanted to hunt moths, but she was timid about making a wrong movement, so she wisely sat on a log and watched Philip and Elnora to learn how they proceeded. Back in the deep woods a hermit thrush was singing his chant to the rising sun. Orioles were sowing the pure, sweet air with notes of gold, poured out while on wing. The robins were only chirping now, for their morning songs had awakened all the other birds an hour ago. Scolding red-wings tilted on half the bushes. Excepting late species of haws, tree bloom was almost gone, but wild flowers made the path border and all the wood floor a riot of colour. Elnora, born among such scenes, worked eagerly, but to the city man, recently from a hospital, they seemed too good to miss. He frequently stooped to examine a flower face, paused to listen intently to the thrush or lifted his head to see the gold flash which accompanied the oriole's trailing notes. So Elnora uttered the first cry, as she softly lifted branches and peered among the grasses.

"My find!" she called. "Bring the box, mother!"

Philip came hurrying also. When they reached her she stood on the path holding a pair of moths. Her eyes were wide with excitement, her cheeks pink, her red lips parted, and on the hand she held out to them clung a pair of delicate blue-green moths, with white bodies, and touches of lavender and straw colour. All around her lay flower-brocaded grasses, behind the deep green background of the forest, while the sun slowly sifted gold from heaven to burnish her hair. Mrs. Comstock heard a sharp breath behind her.

"Oh, what a picture!" exulted Philip at her shoulder. "She is absolutely and altogether lovely! I'd give a small fortune for that faithfully set on canvas!"

He picked the box from Mrs. Comstock's fingers and slowly advanced with it. Elnora held down her hand and transferred the moths. Philip closed the box carefully, but the watching mother saw that his eyes were following the girl's face. He was not making the slightest attempt to conceal his admiration.

"I wonder if a woman ever did anything lovelier than to find a pair of Luna moths on a forest path, early on a perfect June morning," he said to Mrs. Comstock, when he returned the box.

She glanced at Elnora who was intently searching the bushes.

"Look here, young man," said Mrs. Comstock. "You seem to find that girl of mine about right."

"I could suggest no improvement," said Philip. "I never saw a more attractive girl anywhere. She seems absolutely perfect to me."

"Then suppose you don't start any scheme calculated to spoil her!" proposed Mrs. Comstock dryly. "I don't think you can, or that any man could, but I'm not taking any risks. You asked to come here to help in this work. We are both glad to have you, if you confine yourself to work; but it's the least you can do to leave us as you find us."

"I beg your pardon!" said Philip. "I intended no offence. I admire her as I admire any perfect creation."

"And nothing in all this world spoils the average girl so quickly and so surely," said Mrs. Comstock. She raised her voice. "Elnora, fasten up that tag of hair over your left ear. These bushes muss you so you remind me of a sheep poking its nose through a hedge fence."

Mrs. Comstock started down the path toward the log again, when she reached it she called sharply: "Elnora, come here! I believe I have found something myself."

The "something" was a Citheronia Regalis which had emerged from its case on the soft earth under the log. It climbed up the wood, its stout legs dragging a big pursy body, while it wildly flapped tiny wings the size of a man's thumb-nail. Elnora gave one look and a cry which brought Philip.

"That's the rarest moth in America!" he announced. "Mrs. Comstock, you've gone up head. You can put that in a box with a screen cover to-night, and attract half a dozen, possibly."

"Is it rare, Elnora?" inquired Mrs. Comstock, as if no one else knew.

"It surely is," answered Elnora. "If we can find it a mate to-night, it will lay from two hundred and fifty to three hundred eggs to-morrow. With any luck at all I can raise two hundred caterpillars from them. I did once before. And they are worth a dollar apiece."

"Was the one I killed like that?"

"No. That was a different moth, but its life processes were the same as this. The Bird Woman calls this the King of the Poets."

"Why does she?"

"Because it is named for Citheron who was a poet, and regalis refers to a king. You mustn't touch it or you may stunt wing development. You watch and don't let that moth out of sight, or anything touch it. When the wings are expanded and hardened we will put it in a box."

"I am afraid it will race itself to death," objected Mrs. Comstock.

"That's a part of the game," said Philip. "It is starting circulation now. When the right moment comes, it will stop and expand its wings. If you watch closely you can see them expand."

Presently the moth found a rough projection of bark and clung with its feet, back down, its wings hanging. The body was an unusual orange red, the tiny wings were gray, striped with the red and splotched here and there with markings of canary yellow. Mrs. Comstock watched breathlessly. Presently she slipped from the log and knelt to secure a better view.

"Are its wings developing?" called Elnora.

"They are growing larger and the markings coming stronger every minute."

"Let's watch, too," said Elnora to Philip.

They came and looked over Mrs. Comstock's shoulder. Lower drooped the gay wings, wider they spread, brighter grew the markings as if laid off in geometrical patterns. They could hear Mrs. Comstock's tense breath and see her absorbed expression.

"Young people," she said solemnly, "if your studying science and the elements has ever led you to feel that things just happen, kind of evolve by chance, as it were, this sight will be good for you. Maybe earth and air accumulate, but it takes the wisdom of the Almighty God to devise the wing of a moth. If there ever was a miracle, this whole process is one. Now, as I understand it, this creature is going to keep on spreading those wings, until they grow to size and harden to strength sufficient to bear its body. Then it flies away, mates with its kind, lays its eggs on the leaves of a certain tree, and the eggs hatch tiny caterpillars which eat just that kind of leaves, and the worms grow and grow, and take on different forms and colours until at last they are big caterpillars six inches long, with large horns. Then they burrow into the earth, build a water-proof house around themselves from material which is inside them, and lie through rain and freezing cold for months. A year from egg laying they come out like this, and begin the process all over again. They don't eat, they don't see distinctly, they live but a few days, and fly only at night; then they drop off easy, but the process goes on."

A shivering movement went over the moth. The wings drooped and spread wider. Mrs. Comstock sank into soft awed tones.

"There never was a moment in my life," she said, "when I felt so in the Presence, as I do now. I feel as if the Almighty were so real, and so near, that I could reach out and touch Him, as I could this wonderful work of His, if I dared. I feel like saying to Him: 'To the extent of my brain power I realize Your presence, and all it is in me to comprehend of Your power. Help me to learn, even this late, the lessons of Your wonderful creations. Help me to unshackle and expand my soul to the fullest realization of Your wonders. Almighty God, make me bigger, make me broader!'"

The moth climbed to the end of the projection, up it a little way, then suddenly reversed its wings, turned the hidden sides out and dropped them beside its abdomen, like a large fly. The upper side of the wings, thus exposed, was far richer colour, more exquisite texture than the under, and they slowly half lifted and drooped again. Mrs. Comstock turned her face to Philip.

"Am I an old fool, or do you feel it, too?" she half whispered.

"You are wiser than you ever have been before," answered he. "I feel it, also."

"And I," breathed Elnora.

The moth spread its wings, shivered them tremulously, opening and closing them rapidly. Philip handed the box to Elnora.

She shook her head.

"I can't take that one," she said. "Give her freedom."

"But, Elnora," protested Mrs. Comstock, "I don't want to let her go. She's mine. She's the first one I ever found this way. Can't you put her in a big box, and let her live, without hurting her? I can't bear to let her go. I want to learn all about her."

"Then watch while we gather these on the trees," said Elnora. "We will take her home until night and then decide what to do. She won't fly for a long time yet."

Mrs. Comstock settled on the ground, gazing at the moth. Elnora and Philip went to the baited trees, placing several large moths and a number of smaller ones in the cyanide jar, and searching the bushes beyond where they found several paired specimens of differing families. When they returned Elnora showed her mother how to hold her hand before the moth so that it would climb upon her fingers. Then they started back to the cabin, Elnora and Philip leading the way; Mrs. Comstock followed slowly, stepping with great care lest she stumble and injure the moth. Her face wore a look of comprehension, in her eyes was an exalted light. On she came to the blue-bordered pool lying beside her path.

A turtle scrambled from a log and splashed into the water, while a red-wing shouted, "O-ka-lee!" to her. Mrs. Comstock paused and looked intently at the slime-covered quagmire, framed in a flower riot and homed over by sweet-voiced birds. Then she gazed at the thing of incomparable beauty clinging to her fingers and said softly: "If you had known about wonders like these in the days of your youth, Robert Comstock, could you ever have done what you did?"

Elnora missed her mother, and turning to look for her, saw her standing beside the pool. Would the old fascination return? A panic of fear seized the girl. She went back swiftly.

"Are you afraid she is going?" Elnora asked. "If you are, cup your other hand over her for shelter. Carrying her through this air and in the hot sunshine will dry her wings and make them ready for flight very quickly. You can't trust her in such air and light as you can in the cool dark woods."

While she talked she took hold of her mother's sleeve, anxiously smiling a pitiful little smile that Mrs. Comstock understood. Philip set his load at the back door, returning to hold open the garden gate for Elnora and Mrs. Comstock. He reached it in time to see them standing together beside the pool. The mother bent swiftly and kissed the girl on the lips. Philip turned and was busily hunting moths on the raspberry bushes when they reached the gate. And so excellent are the rewards of attending your own business, that he found a Promethea on a lilac in a corner; a moth of such rare wine-coloured, velvety shades that it almost sent Mrs. Comstock to her knees again. But this one was fully developed, able to fly, and had to be taken into the cabin hurriedly. Mrs. Comstock stood in the middle of the room holding up her Regalis.

"Now what must I do?" she asked.

Elnora glanced at Philip Ammon. Their eyes met and both of them smiled; he with amusement at the tall, spare figure, with dark eyes and white crown, asking the childish question so confidingly; and Elnora with pride. She was beginning to appreciate the character of her mother.

"How would you like to sit and see her finish development? I'll get dinner," proposed the girl.

After they had dined, Philip and Elnora carried the dishes to the kitchen, brought out boxes, sheets of cork, pins, ink, paper slips and everything necessary for mounting and classifying the moths they had taken. When the housework was finished Mrs. Comstock with her ruffle sat near, watching and listening. She remembered all they said that she understood, and when uncertain she asked questions. Occasionally she laid down her work to straighten some flower which needed attention or to search the garden for a bug for the grosbeak. In one of these absences Elnora said to Philip: "These replace quite a number of the moths I lost for the man of India. With a week of such luck, I could almost begin to talk college again."

"There is no reason why you should not have the week and the luck," said he. "I have taken moths until the middle of August, though I suspect one is more likely to find late ones in the north where it is colder than here. The next week is hay-time, but we can count on a few double-brooders and strays, and by working the exchange method for all it is worth, I think we can complete the collection again."

"You almost make me hope," said Elnora, "but I must not allow myself. I don't truly think I can replace all I lost, not even with your help. If I could, I scarcely see my way clear to leave mother this winter. I have found her so recently, and she is so precious, I can't risk losing her again. I am going to take the nature position in the Onabasha schools, and I shall be most happy doing the work. Only, these are a temptation."

"I wish you might go to college this fall with the other girls," said Philip. "I feel that if you don't you never will. Isn't there some way?"

"I can't see it if there is, and I really don't want to leave mother."

"Well, mother is mighty glad to hear it," said Mrs. Comstock, entering the arbour.

Philip noticed that her face was pale, her lips quivering, her voice cold.

"I was telling your daughter that she should go to college this winter," he explained, "but she says she doesn't want to leave you."

"If she wants to go, I wish she could," said Mrs. Comstock, a look of relief spreading over her face.

"Oh, all girls want to go to college," said Philip. "It's the only proper place to learn bridge and embroidery; not to mention midnight lunches of mixed pickles and fruit cake, and all the delights of the sororities."

"I have thought for years of going to college," said Elnora, "but I never thought of any of those things."

"That is because your education in fudge and bridge has been sadly neglected," said Philip. "You should hear my sister Polly! This was her final year! Lunches and sororities were all I heard her mention, until Tom Levering came on deck; now he is the leading subject. I can't see from her daily conversation that she knows half as much really worth knowing as you do, but she's ahead of you miles on fun."

"Oh, we had some good times in the high school," said Elnora. "Life hasn't been all work and study. Is Edith Carr a college girl?"

"No. She is the very selectest kind of a private boarding-school girl."

"Who is she?" asked Mrs. Comstock.

Philip opened his lips.

"She is a girl in Chicago, that Mr. Ammon knows very well," said Elnora. "She is beautiful and rich, and a friend of his sister's. Or, didn't you say that?"

"I don't remember, but she is," said Philip. "This moth needs an alcohol bath to remove the dope."

"Won't the down come, too?" asked Elnora anxiously.

"No. You watch and you will see it come out, as Polly would say, 'a perfectly good' moth."

"Is your sister younger than you?" inquired Elnora.

"Yes," said Philip, "but she is three years older than you. She is the dearest sister in all the world. I'd love to see her now."

"Why don't you send for her," suggested Elnora. "Perhaps she'd like to help us catch moths."

"Yes, I think Polly in a Virot hat, Picot embroidered frock and three-inch heels would take more moths than any one who ever tried the Limberlost," laughed Philip.

"Well, you find many of them, and you are her brother."

"Yes, but that is different. Father was reared in Onabasha, and he loved the country. He trained me his way and mother took charge of Polly. I don't quite understand it. Mother is a great home body herself, but she did succeed in making Polly strictly ornamental."

"Does Tom Levering need a 'strictly ornamental' girl?"

"You are too matter of fact! Too 'strictly' material. He needs a darling girl who will love him plenty, and Polly is that."

"Well, then, does the Limberlost need a 'strictly ornamental' girl?"

"No!" cried Philip. "You are ornament enough for the Limberlost. I have changed my mind. I don't want Polly here. She would not enjoy catching moths, or anything we do."

"She might," persisted Elnora. "You are her brother, and surely you care for these things."

"The argument does not hold," said Philip. "Polly and I do not like the same things when we are at home, but we are very fond of each other. The member of my family who would go crazy about this is my father. I wish he could come, if only for a week. I'd send for him, but he is tied up in preparing some papers for a great corporation case this summer. He likes the country. It was his vote that brought me here."

Philip leaned back against the arbour, watching the grosbeak as it hunted food between a tomato vine and a day lily. Elnora set him to making labels, and when he finished them he asked permission to write a letter. He took no pains to conceal his page, and from where she sat opposite him, Elnora could not look his way without reading: "My dearest Edith." He wrote busily for a time and then sat staring across the garden.

"Have you run out of material so quickly?" asked Elnora.

"That's about it," said Philip. "I have said that I am getting well as rapidly as possible, that the air is fine, the folks at Uncle Doc's all well, and entirely too good to me; that I am spending most of my time in the country helping catch moths for a collection, which is splendid exercise; now I can't think of another thing that will be interesting."

There was a burst of exquisite notes in the maple.

"Put in the grosbeak," suggested Elnora. "Tell her you are so friendly with him you feed him potato bugs."

Philip lowered the pen to the sheet, bent forward, then hesitated.

"Blest if I do!" he cried. "She'd think a grosbeak was a depraved person with a large nose. She'd never dream that it was a black-robed lover, with a breast of snow and a crimson heart. She doesn't care for hungry babies and potato bugs. I shall write that to father. He will find it delightful."

Elnora deftly picked up a moth, pinned it and placed its wings. She straightened the antennae, drew each leg into position and set it in perfectly lifelike manner. As she lifted her work to see if she had it right, she glanced at Philip. He was still frowning and hesitating over the paper.

"I dare you to let me dictate a couple of paragraphs."

"Done!" cried Philip. "Go slowly enough that I can write it."

Elnora laughed gleefully.

"I am writing this," she began, "in an old grape arbour in the country, near a log cabin where I had my dinner. From where I sit I can see directly into the home of the next-door neighbour on the west. His name is R. B. Grosbeak. From all I have seen of him, he is a gentleman of the old school; the oldest school there is, no doubt. He always wears a black suit and cap and a white vest, decorated with one large red heart, which I think must be the emblem of some ancient order. I have been here a number of times, and I never have seen him wear anything else, or his wife appear in other than a brown dress with touches of white.

"It has appealed to me at times that she was a shade neglectful of her home duties, but he does not seem to feel that way. He cheerfully stays in the sitting-room, while she is away having a good time, and sings while he cares for the four small children. I must tell you about his music. I am sure he never saw inside a conservatory. I think he merely picked up what he knows by ear and without vocal training, but there is a tenderness in his tones, a depth of pure melody, that I never have heard surpassed. It may be that I think more of his music than that of some other good vocalists hereabout, because I see more of him and appreciate his devotion to his home life.

"I just had an encounter with him at the west fence, and induced him to carry a small gift to his children. When I see the perfect harmony in which he lives, and the depth of content he and the brown lady find in life, I am almost persuaded to— Now this is going to be poetry," said Elnora. "Move your pen over here and begin with a quote and a cap."

Philip's face had been an interesting study while he wrote her sentences. Now he gravely set the pen where she indicated, and Elnora dictated—

"Buy a nice little home in the country,
And settle down there for life."

"That's the truth!" cried Philip. "It's as big a temptation as I ever had. Go on!"

"That's all," said Elnora. "You can finish. The moths are done. I am going hunting for whatever I can find for the grades."

"Wait a minute," begged Philip. "I am going, too."

"No. You stay with mother and finish your letter."

"It is done. I couldn't add anything to that."

"Very well! Sign your name and come on. But I forgot to tell you all the bargain. Maybe you won't send the letter when you hear that. The remainder is that you show me the reply to my part of it."

"Oh, that's easy! I wouldn't have the slightest objection to showing you the whole letter."

He signed his name, folded the sheets and slipped them into his pocket.

"Where are we going and what do we take?"

"Will you go, mother?" asked Elnora.

"I have a little work that should be done," said Mrs. Comstock. "Could you spare me? Where do you want to go?"

"We will go down to Aunt Margaret's and see her a few minutes and get Billy. We will be back in time for supper."

Mrs. Comstock smiled as she watched them down the road. What a splendid-looking pair of young creatures they were! How finely proportioned, how full of vitality! Then her face grew troubled as she saw them in earnest conversation. Just as she was wishing she had not trusted her precious girl with so much of a stranger, she saw Elnora stoop to lift a branch and peer under. The mother grew content. Elnora was thinking only of her work. She was to be trusted utterly.

CHAPTER XVI. WHEREIN THE LIMBERLOST SINGS FOR PHILIP, AND THE TALKING TREES TELL GREAT SECRETS

A few days later Philip handed Elnora a sheet of paper and she read: "In your condition I should think the moth hunting and life at that cabin would be very good for you, but for any sake keep away from that Grosbeak person, and don't come home with your head full of granger ideas. No doubt he has a remarkable voice, but I can't bear untrained singers, and don't you get the idea that a June song is perennial. You are not hearing the music he will make when the four babies have the scarlet fever and the measles, and the gadding wife leaves him at home to care for them then. Poor soul, I pity her! How she exists where rampant cows bellow at you, frogs croak, mosquitoes consume you, the butter goes to oil in summer and bricks in winter, while the pump freezes every day, and there is no earthly amusement, and no society! Poor things! Can't you influence him to move? No wonder she gads when she has a chance! I should die. If you are thinking of settling in the country, think also of a woman who is satisfied with white and brown to accompany you! Brown! Of all deadly colours! I should go mad in brown."

Elnora laughed while she read. Her face was dimpling, as she returned the sheet. "Who's ahead?" she asked.

"Who do you think?" he parried.

"She is," said Elnora. "Are you going to tell her in your next that R. B. Grosbeak is a bird, and that he probably will spend the winter in a wild plum thicket in Tennessee?"

"No," said Philip. "I shall tell her that I understand her ideas of life perfectly, and, of course, I never shall ask her to deal with oily butter and frozen pumps—"

"—and measley babies," interpolated Elnora.

"Exactly!" said Philip. "At the same time I find so much to counterbalance those things, that I should not object to bearing them myself, in view of the recompense. Where do we go and what do we do to-day?"

"We will have to hunt beside the roads and around the edge of the Limberlost to-day," said Elnora. "Mother is making strawberry preserves, and she can't come until she finishes. Suppose we go down to the swamp and I'll show you what is left of the flower-room that Terence O'More, the big lumber man of Great Rapids, made when he was a homeless boy here. Of course, you have heard the story?"

"Yes, and I've met the O'Mores who are frequently in Chicago society. They have friends there. I think them one ideal couple."

"That sounds as if they might be the only one," said Elnora, "and, indeed, they are not. I know dozens. Aunt Margaret and Uncle Wesley are another, the Brownlees another, and my mathematics professor and his wife. The world is full of happy people, but no one ever hears of them. You must fight and make a scandal to get into the papers. No one knows about all the happy people. I am happy myself, and look how perfectly inconspicuous I am."

"You only need go where you will be seen," began Philip, when he remembered and finished. "What do we take to-day?"

"Ourselves," said Elnora. "I have a vagabond streak in my blood and it's in evidence. I am going to show you where real flowers grow, real birds sing, and if I feel quite right about it, perhaps I shall raise a note or two myself."

"Oh, do you sing?" asked Philip politely.

"At times," answered Elnora. "'As do the birds; because I must,' but don't be scared. The mood does not possess me often. Perhaps I shan't raise a note."

They went down the road to the swamp, climbed the snake fence, followed the path to the old trail and then turned south upon it. Elnora indicated to Philip the trail with remnants of sagging barbed wire.

"It was ten years ago," she said. "I was a little school girl, but I wandered widely even then, and no one cared. I saw him often. He had been in a city institution all his life, when he took the job of keeping timber thieves out of this swamp, before many trees had been cut. It was a strong man's work, and he was a frail boy, but he grew hardier as he lived out of doors. This trail we are on is the path his feet first wore, in those days when he was insane with fear and eaten up with loneliness, but he stuck to his work and won out. I used to come down to the road and creep among the bushes as far as I dared, to watch him pass. He walked mostly, at times he rode a wheel.

"Some days his face was dreadfully sad, others it was so determined a little child could see the force in it, and once he was radiant. That day the Swamp Angel was with him. I can't tell you what she was like. I never saw any one who resembled her. He stopped close here to show her a bird's nest. Then they went on to a sort of flower-room he had made, and he sang for her. By the time he left, I had gotten bold enough to come out on the trail, and I met the big Scotchman Freckles lived with. He saw me catching moths and butterflies, so he took me to the flower-room and gave me everything there. I don't dare come alone often, so I can't keep it up as he did, but you can see something of how it was."

Elnora led the way and Philip followed. The outlines of the room were not distinct, because many of the trees were gone, but Elnora showed how it had been as nearly as she could.

"The swamp is almost ruined now," she said. "The maples, walnuts, and cherries are all gone. The talking trees are the only things left worth while."

"The 'talking trees!' I don't understand," commented Philip.

"No wonder!" laughed Elnora. "They are my discovery. You know all trees whisper and talk during the summer, but there are two that have so much to say they keep on the whole winter, when the others are silent. The beeches and oaks so love to talk, they cling to their dead, dry leaves. In the winter the winds are stiffest and blow most, so these trees whisper, chatter, sob, laugh, and at times roar until the sound is deafening. They never cease until new leaves come out in the spring to push off the old ones. I love to stand beneath them with my ear to the trunks, interpreting what they say to fit my moods. The beeches branch low, and their leaves are small so they only know common earthly things; but the oaks run straight above almost all other trees before they branch, their arms are mighty, their leaves large. They meet the winds that travel around the globe, and from them learn the big things."

Philip studied the girls face. "What do the beeches tell you, Elnora?" he asked gently.

"To be patient, to be unselfish, to do unto others as I would have them do to me."

"And the oaks?"

"They say 'be true,' 'live a clean life,' 'send your soul up here and the winds of the world will teach it what honour achieves.'"

"Wonderful secrets, those!" marvelled Philip. "Are they telling them now? Could I hear?"

"No. They are only gossiping now. This is play-time. They tell the big secrets to a white world, when the music inspires them."

"The music?"

"All other trees are harps in the winter. Their trunks are the frames, their branches the strings, the winds the musicians. When the air is cold and clear, the world very white, and the harp music swelling, then the talking trees tell the strengthening, uplifting things."

"You wonderful girl!" cried Philip. "What a woman you will be!"

"If I am a woman at all worth while, it will be because I have had such wonderful opportunities," said Elnora. "Not every girl is driven to the forest to learn what God has to say there. Here are the remains of Freckles's room. The time the Angel came here he sang to her, and I listened. I never heard music like that. No wonder she loved him. Every one who knew him did, and they do yet. Try that log, it makes a fairly good seat. This old store box was his treasure house, just as it's now mine. I will show you my dearest possession. I do not dare take it home because mother can't overcome her dislike for it. It was my father's, and in some ways I am like him. This is the strongest."

Elnora lifted the violin and began to play. She wore a school dress of green gingham, with the sleeves rolled to the elbows. She seemed a part of the setting all around her. Her head shone like a small dark sun, and her face never had seemed so rose-flushed and fair. From the instant she drew the bow, her lips parted and her eyes turned toward something far away in the swamp, and never did she give more of that impression of feeling for her notes and repeating something audible only to her. Philip was too close to get the best effect. He arose and stepped back several yards, leaning against a large tree, looking and listening intently.

As he changed positions he saw that Mrs. Comstock had followed them, and was standing on the trail, where she could not have helped hearing everything Elnora had said.

So to Philip before her and the mother watching on the trail, Elnora played the Song of the Limberlost. It seemed as if the swamp hushed all its other voices and spoke only through her dancing bow. The mother out on the trail had heard it all, once before from the girl, many times from her father. To the man it was a revelation. He stood so stunned he forgot Mrs. Comstock. He tried to realize what a city audience would say to that music, from such a player, with a similar background, and he could not imagine.

He was wondering what he dared say, how much he might express, when the last note fell and the girl laid the violin in the case, closed the door, locked it and hid the key in the rotting wood at the end of a log. Then she came to him. Philip stood looking at her curiously.

"I wonder," he said, "what people would say to that?"

"I played that in public once," said Elnora. "I think they liked it, fairly well. I had a note yesterday offering me the leadership of the high school orchestra in Onabasha. I can take it as well as not. None of my talks to the grades come the first thing in the morning. I can play a few minutes in the orchestra and reach the rooms in plenty of time. It will be more work that I love, and like finding the money. I would gladly play for nothing, merely to be able to express myself."

"With some people it makes a regular battlefield of the human heart—this struggle for self-expression," said Philip. "You are going to do beautiful work in the world, and do it well. When I realize that your violin belonged to your father, that he played it before you were born, and it no doubt affected your mother strongly, and then couple with that the years you have roamed these fields and swamps finding in nature all you had to lavish your heart upon, I can see how you evolved. I understand what you mean by self-expression. I know something of what you have to express. The world never so wanted your message as it does now. It is hungry for the things you know. I can see easily how your position came to you. What you have to give is taught in no college, and I am not sure but you would spoil yourself if you tried to run your mind through a set groove with hundreds of others. I never thought I should say such a thing to any one, but I do say to you, and I honestly believe it; give up the college idea. Your mind does not need that sort of development. Stick close to your work in the woods. You are becoming so infinitely greater on it, than the best college girl I ever knew, that there is no comparison. When you have money to spend, take that violin and go to one of the world's great masters and let the Limberlost sing to him; if he thinks he can improve it, very well. I have my doubts."

"Do you really mean that you would give up all idea of going to college, in my place?"

"I really mean it," said Philip. "If I now held the money in my hands to send you, and could give it to you in some way you would accept I would not. I do not know why it is the fate of the world always to want something different from what life gives them. If you only could realize it, my girl, you are in college, and have been always. You are in the school of experience, and it has taught you to think, and given you a heart. God knows I envy the man who wins it! You have been in the college of the Limberlost all your life, and I never met a graduate from any other institution who could begin to compare with you in sanity, clarity, and interesting knowledge. I wouldn't even advise you to read too many books on your lines. You acquire your material first hand, and you know that you are right. What you should do is to begin early to practise self-expression. Don't wait too long to tell us about the woods as you know them."

"Follow the course of the Bird Woman, you mean?" asked Elnora.

"In your own way; with your own light. She won't live forever. You are younger, and you will be ready to begin where she ends. The swamp has given you all you need so far; now you give it to the world in payment. College be confounded! Go to work and show people what there is in you!"

Not until then did he remember Mrs. Comstock.

"Should we go out to the trail and see if your mother is coming?" he asked.

"Here she is now," said Elnora. "Gracious, it's a mercy I got that violin put away in time! I didn't expect her so soon," whispered the girl as she turned and went toward her mother. Mrs. Comstock's expression was peculiar as she looked at Elnora.

"I forgot that you were making sun-preserves and they didn't require much cooking," she said. "We should have waited for you."

"Not at all!" answered Mrs. Comstock. "Have you found anything yet?"

"Nothing that I can show you," said Elnora. "I am almost sure I have found an idea that will revolutionize the whole course of my work, thought, and ambitions."

"'Ambitions!' My, what a hefty word!" laughed Mrs. Comstock. "Now who would suspect a little red-haired country girl of harbouring such a deadly germ in her body? Can you tell mother about it?"

"Not if you talk to me that way, I can't," said Elnora.

"Well, I guess we better let ambition lie. I've always heard it was safest asleep. If you ever get a bona fide attack, it will be time to attend it. Let's hunt specimens. It is June. Philip and I are in the grades. You have an hour to put an idea into our heads that will stick for a lifetime, and grow for good. That's the way I look at your job. Now, what are you going to give us? We don't want any old silly stuff that has been hashed over and over, we want a big new idea to plant in our hearts. Come on, Miss Teacher, what is the boiled-down, double-distilled essence of June? Give it to us strong. We are large enough to furnish it developing ground. Hurry up! Time is short and we are waiting. What is the miracle of June? What one thing epitomizes the whole month, and makes it just a little different from any other?"

"The birth of these big night moths," said Elnora promptly.

Philip clapped his hands. The tears started to Mrs. Comstock's eyes. She took Elnora in her arms, and kissed her forehead.

"You'll do!" she said. "June is June, not because it has bloom, bird, fruit, or flower, exclusive to it alone.

"It's half May and half July in all of them. But to me, it's just June, when it comes to these great, velvet-winged night moths which sweep its moonlit skies, consummating their scheme of creation, and dropping like a bloomed-out flower. Give them moths for June. Then make that the basis of your year's work. Find the distinctive feature of each month, the one thing which marks it a time apart, and hit them squarely between the eyes with it. Even the babies of the lowest grades can comprehend moths when they see a few emerge, and learn their history, as it can be lived before them. You should show your specimens in pairs, then their eggs, the growing caterpillars, and then the cocoons. You want to dig out the red heart of every month in the year, and hold it pulsing before them.

"I can't name all of them off-hand, but I think of one more right now. February belongs to our winter birds. It is then the great horned owl of the swamp courts his mate, the big hawks pair, and even the crows begin to take notice. These are truly our birds. Like the poor we have them always with us. You should hear the musicians of this swamp in February, Philip, on a mellow night. Oh, but they are in earnest! For twenty-one years I've listened by night to the great owls, all the smaller sizes, the foxes, coons, and every resident left in these woods, and by day to the hawks, yellow-hammers, sap-suckers, titmice, crows, and other winter birds. Only just now it's come to me that the distinctive feature of February is not linen bleaching, nor sugar making; it's the love month of our very own birds. Give them hawks and owls for February, Elnora."

With flashing eyes the girl looked at Philip. "How's that?" she said. "Don't you think I will succeed, with such help? You should hear the concert she is talking about! It is simply indescribable when the ground is covered with snow, and the moonlight white."

"It's about the best music we have," said Mrs. Comstock. "I wonder if you couldn't copy that and make a strong, original piece out of it for your violin, Elnora?"

There was one tense breath, then—— "I could try," said Elnora simply.

Philip rushed to the rescue. "We must go to work," he said, and began examining a walnut branch for Luna moth eggs. Elnora joined him while Mrs. Comstock drew her embroidery from her pocket and sat on a log. She said she was tired, they could come for her when they were ready to go. She could hear their voices around her until she called them at supper time. When they came to her she stood waiting on the trail, the sewing in one hand, the violin in the other. Elnora became very white, but followed the trail without a word. Philip, unable to see a woman carry a heavier load than he, reached for the instrument. Mrs. Comstock shook her head. She carried the violin home, took it into her room and closed the door. Elnora turned to Philip.

"If she destroys that, I shall die!" cried the girl.

"She won't!" said Philip. "You misunderstand her. She wouldn't have said what she did about the owls, if she had meant to. She is your mother. No one loves you as she does. Trust her! Myself—I think she's simply great!"

Mrs. Comstock returned with serene face, and all of them helped with the supper. When it was over Philip and Elnora sorted and classified the afternoon's specimens, and made a trip to the woods to paint and light several trees for moths. When they came back Mrs. Comstock sat in the arbour, and they joined her. The moonlight was so intense, print could have been read by it. The damp night air held odours near to earth, making flower and tree perfume strong. A thousand insects were serenading, and in the maple the grosbeak occasionally said a reassuring word to his wife, while she answered that all was well. A whip-poor-will wailed in the swamp and beside the blue-bordered pool a chat complained disconsolately. Mrs. Comstock went into the cabin, but she returned immediately, laying the violin and bow across Elnora's lap. "I wish you would give us a little music," she said.

CHAPTER XVII. WHEREIN MRS. COMSTOCK DANCES IN THE MOONLIGHT, AND ELNORA MAKES A CONFESSION

Billy was swinging in the hammock, at peace with himself and all the world, when he thought he heard something. He sat bolt upright, his eyes staring. Once he opened his lips, then thought again and closed them. The sound persisted. Billy vaulted the fence, and ran down the road with his queer sidewise hop. When he neared the Comstock cabin, he left the warm dust of the highway and stepped softly at slower pace over the rank grasses of the roadside. He had heard aright. The violin was in the grape arbour, singing a perfect jumble of everything, poured out in an exultant tumult. The strings were voicing the joy of a happy girl heart.

Billy climbed the fence enclosing the west woods and crept toward the arbour. He was not a spy and not a sneak. He merely wanted to satisfy his child-heart as to whether Mrs. Comstock was at home, and Elnora at last playing her loved violin with her mother's consent. One peep sufficed. Mrs. Comstock sat in the moonlight, her head leaning against the arbour; on her face was a look of perfect peace and contentment. As he stared at her the bow hesitated a second and Mrs. Comstock spoke:

"That's all very melodious and sweet," she said, "but I do wish you could play Money Musk and some of the tunes I danced as a girl."

Elnora had been carefully avoiding every note that might be reminiscent of her father. At the words she laughed softly and began "Turkey in the Straw." An instant later Mrs. Comstock was dancing in the moon light. Ammon sprang to her side, caught her in his arms, while to Elnora's laughter and the violin's impetus they danced until they dropped panting on the arbour bench.

Billy scarcely knew when he reached the road. His light feet barely touched the soft way, so swiftly he flew. He vaulted the fence and burst into the house.

"Aunt Margaret! Uncle Wesley!" he screamed. "Listen! Listen! She's playing it! Elnora's playing her violin at home! And Aunt Kate is dancing like anything before the arbour! I saw her in the moonlight! I ran down! Oh, Aunt Margaret!"

Billy fled sobbing to Margaret's breast.

"Why Billy!" she chided. "Don't cry, you little dunce! That's what we've all prayed for these many years; but you must be mistaken about Kate. I can't believe it."

Billy lifted his head. "Well, you just have to!" he said. "When I say I saw anything, Uncle

Wesley knows I did. The city man was dancing with her. They danced together and Elnora laughed. But it didn't look funny to me; I was scared."

"Who was it said 'wonders never cease,'" asked Wesley. "You mark my word, once you get Kate Comstock started, you can't stop her. There's a wagon load of penned-up force in her. Dancing in the moonlight! Well, I'll be hanged!"

Billy was at his side instantly. "Whoever does it will have to hang me, too," he cried.

Sinton threw his arm around Billy and drew him closely. "Tell us all about it, son," he said. Billy told. "And when Elnora just stopped a breath, 'Can't you play some of the old things I knew when I was a girl?' said her ma. Then Elnora began to do a thing that made you want to whirl round and round, and quicker 'an scat there was her ma a-whirling. The city man, he ups and grabs her and whirls, too, and back in the woods I was going just like they did. Elnora begins to laugh, and I ran to tell you, cos I knew you'd like to know. Now, all the world is right, ain't it?" ended Billy in supreme satisfaction.

"You just bet it is!" said Wesley.

Billy looked steadily at Margaret. "Is it, Aunt Margaret?"

Margaret Sinton smiled at him bravely.

An hour later when Billy was ready to climb the stairs to his room, he went to Margaret to say good night. He leaned against her an instant, then brought his lips to her ear. "Wish I could get your little girls back for you!" he whispered and dashed toward the stairs.

Down at the Comstock cabin the violin played on until Elnora was so tired she scarcely could lift the bow. Then Philip went home. The women walked to the gate with him, and stood watching him from sight.

"That's what I call one decent young man!" said Mrs. Comstock. "To see him fit in with us, you'd think he'd been brought up in a cabin; but it's likely he's always had the very cream o' the pot."

"Yes, I think so," laughed Elnora, "but it hasn't hurt him. I've never seen anything I could criticise. He's teaching me so much, unconsciously. You know he graduated from Harvard, and has several degrees in law. He's coming in the morning, and we are going to put in a big day on Catocalae."

"Which is——?"

"Those gray moths with wings that fold back like big flies, and they appear as if they had been carved from old wood. Then, when they fly, the lower wings flash out and they are red and black, or gold and black, or pink and black, or dozens of bright, beautiful colours combined with black. No one ever has classified all of them and written their complete history, unless the Bird Woman is doing it now. She wants everything she can get about them."

"I remember," said Mrs. Comstock. "They are mighty pretty things. I've started up slews of them from the vines covering the logs, all my life. I must be cautious and catch them after this, but they seem powerful spry. I might get hold of something rare." She thought intently and added, "And wouldn't know it if I did. It would just be my luck. I've had the rarest thing on earth in reach this many a day and only had the wit to cinch it just as it was going. I'll bet I don't let anything else escape me."

Next morning Philip came early, and he and Elnora went at once to the fields and woods. Mrs. Comstock had come to believe so implicitly in him that she now stayed at home to complete the work before she joined them, and when she did she often sat sewing, leaving them wandering hours at a time. It was noon before she finished, and then she packed a basket of lunch. She found Elnora and Philip near the violet patch, which was still in its prime. They all lunched together in the shade of a wild crab thicket, with flowers spread at their feet, and the gold orioles streaking the air with flashes of light and trailing ecstasy behind them, while the red-wings, as always, asked the most impertinent questions. Then Mrs. Comstock carried the basket back to the cabin, and Philip and Elnora sat on a log, resting a few minutes. They had unexpected luck, and both were eager to continue the search.

"Do you remember your promise about these violets?" asked he. "To-morrow is Edith's birthday, and if I'd put them special delivery on the morning train, she'd get them in the late afternoon. They ought to keep that long. She leaves for the North next day."

"Of course, you may have them," said Elnora. "We will quit long enough before supper to gather a large bunch. They can be packed so they will carry all right. They should be perfectly fresh, especially if we gather them this evening and let them drink all night."

Then they went back to hunt Catocalae. It was a long and a happy search. It led them into new, unexplored nooks of the woods, past a red-poll nest, and where goldfinches prospected for thistledown for the cradles they would line a little later. It led them into real forest, where deep, dark pools lay, where the hermit thrush and the wood robin extracted the essence from all other bird melody, and poured it out in their pure bell-tone notes. It seemed as if every old gray tree-trunk, slab of loose bark, and prostrate log yielded the flashing gray treasures; while of all others they seemed to take alarm most easily, and be most difficult to capture.

Philip came to Elnora at dusk, daintily holding one by the body, its dark wings showing and its long slender legs trying to clasp his fingers and creep from his hold.

"Oh for mercy's sake!" cried Elnora, staring at him.

"I half believe it!" exulted Ammon.

"Did you ever see one?"

"Only in collections, and very seldom there."

Elnora studied the black wings intently. "I surely believe that's Sappho," she marvelled. "The Bird Woman will be overjoyed."

"We must get the cyanide jar quickly," said Philip.

"I wouldn't lose her for anything. Such a chase as she led me!"

Elnora brought the jar and began gathering up paraphernalia.

"When you make a find like that," she said, "it's the right time to quit and feel glorious all the rest of that day. I tell you I'm proud! We will go now. We have barely time to carry out our plans before supper. Won't mother be pleased to see that we have a rare one?"

"I'd like to see any one more pleased than I am!" said Philip Ammon. "I feel as if I'd earned my supper to-night. Let's go."

He took the greater part of the load and stepped aside for Elnora to precede him. She followed the path, broken by the grazing cattle, toward the cabin and nearest the violet patch she stopped, laid down her net, and the things she carried. Philip passed her and hurried straight toward the back gate.

"Aren't you going to——?" began Elnora.

"I'm going to get this moth home in a hurry," he said. "This cyanide has lost its strength, and it's not working well. We need some fresh in the jar."

He had forgotten the violets! Elnora stood looking after him, a curious expression on her face. One second so—then she picked up the net and followed. At the blue-bordered pool she paused and half turned back, then she closed her lips firmly and went on. It was nine o'clock when Philip said good-bye, and started to town. His gay whistle floated to them from the farthest corner of the Limberlost. Elnora complained of being tired, so she went to her room and to bed.

But sleep would not come. Thought was racing in her brain and the longer she lay the wider awake she grew. At last she softly slipped from bed, lighted her lamp and began opening boxes. Then she went to work. Two hours later a beautiful birch bark basket, strongly and artistically made, stood on her table. She set a tiny alarm clock at three, returned to bed and fell asleep instantly with a smile on her lips.

She was on the floor with the first tinkle of the alarm, and hastily dressing, she picked up the basket and a box to fit it, crept down the stairs, and out to the violet patch. She was unafraid as it was growing light, and lining the basket with damp mosses she swiftly began picking, with practised hands, the best of the flowers. She scarcely could tell which were freshest at times, but day soon came creeping over the Limberlost and peeped at her. The robins awoke all their neighbours, and a babel of bird notes filled the air. The dew was dripping, while the first strong rays of light fell on a world in which Elnora worshipped. When the basket was filled to overflowing, she set it in the stout pasteboard box, packed it solid with mosses, tied it firmly and slipped under the cord a note she had written the previous night.

Then she took a short cut across the woods and walked swiftly to Onabasha. It was after six o'clock, but all of the city she wished to avoid were asleep. She had no trouble in finding a small boy out, and she stood at a distance waiting while he rang Dr. Ammon's bell and delivered the package for Philip to a maid, with the note which was to be given him at once.

On the way home through the woods passing some baited trees she collected the captive moths. She entered the kitchen with them so naturally that Mrs. Comstock made no comment. After breakfast Elnora went to her room, cleared away all trace of the night's work and was out in the arbour mounting moths when Philip came down the road. "I am tired sitting," she said to her mother. "I think I will walk a few rods and meet him."

"Who's a trump?" he called from afar.

"Not you!" retorted Elnora. "Confess that you forgot!"

"Completely!" said Philip. "But luckily it would not have been fatal. I wrote Polly last week to send Edith something appropriate to-day, with my card. But that touch from the woods will be very effective. Thank you more than I can say. Aunt Anna and I unpacked it to see the basket, and it was a beauty. She says you are always doing such things."

"Well, I hope not!" laughed Elnora. "If you'd seen me sneaking out before dawn, not to awaken mother and coming in with moths to make her think I'd been to the trees, you'd know it was a most especial occasion."

"Then Philip understood two things: Elnora's mother did not know of the early morning trip to the city, and the girl had come to meet him to tell him so.

"You were a brick to do it!" he whispered as he closed the gate behind them. "I'll never forget you for it. Thank you ever so much."

"I did not do that for you," said Elnora tersely. "I did it mostly to preserve my own self-respect. I saw you were forgetting. If I did it for anything besides that, I did it for her."

"Just look what I've brought!" said Philip, entering the arbour and greeting Mrs. Comstock. "Borrowed it of the Bird Woman. And it isn't hers. A rare edition of Catocalae with coloured plates. I told her the best I could, and she said to try for Sappho here. I suspect the Bird Woman will be out presently. She was all excitement."

Then they bent over the book together and with the mounted moth before them determined her family. The Bird Woman did come later, and carried the moth away, to put into a book and Elnora and Philip were freshly filled with enthusiasm.

So these days were the beginning of the weeks that followed. Six of them flying on Time's wings, each filled to the brim with interest. After June, the moth hunts grew less frequent; the fields and woods were searched for material for Elnora's grade work. The most absorbing occupation they found was in carrying out Mrs. Comstock's suggestion to learn the vital thing for which each month was distinctive, and make that the key to the nature work. They wrote out a list of the months, opposite each the things all of them could suggest which seemed to pertain to that month alone, and then tried to sift until they found something typical. Mrs. Comstock was a great help. Her mother had been Dutch and had brought from Holland numerous quaint sayings and superstitions easily traceable to Pliny's Natural History; and in Mrs. Comstock's early years in Ohio she had heard much Indian talk among her elders, so she knew the signs of each season, and sometimes they helped. Always her practical thought and sterling common sense were useful. When they were afield until exhausted they came back to the cabin for food, to prepare specimens and classify them, and to talk over the day. Sometimes Philip brought books and read while Elnora and her mother worked, and every night Mrs. Comstock asked for the violin. Her perfect hunger for music was sufficient evidence of how she had suffered without it. So the days crept by, golden, filled with useful work and pure pleasure.

The grosbeak had led the family in the maple abroad and a second brood, in a wild grape vine clambering over the well, was almost ready for flight. The dust lay thick on the country roads, the days grew warmer; summer was just poising to slip into fall, and Philip remained, coming each day as if he had belonged there always.

One warm August afternoon Mrs. Comstock looked up from the ruffle on which she was engaged to see a blue-coated messenger enter the gate.

"Is Philip Ammon here?" asked the boy.

"He is," said Mrs. Comstock.

"I have a message for him."

"He is in the woods back of the cabin. I will ring the bell. Do you know if it is important?"

"Urgent," said the boy; "I rode hard."

Mrs. Comstock stepped to the back door and clanged the dinner bell sharply, paused a second, and rang again. In a short time Philip and Elnora ran down the path.

"Are you ill, mother?" cried Elnora.

Mrs. Comstock indicated the boy. "There is an important message for Philip," she said.

He muttered an excuse and tore open the telegram. His colour faded slightly. "I have to take the first train," he said. "My father is ill and I am needed."

He handed the sheet to Elnora. "I have about two hours, as I remember the trains north, but my things are all over Uncle Doc's house, so I must go at once."

"Certainly," said Elnora, giving back the message. "Is there anything I can do to help? Mother, bring Philip a glass of buttermilk to start on. I will gather what you have here."

"Never mind. There is nothing of importance. I don't want to be hampered. I'll send for it if I miss anything I need."

Philip drank the milk, said good-bye to Mrs. Comstock; thanked her for all her kindness, and turned to Elnora.

"Will you walk to the edge of the Limberlost with me?" he asked. Elnora assented. Mrs. Comstock followed to the gate, urged him to come again soon, and repeated her good-bye. Then she went back to the arbour to await Elnora's return. As she watched down the road she smiled softly.

"I had an idea he would speak to me first," she thought, "but this may change things some. He hasn't time. Elnora will come back a happy girl, and she has good reason. He is a model young man. Her lot will be very different from mine."

She picked up her embroidery and began setting dainty precise little stitches, possible only to certain women.

On the road Elnora spoke first. "I do hope it is nothing serious," she said. "Is he usually strong?"

"Quite strong," said Philip. "I am not at all alarmed but I am very much ashamed. I have been well enough for the past month to have gone home and helped him with some critical cases that were keeping him at work in this heat. I was enjoying myself so I wouldn't offer to go, and he would not ask me to come, so long as he could help it. I have allowed him to overtax himself until he is down, and mother and Polly are north at our cottage. He's never been sick before, and it's probable I am to blame that he is now."

"He intended you to stay this long when you came," urged Elnora.

"Yes, but it's hot in Chicago. I should have remembered him. He is always thinking of me. Possibly he has needed me for days. I am ashamed to go to him in splendid condition and admit that I was having such a fine time I forgot to come home."

"You have had a fine time, then?" asked Elnora.

They had reached the fence. Philip vaulted over to take a short cut across the fields. He turned and looked at her.

"The best, the sweetest, and most wholesome time any man ever had in this world," he said. "Elnora, if I talked hours I couldn't make you understand what a girl I think you are. I never in all my life hated anything as I hate leaving you. It seems to me that I have not strength to do it."

"If you have learned anything worth while from me," said Elnora, "that should be it. Just to have strength to go to your duty, and to go quickly."

He caught the hand she held out to him in both his. "Elnora, these days we have had together, have they been sweet to you?"

"Beautiful days!" said Elnora. "Each like a perfect dream to be thought over and over all my life. Oh, they have been the only really happy days I've ever known; these days rich with mother's love, and doing useful work with your help. Good-bye! You must hurry!"

Philip gazed at her. He tried to drop her hand, only clutched it closer. Suddenly he drew her toward him. "Elnora," he whispered, "will you kiss me good-bye?"

Elnora drew back and stared at him with wide eyes. "I'd strike you sooner!" she said. "Have I ever said or done anything in your presence that made you feel free to ask that, Philip Ammon?"

"No!" panted Philip. "No! I think so much of you I wanted to touch your lips once before I left you. You know, Elnora——"

"Don't distress yourself," said Elnora calmly. "I am broad enough to judge you sanely. I know what you mean. It would be no harm to you. It would not matter to me, but here we will think of some one else. Edith Carr would not want your lips to-morrow if she knew they had touched mine to-day. I was wise to say: 'Go quickly!'"

Philip still clung to her. "Will you write me?" he begged.

"No," said Elnora. "There is nothing to say, save good-bye. We can do that now."

He held on. "Promise that you will write me only one letter," he urged. "I want just one message from you to lock in my desk, and keep always. Promise you will write once, Elnora."

She looked into his eyes, and smiled serenely. "If the talking trees tell me this winter, the secret of how a man may grow perfect, I will write you what it is, Philip. In all the time I have known you, I never have liked you so little. Good-bye."

She drew away her hand and swiftly turned back to the road. Philip Ammon, wordless, started toward Onabasha on a run.

Elnora crossed the road, climbed the fence and sought the shelter of their own woods. She chose a diagonal course and followed it until she came to the path leading past the violet patch. She went down this hurriedly. Her hands were clenched at her side, her eyes dry and bright, her cheeks red-flushed, and her breath coming fast. When she reached the patch she turned into it and stood looking around her.

The mosses were dry, the flowers gone, weeds a foot high covered it. She turned away and went on down the path until she was almost in sight of the cabin.

Mrs. Comstock smiled and waited in the arbour until it occurred to her that Elnora was a long time coming, so she went to the gate. The road stretched away toward the Limberlost empty and lonely. Then she knew that Elnora had gone into their own woods and would come in the back way. She could not understand why the girl did not hurry to her with what she would have to tell. She went out and wandered around the garden. Then she stepped into the path and started along the way leading to the woods, past the pool now framed in a thick setting of yellow lilies. Then she saw, and stopped, gasping for breath. Her hands flew up and her lined face grew ghastly. She stared at the sky and then at the prostrate girl figure. Over and over she tried to speak, but only a dry breath came. She turned and fled back to the garden.

In the familiar enclosure she gazed around her like a caged animal seeking escape. The sun beat down on her bare head mercilessly, and mechanically she moved to the shade of a half-grown hickory tree that voluntarily had sprouted beside the milk house. At her feet lay an axe with which she made kindlings for fires. She stooped and picked it up. The memory of that prone figure sobbing in the grass caught her with a renewed spasm. She shut her eyes as if to close it out. That made hearing so acute she felt certain she heard Elnora moaning beside the path. The eyes flew open. They looked straight at a few spindling tomato plants set too near the tree and stunted by its shade. Mrs. Comstock whirled on the hickory and swung the axe. Her hair shook down, her clothing became disarranged, in the heat the perspiration streamed, but stroke fell on stroke until the tree crashed over, grazing a corner of the milk house and smashing the garden fence on the east.

At the sound Elnora sprang to her feet and came running down the garden walk. "Mother!" she cried. "Mother! What in the world are you doing?"

Mrs. Comstock wiped her ghastly face on her apron. "I've laid out to cut that tree for years," she said. "It shades the beets in the morning, and the tomatoes in the afternoon!"

Elnora uttered one wild little cry and fled into her mother's arms. "Oh mother!" she sobbed. "Will you ever forgive me?"

Mrs. Comstock's arms swept together in a tight grip around Elnora.

"There isn't a thing on God's footstool from a to izzard I won't forgive you, my precious girl!" she said. "Tell mother what it is!"

Elnora lifted her wet face. "He told me," she panted, "just as soon as he decently could—that second day he told me. Almost all his life he's been engaged to a girl at home. He never cared anything about me. He was only interested in the moths and growing strong."

Mrs. Comstock's arms tightened. With a shaking hand she stroked the bright hair.

"Tell me, honey," she said. "Is he to blame for a single one of these tears?"

"Not one!" sobbed Elnora. "Oh mother, I won't forgive you if you don't believe that. Not one! He never said, or looked, or did anything all the world might not have known. He likes me very much as a friend. He hated to go dreadfully!"

"Elnora!" the mother's head bent until the white hair mingled with the brown. "Elnora, why didn't you tell me at first?"

Elnora caught her breath in a sharp snatch. "I know I should!" she sobbed. "I will bear any punishment for not, but I didn't feel as if I possibly could. I was afraid."

"Afraid of what?" the shaking hand was on the hair again.

"Afraid you wouldn't let him come!" panted Elnora. "And oh, mother, I wanted him so!"

CHAPTER XVIII. WHEREIN MRS. COMSTOCK EXPERIMENTS WITH REJUVENATION, AND ELNORA TEACHES NATURAL HISTORY

For the following week Mrs. Comstock and Elnora worked so hard there was no time to talk, and they were compelled to sleep from physical exhaustion. Neither of them made any pretence of eating, for they could not swallow without an effort, so they drank milk and worked. Elnora kept on setting bait for Catacolae and Sphinginae, which, unlike the big moths of June, live several months. She took all the dragonflies and butterflies she could, and when she went over the list for the man of India, she found, to her amazement, that with Philip's help she once more had it complete save a pair of Yellow Emperors.

This circumstance was so surprising she had a fleeting thought of writing Philip and asking him to see if he could not secure her a pair. She did tell the Bird Woman, who from every source at her command tried to complete the series with these moths, but could not find any for sale.

"I think the mills of the Gods are grinding this grist," said Elnora, "and we might as well wait patiently until they choose to send a Yellow Emperor."

Mrs. Comstock invented work. When she had nothing more to do, she hoed in the garden although the earth was hard and dry and there were no plants that really needed attention. Then came a notification that Elnora would be compelled to attend a week's session of the Teachers' Institute held at the county seat twenty miles north of Onabasha the following week. That gave them something of which to think and real work to do. Elnora was requested to bring her violin. As she was on the programme of one of the most important sessions for a talk on nature work in grade schools, she was driven to prepare her speech, also to select and practise some music. Her mother turned her attention to clothing.

They went to Onabasha together and purchased a simple and appropriate fall suit and hat, goods for a dainty little coloured frock, and a dress skirt and several fancy waists. Margaret Sinton came down and the sewing began. When everything was finished and packed, Elnora kissed her mother good-bye at the depot, and entered the train. Mrs. Comstock went into the waiting-room and dropped into a seat to rest. Her heart was so sore her whole left side felt tender. She was half starved for the food she had no appetite to take. She had worked in dogged determination until she was exhausted. For a time she simply sat and rested. Then she began to think. She was glad Elnora had gone where she would be compelled to fix her mind on other matters for a few days. She remembered the girl had said she wanted to go.

School would begin the following week. She thought over what Elnora would have to do to accomplish her work successfully. She would be compelled to arise at six o'clock, walk three miles through varying weather, lead the high school orchestra, and then put in the remainder of the day travelling from building to building over the city, teaching a specified length of time every week in each room. She must have her object lessons ready, and she must do a certain amount of practising with the orchestra. Then a cold lunch at noon, and a three-mile walk at night.

"Humph!" said Mrs. Comstock, "to get through that the girl would have to be made of cast-iron. I wonder how I can help her best?"

She thought deeply.

"The less she sees of what she's been having all summer, the sooner she'll feel better about it," she muttered.

She arose, went to the bank and inquired for the cashier.

"I want to know just how I am fixed here," she said.

The cashier laughed. "You haven't been in a hurry," he replied. "We have been ready for you any time these twenty years, but you didn't seem to pay much attention. Your account is rather flourishing. Interest, when it gets to compounding, is quite a money breeder. Come back here to a table and I will show you your balances."

Mrs. Comstock sank into a chair and waited while the cashier read a jumble of figures to her. It meant that her deposits had exceeded her expenses from one to three hundred dollars a year, according to the cattle, sheep, hogs, poultry, butter, and eggs she had sold. The aggregate of these sums had been compounding interest throughout the years. Mrs. Comstock stared at the total with dazed and unbelieving eyes. Through her sick heart rushed the realization, that if she merely had stood before that wicket and asked one question, she would have known that all those bitter years of skimping for Elnora and herself had been unnecessary. She arose and went back to the depot.

"I want to send a message," she said. She picked up the pencil, and with rash extravagance, wrote, "Found money at bank didn't know about. If you want to go to college, come on first train and get ready." She hesitated a second and then she said to herself grimly, "Yes, I'll pay for that, too," and recklessly added, "With love, Mother." Then she sat waiting for the answer. It came in less than an hour. "Will teach this winter. With dearest love, Elnora."

Mrs. Comstock held the message a long time. When she arose she was ravenously hungry, but the pain in her heart was a little easier. She went to a restaurant and ate some food, then to a dressmaker where she ordered four dresses: two very plain every-day ones, a serviceable dark gray cloth suit, and a soft light gray silk with touches of lavender and lace. She made a heavy list of purchases at Brownlee's, and the remainder of the day she did business in her direct and spirited way. At night she was so tired she scarcely could walk home, but she built a fire and cooked and ate a hearty meal.

Later she went out beside the west fence and gathered an armful of tansy which she boiled to a thick green tea. Then she stirred in oatmeal until it was a stiff paste. She spread a sheet over her bed and began tearing strips of old muslin. She bandaged each hand and arm with the mixture and plastered the soggy, evil-smelling stuff in a thick poultice over her face and neck. She was so tired she went to sleep, and when she awoke she was half skinned. She bathed her face and hands, did the work and went back to town, coming home at night to go through the same process.

By the third morning she was a raw even red, the fourth she had faded to a brilliant pink under the soothing influence of a cream recommended. That day came a letter from Elnora saying that she would remain where she was until Saturday morning, and then come to Ellen Brownlee's at Onabasha and stay for the Saturday's session of teachers to arrange their year's work. Sunday was Ellen's last day at home, and she wanted Elnora very much. She had to call together the orchestra and practise them Sunday; and could not come home until after school Monday night. Mrs. Comstock at once answered the letter saying those arrangements suited her.

The following day she was a pale pink, later a delicate porcelain white. Then she went to a hairdresser and had the rope of snowy hair which covered her scalp washed, dressed, and fastened with such pins and combs as were decided to be most becoming. She took samples of her dresses, went to a milliner, and bought a street hat to match her suit, and a gray satin with lavender orchids to wear with the silk dress. Her last investment was a loose coat of soft gray broadcloth with white lining, and touches of lavender on the embroidered collar, and gray gloves to match.

Then she went home, rested and worked by turns until Monday. When school closed on that evening, Elnora, so tired she almost trembled, came down the long walk after a late session of teachers' meeting, to be stopped by a messenger boy.

"There's a lady wants to see you most important. I am to take you to the place," he said.

Elnora groaned. She could not imagine who wanted her, but there was nothing to do but find out; tired and anxious to see her mother as she was.

"This is the place," said the boy, and went his way whistling. Elnora was three blocks from the high school building on the same street. She was before a quaint old house, fresh with paint and covered with vines. There was a long wide lot, grass-covered, closely set with trees, and a barn and chicken park at the back that seemed to be occupied. Elnora stepped on the veranda which was furnished with straw rugs, bent-hickory chairs, hanging baskets, and a table with a work-box and magazines, and knocked at the screen door.

Inside she could see polished floors, walls freshly papered in low-toned harmonious colours, straw rugs and madras curtains. It seemed to be a restful, homelike place to which she had come. A second later down an open stairway came a tall, dark-eyed woman with cheeks faintly pink and a crown of fluffy snow-white hair. She wore a lavender gingham dress with white collar and cuffs, and she called as she advanced: "That screen isn't latched! Open it and come see your brand-new mother, my girl."

Elnora stepped inside the door. "Mother!" she cried. "You my mother! I don't believe it!"

"Well, you better!" said Mrs. Comstock, "because it's true! You said you wished I were like the other girls' mothers, and I've shot as close the mark as I could without any practice. I thought that walk would be too much for you this winter, so I just rented this house and moved in, to be near you, and help more in case I'm needed. I've only lived here a day, but I like it so well I've a mortal big notion to buy the place."

"But mother!" protested Elnora, clinging to her wonderingly. "You are perfectly beautiful, and this house is a little paradise, but how will we ever pay for it? We can't afford it!"

"Humph! Have you forgotten I telegraphed you I'd found some money I didn't know about? All I've done is paid for, and plenty more to settle for all I propose to do."

Mrs. Comstock glanced around with satisfaction.

"I may get homesick as a pup before spring," she said, "but if I do I can go back. If I don't, I'll sell some timber and put a few oil wells where they don't show much. I can have land enough cleared for a few fields and put a tenant on our farm, and we will buy this and settle here. It's for sale."

"You don't look it, but you've surely gone mad!"

"Just the reverse, my girl," said Mrs. Comstock, "I've gone sane. If you are going to undertake this work, you must be convenient to it. And your mother should be where she can see that you are properly dressed, fed, and cared for. This is our—let me think—reception-room. How do you like it? This door leads to your workroom and study. I didn't do much there because I wasn't sure of my way. But I knew you would want a rug, curtains, table, shelves for books, and a case for your specimens, so I had a carpenter shelve and enclose that end of it. Looks pretty neat to me. The dining-room and kitchen are back, one of the cows in the barn, and some chickens in the coop. I understand that none of the other girls' mothers milk a cow, so a neighbour boy will tend to ours for a third of the milk. There are three bedrooms, and a bath upstairs. Go take one, put on some fresh clothes, and come to supper. You can find your room because your things are in it."

Elnora kissed her mother over and over, and hurried upstairs. She identified her room by the dressing-case. There were a pretty rug, and curtains, white iron bed, plain and rocking chairs to match her case, a shirtwaist chest, and the big closet was filled with her old clothing and several new dresses. She found the bathroom, bathed, dressed in fresh linen and went down to a supper that was an evidence of Mrs. Comstock's highest art in cooking. Elnora was so hungry she ate her first real meal in two weeks. But the bites went down slowly because she forgot about them in watching her mother.

"How on earth did you do it?" she asked at last. "I always thought you were naturally brown as a nut."

"Oh, that was tan and sunburn!" explained Mrs. Comstock. "I always knew I was white underneath it. I hated to shade my face because I hadn't anything but a sunbonnet, and I couldn't stand for it to touch my ears, so I went bareheaded and took all the colour I accumulated. But when I began to think of moving you in to your work, I saw I must put up an appearance that wouldn't disgrace you, so I thought I'd best remove the crust. It took some time, and I hope I may die before I ever endure the feel and the smell of the stuff I used again, but it skinned me nicely. What you now see is my own with a little dust of rice powder, for protection. I'm sort of tender yet."

"And your lovely, lovely hair?" breathed Elnora.

"Hairdresser did that!" said Mrs. Comstock. "It cost like smoke. But I watched her, and with a little help from you I can wash it alone next time, though it will be hard work. I let her monkey with it until she said she had found 'my style.' Then I tore it down and had her show me how to build it up again three times. I thought my arms would drop. When I paid the bill for her work, the time I'd taken, the pins, and combs she'd used, I nearly had heart failure, but I didn't turn a hair before her. I just smiled at her sweetly and said, 'How reasonable you are!' Come to think of it, she was! She might have charged me ten dollars for what she did quite as well as nine seventy-five. I couldn't have helped myself. I had made no bargain to begin on."

Then Elnora leaned back in her chair and shouted, in a gust of hearty laughter, so a little of the ache ceased in her breast. There was no time to think, the remainder of that evening, she was so tired she had to sleep, while her mother did not awaken her until she barely had time to dress, breakfast and reach school. There was nothing in the new life to remind her of the old. It seemed as if there never came a minute for retrospection, but her mother appeared on the scene with more work, or some entertaining thing to do.

Mrs. Comstock invited Elnora's friends to visit her, and proved herself a bright and interesting hostess. She digested a subject before she spoke; and when she advanced a view, her point was sure to be original and tersely expressed. Before three months people waited to hear what she had to say. She kept her appearance so in mind that she made a handsome and a distinguished figure.

Elnora never mentioned Philip Ammon, neither did Mrs. Comstock. Early in December came a note and a big box from him. It contained several books on nature subjects which would be of much help in school work, a number of conveniences Elnora could not afford, and a pair of glass-covered plaster casts, for each large moth she had. In these the upper and underwings of male and female showed. He explained that she would break her specimens easily, carrying them around in boxes. He had seen these and thought they would be of use. Elnora was delighted with them, and at once began the tedious process of softening the mounted moths and fitting them to the casts moulded to receive them. Her time was so taken in school, she progressed slowly, so her mother undertook this work. After trying one or two very common ones she learned to handle the most delicate with ease. She took keen pride in relaxing the tense moths, fitting them to the cases, polishing the glass covers to the last degree and sealing them. The results were beautiful to behold.

Soon after Elnora wrote to Philip:

DEAR FRIEND:

I am writing to thank you for the books, and the box of conveniences sent me for my work. I can use everything with fine results. Hope I am giving good satisfaction in my position. You will be interested to learn that when the summer's work was classified and pinned, I again had my complete collection for the man of India, save a Yellow Emperor. I have tried everywhere I know, so has the Bird Woman. We cannot find a pair for sale. Fate is against me, at least this season. I shall have to wait until next year and try again.

Thank you very much for helping me with my collection and for the books and cases.

Sincerely yours,

ELNORA COMSTOCK.

Philip was disappointed over that note and instead of keeping it he tore it into bits and dropped them into the waste basket.

That was precisely what Elnora had intended he should do. Christmas brought beautiful cards of greeting to Mrs. Comstock and Elnora, Easter others, and the year ran rapidly toward spring. Elnora's position had been intensely absorbing, while she had worked with all her power. She had made a wonderful success and won new friends. Mrs. Comstock had helped in every way she could, so she was very popular also.

Throughout the winter they had enjoyed the city thoroughly, and the change of life it afforded, but signs of spring did wonderful things to the hearts of the country-bred women. A restlessness began on bright February days, calmed during March storms and attacked full force in April. When neither could bear it any longer they were forced to discuss the matter and admit they were growing ill with pure homesickness. They decided to keep the city house during the summer, but to return to the farm to live as soon as school closed.

So Mrs. Comstock would prepare breakfast and lunch and then slip away to the farm to make up beds in her ploughed garden, plant seeds, trim and tend her flowers, and prepare the cabin for occupancy. Then she would go home and make the evening as cheerful as possible for Elnora; in these days she lived only for the girl.

Both of them were glad when the last of May came and the schools closed. They packed the books and clothing they wished to take into a wagon and walked across the fields to the old cabin. As they approached it, Mrs. Comstock said to Elnora: "You are sure you won't be lonely here?"

Elnora knew what she really meant.

"Quite sure," she said. "For a time last fall I was glad to be away, but that all wore out with the winter. Spring made me homesick as I could be. I can scarcely wait until we get back again."

So they began that summer as they had begun all others—with work. But both of them took a new joy in everything, and the violin sang by the hour in the twilight.

CHAPTER XIX. WHEREIN PHILIP AMMON GIVES A BALL IN HONOUR OF EDITH CARR, AND HART HENDERSON APPEARS ON THE SCENE

Edith Carr stood in a vine-enclosed side veranda of the Lake Shore Club House waiting while Philip Ammon gave some important orders. In a few days she would sail for Paris to select a wonderful trousseau she had planned for her marriage in October. To-night Philip was giving a club dance in her honour. He had spent days in devising new and exquisite effects in decorations, entertainment, and supper. Weeks before the favoured guests had been notified. Days before they had received the invitations asking them to participate in this entertainment by Philip Ammon in honour of Miss Carr. They spoke of it as "Phil's dance for Edith!"

She could hear the rumble of carriages and the panting of automobiles as in a steady stream they rolled to the front entrance. She could catch glimpses of floating draperies of gauze and lace, the flash of jewels, and the passing of exquisite colour. Every one was newly arrayed in her honour in the loveliest clothing, and the most expensive jewels they could command. As she thought of it she lifted her head a trifle higher and her eyes flashed proudly.

She was robed in a French creation suggested and designed by Philip. He had said to her: "I know a competent judge who says the distinctive feature of June is her exquisite big night moths. I want you to be the very essence of June that night, as you will be the embodiment of love. Be a moth. The most beautiful of them is either the pale-green Luna or the Yellow Imperialis. Be my moon lady, or my gold Empress."

He took her to the museum and showed her the moths. She instantly decided on the yellow. Because she knew the shades would make her more startlingly beautiful than any other colour. To him she said: "A moon lady seems so far away and cold. I would be of earth and very near on that night. I choose the Empress."

So she matched the colours exactly, wrote out the idea and forwarded the order to Paquin. To-night when Philip Ammon came for her, he stood speechless a minute and then silently kissed her hands.

For she stood tall, lithe, of grace inborn, her dark waving hair high piled and crossed by gold bands studded with amethyst and at one side an enamelled lavender orchid rimmed with diamonds, which flashed and sparkled. The soft yellow robe of lightest weight velvet fitted her form perfectly, while from each shoulder fell a great velvet wing lined with lavender, and flecked with embroidery of that colour in imitation of the moth. Around her throat was a wonderful necklace and on her arms were bracelets of gold set with amethyst and rimmed with diamonds. Philip had said that her gloves, fan, and slippers must be lavender, because the feet of the moth were that colour. These accessories had been made to order and embroidered with gold. It had been arranged that her mother, Philip's, and a few best friends should receive his guests. She was to appear when she led the grand march with Philip Ammon. Miss Carr was positive that she would be the most beautiful, and most exquisitely gowned woman present. In her heart she thought of herself as "Imperialis Regalis," as the Yellow Empress. In a few moments she would stun her world into feeling it as Philip Ammon had done, for she had taken pains that the history of her costume should be whispered to a few who would give it circulation. She lifted her head proudly and waited, for was not Philip planning something unusual and unsurpassed in her honour? Then she smiled.

But of all the fragmentary thoughts crossing her brain the one that never came was that of Philip Ammon as the Emperor. Philip the king of her heart; at least her equal in all things. She was the Empress—yes, Philip was but a mere man, to devise entertainments, to provide luxuries, to humour whims, to kiss hands!

"Ah, my luck!" cried a voice behind her.

Edith Carr turned and smiled.

"I thought you were on the ocean," she said.

"I only reached the dock," replied the man, "when I had a letter that recalled me by the first limited."

"Oh! Important business?"

"The only business of any importance in all the world to me. I'm triumphant that I came. Edith, you are the most superb woman in every respect that I have ever seen. One glimpse is worth the whole journey."

"You like my dress?" She moved toward him and turned, lifting her arms. "Do you know what it is intended to represent?"

"Yes, Polly Ammon told me. I knew when I heard about it how you would look, so I started a sleuth hunt, to get the first peep. Edith, I can become intoxicated merely with looking at you to-night."

He half-closed his eyes and smilingly stared straight at her. He was taller than she, a lean man, with close-cropped light hair, steel-gray eyes, a square chin and "man of the world" written all over him.

Edith Carr flushed. "I thought you realized when you went away that you were to stop that, Hart Henderson," she cried.

"I did, but this letter of which I tell you called me back to start it all over again."

She came a step closer. "Who wrote that letter, and what did it contain concerning me?" she demanded.

"One of your most intimate chums wrote it. It contained the hazard that possibly I had given up too soon. It said that in a fit of petulance you had broken your engagement with Ammon twice this winter, and he had come back because he knew you did not really mean it. I thought deeply there on the dock when I read that, and my boat sailed without me. I argued that anything so weak as an engagement twice broken and patched up again was a mighty frail affair indeed, and likely to smash completely at any time, so I came on the run. I said once I would not see you marry any other man. Because I could not bear it, I planned to go into exile of any sort to escape that. I have changed my mind. I have come back to haunt you until the ceremony is over. Then I go, not before. I was insane!"

The girl laughed merrily. "Not half so insane as you are now, Hart!" she cried gaily. "You know that Philip Ammon has been devoted to me all my life. Now I'll tell you something else, because this looks serious for you. I love him with all my heart. Not while he lives shall he know it, and I will laugh at him if you tell him, but the fact remains: I intend to marry him, but no doubt I shall tease him constantly. It's good for a man to be uncertain. If you could see Philip's face at the quarterly return of his ring, you would understand the fun of it. You had better have taken your boat."

"Possibly," said Henderson calmly. "But you are the only woman in the world for me, and while you are free, as I now see my light, I remain near you. You know the old adage."

"But I'm not 'free!'" cried Edith Carr. "I'm telling you I am not. This night is my public acknowledgment that Phil and I are promised, as our world has surmised since we were children. That promise is an actual fact, because of what I just have told you. My little fits of temper don't count with Phil. He's been reared on them. In fact, I often invent one in a perfect calm to see him perform. He is the most amusing spectacle. But, please, please, do understand that I love him, and always shall, and that we shall be married."

"Just the same, I'll wait and see it an accomplished fact," said Henderson. "And Edith, because I love you, with the sort of love it is worth a woman's while to inspire, I want your happiness before my own. So I am going to say this to you, for I never dreamed you were capable of the feeling you have displayed for Phil. If you do love him, and have loved him always, a disappointment would cut you deeper than you know. Go careful from now on! Don't strain that patched engagement of yours any further. I've known Philip all my life. I've known him through boyhood, in college, and since. All men respect him. Where the rest of us confess our sins, he stands clean. You can go to his arms with nothing to forgive. Mark this thing! I have heard him say, 'Edith is my slogan,' and I have seen him march home strong in the strength of his love for you, in the face of temptations before which every other man of us fell. Before the gods! that ought to be worth something to a girl, if she really is the delicate, sensitive, refined thing she would have man believe. It would take a woman with the organism of an ostrich to endure some of the men here to-night, if she knew them as I do; but Phil is sound to the core. So this is what I would say to you: first, your instincts are right in loving him, why not let him feel it in the ways a woman knows? Second, don't break your engagement again. As men know the man, any of us would be afraid to the soul. He loves you, yes! He is long-suffering for you, yes! But men know he has a limit. When the limit is reached, he will stand fast, and all the powers can't move him. You don't seem to think it, but you can go too far!"

"Is that all?" laughed Edith Carr sarcastically.

"No, there is one thing more," said Henderson. "Here or here-after, now and so long as I breathe, I am your slave. You can do anything you choose and know that I will kneel before you again. So carry this in the depths of your heart; now or at any time, in any place or condition, merely lift your hand, and I will come. Anything you want of me, that thing will I do. I am going to wait; if you need me, it is not necessary to speak; only give me the faintest sign. All your life I will be somewhere near you waiting for it."

"Idjit! You rave!" laughed Edith Carr. "How you would frighten me! What a bugbear you would raise! Be sensible and go find what keeps Phil. I was waiting patiently, but my patience is going. I won't look nearly so well as I do now when it is gone."

At that instant Philip Ammon entered. He was in full evening dress and exceptionally handsome. "Everything is ready," he said; "they are waiting for us to lead the march. It is formed."

Edith Carr smiled entrancingly. "Do you think I am ready?"

Philip looked what he thought, and offered his arm. Edith Carr nodded carelessly to Hart Henderson, and moved away. Attendants parted the curtains and the Yellow Empress bowing right and left, swept the length of the ballroom and took her place at the head of the formed procession. The large open dancing pavilion was draped with yellow silk caught up with lilac flowers. Every corner was filled with bloom of those colours. The music was played by harpers dressed in yellow and violet, so the ball opened.

The midnight supper was served with the same colours and the last half of the programme was being danced. Never had girl been more complimented and petted in the same length of time than Edith Carr. Every minute she seemed to grow more worthy of praise. A partners' dance was called and the floor was filled with couples waiting for the music. Philip stood whispering delightful things to Edith facing him. From out of the night, in at the wide front entrance to the pavilion, there swept in slow wavering flight a large yellow moth and fluttered toward the centre cluster of glaring electric lights. Philip Ammon and Edith Carr saw it at the same instant.

"Why, isn't that——?" she began excitedly.

"It's a Yellow Emperor! This is fate!" cried Philip. "The last one Elnora needs for her collection. I must have it! Excuse me!"

He ran toward the light. "Hats! Handkerchiefs! Fans! Anything!" he panted. "Every one hold up something and stop that! It's a moth; I've got to catch it!"

"It's yellow! He wants it for Edith!" ran in a murmur around the hall. The girl's face flushed, while she bit her lips in vexation.

Instantly every one began holding up something to keep the moth from flying back into the night. One fan held straight before it served, and the moth gently settled on it.

"Hold steady!" cried Philip. "Don't move for your life!" He rushed toward the moth, made a quick sweep and held it up between his fingers. "All right!" he called. "Thanks, every one! Excuse me a minute."

He ran to the office.

"An ounce of gasolene, quick!" he ordered. "A cigar box, a cork, and the glue bottle."

He poured some glue into the bottom of the box, set the cork in it firmly, dashed the gasolene over the moth repeatedly, pinned it to the cork, poured the remainder of the liquid over it, closed the box, and fastened it. Then he laid a bill on the counter.

"Pack that box with cork around it, in one twice its size, tie securely and express to this address at once."

He scribbled on a sheet of paper and shoved it over.

"On your honour, will you do that faithfully as I say?" he asked the clerk.

"Certainly," was the reply.

"Then keep the change," called Philip as he ran back to the pavilion.

Edith Carr stood where he left her, thinking rapidly. She heard the murmur that arose when Philip started to capture the exquisite golden creature she was impersonating. She saw the flash of surprise that went over unrestrained faces when he ran from the room, without even showing it to her. "The last one Elnora needs," rang in her ears. He had told her that he helped collect moths the previous summer, but she had understood that the Bird Woman, with whose work Miss Carr was familiar, wanted them to put in a book.

He had spoken of a country girl he had met who played the violin wonderfully, and at times, he had shown a disposition to exalt her as a standard of womanhood. Miss Carr had ignored what he said, and talked of something else. But that girl's name had been Elnora. It was she who was collecting moths! No doubt she was the competent judge who was responsible for the yellow costume Philip had devised. Had Edith Carr been in her room, she would have torn off the dress at the thought.

Being in a circle of her best friends, which to her meant her keenest rivals and harshest critics, she grew rigid with anger. Her breath hurt her paining chest. No one thought to speak to the musicians, and seeing the floor filled, they began the waltz. Only part of the guests could see what had happened, and at once the others formed and commenced to dance. Gay couples came whirling past her.

Edith Carr grew very white as she stood alone. Her lips turned pale, while her dark eyes flamed with anger. She stood perfectly still where Philip had left her, and the approaching men guided their partners around her, while the girls, looking back, could be seen making exclamations of surprise.

The idolized only daughter of the Carr family hoped that she would drop dead from mortification, but nothing happened. She was too perverse to step aside and say that she was waiting for Philip. Then came Tom Levering dancing with Polly Ammon. Being in the scales with the Ammon family, Tom scented trouble from afar, so he whispered to Polly: "Edith is standing in the middle of the floor, and she's awful mad about something."

"That won't hurt her," laughed Polly. "It's an old pose of hers. She knows she looks superb when she is angry, so she keeps herself furious half the time on purpose."

"She looks like the mischief!" answered Tom. "Hadn't we better steer over and wait with her? She's the ugliest sight I ever saw!"

"Why, Tom!" cried Polly. "Stop, quickly!"

They hurried to Edith.

"Come dear," said Polly. "We are going to wait with you until Phil returns. Let's go after a drink. I am so thirsty!"

"Yes, do!" begged Tom, offering his arm. "Let's get out of here until Phil comes."

There was the opportunity to laugh and walk away, but Edith Carr would not accept it.

"My betrothed left me here," she said. "Here I shall remain until he returns for me, and then—he will be my betrothed no longer!"

Polly grasped Edith's arm.

"Oh, Edith!" she implored. "Don't make a scene here, and to-night. Edith, this has been the loveliest dance ever given at the club house. Every one is saying so. Edith! Darling, do come! Phil will be back in a second. He can explain! It's only a breath since I saw him go out. I thought he had returned."

As Polly panted these disjointed ejaculations, Tom Levering began to grow angry on her account.

"He has been gone just long enough to show every one of his guests that he will leave me standing alone, like a neglected fool, for any passing whim of his. Explain! His explanation would sound well! Do you know for whom he caught that moth? It is being sent to a girl he flirted with all last summer. It has just occurred to me that the dress I am wearing is her suggestion. Let him try to explain!"

Speech unloosed the fountain. She stripped off her gloves to free her hands. At that instant the dancers parted to admit Philip. Instinctively they stopped as they approached and with wondering faces walled in Edith and Philip, Polly and Tom.

"Mighty good of you to wait!" cried Philip, his face showing his delight over his success in capturing the Yellow Emperor. "I thought when I heard the music you were going on."

"How did you think I was going on?" demanded Edith Carr in frigid tones.

"I thought you would step aside and wait a few seconds for me, or dance with Henderson. It was most important to have that moth. It completes a valuable collection for a person who needs the money. Come!"

He held out his arms.

"I 'step aside' for no one!" stormed Edith Carr. "I await no other girl's pleasure! You may 'complete the collection' with that!"

She drew her engagement ring from her finger and reached to place it on one of Philip's outstretched hands. He saw and drew back. Instantly Edith dropped the ring. As it fell, almost instinctively Philip caught it in air. With amazed face he looked closely at Edith Carr. Her distorted features were scarcely recognizable. He held the ring toward her.

"Edith, for the love of mercy, wait until I can explain," he begged. "Put on your ring and let me tell you how it is."

"I know perfectly 'how it is,'" she answered. "I never shall wear that ring again."

"You won't even hear what I have to say? You won't take back your ring?" he cried.

"Never! Your conduct is infamous!"

"Come to think of it," said Philip deliberately, "it is 'infamous' to cut a girl, who has danced all her life, out of a few measures of a waltz. As for asking forgiveness for so black a sin as picking up a moth, and starting it to a friend who lives by collecting them, I don't see how I could! I have not been gone three minutes by the clock, Edith. Put on your ring and finish the dance like a dear girl."

He thrust the glittering ruby into her fingers and again held out his arms. She dropped the ring, and it rolled some distance from them. Hart Henderson followed its shining course, and caught it before it was lost.

"You really mean it?" demanded Philip in a voice as cold as hers ever had been.

"You know I mean it!" cried Edith Carr.

"I accept your decision in the presence of these witnesses," said Philip Ammon. "Where is my father?" The elder Ammon with a distressed face hurried to him. "Father, take my place," said Philip. "Excuse me to my guests. Ask all my friends to forgive me. I am going away for awhile."

He turned and walked from the pavilion. As he went Hart Henderson rushed to Edith Carr and forced the ring into her fingers. "Edith, quick. Come, quick!" he implored. "There's just time to catch him. If you let him go that way, he never will return in this world. Remember what I told you."

"Great prophet! aren't you, Hart?" she sneered. "Who wants him to return? If that ring is thrust upon me again I shall fling it into the lake. Signal the musicians to begin, and dance with me."

Henderson put the ring into his pocket, and began the dance. He could feel the muscular spasms of the girl in his arms, her face was cold and hard, but her breath burned with the scorch of fever. She finished the dance and all others, taking Phil's numbers with Henderson, who had arrived too late to arrange a programme. She left with the others, merely inclining her head as she passed Ammon's father taking his place, and entered the big touring car for which Henderson had telephoned. She sank limply into a seat and moaned softly.

"Shall I drive awhile in the night air?" asked Henderson.

She nodded. He instructed the chauffeur.

She raised her head in a few seconds. "Hart, I'm going to pieces," she said. "Won't you put your arm around me a little while?"

Henderson gathered her into his arms and her head fell on his shoulder. "Closer!" she cried.

Henderson held her until his arms were numb, but he did not know it. The tricks of fate are cruel enough, but there scarcely could have been a worse one than that: To care for a woman as he loved Edith Carr and have her given into his arms because she was so numb with misery over her trouble with another man that she did not know or care what she did. Dawn was streaking the east when he spoke to her.

"Edith, it is growing light."

"Take me home," she said.

Henderson helped her up the steps and rang the bell.

"Miss Carr is ill," he said to the footman. "Arouse her maid instantly, and have her prepare something hot as quickly as possible."

"Edith," he cried, "just a word. I have been thinking. It isn't too late yet. Take your ring and put it on. I will go find Phil at once and tell him you have, that you are expecting him, and he will come."

"Think what he said!" she cried. "He accepted my decision as final, 'in the presence of witnesses,' as if it were court. He can return it to me, if I ever wear it again."

"You think that now, but in a few days you will find that you feel very differently. Living a life of heartache is no joke, and no job for a woman. Put on your ring and send me to tell him to come."

"No."

"Edith, there was not a soul who saw that, but sympathized with Phil. It was ridiculous for you to get so angry over a thing which was never intended for the slightest offence, and by no logical reasoning could have been so considered."

"Do you think that?" she demanded.

"I do!" said Henderson. "If you had laughed and stepped aside an instant, or laughed and stayed where you were, Phil would have been back; or, if he needed punishment in your eyes, to have found me having one of his dances would have been enough. I was waiting. You could have called me with one look. But to publicly do and say what you did, my lady—I know Phil, and I know you went too far. Put on that ring, and send him word you are sorry, before it is too late."

"I will not! He shall come to me."

"Then God help you!" said Henderson, "for you are plunging into misery whose depth you do not dream. Edith, I beg of you——"

She swayed where she stood. Her maid opened the door and caught her. Henderson went down the hall and out to his car.

CHAPTER XX. WHEREIN THE ELDER AMMON OFFERS ADVICE, AND EDITH CARR EXPERIENCES REGRETS

Philip Ammon walked from among his friends a humiliated and a wounded man. Never before had Edith Carr appeared quite so beautiful. All evening she had treated him with unusual consideration. Never had he loved her so deeply. Then in a few seconds everything was different. Seeing the change in her face, and hearing her meaningless accusations, killed something in his heart. Warmth went out and a cold weight took its place. But even after that, he had offered the ring to her again, and asked her before others to reconsider. The answer had been further insult.

He walked, paying no heed to where he went. He had traversed many miles when he became aware that his feet had chosen familiar streets. He was passing his home. Dawn was near, but the first floor was lighted. He staggered up the steps and was instantly admitted. The library door stood open, while his father sat with a book pretending to read. At Philip's entrance the father scarcely glanced up.

"Come on!" he called. "I have just told Banks to bring me a cup of coffee before I turn in. Have one with me!"

Philip sat beside the table and leaned his head on his hands, but he drank a cup of steaming coffee and felt better.

"Father," he said, "father, may I talk with you a little while?"

"Of course," answered Mr. Ammon. "I am not at all tired. I think I must have been waiting in the hope that you would come. I want no one's version of this but yours. Tell me the straight of the thing, Phil."

Philip told all he knew, while his father sat in deep thought.

"On my life I can't see any occasion for such a display of temper, Phil. It passed all bounds of reason and breeding. Can't you think of anything more?"

"I cannot!"

"Polly says every one expected you to carry the moth you caught to Edith. Why didn't you?"

"She screams if a thing of that kind comes near her. She never has taken the slightest interest in them. I was in a big hurry. I didn't want to miss one minute of my dance with her. The moth was not so uncommon, but by a combination of bad luck it had become the rarest in America for a friend of mine, who is making a collection to pay college expenses. For an instant last June the series was completed; when a woman's uncontrolled temper ruined this specimen and the search for it began over. A few days later a pair was secured, and again the money was in sight for several hours. Then an accident wrecked one-fourth of the collection. I helped replace those last June, all but this Yellow Emperor which we could not secure, and we haven't been able to find, buy or trade for one since. So my friend was compelled to teach this past winter instead of going to college. When that moth came flying in there to-night, it seemed to me like fate. All I thought of was, that to secure it would complete the collection and secure the money. So I caught the Emperor and started it to Elnora. I declare to you that I was not out of the pavilion over three minutes at a liberal estimate. If I only had thought to speak to the orchestra! I was sure I would be back before enough couples gathered and formed for the dance."

The eyes of the father were very bright.

"The friend for whom you wanted the moth is a girl?" he asked indifferently, as he ran the book leaves through his fingers.

"The girl of whom I wrote you last summer, and told you about in the fall. I helped her all the time I was away."

"Did Edith know of her?"

"I tried many times to tell her, to interest her, but she was so indifferent that it was insulting. She would not hear me."

"We are neither one in any condition to sleep. Why don't you begin at the first and tell me about this girl? To think of other matters for a time may clear our vision for a sane solution of this. Who is she, just what is she doing, and what is she like? You know I was reared among those Limberlost people, I can understand readily. What is her name and where does she live?"

Philip gave a man's version of the previous summer, while his father played with the book industriously.

"You are very sure as to her refinement and education?"

"In almost two months' daily association, could a man be mistaken? She can far and away surpass Polly, Edith, or any girl of our set on any common, high school, or supplementary branch, and you know high schools have French, German, and physics now. Besides, she is a graduate of two other institutions. All her life she has been in the school of Hard Knocks. She has the biggest, tenderest, most human heart I ever knew in a girl. She has known life in its most cruel phases, and instead of hardening her, it has set her trying to save other people suffering. Then this nature position of which I told you; she graduated in the School of the Woods, before she secured that. The Bird Woman, whose work you know, helped her there. Elnora knows more interesting things in a minute than any other girl I ever met knew in an hour, provided you are a person who cares to understand plant and animal life."

The book leaves slid rapidly through his fingers as the father drawled: "What sort of looking girl is she?"

"Tall as Edith, a little heavier, pink, even complexion, wide open blue-gray eyes with heavy black brows, and lashes so long they touch her cheeks. She has a rope of waving, shining hair that makes a real crown on her head, and it appears almost red in the light. She is as handsome as any fair woman I ever saw, but she doesn't know it. Every time any one pays her a compliment, her mother, who is a caution, discovers that, for some reason, the girl is a fright, so she has no appreciation of her looks."

"And you were in daily association two months with a girl like that! How about it, Phil?"

"If you mean, did I trifle with her, no!" cried Philip hotly. "I told her the second time I met her all about Edith. Almost every day I wrote to Edith in her presence. Elnora gathered violets and made a fancy basket to put them in for Edith's birthday. I started to err in too open admiration for Elnora, but her mother brought me up with a whirl I never forgot. Fifty times a day in the swamps and forests Elnora made a perfect picture, but I neither looked nor said anything. I never met any girl so downright noble in bearing and actions. I never hated anything as I hated leaving her, for we were dear friends, like two wholly congenial men. Her mother was almost always with us. She knew how much I admired Elnora, but so long as I concealed it from the girl, the mother did not care."

"Yet you left such a girl and came back whole-hearted to Edith Carr!"

"Surely! You know how it has been with me about Edith all my life."

"Yet the girl you picture is far her superior to an unprejudiced person, when thinking what a man would require in a wife to be happy."

"I never have thought what I would 'require' to be happy! I only thought whether I could make Edith happy. I have been an idiot! What I've borne you'll never know! To-night is only one of many outbursts like that, in varying and lesser degrees."

"Phil, I love you, when you say you have thought only of Edith! I happen to know that it is true. You are my only son, and I have had a right to watch you closely. I believe you utterly. Any one who cares for you as I do, and has had my years of experience in this world over yours, knows that in some ways, to-night would be a blessed release, if you could take it; but you cannot! Go to bed now, and rest. To-morrow, go back to her and fix it up."

"You heard what I said when I left her! I said it because something in my heart died a minute before that, and I realized that it was my love for Edith Carr. Never again will I voluntarily face such a scene. If she can act like that at a ball, before hundreds, over a thing of which I thought nothing at all, she would go into actual physical fits and spasms, over some of the household crises I've seen the mater meet with a smile. Sir, it is truth that I have thought only of her up to the present. Now, I will admit I am thinking about myself. Father, did you see her? Life is too short, and it can be too sweet, to throw it away in a battle with an unrestrained woman. I am no fighter—where a girl is concerned, anyway. I respect and love her or I do nothing. Never again is either respect or love possible between me and Edith Carr. Whenever I think of her in the future,

I will see her as she was to-night. But I can't face the crowd just yet. Could you spare me a few days?"

"It is only ten days until you were to go north for the summer, go now."

"I don't want to go north. I don't want to meet people I know. There, the story would precede me. I do not need pitying glances or rough condolences. I wonder if I could not hide at Uncle Ed's in Wisconsin for awhile?"

The book closed suddenly. The father leaned across the table and looked into the son's eyes.

"Phil, are you sure of what you just have said?"

"Perfectly sure!"

"Do you think you are in any condition to decide to-night?"

"Death cannot return to life, father. My love for Edith Carr is dead. I hope never to see her again."

"If I thought you could be certain so soon! But, come to think of it, you are very like me in many ways. I am with you in this. Public scenes and disgraces I would not endure. It would be over with me, were I in your position, that I know."

"It is done for all time," said Philip Ammon. "Let us not speak of it further."

"Then, Phil," the father leaned closer and looked at the son tenderly, "Phil, why don't you go to the Limberlost?"

"Father!"

"Why not? No one can comfort a hurt heart like a tender woman; and, Phil, have you ever stopped to think that you may have a duty in the Limberlost, if you are free? I don't know! I only suggest it. But, for a country schoolgirl, unaccustomed to men, two months with a man like you might well awaken feelings of which you do not think. Because you were safe-guarded is no sign the girl was. She might care to see you. You can soon tell. With you, she comes next to Edith, and you have made it clear to me that you appreciate her in many ways above. So I repeat it, why not go to the Limberlost?"

A long time Philip Ammon sat in deep thought. At last he raised his head.

"Well, why not!" he said. "Years could make me no surer than I am now, and life is short. Please ask Banks to get me some coffee and toast, and I will bathe and dress so I can take the early train."

"Go to your bath. I will attend to your packing and everything. And Phil, if I were you, I would leave no addresses."

"Not an address!" said Philip. "Not even Polly."

When the train pulled out, the elder Ammon went home to find Hart Henderson waiting.

"Where is Phil?" he demanded.

"He did not feel like facing his friends at present, and I am just back from driving him to the station. He said he might go to Siam, or Patagonia. He would leave no address."

Henderson almost staggered. "He's not gone? And left no address? You don't mean it! He'll never forgive her!"

"Never is a long time, Hart," said Mr. Ammon. "And it seems even longer to those of us who are well acquainted with Phil. Last night was not the last straw. It was the whole straw-stack. It crushed Phil so far as she is concerned. He will not see her again voluntarily, and he will not forget if he does. You can take it from him, and from me, we have accepted the lady's decision. Will you have a cup of coffee?"

Twice Henderson opened his lips to speak of Edith Carr's despair. Twice he looked into the stern, inflexible face of Mr. Ammon and could not betray her. He held out the ring.

"I have no instructions as to that," said the elder Ammon, drawing back. "Possibly Miss Carr would have it as a keepsake."

"I am sure not," said Henderson curtly.

"Then suppose you return it to Peacock. I will phone him. He will give you the price of it, and you might add it to the children's Fresh Air Fund. We would be obliged if you would do that. No one here cares to handle the object."

"As you choose," said Henderson. "Good morning!"

Then he went to his home, but he could not think of sleep. He ordered breakfast, but he could not eat. He paced the library for a time, but it was too small. Going on the streets he walked until exhausted, then he called a hansom and was driven to his club. He had thought himself familiar with every depth of suffering; that night had taught him that what he felt for himself was not to be compared with the anguish which wrung his heart over the agony of Edith Carr. He tried to blame Philip Ammon, but being an honest man, Henderson knew that was unjust. The fault lay wholly with her, but that only made it harder for him, as he realized it would in time for her.

As he sauntered into the room an attendant hurried to him.

"You are wanted most urgently at the 'phone, Mr. Henderson," he said. "You have had three calls from Main 5770."

Henderson shivered as he picked down the receiver and gave the call.

"Is that you, Hart?" came Edith's voice.

"Yes."

"Did you find Phil?"

"No."

"Did you try?"

"Yes. As soon as I left you I went straight there."

"Wasn't he home yet?"

"He has been home and gone again."

"Gone!"

The cry tore Henderson's heart.

"Shall I come and tell you, Edith?"

"No! Tell me now."

"When I reached the house Banks said Mr. Ammon and Phil were out in the motor, so I waited. Mr. Ammon came back soon. Edith, are you alone?"

"Yes. Go on!"

"Call your maid. I can't tell you until some one is with you."

"Tell me instantly!"

"Edith, he said he had been to the station. He said Phil had started to Siam or Patagonia, he didn't know which, and left no address. He said——"

Distinctly Henderson heard her fall. He set the buzzer ringing, and in a few seconds heard voices, so he knew she had been found. Then he crept into a private den and shook with a hard, nervous chill.

The next day Edith Carr started on her trip to Europe. Henderson felt certain she hoped to meet Philip there. He was sure she would be disappointed, though he had no idea where Ammon could have gone. But after much thought he decided he would see Edith soonest by remaining at home, so he spent the summer in Chicago.

CHAPTER XXI. WHEREIN PHILIP AMMON RETURNS TO THE LIMBERLOST, AND ELNORA STUDIES THE SITUATION

"We must be thinking about supper, mother," said Elnora, while she set the wings of a Cecropia with much care. "It seems as if I can't get enough to eat, or enough of being at home. I enjoyed that city house. I don't believe I could have done my work if I had been compelled to walk back and forth. I thought at first I never wanted to come here again. Now, I feel as if I could not live anywhere else."

"Elnora," said Mrs. Comstock, "there's some one coming down the road."

"Coming here, do you think?"

"Yes, coming here, I suspect."

Elnora glanced quickly at her mother and then turned to the road as Philip Ammon reached the gate.

"Careful, mother!" the girl instantly warned. "If you change your treatment of him a hair's breadth, he will suspect. Come with me to meet him."

She dropped her work and sprang up.

"Well, of all the delightful surprises!" she cried.

She was a trifle thinner than during the previous summer. On her face there was a more mature, patient look, but the sun struck her bare head with the same ray of red gold. She wore one of the old blue gingham dresses, open at the throat and rolled to the elbows. Mrs. Comstock did not appear at all the same woman, but Philip saw only Elnora; heard only her greeting. He caught both hands where she offered but one.

"Elnora," he cried, "if you were engaged to me, and we were at a ball, among hundreds, where I offended you very much, and didn't even know I had done anything, and if I asked you before all of them to allow me to explain, to forgive me, to wait, would your face grow distorted and unfamiliar with anger? Would you drop my ring on the floor and insult me repeatedly? Oh Elnora, would you?"

Elnora's big eyes seemed to leap, while her face grew very white. She drew away her hands.

"Hush, Phil! Hush!" she protested. "That fever has you again! You are dreadfully ill. You don't know what you are saying."

"I am sleepless and exhausted; I'm heartsick; but I am well as I ever was. Answer me, Elnora, would you?"

"Answer nothing!" cried Mrs. Comstock. "Answer nothing! Hang your coat there on your nail, Phil, and come split some kindling. Elnora, clean away that stuff, and set the table. Can't you see the boy is starved and tired? He's come home to rest and eat a decent meal. Come on, Phil!"

Mrs. Comstock marched away, and Philip hung his coat in its old place and followed. Out of sight and hearing she turned on him.

"Do you call yourself a man or a hound?" she flared.

"I beg your pardon——" stammered Philip Ammon.

"I should think you would!" she ejaculated. "I'll admit you did the square thing and was a man last summer, though I'd liked it better if you'd faced up and told me you were promised;

but to come back here babying, and take hold of Elnora like that, and talk that way because you have had a fuss with your girl, I don't tolerate. Split that kindling and I'll get your supper, and then you better go. I won't have you working on Elnora's big heart, because you have quarrelled with some one else. You'll have it patched up in a week and be gone again, so you can go right away."

"Mrs. Comstock, I came to ask Elnora to marry me."

"The more fool you, then!" cried Mrs. Comstock. "This time yesterday you were engaged to another woman, no doubt. Now, for some little flare-up you come racing here to use Elnora as a tool to spite the other girl. A week of sane living, and you will be sorry and ready to go back to Chicago, or, if you really are man enough to be sure of yourself, she will come to claim you. She has her rights. An engagement of years is a serious matter, and not broken for a whim. If you don't go, she'll come. Then, when you patch up your affairs and go sailing away together, where does my girl come in?"

"I am a lawyer, Mrs. Comstock," said Philip. "It appeals to me as beneath your ordinary sense of justice to decide a case without hearing the evidence. It is due me that you hear me first."

"Hear your side!" flashed Mrs. Comstock. "I'd a heap sight rather hear the girl!"

"I wish to my soul that you had heard and seen her last night, Mrs. Comstock," said Ammon. "Then, my way would be clear. I never even thought of coming here to-day. I'll admit I would have come in time, but not for many months. My father sent me."

"Your father sent you! Why?"

"Father, mother, and Polly were present last night. They, and all my friends, saw me insulted and disgraced in the worst exhibition of uncontrolled temper any of us ever witnessed. All of them knew it was the end. Father liked what I had told him of Elnora, and he advised me to come here, so I came. If she does not want me, I can leave instantly, but, oh I hoped she would understand!"

"You people are not splitting wood," called Elnora.

"Oh yes we are!" answered Mrs. Comstock. "You set out the things for biscuit, and lay the table." She turned again to Philip. "I know considerable about your father," she said. "I have met your Uncle's family frequently this winter. I've heard your Aunt Anna say that she didn't at all like Miss Carr, and that she and all your family secretly hoped that something would happen to prevent your marrying her. That chimes right in with your saying that your father sent you here. I guess you better speak your piece."

Philip gave his version of the previous night.

"Do you believe me?" he finished.

"Yes," said Mrs. Comstock.

"May I stay?"

"Oh, it looks all right for you, but what about her?"

"Nothing, so far as I am concerned. Her plans were all made to start to Europe to-day. I suspect she is on the way by this time. Elnora is very sensible, Mrs. Comstock. Hadn't you better let her decide this?"

"The final decision rests with her, of course," admitted Mrs. Comstock. "But look you one thing! She's all I have. As Solomon says, 'she is the one child, the only child of her mother.' I've suffered enough in this world that I fight against any suffering which threatens her. So far as I know you've always been a man, and you may stay. But if you bring tears and heartache to her, don't have the assurance to think I'll bear it tamely. I'll get right up and fight like a catamount, if things go wrong for Elnora!"

"I have no doubt but you will," replied Philip, "and I don't blame you in the least if you do. I have the utmost devotion to offer Elnora, a good home, fair social position, and my family will love her dearly. Think it over. I know it is sudden, but my father advised it."

"Yes, I reckon he did!" said Mrs. Comstock dryly. "I guess instead of me being the catamount, you had the genuine article up in Chicago, masquerading in peacock feathers, and posing as a fine lady, until her time came to scratch. Human nature seems to be the same the world over. But I'd give a pretty to know that secret thing you say you don't, that set her raving over your just catching a moth for Elnora. You might get that crock of strawberries in the spring house."

They prepared and ate supper. Afterward they sat in the arbour and talked, or Elnora played until time for Philip to go.

"Will you walk to the gate with me?" he asked Elnora as he arose.

"Not to-night," she answered lightly. "Come early in the morning if you like, and we will go over to Sleepy Snake Creek and hunt moths and gather dandelions for dinner."

Philip leaned toward her. "May I tell you to-morrow why I came?" he asked.

"I think not," replied Elnora. "The fact is, I don't care why you came. It is enough for me that we are your very good friends, and that in trouble, you have found us a refuge. I fancy we had better live a week or two before you say anything. There is a possibility that what you have to say may change in that length of time.

"It will not change one iota!" cried Philip.

"Then it will have the grace of that much age to give it some small touch of flavour," said the girl. "Come early in the morning."

She lifted the violin and began to play.

"Well bless my soul!" ejaculated the astounded Mrs. Comstock. "To think I was worrying for fear you couldn't take care of yourself!"

Elnora laughed while she played.

"Shall I tell you what he said?"

"Nope! I don't want to hear it!" said Elnora. "He is only six hours from Chicago. I'll give her a week to find him and fix it up, if he stays that long. If she doesn't put in an appearance then, he can tell me what he wants to say, and I'll take my time to think it over. Time in plenty, too! There are three of us in this, and one must be left with a sore heart for life. If the decision rests with me I propose to be very sure that it is the one who deserves such hard luck."

The next morning Philip came early, dressed in the outing clothing he had worn the previous summer, and aside from a slight paleness seemed very much the same as when he left. Elnora met him on the old footing, and for a week life went on exactly as it had the previous summer. Mrs. Comstock made mental notes and watched in silence. She could see that Elnora was on a strain, though she hoped Philip would not. The girl grew restless as the week drew to a close. Once when the gate clicked she suddenly lost colour and moved nervously. Billy came down the walk.

Philip leaned toward Mrs. Comstock and said: "I am expressly forbidden to speak to Elnora as I would like. Would you mind telling her for me that I had a letter from my father this morning saying that Miss Carr is on her way to Europe for the summer?"

"Elnora," said Mrs. Comstock promptly, "I have just heard that Carr woman is on her way to Europe, and I wish to my gracious stars she'd stay there!"

Philip Ammon shouted, but Elnora arose hastily and went to meet Billy. They came into the arbour together and after speaking to Mrs. Comstock and Philip, Billy said: "Uncle Wesley and I found something funny, and we thought you'd like to see."

"I don't know what I should do without you and Uncle Wesley to help me," said Elnora. "What have you found now?"

"Something I couldn't bring. You have to come to it. I tried to get one and I killed it. They are a kind of insecty things, and they got a long tail that is three fine hairs. They stick those hairs right into the hard bark of trees, and if you pull, the hairs stay fast and it kills the bug."

"We will come at once," laughed Elnora. "I know what they are, and I can use some in my work."

"Billy, have you been crying?" inquired Mrs. Comstock.

Billy lifted a chastened face. "Yes, ma'am," he replied. "This has been the worst day."

"What's the matter with the day?"

"The day is all right," admitted Billy. "I mean every single thing has gone wrong with me."

"Now that is too bad!" sympathized Mrs. Comstock.

"Began early this morning," said Billy. "All Snap's fault, too."

"What has poor Snap been doing?" demanded Mrs. Comstock, her eyes beginning to twinkle.

"Digging for woodchucks, like he always does. He gets up at two o'clock to dig for them. He was coming in from the woods all tired and covered thick with dirt. I was going to the barn with the pail of water for Uncle Wesley to use in milking. I had to set down the pail to shut the gate so the chickens wouldn't get into the flower beds, and old Snap stuck his dirty nose into the water and began to lap it down. I knew Uncle Wesley wouldn't use that, so I had to go 'way back to the cistern for more, and it pumps awful hard. Made me mad, so I threw the water on Snap."

"Well, what of it?"

"Nothing, if he'd stood still. But it scared him awful, and when he's afraid he goes a-humping for Aunt Margaret. When he got right up against her he stiffened out and gave a big shake. You oughter seen the nice blue dress she had put on to go to Onabasha!"

Mrs. Comstock and Philip laughed, but Elnora put her arms around the boy. "Oh Billy!" she cried. "That was too bad!"

"She got up early and ironed that dress to wear because it was cool. Then, when it was all dirty, she wouldn't go, and she wanted to real bad." Billy wiped his eyes. "That ain't all, either," he added.

"We'd like to know about it, Billy," suggested Mrs. Comstock, struggling with her face.

"Cos she couldn't go to the city, she's most worked herself to death. She's done all the dirty, hard jobs she could find. She's fixing her grape juice now."

"Sure!" cried Mrs. Comstock. "When a woman is disappointed she always works like a dog to gain sympathy!"

"Well, Uncle Wesley and I are sympathizing all we know how, without her working so. I've squeezed until I almost busted to get the juice out from the seeds and skins. That's the hard part. Now, she has to strain it through white flannel and seal it in bottles, and it's good for sick folks. Most wish I'd get sick myself, so I could have a glass. It's so good!"

Elnora glanced swiftly at her mother.

"I worked so hard," continued Billy, "that she said if I would throw the leavings in the woods, then I could come after you to see about the bugs. Do you want to go?"

"We will all go," said Mrs. Comstock. "I am mightily interested in those bugs myself."

From afar commotion could be seen at the Sinton home. Wesley and Margaret were running around wildly and peculiar sounds filled the air.

"What's the trouble?" asked Philip, hurrying to Wesley.

"Cholera!" groaned Sinton. "My hogs are dying like flies."

Margaret was softly crying. "Wesley, can't I fix something hot? Can't we do anything? It means several hundred dollars and our winter meat."

"I never saw stock taken so suddenly and so hard," said Wesley. "I have 'phoned for the veterinary to come as soon as he can get here."

All of them hurried to the feeding pen into which the pigs seemed to be gathering from the woods. Among the common stock were big white beasts of pedigree which were Wesley's pride at county fairs. Several of these rolled on their backs, pawing the air feebly and emitting little squeaks. A huge Berkshire sat on his haunches, slowly shaking his head, the water dropping from his eyes, until he, too, rolled over with faint grunts. A pair crossing the yard on wavering legs collided, and attacked each other in anger, only to fall, so weak they scarcely could squeal. A fine snowy Plymouth Rock rooster, after several attempts, flew to the fence, balanced with great effort, wildly flapped his wings and started a guttural crow, but fell sprawling among the pigs, too helpless to stand.

"Did you ever see such a dreadful sight?" sobbed Margaret.

Billy climbed on the fence, took one long look and turned an astounded face to Wesley.

"Why them pigs is drunk!" he cried. "They act just like my pa!"

Wesley turned to Margaret.

"Where did you put the leavings from that grape juice?" he demanded.

"I sent Billy to throw it in the woods."

"Billy——" began Wesley.

"Threw it just where she told me to," cried Billy. "But some of the pigs came by there coming into the pen, and some were close in the fence corners."

"Did they eat it?" demanded Wesley.

"They just chanked into it," replied Billy graphically. "They pushed, and squealed, and fought over it. You couldn't blame 'em! It was the best stuff I ever tasted!"

"Margaret," said Wesley, "run 'phone that doctor he won't be needed. Billy, take Elnora and Mr. Ammon to see the bugs. Katharine, suppose you help me a minute."

Wesley took the clothes basket from the back porch and started in the direction of the cellar. Margaret returned from the telephone.

"I just caught him," she said. "There's that much saved. Why Wesley, what are you going to do?"

"You go sit on the front porch a little while," said Wesley. "You will feel better if you don't see this."

"Wesley," cried Margaret aghast. "Some of that wine is ten years old. There are days and days of hard work in it, and I couldn't say how much sugar. Dr. Ammon keeps people alive with it when nothing else will stay on their stomachs."

"Let 'em die, then!" said Wesley. "You heard the boy, didn't you?"

"It's a cold process. There's not a particle of fermentation about it."

"Not a particle of fermentation! Great day, Margaret! Look at those pigs!"

Margaret took a long look. "Leave me a few bottles for mince-meat," she wavered.

"Not a smell for any use on this earth! You heard the boy! He shan't say, when he grows to manhood, that he learned to like it here!"

Wesley threw away the wine, Mrs. Comstock cheerfully assisting. Then they walked to the woods to see and learn about the wonderful insects. The day ended with a big supper at Sintons', and then they went to the Comstock cabin for a concert. Elnora played beautifully that night. When the Sintons left she kissed Billy with particular tenderness. She was so moved that she was kinder to Philip than she had intended to be, and Elnora as an antidote to a disappointed lover was a decided success in any mood.

However strong the attractions of Edith Carr had been, once the bond was finally broken, Philip Ammon could not help realizing that Elnora was the superior woman, and that he was fortunate to have escaped, when he regarded his ties strongest. Every day, while working with Elnora, he saw more to admire. He grew very thankful that he was free to try to win her, and impatient to justify himself to her.

Elnora did not evince the slightest haste to hear what he had to say, but waited the week she had set, in spite of Philip's hourly manifest impatience. When she did consent to listen, Philip felt before he had talked five minutes, that she was putting herself in Edith Carr's place, and judging him from what the other girl's standpoint would be. That was so disconcerting, he did not plead his cause nearly so well as he had hoped, for when he ceased Elnora sat in silence.

"You are my judge," he said at last. "What is your verdict?"

"If I could hear her speak from her heart as I just have heard you, then I could decide," answered Elnora.

"She is on the ocean," said Philip. "She went because she knew she was wholly in the wrong. She had nothing to say, or she would have remained."

"That sounds plausible," reasoned Elnora, "but it is pretty difficult to find a woman in an affair that involves her heart with nothing at all to say. I fancy if I could meet her, she would say several things. I should love to hear them. If I could talk with her three minutes, I could tell what answer to make you."

"Don't you believe me, Elnora?"

"Unquestioningly," answered Elnora. "But I would believe her also. If only I could meet her I soon would know."

"I don't see how that is to be accomplished," said Philip, "but I am perfectly willing. There is no reason why you should not meet her, except that she probably would lose her temper and insult you."

"Not to any extent," said Elnora calmly. "I have a tongue of my own, while I am not without some small sense of personal values."

Philip glanced at her and began to laugh. Very different of facial formation and colouring, Elnora at times closely resembled her mother. She joined in his laugh ruefully.

"The point is this," she said. "Some one is going to be hurt, most dreadfully. If the decision as to whom it shall be rests with me, I must know it is the right one. Of course, no one ever hinted it to you, but you are a very attractive man, Philip. You are mighty good to look at, and you have a trained, refined mind, that makes you most interesting. For years Edith Carr has felt that you were hers. Now, how is she going to change? I have been thinking—thinking deep and long, Phil. If I were in her place, I simply could not give you up, unless you had made yourself unworthy of love. Undoubtedly, you never seemed so desirable to her as just now, when she is told she can't have you. What I think is that she will come to claim you yet."

"You overlook the fact that it is not in a woman's power to throw away a man and pick him up at pleasure," said Philip with some warmth. "She publicly and repeatedly cast me off. I accepted her decision as publicly as it was made. You have done all your thinking from a wrong viewpoint. You seem to have an idea that it lies with you to decide what I shall do, that if you say the word, I shall return to Edith. Put that thought out of your head! Now, and for all time to come, she is a matter of indifference to me. She killed all feeling in my heart for her so completely that I do not even dread meeting her.

"If I hated her, or was angry with her, I could not be sure the feeling would not die. As it is, she has deadened me into a creature of indifference. So you just revise your viewpoint a little, Elnora. Cease thinking it is for you to decide what I shall do, and that I will obey you. I make my own decisions in reference to any woman, save you. The question you are to decide is whether I may remain here, associating with you as I did last summer; but with the difference that it is understood that I am free; that it is my intention to care for you all I please, to make you return my feeling for you if I can. There is just one question for you to decide, and it is not triangular. It is between us. May I remain? May I love you? Will you give me the chance to prove what I think of you?"

"You speak very plainly," said Elnora.

"This is the time to speak plainly," said Philip Ammon. "There is no use in allowing you to go on threshing out a problem which does not exist. If you do not want me here, say so and I will go. Of course, I warn you before I start, that I will come back. I won't yield without the stiffest fight it is in me to make. But drop thinking it lies in your power to send me back to Edith Carr. If she were the last woman in the world, and I the last man, I'd jump off the planet before I would give her further opportunity to exercise her temper on me. Narrow this to us, Elnora. Will you take the place she vacated? Will you take the heart she threw away? I'd give my right hand and not flinch, if I could offer you my life, free from any contact with hers, but that is not possible. I can't undo things which are done. I can only profit by experience and build better in the future."

"I don't see how you can be sure of yourself," said Elnora. "I don't see how I could be sure of you. You loved her first, you never can care for me anything like that. Always I'd have to be afraid you were thinking of her and regretting."

"Folly!" cried Philip. "Regretting what? That I was not married to a woman who was liable to rave at me any time or place, without my being conscious of having given offence? A man does relish that! I am likely to pine for more!"

"You'd be thinking she'd learned a lesson. You would think it wouldn't happen again."

"No, I wouldn't be 'thinking,'" said, Philip. "I'd be everlastingly sure! I wouldn't risk what I went through that night again, not to save my life! Just you and me, Elnora. Decide for us."

"I can't!" cried Elnora. "I am afraid!"

"Very well," said Philip. "We will wait until you feel that you can. Wait until fear vanishes. Just decide now whether you would rather have me go for a few months, or remain with you. Which shall it be, Elnora?"

"You can never love me as you did her," wailed Elnora.

"I am happy to say I cannot," replied he. "I've cut my matrimonial teeth. I'm cured of wanting to swell in society. I'm over being proud of a woman for her looks alone. I have no further use for lavishing myself on a beautiful, elegantly dressed creature, who thinks only of self. I have learned that I am a common man. I admire beauty and beautiful clothing quite as much as I ever did; but, first, I want an understanding, deep as the lowest recess of my soul, with the woman I marry. I want to work for you, to plan for you, to build you a home with every comfort, to give you all good things I can, to shield you from every evil. I want to interpose my body between yours and fire, flood, or famine. I want to give you everything; but I hate the idea of getting nothing at all on which I can depend in return. Edith Carr had only good looks to offer, and when anger overtook her, beauty went out like a snuffed candle.

"I want you to love me. I want some consideration. I even crave respect. I've kept myself clean. So far as I know how to be, I am honest and scrupulous. It wouldn't hurt me to feel that you took some interest in these things. Rather fierce temptations strike a man, every few days, in this world. I can keep decent, for a woman who cares for decency, but when I do, I'd like to have the fact recognized, by just enough of a show of appreciation that I could see it. I am tired of this one-sided business. After this, I want to get a little in return for what I give. Elnora, you have love, tenderness, and honest appreciation of the finest in life. Take what I offer, and give what I ask."

"You do not ask much," said Elnora.

"As for not loving you as I did Edith," continued Philip, "as I said before, I hope not! I have a newer and a better idea of loving. The feeling I offer you was inspired by you. It is a Limberlost product. It is as much bigger, cleaner, and more wholesome than any feeling I ever had for Edith Carr, as you are bigger than she, when you stand before your classes and in calm dignity explain the marvels of the Almighty, while she stands on a ballroom floor, and gives way to uncontrolled temper. Ye gods, Elnora, if you could look into my soul, you would see it leap and rejoice over my escape! Perhaps it isn't decent, but it's human; and I'm only a common human being. I'm the gladdest man alive that I'm free! I would turn somersaults and yell if I dared. What an escape! Stop straining after Edith Carr's viewpoint and take a look from mine. Put yourself in my place and try to study out how I feel.

"I am so happy I grow religious over it. Fifty times a day I catch myself whispering, 'My soul is escaped!' As for you, take all the time you want. If you prefer to be alone, I'll take the next train and stay away as long as I can bear it, but I'll come back. You can be most sure of that. Straight as your pigeons to their loft, I'll come back to you, Elnora. Shall I go?"

"Oh, what's the use to be extravagant?" murmured Elnora.

CHAPTER XXII. WHEREIN PHILIP AMMON KNEELS TO ELNORA, AND STRANGERS COME TO THE LIMBERLOST

The month which followed was a reproduction of the previous June. There were long moth hunts, days of specimen gathering, wonderful hours with great books, big dinners all of them helped to prepare, and perfect nights filled with music. Everything was as it had been, with the difference that Philip was now an avowed suitor. He missed no opportunity to advance himself in Elnora's graces. At the end of the month he was no nearer any sort of understanding with her than he had been at the beginning. He revelled in the privilege of loving her, but he got no response. Elnora believed in his love, yet she hesitated to accept him, because she could not forget Edith Carr.

One afternoon early in July, Philip came across the fields, through the Comstock woods, and entered the garden. He inquired for Elnora at the back door and was told that she was reading under the willow. He went around the west end of the cabin to her. She sat on a rustic bench they had made and placed beneath a drooping branch. He had not seen her before in the dress she was wearing. It was clinging mull of pale green, trimmed with narrow ruffles and touched with knots of black velvet; a simple dress, but vastly becoming. Every tint of her bright hair, her luminous eyes, her red lips, and her rose-flushed face, neck, and arms grew a little more vivid with the delicate green setting.

He stopped short. She was so near, so temptingly sweet, he lost control. He went to her with a half-smothered cry after that first long look, dropped on one knee beside her and reached an arm behind her to the bench back, so that he was very near. He caught her hands.

"Elnora!" he cried tensely, "end it now! Say this strain is over. I pledge you that you will be happy. You don't know! If you only would say the word, you would awake to new life and great joy! Won't you promise me now, Elnora?"

The girl sat staring into the west woods, while strong in her eyes was her father's look of seeing something invisible to others. Philip's arm slipped from the bench around her. His fingers closed firmly over hers. "Elnora," he pleaded, "you know me well enough. You have had time in plenty. End it now. Say you will be mine!" He gathered her closer, pressing his face against hers, his breath on her cheek. "Can't you quite promise yet, my girl of the Limberlost?"

Elnora shook her head. Instantly he released her.

"Forgive me," he begged. "I had no intention of thrusting myself upon you, but, Elnora, you are the veriest Queen of Love this afternoon. From the tips of your toes to your shining crown, I worship you. I want no woman save you. You are so wonderful this afternoon, I couldn't help urging. Forgive me. Perhaps it was something that came this morning for you. I wrote Polly to send it. May we try if it fits? Will you tell me if you like it?"

He drew a little white velvet box from his pocket and showed her a splendid emerald ring.

"It may not be right," he said. "The inside of a glove finger is not very accurate for a measure, but it was the best I could do. I wrote Polly to get it, because she and mother are home from the East this week, but next they will go on to our cottage in the north, and no one knows what is right quite so well as Polly." He laid the ring in Elnora's hand. "Dearest," he said, "don't slip that on your finger; put your arms around my neck and promise me, all at once and abruptly, or I'll keel over and die of sheer joy."

Elnora smiled.

"I won't! Not all those venturesome things at once; but, Phil, I'm ashamed to confess that ring simply fascinates me. It is the most beautiful one I ever saw, and do you know that I never owned a ring of any kind in my life? Would you think me unwomanly if I slip it on for a second, before I can say for sure? Phil, you know I care! I care very much! You know I will tell you the instant I feel right about it."

"Certainly you will," agreed Philip promptly. "It is your right to take all the time you choose. I can't put that ring on you until it means a bond between us. I'll shut my eyes and you try it on, so we can see if it fits." Philip turned his face toward the west woods and tightly closed his eyes. It was a boyish thing to do, and it caught the hesitating girl in the depths of her heart as the boy element in a man ever appeals to a motherly woman. Before she quite realized what she was doing, the ring slid on her finger. With both arms she caught Philip and drew him to her breast, holding him closely. Her head drooped over his, her lips were on his hair. So an instant, then her arms dropped. He lifted a convulsed, white face.

"Dear Lord!" he whispered. "You—you didn't mean that, Elnora! You—— What made you do it?"

"You—you looked so boyish!" panted Elnora. "I didn't mean it! I—I forgot that you were older than Billy. Look—look at the ring!"

"'The Queen can do no wrong,'" quoted Philip between his set teeth. "But don't you do that again, Elnora, unless you do mean it. Kings are not so good as queens, and there is a limit with all men. As you say, we will look at your ring. It seems very lovely to me. Suppose you leave it on until time for me to go. Please do! I have heard of mute appeals; perhaps it will plead for me. I am wild for your lips this afternoon. I am going to take your hands."

He caught both of them and covered them with kisses.

"Elnora," he said, "Will you be my wife?"

"I must have a little more time," she whispered. "I must be absolutely certain, for when I say yes, and give myself to you, only death shall part us. I would not give you up. So I want a little more time—but, I think I will."

"Thank you," said Philip. "If at any time you feel that you have reached a decision, will you tell me? Will you promise me to tell me instantly, or shall I keep asking you until the time comes?"

"You make it difficult," said Elnora. "But I will promise you that. Whenever the last doubt vanishes, I will let you know instantly—if I can."

"Would it be difficult for you?" whispered Ammon.

"I—I don't know," faltered Elnora.

"It seems as if I can't be man enough to put this thought aside and give up this afternoon," said Philip. "I am ashamed of myself, but I can't help it. I am going to ask God to make that last doubt vanish before I go this night. I am going to believe that ring will plead for me. I am going to hope that doubt will disappear suddenly. I will be watching. Every second I will be watching. If it happens and you can't speak, give me your hand. Just the least movement toward me, I will understand. Would it help you to talk this over with your mother? Shall I call her? Shall I——?"

Honk! Honk! Honk! Hart Henderson set the horn of the big automobile going as it shot from behind the trees lining the Brushwood road. The picture of a vine-covered cabin, a large drooping tree, a green-clad girl and a man bending over her very closely flashed into view. Edith Carr caught her breath with a snap. Polly Ammon gave Tom Levering a quick touch and wickedly winked at him.

Several days before, Edith had returned from Europe suddenly. She and Henderson had called at the Ammon residence saying that they were going to motor down to the Limberlost to see Philip a few hours, and urged that Polly and Tom accompany them. Mrs. Ammon knew that her husband would disapprove of the trip, but it was easy to see that Edith Carr had determined on going. So the mother thought it better to have Polly along to support Philip than to allow him to confront Edith unexpectedly and alone. Polly was full of spirit. She did not relish the thought of Edith as a sister. Always they had been in the same set, always Edith, because of greater beauty and wealth, had patronized Polly. Although it had rankled, she had borne it sweetly. But two days before, her father had extracted a promise of secrecy, given her Philip's address and told her to send him the finest emerald ring she could select. Polly knew how that ring would be used. What she did not know was that the girl who accompanied her went back to the store afterward, made an excuse to the clerk that she had been sent to be absolutely sure that the address was right, and so secured it for Edith Carr.

Two days later Edith had induced Hart Henderson to take her to Onabasha. By the aid of maps they located the Comstock land and passed it, merely to see the place. Henderson hated that trip, and implored Edith not to take it, but she made no effort to conceal from him what she suffered, and it was more than he could endure. He pointed out that Philip had gone away without leaving an address, because he did not wish to see her, or any of them. But Edith was so sure of her power, she felt certain Philip needed only to see her to succumb to her beauty as he always had done, while now she was ready to plead for forgiveness. So they came down the Brushwood road, and Henderson had just said to Edith beside him: "This should be the Comstock land on our left."

A minute later the wood ended, while the sunlight, as always pitiless, etched with distinctness the scene at the west end of the cabin. Instinctively, to save Edith, Henderson set the horn blowing. He had thought to drive to the city, but Polly Ammon arose crying: "Phil! Phil!" Tom Levering was on his feet shouting and waving, while Edith in her most imperial manner ordered him to turn into the lane leading through the woods beside the cabin.

"Find some way for me to have a minute alone with her," she commanded as he stopped the car.

"That is my sister Polly, her fiance Tom Levering, a friend of mine named Henderson, and——" began Philip,

"—and Edith Carr," volunteered Elnora.

"And Edith Carr," repeated Philip Ammon. "Elnora, be brave, for my sake. Their coming can make no difference in any way. I won't let them stay but a few minutes. Come with me!"

"Do I seem scared?" inquired Elnora serenely. "This is why you haven't had your answer. I have been waiting just six weeks for that motor. You may bring them to me at the arbour."

Philip glanced at her and broke into a laugh. She had not lost colour. Her self-possession was perfect. She deliberately turned and walked toward the grape arbour, while he sprang over the west fence and ran to the car.

Elnora standing in the arbour entrance made a perfect picture, framed in green leaves and tendrils. No matter how her heart ached, it was good to her, for it pumped steadily, and kept her cheeks and lips suffused with colour. She saw Philip reach the car and gather his sister into his arms. Past her he reached a hand to Levering, then to Edith Carr and Henderson. He lifted his sister to the ground, and assisted Edith to alight. Instantly, she stepped beside him, and Elnora's heart played its first trick.

She could see that Miss Carr was splendidly beautiful, while she moved with the hauteur and grace supposed to be the prerogatives of royalty. And she had instantly taken possession of Philip. But he also had a brain which was working with rapidity. He knew Elnora was watching, so he turned to the others.

"Give her up, Tom!" he cried. "I didn't know I wanted to see the little nuisance so badly, but I do. How are father and mother? Polly, didn't the mater send me something?"

"She did!" said Polly Ammon, stopping on the path and lifting her chin as a little child, while she drew away her veil.

Philip caught her in his arms and stooped for his mother's kiss.

"Be good to Elnora!" he whispered.

"Umhu!" assented Polly. And aloud—"Look at that ripping green and gold symphony! I never saw such a beauty! Thomas Asquith Levering, you come straight here and take my hand!"

Edith's move to compel Philip to approach Elnora beside her had been easy to see; also its failure. Henderson stepped into Philip's place as he turned to his sister. Instead of taking Polly's hand Levering ran to open the gate. Edith passed through first, but Polly darted in front of her on the run, with Phil holding her arm, and swept up to Elnora. Polly looked for the ring and saw it. That settled matters with her.

"You lovely, lovely, darling girl!" she cried, throwing her arms around Elnora and kissing her. With her lips close Elnora's ear, Polly whispered, "Sister! Dear, dear sister!"

Elnora drew back, staring at Polly in confused amazement. She was a beautiful girl, her eyes were sparkling and dancing, and as she turned to make way for the others, she kept one of Elnora's hands in hers. Polly would have dropped dead in that instant if Edith Carr could have killed with a look, for not until then did she realize that Polly would even many a slight, and that it had been a great mistake to bring her.

Edith bowed low, muttered something and touched Elnora's fingers. Tom took his cue from Polly.

"I always follow a good example," he said, and before any one could divine his intention he kissed Elnora as he gripped her hand and cried: "Mighty glad to meet you! Like to meet you a dozen times a day, you know!"

Elnora laughed and her heart pumped smoothly. They had accomplished their purpose. They had let her know they were there through compulsion, but on her side. In that instant only pity was in Elnora's breast for the flashing dark beauty, standing with smiling face while her heart must have been filled with exceeding bitterness. Elnora stepped back from the entrance.

"Come into the shade," she urged. "You must have found it warm on these country roads. Won't you lay aside your dust-coats and have a cool drink? Philip, would you ask mother to come, and bring that pitcher from the spring house?"

They entered the arbour exclaiming at the dim, green coolness. There was plenty of room and wide seats around the sides, a table in the centre, on which lay a piece of embroidery, magazines, books, the moth apparatus, and the cyanide jar containing several specimens. Polly rejoiced in the cooling shade, slipped off her duster, removed her hat, rumpled her pretty hair and seated herself to indulge in the delightful occupation of paying off old scores. Tom Levering followed her example. Edith took a seat but refused to remove her hat and coat, while Henderson stood in the entrance.

"There goes something with wings! Should you have that?" cried Levering.

He seized a net from the table and raced across the garden after a butterfly. He caught it and came back mightily pleased with himself. As the creature struggled in the net, Elnora noted a repulsed look on Edith Carr's face. Levering helped the situation beautifully.

"Now what have I got?" he demanded. "Is it just a common one that every one knows and you don't keep, or is it the rarest bird off the perch?"

"You must have had practice, you took that so perfectly," said Elnora. "I am sorry, but it is quite common and not of a kind I keep. Suppose all of you see how beautiful it is and then it may go nectar hunting again."

She held the butterfly where all of them could see, showed its upper and under wing colours, answered Polly's questions as to what it ate, how long it lived, and how it died. Then she put it into Polly's hand saying: "Stand there in the light and loosen your hold slowly and easily."

Elnora caught a brush from the table and began softly stroking the creature's sides and wings. Delighted with the sensation the butterfly opened and closed its wings, clinging to Polly's soft little fingers, while every one cried out in surprise. Elnora laid aside the brush, and the butterfly sailed away.

"Why, you are a wizard! You charm them!" marvelled Levering.

"I learned that from the Bird Woman," said Elnora. "She takes soft brushes and coaxes butterflies and moths into the positions she wants for the illustrations of a book she is writing. I have helped her often. Most of the rare ones I find go to her."

"Then you don't keep all you take?" questioned Levering.

"Oh, dear, no!" cried Elnora. "Not a tenth! For myself, a pair of each kind to use in illustrating the lectures I give in the city schools in the winter, and one pair for each collection I make. One might as well keep the big night moths of June, for they only live four or five days anyway. For the Bird Woman, I only save rare ones she has not yet secured. Sometimes I think it is cruel to take such creatures from freedom, even for an hour, but it is the only way to teach the masses of people how to distinguish the pests they should destroy, from the harmless ones of great beauty. Here comes mother with something cool to drink."

Mrs. Comstock came deliberately, talking to Philip as she approached. Elnora gave her one searching look, but could discover only an extreme brightness of eye to denote any unusual feeling. She wore one of her lavender dresses, while her snowy hair was high piled. She had taken care of her complexion, and her face had grown fuller during the winter. She might have been any one's mother with pride, and she was perfectly at ease.

Polly instantly went to her and held up her face to be kissed. Mrs. Comstock's eyes twinkled and she made the greeting hearty.

The drink was compounded of the juices of oranges and berries from the garden. It was cool enough to frost glasses and pitcher and delicious to dusty tired travellers. Soon the pitcher was empty, and Elnora picked it up and went to refill it. While she was gone Henderson asked Philip about some trouble he was having with his car. They went to the woods and began a minute examination to find a defect which did not exist. Polly and Levering were having an animated conversation with Mrs. Comstock. Henderson saw Edith arise, follow the garden path next the woods and stand waiting under the willow which Elnora would pass on her return. It was for that meeting he had made the trip. He got down on the ground, tore up the car, worked, asked for help, and kept Philip busy screwing bolts and applying the oil can. All the time Henderson kept an eye on Edith and Elnora under the willow. But he took pains to lay the work he asked Philip to do where that scene would be out of his sight. When Elnora came around the corner with the pitcher, she found herself facing Edith Carr.

"I want a minute with you," said Miss Carr.

"Very well," replied Elnora, walking on.

"Set the pitcher on the bench there," commanded Edith Carr, as if speaking to a servant.

"I prefer not to offer my visitors a warm drink," said Elnora. "I'll come back if you really wish to speak with me."

"I came solely for that," said Edith Carr.

"It would be a pity to travel so far in this dust and heat for nothing. I'll only be gone a second."

Elnora placed the pitcher before her mother. "Please serve this," she said. "Miss Carr wishes to speak with me."

"Don't you pay the least attention to anything she says," cried Polly. "Tom and I didn't come here because we wanted to. We only came to checkmate her. I hoped I'd get the opportunity to say a word to you, and now she has given it to me. I just want to tell you that she threw Phil over in perfectly horrid way. She hasn't any right to lay the ghost of a claim to him, has she, Tom?"

"Nary a claim," said Tom Levering earnestly. "Why, even you, Polly, couldn't serve me as she did Phil, and ever get me back again. If I were you, Miss Comstock, I'd send my mother to talk with her and I'd stay here."

Tom had gauged Mrs. Comstock rightly. Polly put her arms around Elnora. "Let me go with you, dear," she begged.

"I promised I would speak with her alone," said Elnora, "and she must be considered. But thank you, very much."

"How I shall love you!" exulted Polly, giving Elnora a parting hug.

The girl slowly and gravely walked back to the willow. She could not imagine what was coming, but she was promising herself that she would be very patient and control her temper.

"Will you be seated?" she asked politely.

Edith Carr glanced at the bench, while a shudder shook her.

"No. I prefer to stand," she said. "Did Mr. Ammon give you the ring you are wearing, and do you consider yourself engaged to him?"

"By what right do you ask such personal questions as those?" inquired Elnora.

"By the right of a betrothed wife. I have been promised to Philip Ammon ever since I wore short skirts. All our lives we have expected to marry. An agreement of years cannot be broken in one insane moment. Always he has loved me devotedly. Give me ten minutes with him and he will be mine for all time."

"I seriously doubt that," said Elnora. "But I am willing that you should make the test. I will call him."

"Stop!" commanded Edith Carr. "I told you that it was you I came to see."

"I remember," said Elnora.

"Mr. Ammon is my betrothed," continued Edith Carr. "I expect to take him back to Chicago with me."

"You expect considerable," murmured Elnora. "I will raise no objection to your taking him, if you can—but, I tell you frankly, I don't think it possible."

"You are so sure of yourself as that," scoffed Edith Carr. "One hour in my presence will bring back the old spell, full force. We belong to each other. I will not give him up."

"Then it is untrue that you twice rejected his ring, repeatedly insulted him, and publicly renounced him?"

"That was through you!" cried Edith Carr. "Phil and I never had been so near and so happy as we were on that night. It was your clinging to him for things that caused him to desert me among his guests, while he tried to make me await your pleasure. I realize the spell of this place, for a summer season. I understand what you and your mother have done to inveigle him. I know that your hold on him is quite real. I can see just how you have worked to ensnare him!"

"Men would call that lying," said Elnora calmly. "The second time I met Philip Ammon he told me of his engagement to you, and I respected it. I did by you as I would want you to do by me. He was here parts of each day, almost daily last summer. The Almighty is my witness that never once, by word or look, did I ever make the slightest attempt to interest him in my person or personality. He wrote you frequently in my presence. He forgot the violets for which he asked to send you. I gathered them and carried them to him. I sent him back to you in unswerving devotion, and the Almighty is also my witness that I could have changed his heart last summer, if I had tried. I wisely left that work for you. All my life I shall be glad that I lived and worked on the square. That he ever would come back to me free, by your act, I never dreamed. When he left me I did not hope or expect to see him again," Elnora's voice fell soft and low, "and, behold! You sent him—and free!"

"You exult in that!" cried Edith Carr. "Let me tell you he is not free! We have belonged for years. We always shall. If you cling to him, and hold him to rash things he has said and done, because he thought me still angry and unforgiving with him, you will ruin all our lives. If he married you, before a month you would read heart-hunger for me in his eyes. He could not love me as he has done, and give me up for a little scene like that!"

"There is a great poem," said Elnora, "one line of which reads, 'For each man kills the thing he loves.' Let me tell you that a woman can do that also. He did love you—that I concede. But you killed his love everlastingly, when you disgraced him in public. Killed it so completely he does not even feel resentment toward you. To-day, he would do you a favour, if he could; but love you, no! That is over!"

Edith Carr stood truly regal and filled with scorn. "You are mistaken! Nothing on earth could kill that!" she cried, and Elnora saw that the girl really believed what she said.

"You are very sure of yourself!" said Elnora.

"I have reason to be sure," answered Edith Carr.

"We have lived and loved too long. I have had years with him to match against your days. He is mine! His work, his ambitions, his friends, his place in society are with me. You may have a summer charm for a sick man in the country; if he tried placing you in society, he soon would see you as others will. It takes birth to position, schooling, and endless practice to meet social demands gracefully. You would put him to shame in a week."

"I scarcely think I should follow your example so far," said Elnora dryly. "I have a feeling for Philip that would prevent my hurting him purposely, either in public or private. As for managing a social career for him he never mentioned that he desired such a thing. What he asked of me was that I should be his wife. I understood that to mean that he desired me to keep him a clean house, serve him digestible food, mother his children, and give him loving sympathy and tenderness."

"Shameless!" cried Edith Carr.

"To which of us do you intend that adjective to apply?" inquired Elnora. "I never was less ashamed in all my life. Please remember I am in my own home, and your presence here is not on my invitation."

Miss Carr lifted her head and struggled with her veil. She was very pale and trembling violently, while Elnora stood serene, a faint smile on her lips.

"Such vulgarity!" panted Edith Carr. "How can a man like Philip endure it?"

"Why don't you ask him?" inquired Elnora. "I can call him with one breath; but, if he judged us as we stand, I should not be the one to tremble at his decision. Miss Carr, you have been quite plain. You have told me in carefully selected words what you think of me. You insult my birth, education, appearance, and home. I assure you I am legitimate. I will pass a test examination with you on any high school or supplementary branch, or French or German. I will take a physical examination beside you. I will face any social emergency you can mention with you. I am acquainted with a whole world in which Philip Ammon is keenly interested, that you scarcely know exists. I am not afraid to face any audience you can get together anywhere with my violin. I am not repulsive to look at, and I have a wholesome regard for the proprieties and civilities of life. Philip Ammon never asked anything more of me, why should you?"

"It is plain to see," cried Edith Carr, "that you took him when he was hurt and angry and kept his wound wide open. Oh, what have you not done against me?"

"I did not promise to marry him when an hour ago he asked me, and offered me this ring, because there was so much feeling in my heart for you, that I knew I never could be happy, if I felt that in any way I had failed in doing justice to your interests. I did slip on this ring, which he had just brought, because I never owned one, and it is very beautiful, but I made him no promise, nor shall I make any, until I am quite, quite sure, that you fully realize he never would marry you if I sent him away this hour."

"You know perfectly that if your puny hold on him were broken, if he were back in his home, among his friends, and where he was meeting me, in one short week he would be mine again, as he always has been. In your heart you don't believe what you say. You don't dare trust him in my presence. You are afraid to allow him out of your sight, because you know what the results would be. Right or wrong, you have made up your mind to ruin him and me, and you are going to be selfish enough to do it. But——"

"That will do!" said Elnora. "Spare me the enumeration of how I will regret it. I shall regret nothing. I shall not act until I know there will be nothing to regret. I have decided on my course. You may return to your friends."

"What do you mean?" demanded Edith Carr.

"That is my affair," replied Elnora. "Only this! When your opportunity comes, seize it! Any time you are in Philip Ammon's presence, exert the charms of which you boast, and take him. I grant you are justified in doing it if you can. I want nothing more than I want to see you marry Philip if he wants you. He is just across the fence under that automobile. Go spread your meshes and exert your wiles. I won't stir to stop you. Take him to Onabasha, and to Chicago with you. Use every art you possess. If the old charm can be revived I will be the first to wish both of you well. Now, I must return to my visitors. Kindly excuse me."

Elnora turned and went back to the arbour. Edith Carr followed the fence and passed through the gate into the west woods where she asked Henderson about the car. As she stood near him she whispered: "Take Phil back to Onabasha with us."

"I say, Ammon, can't you go to the city with us and help me find a shop where I can get this pinion fixed?" asked Henderson. "We want to lunch and start back by five. That will get us home about midnight. Why don't you bring your automobile here?"

"I am a working man," said Philip. "I have no time to be out motoring. I can't see anything the matter with your car, myself; but, of course you don't want to break down in the night, on strange roads, with women on your hands. I'll see."

Philip went into the arbour, where Polly took possession of his lap, fingered his hair, and kissed his forehead and lips.

"When are you coming to the cottage, Phil?" she asked. "Come soon, and bring Miss Comstock for a visit. All of us will be so glad to have her."

Philip beamed on Polly. "I'll see about that," he said. "Sounds pretty good. Elnora, Henderson is in trouble with his automobile. He wants me to go to Onabasha with him to show him where the doctor lives, and make repairs so he can start back this evening. It will take about two hours. May I go?"

"Of course, you must go," she said, laughing lightly. "You can't leave your sister. Why don't you return to Chicago with them? There is plenty of room, and you could have a fine visit."

"I'll be back in just two hours," said Philip. "While I am gone, you be thinking over what we were talking of when the folks came."

"Miss Comstock can go with us as well as not," said Polly. "That back seat was made for three, and I can sit on your lap."

"Come on! Do come!" urged Philip instantly, and Tom Levering joined him, but Henderson and Edith silently waited at the gate.

"No, thank you," laughed Elnora. "That would crowd you, and it's warm and dusty. We will say good-bye here."

She offered her hand to all of them, and when she came to Philip she gave him one long steady look in the eyes, then shook hands with him also.

CHAPTER XXIII. WHEREIN ELNORA REACHES A DECISION, AND FRECKLES AND THE ANGEL APPEAR

"Well, she came, didn't she?" remarked Mrs. Comstock to Elnora as they watched the automobile speed down the road. As it turned the Limberlost corner, Philip arose and waved to them.

"She hasn't got him yet, anyway," said Mrs. Comstock, taking heart. "What's that on your finger, and what did she say to you?"

Elnora explained about the ring as she drew it off.

"I have several letters to write, then I am going to change my dress and walk down toward Aunt Margaret's for a little exercise. I may meet some of them, and I don't want them to see this ring. You keep it until Philip comes," said Elnora. "As for what Miss Carr said to me, many things, two of importance: one, that I lacked every social requirement necessary for the happiness of Philip Ammon, and that if I married him I would see inside a month that he was ashamed of me——"

"Aw, shockins!" scorned Mrs. Comstock. "Go on!"

"The other was that she has been engaged to him for years, that he belongs to her, and she refuses to give him up. She said that if he were in her presence one hour, she would have him under a mysterious thing she calls 'her spell' again; if he were where she could see him for one week, everything would be made up. It is her opinion that he is suffering from wounded pride, and that the slightest concession on her part will bring him to his knees before her."

Mrs. Comstock giggled. "I do hope the boy isn't weak-kneed," she said. "I just happened to be passing the west window this afternoon——"

Elnora laughed. "Nothing save actual knowledge ever would have made me believe there was a girl in all this world so infatuated with herself. She speaks casually of her power over men, and boasts of 'bringing a man to his knees' as complacently as I would pick up a net and say: 'I am going to take a butterfly.' She honestly believes that if Philip were with her a short time she could rekindle his love for her and awaken in him every particle of the old devotion. Mother, the girl is honest! She is absolutely sincere! She so believes in herself and the strength of Phil's love for her, that all her life she will believe in and brood over that thought, unless she is taught differently. So long as she thinks that, she will nurse wrong ideas and pine over her blighted life. She must be taught that Phil is absolutely free, and yet he will not go to her."

"But how on earth are you proposing to teach her that?"

"The way will open."

"Lookey here, Elnora!" cried Mrs. Comstock. "That Carr girl is the handsomest dark woman I ever saw. She's got to the place where she won't stop at anything. Her coming here proves that. I don't believe there was a thing the matter with that automobile. I think that was a scheme she fixed up to get Phil where she could see him alone, as she worked to see you. If you are going deliberately to put Philip under her influence again, you've got to brace yourself for the possibility that she may win. A man is a weak mortal, where a lovely woman is concerned, and he never denied that he loved her once. You may make yourself downright miserable."

"But mother, if she won, it wouldn't make me half so miserable as to marry Phil myself, and then read hunger for her in his eyes! Some one has got to suffer over this. If it proves to be me, I'll bear it, and you'll never hear a whisper of complaint from me. I know the real Philip Ammon better in our months of work in the fields than she knows him in all her years of society engagements. So she shall have the hour she asked, many, many of them, enough to make her acknowledge that she is wrong. Now I am going to write my letters and take my walk."

Elnora threw her arms around her mother and kissed her repeatedly. "Don't you worry about me," she said. "I will get along all right, and whatever happens, I always will be your girl and you my darling mother."

She left two sealed notes on her desk. Then she changed her dress, packed a small bundle which she dropped with her hat from the window beside the willow, and softly went down stairs. Mrs. Comstock was in the garden. Elnora picked up the hat and bundle, hurried down the road a few rods, then climbed the fence and entered the woods. She took a diagonal course, and after a long walk reached a road two miles west and one south. There she straightened her clothing, put on her hat and a thin dark veil and waited the passing of the next trolley. She left it at the first town and took a train for Fort Wayne. She made that point just in time to climb on the evening train north, as it pulled from the station. It was after midnight when she left the car at

Grand Rapids, and went into the depot to await the coming of day.

Tired out, she laid her head on her bundle and fell asleep on a seat in the women's waiting-room. Long after light she was awakened by the roar and rattle of trains. She washed, re-arranged her hair and clothing, and went into the general waiting-room to find her way to the street. She saw him as he entered the door. There was no mistaking the tall, lithe figure, the bright hair, the lean, brown-splotched face, the steady gray eyes. He was dressed for travelling, and carried a light overcoat and a bag. Straight to him Elnora went speeding.

"Oh, I was just starting to find you!" she cried.

"Thank you!" he said.

"You are going away?" she panted.

"Not if I am needed. I have a few minutes. Can you be telling me briefly?"

"I am the Limberlost girl to whom your wife gave the dress for Commencement last spring, and both of you sent lovely gifts. There is a reason, a very good reason, why I must be hidden for a time, and I came straight to you—as if I had a right."

"You have!" answered Freckles. "Any boy or girl who ever suffered one pang in the Limberlost has a claim to the best drop of blood in my heart. You needn't be telling me anything more. The Angel is at our cottage on Mackinac. You shall tell her and play with the babies while you want shelter. This way!"

They breakfasted in a luxurious car, talked over the swamp, the work of the Bird Woman; Elnora told of her nature lectures in the schools, and soon they were good friends. In the evening they left the train at Mackinaw City and crossed the Straits by boat. Sheets of white moonlight flooded the water and paved a molten path across the breast of it straight to the face of the moon.

The island lay a dark spot on the silver surface, its tall trees sharply outlined on the summit, and a million lights blinked around the shore. The night guns boomed from the white fort and a dark sentinel paced the ramparts above the little city tucked down close to the water. A great tenor summering in the north came out on the upper deck of the big boat, and baring his head, faced the moon and sang: "Oh, the moon shines bright on my old Kentucky home!" Elnora thought of the Limberlost, of Philip, and her mother, and almost choked with the sobs that would arise in her throat. On the dock a woman of exquisite beauty swept into the arms of Terence O'More.

"Oh, Freckles!" she cried. "You've been gone a month!"

"Four days, Angel, only four days by the clock," remonstrated Freckles. "Where are the children?"

"Asleep! Thank goodness! I'm worn to a thread. I never saw such inventive, active children. I can't keep track of them!"

"I have brought you help," said Freckles. "Here is the Limberlost girl in whom the Bird Woman is interested. Miss Comstock needs a rest before beginning her school work for next year, so she came to us."

"You dear thing! How good of you!" cried the Angel. "We shall be so happy to have you!"

In her room that night, in a beautiful cottage furnished with every luxury, Elnora lifted a tired face to the Angel.

"Of course, you understand there is something back of this?" she said. "I must tell you."

"Yes," agreed the Angel. "Tell me! If you get it out of your system, you will stand a better chance of sleeping."

Elnora stood brushing the copper-bright masses of her hair as she talked. When she finished the Angel was almost hysterical.

"You insane creature!" she cried. "How crazy of you to leave him to her! I know both of them. I have met them often. She may be able to make good her boast. But it is perfectly splendid of you! And, after all, really it is the only way. I can see that. I think it is what I should have done myself, or tried to do. I don't know that I could have done it! When I think of walking away and leaving Freckles with a woman he once loved, to let her see if she can make him love her again, oh, it gives me a graveyard heart. No, I never could have done it! You are bigger than I ever was. I should have turned coward, sure."

"I am a coward," admitted Elnora. "I am soul-sick! I am afraid I shall lose my senses before this is over. I didn't want to come! I wanted to stay, to go straight into his arms, to bind myself with his ring, to love him with all my heart. It wasn't my fault that I came. There was something inside that just pushed me. She is beautiful——"

"I quite agree with you!"

"You can imagine how fascinating she can be. She used no arts on me. Her purpose was to cower me. She found she could not do that, but she did a thing which helped her more: she proved that she was honest, perfectly sincere in what she thought. She believes that if she merely beckons to Philip, he will go to her. So I am giving her the opportunity to learn from him what he will do. She never will believe it from any one else. When she is satisfied, I shall be also."

"But, child! Suppose she wins him back!"

"That is the supposition with which I shall eat and sleep for the coming few weeks. Would one dare ask for a peep at the babies before going to bed?"

"Now, you are perfect!" announced the Angel. "I never should have liked you all I can, if you had been content to go to sleep in this house without asking to see the babies. Come this way. We named the first boy for his father, of course, and the girl for Aunt Alice. The next boy is named for my father, and the baby for the Bird Woman. After this we are going to branch out."

Elnora began to laugh.

"Oh, I suspect there will be quite a number of them," said the Angel serenely. "I am told the more there are the less trouble they make. The big ones take care of the little ones. We want a large family. This is our start."

She entered a dark room and held aloft a candle. She went to the side of a small white iron bed in which lay a boy of eight and another of three. They were perfectly formed, rosy children, the elder a replica of his mother, the other very like. Then they came to a cradle where a baby girl of almost two slept soundly, and made a picture.

"But just see here!" said the Angel. She threw the light on a sleeping girl of six. A mass of red curls swept the pillow. Line and feature the face was that of Freckles. Without asking, Elnora knew the colour and expression of the closed eyes. The Angel handed Elnora the candle, and stooping, straightened the child's body. She ran her fingers through the bright curls, and lightly touched the aristocratic little nose.

"The supply of freckles holds out in my family, you see!" she said. "Both of the girls will have them, and the second boy a few."

She stood an instant longer, then bending, ran her hand caressingly down a rosy bare leg, while she kissed the babyish red mouth. There had been some reason for touching all of them, the kiss fell on the lips which were like Freckles's.

To Elnora she said a tender good-night, whispering brave words of encouragement and making plans to fill the days to come. Then she went away. An hour later there was a light tap on the girl's door.

"Come!" she called as she lay staring into the dark.

The Angel felt her way to the bedside, sat down and took Elnora's hands.

"I just had to come back to you," she said. "I have been telling Freckles, and he is almost hurting himself with laughing. I didn't think it was funny, but he does. He thinks it's the funniest thing that ever happened. He says that to run away from Mr. Ammon, when you had made him no promise at all, when he wasn't sure of you, won't send him home to her; it will set him hunting you! He says if you had combined the wisdom of Solomon, Socrates, and all the remainder of the wise men, you couldn't have chosen any course that would have sealed him to you so surely. He feels that now Mr. Ammon will perfectly hate her for coming down there and driving you away. And you went to give her the chance she wanted. Oh, Elnora! It is becoming funny! I see it, too!"

The Angel rocked on the bedside. Elnora faced the dark in silence.

"Forgive me," gulped the Angel. "I didn't mean to laugh. I didn't think it was funny, until all at once it came to me. Oh, dear! Elnora, it *is* funny! I've got to laugh!"

"Maybe it is," admitted Elnora "to others; but it isn't very funny to me. And it won't be to Philip, or to mother."

That was very true. Mrs. Comstock had been slightly prepared for stringent action of some kind, by what Elnora had said. The mother instantly had guessed where the girl would go, but nothing was said to Philip. That would have been to invalidate Elnora's test in the beginning, and Mrs. Comstock knew her child well enough to know that she never would marry Philip unless she felt it right that she should. The only way was to find out, and Elnora had gone to seek the information. There was nothing to do but wait until she came back, and her mother was not in the least uneasy but that the girl would return brave and self-reliant, as always.

Philip Ammon hurried back to the Limberlost, strong in the hope that now he might take Elnora into his arms and receive her promise to become his wife. His first shock of disappointment came when he found her gone. In talking with Mrs. Comstock he learned that Edith Carr had made an opportunity to speak with Elnora alone. He hastened down the road to meet her, coming back alone, an agitated man. Then search revealed the notes. His read:

DEAR PHILIP:

I find that I am never going to be able to answer your question of this afternoon fairly to all of us, when you are with me. So I am going away a few weeks to think over matters alone. I shall not tell you, or even mother, where I am going, but I shall be safe, well cared for, and happy. Please go back home and live among your friends, just as you always have done, and on or before the first of September, I will write you where I am, and what I have decided. Please do not blame Edith Carr for this, and do not avoid her. I hope you will call on her and be friends. I think she is very sorry, and covets your friendship at least. Until September, then, as ever,

ELNORA.

Mrs. Comstock's note was much the same. Philip was ill with disappointment. In the arbour he laid his head on the table, among the implements of Elnora's loved work, and gulped down dry sobs he could not restrain. Mrs. Comstock never had liked him so well. Her hand involuntarily crept toward his dark head, then she drew back. Elnora would not want her to do anything whatever to influence him.

"What am I going to do to convince Edith Carr that I do not love her, and Elnora that I am hers?" he demanded.

"I guess you have to figure that out yourself," said Mrs. Comstock. "I'd be glad to help you if I could, but it seems to be up to you."

Philip sat a long time in silence. "Well, I have decided!" he said abruptly. "Are you perfectly sure Elnora had plenty of money and a safe place to go?"

"Absolutely!" answered Mrs. Comstock. "She has been taking care of herself ever since she was born, and she always has come out all right, so far; I'll stake all I'm worth on it, that she always will. I don't know where she is, but I'm not going to worry about her safety."

"I can't help worrying!" cried Philip. "I can think of fifty things that may happen to her when she thinks she is safe. This is distracting! First, I am going to run up to see my father. Then, I'll let you know what we have decided. Is there anything I can do for you?"

"Nothing!" said Mrs. Comstock.

But the desire to do something for him was so strong with her she scarcely could keep her lips closed or her hands quiet. She longed to tell him what Edith Carr had said, how it had affected Elnora, and to comfort him as she felt she could. But loyalty to the girl held her. If Elnora truly felt that she could not decide until Edith Carr was convinced, then Edith Carr would have to yield or triumph. It rested with Philip. So Mrs. Comstock kept silent, while Philip took the night limited, a bitterly disappointed man.

By noon the next day he was in his father's offices. They had a long conference, but did not arrive at much until the elder Ammon suggested sending for Polly. Anything that might have happened could be explained after Polly had told of the private conference between Edith and Elnora.

"Talk about lovely woman!" cried Philip Ammon. "One would think that after such a dose as Edith gave me, she would be satisfied to let me go my way, but no! Not caring for me enough herself to save me from public disgrace, she must now pursue me to keep any other woman from loving me. I call that too much! I am going to see her, and I want you to go with me, father."

"Very well," said Mr. Ammon, "I will go."

When Edith Carr came into her reception-room that afternoon, gowned for conquest, she expected only Philip, and him penitent. She came hurrying toward him, smiling, radiant, ready to use every allurement she possessed, and paused in dismay when she saw his cold face and his father. "Why, Phil!" she cried. "When did you come home?"

"I am not at home," answered Philip. "I merely ran up to see my father on business, and to inquire of you what it was you said to Miss Comstock yesterday that caused her to disappear before I could return to the Limberlost."

"Miss Comstock disappear! Impossible!" cried Edith Carr. "Where could she go?"

"I thought perhaps you could answer that, since it was through you that she went."

"Phil, I haven't the faintest idea where she is," said the girl gently.

"But you know perfectly why she went! Kindly tell me that."

"Let me see you alone, and I will."

"Here and now, or not at all."

"Phil!"

"What did you say to the girl I love?"

Then Edith Carr stretched out her arms.

"Phil, I am the girl you love!" she cried. "All your life you have loved me. Surely it cannot be all gone in a few weeks of misunderstanding. I was jealous of her! I did not want you to leave me an instant that night for any other girl living. That was the moth I was representing. Every one knew it! I wanted you to bring it to me. When you did not, I knew instantly it had been for her that you worked last summer, she who suggested my dress, she who had power to take you from me, when I wanted you most. The thought drove me mad, and I said and did those insane things. Phil, I beg your pardon! I ask your forgiveness. Yesterday she said that you had told her of me at once. She vowed both of you had been true to me and Phil, I couldn't look into her eyes and not see that it was the truth. Oh, Phil, if you understood how I have suffered you would forgive me. Phil, I never knew how much I cared for you! I will do anything—anything!"

"Then tell me what you said to Elnora yesterday that drove her, alone and friendless, into the night, heaven knows where!"

"You have no thought for any one save her?"

"Yes," said Philip. "I have. Because I once loved you, and believed in you, my heart aches for you. I will gladly forgive anything you ask. I will do anything you want, except to resume our former relations. That is impossible. It is hopeless and useless to ask it."

"You truly mean that!"

"Yes."

"Then find out from her what I said!"

"Come, father," said Philip, rising.

"You were going to show Miss Comstock's letter to Edith!" suggested Mr. Ammon.

"I have not the slightest interest in Miss Comstock's letter," said Edith Carr.

"You are not even interested in the fact that she says you are not responsible for her going, and that I am to call on you and be friends with you?"

"That is interesting, indeed!" sneered Miss Carr.

She took the letter, read and returned it.

"She has done what she could for my cause, it seems," she said coldly. "How very generous of her! Do you propose calling out Pinkertons and instituting a general search?"

"No," replied Philip. "I simply propose to go back to the Limberlost and live with her mother, until Elnora becomes convinced that I am not courting you, and never shall be. Then, perhaps, she will come home to us. Good-bye. Good luck to you always!"

CHAPTER XXIV. WHEREIN EDITH CARR WAGES A BATTLE, AND HART HENDERSON STANDS GUARD

Many people looked, a few followed, when Edith Carr slowly came down the main street of Mackinac, pausing here and there to note the glow of colour in one small booth after another, overflowing with gay curios. That street of packed white sand, winding with the curves of the shore, outlined with brilliant shops, and thronged with laughing, bare-headed people in outing costumes was a picturesque and fascinating sight. Thousands annually made long journeys and paid exorbitant prices to take part in that pageant.

As Edith Carr passed, she was the most distinguished figure of the old street. Her clinging black gown was sufficiently elaborate for a dinner dress. On her head was a large, wide, drooping-brimmed black hat, with immense floating black plumes, while on the brim, and among the laces on her breast glowed velvety, deep red roses. Some way these made up for the lack of colour in her cheeks and lips, and while her eyes seemed unnaturally bright, to a close observer they appeared weary. Despite the effort she made to move lightly she was very tired, and dragged her heavy feet with an effort.

She turned at the little street leading to the dock, and went to meet the big lake steamer ploughing up the Straits from Chicago. Past the landing place, on to the very end of the pier she went, then sat down, leaned against a dock support and closed her tired eyes. When the steamer came very close she languidly watched the people lining the railing. Instantly she marked one lean anxious face turned toward hers, and with a throb of pity she lifted a hand and waved to

Hart Henderson. He was the first man to leave the boat, coming to her instantly. She spread her trailing skirts and motioned him to sit beside her. Silently they looked across the softly lapping water. At last she forced herself to speak to him.

"Did you have a successful trip?"

"I accomplished my purpose."

"You didn't lose any time getting back."

"I never do when I am coming to you."

"Do you want to go to the cottage for anything?"

"No."

"Then let us sit here and wait until the Petoskey steamer comes in. I like to watch the boats. Sometimes I study the faces, if I am not too tired."

"Have you seen any new types to-day?"

She shook her head. "This has not been an easy day, Hart."

"And it's going to be worse," said Henderson bitterly. "There's no use putting it off. Edith, I saw some one to-day."

"You should have seen thousands," she said lightly.

"I did. But of them all, only one will be of interest to you."

"Man or woman?"

"Man."

"Where?"

"Lake Shore private hospital."

"An accident?"

"No. Nervous and physical breakdown."

"Phil said he was going back to the Limberlost."

"He went. He was there three weeks, but the strain broke him. He has an old letter in his hands that he has handled until it is ragged. He held it up to me and said: 'You can see for yourself that she says she will be well and happy, but we can't know until we see her again, and that may never be. She may have gone too near that place her father went down, some of that Limberlost gang may have found her in the forest, she may lie dead in some city morgue this instant, waiting for me to find her body.'"

"Hart! For pity sake stop!"

"I can't," cried Henderson desperately. "I am forced to tell you. They are fighting brain fever. He did go back to the swamp and he prowled it night and day. The days down there are hot now, and the nights wet with dew and cold. He paid no attention and forgot his food. A fever started and his uncle brought him home. They've never had a word from her, or found a trace of her. Mrs. Comstock thought she had gone to O'Mores' at Great Rapids, so when Phil broke down she telegraphed there. They had been gone all summer, so her mother is as anxious as Phil."

"The O'Mores are here," said Edith. "I haven't seen any of them, because I haven't gone out much in the few days since we came, but this is their summer home."

"Edith, they say at the hospital that it will take careful nursing to save Phil. He is surrounded by stacks of maps and railroad guides. He is trying to frame up a plan to set the entire detective agency of the country to work. He says he will stay there just two days longer. The doctors say he will kill himself when he goes. He is a sick man, Edith. His hands are burning and shaky and his breath was hot against my face."

"Why are you telling me?" It was a cry of acute anguish.

"He thinks you know where she is."

"I do not! I haven't an idea! I never dreamed she would go away when she had him in her hand! I should not have done it!"

"He said it was something you said to her that made her go."

"That may be, but it doesn't prove that I know where she went."

Henderson looked across the water and suffered keenly. At last he turned to Edith and laid a firm, strong hand over hers.

"Edith," he said, "do you realize how serious this is?"

"I suppose I do."

"Do you want as fine a fellow as Philip driven any further? If he leaves that hospital now, and goes out to the exposure and anxiety of a search for her, there will be a tragedy that no after regrets can avert. Edith, what did you say to Miss Comstock that made her run away from Phil?"

The girl turned her face from him and sat still, but the man gripping her hands and waiting in agony could see that she was shaken by the jolting of the heart in her breast.

"Edith, what did you say?"

"What difference can it make?"

"It might furnish some clue to her action."

"It could not possibly."

"Phil thinks so. He has thought so until his brain is worn enough to give way. Tell me, Edith!"

"I told her Phil was mine! That if he were away from her an hour and back in my presence, he would be to me as he always has been."

"Edith, did you believe that?"

"I would have staked my life, my soul on it!"

"Do you believe it now?"

There was no answer. Henderson took her other hand and holding both of them firmly he said softly: "Don't mind me, dear. I don't count! I'm just old Hart! You can tell me anything. Do you still believe that?"

The beautiful head barely moved in negation. Henderson gathered both her hands in one of his and stretched an arm across her shoulders to the post to support her. She dragged her hands from him and twisted them together.

"Oh, Hart!" she cried. "It isn't fair! There is a limit! I have suffered my share. Can't you see? Can't you understand?"

"Yes," he panted. "Yes, my girl! Tell me just this one thing yet, and I'll cheerfully kill any one who annoys you further. Tell me, Edith!"

Then she lifted her big, dull, pain-filled eyes to his and cried: "No! I do not believe it now! I know it is not true! I killed his love for me. It is dead and gone forever. Nothing will revive it! Nothing in all this world. And that is not all. I did not know how to touch the depths of his nature. I never developed in him those things he was made to enjoy. He admired me. He was proud to be with me. He thought, and I thought, that he worshipped me; but I know now that he never did care for me as he cares for her. Never! I can see it! I planned to lead society, to make his home a place sought for my beauty and popularity. She plans to advance his political ambitions, to make him comfortable physically, to stimulate his intellect, to bear him a brood of red-faced children. He likes her and her plans as he never did me and mine. Oh, my soul! Now, are you satisfied?"

She dropped back against his arm exhausted. Henderson held her and learned what suffering truly means. He fanned her with his hat, rubbed her cold hands and murmured broken, incoherent things. By and by slow tears slipped from under her closed lids, but when she opened them her eyes were dull and hard.

"What a rag one is when the last secret of the soul is torn out and laid bare!" she cried.

Henderson thrust his handkerchief into her fingers and whispered, "Edith, the boat has been creeping up. It's very close. Maybe some of our crowd are on it. Hadn't we better slip away from here before it lands?"

"If I can walk," she said. "Oh, I am so dead tired, Hart!

"Yes, dear," said Henderson soothingly. "Just try to pass the landing before the boat anchors. If I only dared carry you!"

They struggled through the waiting masses, but directly opposite the landing there was a backward movement in the happy, laughing crowd, the gang-plank came down with a slam, and people began hurrying from the boat. Crowded against the fish house on the dock, Henderson could only advance a few steps at a time. He was straining every nerve to protect and assist Edith. He saw no one he recognized near them, so he slipped his arm across her back to help support her. He felt her stiffen against him and catch her breath. At the same instant, the clearest, sweetest male voice he ever had heard called: "Be careful there, little men!"

Henderson sent a swift glance toward the boat. Terence O'More had stepped from the gang-plank, leading a little daughter, so like him, it was comical. There followed a picture not easy to describe. The Angel in the full flower of her beauty, richly dressed, a laugh on her cameo face, the setting sun glinting on her gold hair, escorted by her eldest son, who held her hand tightly and carefully watched her steps. Next came Elnora, dressed with equal richness, a trifle taller and slenderer, almost the same type of colouring, but with different eyes and hair, facial lines and expression. She was led by the second O'More boy who convulsed the crowd by saying: "Tareful, Elnora! Don't 'oo be 'teppin' in de water!"

People surged around them, purposely closing them in.

"What lovely women! Who are they? It's the O'Mores. The lightest one is his wife. Is that her sister? No, it is his! They say he has a title in England."

Whispers ran fast and audible. As the crowd pressed around the party an opening was left beside the fish sheds. Edith ran down the dock. Henderson sprang after her, catching her arm and assisting her to the street.

"Up the shore! This way!" she panted. "Every one will go to dinner the first thing they do."

They left the street and started around the beach, but Edith was breathless from running, while the yielding sand made difficult walking.

"Help me!" she cried, clinging to Henderson. He put his arm around her, almost carrying her from sight into a little cove walled by high rocks at the back, while there was a clean floor of white sand, and logs washed from the lake for seats. He found one of these with a back rest, and hurrying down to the water he soaked his handkerchief and carried it to her. She passed it across her lips, over her eyes, and then pressed the palms of her hands upon it. Henderson removed the heavy hat, fanned her with his, and wet the handkerchief again.

"Hart, what makes you?" she said wearily. "My mother doesn't care. She says this is good for me. Do you think this is good for me, Hart?"

"Edith, you know I would give my life if I could save you this," he said, and could not speak further.

She leaned against him, closed her eyes and lay silent so long the man fell into panic.

"Edith, you are not unconscious?" he whispered, touching her.

"No, just resting. Please don't leave me."

He held her carefully, gently fanning her. She was suffering almost more than either of them could endure.

"I wish you had your boat," she said at last. "I want to sail with the wind in my face."

"There is no wind. I can bring my motor around in a few minutes."

"Then get it."

"Lie on the sand. I can 'phone from the first booth. It won't take but a little while."

Edith lay on the white sand, and Henderson covered her face with her hat. Then he ran to the nearest booth and talked imperatively. Presently he was back bringing a hot drink that was stimulating. Shortly the motor ran close to the beach and stopped. Henderson's servant brought a row-boat ashore and took them to the launch. It was filled with cushions and wraps. Henderson made a couch and soon, warmly covered, Edith sped out over the water in search of peace.

Hour after hour the boat ran up and down the shore. The moon arose and the night air grew very chilly. Henderson put on an overcoat and piled more covers on Edith.

"You must take me home," she said at last. "The folks will be uneasy."

He was compelled to take her to the cottage with the battle still raging. He went back early the next morning, but already she had wandered out over the island. Instinctively Henderson felt that the shore would attract her. There was something in the tumult of rough little Huron's waves that called to him. It was there he found her, crouching so close the water the foam was dampening her skirts.

"May I stay?" he asked.

"I have been hoping you would come," she answered. "It's bad enough when you are here, but it is a little easier than bearing it alone."

"Thank God for that!" said Henderson sitting beside her. "Shall I talk to you?"

She shook her head. So they sat by the hour. At last she spoke: "Of course, you know there is something I have got to do, Hart!"

"You have not!" cried Henderson, violently. "That's all nonsense! Give me just one word of permission. That is all that is required of you."

"'Required?' You grant, then, that there is something 'required?'"

"One word. Nothing more."

"Did you ever know one word could be so big, so black, so desperately bitter? Oh, Hart!"

"No."

"But you know it now, Hart!"

"Yes."

"And still you say that it is 'required?'"

Henderson suffered unspeakably. At last he said: "If you had seen and heard him, Edith, you, too, would feel that it is 'required.' Remember——"

"No! No! No!" she cried. "Don't ask me to remember even the least of my pride and folly. Let me forget!"

She sat silent for a long time.

"Will you go with me?" she whispered.

"Of course."

At last she arose.

"I might as well give up and have it over," she faltered.

That was the first time in her life that Edith Carr ever had proposed to give up anything she wanted.

"Help me, Hart!"

Henderson started around the beach assisting her all he could. Finally he stopped.

"Edith, there is no sense in this! You are too tired to go. You know you can trust me. You wait in any of these lovely places and send me. You will be safe, and I'll run. One word is all that is necessary."

"But I've got to say that word myself, Hart!"

"Then write it, and let me carry it. The message is not going to prove who went to the office and sent it."

"That is quite true," she said, dropping wearily, but she made no movement to take the pen and paper he offered.

"Hart, you write it," she said at last.

Henderson turned away his face. He gripped the pen, while his breath sucked between his dry teeth.

"Certainly!" he said when he could speak. "Mackinac, August 27, 1908. Philip Ammon, Lake Shore Hospital, Chicago." He paused with suspended pen and glanced at Edith. Her white lips were working, but no sound came. "Miss Comstock is with the Terence O'Mores, on Mackinac Island," prompted Henderson.

Edith nodded.

"Signed, Henderson," continued the big man.

Edith shook her head.

"Say, 'She is well and happy,' and sign, Edith Carr!" she panted.

"Not on your life!" flashed Henderson.

"For the love of mercy, Hart, don't make this any harder! It is the least I can do, and it takes every ounce of strength in me to do it."

"Will you wait for me here?" he asked.

She nodded, and, pulling his hat lower over his eyes, Henderson ran around the shore. In less than an hour he was back. He helped her a little farther to where the Devil's Kitchen lay cut into the rocks; it furnished places to rest, and cool water. Before long his man came with the boat. From it they spread blankets on the sand for her, and made chafing-dish tea. She tried to refuse it, but the fragrance overcame her for she drank ravenously. Then Henderson cooked several dishes and spread an appetizing lunch. She was young, strong, and almost famished for food. She was forced to eat. That made her feel much better. Then Henderson helped her into the boat and ran it through shady coves of the shore, where there were refreshing breezes. When she fell asleep the girl did not know, but the man did. Sadly in need of rest himself, he ran that boat for five hours through quiet bays, away from noisy parties, and where the shade was cool and deep. When she awoke he took her home, and as they went she knew that she had been mistaken. She would not die. Her heart was not even broken. She had suffered horribly; she would suffer more; but eventually the pain must wear out. Into her head crept a few lines of an old opera:

"Hearts do not break, they sting and ache,

For old love's sake, but do not die,
As witnesseth the living I."

That evening they were sailing down the Straits before a stiff breeze and Henderson was busy with the tiller when she said to him: "Hart, I want you to do something more for me."

"You have only to tell me," he said.

"Have I only to tell you, Hart?" she asked softly.

"Haven't you learned that yet, Edith?"

"I want you to go away."

"Very well," he said quietly, but his face whitened visibly.

"You say that as if you had been expecting it."

"I have. I knew from the beginning that when this was over you would dislike me for having seen you suffer. I have grown my Gethsemane in a full realization of what was coming, but I could not leave you, Edith, so long as it seemed to me that I was serving you. Does it make any difference to you where I go?"

"I want you where you will be loved, and good care taken of you."

"Thank you!" said Henderson, smiling grimly. "Have you any idea where such a spot might be found?"

"It should be with your sister at Los Angeles. She always has seemed very fond of you."

"That is quite true," said Henderson, his eyes brightening a little. "I will go to her. When shall I start?"

"At once."

Henderson began to tack for the landing, but his hands shook until he scarcely could manage the boat. Edith Carr sat watching him indifferently, but her heart was throbbing painfully. "Why is there so much suffering in the world?" she kept whispering to herself. Inside her door Henderson took her by the shoulders almost roughly.

"For how long is this, Edith, and how are you going to say good-bye to me?"

She raised tired, pain-filled eyes to his.

"I don't know for how long it is," she said. "It seems now as if it had been a slow eternity. I wish to my soul that God would be merciful to me and make something 'snap' in my heart, as there did in Phil's, that would give me rest. I don't know for how long, but I'm perfectly shameless with you, Hart. If peace ever comes and I want you, I won't wait for you to find it out yourself, I'll cable, Marconigraph, anything. As for how I say good-bye; any way you please, I don't care in the least what happens to me."

Henderson studied her intently.

"In that case, we will shake hands," he said. "Good-bye, Edith. Don't forget that every hour I am thinking of you and hoping all good things will come to you soon."

CHAPTER XXV. WHEREIN PHILIP FINDS ELNORA, AND EDITH CARR OFFERS A YELLOW EMPEROR

"Oh, I need my own violin," cried Elnora. "This one may be a thousand times more expensive, and much older than mine; but it wasn't inspired and taught to sing by a man who knew how. It doesn't know 'beans,' as mother would say, about the Limberlost."

The guests in the O'More music-room laughed appreciatively.

"Why don't you write your mother to come for a visit and bring yours?" suggested Freckles.

"I did that three days ago," acknowledged Elnora. "I am half expecting her on the noon boat. That is one reason why this violin grows worse every minute. There is nothing at all the matter with me."

"Splendid!" cried the Angel. "I've begged and begged her to do it. I know how anxious these mothers become. When did you send? What made you? Why didn't you tell me?"

"'When?' Three days ago. 'What made me?' You. 'Why didn't I tell you?' Because I can't be sure in the least that she will come. Mother is the most individual person. She never does what every one expects she will. She may not come, and I didn't want you to be disappointed."

"How did I make you?" asked the Angel.

"Loving Alice. It made me realize that if you cared for your girl like that, with Mr. O'More and three other children, possibly my mother, with no one, might like to see me. I know I want to see her, and you had told me to so often, I just sent for her. Oh, I do hope she comes! I want her to see this lovely place."

"I have been wondering what you thought of Mackinac," said Freckles.

"Oh, it is a perfect picture, all of it! I should like to hang it on the wall, so I could see it whenever I wanted to; but it isn't real, of course; it's nothing but a picture."

"These people won't agree with you," smiled Freckles.

"That isn't necessary," retorted Elnora. "They know this, and they love it; but you and I are acquainted with something different. The Limberlost is life. Here it is a carefully kept park. You motor, sail, and golf, all so secure and fine. But what I like is the excitement of choosing a path carefully, in the fear that the quagmire may reach out and suck me down; to go into the swamp naked-handed and wrest from it treasures that bring me books and clothing, and I like enough of a fight for things that I always remember how I got them. I even enjoy seeing a canny old vulture eyeing me as if it were saying: 'Ware the sting of the rattler, lest I pick your bones as I did old Limber's.' I like sufficient danger to put an edge on life. This is so tame. I should have loved it when all the homes were cabins, and watchers for the stealthy Indian canoes patrolled the shores. You wait until mother comes, and if my violin isn't angry with me for leaving it, to-night we shall sing you the Song of the Limberlost. You shall hear the big gold bees over the red, yellow, and purple flowers, bird song, wind talk, and the whispers of Sleepy Snake Creek, as it goes past you. You will know!" Elnora turned to Freckles.

He nodded. "Who better?" he asked. "This is secure while the children are so small, but when they grow larger, we are going farther north, into real forest, where they can learn self-reliance and develop backbone."

Elnora laid away the violin. "Come along, children," she said. "We must get at that backbone business at once. Let's race to the playhouse."

With the brood at her heels Elnora ran, and for an hour lively sounds stole from the remaining spot of forest on the Island, which lay beside the O'More cottage. Then Terry went to the playroom to bring Alice her doll. He came racing back, dragging it by one leg, and crying:

"There's company! Someone has come that mamma and papa are just tearing down the house over. I saw through the window."

"It could not be my mother, yet," mused Elnora. "Her boat is not due until twelve. Terry, give Alice that doll——"

"It's a man-person, and I don't know him, but my father is shaking his hand right straight along, and my mother is running for a hot drink and a cushion. It's a kind of a sick person, but they are going to make him well right away, any one can see that. This is the best place.

"I'll go tell him to come lie on the pine needles in the sun and watch the sails go by. That will fix him!"

"Watch sails go by," chanted Little Brother. "'A fix him! Elnora fix him, won't you?"

"I don't know about that," answered Elnora. "What sort of person is he, Terry?"

"A beautiful white person; but my father is going to 'colour him up,' I heard him say so. He's just out of the hospital, and he is a bad person, 'cause he ran away from the doctors and made them awful angry. But father and mother are going to doctor him better. I didn't know they could make sick people well."

"'Ey do anyfing!" boasted Little Brother.

Before Elnora missed her, Alice, who had gone to investigate, came flying across the shadows and through the sunshine waving a paper. She thurst it into Elnora's hand.

"There is a man-person—a stranger-person!" she shouted. "But he knows you! He sent you that! You are to be the doctor! He said so! Oh, do hurry! I like him heaps!"

Elnora read Edith Carr's telegram to Philip Ammon and understood that he had been ill, that she had been located by Edith who had notified him. In so doing she had acknowledged defeat. At last Philip was free. Elnora looked up with a radiant face.

"I like him 'heaps' myself!" she cried. "Come on children, we will go tell him so."

Terry and Alice ran, but Elnora had to suit her steps to Little Brother, who was her loyal esquire, and would have been heartbroken over desertion and insulted at being carried. He was rather dragged, but he was arriving, and the emergency was great, he could see that.

"She's coming!" shouted Alice.

"She's going to be the doctor!" cried Terry.

"She looked just like she'd seen angels when she read the letter," explained Alice.

"She likes you 'heaps!' She said so!" danced Terry. "Be waiting! Here she is!"

Elnora helped Little Brother up the steps, then deserted him and came at a rush. The stranger-person stood holding out trembling arms.

"Are you sure, at last, runaway?" asked Philip Ammon.

"Perfectly sure!" cried Elnora.

"Will you marry me now?"

"This instant! That is, any time after the noon boat comes in."

"Why such unnecessary delay?" demanded Ammon.

"It is almost September," explained Elnora. "I sent for mother three days ago. We must wait until she comes, and we either have to send for Uncle Wesley and Aunt Margaret, or go to them. I couldn't possibly be married properly without those dear people."

"We will send," decided Ammon. "The trip will be a treat for them. O'More, would you get off a message at once?"

Every one met the noon boat. They went in the motor because Philip was too weak to walk so far. As soon as people could be distinguished at all Elnora and Philip sighted an erect figure, with a head like a snowdrift. When the gang-plank fell the first person across it was a lean, red-haired boy of eleven, carrying a violin in one hand and an enormous bouquet of yellow marigolds and purple asters in the other. He was beaming with broad smiles until he saw Philip. Then his expression changed.

"Aw, say!" he exclaimed reproachfully. "I bet you Aunt Margaret is right. He is going to be your beau!"

Elnora stooped to kiss Billy as she caught her mother.

"There, there!" cried Mrs. Comstock. "Don't knock my headgear into my eye. I'm not sure I've got either hat or hair. The wind blew like bizzem coming up the river."

She shook out her skirts, straightened her hat, and came forward to meet Philip, who took her into his arms and kissed her repeatedly. Then he passed her along to Freckles and the Angel to whom her greetings were mingled with scolding and laughter over her wind-blown hair.

"No doubt I'm a precious spectacle!" she said to the Angel. "I saw your pa a little before I started, and he sent you a note. It's in my satchel. He said he was coming up next week. What a lot of people there are in this world! And what on earth are all of them laughing about? Did none of them ever hear of sickness, or sorrow, or death? Billy, don't you go to playing Indian or chasing woodchucks until you get out of those clothes. I promised Margaret I'd bring back that suit good as new."

Then the O'More children came crowding to meet Elnora's mother.

"Merry Christmas!" cried Mrs. Comstock, gathering them in. "Got everything right here but the tree, and there seems to be plenty of them a little higher up. If this wind would stiffen just enough more to blow away the people, so one could see this place, I believe it would be right decent looking."

"See here," whispered Elnora to Philip. "You must fix this with Billy. I can't have his trip spoiled."

"Now, here is where I dust the rest of 'em!" complacently remarked Mrs. Comstock, as she climbed into the motor car for her first ride, in company with Philip and Little Brother. "I have been the one to trudge the roads and hop out of the way of these things for quite a spell."

She sat very erect as the car rolled into the broad main avenue, where only stray couples were walking. Her eyes began to twinkle and gleam. Suddenly she leaned forward and touched the driver on the shoulder.

"Young man," she said, "just you toot that horn suddenly and shave close enough a few of those people, so that I can see how I look when I leap for ragweed and snake fences."

The amazed chauffeur glanced questioningly at Philip who slightly nodded. A second later there was a quick "honk!" and a swerve at a corner. A man engrossed in conversation grabbed the woman to whom he was talking and dashed for the safety of a lawn. The woman tripped in her skirts, and as she fell the man caught and dragged her. Both of them turned red faces to the car and berated the driver. Mrs. Comstock laughed in unrestrained enjoyment. Then she touched the chauffeur again.

"That's enough," she said. "It seems a mite risky." A minute later she added to Philip, "If only they had been carrying six pounds of butter and ten dozen eggs apiece, wouldn't that have been just perfect?"

Billy had wavered between Elnora and the motor, but his loyal little soul had been true to her, so the walk to the cottage began with him at her side. Long before they arrived the little O'Mores had crowded around and captured Billy, and he was giving them an expurgated version of Mrs. Comstock's tales of Big Foot and Adam Poe, boasting that Uncle Wesley had been in the camps of Me-shin-go-me-sia and knew Wa-ca-co-nah before he got religion and dressed like white men; while the mighty prowess of Snap as a woodchuck hunter was done full justice. When they reached the cottage Philip took Billy aside, showed him the emerald ring and gravely asked his permission to marry Elnora. Billy struggled to be just, but it was going hard with him, when Alice, who kept close enough to hear, intervened.

"Why don't you let them get married?" she asked. "You are much too small for her. You wait for me!"

Billy studied her intently. At last he turned to Ammon. "Aw, well! Go on, then!" he said gruffly. "I'll marry Alice!"

Alice reached her hand. "If you got that settled let's put on our Indian clothes, call the boys, and go to the playhouse."

"I haven't got any Indian clothes," said Billy ruefully.

"Yes, you have," explained Alice. "Father bought you some coming from the dock. You can put them on in the playhouse. The boys do."

Billy examined the playhouse with gleaming eyes.

Never had he encountered such possibilities. He could see a hundred amusing things to try, and he could not decide which to do first. The most immediate attraction seemed to be a dead pine, held perpendicularly by its fellows, while its bark had decayed and fallen, leaving a bare, smooth trunk.

"If we just had some grease that would make the dandiest pole to play Fourth of July with!" he shouted.

The children remembered the Fourth. It had been great fun.

"Butter is grease. There is plenty in the 'frigerator," suggested Alice, speeding away.

Billy caught the cold roll and began to rub it against the tree excitedly.

"How are you going to get it greased to the top?" inquired Terry.

Billy's face lengthened. "That's so!" he said. "The thing is to begin at the top and grease down. I'll show you!"

Billy put the butter in his handkerchief and took the corners between his teeth. He climbed the pole, greasing it as he slid down.

"Now, I got to try first," he said, "because I'm the biggest and so I have the best chance; only the one that goes first hasn't hardly any chance at all, because he has to wipe off the grease on himself, so the others can get up at last. See?"

"All right!" said Terry. "You go first and then I will and then Alice. Phew! It's slick. He'll never get up."

Billy wrestled manfully, and when he was exhausted he boosted Terry, and then both of them helped Alice, to whom they awarded a prize of her own doll. As they rested Billy remembered.

"Do your folks keep cows?" he asked.

"No, we buy milk," said Terry.

"Gee! Then what about the butter? Maybe your ma needs it for dinner!"

"No, she doesn't!" cried Alice. "There's stacks of it! I can have all the butter I want."

"Well, I'm mighty glad of it!" said Billy. "I didn't just think. I'm afraid we've greased our clothes, too."

"That's no difference," said Terry. "We can play what we please in these things."

"Well, we ought to be all dirty, and bloody, and have feathers on us to be real Indians," said Billy.

Alice tried a handful of dirt on her sleeve and it streaked beautifully. Instantly all of them began smearing themselves.

"If we only had feathers," lamented Billy.

Terry disappeared and shortly returned from the garage with a feather duster. Billy fell on it with a shriek. Around each one's head he firmly tied a twisted handkerchief, and stuck inside it a row of stiffly upstanding feathers.

"Now, if we just only had some pokeberries to paint us red, we'd be real, for sure enough Indians, and we could go on the warpath and fight all the other tribes and burn a lot of them at the stake."

Alice sidled up to him. "Would huckleberries do?" she asked softly.

"Yes!" shouted Terry, wild with excitement. "Anything that's a colour."

Alice made another trip to the refrigerator. Billy crushed the berries in his hands and smeared and streaked all their faces liberally.

"Now are we ready?" asked Alice.

Billy collapsed. "I forgot the ponies! You got to ride ponies to go on the warpath!"

"You ain't neither!" contradicted Terry. "It's the very latest style to go on the warpath in a motor. Everybody does! They go everywhere in them. They are much faster and better than any old ponies."

Billy gave one genuine whoop. "Can we take your motor?"

Terry hesitated.

"I suppose you are too little to run it?" said Billy.

"I am not!" flashed Terry. "I know how to start and stop it, and I drive lots for Stephens. It is hard to turn over the engine when you start."

"I'll turn it," volunteered Billy. "I'm strong as anything."

"Maybe it will start without. If Stephens has just been running it, sometimes it will. Come on, let's try."

Billy straightened up, lifted his chin and cried: "Houpe! Houpe! Houpe!"

The little O'Mores stared in amazement.

"Why don't you come on and whoop?" demanded Billy. "Don't you know how? You are great Indians! You got to whoop before you go on the warpath. You ought to kill a bat, too, and see if the wind is right. But maybe the engine won't run if we wait to do that. You can whoop, anyway. All together now!"

They did whoop, and after several efforts the cry satisfied Billy, so he led the way to the big motor, and took the front seat with Terry. Alice and Little Brother climbed into the back.

"Will it go?" asked Billy, "or do we have to turn it?"

"It will go," said Terry as the machine gently slid out into the avenue and started under his guidance.

"This is no warpath!" scoffed Billy. "We got to go a lot faster than this, and we got to whoop. Alice, why don't you whoop?"

Alice arose, took hold of the seat in front and whooped.

"If I open the throttle, I can't squeeze the bulb to scare people out of our way," said Terry. "I can't steer and squeeze, too."

"We'll whoop enough to get them out of the way. Go faster!" urged Billy.

Billy also stood, lifted his chin and whooped like the wildest little savage that ever came out of the West. Alice and Little Brother added their voices, and when he was not absorbed with the steering gear, Terry joined in.

"Faster!" shouted Billy.

Intoxicated with the speed and excitement, Terry threw the throttle wider and the big car leaped forward and sped down the avenue. In it four black, feather-bedecked children whooped in wild glee until suddenly Terry's war cry changed to a scream of panic.

"The lake is coming!"

"Stop!" cried Billy. "Stop! Why don't you stop?"

Paralyzed with fear Terry clung to the steering gear and the car sped onward.

"You little fool! Why don't you stop?" screamed Billy, catching Terry's arm. "Tell me how to stop!"

A bicycle shot beside them and Freckles standing on the pedals shouted: "Pull out the pin in that little circle at your feet!"

Billy fell on his knees and tugged and the pin yielded at last. Just as the wheels struck the white sand the bicycle sheered close, Freckles caught the lever and with one strong shove set the brake. The water flew as the car struck Huron, but luckily it was shallow and the beach smooth. Hub deep the big motor stood quivering as Freckles climbed in and backed it to dry sand.

Then he drew a deep breath and stared at his brood.

"Terence, would you kindly be explaining?" he said at last.

Billy looked at the panting little figure of Terry.

"I guess I better," he said. "We were playing Indians on the warpath, and we hadn't any ponies, and Terry said it was all the style to go in automobiles now, so we——"

Freckles's head went back, and he did some whooping himself.

"I wonder if you realize how nearly you came to being four drowned children?" he said gravely, after a time.

"Oh, I think I could swim enough to get most of us out," said Billy. "Anyway, we need washing."

"You do indeed," said Freckles. "I will head this procession to the garage, and there we will remove the first coat." For the remainder of Billy's visit the nurse, chauffeur, and every servant of the O'More household had something of importance on their minds, and Billy's every step was shadowed.

"I have Billy's consent," said Philip to Elnora, "and all the other consent you have stipulated. Before you think of something more, give me your left hand, please."

Elnora gave it gladly, and the emerald slipped on her finger. Then they went together into the forest to tell each other all about it, and talk it over.

"Have you seen Edith?" asked Philip.

"No," answered Elnora. "But she must be here, or she may have seen me when we went to Petoskey a few days ago. Her people have a cottage over on the bluff, but the Angel never told me until to-day. I didn't want to make that trip, but the folks were so anxious to entertain me, and it was only a few days until I intended to let you know myself where I was."

"And I was going to wait just that long, and if I didn't hear then I was getting ready to turn over the country. I can scarcely realize yet that Edith sent me that telegram."

"No wonder! It's a difficult thing to believe. I can't express how I feel for her."

"Let us never speak of it again," said Philip. "I came nearer feeling sorry for her last night than I have yet. I couldn't sleep on that boat coming over, and I couldn't put away the thought of what sending that message cost her. I never would have believed it possible that she would do it. But it is done. We will forget it."

"I scarcely think I shall," said Elnora. "It is something I like to remember. How suffering must have changed her! I would give anything to bring her peace."

"Henderson came to see me at the hospital a few days ago. He's gone a rather wild pace, but if he had been held from youth by the love of a good woman he might have lived differently. There are things about him one cannot help admiring."

"I think he loves her," said Elnora softly.

"He does! He always has! He never made any secret of it. He will cut in now and do his level best, but he told me that he thought she would send him away. He understands her thoroughly."

Edith Carr did not understand herself. She went to her room after her good-bye to Henderson, lay on her bed and tried to think why she was suffering as she was.

"It is all my selfishness, my unrestrained temper, my pride in my looks, my ambition to be first," she said. "That is what has caused this trouble."

Then she went deeper.

"How does it happen that I am so selfish, that I never controlled my temper, that I thought beauty and social position the vital things of life?" she muttered. "I think that goes a little past me. I think a mother who allows a child to grow up as I did, who educates it only for the frivolities of life, has a share in that child's ending. I think my mother has some responsibility in this," Edith Carr whispered to the night. "But she will recognize none. She would laugh at me if I tried to tell her what I have suffered and the bitter, bitter lesson I have learned. No one really cares, but Hart. I've sent him away, so there is no one! No one!"

Edith pressed her fingers across her burning eyes and lay still.

"He is gone!" she whispered at last. "He would go at once. He would not see me again. I should think he never would want to see me any more. But I will want to see him! My soul! I want him now! I want him every minute! He is all I have. And I've sent him away. Oh, these dreadful days to come, alone! I can't bear it. Hart! Hart!" she cried aloud. "I want you! No one cares but you. No one understands but you. Oh, I want you!"

She sprang from her bed and felt her way to her desk.

"Get me some one at the Henderson cottage," she said to Central, and waited shivering.

"They don't answer."

"They are there! You must get them. Turn on the buzzer."

After a time the sleepy voice of Mrs. Henderson answered.

"Has Hart gone?" panted Edith Carr.

"No! He came in late and began to talk about starting to California. He hasn't slept in weeks to amount to anything. I put him to bed. There is time enough to start to California when he awakens. Edith, what are you planning to do next with that boy of mine?"

"Will you tell him I want to see him before he goes?"

"Yes, but I won't wake him."

"I don't want you to. Just tell him in the morning."

"Very well."

"You will be sure?"

"Sure!"

Hart was not gone. Edith fell asleep. She arose at noon the next day, took a cold bath, ate her breakfast, dressed carefully, and leaving word that she had gone to the forest, she walked slowly across the leaves. It was cool and quiet there, so she sat where she could see him coming, and waited. She was thinking deep and fast.

Henderson came swiftly down the path. A long sleep, food, and Edith's message had done him good. He had dressed in new light flannels that were becoming. Edith arose and went to meet him.

"Let us walk in the forest," she said.

They passed the old Catholic graveyard, and entered the deepest wood of the Island, where all shadows were green, all voices of humanity ceased, and there was no sound save the whispering of the trees, a few bird notes and squirrel rustle. There Edith seated herself on a mossy old log, and Henderson studied her. He could detect a change. She was still pale and her eyes tired, but the dull, strained look was gone. He wanted to hope, but he did not dare. Any other man would have forced her to speak. The mighty tenderness in Henderson's heart shielded her in every way.

"What have you thought of that you wanted yet, Edith?" he asked lightly as he stretched himself at her feet.

"You!"

Henderson lay tense and very still.

"Well, I am here!"

"Thank Heaven for that!"

Henderson sat up suddenly, leaning toward her with questioning eyes. Not knowing what he dared say, afraid of the hope which found birth in his heart, he tried to shield her and at the same time to feel his way.

"I am more thankful than I can express that you feel so," he said. "I would be of use, of comfort, to you if I knew how, Edith."

"You are my only comfort," she said. "I tried to send you away. I thought I didn't want you. I thought I couldn't bear the sight of you, because of what you have seen me suffer. But I went to the root of this thing last night, Hart, and with self in mind, as usual, I found that I could not live without you."

Henderson began breathing lightly. He was afraid to speak or move.

"I faced the fact that all this is my own fault," continued Edith, "and came through my own selfishness. Then I went farther back and realized that I am as I was reared. I don't want to blame my parents, but I was carefully trained into what I am. If Elnora Comstock had been like me, Phil would have come back to me. I can see how selfish I seem to him, and how I appear to you, if you would admit it."

"Edith," said Henderson desperately, "there is no use to try to deceive you. You have known from the first that I found you wrong in this. But it's the first time in your life I ever thought you wrong about anything—and it's the only time I ever shall. Understand, I think you the bravest, most beautiful woman on earth, the one most worth loving."

"I'm not to be considered in the same class with her."

"I don't grant that, but if I did, you, must remember how I compare with Phil. He's my superior at every point. There's no use in discussing that. You wanted to see me, Edith. What did you want?"

"I wanted you to not go away."

"Not at all?"

"Not at all! Not ever! Not unless you take me with you, Hart."

She slightly extended one hand to him. Henderson took that hand, kissing it again and again.

"Anything you want, Edith," he said brokenly. "Just as you wish it. Do you want me to stay here, and go on as we have been?"

"Yes, only with a difference."

"Can you tell me, Edith?"

"First, I want you to know that you are the dearest thing on earth to me, right now. I would give up everything else, before I would you. I can't honestly say that I love you with the love you deserve. My heart is too sore. It's too soon to know. But I love you some way. You are necessary to me. You are my comfort, my shield. If you want me, as you know me to be, Hart, you may consider me yours. I give you my word of honour I will try to be as you would have me, just as soon as I can."

Henderson kissed her hand passionately. "Don't, Edith," he begged. "Don't say those things. I can't bear it. I understand. Everything will come right in time. Love like mine must bring a reward. You will love me some day. I can wait. I am the most patient fellow."

"But I must say it," cried Edith. "I—I think, Hart, that I have been on the wrong road to find happiness. I planned to finish life as I started it with Phil; and you see how glad he was to change. He wanted the other sort of girl far more than he ever wanted me. And you, Hart, honest, now—I'll know if you don't tell me the truth! Would you rather have a wife as I planned to live life with Phil, or would you rather have her as Elnora Comstock intends to live with him?"

"Edith!" cried the man, "Edith!"

"Of course, you can't say it in plain English," said the girl. "You are far too chivalrous for that. You needn't say anything. I am answered. If you could have your choice you wouldn't have a society wife, either. In your heart you'd like the smaller home of comfort, the furtherance of your ambitions, the palatable meals regularly served, and little children around you. I am sick of all we have grown up to, Hart. When your hour of trouble comes, there is no comfort for you. I am tired to death. You find out what you want to do, and be, that is a man's work in the world, and I will plan our home, with no thought save your comfort. I'll be the other kind of a girl, as fast as I can learn. I can't correct all my faults in one day, but I'll change as rapidly as I can."

"God knows, I will be different, too, Edith. You shall not be the only generous one. I will make all the rest of life worthy of you. I will change, too!"

"Don't you dare!" said Edith Carr, taking his head between her hands and holding it against her knees, while the tears slid down her cheeks. "Don't you dare change, you big-hearted, splendid lover! I am little and selfish. You are the very finest, just as you are!"

Henderson was not talking then, so they sat through a long silence. At last he heard Edith draw a quick breath, and lifting his head he looked where she pointed. Up a fern stalk climbed a curious looking object. They watched breathlessly. By lavender feet clung a big, pursy, lavender-splotched, yellow body. Yellow and lavender wings began to expand and take on colour. Every instant great beauty became more apparent. It was one of those double-brooded freaks, which do occur on rare occasions, or merely an Eacles Imperialis moth that in the cool damp northern forest had failed to emerge in June. Edith Carr drew back with a long, shivering breath. Henderson caught her hands and gripped them firmly. Steadily she looked the thought of her heart into his eyes.

"By all the powers, you shall not!" swore the man. "You have done enough. I will smash that thing!"

"Oh no you won't!" cried the girl, clinging to his hands. "I am not big enough yet, Hart, but before I leave this forest I shall have grown to breadth and strength to carry that to her. She needs two of each kind. Phil only sent her one!"

"Edith I can't bear it! That's not demanded! Let me take it!"

"You may go with me. I know where the O'More cottage is. I have been there often."

"I'll say you sent it!"

"You may watch me deliver it!"

"Phil may be there by now."

"I hope he is! I should like him to see me do one decent thing by which to remember me."

"I tell you that is not necessary!"

"'Not necessary!'" cried the girl, her big eyes shining. "Not necessary? Then what on earth is the thing doing here? I just have boasted that I would change, that I would be like her, that I would grow bigger and broader. As the words are spoken God gives me the opportunity to prove whether I am sincere. This is my test, Hart! Don't you see it? If I am big enough to carry that to her, you will believe that there is some good in me. You will not be loving me in vain. This is an especial Providence, man! Be my strength! Help me, as you always have done!"

Henderson arose and shook the leaves from his clothing. He drew Edith Carr to her feet and carefully picked the mosses from her skirts. He went to the water and moistened his handkerchief to bathe her face.

"Now a dust of powder," he said when the tears were washed away.

From a tiny book Edith tore leaves that she passed over her face.

"All gone!" cried Henderson, critically studying her. "You look almost half as lovely as you really are!"

Edith Carr drew a wavering breath. She stretched one hand to him.

"Hold tight, Hart!" she said. "I know they handle these things, but I would quite as soon touch a snake."

Henderson clenched his teeth and held steadily. The moth had emerged too recently to be troublesome. It climbed on her fingers quietly and obligingly clung there without moving. So hand in hand they went down the dark forest path. When they came to the avenue, the first person they met paused with an ejaculation of wonder. The next stopped also, and every one following. They could make little progress on account of marvelling, interested people. A strange excitement took possession of Edith. She began to feel proud of the moth.

"Do you know," she said to Henderson, "this is growing easier every step. Its clinging is not disagreeable as I thought it would be. I feel as if I were saving it, protecting it. I am proud that we are taking it to be put into a collection or a book. It seems like doing a thing worth while. Oh, Hart, I wish we could work together at something for which people would care as they seem to for this. Hear what they say! See them lift their little children to look at it!"

"Edith, if you don't stop," said Henderson, "I will take you in my arms here on the avenue. You are adorable!"

"Don't you dare!" laughed Edith Carr. The colour rushed to her cheeks and a new light leaped in her eyes.

"Oh, Hart!" she cried. "Let's work! Let's do something! That's the way she makes people love her so. There's the place, and thank goodness, there is a crowd."

"You darling!" whispered Henderson as they passed up the walk. Her face was rose-flushed with excitement and her eyes shone.

"Hello, everyone!" she cried as she came on the wide veranda. "Only see what we found up in the forest! We thought you might like to have it for some of your collections."

She held out the moth as she walked straight to Elnora, who arose to meet her, crying: "How perfectly splendid! I don't even know how to begin to thank you."

Elnora took the moth. Edith shook hands with all of them and asked Philip if he were improving. She said a few polite words to Freckles and the Angel, declined to remain on account of an engagement, and went away, gracefully.

"Well bully for her!" said Mrs. Comstock. "She's a little thoroughbred after all!"

"That was a mighty big thing for her to be doing," said Freckles in a hushed voice.

"If you knew her as well as I do," said Philip Ammon, "you would have a better conception of what that cost."

"It was a terror!" cried the Angel. "I never could have done it."

"'Never could have done it!'" echoed Freckles. "Why, Angel, dear, that is the one thing of all the world you would have done!"

"I have to take care of this," faltered Elnora, hurrying toward the door to hide the tears which were rolling down her cheeks.

"I must help," said Philip, disappearing also. "Elnora," he called, catching up with her, "take me where I may cry, too. Wasn't she great?"

"Superb!" exclaimed Elnora. "I have no words. I feel so humbled!"

"So do I," said Philip. "I think a brave deed like that always makes one feel so. Now are you happy?"

"Unspeakably happy!" answered Elnora.

BOOK THREE

AT THE FOOT OF THE RAINBOW

"And the bow shall be set in the cloud; and I will look upon it,
that I may remember the everlasting covenant between God and
every living creature of all flesh that is upon the earth."
—GENESIS, ix-16.

CHAPTER 1

THE RAT-CATCHERS OF THE WABASH

"Hey, you swate-scented little heart-warmer!" cried Jimmy Malone, as he lifted his tenth trap, weighted with a struggling muskrat, from the Wabash. "Varmint you may be to all the rist of creation, but you mane a night at Casey's to me."

Jimmy whistled softly as he reset the trap. For the moment he forgot that he was five miles from home, that it was a mile farther to the end of his line at the lower curve of Horseshoe Bend, that his feet and fingers were almost freezing, and that every rat of the ten now in the bag on his back had made him thirstier. He shivered as the cold wind sweeping the curves of the river struck him; but when an unusually heavy gust dropped the ice and snow from a branch above him on the back of his head, he laughed, as he ducked and cried: "Kape your snowballing till the Fourth of July, will you!"

"Chick-a-dee-dee-dee!" remarked a tiny gray bird on the tree above him. Jimmy glanced up. "Chickie, Chickie, Chickie," he said. "I can't till by your dress whether you are a hin or a rooster. But I can till by your employmint that you are working for grub. Have to hustle lively for every worm you find, don't you, Chickie? Now me, I'm hustlin' lively for a drink, and I be domn if it seems nicessary with a whole river of drinkin' stuff flowin' right under me feet. But the old Wabash ain't runnin "wine and milk and honey" not by the jug-full. It seems to be compounded of aquil parts of mud, crude ile, and rain water. If 'twas only runnin' Melwood, be gorry, Chickie, you'd see a mermaid named Jimmy Malone sittin' on the Kingfisher Stump, combin' its auburn hair with a breeze, and scoopin' whiskey down its gullet with its tail fin. No, hold on, Chickie, you wouldn't either. I'm too flat-chisted for a mermaid, and I'd have no time to lave off gurglin' for the hair-combin' act, which, Chickie, to me notion is as issential to a mermaid as the curves. I'd be a sucker, the biggest sucker in the Gar-hole, Chickie bird. I'd be an all-day sucker, be gobs; yis, and an all-night sucker, too. Come to think of it, Chickie, be domn if I'd be a sucker at all. Look at the mouths of thim! Puckered up with a drawstring! Oh, Hell on the Wabash, Chickie, think of Jimmy Malone lyin' at the bottom of a river flowin' with Melwood, and a puckerin'-string mouth! Wouldn't that break the heart of you? I know what I'd be. I'd be the Black Bass of Horseshoe Bend, Chickie, and I'd locate just below the shoals headin' up stream, and I'd hold me mouth wide open till I paralyzed me jaws so I couldn't shut thim. I'd just let the pure stuff wash over me gills constant, world without end. Good-by, Chickie. Hope you got your grub, and pretty soon I'll have enough drink to make me feel like I was the Bass for one night, anyway."

Jimmy hurried to his next trap, which was empty, but the one after that contained a rat, and there were footprints in the snow. "That's where the porrage-heart of the Scotchman comes in," said Jimmy, as he held up the rat by one foot, and gave it a sharp rap over the head with the trap to make sure it was dead. "Dannie could no more hear a rat fast in one of me traps and not come over and put it out of its misery, than he could dance a hornpipe. And him only sicond hand from hornpipe land, too! But his feet's like lead. Poor Dannie! He gets just about half the rats I do. He niver did have luck."

Jimmy's gay face clouded for an instant. The twinkle faded from his eyes, and a look of unrest swept into them. He muttered something, and catching up his bag, shoved in the rat. As he reset the trap, a big crow dropped from branch to branch on a sycamore above him, and his back scarcely was turned before it alighted on the ice, and ravenously picked at three drops of blood purpling there.

Away down the ice-sheeted river led Dannie's trail, showing plainly across the snow blanket. The wind raved through the trees, and around the curves of the river. The dark earth of the banks peeping from under overhanging ice and snow, looked like the entrance to deep mysterious caves. Jimmy's superstitious soul readily peopled them with goblins and devils. He shuddered, and began to talk aloud to cheer himself. "Elivin muskrat skins, times fifteen cints apiece, one dollar sixty-five. That will buy more than I can hold. Hagginy! Won't I be takin' one long fine gurgle of the pure stuff! And there's the boys! I might do the grand for once. One on me for the house! And I might pay something on my back score, but first I'll drink till I swell like a poisoned pup. And I ought to get Mary that milk pail she's been kickin' for this last month. Women and cows are always kickin'! If the blarsted cow hadn't kicked a hole in the pail, there'd be no need of Mary kicking for a new one. But dough IS dubious soldering. Mary says it's bad enough on the dish pan, but it positively ain't hilthy about the milk pail, and she is right. We ought to have a new pail. I guess I'll get it first, and fill up on what's left. One for a quarter will do. And I've several traps yet, I may get a few more rats."

The virtuous resolve to buy a milk pail before he quenched the thirst which burned him, so elated Jimmy with good opinion of himself that he began whistling gayly as he strode toward his next trap. And by that token, Dannie Macnoun, resetting an empty trap a quarter of a mile below, knew that Jimmy was coming, and that as usual luck was with him. Catching his blood and water dripping bag, Dannie dodged a rotten branch that came crashing down under the weight of its icy load, and stepping out on the river, he pulled on his patched wool-lined mittens as he waited for Jimmy.

"How many, Dannie?" called Jimmy from afar.

"Seven," answered Dannie. "What for ye?"

"Elivin," replied Jimmy, with a bit of unconscious swagger. "I am havin' poor luck to-day."

"How mony wad satisfy ye?" asked Dannie sarcastically.

"Ain't got time to figure that," answered Jimmy, working in a double shuffle as he walked. "Thrash around a little, Dannie. It will warm you up."

"I am no cauld," answered Dannie.

"No cauld!" imitated Jimmy. "No cauld! Come to observe you closer, I do detect symptoms of sunstroke in the ridness of your face, and the whiteness about your mouth; but the frost on your neck scarf, and the icicles fistooned around the tail of your coat, tell a different story.

"Dannie, you remind me of the baptizin' of Pete Cox last winter. Pete's nothin' but skin and bone, and he niver had a square meal in his life to warm him. It took pushin' and pullin' to get him in the water, and a scum froze over while he was under. Pete came up shakin' like the feeder on a thrashin' machine, and whin he could spake at all, 'Bless Jasus,' says he, 'I'm jist as wa-wa-warm as I wa-wa-want to be.' So are you, Dannie, but there's a difference in how warm folks want to be. For meself, now, I could aisily bear a little more hate."

"It's honest, I'm no cauld," insisted Dannie; and he might have added that if Jimmy would not fill his system with Casey's poisons, that degree of cold would not chill and pinch him either. But being Dannie, he neither thought nor said it. "'Why, I'm frozen to me sowl!" cried Jimmy, as he changed the rat bag to his other hand, and beat the empty one against his leg. "Say, Dannie, where do you think the Kingfisher is wintering?"

"And the Black Bass," answered Dannie. "Where do ye suppose the Black Bass is noo?"

"Strange you should mintion the Black Bass," said Jimmy. "I was just havin' a little talk about him with a frind of mine named Chickie-dom, no, Chickie-dee, who works a grub stake back there. The Bass might be lyin' in the river bed right under our feet. Don't you remimber the time whin I put on three big cut-worms, and skittered thim beyond the log that lays across here, and he lept from the water till we both saw him the best we ever did, and nothin' but my old rotten line ever saved him? Or he might be where it slumps off just below the Kingfisher stump. But I know where he is all right. He's down in the Gar-hole, and he'll come back here spawning time, and chase minnows when the Kingfisher comes home. But, Dannie, where the nation do you suppose the Kingfisher is?"

"No' so far away as ye might think," replied Dannie. "Doc Hues told me that coming on the train frae Indianapolis on the fifteenth of December, he saw one fly across a little pond juist below Winchester. I believe they go south slowly, as the cold drives them, and stop near as they can find guid fishing. Dinna that stump look lonely wi'out him?"

"And sound lonely without the Bass slashing around! I am going to have that Bass this summer if I don't do a thing but fish!" vowed Jimmy.

"I'll surely have a try at him," answered Dannie, with a twinkle in his gray eyes. "We've caught most everything else in the Wabash, and our reputation fra taking guid fish is ahead of any one on the river, except the Kingfisher. Why the Diel dinna one of us haul out that Bass?"

"Ain't I just told you that I am going to hook him this summer?" shivered Jimmy.

"Dinna ye hear me mention that I intended to take a try at him mysel'?" questioned Dannie. "Have ye forgotten that I know how to fish?"

"'Nough breeze to-day without starting a Highlander," interposed Jimmy hastily. "I believe I hear a rat in my next trap. That will make me twilve, and it's good and glad of it I am for I've to walk to town when my line is reset. There's something Mary wants."

"If Mary wants ye to go to town, why dinna ye leave me to finish your traps, and start now?" asked Dannie. "It's getting dark, and if ye are so late ye canna see the drifts, ye never can cut across the fields; fra the snow is piled waist high, and it's a mile farther by the road."

"I got to skin my rats first, or I'll be havin' to ask credit again," replied Jimmy.

"That's easy," answered Dannie. "Turn your rats over to me richt noo. I'll give ye market price fra them in cash."

"But the skinnin' of them," objected Jimmy for decency sake, though his eyes were beginning to shine and his fingers to tremble.

"Never ye mind about that," retorted Dannie. "I like to take my time to it, and fix them up nice. Elivin, did ye say?"

"Elivin," answered Jimmy, breaking into a jig, supposedly to keep his feet warm, in reality because he could not stand quietly while Dannie pulled off his mittens, got out and unstrapped his wallet, and carefully counted out the money. "Is that all ye need?" he asked.

For an instant Jimmy hesitated. Missing a chance to get even a few cents more meant a little shorter time at Casey's. "That's enough, I think," he said. "I wish I'd staid out of matrimony, and then maybe I could iver have a cint of me own. You ought to be glad you haven't a woman to consume ivery penny you earn before it reaches your pockets, Dannie Micnoun."

"I hae never seen Mary consume much but calico and food," Dannie said dryly.

"Oh, it ain't so much what a woman really spinds," said Jimmy, peevishly, as he shoved the money into his pocket, and pulled on his mittens. "It's what you know she would spind if she had the chance."

"I dinna think ye'll break up on that," laughed Dannie.

And that was what Jimmy wanted. So long as he could set Dannie laughing, he could mold him.

"No, but I'll break down," lamented Jimmy in sore self-pity, as he remembered the quarter sacred to the purchase of the milk pail.

"Ye go on, and hurry," urged Dannie. "If ye dinna start home by seven, I'll be combing the drifts fra ye before morning."

"Anything I can do for you?" asked Jimmy, tightening his old red neck scarf.

"Yes," answered Dannie. "Do your errand and start straight home, your teeth are chattering noo. A little more exposure, and the rheumatism will be grinding ye again. Ye will hurry, Jimmy?"

"Sure!" cried Jimmy, ducking under a snow slide, and breaking into a whistle as he turned toward the road.

Dannie's gaze followed Jimmy's retreating figure until he climbed the bank, and was lost in the woods, and the light in his eyes was the light of love. He glanced at the sky, and hurried down the river. First across to Jimmy's side to gather his rats and reset his traps, then to his own. But luck seemed to have turned, for all the rest of Dannie's were full, and all of Jimmy's were empty. But as he was gone, it was not necessary for Dannie to slip across and fill them, as was his custom when they worked together. He would divide the rats at skinning time, so that Jimmy would have just twice as many as he, because Jimmy had a wife to support. The last trap of the line lay a little below the curve of Horseshoe Bend, and there Dannie twisted the tops of the bags together, climbed the bank, and struck across Rainbow Bottom. He settled his load to his shoulders, and glanced ahead to choose the shortest route. He stopped suddenly with a quick intake of breath.

"God!" he cried reverently. "Hoo beautifu' are Thy works."

The ice-covered Wabash circled Rainbow Bottom like a broad white frame, and inside it was a perfect picture wrought in crystal white and snow shadows. The blanket on the earth lay smoothly in even places, rose with knolls, fell with valleys, curved over prostrate logs, heaped in mounds where bushes grew thickly, and piled high in drifts where the wind blew free. In the shelter of the bottom the wind had not stripped the trees of their loads as it had those along the river. The willows, maples, and soft woods bent almost to earth with their shining burden; but the stout, stiffly upstanding trees, the oaks, elms, and cottonwoods defied the elements to bow their proud heads. While the three mighty trunks of the great sycamore in the middle looked white as the snow, and dwarfed its companions as it never had in summer; its wide-spreading branches were sharply cut against the blue background, and they tossed their frosted balls in the face of Heaven. The giant of Rainbow Bottom might be broken, but it never would bend. Every clambering vine, every weed and dried leaf wore a coat of lace-webbed frostwork. The wind swept a mist of tiny crystals through the air, and from the shelter of the deep woods across the river a Cardinal whistled gayly.

The bird of Good Cheer, whistling no doubt on an empty crop, made Dannie think of Jimmy, and his unfailing fountain of mirth. Dear Jimmy! Would he ever take life seriously? How good he was to tramp to town and back after five miles on the ice. He thought of Mary with almost a touch of impatience. What did the woman want that was so necessary as to send a man to town after a day on the ice? Jimmy would be dog tired when he got home. Dannie decided to hurry, and do the feeding and get in the wood before he began to skin the rats.

He found walking uncertain. He plunged into unsuspected hollows, and waded drifts, so that he was panting when he reached the lane. From there he caught the gray curl of smoke against the sky from one of two log cabins side by side at the top of the embankment, and he almost ran toward them. Mary might think they were late at the traps, and be out doing the feeding, and it would be cold for a woman.

On reaching his own door, he dropped the rat bags inside, and then hurried to the yard of the other cabin. He gathered a big load of wood in his arms, and stamping the snow from his feet, called "Open!" at the door. Dannie stepped inside and filled the empty box. With smiling eyes he turned to Mary, as he brushed the snow and moss from his sleeves.

"Nothing but luck to-day," he said. "Jimmy took elivin fine skins frae his traps before he started to town, and I got five more that are his, and I hae eight o' my own."

Mary looked such a dream to Dannie, standing there all pink and warm and tidy in her fresh blue dress, that he blinked and smiled, half bewildered.

"What did Jimmy go to town for?" she asked.

"Whatever it was ye wanted," answered Dannie.

"What was it I wanted?" persisted Mary.

"He dinna tell me," replied Dannie, and the smile wavered.

"Me, either," said Mary, and she stooped and picked up her sewing.

Dannie went out and gently closed the door. He stood for a second on the step, forcing himself to take an inventory of the work. There were the chickens to feed, and the cows to milk, feed, and water. Both the teams must be fed and bedded, a fire in his own house made, and two dozen rats skinned, and the skins put to stretch and cure. And at the end of it all, instead of a bed and rest, there was every probability that he must drive to town after Jimmy; for Jimmy could get helpless enough to freeze in a drift on a dollar sixty-five.

"Oh, Jimmy, Jimmy!" muttered Dannie. "I wish ye wadna." And he was not thinking of himself, but of the eyes of the woman inside.

So Dannie did all the work, and cooked his supper, because he never ate in Jimmy's cabin when Jimmy was not there. Then he skinned rats, and watched the clock, because if Jimmy did not come by eleven, it meant he must drive to town and bring him home. No wonder Jimmy chilled at the trapping when he kept his blood on fire with whiskey. At half-past ten, Dannie, with scarcely half the rats finished, went out into the storm and hitched to the single buggy. Then he tapped at Mary Malone's door, quite softly, so that he would not disturb her if she had gone to bed. She was not sleeping, however, and the loneliness of her slight figure, as she stood with the lighted room behind her, struck Dannie forcibly, so that his voice trembled with pity as he said: "Mary, I've run out o' my curing compound juist in the midst of skinning the finest bunch o' rats we've taken frae the traps this winter. I am going to drive to town fra some more before the stores close, and we will be back in less than an hour. I thought I'd tell ye, so if ye wanted me ye wad know why I dinna answer. Ye winna be afraid, will ye?"

"No," replied Mary, "I won't be afraid."

"Bolt the doors, and pile on plenty of wood to keep ye warm," said Dannie as he turned away.

Just for a minute Mary stared out into the storm. Then a gust of wind nearly swept her from her feet, and she pushed the door shut, and slid the heavy bolt into place. For a little while she leaned and listened to the storm outside. She was a clean, neat, beautiful Irish woman. Her eyes were wide and blue, her cheeks pink, and her hair black and softly curling about her face and neck. The room in which she stood was neat as its keeper. The walls were whitewashed, and covered with prints, pictures, and some small tanned skins. Dried grasses and flowers filled the vases on the mantle. The floor was neatly carpeted with a striped rag carpet, and in the big open fireplace a wood fire roared. In an opposite corner stood a modern cooking stove, the pipe passing through a hole in the wall, and a door led into a sleeping room beyond.

As her eyes swept the room they rested finally on a framed lithograph of the Virgin, with the Infant in her arms. Slowly Mary advanced, her gaze fast on the serene pictured face of the mother clasping her child. Before it she stood staring. Suddenly her breast began to heave, and the big tears brimmed from her eyes and slid down her cheeks.

"Since you look so wise, why don't you tell me why?" she demanded. "Oh, if you have any mercy, tell me why!"

Then before the steady look in the calm eyes, she hastily made the sign of the cross, and slipping to the floor, she laid her head on a chair, and sobbed aloud.

CHAPTER II

RUBEN O'KHAYAM AND THE MILK PAIL

Jimmy Malone, carrying a shinning tin milk pail, stepped into Casey's saloon and closed the door behind him.

"E' much as wine has played the Infidel, And robbed me of my robe of Honor—well, I wonder what the Vinters buy One-half so precious as the stuff they sell."

Jimmy stared at the back of a man leaning against the bar, and gazing lovingly at a glass of red wine, as he recited in mellow, swinging tones. Gripping the milk pail, Jimmy advanced a step. The man stuck a thumb in the belt of his Norfolk jacket, and the verses flowed on:

"The grape that can with logic absolute

The two and seventy jarring sects confute:

The sovereign Alchemist that in a trice

Life's leaden metal into Gold transmute."

Jimmy's mouth fell open, and he slowly nodded indorsement of the sentiment. The man lifted his glass.

"Ah, make the most of what we yet may spend,

Before we too into the Dust descend;

Yesterday this Day's Madness did prepare;

To-morrow's Silence, Triumph, or Despair:

Drink! for you know not whence you came nor why:

Drink! for you know not why you go nor where."

Jimmy set the milk pail on the bar and faced the man.

"'Fore God, that's the only sensible word I ever heard on my side of the quistion in all me life. And to think that it should come from the mouth of a man wearing such a Go-to-Hell coat!"

Jimmy shoved the milk pail in front of the stranger. "In the name of humanity, impty yourself of that," he said. "Fill me pail with the stuff and let me take it home to Mary. She's always got the bist of the argumint, but I'm thinkin' that would cork her. You won't?" questioned Jimmy resentfully. "Kape it to yoursilf, thin, like you did your wine." He shoved the bucket toward the barkeeper, and emptied his pocket on the bar. "There, Casey, you be the Sovereign Alchemist, and transmute that metal into Melwood pretty quick, for I've not wet me whistle in three days, and the belly of me is filled with burnin' autumn leaves. Gimme a loving cup, and come on boys, this is on me while it lasts."

The barkeeper swept the coin into the till, picked up the bucket, and started back toward a beer keg.

"Oh, no you don't!" cried Jimmy. "Come back here and count that 'leaden metal,' and then be transmutin' it into whiskey straight, the purest gold you got. You don't drown out a three-days' thirst with beer. You ought to give me 'most two quarts for that."

The barkeeper was wise. He knew that what Jimmy started would go on with men who could pay, and he filled the order generously.

Jimmy picked up the pail. He dipped a small glass in the liquor, and held near an ounce aloft.

"I wonder what the Vinters buy

One-half so precious as the stuff they sell?"

he quoted. "Down goes!" and he emptied the glass at a draft. Then he walked to the group at the stove, and began dipping a drink for each.

When Jimmy came to a gray-haired man, with a high forehead and an intellectual face, he whispered: "Take your full time, Cap. Who's the rhymin' inkybator?"

"Thread man, Boston," mouthed the Captain, as he reached for the glass with trembling fingers. Jimmy held on. "Do you know that stuff he's giving off?" The Captain nodded, and rose to his feet. He always declared he could feel it farther if he drank standing.

"What's his name?" whispered Jimmy, releasing the glass. "Rubaiyat, Omar Khayyam," panted the Captain, and was lost. Jimmy finished the round of his friends, and then approached the bar.

His voice was softening. "Mister Ruben O'Khayam," he said, "it's me private opinion that ye nade lace-trimmed pantalettes and a sash to complate your costume, but barrin' clothes, I'm entangled in the thrid of your discourse. Bein' a Boston man meself, it appeals to me, that I detict the refinemint of the East in yer voice. Now these, me frinds, that I've just been tratin', are men of these parts; but we of the middle East don't set up to equal the culture of the extreme East. So, Mr. O'Khayam, solely for the benefit you might be to us, I'm askin' you to join me and me frinds in the momenchous initiation of me new milk pail."

Jimmy lifted a brimming glass, and offered it to the Thread Man. "Do you transmute?" he asked. Now if the Boston man had looked Jimmy in the eye, and said "I do," this book would not have been written. But he did not. He looked at the milk pail, and the glass, which had passed through the hands of a dozen men in a little country saloon away out in the wilds of Indiana, and said: "I do not care to partake of further refreshment; if I can be of intellectual benefit, I might remain for a time."

For a flash Jimmy lifted the five feet ten of his height to six; but in another he shrank below normal. What appeared to the Thread Man to be a humble, deferential seeker after wisdom, led him to one of the chairs around the big coal base burner. But the boys who knew Jimmy were watching the whites of his eyes, as they drank the second round. At this stage Jimmy was on velvet. How long he remained there depended on the depth of Melwood in the milk pail between his knees. He smiled winningly on the Thread Man.

"Ye know, Mister O'Khayam," he said, "at the present time you are located in one of the wooliest parts of the wild East. I don't suppose anything woolier could be found on the plains of Nebraska where I am reliably informed they've stuck up a pole and labeled it the cinter of the United States. Being a thousand miles closer that pole than you are in Boston, naturally we come by that distance closer to the great wool industry. Most of our wool here grows on our tongues, and we shear it by this transmutin' process, concerning which you have discoursed so beautiful. But barrin' the shearin' of our wool, we are the mildest, most sheepish fellows you could imagine. I don't reckon now there is a man among us who could be induced to blat or to butt, under the most tryin' circumstances. My Mary's got a little lamb, and all the rist of the boys are lambs. But all the lambs are waned, and clusterin' round the milk pail. Ain't that touchin'? Come on, now, Ruben, ile up and edify us some more!"

"On what point do you seek enlightenment?" inquired the Thread Man.

Jimmy stretched his long legs, and spat against the stove in pure delight.

"Oh, you might loosen up on the work of a man," he suggested. "These lambs of Casey's fold may larn things from you to help thim in the striss of life. Now here's Jones, for instance, he's holdin' togither a gang of sixty gibbering Atalyans; any wan of thim would cut his throat and skip in the night for a dollar, but he kapes the beast in thim under, and they're gettin' out gravel for the bed of a railway. Bingham there is oil. He's punchin' the earth full of wan thousand foot holes, and sendin' off two hundred quarts of nitroglycerine at the bottom of them, and pumpin' the accumulation across continents to furnish folks light and hate. York here is runnin' a field railway between Bluffton and Celina, so that I can get to the river and the resurvoir to fish without walkin'. Haines is bossin' a crew of forty Canadians and he's takin' the timber from the woods hereabouts, and sending it to be made into boats to carry stuff across sea. Meself, and me partner, Dannie Micnoun, are the lady-likest lambs in the bunch. We grow grub to feed folks in summer and trap for skins to cover 'em in winter. Corn is our great commodity. Plowin' and hoein' it in summer, and huskin' it in the fall is sich lamb-like work. But don't mintion it in the same brith with tendin' our four dozen fur traps on a twenty-below-zero day. Freezing hands and fate, and fallin' into air bubbles, and building fires to thaw out our frozen grub. Now here among us poor little, transmutin', lambs you come, a raging lion, ripresentin' the cultour and rayfinement of the far East. By the pleats on your breast you show us the style. By the thrid case in your hand you furnish us material so that our women can tuck their petticoats so fancy, and by the book in your head you teach us your sooperiority. By the same token, I wish I had that book in me head, for I could just squelch Dannie and Mary with it complate. Say, Mister O'Khayam, next time you come this way bring me a copy. I'm wantin' it bad. I got what you gave off all secure, but I take it there's more. No man goin' at that clip could shut off with thim few lines. Do you know the rist?"

The Thread Man knew the most of it, and although he was very uncomfortable, he did not know just how to get away, so he recited it. The milk pail was empty now, and Jimmy had almost forgotten that it was a milk pail, and seemed inclined to resent the fact that it had gone empty. He beat time on the bottom of it, and frequently interrupted the Thread Man to repeat a couplet which particularly suited him. By and by he got to his feet and began stepping off a slow dance to a sing-song repetition of lines that sounded musical to him, all the time marking the measures vigorously on the pail. When he tired of a couplet, he pounded the pail over the bar, stove, or chairs in encore, until the Thread Man could think up another to which he could dance.

"Wine! Wine! Wine! Red Wine!

The Nightingale cried to the rose,"

chanted Jimmy, thumping the pail in time, and stepping off the measures with feet that scarcely seemed to touch the floor. He flung his hat to the barkeeper, and his coat on a chair, ruffled his fingers through his thick auburn hair, and holding the pail under one arm, he paused, panting for breath and begging for more. The Thread Man sat on the edge of his chair, and the eyes he fastened on Jimmy were beginning to fill with interest.

"Come fill the Cup and in the fire of Spring

Your Winter-Garment of Repentance fling.

The bird of time has but a little way to flutter

And the bird is on the wing."

Smash came the milk pail across the bar. "Hooray!" shouted Jimmy. "Besht yet!" Bang! Bang! He was off. "ird ish on the wing," he chanted, and his feet flew. "Come fill the cup, and in the firesh of spring—Firesh of Spring, Bird ish on the Wing!" Between the music of the milk pail, the brogue of the panted verses, and the grace of Jimmy's flying feet, the Thread Man was almost prostrate. It suddenly came to him that here might be a chance to have a great time.

"More!" gasped Jimmy. "Me some more!" The Thread Man wiped his eyes.

"Wether the cup with sweet or bitter run,

The wine of life keeps oozing drop by drop,

The leaves of life keep falling one by one."

Away went Jimmy.

"Swate or bitter run,

Laves of life kape falling one by one."

Bang! Bang! sounded a new improvision on the sadly battered pail, and to a new step Jimmy flashed back and forth the length of the saloon. At last he paused to rest a second. "One more! Just one more!" he begged.

"A Book of Verses underneath the Bough,

A jug of wine, a Loaf of Bread and Thou

Beside me singing in the Wilderness.

Oh, wilderness were Paradise enough!"

Jimmy's head dropped an instant. His feet slowly shuffled in improvising a new step, and then he moved away, thumping the milk pail and chanting:

"A couple of fish poles underneath a tree,

A bottle of Rye and Dannie beside me

A fishing in the Wabash.

Were the Wabash Paradise? HULLY GEE!

Tired out, he dropped across a chair facing the back and folded his arms. He regained breath to ask the Thread Man: "Did you iver have a frind?"

He had reached the confidential stage.

The Boston man was struggling to regain his dignity. He retained the impression that at the wildest of the dance he had yelled and patted time for Jimmy.

"I hope I have a host of friends," he said, settling his pleated coat.

"Damn hosht!" said Jimmy. "Jisht in way. Now I got one frind, hosht all by himself. Be here pretty soon now. Alwaysh comesh nights like thish."

"Comes here?" inquired the Thread Man. "Am I to meet another interesting character?"

"Yesh, comesh here. Comesh after me. Comesh like the clock sthriking twelve. Don't he, boys?" inquired Jimmy. "But he ain't no interesting character. Jisht common man, Dannie is. Honest man. Never told a lie in his life. Yesh, he did, too. I forgot. He liesh for me. Jish liesh and liesh. Liesh to Mary. Tells her any old liesh to keep me out of schrape. You ever have frind hish up and drive ten milesh for you night like thish, and liesh to get you out of schrape?"

"I never needed any one to lie and get me out of a scrape," answered the Thread Man.

Jimmy sat straight and solemnly batted his eyes. "Gee! You musht misshed mosht the fun!" he said. "Me, I ain't ever misshed any. Always in schrape. But Dannie getsh me out. Good old Dannie. Jish like dog. Take care me all me life. See? Old folks come on same boat. Women get thick. Shettle beside. Build cabinsh together. Work together, and domn if they didn't get shmall pox and die together. Left me and Dannie. So we work together jish shame, and we fallsh in love with the shame girl. Dannie too slow. I got her." Jimmy wiped away great tears.

"How did you get her, Jimmy?" asked a man who remembered a story.

"How the nation did I get her?" Jimmy scratched his head, and appealed to the Thread Man. "Dannie besht man. Milesh besht man! Never lie—'cept for me. Never drink—'cept for me. Alwaysh save his money—'cept for me. Milesh besht man! Isn't he besht man, Spooley?"

"Ain't it true that you served Dannie a mean little trick?" asked the man who remembered.

Jimmy wasn't quite drunk enough, and the violent exercise of the dance somewhat sobered him. He glared at the man. "Whatsh you talkin' about?" he demanded.

"I'm just asking you," said the man, "why, if you played straight with Dannie about the girl, you never have had the face to go to confession since you married her."

"Alwaysh send my wife," said Jimmy grandly. "Domsh any woman that can't confiss enough for two!"

Then he hitched his chair closer to the Thread Man, and grew more confidential. "Shee here," he said. "Firsht I see your pleated coat, didn't like. But head's all right. Great head! Sthuck on frillsh there! Want to be let in on something? Got enough city, clubsh, an' all that? Want to taste real thing? Lesh go coon huntin'. Theysh tree down Canoper, jish short pleashant walk, got fify coons in it! Nobody knowsh the tree but me, shee? Been good to ush boys. Sat on same kind of chairs we do. Educate ush up lot. Know mosht that poetry till I die, shee? 'Wonner wash vinters buy, halfsh precious ash sthuff shell,' shee? I got it! Let you in on real thing. Take grand big coon skinch back to Boston with you. Ringsh on tail. Make wife fine muff, or fur trimmingsh. Good to till boysh at club about, shee?"

"Are you asking me to go on a coon hunt with you?" demanded the Thread Man. "When? Where?"

"Corshally invited," answered Jimmy. "To-morrow night. Canoper. Show you plashe. Bill Duke's dogs. My gunsh. Moonsh shinin'. Dogs howlin'. Shnow flying! Fify coonsh rollin' out one hole! Shoot all dead! Take your pick! Tan skin for you myself! Roaring big firesh warm by. Bag finesh sandwiches ever tasted. Milk pail pure gold drink. No stop, slop out going over bridge. Take jug. Big jug. Toss her up an' let her gurgle. Dogsh bark. Fire pop. Guns bang. Fifty coons drop. Boysh all go. Want to get more education. Takes culture to get woolsh off. Shay, will you go?"

"I wouldn't miss it for a thousand dollars," said the Thread Man. "But what will I say to my house for being a day late?"

"Shay gotter grip," suggested Jimmy. "Never too late to getter grip. Will you all go, boysh?"

There were not three men in the saloon who knew of a tree that had contained a coon that winter, but Jimmy was Jimmy, and to be trusted for an expedition of that sort; and all of them agreed to be at the saloon ready for the hunt at nine o'clock the next night. The Thread Man felt that he was going to see Life. He immediately invited the boys to the bar to drink to the success of the hunt.

"You shoot own coon yourself," offered the magnanimous Jimmy. "You may carrysh my gunsh, take first shot. First shot to Missher O'Khayam, boysh, 'member that. Shay, can you hit anything? Take a try now." Jimmy reached behind him, and shoved a big revolver into the hand of the Thread Man. "Whersh target?" he demanded.

As he turned from the bar, the milk pail which he still carried under his arm caught on an iron rod. Jimmy gave it a jerk, and ripped the rim from the bottom. "Thish do," he said. "Splendid marksh. Shinesh jish like coon's eyesh in torch light."

He carried the pail to the back wall and hung it over a nail. The nail was straight, and the pail flaring. The pail fell. Jimmy kicked it across the room, and then gathered it up, and drove a dent in it with his heel that would hold over the nail. Then he went back to the Thread Man. "Theresh mark, Ruben. Blash away!" he said.

The Boston man hesitated. "Whatsh the matter? Cansh shoot off nothing but your mouth?" demanded Jimmy. He caught the revolver and fired three shots so rapidly that the sounds came almost as one. Two bullets pierced the bottom of the pail, and the other the side as it fell.

The door opened, and with the rush of cold air Jimmy gave just one glance toward it, and slid the revolver into his pocket, reached for his hat, and started in the direction of his coat. "Glad to see you, Micnoun," he said. "If you are goingsh home, I'll jish ride out with you. Good night, boysh. Don't forgetsh the coon hunt," and Jimmy was gone.

A minute later the door opened again, and this time a man of nearly forty stepped inside. He had a manly form, and a manly face, was above the average in looks, and spoke with a slight Scotch accent.

"Do any of ye boys happen to know what it was Jimmy had with him when he came in here?"

A roar of laughter greeted the query. The Thread Man picked up the pail. As he handed it to Dannie, he said: "Mr. Malone said he was initiating a new milk pail, but I am afraid he has overdone the job."

"Thank ye," said Dannie, and taking the battered thing, he went out into the night.

Jimmy was asleep when he reached the buggy. Dannie had long since found it convenient to have no fence about his dooryard. He drove to the door, dragged Jimmy from the buggy, and stabled the horse. By hard work he removed Jimmy's coat and boots, laid him across the bed, and covered him. Then he grimly looked at the light in the next cabin. "Why doesna she go to bed?" he said. He summoned courage, and crossing the space between the two buildings, he tapped on the window. "It's me, Mary," he called. "The skins are only half done, and Jimmy is going to help me finish. He will come over in the morning. Ye go to bed. Ye needna be afraid. We will hear ye if ye even snore." There was no answer, but by a movement in the cabin Dannie knew that Mary was still dressed and waiting. He started back, but for an instant, heedless of the scurrying snow and biting cold, he faced the sky.

"I wonder if ye have na found a glib tongue and light feet the least part o' matrimony," he said. "Why in God's name couldna ye have married me? I'd like to know why."

As he closed the door, the cold air roused Jimmy.

"Dannie," he said, "donsh forget the milk pail. All 'niciate good now."

CHAPTER III

THE FIFTY COONS OF THE CANOPER

Near noon of the next day, Jimmy opened his eyes and stretched himself on Dannie's bed. It did not occur to him that he was sprawled across it in such a fashion that if Dannie had any sleep that night, he had taken it on chairs before the fireplace. At first Jimmy decided that he had a head on him, and would turn over and go back where he came from. Then he thought of the coon hunt, and sitting on the edge of the bed he laughed, as he looked about for his boots.

"I am glad ye are feeling so fine," said Dannie at the door, in a relieved voice. "I had a notion that ye wad be crosser than a badger when ye came to."

Jimmy laughed on.

"What's the fun?" inquired Dannie.

Jimmy thought hard a minute. Here was one instance where the truth would serve better than any invention, so he virtuously told Dannie all about it. Dannie thought of the lonely little woman next door, and rebelled.

"But, Jimmy!" he cried, "ye canna be gone all nicht again. It's too lonely fra Mary, and there's always a chance I might sleep sound and wadna hear if she should be sick or need ye."

"Then she can just yell louder, or come after you, or get well, for I am going, see? He was a thrid peddler in a dinky little pleated coat, Dannie. He laid up against the counter with his feet crossed at a dancing-girl angle. But I will say for him that he was running at the mouth with the finest flow of language I iver heard. I learned a lot of it, and Cap knows the stuff, and I'm goin' to have him get you the book. But, Dannie, he wouldn't drink with us, but he stayed to iducate us up a little. That little spool man, Dannie, iducatin' Jones of the gravel gang, and Bingham of the Standard, and York of the 'lectric railway, and Haines of the timber gang, not to mintion the champeen rat-catcher of the Wabash."

Jimmy hugged himself, and rocked on the edge of the bed.

"Oh, I can just see it, Dannie," he cried. "I can just see it now! I was pretty drunk, but I wasn't too drunk to think of it, and it came to me sudden like."

Dannie stared at Jimmy wide-eyed, while he explained the details, and then he too began to laugh, and the longer he laughed the funnier it grew.

"I've got to start," said Jimmy. "I've an awful afternoon's work. I must find him some rubber boots. He's to have the inestimable privilege of carryin' me gun, Dannie, and have the first shot at the coons, fifty, I'm thinkin' I said. And if I don't put some frills on his cute little coat! Oh, Dannie, it will break the heart of me if he don't wear that pleated coat!"

Dannie wiped his eyes.

"Come on to the kitchen," he said, "I've something ready fra ye to eat. Wash, while I dish it."

"I wish to Heaven you were a woman, Dannie," said Jimmy. "A fellow could fall in love with you, and marry you with some satisfaction. Crimminy, but I'm hungry!"

Jimmy ate greedily, and Dannie stepped about setting the cabin to rights. It lacked many feminine touches that distinguished Jimmy's as the abode of a woman; but it was neat and clean, and there seemed to be a place where everything belonged.

"Now, I'm off," said Jimmy, rising. "I'll take your gun, because I ain't goin' to see Mary till I get back."

"Oh, Jimmy, dinna do that!" pleaded Dannie. "I want my gun. Go and get your own, and tell her where ye are going and what ye are going to do. She'd feel less lonely."

"I know how she would feel better than you do," retorted Jimmy. "I am not going. If you won't give me your gun, I'll borrow one; or have all my fun spoiled."

Dannie took down the shining gun and passed it over. Jimmy instantly relented. He smiled an old boyish smile, that always caught Dannie in his softest spot.

"You are the bist frind I have on earth, Dannie," he said winsomely. "You are a man worth tying to. By gum, there's NOTHING I wouldn't do for you! Now go on, like the good fellow you are, and fix it up with Mary."

So Dannie started for the wood pile. In summer he could stand outside and speak through the screen. In winter he had to enter the cabin for errands like this, and as Jimmy's wood box was as heavily weighted on his mind as his own, there was nothing unnatural in his stamping snow on Jimmy's back stoop, and calling "Open!" to Mary at any hour of the day he happened to be passing the wood pile.

He stood at a distance, and patiently waited until a gray and black nut-hatch that foraged on the wood covered all the new territory discovered by the last disturbance of the pile. From loosened bark Dannie watched the bird take several good-sized white worms and a few dormant ants. As it flew away he gathered an armload of wood. He was very careful to clean his feet on the stoop, place the wood without tearing the neat covering of wall paper, and brush from his coat the snow and moss so that it fell in the box. He had heard Mary tell the careless Jimmy to do all these things, and Dannie knew that they saved her work. There was a whiteness on her face that morning that startled him, and long after the last particle of moss was cleaned from his sleeve he bent over the box trying to get something said. The cleaning took such a length of time that the glint of a smile crept into the grave eyes of the woman, and the grim line of her lips softened.

"Don't be feeling so badly about it, Dannie," she said. "I could have told you when you went after him last night that he would go back as soon as he wakened to-day. I know he is gone. I watched him lave."

Dannie brushed the other sleeve, on which there had been nothing at the start, and answered: "Noo, dinna ye misjudge him, Mary. He's goin' to a coon hunt to-nicht. Dinna ye see him take my gun?"

This evidence so bolstered Dannie that he faced Mary with confidence.

"There's a traveling man frae Boston in town, Mary, and he was edifying the boys a little, and Jimmy dinna like it. He's going to show him a little country sport to-nicht to edify him."

Dannie outlined the plan of Jimmy's campaign. Despite disapproval, and a sore heart, Mary Malone had to smile—perhaps as much over Dannie's eagerness in telling what was contemplated as anything.

"Why don't you take Jimmy's gun and go yoursilf?" she asked. "You haven't had a day off since fishing was over."

"But I have the work to do," replied Dannie, "and I couldna leave—" He broke off abruptly, but the woman supplied the word.

"Why can't you lave me, if Jimmy can? I'm not afraid. The snow and the cold will furnish me protiction to-night. There'll be no one to fear. Why should you do Jimmy's work, and miss the sport, to guard the thing he holds so lightly?"

The red flushed Dannie's cheeks. Mary never before had spoken like that. He had to say something for Jimmy quickly, and quickness was not his forte. His lips opened, but nothing came; for as Jimmy had boasted, Dannie never lied, except for him, and at those times he had careful preparation before he faced Mary. Now, he was overtaken unawares. He looked so boyish in his confusion, the mother in Mary's heart was touched.

"I'll till you what we'll do, Dannie," she said. "You tind the stock, and get in wood enough so that things won't be frazin' here; and then you hitch up and I'll go with you to town, and stay all night with Mrs. Dolan. You can put the horse in my sister's stable, and whin you and Jimmy get back, you'll be tired enough that you'll be glad to ride home. A visit with Katie will be good for me; I have been blue the last few days, and I can see you are just aching to go with the boys. Isn't that a fine plan?"

"I should say that IS a guid plan," answered the delighted Dannie. Anything to save Mary another night alone was good, and then—that coon hunt did sound alluring.

And that was how it happened that at nine o'clock that night, just as arrangements were being completed at Casey's, Dannie Macnoun stepped into the group and said to the astonished Jimmy: "Mary wanted to come to her sister's over nicht, so I fixed everything, and I'm going to the coon hunt, too, if you boys want me."

The crowd closed around Dannie, patted his back and cheered him, and he was introduced to Mister O'Khayam, of Boston, who tried to drown the clamor enough to tell what his name really was, "in case of accident"; but he couldn't be heard for Jimmy yelling that a good old Irish name like O'Khayam couldn't be beat in case of anything. And Dannie took a hasty glance at the Thread Man, to see if he wore that hated pleated coat, which lay at the bottom of Jimmy's anger.

Then they started. Casey's wife was to be left in charge of the saloon, and the Thread Man half angered Casey by a whispered conversation with her in a corner. Jimmy cut his crowd as low as he possibly could, but it numbered fifteen men, and no one counted the dogs. Jimmy led the way, the Thread Man beside him, and the crowd followed. The walking would be best to follow the railroad to the Canoper, and also they could cross the railroad bridge over the river and save quite a distance.

Jimmy helped the Thread Man into a borrowed overcoat and mittens, and loaded him with a twelve-pound gun, and they started. Jimmy carried a torch, and as torch bearer he was a rank failure, for he had a careless way of turning it and flashing it into people's faces that compelled them to jump to save themselves. Where the track lay clear and straight ahead the torch seemed to light it like day; but in dark places it was suddenly lowered or wavering somewhere else. It was through this carelessness of Jimmy's that at the first cattle-guard north of the village the torch flickered backward, ostensibly to locate Dannie, and the Thread Man went crashing down between the iron bars, and across the gun. Instantly Jimmy sprawled on top of him, and the next two men followed suit. The torch plowed into the snow and went out, and the yells of Jimmy alarmed the adjoining village.

He was hurt the worst of all, and the busiest getting in marching order again. "Howly smoke!" he panted. "I was havin' the time of me life, and plum forgot that cow-kitcher. Thought it was a quarter of a mile away yet. And liked to killed meself with me carelessness. But that's always the way in true sport. You got to take the knocks with the fun." No one asked the Thread Man if he was hurt, and he did not like to seem unmanly by mentioning a skinned shin, when Jimmy Malone seemed to have bursted most of his inside; so he shouldered his gun and limped along, now slightly in the rear of Jimmy. The river bridge was a serious matter with its icy coat, and danger of specials, and the torches suddenly flashed out from all sides; and the Thread Man gave thanks for Dannie Macnoun, who reached him a steady hand across the ties. The walk was three miles, and the railroad lay at from twenty to thirty feet elevation along the river and through the bottom land. The Boston man would have been thankful for the light, but as the last man stepped from the ties of the bridge all the torches went out save one. Jimmy explained they simply had to save them so that they could see where the coon fell when they began to shake the coon tree.

Just beside the water tank, and where the embankment was twenty feet sheer, Jimmy was cautioning the Boston man to look out, when the hunter next behind him gave a wild yell and plunged into his back. Jimmy's grab for him seemed more a push than a pull, and the three rolled to the bottom, and half way across the flooded ditch. The ditch was frozen over, but they were shaken, and smothered in snow. The whole howling party came streaming down the embankment. Dannie held aloft his torch and discovered Jimmy lying face down in a drift, making no effort to rise, and the Thread Man feebly tugging at him and imploring some one to come and help get Malone out. Then Dannie slunk behind the others and yelled until he was tired.

By and by Jimmy allowed himself to be dragged out.

"Who the thunder was that come buttin' into us?" he blustered. "I don't allow no man to butt into me when I'm on an imbankmint. Send the fool back here till I kill him."

The Thread Man was pulling at Jimmy's arm. "Don't mind, Jimmy," he gasped. "It was an accident! The man slipped. This is an awful place. I will be glad when we reach the woods. I'll feel safer with ground that's holding up trees under my feet. Come on, now! Are we not almost there? Should we not keep quiet from now on? Will we not alarm the coons?"

"Sure," said Jimmy. "Boys, don't hollo so much. Every blamed coon will be scared out of its hollow!"

"Amazing!" said the Thread Man. "How clever! Came on the spur of the moment. I must remember that to tell the Club. Do not hollo. Scare the coon out of its hollow!"

"Oh, I do miles of things like that," said Jimmy dryly, "and mostly I have to do thim before the spur of the moment; because our moments go so domn fast out here mighty few of thim have time to grow their spurs before they are gone. Here's where we turn. Now, boys, they've been trying to get this biler across the tracks here, and they've broke the ice. The water in this ditch is three feet deep and freezing cold. They've stuck getting the biler over, but I wonder if we can't cross on it, and hit the wood beyond. Maybe we can walk it."

Jimmy set a foot on the ice-covered boiler, howled, and fell back on the men behind him. "Jimminy crickets, we niver can do that!" he yelled. "It's a glare of ice and roundin'. Let's crawl through it! The rist of you can get through if I can. We'd better take off our overcoats, to make us smaller. We can roll thim into a bundle, and the last man can pull it through behind him."

Jimmy threw off his coat and entered the wrecked oil engine. He knew how to hobble through on his toes, but the pleated coat of the Boston man, who tried to pass through by stooping, got almost all Jimmy had in store for it. Jimmy came out all right with a shout. The Thread Man did not step half so far, and landed knee deep in the icy oil-covered slush of the ditch. That threw him off his balance, and Jimmy let him sink one arm in the pool, and then grabbed him, and scooped oil on his back with the other hand as he pulled. During the excitement and struggles of Jimmy and the Thread Man, the rest of the party jumped the ditch and gathered about, rubbing soot and oil on the Boston man, and he did not see how they crossed.

Jimmy continued to rub oil and soot into the hated coat industriously. The dogs leaped the ditch, and the instant they struck the woods broke away baying over fresh tracks. The men yelled like mad. Jimmy struggled into his overcoat, and helped the almost insane Boston man into his and then they hurried after the dogs.

The scent was so new and clear the dogs simply raged. The Thread Man was wild, Jimmy was wilder, and the thirteen contributed all they could for laughing. Dannie forgot to be ashamed of himself and followed the example of the crowd. Deeper and deeper into the wild, swampy Canoper led the chase. With a man on either side to guide him into the deepest holes and to shove him into bushy thickets, the skinned, soot-covered, oil-coated Boston man toiled and sweated. He had no time to think, the excitement was so intense. He scrambled out of each pitfall set for him, and plunged into the next with such uncomplaining bravery that Dannie very shortly grew ashamed, and crowding up beside him he took the heavy gun and tried to protect him all he could without falling under the eye of Jimmy, who was keeping close watch on the Boston man.

Wild yelling told that the dogs had treed, and with shaking fingers the Thread Man pulled off the big mittens he wore and tried to lift the gun. Jimmy flashed a torch, and sure enough, in the top of a medium hickory tree, the light was reflected in streams from the big shining eyes of a coon. "Treed!" yelled Jimmy frantically. "Treed! and big as an elephant. Company's first shot. Here, Mister O'Khayam, here's a good place to stand. Gee, what luck! Coon in sight first thing, and Mellen's food coon at that! Shoot, Mister O'Khayam, shoot!"

The Thread Man lifted the wavering gun, but it was no use.

"Tell you what, Ruben," said Jimmy. "You are too tired to shoot straight. Let's take a rist, and ate our lunch. Then we'll cut down the tree and let the dogs get cooney. That way there won't be any shot marks in his skin. What do you say? Is that a good plan?"

They all said that was the proper course, so they built a fire, and placed the Thread Man where he could see the gleaming eyes of the frightened coon, and where all of them could feast on his soot and oil-covered face. Then they opened the bag and passed the sandwiches.

"I really am hungry," said the weary Thread Man, biting into his with great relish. His jaws moved once or twice experimentally, and then he lifted his handkerchief to his lips.

"I wish 'twas as big as me head," said Jimmy, taking a great bite, and then he began to curse uproariously.

"What ails the things?" inquired Dannie, ejecting a mouthful. And then all of them began to spit birdshot, and started an inquest simultaneously. Jimmy raged. He swore some enemy had secured the bag and mined the feast; but the boys who knew him laughed until it seemed the Thread Man must suspect. He indignantly declared it was a dirty trick. By the light of the fire he knelt and tried to free one of the sandwiches from its sprinkling of birdshot, so that it would be fit for poor Jimmy, who had worked so hard to lead them there and tree the coon. For the first time Jimmy looked thoughtful.

But the sight of the Thread Man was too much for him, and a second later he was thrusting an ax into the hands accustomed to handling a thread case. Then he led the way to the tree, and began chopping at the green hickory. It was slow work, and soon the perspiration streamed. Jimmy pulled off his coat and threw it aside. He assisted the Thread Man out of his and tossed it behind him. The coat alighted in the fire, and was badly scorched before it was rescued. But the Thread Man was game. Fifty times that night it had been said that he was to have the first coon, of course he should work for it. So with the ax with which Casey chopped ice for his refrigerator, the Boston man banged against the hickory, and swore to himself because he could not make the chips fly as Jimmy did.

"Iverybody clear out!" cried Jimmy. "Number one is coming down. Get the coffee sack ready. Baste cooney over the head and shove him in before the dogs tear the skin. We want a dandy big pelt out of this!"

There was a crack, and the tree fell with a crash. All the Boston man could see was that from a tumbled pile of branches, dogs, and men, some one at last stepped back, gripping a sack, and cried: "Got it all right, and it's a buster."

"Now for the other forty-nine!" shouted Jimmy, straining into his coat.

"Come on, boys, we must secure a coon for every one," cried the Thread Man, heartily as any member of the party might have said it. But the rest of the boys suddenly grew tired. They did not want any coons, and after some persuasion the party agreed to go back to Casey's to warm up. The Thread Man got into his scorched, besooted, oil-smeared coat, and the overcoat which had been loaned him, and shouldered the gun. Jimmy hesitated. But Dannie came up to the Boston man and said: "There's a place in my shoulder that gun juist fits, and it's lonesome without it. Pass it over." Only the sorely bruised and strained Thread Man knew how glad he was to let it go.

It was Dannie, too, who whispered to the Thread Man to keep close behind him; and when the party trudged back to Casey's it was so surprising how much better he knew the way going back than Jimmy had known it coming out, that the Thread Man did remark about it. But Jimmy explained that after one had been out a few hours their eyes became accustomed to the darkness and they could see better. That was reasonable, for the Thread Man knew it was true in his own experience.

So they got back to Casey's, and found a long table set, and a steaming big oyster supper ready for them; and that explained the Thread Man's conference with Mrs. Casey. He took the head of the table, with his back to the wall, and placed Jimmy on his right and Dannie on his left. Mrs. Casey had furnished soap and towels, and at least part of the Boston man's face was clean. The oysters were fine, and well cooked. The Thread Man recited more of the wonderful poem for Dannie's benefit, and told jokes and stories. They laughed until they were so weak they could only pound the table to indicate how funny it was. And at the close, just as they were making a movement to rise, Casey proposed that he bring in the coon, and let all of them get a good look at their night's work. The Thread Man applauded, and Casey brought in the bag and shook it bottom up over the floor. Therefrom there issued a poor, frightened, maltreated little pet coon of Mrs. Casey's, and it dexterously ran up Casey's trouser leg and hid its nose in his collar, its chain dragging behind. And that was so funny the boys doubled over the table, and laughed and screamed until a sudden movement brought them to their senses.

The Thread Man was on his feet, and his eyes were no laughing matter. He gripped his chair back, and leaned toward Jimmy. "You walked me into that cattle-guard on purpose!" he cried.

Silence.

"You led me into that boiler, and fixed the oil at the end!"

No answer.

"You mauled me all over the woods, and loaded those sandwiches yourself, and sored me for a week trying to chop down a tree with a pet coon chained in it! You——! You——! What had I done to you?"

"You wouldn't drink with me, and I didn't like the domned, dinky, little pleated coat you wore," answered Jimmy.

One instant amazement held sway on the Thread Man's face; the next, "And damned if I like yours!" he cried, and catching up a bowl half filled with broth he flung it squarely into Jimmy's face.

Jimmy, with a great oath, sprang at the Boston man. But once in his life Dannie was quick. For the only time on record he was ahead of Jimmy, and he caught the uplifted fist in a grip that Jimmy's use of whiskey and suffering from rheumatism had made his master.

"Steady—Jimmy, wait a minute," panted Dannie. "This mon is na even wi' ye yet. When every muscle in your body is strained, and every inch of it bruised, and ye are daubed wi' soot, and bedraggled in oil, and he's made ye the laughin' stock fra strangers by the hour, ye will be juist even, and ready to talk to him. Every minute of the nicht he's proved himself a mon, and right now he's showed he's na coward. It's up to ye, Jimmy. Do it royal. Be as much of a mon as he is. Say ye are sorry!"

One tense instant the two friends faced each other.

Then Jimmy's fist unclenched, and his arms dropped. Dannie stepped back, trying to breathe lightly, and it was between Jimmy and the Thread Man.

"I am sorry," said Jimmy. "I carried my objictions to your wardrobe too far. If you'll let me, I'll clean you up. If you'll take it, I'll raise you the price of a new coat, but I'll be domn if I'll hilp put such a man as you are into another of the fiminine ginder."

The Thread Man laughed, and shook Jimmy's hand; and then Jimmy proved why every one liked him by turning to Dannie and taking his hand. "Thank you, Dannie," he said. "You sure hilped me to mesilf that time. If I'd hit him, I couldn't have hild up me head in the morning."

CHAPTER IV

WHEN THE KINGFISHER AND THE BLACK BASS CAME HOME

"Crimminy, but you are slow." Jimmy made the statement, not as one voices a newly discovered fact, but as one iterates a time-worn truism. He sat on a girder of the Limberlost bridge, and scraped the black muck from his boots in a little heap. Then he twisted a stick into the top of his rat sack, preparatory to his walk home. The ice had broken on the river, and now the partners had to separate at the bridge, each following his own line of traps to the last one, and return to the bridge so that Jimmy could cross to reach home. Jimmy was always waiting, after the river opened, and it was a remarkable fact to him that as soon as the ice was gone his luck failed him. This evening the bag at his feet proved by its bulk that it contained just about one-half the rats Dannie carried.

"I must set my traps in my own way," answered Dannie calmly. "If I stuck them into the water ony way and went on, so would the rats. A trap is no a trap unless it is concealed."

"That's it! Go on and give me a sarmon!" urged Jimmy derisively. "Who's got the bulk of the rats all winter? The truth is that my side of the river is the best catching in the extrame cold, and you get the most after the thaws begin to come. The rats seem to have a lot of burrows and shift around among thim. One time I'm ahead, and the nixt day they go to you: But it don't mane that you are any better TRAPPER than I am. I only got siven to-night. That's a sweet day's work for a whole man. Fifteen cints apace for sivin rats. I've a big notion to cut the rat business, and compete with Rocky in ile."

Dannie laughed. "Let's hurry home, and get the skinning over before nicht," he said. "I think the days are growing a little longer. I seem to scent spring in the air to-day."

Jimmy looked at Dannie's mud-covered, wet clothing, his blood-stained mittens and coat back, and the dripping bag he had rested on the bridge. "I've got some music in me head, and some action in me feet," he said, "but I guess God forgot to put much sintimint into me heart. The breath of spring niver got so strong with me that I could smell it above a bag of muskrats and me trappin' clothes."

He arose, swung his bag to his shoulder, and together they left the bridge, and struck the road leading to Rainbow Bottom. It was late February. The air was raw, and the walking heavy. Jimmy saw little around him, and there was little Dannie did not see. To him, his farm, the river, and the cabins in Rainbow Bottom meant all there was of life, for all he loved on earth was there. But loafing in town on rainy days, when Dannie sat with a book; hearing the talk at Casey's, at the hotel, and on the streets, had given Jimmy different views of life, and made his lot seem paltry compared with that of men who had greater possessions. On days when Jimmy's luck was bad, or when a fever of thirst burned him, he usually discoursed on some sort of intangible experience that men had, which he called "seeing life." His rat bag was unusually light that night, and in a vague way he connected it with the breaking up of the ice. When the river lay solid he usually carried home just twice the rats Dannie had, and as he had patronized Dannie all his life, it fretted Jimmy to be behind even one day at the traps.

"Be Jasus, I get tired of this!" he said. "Always and foriver the same thing. I kape goin' this trail so much that I've got a speakin' acquaintance with meself. Some of these days I'm goin' to take a trip, and have a little change. I'd like to see Chicago, and as far west as the middle, anyway."

"Well, ye canna go," said Dannie. "Ye mind the time when ye were married, and I thought I'd be best away, and packed my trunk? When ye and Mary caught me, ye got mad as fire, and she cried, and I had to stay. Just ye try going, and I'll get mad, and Mary will cry, and ye will stay at home, juist like I did."

There was a fear deep in Dannie's soul that some day Jimmy would fulfill this long-time threat of his. "I dinna think there is ony place in all the world so guid as the place ye own," Dannie said earnestly. "I dinna care a penny what anybody else has, probably they have what they want. What *I* want is the land that my feyther owned before me, and the house that my mither kept. And they'll have to show me the place they call Eden before I'll give up that it beats Rainbow Bottom—Summer, Autumn, or Winter. I dinna give twa hoops fra the palaces men rig up, or the thing they call 'landscape gardening'. When did men ever compete with the work of God? All the men that have peopled the earth since time began could have their brains rolled into one, and he would stand helpless before the anatomy of one of the rats in these bags. The thing God does is guid enough fra me."

"Why don't you take a short cut to the matin'-house?" inquired Jimmy.

"Because I wad have nothing to say when I got there," retorted Dannie. "I've a meetin'-house of my ain, and it juist suits me; and I've a God, too, and whether He is spirit or essence, He suits me. I dinna want to be held to sharper account than He faces me up to, when I hold communion with mesel'. I dinna want any better meetin'-house than Rainbow Bottom. I dinna care for better talkin' than the 'tongues in the trees'; sounder preachin' than the 'sermons in the stones'; finer readin' than the books in the river; no, nor better music than the choir o' the birds, each singin' in its ain way fit to burst its leetle throat about the mate it won, the nest they built, and the babies they are raising. That's what I call the music o' God, spontaneous, and the soul o' joy. Give it me every time compared with notes frae a book. And all the fine places that the wealth o' men ever evolved winna begin to compare with the work o' God, and I've got that around me every day."

"But I want to see life," wailed Jimmy.

"Then open your eyes, mon, fra the love o' mercy, open your eyes! There's life sailing over your heid in that flock o' crows going home fra the night. Why dinna ye, or some other mon, fly like that? There's living roots, and seeds, and insects, and worms by the million wherever ye are setting foot. Why dinna ye creep into the earth and sleep through the winter, and renew your life with the spring? The trouble with ye, Jimmy, is that ye've always followed your heels. If ye'd stayed by the books, as I begged ye, there now would be that in your heid that would teach ye that the old story of the Rainbow is true. There is a pot of gold, of the purest gold ever smelted, at its foot, and we've been born, and own a good living richt there. An' the gold is there; that I know, wealth to shame any bilious millionaire, and both of us missing the pot when we hold the location. Ye've the first chance, mon, fra in your life is the great prize mine will forever lack. I canna get to the bottom of the pot, but I'm going to come close to it as I can; and as for ye, empty it! Take it all! It's yours! It's fra the mon who finds it, and we own the location."

"Aha! We own the location," repeated Jimmy. "I should say we do! Behold our hotbed of riches! I often lay awake nights thinkin' about my attachmint to the place.

"How dear to me heart are the scanes of me childhood,

Fondly gaze on the cabin where I'm doomed to dwell,

Those chicken-coop, thim pig-pen, these highly piled-wood

Around which I've always raised Hell."

Jimmy turned in at his own gate, while Dannie passed to the cabin beyond. He entered, set the dripping rat bag in a tub, raked open the buried fire and threw on a log. He always ate at Jimmy's when Jimmy was at home, so there was no supper to get. He went out to the barn, wading mud ankle deep, fed and bedded his horses, and then went over to Jimmy's barn, and completed his work up to milking. Jimmy came out with the pail, and a very large hole in the bottom of it was covered with dried dough. Jimmy looked at it disapprovingly.

"I bought a new milk pail the other night. I know I did," he said. "Mary was kicking for one a month ago, and I went after it the night I met Ruben O'Khayam. Now what the nation did I do with that pail?"

"I have wondered mysel'," answered Dannie, as he leaned over and lifted a strange looking object from a barrel. "This is what ye brought home, Jimmy."

Jimmy stared at the shining, battered, bullet-punctured pail in amazement. Slowly he turned it over and around, and then he lifted bewildered eyes to Dannie.

"Are you foolin'?" he asked. "Did I bring that thing home in that shape?"

"Honest!" said Dannie.

"I remember buyin' it," said Jimmy slowly. "I remember hanging on to it like grim death, for it was the wan excuse I had for goin', but I don't just know how—!" Slowly he revolved the pail, and then he rolled over in the hay and laughed until he was tired. Then he sat up and wiped his eyes. "Great day! What a lot of fun I must have had before I got that milk pail into that shape," he said. "Domned if I don't go straight to town and buy another one; yes, bedad! I'll buy two!"

In the meantime Dannie milked, fed and watered the cattle, and Jimmy picked up the pail of milk and carried it to the house. Dannie came by the wood pile and brought in a heavy load. Then they washed, and sat down to supper.

"Seems to me you look unusually perky," said Jimmy to his wife. "Had any good news?"

"Splendid!" said Mary. "I am so glad! And I don't belave you two stupids know!"

"You niver can tell by lookin' at me what I know," said Jimmy. "Whin I look the wisest I know the least. Whin I look like a fool, I'm thinkin' like a philosopher."

"Give it up," said Dannie promptly. You would not catch him knowing anything it would make Mary's eyes shine to tell.

"Sap is running!" announced Mary.

"The Divil you say!" cried Jimmy.

"It is!" beamed Mary. "It will be full in three days. Didn't you notice how green the maples are? I took a little walk down to the bottom to-day. I niver in all my life was so tired of winter, and the first thing I saw was that wet look on the maples, and on the low land, where they are sheltered and yet get the sun, several of them are oozing!"

"Grand!" cried Dannie. "Jimmy, we must peel those rats in a hurry, and then clean the spiles, and see how mony new ones we will need. To-morrow we must come frae the traps early and look up our troughs."

"Oh, for pity sake, don't pile up work enough to kill a horse," cried Jimmy. "Ain't you ever happy unless you are workin'?"

"Yes," said Dannie. "Sometimes I find a book that suits me, and sometimes the fish bite, and sometimes it's in the air."

"Git the condinser" said Jimmy. "And that reminds me, Mary, Dannie smelled spring in the air to-day."

"Well, what if he did?" questioned Mary. "I can always smell it. A little later, when the sap begins to run in all the trees, and the buds swell, and the ice breaks up, and the wild geese go over, I always scent spring; and when the catkins bloom, then it comes strong, and I just love it. Spring is my happiest time. I have more news, too!"

"Don't spring so much at wance!" cried Jimmy, "you'll spoil my appetite."

"I guess there's no danger," replied Mary.

"There is," said Jimmy. "At laste in the fore siction. 'Appe' is Frinch, and manes atin'. 'Tite' is Irish, and manes drinkin'. Appetite manes atin' and drinkin' togither. 'Tite' manes drinkin' without atin', see?"

"I was just goin' to mintion it meself," said Mary, "it's where you come in strong. There's no danger of anybody spoilin' your drinkin', if they could interfere with your atin'. You guess, Dannie."

"The dominick hen is setting," ventured Dannie, and Mary's face showed that he had blundered on the truth.

"She is," affirmed Mary, pouring the tea, "but it is real mane of you to guess it, when I've so few new things to tell. She has been setting two days, and she went over fifteen fresh eggs to-day. In just twinty-one days I will have fiftane the cunningest little chickens you ever saw, and there is more yet. I found the nest of the gray goose, and there are three big eggs in it, all buried in feathers. She must have stripped her breast almost bare to cover them. And I'm the happiest I've been all winter. I hate the long, lonely, shut-in time. I am going on a delightful spree. I shall help boil down sugar-water and make maple syrup. I shall set hins, and geese, and turkeys. I shall make soap, and clane house, and plant seed, and all my flowers will bloom again. Goody for summer; it can't come too soon to suit me."

"Lord! I don't see what there is in any of those things," said Jimmy. "I've got just one sign of spring that interests me. If you want to see me caper, somebody mention to me the first rattle of the Kingfisher. Whin he comes home, and house cleans in his tunnel in the embankment, and takes possession of his stump in the river, the nixt day the Black Bass locates in the deep water below the shoals. THIN you can count me in. There is where business begins for Jimmy boy. I am going to have that Bass this summer, if I don't plant an acre of corn."

"I bet you that's the truth!" said Mary, so quickly that both men laughed.

"Ahem!" said Dannie. "Then I will have to do my plowing by a heidlicht, so I can fish as much as ye do in the day time. I hereby make, enact, and enforce a law that neither of us is to fish in the Bass hole when the other is not there to fish also. That is the only fair way. I've as much richt to him as ye have."

"Of course!" said Mary. "That is a fair way. Make that a rule, and kape it. If you both fish at once, it's got to be a fair catch for the one that lands it; but whoever catches it,*I* shall ate it, so it don't much matter to me."

"You ate it!" howled Jimnmy. "I guess not. Not a taste of that fish, when he's teased me for years? He's as big as a whale. If Jonah had had the good fortune of falling in the Wabash, and being swallowed by the Black Bass, he could have ridden from Peru to Terre Haute, and suffered no inconvanience makin' a landin'. Siven pounds he'll weigh by the steelyard I'll wager you."

"Five, Jimmy, five," corrected Dannie.

"Siven!" shouted Jimmy. "Ain't I hooked him repeated? Ain't I seen him broadside? I wonder if thim domn lines of mine have gone and rotted."

He left his supper, carrying his chair, and standing on it he began rummaging the top shelf of the cupboard for his box of tackle. He knocked a bottle from the shelf, but caught it in mid-air with a dexterous sweep.

"Spirits are movin'," cried Jimmy, as he restored the camphor to its place. He carried the box to the window, and became so deeply engrossed in its contents that he did not notice when Dannie picked up his rat bag and told him to come on and help skin their day's catch. Mary tried to send him, and he was going in a minute, but the minute stretched and stretched, and both of them were surprised when the door opened and Dannie entered with an armload of spiles, and the rat-skinning was all over. So Jimmy went on unwinding lines, and sharpening hooks, and talking fish; while Dannie and Mary cleaned the spiles, and figured on how many new elders must be cut and prepared for more on the morrow; and planned the sugar making.

When it was bedtime, and Dannie had gone an Jimmy and Mary closed their cabin for the night, Mary stepped to the window that looked on Dannie's home to see if his light was burning. It was, and clear in its rays stood Dannie, stripping yard after yard of fine line through his fingers, and carefully examining it. Jimmy came and stood beside her as she wondered.

"Why, the domn son of the Rainbow," he cried, "if he ain't testing his fish lines!"

The next day Mary Malone was rejoicing when the men returned from trapping, and gathering and cleaning the sugar-water troughs. There had been a robin at the well.

"Kape your eye on, Mary" advised Jimmy. "If she ain't watched close from this time on, she'll be settin' hins in snowdrifts, and pouring biling water on the daffodils to sprout them."

On the first of March, five killdeers flew over in a flock, and a half hour later one straggler crying piteously followed in their wake.

"Oh, the mane things!" almost sobbed Mary. "Why don't they wait for it?"

She stood by a big kettle of boiling syrup at the sugar camp, almost helpless in Jimmy's boots and Dannie's great coat. Jimmy cut and carried wood, and Dannie hauled sap. All the woods were stirred by the smell of the curling smoke and the odor of the boiling sap, fine as the fragrance of flowers. Bright-eyed deer mice peeped at her from under old logs, the chickadees, nuthatches, and jays started an investigating committee to learn if anything interesting to them was occurring. One gayly-dressed little sapsucker hammered a tree near by and scolded vigorously.

"Right you are!" said Mary. "It's a pity you're not big enough to drive us from the woods, for into one kittle goes enough sap to last you a lifetime."

The squirrels were sure it was an intrusion, and raced among the branches overhead, barking loud defiance. At night the three rode home on the sled, with the syrup jugs beside them, and Mary's apron was filled with big green rolls of pungent woolly-dog moss.

Jimmy built the fires, Dannie fed the stock, and Mary cooked the supper. When it was over, while the men warmed chilled feet and fingers by the fire, Mary poured some syrup into a kettle, and just as it "sugared off" she dipped streams of the amber sweetness into cups of water. All of them ate it like big children, and oh, but it was good! Two days more of the same work ended sugar making, but for the next three days Dannie gathered the rapidly diminishing sap for the vinegar barrel.

Then there were more hens ready to set, water must be poured hourly into the ash hopper to start the flow of lye for soap making, and the smoke house must be gotten ready to cure the hams and pickled meats, so that they would keep during warm weather. The bluebells were pushing through the sod in a race with the Easter and star flowers. One morning Mary aroused Jimmy with a pull at his arm.

"Jimmy, Jimmy," she cried. "Wake up!"

"Do you mane, wake up, or get up?" asked Jimmy sleepily.

"Both," cried Mary. "The larks are here!"

A little later Jimmy shouted from the back door to the barn: "Dannie, do you hear the larks?"

"Ye bet I do," answered Dannie. "Heard ane goin' over in the nicht. How long is it now till the Kingfisher comes?"

"Just a little while," said Jimmy. "If only these March storms would let up 'stid of down! He can't come until he can fish, you know. He's got to have crabs and minnies to live on."

A few days later the green hylas began to pipe in the swamps, the bullfrogs drummed among the pools in the bottom, the doves cooed in the thickets, and the breath of spring was in the nostrils of all creation, for the wind was heavy with the pungent odor of catkin pollen. The spring flowers were two inches high. The peonies and rhubarb were pushing bright yellow and red cones through the earth. The old gander, leading his flock along the Wabash, had hailed passing flocks bound northward until he was hoarse; and the Brahma rooster had threshed the yellow dorkin until he took refuge under the pig pen, and dare not stick out his unprotected head.

The doors had stood open at supper time, and Dannie staid up late, mending and oiling the harness. Jimmy sat by cleaning his gun, for to his mortification he had that day missed killing a crow which stole from the ash hopper the egg with which Mary tested the strength of the lye. In a basket behind the kitchen stove fifteen newly hatched yellow chickens, with brown stripes on their backs, were peeping and nestling; and on wing the killdeers cried half the night. At two o'clock in the morning came a tap on the Malone's bedroom window.

"Dannie?" questioned Mary, half startled.

"Tell Jimmy!" cried Dannie's breathless voice outside. "Tell him the Kingfisher has juist struck the river!"

Jimmy sat straight up in bed.

"Then glory be!" he cried. "To-morrow the Black Bass comes home!"

CHAPTER V

WHEN THE RAINBOW SET ITS ARCH IN THE SKY

"Where did Jimmy go?" asked Mary.

Jimmy had been up in time to feed the chickens and carry in the milk, but he disappeared shortly after breakfast.

Dannie almost blushed as he answered: "He went to take a peep at the river. It's going down fast. When it gets into its regular channel, spawning will be over and the fish will come back to their old places. We figure that the Black Bass will be home to-day."

"When you go digging for bait," said Mary, "I wonder if the two of you could make it convanient to spade an onion bed. If I had it spaded I could stick the sets mesilf."

"Now, that amna fair, Mary," said Dannie. "We never went fishing till the garden was made, and the crops at least wouldna suffer. We'll make the beds, of course, juist as soon as they can be spaded, and plant the seed, too."

"I want to plant the seeds mesilf," said Mary.

"And we dinna want ye should," replied Dannie. "All we want ye to do, is to boss."

"But I'm going to do the planting mesilf," Mary was emphatic. "It will be good for me to be in the sunshine, and I do enjoy working in the dirt, so that for a little while I'm happy."

"If ye want to put the onions in the highest place, I should think I could spade ane bed now, and enough fra lettuce and radishes."

Dannie went after a spade, and Mary Malone laughed softly as she saw that he also carried an old tin can. He tested the earth in several places, and then called to her: "All right, Mary! Ground in prime shape. Turns up dry and mellow. We will have the garden started in no time."

He had spaded but a minute when Mary saw him run past the window, leap the fence, and go hurrying down the path to the river. She went to the door. At the head of the lane stood Jimmy, waving his hat, and the fresh morning air carried his cry clearly: "Gee, Dannie! Come hear him splash!"

Just why that cry, and the sight of Dannie Macnoun racing toward the river, his spade lying on the upturned earth of her scarcely begun onion bed, should have made her angry, it would be hard to explain. He had no tackle or bait, and reason easily could have told her that he would return shortly, and finish anything she wanted done; but when was a lonely, disappointed woman ever reasonable?

She set the dish water on the stove, wiped her hands on her apron, and walking to the garden, picked up the spade and began turning great pieces of earth. She had never done rough farm work, such as women all about her did; she had little exercise during the long, cold winter, and the first half dozen spadefuls tired her until the tears of self-pity rolled.

"I wish there was a turtle as big as a wash tub in the river" she sobbed, "and I wish it would eat that old Black Bass to the last scale. And I'm going to take the shotgun, and go over to the embankment, and poke it into the tunnel, and blow the old Kingfisher through into the cornfield. Then maybe Dannie won't go off too and leave me. I want this onion bed spaded right away, so I do."

"Drop that! Idjit! What you doing?" yelled Jimmy.

"Mary, ye goose!" panted Dannie, as he came hurrying across the yard. "Wha' do ye mean? Ye knew I'd be back in a minute! Jimmy juist called me to hear the Bass splash. I was comin' back. Mary, this amna fair."

Dannie took the spade from her hand, and Mary fled sobbing to the house.

"What's the row?" demanded Jimmy of the suffering Dannie.

"I'd juist started spadin' this onion bed," explained Dannie. "Of course, she thought we were going to stay all day."

"With no poles, and no bait, and no grub? She didn't think any such a domn thing," said Jimmy. "You don't know women! She just got to the place where it's her time to spill brine, and raise a rumpus about something, and aisy brathin' would start her. Just let her bawl it out, and thin—we'll get something dacent for dinner."

Dannie turned a spadeful of earth and broke it open, and Jimmy squatted by the can, and began picking out the angle worms.

"I see where we dinna fish much this summer," said Dannie, as he waited. "And where we fish close home when we do, and where all the work is done before we go."

"Aha, borrow me rose-colored specks!" cried Jimmy. "I don't see anything but what I've always seen. I'll come and go as I please, and Mary can do the same. I don't throw no 'jeminy fit' every time a woman acts the fool a little, and if you'd lived with one fiftane years you wouldn't either. Of course we'll make the garden. Wish to goodness it was a beer garden! Wouldn't I like to plant a lot of hop seed and see rows of little green beer bottles humpin' up the dirt. Oh, my! What all does she want done?"

Dannie turned another spadeful of earth and studied the premises, while Jimmy gathered the worms.

"Palins all on the fence?" asked Dannie.

"Yep," said Jimmy.

"Well, the yard is to be raked."

"Yep."

"The flooer beds spaded."

"Yep."

"Stones around the peonies, phlox, and hollyhocks raised and manure worked in. All the trees must be pruned, the bushes and vines trimmed, and the gooseberries, currants, and raspberries thinned. The strawberry bed must be fixed up, and the rhubarb and asparagus spaded around and manured. This whole garden must be made——"

"And the road swept, and the gate sandpapered, and the barn whitewashed! Return to grazing, Nebuchadnezzar," said Jimmy. "We do what's raisonable, and then we go fishin'. See?"

Three beds spaded, squared, and ready for seeding lay in the warm spring sunshine before noon. Jimmy raked the yard, and Dannie trimmed the gooseberries. Then he wheeled a barrel of swamp loam for a flower bed by the cabin wall, and listened intently between each shovelful he threw. He could not hear a sound. What was more, he could not bear it. He went to Jimmy.

"Say, Jimmy," he said. "Dinna ye have to gae in fra a drink?"

"House or town?" inquired Jimmy sweetly.

"The house!" exploded Dannie. "I dinna hear a sound yet. Ye gae in fra a drink, and tell Mary I want to know where she'd like the new flooer bed she's been talking about."

Jimmy leaned the rake against a tree, and started.

"And Jimmy," said Dannie. "If she's quit crying, ask her what was the matter. I want to know."

Jimmy vanished. Presently he passed Dannie where he worked.

"Come on," whispered Jimmy.

The bewildered Dannie followed. Jimmy passed the wood pile, and pig pen, and slunk around behind the barn, where he leaned against the logs and held his sides. Dannie stared at him.

"She says," wheezed Jimmy, "that she guesses SHE wanted to go and hear the Bass splash, too!"

Dannie's mouth fell open, and then closed with a snap.

"Us fra the fool killer!" he said. "Ye dinna let her see ye laugh?"

"Let her see me laugh!" cried Jimmy. "Let her see me laugh! I told her she wasn't to go for a few days yet, because we were sawin' the Kingfisher's stump up into a rustic sate for her, and we were goin' to carry her out to it, and she was to sit there and sew, and umpire the fishin', and whichiver bait she told the Bass to take, that one of us would be gettin' it. And she was pleased as anything, me lad, and now it's up to us to rig up some sort of a dacint sate, and tag a woman along half the time. You thick-tongued descindint of a bagpipe baboon, what did you sind me in there for?"

"Maybe a little of it will tire her," groaned Dannie.

"It will if she undertakes to follow me," Jimmy said. "I know where horse-weeds grow giraffe high."

Then they went back to work, and presently many savory odors began to steal from the cabin. Whereat Jimmy looked at Dannie, and winked an 'I-told-you-so' wink. A garden grows fast under the hands of two strong men really working, and by the time the first slice of sugar-cured ham from the smoke house for that season struck the sizzling skillet, and Mary very meekly called from the back door to know if one of them wanted to dig a little horse radish, the garden was almost ready for planting. Then they went into the cabin and ate fragrant, thick slices of juicy fried ham, seasoned with horse radish; fried eggs, freckled with the ham fat in which they were cooked; fluffy mashed potatoes, with a little well of melted butter in the center of the mound overflowing the sides; raisin pie, soda biscuit, and their own maple syrup.

"Ohumahoh!" said Jimmy. "I don't know as I hanker for city life so much as I sometimes think I do. What do you suppose the adulterated stuff we read about in papers tastes like?"

"I've often wondered," answered Dannie. "Look at some of the hogs and cattle that we see shipped from here to city markets. The folks that sell them would starve before they'd eat a bit o' them, yet somebody eats them, and what do ye suppose maple syrup made from hickory bark and brown sugar tastes like?"

"And cold-storage eggs, and cotton-seed butter, and even horse radish half turnip," added Mary. "Bate up the cream a little before you put it in your coffee, or it will be in lumps. Whin the cattle are on clover it raises so thick."

Jimmy speared a piece of salt-rising bread crust soaked in ham gravy made with cream, and said: "I wish I could bring that Thrid Man home with me to one meal of the real thing nixt time he strikes town. I belave he would injoy it. May I, Mary?"

Mary's face flushed slightly. "Depends on whin he comes," she said. "Of course, if I am cleaning house, or busy with something I can't put off——"

"Sure!" cried Jimmy. "I'd ask you before I brought him, because I'd want him to have something spicial. Some of this ham, and horse radish, and maple syrup to begin with, and thin your fried spring chicken and your stewed squirrel is a drame, Mary. Nobody iver makes turtle soup half so rich as yours, and your green peas in cream, and asparagus on toast is a rivilation—don't you rimimber 'twas Father Michael that said it? I ought to be able to find mushrooms in a few weeks, and I can taste your rhubarb pie over from last year. Gee! But I wish he'd come in strawberrying! Berries from the vines, butter in the crust, crame you have to bate to make it smooth—talk about shortcake!"

"What's wrong wi' cherry cobbler?" asked Dannie.

"Or blackberry pie?"

"Or greens cooked wi' bacon?"

"Or chicken pie?"

"Or catfish, rolled in cornmeal and fried in ham fat?"

"Or guineas stewed in cream, with hard-boiled eggs in the gravy?"

"Oh, stop!" cried the delighted Mary. "It makes me dead tired thinkin' how I'll iver be cookin' all you'll want. Sure, have him come, and both of you can pick out the things you like the best, and I'll fix thim for him. Pure, fresh stuff might be a trate to a city man. When Dolan took sister Katie to New York with him, his boss sent them to a five-dollar-a-day house, and they thought they was some up. By the third day poor Katie was cryin' for a square male. She couldn't touch the butter, the eggs made her sick, and the cold-storage meat and chicken never got nearer her stomach than her nose. So she just ate fish, because they were fresh, and she ate, and she ate, till if you mintion New York to poor Katie she turns pale, and tastes fish. She vows and declares that she feeds her chickens and hogs better food twice a day than people fed her in New York."

"I'll bet my new milk pail the grub we eat ivery day would be a trate that would raise him," said Jimmy. "Provided his taste ain't so depraved with saltpeter and chalk he don't know fresh, pure food whin he tastes it. I understand some of the victims really don't."

"Your new milk pail?" questioned Mary.

"That's what!" said Jimmy. "The next time I go to town I'm goin' to get you two."

"But I only need one," protested Mary. "Instead of two, get me a new dishpan. Mine leaks, and smears the stove and table."

"Be Gorry!" sighed Jimmy. "There goes me tongue, lettin' me in for it again. I'll look over the skins, and if any of thim are ripe, I'll get you a milk pail and a dishpan the nixt time I go to town. And, by gee! If that dandy big coon hide I got last fall looks good, I'm going to comb it up, and work the skin fine, and send it to the Thrid Man, with me complimints. I don't feel right about him yet. Wonder what his name railly is, and where he lives, or whether I killed him complate."

"Any dry goods man in town can tell ye," said Dannie.

"Ask the clerk in the hotel," suggested Mary.

"You've said it," cried Jimmy. "That's the stuff! And I can find out whin he will be here again."

Two hours more they faithfully worked on the garden, and then Jimmy began to grow restless.

"Ah, go on!" cried Mary. "You have done all that is needed just now, and more too. There won't any fish bite to-day, but you can have the pleasure of stringin' thim poor sufferin' worms on a hook and soaking thim in the river."

"'Sufferin' worms!' Sufferin' Job!" cried Jimmy. "What nixt? Go on, Dannie, get your pole!"

Dannie went. As he came back Jimmy was sprinkling a thin layer of earth over the bait in the can. "Why not come along, Mary?" he suggested.

"I'm not done planting my seeds," she answered. "I'll be tired when I am, and I thought that place wasn't fixed for me yet."

"We can't fix that till a little later," said Jimmy. "We can't tell where it's going to be grassy and shady yet, and the wood is too wet to fix a sate."

"Any kind of a sate will do," said Mary. "I guess you better not try to make one out of the Kingfisher stump. If you take it out it may change the pool and drive away the Bass."

"Sure!" cried Jimmy. "What a head you've got! We'll have to find some other stump for a sate."

"I don't want to go until it gets dry under foot, and warmer" said Mary. "You boys go on. I'll till you whin I am riddy to go."

"There!" said Jimmy, when well on the way to the river. "What did I tell you? Won't go if she has the chance! Jist wants to be ASKED."

"I dinna pretend to know women," said Dannie gravely. "But whatever Mary does is all richt with me."

"So I've obsarved," remarked Jimmy. "Now, how will we get at this fishin' to be parfectly fair?"

"Tell ye what I think," said Dannie. "I think we ought to pick out the twa best places about the Black Bass pool, and ye take ane fra yours and I'll take the ither fra mine, and then we'll each fish from his own place."

"Nothing fair about that," answered Jimmy. "You might just happen to strike the bed where he lays most, and be gettin' bites all the time, and me none; or I might strike it and you be left out. And thin there's days whin the wind has to do, and the light. We ought to change places ivery hour."

"There's nothing fair in that either," broke in Dannie. "I might have him tolled up to my place, and juist be feedin' him my bait, and here you'd come along and prove by your watch that my time was up, and take him when I had him all ready to bite."

"That's so for you!" hurried in Jimmy. "I'll be hanged if I'd leave a place by the watch whin I had a strike!"

"Me either," said Dannie. "'Tis past human nature to ask it. I'll tell ye what we'll do. We'll go to work and rig up a sort of a bridge where it's so narrow and shallow, juist above Kingfisher shoals, and then we'll toss up fra sides. Then each will keep to his side. With a decent pole either of us can throw across the pool, and both of us can fish as we please. Then each fellow can pick his bait, and cast or fish deep as he thinks best. What d'ye say to that?"

"I don't see how anything could be fairer than that," said Jimmy. "I don't want to fish for anything but the Bass. I'm goin' back and get our rubber boots, and you be rollin' logs, and we'll build that crossing right now."

"All richt," said Dannie.

So they laid aside their poles and tackle, and Dannie rolled logs and gathered material for the bridge, while Jimmy went back after their boots. Then both of them entered the water and began clearing away drift and laying the foundations. As the first log of the crossing lifted above the water Dannie paused.

"How about the Kingfisher?" he asked. "Winna this scare him away?"

"Not if he ain't a domn fool," said Jimmy; "and if he is, let him go!"

"Seems like the river would no be juist richt without him," said Dannie, breaking off a spice limb and nibbling the fragrant buds. "Let's only use what we bare need to get across. And where will we fix fra Mary?"

"Oh, git out!" said Jimmy. "I ain't goin' to fool with that."

"Well, we best fix a place. Then we can tell her we fixed it, and it's all ready."

"Sure!" cried Jimmy. "You are catchin' it from your neighbor. Till her a place is all fixed and watin', and you couldn't drag her here with a team of oxen. Till her you are GOING to fix it soon, and she'll come to see if you've done it, if she has to be carried on a stritcher."

So they selected a spot that they thought would be all right for Mary, and not close enough to disturb the Bass and the Kingfisher, rolled two logs, and fished a board that had been carried by a freshet from the water and laid it across them, and decided that would have to serve until they could do better.

Then they sat astride the board, Dannie drew out a coin, and they tossed it to see which was heads and tails. Dannie won heads. Then they tossed to see which bank was heads or tails, and the right, which was on Rainbow side, came heads. So Jimmy was to use the bridge. Then they went home, and began the night work. The first thing Jimmy espied was the barrel containing the milk pail. He fished out the pail, and while Dannie fed the stock, shoveled manure, and milked, Jimmy pounded out the dents, closed the bullet holes, emptied the bait into it, half filled it with mellow earth, and went to Mary for some corn meal to sprinkle on the top to feed the worms.

At four o'clock the next morning, Dannie was up feeding, milking, scraping plows, and setting bolts. After breakfast they piled their implements on a mudboat, which Dannie drove, while Jimmy rode one of his team, and led the other, and opened the gates. They began on Dannie's field, because it was closest, and for the next two weeks, unless it were too rainy to work, they plowed, harrowed, lined off, and planted the seed.

The blackbirds followed along the furrows picking up grubs, the crows cawed from high tree tops, the bluebirds twittered about hollow stumps and fence rails, the wood thrushes sang out their souls in the thickets across the river, and the King Cardinal of Rainbow Bottom whistled to split his throat from the giant sycamore. Tender greens were showing along the river and in the fields, and the purple of red-bud mingled with the white of wild plum all along the Wabash.

The sunny side of the hill that sloped down to Rainbow Bottom was a mass of spring beauties, anemones, and violets; thread-like ramps rose rank to the scent among them, and round ginger leaves were thrusting their folded heads through the mold. The Kingfisher was cleaning his house and fishing from his favorite stump in the river, while near him, at the fall of every luckless worm that missed its hold on a blossom-whitened thorn tree, came the splash of the great Black Bass. Every morning the Bass took a trip around Horseshoe Bend food hunting, and the small fry raced for life before his big, shear-like jaws. During the heat of noon he lay in the deep pool below the stump, and rested; but when evening came he set out in search of supper, and frequently he felt so good that he leaped clear of the water, and fell back with a splash that threw shining spray about him, or lashed out with his tail and sent widening circles of waves rolling from his lurking place. Then the Kingfisher rattled with all his might, and flew for the tunnel in the embankment.

Some of these days the air was still, the earth warmed in the golden sunshine, and murmured a low song of sleepy content. Some days the wind raised, whirling dead leaves before it, and covering the earth with drifts of plum, cherry, and apple bloom, like late falling snow. Then great black clouds came sweeping across the sky, and massed above Rainbow Bottom. The lightning flashed as if the heavens were being cracked open, and the rolling thunder sent terror to the hearts of man and beast. When the birds flew for shelter, Dannie and Jimmy unhitched their horses, and raced for the stables to escape the storm, and to be with Mary, whom electricity made nervous.

They would sit on the little front porch, and watch the greedy earth drink the downpour. They could almost see the grass and flowers grow. When the clouds scattered, the thunder grew fainter; and the sun shone again between light sprinkles of rain. Then a great, glittering rainbow set its arch in the sky, and it planted one of its feet in Horseshoe Bend, and the other so far away they could not even guess where.

If it rained lightly, in a little while Dannie and Jimmy could go back to their work afield. If the downpour was heavy, and made plowing impossible, they pulled weeds, and hoed in the garden. Dannie discoursed on the wholesome freshness of the earth, and Jimmy ever waited a chance to twist his words, and ring in a laugh on him. He usually found it. Sometimes, after a rain, they took their bait cans, and rods, and went down to the river to fish.

If one could not go, the other religiously refrained from casting bait into the pool where the Black Bass lay. Once, when they were fishing together, the Bass rose to a white moth, skittered over the surface by Dannie late in the evening, and twice Jimmy had strikes which he averred had taken the arm almost off him, but neither really had the Bass on his hook. They kept to their own land, and fished when they pleased, for game laws and wardens were unknown to them.

Truth to tell, neither of them really hoped to get the Bass before fall. The water was too high in the spring. Minnows were plentiful, and as Jimmy said, "It seemed as if the domn plum tree just rained caterpillars." So they bided their time, and the signs prohibiting trespass on all sides of their land were many and emphatic, and Mary had instructions to ring the dinner bell if she caught sight of any strangers.

The days grew longer, and the sun was insistent. Untold miles they trudged back and forth across their land, guiding their horses, jerked about with plows, their feet weighted with the damp, clinging earth, and their clothing pasted to their wet bodies. Jimmy was growing restless. Never in all his life had he worked so faithfully as that spring, and never had his visits to Casey's so told on him. No matter where they started, or how hard they worked, Dannie was across the middle of the field, and helping Jimmy before the finish. It was always Dannie who plowed on, while Jimmy rode to town for the missing bolt or buckle, and he generally rolled from his horse into a fence corner, and slept the remainder of the day on his return.

The work and heat were beginning to tire him, and his trips to Casey's had been much less frequent than he desired. He grew to feel that between them Dannie and Mary were driving him, and a desire to balk at slight cause, gathered in his breast. He deliberately tied his team in a fence corner, lay down, and fell asleep. The clanging of the supper bell aroused him. He opened his eyes, and as he rose, found that Dannie had been to the barn, and brought a horse blanket to cover him. Well as he knew anything, Jimmy knew that he had no business sleeping in fence corners so early in the season. With candor he would have admitted to himself that a part of his brittle temper came from aching bones and rheumatic twinges. Some way, the sight of Dannie swinging across the field, looking as fresh as in the early morning, and the fact that he had carried a blanket to cover him, and the further fact that he was wild for drink, and could think of no excuse on earth for going to town, brought him to a fighting crisis.

Dannie turned his horses at Jimmy's feet.

"Come on, Jimmy, supper bell has rung," he cried. "We mustn't keep Mary waiting. She wants us to help her plant the sweet potatoes to-nicht."

Jimmy rose, and his joints almost creaked. The pain angered him. He leaned forward and glared at Dannie.

"Is there one minute of the day whin you ain't thinkin' about my wife?" he demanded, oh, so slowly, and so ugly!

Dannie met his hateful gaze squarely. "Na a minute," he answered, "excepting when I am thinking about ye."

"The Hell you say!" exploded the astonished Jimmy.

Dannie stepped out of the furrow, and came closer. "See here, Jimmy Malone," he said. "Ye ain't forgot the nicht when I told ye I loved Mary, with all my heart, and that I'd never love another woman. I sent ye to tell her fra me, and to ask if I might come to her. And ye brought me her answer. It's na your fault that she preferred ye. Everybody did. But it IS your fault that I've stayed on here. I tried to go, and ye wouldna let me. So for fifteen years, ye have lain with the woman I love, and I have lain alone in a few rods of ye. If that ain't Man-Hell, try some other on me, and see if it will touch me! I sent ye to tell her that I loved her; have I ever sent ye to tell her that I've quit? I should think you'd know, by this time, that I'm na quitter. Love her! Why, I love her till I can see her standin' plain before me, when I know she's a mile away. Love her! Why, I can smell her any place I am, sweeter than any flower I ever held to my face. Love her! Till the day I dee I'll love her. But it ain't any fault of yours, and if ye've come to the place where I worry ye, that's the place where I go, as I wanted to on the same day ye brought Mary to Rainbow Bottom."

Jimmy's gray jaws fell open. Jimmy's sullen eyes cleared. He caught Dannie by the arm.

"For the love of Hivin, what did I say, Dannie?" he panted. "I must have been half asleep. Go! You go! You leave Rainbow Bottom! Thin, by God, I go too! I won't stay here without you, not a day. If I had to take my choice between you, I'd give up Mary before I'd give up the best frind I iver had. Go! I guess not, unless I go with you! She can go to——"

"Jimmy! Jimmy!" cautioned Dannie.

"I mane ivery domn word of it," said Jimmy. "I think more of you, than I iver did of any woman."

Dannie drew a deep breath. "Then why in the name of God did ye SAY that thing to me? I have na betrayed your trust in me, not ever, Jimmy, and ye know it. What's the matter with ye?"

Jimmy heaved a deep sigh, and rubbed his hands across his hot, angry face. "Oh, I'm just so domn sore!" he said. "Some days I get about wild. Things haven't come out like I thought they would."

"Jimmy, if ye are in trouble, why do ye na tell me? Canna I help ye? Have'nt I always helped ye if I could?"

"Yes, you have," said Jimmy. "Always, been a thousand times too good to me. But you can't help here. I'm up agin it alone, but put this in your pipe, and smoke it good and brown, if you go, I go. I don't stay here without you."

"Then it's up to ye na to make it impossible for me to stay," said Dannie. "After this, I'll try to be carefu'. I've had no guard on my lips. I've said whatever came into my heid."

The supper bell clanged sharply a second time.

"That manes more Hivin on the Wabash," said Jimmy. "Wish I had a bracer before I face it."

"How long has it been, Jimmy?" asked Dannie.

"Etarnity!" replied Jimmy briefly.

Dannie stood thinking, and then light broke. Jimmy was always short of money in summer. When trapping was over, and before any crops were ready, he was usually out of funds. Dannie hesitated, and then he said, "Would a small loan be what ye need, Jimmy?"

Jimmy's eyes gleamed. "It would put new life into me," he cried. "Forgive me, Dannie. I am almost crazy."

Dannie handed over a coin, and after supper Jimmy went to town. Then Dannie saw his mistake. He had purchased peace for himself, but what about Mary?

CHAPTER VI

THE HEART OF MARY MALONE

"This is the job that was done with the reaper,

If we hustle we can do it ourselves,

Thus securing to us a little cheaper,

The bread and pie upon our pantry shelves.

Eat this wheat, by and by,

On this beautiful Wabash shore,

Drink this rye, by and by,

Eat and drink on this beautiful shore."

So sang Jimmy as he drove through the wheat, oats and rye accompanied by the clacking machinery. Dannie stopped stacking sheaves to mop his warm, perspiring face and to listen. Jimmy always with an eye to the effect he was producing immediately broke into wilder parody:

"Drive this mower, a little slower,

On this beautiful Wabash shore,

Cuttin' wheat to buy our meat,

Cuttin' oats, to buy our coats,

Also pants, if we get the chance.

By and by, we'll cut the rye,

But I bet my hat I drink that, I drink that.

Drive this mower a little slower,

In this wheat, in this wheat, by and by."

The larks scolded, fluttering over head, for at times the reaper overtook their belated broods. The bobolinks danced and chattered on stumps and fences, in an agony of suspense, when their nests were approached, and cried pitifully if they were destroyed. The chewinks flashed from the ground to the fences and trees, and back, crying "Che-wink?" "Che-wee!" to each other, in such excitement that they appeared to be in danger of flirting off their long tails. The quail ran about the shorn fields, and excitedly called from fence riders to draw their flocks into the security of Rainbow Bottom.

Frightened hares bounded through the wheat, and if the cruel blade sheared into their nests, Dannie gathered the wounded and helpless of the scattered broods in his hat, and carried them to Mary.

Then came threshing, which was a busy time, but after that, through the long hot days of late July and August, there was little to do afield, and fishing was impossible. Dannie grubbed fence corners, mended fences, chopped and corded wood for winter, and in spare time read his books. For the most part Jimmy kept close to Dannie. Jimmy's temper never had been so variable. Dannie was greatly troubled, for despite Jimmy's protests of devotion, he flared at a word, and sometimes at no word at all. The only thing in which he really seemed interested was the coon skin he was dressing to send to Boston. Over that he worked by the hour, sometimes with earnest face, and sometimes he raised his head, and let out a whoop that almost frightened Mary. At such times he was sure to go on and give her some new detail of the hunt for the fifty coons, that he had forgotten to tell her before.

He had been to the hotel, and learned the Thread Man's name and address, and found that he did not come regularly, and no one knew when to expect him; so when he had combed and brushed the fur to its finest point, and worked the skin until it was velvet soft, and bleached it until it was muslin white, he made it into a neat package and sent it with his compliments to the Boston man. After he had waited for a week, he began going to town every day to the post office for the letter he expected, and coming home much worse for a visit to Casey's. Since plowing time he had asked Dannie for money as he wanted it, telling him to keep an account, and he would pay him in the fall. He seemed to forget or not to know how fast his bills grew.

Then came a week in August when the heat invaded even the cool retreat along the river. Out on the highway passing wheels rolled back the dust like water, and raised it in clouds after them. The rag weeds hung wilted heads along the road. The goldenrod and purple ironwort were dust-colored and dust-choked. The trees were thirsty, and their leaves shriveling. The river bed was bare its width in places, and while the Kingfisher made merry with his family, and rattled, feasting from Abram Johnson's to the Gar-hole, the Black Bass sought its deep pool, and lay still. It was a rare thing to hear it splash in those days.

The prickly heat burned until the souls of men were tried. Mary slipped listlessly about or lay much of the time on a couch beside a window, where a breath of air stirred. Despite the good beginning he had made in the spring, Jimmy slumped with the heat and exposures he had risked, and was hard to live with.

Dannie was not having a good time himself. Since Jimmy's wedding, life had been all grind to Dannie, but he kept his reason, accepted his lot, and ground his grist with patience and such cheer as few men could have summoned to the aid of so poor a cause.

Had there been any one to notice it, Dannie was tired and heat-ridden also, but as always, Dannie sank self, and labored uncomplainingly with Jimmy's problems. On a burning August morning Dannie went to breakfast, and found Mary white and nervous, little prepared to eat, and no sign of Jimmy.

"Jimmy sleeping?" he asked.

"I don't know where Jimmy is," Mary answered coldly.

"Since when?" asked Dannie, gulping coffee, and taking hasty bites, for he had begun his breakfast supposing that Jimmy would come presently.

"He left as soon as you went home last night," she said, "and he has not come back yet."

Dannie did not know what to say. Loyal to the bone to Jimmy, loving each hair on the head of Mary Malone, and she worn and neglected; the problem was heartbreaking in any solution he attempted, and he felt none too well himself. He arose hastily, muttering something about getting the work done. He brought in wood and water, and asked if there was anything more he could do.

"Sure!" said Mary, in a calm, even voice. "Go to the barn, and shovel manure for Jimmy Malone, and do all the work he shirks, before you do anything for yoursilf."

Dannie always had admitted that he did not understand women, but he understood a plain danger signal, and he almost ran from the cabin. In the fear that Mary might think he had heeded her hasty words, he went to his own barn first, just to show her that he did not do Jimmy's work. The flies and mosquitoes were so bad he kept his horses stabled through the day, and turned them to pasture at night. So their stalls were to be cleaned, and he set to work. When he had finished his own barn, as he had nothing else to do, he went on to Jimmy's. He had finished the stalls, and was sweeping when he heard a sound at the back door, and turning saw Jimmy clinging to the casing, unable to stand longer. Dannie sprang to him, and helped him inside. Jimmy sank to the floor. Dannie caught up several empty grain sacks, folded them, and pushed them under Jimmy's head for a pillow.

"Dannish, didsh shay y'r nash'nal flowerish wash shisle?" asked Jimmy.

"Yes," said Dannie, lifting the heavy auburn head to smooth the folds from the sacks.

"Whysh like me?"

"I dinna," answered Dannie wearily.

"Awful jagsh on," murmured Jimmy, sighed heavily, and was off. His clothing was torn and dust-covered, his face was purple and bloated, and his hair was dusty and disordered. He was a repulsive sight. As Dannie straightened Jimmy's limbs he thought he heard a step. He lifted his head and leaned forward to listen.

"Dannie Micnoun?" called the same even, cold voice he had heard at breakfast. "Have you left me, too?"

Dannie sprang for a manger. He caught a great armload of hay, and threw it over Jimmy. He gave one hurried toss to scatter it, for Mary was in the barn. As he turned to interpose his body between her and the manger, which partially screened Jimmy, his heart sickened. He was too late. She had seen. Frightened to the soul, he stared at her.

She came a step closer, and with her foot gave a hand of Jimmy's that lay exposed a contemptuous shove.

"You didn't get him complately covered," she said. "How long have you had him here?"

Dannie was frightened into speech. "Na a minute, Mary; he juist came in when I heard ye. I was trying to spare ye."

"Him, you mane," she said, in that same strange voice. "I suppose you give him money, and he has a bottle, and he's been here all night."

"Mary," said Dannie, "that's na true. I have furnished him money. He'd mortgage the farm, or do something worse if I didna; but I dinna WHERE he has been all nicht, and in trying to cover him, my only thought was to save ye pain."

"And whin you let him spind money you know you'll never get back, and loaf while you do his work, and when you lie mountain high, times without number, who is it for?"

Then fifteen years' restraint slid from Dannie like a cloak, and in the torture of his soul his slow tongue outran all its previous history.

"Ye!" he shouted. "It's fra Jimmy, too, but ye first. Always ye first!" Mary began to tremble. Her white cheeks burned red. Her figure straightened, and her hands clenched.

"On the cross! Will you swear it?" she cried.

"On the sacred body of Jesus Himself, if I could face Him," answered Dannie. "Anything! Everything is fra ye first, Mary!"

"Then why?" she panted between gasps for breath. "Tell me why? If you have cared for me enough to stay here all these years and see that I had the bist tratemint you could get for me, why didn't you care for me enough more to save me this? Oh, Dannie, tell me why?"

And then she shook with strangled sobs until she scarce could stand alone. Dannie Macnoun cleared the space between them and took her in his arms. Her trembling hands clung to him, her head dropped on his breast, and the perfume of her hair in his nostrils drove him mad. Then the tense bulk of her body struck against him, and horror filled his soul. One second he held her, the next, Jimmy smothering under the hay, threw up an arm, and called like a petulant child, "Dannie! Make shun quit shinish my fashe!"

And Dannie awoke to the realization that Mary was another man's, and that man, one who trusted him completely. The problem was so much too big for poor Dannie that reason kindly slipped a cog. He broke from the grasp of the woman, fled through the back door, and took to the woods.

He ran as if fiends were after him, and he ran and ran. And when he could run no longer, he walked, but he went on. Just on and on. He crossed forests and fields, orchards and highways, streams and rivers, deep woods and swamps, and on, and on he went. He felt nothing, and saw nothing, and thought nothing, save to go on, always on. In the dark he stumbled on and through the day he staggered on, and he stopped for nothing, save at times to lift water to his parched lips.

The bushes took his hat, the thorns ripped his shirt, the water soaked his shoes and they spread and his feet came through and the stones cut them until they bled. Leaves and twigs stuck in his hair, and his eyes grew bloodshot, his lips and tongue swollen, and when he could go no further on his feet, he crawled on his knees, until at last he pitched forward on his face and lay still. The tumult was over and Mother Nature set to work to see about repairing damages.

Dannie was so badly damaged, soul, heart, and body, that she never would have been equal to the task, but another woman happened that way and she helped. Dannie was carried to a house and a doctor dressed his hurts. When the physician got down to first principles, and found a big, white-bodied, fine-faced Scotchman in the heart of the wreck, he was amazed. A wild man, but not a whiskey bloat. A crazy man, but not a maniac. He stood long beside Dannie as he lay unconscious.

"I'll take oath that man has wronged no one," he said. "What in the name of God has some woman been doing to him?"

He took money from Dannie's wallet and bought clothing to replace the rags he had burned. He filled Dannie with nourishment, and told the woman who found him that when he awoke, if he did not remember, to tell him that his name was Dannie Macnoun, and that he lived in Rainbow Bottom, Adams County. Because just at that time Dannie was halfway across the state.

A day later he awoke, in a strange room and among strange faces. He took up life exactly where he left off. And in his ears, as he remembered his flight, rang the awful cry uttered by Mary Malone, and not until then did there come to Dannie the realization that she had been driven to seek him for help, because her woman's hour was upon her. Cold fear froze Dannie's soul.

He went back by railway and walked the train most of the way. He dropped from the cars at the water tank and struck across country, and again he ran. But this time it was no headlong flight. Straight as a homing bird went Dannie with all speed, toward the foot of the Rainbow and Mary Malone.

The Kingfisher sped rattling down the river when Dannie came crashing along the bank.

"Oh, God, let her be alive!" prayed Dannie as he leaned panting against a tree for an instant, because he was very close now and sickeningly afraid. Then he ran on. In a minute it would be over. At the next turn he could see the cabins. As he dashed along, Jimmy Malone rose from a log and faced him. A white Jimmy, with black-ringed eyes and shaking hands.

"Where the Hell have you been?" Jimmy demanded.

"Is she dead?" cried Dannie.

"The doctor is talking scare," said Jimmy. "But I don't scare so easy. She's never been sick in her life, and she has lived through it twice before, why should she die now? Of course the kid is dead again," he added angrily.

Dannie shut his eyes and stood still. He had helped plant star-flowers on two tiny cross-marked mounds at Five Mile Hill. Now, there were three. Jimmy had worn out her love for him, that was plain. "Why should she die now?" To Dannie it seemed that question should have been, "Why should she live?"

Jimmy eyed him belligerently. "Why in the name of sinse did you cut out whin I was off me pins?" he growled. "Of course I don't blame you for cutting that kind of a party, me for the woods, all right, but what I can't see is why you couldn't have gone for the doctor and waited until I'd slept it off before you wint."

"I dinna know she was sick," answered Dannie. "I deserve anything ony ane can say to me, and it's all my fault if she dees, but this ane thing ye got to say ye know richt noo, Jimmy. Ye got to say ye know that I dinna understand Mary was sick when I went."

"Sure! I've said that all the time," agreed Jimmy. "But what I don't understand is, WHY you went! I guess she thinks it was her fault. I came out here to try to study it out. The nurse-woman, domn pretty girl, says if you don't get back before midnight, it's all up. You're just on time, Dannie. The talk in the house is that she'll wink out if you don't prove to her that she didn't drive you away. She is about crazy over it. What did she do to you?"

"Nothing!" exclaimed Dannie. "She was so deathly sick she dinna what she was doing. I can see it noo, but I dinna understand then."

"That's all right," said Jimmy. "She didn't! She kapes moaning over and over 'What did I do?' You hustle in and fix it up with her. I'm getting tired of all this racket."

All Dannie heard was that he was to go to Mary. He went up the lane, across the garden, and stepped in at the back door. Beside the table stood a comely young woman, dressed in blue and white stripes. She was doing something with eggs and milk. She glanced at Dannie, and finished filling a glass. As she held it to the light, "Is your name Macnoun?" she inquired.

"Yes," said Dannie.

"Dannie Macnoun?" she asked.

"Yes," said Dannie.

"Then you are the medicine needed here just now," she said, as if that were the most natural statement in the world. "Mrs. Malone seems to have an idea that she offended you, and drove you from home, just prior to her illness, and as she has been very sick, she is in no condition to bear other trouble. You understand?"

"Do ye understand that I couldna have gone if I had known she was ill?" asked Dannie in turn.

"From what she has said in delirium I have been sure of that," replied the nurse. "It seems you have been the stay of the family for years. I have a very high opinion of you, Mr. Macnoun. Wait until I speak to her."

The nurse vanished, presently returned, and as Dannie passed through the door, she closed it after him, and he stood still, trying to see in the dim light. That great snowy stretch, that must be the bed. That tumbled dark circle, that must be Mary's hair. That dead white thing beneath it, that must be Mary's face. Those burning lights, flaming on him, those must be Mary's eyes. Dannie stepped softly across the room, and bent over the bed. He tried hard to speak naturally.

"Mary" he said, "oh, Mary, I dinna know ye were ill! Oh, believe me, I dinna realize ye were suffering pain."

She smiled faintly, and her lips moved. Dannie bent lower.

"Promise," she panted. "Promise you will stay now."

Her hand fumbled at her breast, and then she slipped on the white cover a little black cross. Dannie knew what she meant. He laid his hand on the emblem precious to her, and said softly, "I swear I never will leave ye again, Mary Malone."

A great light swept into her face, and she smiled happily.

"Now ye," said Dannie. He slipped the cross into her hand. "Repeat after me," he said. "I promise I will get well, Dannie."

"I promise I will get well, Dannie, if I can," said Mary.

"Na," said Dannie. "That winna do. Repeat what I said, and remember it is on the cross. Life hasna been richt for ye, Mary, but if ye will get well, before the Lord in some way we will make it happier. Ye will get well?"

"I promise I will get well, Dannie," said Mary Malone, and Dannie softly left the room.

Outside he said to the nurse, "What can I do?"

She told him everything of which she could think that would be of benefit.

"Now tell me all ye know of what happened," commanded Dannie.

"After you left," said the nurse, "she was in labor, and she could not waken her husband, and she grew frightened and screamed. There were men passing out on the road. They heard her, and came to see what was the matter."

"Strangers?" shuddered Dannie, with dry lips.

"No, neighbors. One man went for the nearest woman, and the other drove to town for a doctor. They had help here almost as soon as you could. But, of course, the shock was a very dreadful thing, and the heat of the past few weeks has been enervating."

"Ane thing more," questioned Dannie. "Why do her children dee?"

"I don't know about the others," answered the nurse. "This one simply couldn't be made to breathe. It was a strange thing. It was a fine big baby, a boy, and it seemed perfect, but we couldn't save it. I never worked harder. They told me she had lost two others, and we tried everything of which we could think. It just seemed as if it had grown a lump of flesh, with no vital spark in it."

Dannie turned, went out of the door, and back along the lane to the river where he had left Jimmy. "'A lump of flesh with na vital spark in it,'" he kept repeating. "I dinna but that is the secret. She is almost numb with misery. All these days when she's been without hope, and these awful nichts, when she's watched and feared alone, she has no wished to perpetuate him in children who might be like him, and so at their coming the 'vital spark' is na in them. Oh, Jimmy, Jimmy, have ye Mary's happiness and those three little graves to answer for?"

He found Jimmy asleep where he had left him. Dannie shook him awake. "I want to talk with ye," he said.

Jimmy sat up, and looked into Dannie's face. He had a complaint on his lips but it died there. He tried to apologize. "I am almost dead for sleep," he said. "There has been no rest for anyone here. What do you think?"

"I think she will live," said Dannie dryly. "In spite of your neglect, and my cowardice, I think she will live to suffer more frae us."

Jimmy's mouth opened, but for once no sound issued. The drops of perspiration raised on his forehead.

Dannie sat down, and staring at him Jimmy saw that there were patches of white hair at his temples that had been brown a week before; his colorless face was sunken almost to the bone, and there was a peculiar twist about his mouth. Jimmy's heart weighed heavily, his tongue stood still, and he was afraid to the marrow in his bones.

"I think she will live," repeated Dannie. "And about the suffering more, we will face that like men, and see what can be done about it. This makes three little graves on the hill, Jimmy, what do they mean to ye?"

"Domn bad luck," said Jimmy promptly.

"Nothing more?" asked Dannie. "Na responsibility at all. Ye are the father of those children. Have ye never been to the doctor, and asked why ye lost them?"

"No, I haven't," said Jimmy.

"That is ane thing we will do now," said Dannie, "and then we will do more, much more."

"What are you driving at?" asked Jimmy.

"The secret of Mary's heart," said Dannie.

The cold sweat ran from the pores of Jimmy's body. He licked his dry lips, and pulled his hat over his eyes, that he might watch Dannie from under the brim.

"We are twa big, strong men," said Dannie. "For fifteen years we have lived here wi' Mary. The night ye married her, the licht of happiness went out for me. But I shut my mouth, and shouldered my burden, and went on with my best foot first; because if she had na refused me, I should have married her, and then ye would have been the one to suffer. If she had chosen me, I should have married her, juist as ye did. Oh, I've never forgotten that! So I have na been a happy mon, Jimmy. We winna go into that any further, we've been over it once. It seems to be a form of torture especially designed fra me, though at times I must confess, it seems rough, and I canna see why, but we'll cut that off with this: life has been Hell's hottest sweat-box fra me these fifteen years."

Jimmy groaned aloud. Dannie's keen gray eyes seemed boring into the soul of the man before him, as he went on.

"Now how about ye? Ye got the girl ye wanted. Ye own a guid farm that would make ye a living, and save ye money every year. Ye have done juist what ye pleased, and as far as I could, I have helped ye. I've had my eye on ye pretty close, Jimmy, and if YE are a happy mon, I dinna but I'm content as I am. What's your trouble? Did ye find ye dinna love Mary after ye won her? Did ye murder your mither or blacken your soul with some deadly sin? Mon! If I had in my life what ye every day neglect and torture, Heaven would come doon, and locate at the foot of the Rainbow fra me. But, ye are no happy, Jimmy. Let's get at the root of the matter. While ye are unhappy, Mary will be also. We are responsible to God for her, and between us, she is empty armed, near to death, and almost dumb with misery. I have juist sworn to her on the cross she loves that if she will make ane more effort, and get well, we will make her happy. Now, how are we going to do it?"

Another great groan burst from Jimmy, and he shivered as if with a chill.

"Let us look ourselves in the face," Dannie went on, "and see what we lack. What can we do fra her? What will bring a song to her lips, licht to her beautiful eyes, love to her heart, and a living child to her arms? Wake up, mon! By God, if ye dinna set to work with me and solve this problem, I'll shake a solution out of ye! What I must suffer is my own, but what's the matter with ye, and why, when she loved and married ye, are ye breakin' Mary's heart? Answer me, mon!"

Dannie reached over and snatched the hat from Jimmy's forehead, and stared at an inert heap. Jimmy lay senseless, and he looked like death. Dannie rushed down to the water with the hat, and splashed drops into Jimmy's face until he gasped for breath. When he recovered a little, he shrank from Dannie, and began to sob, as if he were a sick ten-year-old child.

"I knew you'd go back on me, Dannie," he wavered. "I've lost the only frind I've got, and I wish I was dead."

"I havena gone back on ye," persisted Dannie, bathing Jimmy's face. "Life means nothing to me, save as I can use it fra Mary, and fra ye. Be quiet, and sit up here, and help me work this thing out. Why are ye a discontented mon, always wishing fra any place save home? Why do ye spend all ye earn foolishly, so that ye are always hard up, when ye might have affluence? Why does Mary lose her children, and why does she noo wish she had na married ye?"

"Who said she wished she hadn't married me?" cried Jimmy.

"Do ye mean to say ye think she doesn't?" blazed Dannie.

"I ain't said anything!" exclaimed Jimmy.

"Na, and I seem to have damn poor luck gettin' ye TO say anything. I dinna ask fra tears, nor faintin' like a woman. Be a mon, and let me into the secret of this muddle. There is a secret, and ye know it. What is it? Why are ye breaking the heart o' Mary Malone? Answer me, or 'fore God I'll wring the answer fra your body!"

And Jimmy keeled over again. This time he was gone so far that Dannie was frightened into a panic, and called the doctor coming up the lane to Jimmy before he had time to see Mary. The doctor soon brought Jimmy around, prescribed quiet and sleep; talked about heart trouble developing, and symptoms of tremens, and Dannie poured on water, and gritted his teeth. And it ended by Jimmy being helped to Dannie's cabin, undressed, and put into bed, and then Dannie went over to see what he could do for the nurse. She looked at him searchingly.

"Mr. Macnoun, when were you last asleep?" she asked.

"I forget," answered Dannie.

"When did you last have a good hot meal?"

"I dinna know," replied Dannie.

"Drink that," said the nurse, handing him the bowl of broth she carried, and going back to the stove for another. "When I have finished making Mrs. Malone comfortable, I'm going to get you something to eat, and you are going to eat it. Then you are going to lie down on that cot where I can call you if I need you, and sleep six hours, and then you're going to wake up and watch by this door while I sleep my six. Even nurses must have some rest, you know."

"Ye first," said Dannie. "I'll be all richt when I get food. Since ye mention it, I believe I am almost mad with hunger."

The nurse handed him another bowl of broth. "Just drink that, and drink slowly," she said, as she left the room.

Dannie could hear her speaking softly to Mary, and then all was quiet, and the girl came out and closed the door. She deftly prepared food for Dannie, and he ate all she would allow him, and begged for more; but she firmly told him her hands were full now, and she had no one to depend on but him to watch after the turn of the night. So Dannie lay down on the cot. He had barely touched it when he thought of Jimmy, so he got up quietly and started home. He had almost reached his back door when it opened, and Jimmy came out. Dannie paused, amazed at Jimmy's wild face and staring eyes.

"Don't you begin your cursed gibberish again," cried Jimmy, at sight of him. "I'm burning in all the tortures of fire now, and I'll have a drink if I smash down Casey's and steal it."

Dannie jumped for him, and Jimmy evaded him and fled. Dannie started after. He had reached the barn before he began to think. "I depend on you," the nurse had said. "Jimmy, wait!" he called. "Jimmy, have ye any money?" Jimmy was running along the path toward town. Dannie stopped. He stood staring after Jimmy for a second, and then he deliberately turned, went back, and lay down on the cot, where the nurse expected to find him when she wanted him to watch by the door of Mary Malone.

CHAPTER VII

THE APPLE OF DISCORD BECOMES A JOINTED ROD

"What do you think about fishing, Dannie?" asked Jimmy Malone.

"There was a licht frost last nicht," said Dannie. "It begins to look that way. I should think a week more, especially if there should come a guid rain."

Jimmy looked disappointed. His last trip to town had ended in a sodden week in the barn, and at Dannie's cabin. For the first time he had carried whiskey home with him. He had insisted on Dannie drinking with him, and wanted to fight when he would not. He addressed the bottle, and Dannie, as the Sovereign Alchemist by turns, and "transmuted the leaden metal of life into pure gold" of a glorious drunk, until his craving was satisfied. Then he came back to work and reason one morning, and by the time Mary was about enough to notice him, he was Jimmy at his level best, and doing more than he had in years to try to interest and please her.

Mary had fully recovered, and appeared as strong as she ever had been, but there was a noticeable change in her. She talked and laughed with a gayety that seemed forced, and in the midst of it her tongue turned bitter, and Jimmy and Dannie fled before it.

The gray hairs multiplied on Dannie's head with rapidity. He had gone to the doctor, and to Mary's sister, and learned nothing more than the nurse could tell him. Dannie was willing to undertake anything in the world for Mary, but just how to furnish the "vital spark," to an unborn babe, was too big a problem for him. And Jimmy Malone was growing to be another. Heretofore, Dannie had borne the brunt of the work, and all of the worry. He had let Jimmy feel that his was the guiding hand. Jimmy's plans were followed whenever it was possible, and when it was not, Dannie started Jimmy's way, and gradually worked around to his own. But, there never had been a time between them, when things really came to a crisis, and Dannie took the lead, and said matters must go a certain way, that Jimmy had not acceded. In reality, Dannie always had been master.

Now he was not. Where he lost control he did not know. He had tried several times to return to the subject of how to bring back happiness to Mary, and Jimmy immediately developed symptoms of another attack of heart disease, a tendency to start for town, or openly defied him by walking away. Yet, Jimmy stuck to him closer than he ever had, and absolutely refused to go anywhere, or to do the smallest piece of work alone. Sometimes he grew sullen and morose when he was not drinking, and that was very unlike the gay Jimmy. Sometimes he grew wildly hilarious, as if he were bound to make such a racket that he could hear no sound save his own voice. So long as he stayed at home, helped with the work, and made an effort to please Mary, Dannie hoped for the best, but his hopes never grew so bright that they shut out an awful fear that was beginning to loom in the future. But he tried in every way to encourage Jimmy, and help him in the struggle he did not understand, so when he saw that Jimmy was disappointed about the fishing, he suggested that he should go alone.

"I guess not!" said Jimmy. "I'd rather go to confission than to go alone. What's the fun of fishin' alone? All the fun there is to fishin' is to watch the other fellow's eyes when you pull in a big one, and try to hide yours from him when he gets it. I guess not! What have we got to do?"

"Finish cutting the corn, and get in the pumpkins before there comes frost enough to hurt them."

"Well, come along!" said Jimmy. "Let's get it over. I'm going to begin fishing for that Bass the morning after the first black frost, if I do go alone. I mean it!"

"But ye said—" began Dannie.

"Hagginy!" cried Jimmy. "What a lot of time you've wasted if you've been kaping account of all the things I've said. Haven't you learned by this time that I lie twice to the truth once?"

Dannie laughed. "Dinna say such things, Jimmy. I hate to hear ye. Of course, I know about the fifty coons of the Canoper, and things like that; honest, I dinna believe ye can help it. But na man need lie about a serious matter, and when he knows he is deceiving another who trusts him." Jimmy became so white that he felt the color receding, and turned to hide his face. "Of course, about those fifty coons noo, what was the harm in that? Nobody believed it. That wasna deceiving any ane."

"Yes, but it was," answered Jimmy. "The Boston man belaved it, and I guiss he hasn't forgiven me, if he did take my hand, and drink with me. You know I haven't had a word from him about that coon skin. I worked awful hard on that skin. Some way, I tried to make it say to him again that I was sorry for that night's work. Sometimes I am afraid I killed the fellow."

"O-ho!" scoffed Dannie. "Men ain't so easy killed. I been thinkin' about it, too, and I'll tell ye what I think. I think he goes on long trips, and only gets home every four or five months. The package would have to wait. His folks wouldna try to send it after him. He was a monly fellow, all richt, and ye will hear fra him yet."

"I'd like to," said Jimmy, absently, beating across his palm a spray of goldenrod he had broken. "Just a line to tell me that he don't bear malice."

"Ye will get it," said Dannie. "Have a little patience. But that's your greatest fault, Jimmy. Ye never did have ony patience."

"For God's sake, don't begin on me faults again," snapped Jimmy. "I reckon I know me faults about as well as the nixt fellow. I'm so domn full of faults that I've thought a lot lately about fillin' up, and takin' a sleep on the railroad."

A new fear wrung Dannie's soul. "Ye never would, Jimmy," he implored.

"Sure not!" cried Jimmy. "I'm no good Catholic livin', but if it come to dyin', bedad I niver could face it without first confissin' to the praste, and that would give the game away. Let's cut out dyin', and cut corn!"

"That's richt," agreed Dannie. "And let's work like men, and then fish fra a week or so, before ice and trapping time comes again. I'll wager I can beat ye the first row."

"Bate!" scoffed Jimmy. "Bate! With them club-footed fingers of yours? You couldn't bate an egg. Just watch me! If you are enough of a watch to keep your hands runnin' at the same time."

Jimmy worked feverishly for an hour, and then he straightened and looked about him. On the left lay the river, its shores bordered with trees and bushes. Behind them was deep wood. Before them lay their open fields, sloping down to the bottom, the cabins on one side, and the kingfisher embankment on the other. There was a smoky haze in the air. As always the blackbirds clamored along the river. Some crows followed the workers at a distance, hunting for grains of corn, and over in the woods, a chewink scratched and rustled among the deep leaves as it searched for grubs. From time to time a flock of quail arose before them with a whirr and scattered down the fields, reassembling later at the call of their leader, from a rider of the snake fence, which inclosed the field.

"Bob, Bob White," whistled Dannie.

"Bob, Bob White," answered the quail.

"I got my eye on that fellow," said Jimmy. "When he gets a little larger, I'm going after him."

"Seems an awful pity to kill him," said Dannie. "People rave over the lark, but I vow I'd miss the quail most if they were both gone. They are getting scarce."

"Well, I didn't say I was going to kill the whole flock," said Jimmy. "I was just going to kill a few for Mary, and if I don't, somebody else will."

"Mary dinna need onything better than ane of her own fried chickens," said Dannie. "And its no true about hunters. We've the river on ane side, and the bluff on the other. If we keep up our fishing signs, and add hunting to them, and juist shut the other fellows out, the birds will come here like everything wild gathers in National Park, out West. Ye bet things know where they are taken care of, well enough."

Jimmy snipped a spray of purple ironwort with his corn-cutter, and stuck it through his suspender buckle. "I think that would be more fun than killin' them. If you're a dacint shot, and your gun is clane" (Jimmy remembered the crow that had escaped with the eggs at soap-making), "you pretty well know you're goin' to bring down anything you aim at. But it would be a dandy joke to shell a little corn as we husk it, and toll all the quail into Rainbow Bottom, and then kape the other fellows out. Bedad! Let's do it."

Jimmy addressed the quail:

"Quailie, quailie on the fince,

We think your singin's just imminse.

Stay right here, and live with us,

And the fellow that shoots you will strike a fuss."

"We can protect them all richt enough," laughed Dannie. "And when the snow comes we can feed Cardinals like cheekens. Wish when we threshed, we'd saved a few sheaves of wheat. They do that in Germany, ye know. The last sheaf of the harvest they put up on a long pole at Christmas, as a thank-offering to the birds fra their care of the crops. My father often told of it."

"That would be great," said Jimmy. "Now look how domn slow you are! Why didn't you mintion it at harvest? I'd like things comin' for me to take care of them. Gee! Makes me feel important just to think about it. Next year we'll do it, sure. They'd be a lot of company. A man could work in this field to-day, with all the flowers around him, and the colors of the leaves like a garden, and a lot of birds talkin' to him, and not feel afraid of being alone."

"Afraid?" quoted Dannie, in amazement.

For an instant Jimmy looked startled. Then his love of proving his point arose. "Yes, afraid!" he repeated stubbornly. "Afraid of being away from the sound of a human voice, because whin you are, the voices of the black divils of conscience come twistin' up from the ground in a little wiry whisper, and moanin' among the trees, and whistlin' in the wind, and rollin' in the thunder, and above all in the dark they screech, and shout, and roar,'We're after you, Jimmy Malone! We've almost got you, Jimmy Malone! You're going to burn in Hell, Jimmy Malone!'"

Jimmy leaned toward Dannie, and began in a low voice, but he grew so excited as he tried to picture the thing that he ended in a scream, and even then Dannie's horrified eyes failed to recall him. Jimmy straightened, stared wildly behind him, and over the open, hazy field, where flowers bloomed, and birds called, and the long rows of shocks stood unconscious auditors of the strange scene. He lifted his hat, and wiped the perspiration from his dripping face with the sleeve of his shirt, and as he raised his arm, the corn-cutter flashed in the light.

"My God, it's awful, Dannie! It's so awful, I can't begin to tell you!"

Dannie's face was ashen. "Jimmy, dear auld fellow," he said, "how long has this been going on?"

"A million years," said Jimmy, shifting the corn-cutter to the hand that held his hat, that he might moisten his fingers with saliva and rub it across his parched lips.

"Jimmy, dear," Dannie's hand was on Jimmy's sleeve. "Have ye been to town in the nicht, or anything like that lately?"

"No, Dannie, dear, I ain't," sneered Jimmy, setting his hat on the back of his head and testing the corn-cutter with his thumb. "This ain't Casey's, me lad. I've no more call there, at this minute, than you have."

"It is Casey's, juist the same," said Dannie bitterly. "Dinna ye know the end of this sort of thing?"

"No, bedad, I don't!" said Jimmy. "If I knew any way to ind it, you can bet I've had enough. I'd ind it quick enough, if I knew how. But the railroad wouldn't be the ind. That would just be the beginnin'. Keep close to me, Dannie, and talk, for mercy sake, talk! Do you think we could finish the corn by noon?"

"Let's try!" said Dannie, as he squared his shoulders to adjust them to his new load. "Then we'll get in the pumpkins this afternoon, and bury the potatoes, and the cabbage and turnips, and then we're aboot fixed fra winter."

"We must take one day, and gather our nuts," suggested Jimmy, struggling to make his voice sound natural, "and you forgot the apples. We must bury thim too."

"That's so," said Dannie, "and when that's over, we'll hae nothing left to do but catch the Bass, and say farewell to the Kingfisher."

"I've already told you that I would relave you of all responsibility about the Bass," said Jimmy, "and when I do, you won't need trouble to make your adieus to the Kingfisher of the Wabash. He'll be one bird that won't be migrating this winter."

Dannie tried to laugh. "I'd like fall as much as any season of the year," he said, "if it wasna for winter coming next."

"I thought you liked winter, and the trampin' in the white woods, and trappin', and the long evenings with a book."

"I do," said Dannie. "I must have been thinkin' of Mary. She hated last winter so. Of course, I had to go home when ye were away, and the nichts were so long, and so cold, and mony of them alone. I wonder if we canna arrange fra one of her sister's girls to stay with her this winter?"

"What's the matter with me?" asked Jimmy.

"Nothing, if only ye'd stay," answered Dannie.

"All I'll be out of nights, you could put in one eye," said Jimmy. "I went last winter, and before, because whin they clamored too loud, I could be drivin' out the divils that way, for a while, and you always came for me, but even that won't be stopping it now. I wouldn't stick my head out alone after dark, not if I was dying!"

"Jimmy, ye never felt that way before," said Dannie. "Tell me what happened this summer to start ye."

"I've done a domn sight of faleing that you didn't know anything about," answered Jimmy. "I could work it off at Casey's for a while, but this summer things sort of came to a head, and I saw meself for fair, and before God, Dannie, I didn't like me looks."

"Well, then, I like your looks," said Dannie. "Ye are the best company I ever was in. Ye are the only mon I ever knew that I cared fra, and I care fra ye so much, I havna the way to tell ye how much. You're possessed with a damn fool idea, Jimmy, and ye got to shake it off. Such a great-hearted, big mon as ye! I winna have it! There's the dinner bell, and richt glad I am of it!"

That afternoon when pumpkin gathering was over and Jimmy had invited Mary out to separate the "punk" from the pumpkins, there was a wagon-load of good ones above what they would need for their use. Dannie proposed to take them to town and sell them. To his amazement Jimmy refused to go along.

"I told you this morning that Casey wasn't calling me at prisent," he said, "and whin I am not called I'd best not answer. I have promised Mary to top the onions and bury the cilery, and murder the bates."

"Do what wi' the beets?" inquired the puzzled Dannie.

"Kill thim! Kill thim stone dead. I'm too tinder-hearted to be burying anything but a dead bate, Dannie. That's a thousand years old, but laugh, like I knew you would, old Ramphirinkus! No, thank you, I don't go to town!"

Then Dannie was scared. "He's going to be dreadfully seek or go mad," he said.

So he drove to the village, sold the pumpkins, filled Mary's order for groceries, and then went to the doctor, and told him of Jimmy's latest developments.

"It is the drink," said that worthy disciple of Esculapius. "It's the drink! In time it makes a fool sodden and a bright man mad. Few men have sufficient brains to go crazy. Jimmy has. He must stop the drink."

On the street, Dannie encountered Father Michael. The priest stopped him to shake hands.

"How's Mary Malone?" he asked.

"She is quite well noo," answered Dannie, "but she is na happy. I live so close, and see so much, I know. I've thought of ye lately. I have thought of coming to see ye. I'm na of your religion, but Mary is, and what suits her is guid enough for me. I've tried to think of everything under the sun that might help, and among other things I've thought of ye. Jimmy was confirmed in your church, and he was more or less regular up to his marriage."

"Less, Mr. Macnoun, much less!" said the priest. "Since, not at all. Why do you ask?"

"He is sick," said Dannie. "He drinks a guid deal. He has been reckless about sleeping on the ground, and noo, if ye will make this confidential?"—the priest nodded—

"he is talking aboot sleeping on the railroad, and he's having delusions. There are devils after him. He is the finest fellow ye ever knew, Father Michael. We've been friends all our lives. Ye have had much experience with men, and it ought to count fra something. From all ye know, and what I've told ye, could his trouble be cured as the doctor suggests?"

The priest did a queer thing. "You know him as no living man, Dannie," he said. "What do you think?"

Dannie's big hands slowly opened and closed. Then he fell to polishing the nails of one hand on the palm of the other. At last he answered, "If ye'd asked me that this time last year, I'd have said 'it's the drink,' at a jump. But times this summer, this morning, for instance, when he hadna a drop in three weeks, and dinna want ane, when he could have come wi' me to town, and wouldna, and there were devils calling him from the ground, and the trees, and the sky, out in the open cornfield, it looked bad."

The priest's eyes were boring into Dannie's sick face. "How did it look?" he asked briefly.

"It looked," said Dannie, and his voice dropped to a whisper, "it looked like he might carry a damned ugly secret, that it would be better fra him if ye, at least, knew."

"And the nature of that secret?"

Dannie shook his head. "Couldna give a guess at it! Known him all his life. My only friend. Always been togither. Square a mon as God ever made. There's na fault in him, if he'd let drink alone. Got more faith in him than any ane I ever knew. I wouldna trust mon on God's footstool, if I had to lose faith in Jimmy. Come to think of it, that 'secret' business is all old woman's scare. The drink is telling on him. If only he could be cured of that awful weakness, all heaven would come down and settle in Rainbow Bottom."

They shook hands and parted without Dannie realizing that he had told all he knew and learned nothing. Then he entered the post office for the weekly mail. He called for Malone's papers also, and with them came a slip from the express office notifying Jimmy that there was a package for him. Dannie went to see if they would let him have it, and as Jimmy lived in the country, and as he and Dannie were known to be partners, he was allowed to sign the book, and carry away a long, slender, wooden box, with a Boston tag. The Thread Man had sent Jimmy a present, and from the appearance of the box, Dannie made up his mind that it was a cane.

Straightway he drove home at a scandalous rate of speed, and on the way, he dressed Jimmy in a broadcloth suit, patent leathers, and a silk hat. Then he took him to a gold cure, where he learned to abhor whiskey in a week, and then to the priest, to whom he confessed that he had lied about the number of coons in the Canoper. And so peace brooded in Rainbow Bottom, and all of them were happy again. For with the passing of summer, Dannie had learned that heretofore there had been happiness of a sort, for them, and that if they could all get back to the old footing it would be well, or at least far better than it was at present. With Mary's tongue dripping gall, and her sweet face souring, and Jimmy hearing devils, no wonder poor Dannie overheated his team in a race to carry a package that promised to furnish some diversion.

Jimmy and Mary heard the racket, and standing on the celery hill, they saw Dannie come clattering up the lane, and as he saw them, he stood in the wagon, and waved the package over his head.

Jimmy straightened with a flourish, stuck the spade in the celery hill, and descended with great deliberation. "I mintioned to Dannie this morning," he said "that it was about time I was hearin' from the Thrid Man."

"Oh! Do you suppose it is something from Boston?" the eagerness in Mary's voice made it sound almost girlish again.

"Hunt the hatchet!" hissed Jimmy, and walked very leisurely into the cabin.

Dannie was visibly excited as he entered. "I think ye have heard from the Thread Mon," he said, handing Jimmy the package.

Jimmy took it, and examined it carefully. He never before in his life had an express package, the contents of which he did not know. It behooved him to get all there was out of the pride and the joy of it.

Mary laid down the hatchet so close that it touched Jimmy's hand, to remind him. "Now what do you suppose he has sent you?" she inquired eagerly, her hand straying toward the packages.

Jimmy tested the box. "It don't weigh much," he said, "but one end of it's the heaviest."

He set the hatchet in a tiny crack, and with one rip, stripped off the cover. Inside lay a long, brown leather case, with small buckles, and in one end a little leather case, flat on one side, rounding on the other, and it, too, fastened with a buckle. Jimmy caught sight of a paper book folded in the bottom of the box, as he lifted the case. With trembling fingers he unfastened the buckles, the whole thing unrolled, and disclosed a case of leather, sewn in four divisions, from top to bottom, and from the largest of these protruded a shining object. Jimmy caught this, and began to draw, and the shine began to lengthen.

"Just what I thought!" exclaimed Dannie. "He's sent ye a fine cane."

"A hint to kape out of the small of his back the nixt time he goes promenadin' on a cow-kitcher! The divil!" exploded Jimmy.

His quick eyes had caught a word on the cover of the little book in the bottom of the box.

"A cane! A cane! Look at that, will ye?" He flashed six inches of grooved silvery handle before their faces, and three feet of shining black steel, scarcely thicker than a lead pencil. "Cane!" he cried scornfully. Then he picked up the box, and opening it drew out a little machine that shone like a silver watch, and setting it against the handle, slipped a small slide over each end, and it held firmly, and shone bravely.

"Oh, Jimmy, what is it?" cried Mary.

"Me cane!" answered Jimmy. "Me new cane from Boston. Didn't you hear Dannie sayin' what it was? This little arrangemint is my cicly-meter, like they put on wheels, and buggies now, to tell how far you've traveled. The way this works, I just tie this silk thrid to me door knob and off I walks, it a reeling out behind, and whin I turn back it takes up as I come, and whin I get home I take the yardstick and measure me string, and be the same token, it tells me how far I've traveled." As he talked he drew out another shining length and added it to the first, and then another and a last, fine as a wheat straw. "These last jints I'm adding," he explained to Mary, "are so that if I have me cane whin I'm riding I can stritch it out and touch up me horses with it. And betimes, if I should iver break me old cane fish pole, I could take this down to the river, and there, the books call it 'whipping the water.' See! Cane, be Jasus! It's the Jim-dandiest little fishing rod anybody in these parts iver set eyes on. Lord! What a beauty!"

He turned to Dannie and shook the shining, slender thing before his envious eyes.

"Who gets the Black Bass now?" he triumphed in tones of utter conviction.

There is no use in taking time to explain to any fisherman who has read thus far that Dannie, the patient; Dannie, the long-suffering, felt abused. How would you feel yourself?

"The Thread Man might have sent twa," was his thought. "The only decent treatment he got that nicht was frae me, and if I'd let Jimmy hit him, he'd gone through the wall. But there never is anything fra me!"

And that was true. There never was.

Aloud he said, "Dinna bother to hunt the steelyards, Mary. We winna weigh it until he brings it home."

"Yes, and by gum, I'll bring it with this! Look, here is a picture of a man in a boat, pullin' in a whale with a pole just like this," bragged Jimmy.

"Yes," said Dannie. "That's what it's made for. A boat and open water. If ye are going to fish wi' that thing along the river we'll have to cut doon all the trees, and that will dry up the water. That's na for river fishing."

Jimmy was intently studying the book. Mary tried to take the rod from his hand.

"Let be!" he cried, hanging on. "You'll break it!"

"I guess steel don't break so easy," she said aggrievedly. "I just wanted to 'heft' it."

"Light as a feather," boasted Jimmy. "Fish all day and it won't tire a man at all. Done—unjoint it and put it in its case, and not go dragging up everything along the bank like a living stump-puller. This book says this line will bear twinty pounds pressure, and sometimes it's takin' an hour to tire out a fish, if it's a fighter. I bet you the Black Bass is a fighter, from what we know of him."

"Ye can watch me land him and see what ye think about it," suggested Dannie.

Jimmy held the book with one hand and lightly waved the rod with the other, in a way that would have developed nerves in an Indian. He laughed absently.

"With me shootin' bait all over his pool with this?" he asked. "I guess not!"

"But you can't fish for the Bass with that, Jimmy Malone," cried Mary hotly. "You agreed to fish fair for the Bass, and it wouldn't be fair for you to use that, whin Dannie only has his old cane pole. Dannie, get you a steel pole, too," she begged.

"If Jimmy is going to fish with that, there will be all the more glory in taking the Bass from him with the pole I have," answered Dannie.

"You keep out," cried Jimmy angrily to Mary. "It was a fair bargain. He made it himself. Each man was to fish surface or deep, and with his own pole and bait. I guess this IS my pole, ain't it?"

"Yes," said Mary. "But it wasn't yours whin you made that agreemint. You very well know Dannie expected you to fish with the same kind of pole and bait that he did; didn't you, Dannie?"

"Yes," said Dannie, "I did. Because I never dreamed of him havin' any other. But since he has it, I think he's in his rights if he fishes with it. I dinna care. In the first place he will only scare the Bass away from him with the racket that reel will make, and in the second, if he tries to land it with that thing, he will smash it, and lose the fish. There's a longhandled net to land things with that goes with those rods. He'd better sent ye one. Now you'll have to jump into the river and land a fish by hand if ye hook it."

"That's true!" cried Mary. "Here's one in a picture."

She had snatched the book from Jimmy. He snatched it back.

"Be careful, you'll tear that!" he cried. "I was just going to say that I would get some fine wire or mosquito bar and make one."

Dannie's fingers were itching to take the rod, if only for an instant. He looked at it longingly. But Jimmy was impervious. He whipped it softly about and eagerly read from the book.

"Tells here about a man takin' a fish that weighed forty pounds with a pole just like this," he announced. "Scat! Jumpin' Jehosophat! What do you think of that!"

"Couldn't you fish turn about with it?" inquired Mary.

"Na, we couldna fish turn about with it," answered Dannie. "Na with that pole. Jimmy would throw a fit if anybody else touched it. And he's welcome to it. He never in this world will catch the Black Bass with it. If I only had some way to put juist fifteen feet more line on my pole, I'd show him how to take the Bass to-morrow. The way we always have come to lose it is with too short lines. We have to try to land it before it's tired out and it's strong enough to break and tear away. It must have ragged jaws and a dozen pieces of line hanging to it, fra both of us have hooked it time and again. When it strikes me, if I only could give it fifteen feet more line, I could land it."

"Can't you fix some way?" asked Mary.

"I'll try," answered Dannie.

"And in the manetime, I'd just be givin' it twinty off me dandy little reel, and away goes me with Mr. Bass," said Jimmy. "I must take it to town and have its picture took to sind the Thrid Man."

And that was the last straw. Dannie had given up being allowed to touch the rod, and was on his way to unhitch his team and do the evening work. The day had been trying and just for the moment he forgot everything save that his longing fingers had not touched that beautiful little fishing rod.

"The Boston man forgot another thing," he said. "The Dude who shindys 'round with those things in pictures, wears a damn, dinky, little pleated coat!"

CHAPTER VIII

WHEN THE BLACK BASS STRUCK

"Lots of fish down in the brook,

All you need is a rod, and a line, and a hook,"

hummed Jimmy, still lovingly fingering his possessions.

"Did Dannie iver say a thing like that to you before?" asked Mary.

"Oh, he's dead sore," explained Jimmy. "He thinks he should have had a jinted rod, too."

"And so he had," replied Mary. "You said yoursilf that you might have killed that man if Dannie hadn't showed you that you were wrong."

"You must think stuff like this is got at the tin-cint store," said Jimmy.

"Oh, no I don't!" said Mary. "I expect it cost three or four dollars."

"Three or four dollars," sneered Jimmy. "All the sinse a woman has! Feast your eyes on this book and rade that just this little reel alone cost fifteen, and there's no telling what the rod is worth. Why it's turned right out of pure steel, same as if it were wood. Look for yoursilf."

"Thanks, no! I'm afraid to touch it," said Mary.

"Oh, you are sore too!" laughed Jimmy. "With all that money in it, I should think you could see why I wouldn't want it broke."

"You've sat there and whipped it around for an hour. Would it break it for me or Dannie to do the same thing? If it had been his, you'd have had a worm on it and been down to the river trying it for him by now."

"Worm!" scoffed Jimmy. "A worm! That's a good one! Idjit! You don't fish with worms with a jinted rod."

"Well what do you fish with? Humming birds?"

"No. You fish with—" Jimmy stopped and eyed Mary dubiously. "You fish with a lot of things," he continued. "Some of thim come in little books and they look like moths, and some like snake-faders, and some of them are buck-tail and bits of tin, painted to look shiny. Once there was a man in town who had a minnie made of rubber and all painted up just like life. There were hooks on its head, and on its back, and its belly, and its tail, so's that if a fish snapped at it anywhere it got hooked."

"I should say so!" exclaimed Mary. "It's no fair way to fish, to use more than one hook. You might just as well take a net and wade in and seine out the fish as to take a lot of hooks and rake thim out."

"Well, who's going to take a lot of hooks and rake thim out?"

"I didn't say anybody was. I was just saying it wouldn't be fair to the fish if they did."

"Course I wouldn't fish with no riggin' like that, when Dannie only has one old hook. Whin we fish for the Bass, I won't use but one hook either. All the same, I'm going to have some of those fancy baits. I'm going to get Jim Skeels at the drug store to order thim for me. I know just how you do," said Jimmy flourishing the rod. "You put on your bait and quite a heavy sinker, and you wind it up to the ind of your rod, and thin you stand up in your boat——"

"Stand up in your boat!"

"I wish you'd let me finish!—or on the bank, and you take this little whipper-snapper, and you touch the spot on the reel that relases the thrid, and you give the rod a little toss, aisy as throwin' away chips, and off maybe fifty feet your bait hits the water, 'spat!' and 'snap!' goes Mr. Bass, and 'stick!' goes the hook. See?"

"What I see is that if you want to fish that way in the Wabash, you'll have to wait until the dredge goes through and they make a canal out of it; for be the time you'd throwed fifty feet, and your fish had run another fifty, there'd be just one hundred snags, and logs, and stumps between you; one for every foot of the way. It must look pretty on deep water, where it can be done right, but I bet anything that if you go to fooling with that on our river, Dannie gets the Bass."

"Not much, Dannie don't 'gets the Bass,'" said Jimmy confidently. "Just you come out here and let me show you how this works. Now you see, I put me sinker on the ind of the thrid, no hook of course, for practice, and I touch this little spring here, and give me little rod a whip and away goes me bait, slick as grase. Mr. Bass is layin' in thim bass weeds right out there, foreninst the pie-plant bed, and the bait strikes the water at the idge, see! and 'snap,' he takes it and sails off slow, to swally it at leisure. Here's where I don't pull a morsel. Jist let him rin and swally, and whin me line is well out and he has me bait all digistid, 'yank,' I give him the round-up, and THIN, the fun begins. He leps clear of the water and I see he's tin pound. If he rins from me, I give him rope, and if he rins to, I dig in, workin' me little machane for dear life to take up the thrid before it slacks. Whin he sees me, he makes a dash back, and I just got to relase me line and let him go, because he'd bust this little silk thrid all to thunder if I tried to force him onpleasant to his intintions, and so we kape it up until he's plum wore out and comes a promenadin' up to me boat, bank I mane, and I scoops him in, and that's sport, Mary! That's MAN'S fishin'! Now watch! He's in thim bass weeds before the pie-plant, like I said, and I'm here on the bank, and I THINK he's there, so I give me little jinted rod a whip and a swing——"

Jimmy gave the rod a whip and a swing. The sinker shot in air, struck the limb of an apple tree and wound a dozen times around it. Jimmy said things and Mary giggled. She also noticed that Dannie had stopped work and was standing in the barn door watching intently. Jimmy climbed the tree, unwound the line and tried again.

"I didn't notice that domn apple limb stickin' out there," he said. "Now you watch! Right out there among the bass weeds foreninst the pie-plant."

To avoid another limb, Jimmy aimed too low and the sinker shot under the well platform not ten feet from him.

"Lucky you didn't get fast in the bass weeds," said Mary as Jimmy reeled in.

"Will, I got to get me range," explained Jimmy. "This time——"

Jimmy swung too high. The spring slipped from under his unaccustomed thumb. The sinker shot above and behind him and became entangled in the eaves, while yards of the fine silk line flew off the spinning reel and dropped in tangled masses at his feet, and in an effort to do something Jimmy reversed the reel and it wound back on tangles and all until it became completely clogged. Mary had sat down on the back steps to watch the exhibition. Now, she stood up to laugh.

"And THAT'S just what will happen to you at the river," she said. "While you are foolin' with that thing, which ain't for rivers, and which you don't know beans about handlin', Dannie will haul in the Bass, and serve you right, too!"

"Mary," said Jimmy, "I niver struck ye in all me life, but if ye don't go in the house, and shut up, I'll knock the head off ye!"

"I wouldn't be advisin' you to," she said. "Dannie is watching you."

Jimmy glanced toward the barn in time to see Dannie's shaking shoulders as he turned from the door. With unexpected patience, he firmly closed his lips and went after a ladder. By the time he had the sinker loose and the line untangled, supper was ready. By the time he had mastered the reel, and could land the sinker accurately in front of various imaginary beds of bass weeds, Dannie had finished the night work in both stables and gone home. But his back door stood open and therefrom there protruded the point of a long, heavy cane fish pole. By the light of a lamp on his table, Dannie could be seen working with pincers and a ball of wire.

"I wonder what he thinks he can do?" said Jimmy.

"I suppose he is trying to fix some way to get that fifteen feet more line he needs," replied Mary.

When they went to bed the light still burned and the broad shoulders of Dannie bent over the pole. Mary had fallen asleep, but she was awakened by Jimmy slipping from the bed. He went to the window and looked toward Dannie's cabin. Then he left the bedroom and she could hear him crossing to the back window of the next room. Then came a smothered laugh and he softly called her. She went to him.

Dannie's figure stood out clear and strong in the moonlight, in his wood-yard. His black outline looked unusually powerful in the silvery whiteness surrounding it.

He held his fishing pole in both hands and swept a circle about him that would have required considerable space on Lake Michigan, and made a cast toward the barn. The line ran out smoothly and evenly, and through the gloom Mary saw Jimmy's figure straighten and his lips close in surprise. Then Dannie began taking in line. That process was so slow, Jimmy doubled up and laughed again.

"Be lookin' at that, will ye?" he heaved. "What does the domn fool think the Black Bass will be doin' while he is takin' in line on that young windlass?"

"There'd be no room on the river to do that," answered Mary serenely. "Dannie wouldn't be so foolish as to try. All he wants now is to see if his line will run, and it will. Whin he gets to the river, he'll swing his bait where he wants it with his pole, like he always does, and whin the Bass strikes he'll give it the extra fifteen feet more line he said he needed, and thin he'll have a pole and line with which he can land it."

"Not on your life he won't!" said Jimmy.

He opened the back door and stepped out just as Dannie raised the pole again.

"Hey, you! Quit raisin' Cain out there!" yelled Jimmy. "I want to get some sleep."

Across the night, tinged neither with chagrin nor rancor, boomed the big voice of Dannie.

"Believe I have my extra line fixed so it works all right," he said. "Awful sorry if I waked you. Thought I was quiet."

"How much did you make off that?" inquired Mary.

"Two points," answered Jimmy. "Found out that Dannie ain't sore at me any longer and that you are."

Next morning was no sort of angler's weather, but the afternoon gave promise of being good fishing by the morrow. Dannie worked about the farms, preparing for winter; Jimmy worked with him until mid-afternoon, then he hailed a boy passing, and they went away together. At supper time Jimmy had not returned. Mary came to where Dannie worked.

"Where's Jimmy?" she asked.

"I dinna, know" said Dannie. "He went away a while ago with some boy, I didna notice who."

"And he didn't tell you where he was going?"

"No."

"And he didn't take either of his fish poles?"

"No."

Mary's lips thinned to a mere line. "Then it's Casey's," she said, and turned away.

Dannie was silent. Presently Mary came back.

"If Jimmy don't come till morning," she asked, "or comes in shape that he can't fish, will you go without him?"

"To-morrow was the day we agreed on," answered Dannie.

"Will you go without him?" persisted Mary.

"What would HE do if it were me?" asked Dannie.

"When have you iver done to Jimmy Malone what he would do if he were you?"

"Is there any reason why ye na want me to land the Black Bass, Mary?"

"There is a particular reason why I don't want your living with Jimmy to make you like him," answered Mary. "My timper is being wined, and I can see where it's beginning to show on you. Whativer you do, don't do what he would."

"Dinna be hard on him, Mary. He doesna think," urged Dannie.

"You niver said twer words. He don't think. He niver thought about anybody in his life except himself, and he niver will."

"Maybe he didna go to town!"

"Maybe the sun won't rise in the morning, and it will always be dark after this! Come in and get your supper."

"I'd best pick up something to eat at home," said Dannie.

"I have some good food cooked, and it's a pity to be throwin' it away. What's the use? You've done a long day's work, more for us than yoursilf, as usual; come along and get your supper."

Dannie went, and as he was washing at the back door, Jimmy came through the barn, and up the walk. He was fresh, and in fine spirits, and where ever he had been, it was a sure thing that it was nowhere near Casey's.

"Where have you been?" asked Mary wonderingly.

"Robbin' graves," answered Jimmy promptly. "I needed a few stiffs in me business so I just went out to Five Mile and got them."

"What are ye going to do with them, Jimmy?" chuckled Dannie.

"Use thim for Bass bait! Now rattle, old snake!" replied Jimmy.

After supper Dannie went to the barn for the shovel to dig worms for bait, and noticed that Jimmy's rubber waders hanging on the wall were covered almost to the top with fresh mud and water stains, and Dannie's wonder grew.

Early the next morning they started for the river. As usual Jimmy led the way. He proudly carried his new rod. Dannie followed with a basket of lunch Mary had insisted on packing, his big cane pole, a can of worms, and a shovel, in case they ran out of bait.

Dannie had recovered his temper, and was just great-hearted, big Dannie again. He talked about the south wind, and shivered with the frost, and listened for the splash of the Bass. Jimmy had little to say. He seemed to be thinking deeply. No doubt he felt in his soul that they should settle the question of who landed the Bass with the same rods they had used when the contest was proposed, and that was not all.

When they came to the temporary bridge, Jimmy started across it, and Dannie called to him to wait, he was forgetting his worms.

"I don't want any worms," answered Jimmy briefly. He walked on. Dannie stood staring after him, for he did not understand that. Then he went slowly to his side of the river, and deposited his load under a tree where it would be out of the way.

He lay down his pole, took a rude wooden spool of heavy fish cord from his pocket, and passed the line through the loop next the handle and so on the length of the rod to the point. Then he wired on a sharp bass hook, and wound the wire far up the doubled line. As he worked, he kept an eye on Jimmy. He was doing practically the same thing. But just as Dannie had fastened on a light lead to carry his line, a souse in the river opposite attracted his attention. Jimmy hauled from the water a minnow bucket, and opening it, took out a live minnow, and placed it on his hook. "Riddy," he called, as he resank the bucket, and stood on the bank, holding his line in his fingers, and watching the minnow play at his feet.

The fact that Dannie was a Scotchman, and unusually slow and patient, did not alter the fact that he was just a common human being. The lump that rose in his throat was so big, and so hard, he did not try to swallow it. He hurried back into Rainbow Bottom. The first log he came across he kicked over, and grovelling in the rotten wood and loose earth with his hands, he brought up a half dozen bluish-white grubs. He tore up the ground for the length of the log, and then he went to others, cramming the worms and dirt with them into his pockets. When he had enough, he went back, and with extreme care placed three of them on his hook. He tried to see how Jimmy was going to fish, but he could not tell.

So Dannie decided that he would cast in the morning, fish deep at noon, and cast again toward evening.

He rose, turned to the river, and lifted his rod. As he stood looking over the channel, and the pool where the Bass homed, the Kingfisher came rattling down the river, and as if in answer to its cry, the Black Bass gave a leap, that sent the water flying.

"Ready!" cried Dannie, swinging his pole over the water.

As the word left his lips, "whizz," Jimmy's minnow landed in the middle of the circles widening about the rise of the Bass. There was a rush and a snap, and Dannie saw the jaws of the big fellow close within an inch of the minnow, and he swam after it for a yard, as Jimmy slowly reeled in. Dannie waited a second, and then softly dropped his grubs on the water just before where he figured the Bass would be. He could hear Jimmy smothering oaths. Dannie said something himself as his untouched bait neared the bank. He lifted it, swung it out, and slowly trailed it in again. "Spat!" came Jimmy's minnow almost at his feet, and again the Bass leaped for it. Again he missed. As the minnow reeled away the second time, Dannie swung his grubs higher, and struck the water "Spat," as the minnow had done. "Snap," went the Bass. One instant the line strained, the next the hook came up stripped clean of bait.

Then Dannie and Jimmy really went at it, and they were strangers. Not a word of friendly banter crossed the river. They cast until the Bass grew suspicious, and would not rise to the bait; then they fished deep. Then they cast again. If Jimmy fell into trouble with his reel, Dannie had the honesty to stop fishing until it worked again, but he spent the time burrowing for grubs until his hands resembled the claws of an animal. Sometimes they sat, and still-fished. Sometimes, they warily slipped along the bank, trailing bait a few inches under water. Then they would cast and skitter by turns.

The Kingfisher struck his stump, and tilted on again. His mate, and their family of six followed in his lead, so that their rattle was almost constant. A fussy little red-eyed vireo asked questions, first of Jimmy, and then crossing the river besieged Dannie, but neither of the stern-faced fishermen paid it any heed. The blackbirds swung on the rushes, and talked over the season. As always, a few crows cawed above the deep woods, and the chewinks threshed about among the dry leaves. A band of larks were gathering for migration, and the frosty air was vibrant with their calls to each other.

Killdeers were circling above them in flocks. A half dozen robins gathered over a wild grapevine, and chirped cheerfully, as they pecked at the frosted fruit. At times, the pointed nose of a muskrat wove its way across the river, leaving a shining ripple in its wake. In the deep woods squirrels barked and chattered. Frost-loosened crimson leaves came whirling down, settling in a bright blanket that covered the water several feet from the bank, and unfortunate bees that had fallen into the river struggled frantically to gain a footing on them. Water beetles shot over the surface in small shining parties, and schools of tiny minnows played along the banks. Once a black ant assassinated an enemy on Dannie's shoe, by creeping up behind it and puncturing its abdomen.

Noon came, and neither of the fishermen spoke or moved from their work. The lunch Mary had prepared with such care they had forgotten. A little after noon, Dannie got another strike, deep fishing. Mid-afternoon found them still even, and patiently fishing. Then it was not so long until supper time, and the air was steadily growing colder. The south wind had veered to the west, and signs of a black frost were in the air. About this time the larks arose as with one accord, and with a whirr of wings that proved how large the flock was, they sailed straight south.

Jimmy hauled his minnow bucket from the river, poured the water from it, and picked his last minnow, a dead one, from the grass. Dannie was watching him, and rightly guessed that he would fish deep. So Dannie scooped the remaining dirt from his pockets, and found three grubs. He placed them on his hook, lightened his sinker, and prepared to skitter once more.

Jimmy dropped his minnow beside the Kingfisher stump, and let it sink. Dannie hit the water at the base of the stump, where it had not been disturbed for a long time, a sharp "Spat," with his worms. Something seized his bait, and was gone. Dannie planted his feet firmly, squared his jaws, gripped his rod, and loosened his line. As his eye followed it, he saw to his amazement that Jimmy's line was sailing off down the river beside his, and heard the reel singing.

Dannie was soon close to the end of his line. He threw his weight into a jerk enough to have torn the head from a fish, and down the river the Black Bass leaped clear of the water, doubled, and with a mighty shake tried to throw the hook from his mouth.

"Got him fast, by God!" screamed Jimmy in triumph.

Straight toward them rushed the fish. Jimmy reeled wildly; Dannie gathered in his line by yard lengths, and grasped it with the hand that held the rod. Near them the Bass leaped again, and sped back down the river. Jimmy's reel sang, and Dannie's line jerked through his fingers. Back came the fish. Again Dannie gathered in line, and Jimmy reeled frantically. Then Dannie, relying on the strength of his line thought he could land the fish, and steadily drew it toward him. Jimmy's reel began to sing louder, and his line followed Dannie's. Instantly Jimmy went wild.

"Stop pullin' me little silk thrid!" he yelled. "I've got the Black Bass hooked fast as a rock, and your domn clothes line is sawin' across me. Cut there! Cut that domn rope! Quick!"

"He's mine, and I'll land him!" roared Dannie. "Cut yoursel', and let me get my fish!"

So it happened, that when Mary Malone, tired of waiting for the boys to come, and anxious as to the day's outcome, slipped down to the Wabash to see what they were doing, she heard sounds that almost paralyzed her. Shaking with fear, she ran toward the river, and paused at a little thicket behind Dannie.

Jimmy danced and raged on the opposite bank. "Cut!" he yelled. "Cut that domn cable, and let me Bass loose! Cut your line, I say!"

Dannie stood with his feet planted wide apart, and his jaws set. He drew his line steadily toward him, and Jimmy's followed. "Ye see!" exulted Dannie. "Ye're across me. The Bass is mine! Reel out your line till I land him, if ye dinna want it broken."

"If you don't cut your domn line, I will!" raved Jimmy.

"Cut nothin'!" cried Dannie. "Let's see ye try to touch it!"

Into the river went Jimmy; splash went Dannie from his bank. He was nearer the tangled lines, but the water was deepest on his side, and the mud of the bed held his feet. Jimmy reached the crossed lines, knife in hand, by the time Dannie was there.

"Will you cut?" cried Jimmy.

"Na!" bellowed Dannie. "I've give up every damn thing to ye all my life, but I'll no give up the Black Bass. He's mine, and I'll land him!"

Jimmy made a lunge for the lines. Dannie swung his pole backward drawing them his way. Jimmy slashed again. Dannie dropped his pole, and with a sweep, caught the twisted lines in his fingers.

"Noo, let's see ye cut my line! Babby!" he jeered.

Jimmy's fist flew straight, and the blood streamed from Dannie's nose. Dannie dropped the lines, and straightened. "You—" he panted. "You—" And no other words came.

If Jimmy had been possessed of any small particle of reason, he lost it at the sight of blood on Dannie's face.

"You're a domn fish thief!" he screamed.

"Ye lie!" breathed Dannie, but his hand did not lift.

"You are a coward! You're afraid to strike like a man! Hit me! You don't dare hit me!"

"Ye lie!" repeated Dannie.

"You're a dog!" panted Jimmy. "I've used you to wait on me all me life!"

"THAT'S the God's truth!" cried Dannie. But he made no movement to strike. Jimmy leaned forward with a distorted, insane face.

"That time you sint me to Mary for you, I lied to her, and married her meself. NOW, will you fight like a man?"

Dannie made a spring, and Jimmy crumpled up in his grasp.

"Noo, I will choke the miserable tongue out of your heid, and twist the heid off your body, and tear the body to mince-meat," raved Dannie, and he promptly began the job.

With one awful effort Jimmy tore the gripping hands from his throat a little. "Lie!" he gasped. "It's all a lie!"

"It's the truth! Before God it's the truth!" Mary Malone tried to scream behind them. "It's the truth! It's the truth!" And her ears told her that she was making no sound as with dry lips she mouthed it over and over. And then she fainted, and sank down in the bushes.

Dannie's hands relaxed a little, he lifted the weight of Jimmy's body by his throat, and set him on his feet. "I'll give ye juist ane chance," he said. "IS THAT THE TRUTH?"

Jimmy's awful eyes were bulging from his head, his hands were clawing at Dannie's on his throat, and his swollen lips repeated it over and over as breath came, "It's a lie! It's a lie!"

"I think so myself," said Dannie. "Ye never would have dared. Ye'd have known that

I'd find out some day, and on that day, I'd kill ye as I would a copperhead."

"A lie!" panted Jimmy.

"Then WHY did ye tell it?" And Dannie's fingers threatened to renew their grip.

"I thought if I could make you strike back," gasped Jimmy, "my hittin' you wouldn't same so bad."

Then Dannie's hands relaxed. "Oh, Jimmy! Jimmy!" he cried. "Was there ever any other mon like ye?"

Then he remembered the cause of their trouble.

"But, I'm everlastingly damned," Dannie went on, "if I'll gi'e up the Black Bass to ye, unless it's on your line. Get yourself up there on your bank!"

The shove he gave Jimmy almost upset him, and Jimmy waded back, and as he climbed the bank, Dannie was behind him. After him he dragged a tangled mass of lines and poles, and at the last up the bank, and on the grass, two big fish; one, the great Black Bass of Horseshoe Bend; and the other nearly as large, a channel catfish; undoubtedly, one of those which had escaped into the Wabash in an overflow of the Celina reservoir that spring.

"NOO, I'll cut," said Dannie. "Keep your eye on me sharp. See me cut my line at the end o' my pole." He snipped the line in two. "Noo watch," he cautioned, "I dinna want contra deection about this!"

He picked up the Bass, and taking the line by which it was fast at its mouth, he slowly drew it through his fingers. The wiry silk line slipped away, and the heavy cord whipped out free.

"Is this my line?" asked Dannie, holding it up.

Jimmy nodded.

"Is the Black Bass my fish? Speak up!" cried Dannie, dangling the fish from the line.

"It's yours," admitted Jimmy.

"Then I'll be damned if I dinna do what I please wi' my own!" cried Dannie. With trembling fingers he extracted the hook, and dropped it. He took the gasping big fish in both hands, and tested its weight. "Almost seex," he said. "Michty near seex!" And he tossed the Black Bass back into the Wabash.

Then he stooped, and gathered up his pole and line.

With one foot he kicked the catfish, the tangled silk line, and the jointed rod, toward Jimmy. "Take your fish!" he said. He turned and plunged into the river, recrossed it as he came, gathered up the dinner pail and shovel, passed Mary Malone, a tumbled heap in the bushes, and started toward his cabin.

The Black Bass struck the water with a splash, and sank to the mud of the bottom, where he lay joyfully soaking his dry gills, parched tongue, and glazed eyes. He scooped water with his tail, and poured it over his torn jaw. And then he said to his progeny, "Children, let this be a warning to you. Never rise to but one grub at a time. Three is too good to be true! There is always a stinger in their midst." And the Black Bass ruefully shook his sore head and scooped more water.

CHAPTER IX

WHEN JIMMY MALONE CAME TO CONFESSION

Dannie never before had known such anger as possessed him when he trudged homeward across Rainbow Bottom. His brain whirled in a tumult of conflicting passions, and his heart pained worse than his swelling face. In one instant the knowledge that Jimmy had struck him, possessed him with a desire to turn back and do murder. In the next, a sense of profound scorn for the cowardly lie which had driven him to the rage that kills encompassed him, and then in a surge came compassion for Jimmy, at the remberence of the excuse he had offered for saying that thing. How childish! But how like Jimmy! What was the use in trying to deal with him as if he were a man? A great spoiled, selfish baby was all he ever would be.

The fallen leaves rustled about Dannie's feet. The blackbirds above him in chattering debate discussed migration. A stiff breeze swept the fields, topped the embankment, and rushed down circling about Dannie, and setting his teeth chattering, for he was almost as wet as if he had been completely immersed. As the chill struck in, from force of habit he thought of Jimmy. If he was ever going to learn how to take care of himself, a man past thirty-five should know. Would he come home and put on dry clothing? But when had Jimmy taken care of himself? Dannie felt that he should go back, bring him home, and make him dress quickly.

A sharp pain shot across Dannie's swollen face. His lips shut firmly. No! Jimmy had struck him. And Jimmy was in the wrong. The fish was his, and he had a right to it. No man living would have given it up to Jimmy, after he had changed poles. And slipped away with a boy and gotten those minnows, too! And wouldn't offer him even one. Much good they had done him. Caught a catfish on a dead one! Wonder if he would take the catfish to town and have its picture taken! Mighty fine fish, too, that channel cat! If it hadn't been for the Black Bass, they would have wondered and exclaimed over it, and carefully weighed it, and commented on the gamy fight it made. Just the same he was glad, that he landed the Bass. And he got it fairly. If Jimmy's old catfish mixed up with his line, he could not help that. He baited, hooked, played, and landed the Bass all right, and without any minnows either.

When he reached the top of the hill he realized that he was going to look back. In spite of Jimmy's selfishness, in spite of the blow, in spite of the ugly lie, Jimmy had been his lifelong partner, and his only friend, and stiffen his neck as he would, Dannie felt his head turning. He deliberately swung his fish pole into the bushes, and when it caught, as he knew it would, he set down his load, and turned as if to release it. Not a sight of Jimmy anywhere! Dannie started on.

"We are after you, Jimmy Malone!"

A thin, little, wiry thread of a cry, that seemed to come twisting as if wrung from the chill air about him, whispered in his ear, and Dannie jumped, dropped his load, and ran for the river. He couldn't see a sign of Jimmy. He hurried over the shaky little bridge they had built. The catfish lay gasping on the grass, the case and jointed rod lay on a log, but Jimmy was gone.

Dannie gave the catfish a shove that sent it well into the river, and ran for the shoals at the lower curve of Horseshoe Bend. The tracks of Jimmy's crossing were plain, and after him hurried Dannie. He ran up the hill, and as he reached the top he saw Jimmy climb on a wagon out on the road. Dannie called, but the farmer touched up his horses and trotted away without hearing him. "The fool! To ride!" thought Dannie. "Noo he will chill to the bone!".

Dannie cut across the fields to the lane and gathered up his load. With the knowledge that Jimmy had started for town came the thought of Mary. What was he going to say to her? He would have to make a clean breast of it, and he did not like the showing. In fact, he simply could not make a clean breast of it. Tell her? He could not tell her. He would lie to her once more, this one time for himself. He would tell her he fell in the river to account for his wet clothing and bruised face, and wait until Jimmy came home and see what he told her.

He went to the cabin and tapped at the door; there was no answer, so he opened it and set the lunch basket inside. Then he hurried home, built a fire, bathed, and put on dry clothing. He wondered where Mary was. He was ravenously hungry now. He did all the evening work, and as she still did not come, he concluded that she had gone to town, and that Jimmy knew she was there. Of course, that was it! Jimmy could get dry clothing of his brother-in-law. To be sure, Mary had gone to town. That was why Jimmy went.

And he was right. Mary had gone to town. When sense slowly returned to her she sat up in the bushes and stared about her. Then she arose and looked toward the river. The men were gone. Mary guessed the situation rightly. They were too much of river men to drown in a few feet of water; they scarcely would kill each other. They had fought, and Dannie had gone home, and Jimmy to the consolation of Casey's. WHERE SHOULD SHE GO? Mary Malone's lips set in a firm line.

"It's the truth! It's the truth!" she panted over and over, and now that there was no one to hear, she found that she could say it quite plainly. As the sense of her outraged womanhood swept over her she grew almost delirious. "I hope you killed him, Dannie Micnoun," she raved. "I hope you killed him, for if you didn't, I will. Oh! Oh!"

She was almost suffocating with rage. The only thing clear to her was that she never again would live an hour with Jimmy Malone. He might have gone home. Probably he did go for dry clothing. She would go to her sister. She hurried across the bottom, with wavering knees she climbed the embankment, then skirting the fields, she half walked, half ran to the village, and selecting back streets and alleys, tumbled, half distracted, into the home of her sister.

"Holy Vargin!" screamed Katy Dolan. "Whativer do be ailin' you, Mary Malone?"

"Jimmy! Jimmy!" sobbed the shivering Mary.

"I knew it! I knew it! I've ixpicted it for years!" cried Katy.

"They've had a fight——"

"Just what I looked for! I always told you they were too thick to last!"

"And Jimmy told Dannie he'd lied to me and married me himsilf——"

"He did! I saw him do it!" screamed Katy.

"And Dannie tried to kill him——"

"I hope to Hivin he got it done, for if any man iver naded killin'! A carpse named Jimmy Malone would a looked good to me any time these fiftane years. I always said——"

"And he took it back——"

"Just like the rid divil! I knew he'd do it! And of course that mutton-head of a Dannie Micnoun belaved him, whativer he said."

"Of course he did!"

"I knew it! Didn't I say so first?"

"And I tried to scrame and me tongue stuck——"

"Sure! You poor lamb! My tongue always sticks! Just what I ixpicted!"

"And me head just went round and I keeled over in the bushes——"

"I've told Dolan a thousand times! I knew it! It's no news to me!"

"And whin I came to, they were gone, and I don't know where, and I don't care! But I won't go back! I won't go back! I'll not live with him another day. Oh, Katy! Think how you'd feel if some one had siparated you and Dolan before you'd iver been togither!"

Katie Dolan gathered her sister into her arms. "You poor lamb," she wailed. "I've known ivery word of this for fiftane years, and if I'd had the laste idea 'twas so, I'd a busted Jimmy Malone to smithereens before it iver happened!"

"I won't go back! I won't go back!" raved Mary.

"I guess you won't go back," cried Katy, patting every available spot on Mary, or making dashes at her own eyes to stop the flow of tears. "I guess you won't go back! You'll stay right here with me. I've always wanted you! I always said I'd love to have you! I've told thim from the start there was something wrong out there! I've ixpicted you ivry day for years, and I niver was so surprised in all me life as whin you came! Now, don't you shed another tear. The Lord knows this is enough, for anybody. None at all would be too many for Jimmy Malone. You get right into bid, and I'll make you a cup of rid-pipper tay to take the chill out of you. And if Jimmy Malone comes around this house I'll lav him out with the poker, and if Dannie Micnoun comes saft-saddering after him I'll stritch him out too; yis, and if Dolan's got anything to say, he can take his midicine like the rist. The min are all of a pace anyhow! I've always said it! If I wouldn't like to get me fingers on that haythen; never goin' to confission, spindin' ivrything on himself you naded for dacent livin'! Lit him come! Just lit him come!"

Thus forestalled with knowledge, and overwhelmed with kindness, Mary Malone cuddled up in bed and sobbed herself to sleep, and Katy Dolan assured her, as long as she was conscious, that she always had known it, and if Jimmy Malone came near, she had the poker ready.

Dannie did the evening work. When he milked he drank most of it, but that only made him hungrier, so he ate the lunch he had brought back from the river, as he sat before a roaring fire. His heart warmed with his body. Irresponsible Jimmy always had aroused something of the paternal instinct in Dannie. Some one had to be responsible, so Dannie had been. Some way he felt responsible now. With another man like himself, it would have been man to man, but he always had spoiled Jimmy; now who was to blame that he was spoiled?

Dannie was very tired, his face throbbed and ached painfully, and it was a sight to see. His bed never had looked so inviting, and never had the chance to sleep been further away. With a sigh, he buttoned his coat, twisted an old scarf around his neck, and started for the barn. There was going to be a black frost. The cold seemed to pierce him. He hitched to the single buggy, and drove to town. He went to Casey's, and asked for Jimmy.

"He isn't here," said Casey.

"Has he been here?" asked Dannie.

Casey hesitated, and then blurted out, "He said you wasn't his keeper, and if you came after him, to tell you to go to Hell."

Then Dannie was sure that Jimmy was in the back room, drying his clothing. So he drove to Mrs. Dolan's, and asked if Mary were there for the night. Mrs. Dolan said she was, and she was going to stay, and he might tell Jimmy Malone that he need not come near them, unless he wanted his head laid open. She shut the door forcibly.

Dannie waited until Casey closed at eleven, and to his astonishment Jimmy was not among the men who came out. That meant that he had drank lightly after all, slipped from the back door, and gone home. And yet, would he do it, after what he had said about being afraid? If he had not drank heavily, he would not go into the night alone, when he had been afraid in the daytime. Dannie climbed from the buggy once more, and patiently searched the alley and the street leading to the footpath across farms. No Jimmy. Then Dannie drove home, stabled his horse, and tried Jimmy's back door. It was unlocked. If Jimmy were there, he probably would be lying across the bed in his clothing, and Dannie knew that Mary was in town. He made a light, and cautiously entered the sleeping room, intending to undress and cover Jimmy, but Jimmy was not there.

Dannie's mouth fell open. He put out the light, and stood on the back steps. The frost had settled in a silver sheen over the roofs of the barns and the sheds, and a scum of ice had frozen over a tub of drippings at the well. Dannie was bitterly cold. He went home, and hunted out his winter overcoat, lighted his lantern, picked up a heavy cudgel in the corner, and started to town on foot over the path that lay across the fields. He followed it to Casey's back door. He went to Mrs. Dolan's again, but everything was black and silent there. There had been evening trains. He thought of Jimmy's frequent threat to go away. He dismissed that thought grimly. There had been no talk of going away lately, and he knew that Jimmy had little money. Dannie started for home, and for a rod on either side he searched the path. As he came to the back of the barns, he rated himself for not thinking of them first. He searched both of them, and all around them, and then wholly tired, and greatly disgusted, he went home and to bed. He decided that Jimmy HAD gone to Mrs. Dolan's and that kindly woman had relented and taken him in. Of course that was where he was.

Dannie was up early in the morning. He wanted to have the work done before Mary and Jimmy came home. He fed the stock, milked, built a fire, and began cleaning the stables. As he wheeled the first barrow of manure to the heap, he noticed a rooster giving danger signals behind the straw-stack. At the second load it was still there, and Dannie went to see what alarmed it.

Jimmy lay behind the stack, where he had fallen face down, and as Dannie tried to lift him he saw that he would have to cut him loose, for he had frozen fast in the muck of the barnyard. He had pitched forward among the rough cattle and horse tracks and fallen within a few feet of the entrance to a deep hollow eaten out of the straw by the cattle. Had he reached that shelter he would have been warm enough and safe for the night.

Horrified, Dannie whipped out his knife, cut Jimmy's clothing loose and carried him to his bed. He covered him, and hitching up drove at top speed for a doctor. He sent the physician ahead and then rushed to Mrs. Dolan's. She saw him drive up and came to the door.

"Send Mary home and ye come too," Dannie called before she had time to speak. "Jimmy lay oot all last nicht, and I'm afraid he's dead."

Mrs. Dolan hurried in and repeated the message to Mary. She sat speechless while her sister bustled about putting on her wraps.

"I ain't goin'," she said shortly. "If I got sight of him, I'd kill him if he wasn't dead."

"Oh, yis you are goin'," said Katy Dolan. "If he's dead, you know, it will save you being hanged for killing him. Get on these things of mine and hurry. You got to go for decency sake; and kape a still tongue in your head. Dannie Micnoun is waiting for us."

Together they went out and climbed into the carriage. Mary said nothing, but Dannie was too miserable to notice.

"You didn't find him thin, last night?" asked Mrs. Dolan.

"Na!" shivered Dannie. "I was in town twice. I hunted almost all nicht. At last I made sure you had taken him in and I went to bed. It was three o'clock then. I must have passed often, wi'in a few yards of him."

"Where was he?" asked Katy.

"Behind the straw-stack," replied Dannie.

"Do you think he will die?"

"Dee!" cried Dannie. "Jimmy dee! Oh, my God! We mauna let him!"

Mrs. Dolan took a furtive peep at Mary, who, dry-eyed and white, was staring straight ahead. She was trembling and very pale, but if Katy Dolan knew anything she knew that her sister's face was unforgiving and she did not in the least blame her.

Dannie reached home as soon as the horse could take them, and under the doctor's directions all of them began work. Mary did what she was told, but she did it deliberately, and if Dannie had taken time to notice her he would have seen anything but his idea of a woman facing death for any one she ever had loved. Mary's hurt went so deep, Mrs. Dolan had trouble to keep it covered. Some of the neighbors said Mary was cold-hearted, and some of them that she was stupefied with grief.

Without stopping for food or sleep, Dannie nursed Jimmy. He rubbed, he bathed, he poulticed, he badgered the doctor and cursed his inability to do some good. To every one except Dannie, Jimmy's case was hopeless from the first. He developed double pneumonia in its worst form and he was in no condition to endure it in the lightest. His labored breathing could be heard all over the cabin, and he could speak only in gasps. On the third day he seemed a little better, and when Dannie asked what he could do for him, "Father Michael," Jimmy panted, and clung to Dannie's hand.

Dannie sent a man and remained with Jimmy. He made no offer to go when the priest came.

"This is probably in the nature of a last confession," said Father Michael to Dannie, "I shall have to ask you to leave us alone."

Dannie felt the hand that clung to him relax, and the perspiration broke on his temples. "Shall I go, Jimmy?" he asked.

Jimmy nodded. Dannie arose heavily and left the room. He sat down outside the door and rested his head in his hands.

The priest stood beside Jimmy. "The doctor tells me it is difficult for you to speak," he said, "I will help you all I can. I will ask questions and you need only assent with your head or hand. Do you wish the last sacrament administered, Jimmy Malone?"

The sweat rolled off Jimmy's brow. He assented.

"Do you wish to make final confession?"

A great groan shook Jimmy. The priest remembered a gay, laughing boy, flinging back a shock of auburn hair, his feet twinkling in the lead of the dance. Here was ruin to make the heart of compassion ache. The Father bent and clasped the hand of Jimmy firmly. The question he asked was between Jimmy Malone and his God. The answer almost strangled him.

"Can you confess that mortal sin, Jimmy?" asked the priest.

The drops on Jimmy's face merged in one bath of agony. His hands clenched and his breath seemed to go no lower than his throat.

"Lied—Dannie," he rattled. "Sip-rate him—and Mary."

"Are you trying to confess that you betrayed a confidence of Dannie Macnoun and married the girl who belonged to him, yourself?"

Jimmy assented.

His horrified eyes hung on the priest's face and saw it turn cold and stern. Always the thing he had done had tormented him; but not until the past summer had he begun to realize the depth of it, and it had almost unseated his reason. But not until now had come fullest appreciation, and Jimmy read it in the eyes filled with repulsion above him.

"And with that sin on your soul, you ask the last sacrament and the seal of forgiveness! You have not wronged God and the Holy Catholic Church as you have this man, with whom you have lived for years, while you possessed his rightful wife. Now he is here, in deathless devotion, fighting to save you. You may confess to him. If he will forgive you, God and the Church will ratify it, and set the seal on your brow. If not, you die unshriven! I will call Dannie Macnoun."

One gurgling howl broke from the swollen lips of Jimmy.

As Dannie entered the room, the priest spoke a few words to him, stepped out and closed the door. Dannie hurried to Jimmy's side.

"He said ye wanted to tell me something," said Dannie. "What is it? Do you want me to do anything for you?"

Suddenly Jimmy struggled to a sitting posture. His popping eyes almost burst from their sockets as he clutched Dannie with both hands. The perspiration poured in little streams down his dreadful face.

"Mary," the next word was lost in a strangled gasp. Then came "yours" and then a queer rattle. Something seemed to give way. "The Divils!" he shrieked. "The Divils have got me!"

Snap! his heart failed, and Jimmy Malone went out to face his record, unforgiven by man, and unshriven by priest.

CHAPTER X

DANNIE'S RENUNCIATION

So they stretched Jimmy's length on Five Mile Hill beside the three babies that had lacked the "vital spark." Mary went to the Dolans for the winter and Dannie was left, sole occupant of Rainbow Bottom. Because so much fruit and food that would freeze were stored there, he was even asked to live in Jimmy's cabin.

Dannie began the winter stolidly. All day long and as far as he could find anything to do in the night, he worked. He mended everything about both farms, rebuilt all the fences and as a never-failing resource, he cut wood. He cut so much that he began to realize that it would get too dry and the burning of it would become extravagant, so he stopped that and began making some changes he had long contemplated. During fur time he set his line of traps on his side of the river and on the other he religiously set Jimmy's.

But he divided the proceeds from the skins exactly in half, no matter whose traps caught them, and with Jimmy's share of the money he started a bank account for Mary. As he could not use all of them he sold Jimmy's horses, cattle and pigs. With half the stock gone he needed only half the hay and grain stored for feeding. He disposed of the chickens, turkeys, ducks, and geese that Mary wanted sold, and placed the money to her credit. He sent her a beautiful little red bank book and an explanation of all these transactions by Dolan. Mary threw the book across the room because she wanted Dannie to keep her money himself, and then cried herself to sleep that night, because Dannie had sent the book instead of bringing it. But when she fully understood the transactions and realized that if she chose she could spend several hundred dollars, she grew very proud of that book.

About the empty cabins and the barns, working on the farms, wading the mud and water of the river bank, or tingling with cold on the ice went two Dannies. The one a dull, listless man, mechanically forcing a tired, overworked body to action, and the other a self-accused murderer.

"I am responsible for the whole thing," he told himself many times a day. "I always humored Jimmy. I always took the muddy side of the road, and the big end of the log, and the hard part of the work, and filled his traps wi' rats from my own; why in God's name did I let the Deil o' stubbornness in me drive him to his death, noo? Why didna I let him have the Black Bass? Why didna I make him come home and put on dry clothes? I killed him, juist as sure as if I'd taken an ax and broken his heid."

Through every minute of the exposure of winter outdoors and the torment of it inside, Dannie tortured himself. Of Mary he seldom thought at all. She was safe with her sister, and although Dannie did not know when or how it happened, he awoke one day to the realization that he had renounced her. He had killed Jimmy; he could not take his wife and his farm. And Dannie was so numb with long-suffering, that he did not much care. There come times when troubles pile so deep that the edge of human feeling is dulled.

He would take care of Mary, yes, she was as much Jimmy's as his farm, but he did not want her for himself now. If he had to kill his only friend, he would not complete his downfall by trying to win his wife. So through that winter Mary got very little consideration in the remorseful soul of Dannie, and Jimmy grew, as the dead grow, by leaps and bounds, until by spring Dannie had him well-nigh canonized.

When winter broke, Dannie had his future well mapped out. And that future was devotion to Jimmy's memory, with no more of Mary in it than was possible to keep out. He told himself that he was glad she was away and he did not care to have her return. Deep in his soul he harbored the feeling that he had killed Jimmy to make himself look victor in her eyes in such a small matter as taking a fish. And deeper yet a feeling that, everything considered, still she might mourn Jimmy more than she did.

So Dannie definitely settled that he always would live alone on the farms. Mary should remain with her sister, and at his death, everything should be hers. The night he finally reached that decision, the Kingfisher came home. Dannie heard his rattle of exultation as he struck the embankment and the suffering man turned his face to the wall and sobbed aloud, so that for a little time he stifled Jimmy's dying gasps that in wakeful night hours sounded in his ears. Early the next morning he drove through the village on his way to the county seat, with a load of grain. Dolan saw him and running home he told Mary. "He will be gone all day. Now is your chance!" he said.

Mary sprang to her feet, "Hurry!" she panted, "hurry!"

An hour later a loaded wagon, a man and three women drew up before the cabins in Rainbow Bottom. Mary, her sister, Dolan, and a scrub woman entered. Mary pointed out the objects which she wished removed, and Dolan carried them out. They took up the carpets, swept down the walls, and washed the windows. They hung pictures, prints, and lithographs, and curtained the windows in dainty white. They covered the floors with bright carpets, and placed new ornaments on the mantle, and comfortable furniture in the rooms. There was a white iron bed, and several rocking chairs, and a shelf across the window filled with potted hyacinths in bloom. Among them stood a glass bowl, containing three wonderful little gold fish, and from the top casing hung a brass cage, from which a green linnet sang an exultant song.

You should have seen Mary Malone! When everything was finished, she was changed the most of all. She was so sure of Dannie, that while the winter had brought annoyance that he did not come, it really had been one long, glorious rest. She laughed and sang, and grew younger with every passing day. As youth surged back, with it returned roundness of form, freshness of face, and that bred the desire to be daintily dressed. So of pretty light fabrics she made many summer dresses, for wear mourning she would not.

When calmness returned to Mary, she had told the Dolans the whole story. "Now do you ixpict me to grieve for the man?" she asked. "Fiftane years with him, through his lying tongue, whin by ivery right of our souls and our bodies, Dannie Micnoun and I belanged to each other. Mourn for him! I'm glad he's dead! Glad! Glad! If he had not died, I should have killed him, if Dannie did not! It was a happy thing that he died. His death saved me mortal sin. I'm glad, I tell you, and I do not forgive him, and I niver will, and I hope he will burn——"

Katy Dolan clapped her hand over Mary's mouth. "For the love of marcy, don't say that!" she cried. "You will have to confiss it, and you'd be ashamed to face the praste."

"I would not," cried Mary. "Father Michael knows I'm just an ordinary woman, he don't ixpict me to be an angel." But she left the sentence unfinished.

After Mary's cabin was arranged to her satisfaction, they attacked Dannie's; emptying it, cleaning it completely, and refurnishing it from the best of the things that had been in both. Then Mary added some new touches. A comfortable big chair was placed by his fire, new books on his mantle, a flower in his window, and new covers on his bed. While the women worked, Dolan raked the yards, and freshened matters outside as best he could. When everything they had planned to do was accomplished, the wagon, loaded with the ugly old things Mary despised, drove back to the village, and she, with little Tilly Dolan for company, remained.

Mary was tense with excitement. All the woman in her had yearned for these few pretty things she wanted for her home throughout the years that she had been compelled to live in crude, ugly surroundings; because every cent above plainest clothing and food, went for drink for Jimmy, and treats for his friends. Now she danced and sang, and flew about trying a chair here, and another there, to get the best effect. Every little while she slipped into her bedroom, stood before a real dresser, and pulled out its trays to make sure that her fresh, light dresses were really there. She shook out the dainty curtains repeatedly, watered the flowers, and fed the fish when they did not need it. She babbled incessantly to the green linnet, which with swollen throat rejoiced with her, and occasionally she looked in the mirror.

She lighted the fire, and put food to cook. She covered a new table, with a new cloth, and set it with new dishes, and placed a jar of her flowers in the center. What a supper she did cook! When she had waited until she was near crazed with nervousness, she heard the wagon coming up the lane. Peeping from the window, she saw Dannie stop the horses short, and sit staring at the cabins, and she realized that smoke would be curling from the chimney, and the flowers and curtains would change the shining windows outside. She trembled with excitement, and than a great yearning seized her, as he slowly drove closer, for his brown hair was almost white, and the lines on his face seemed indelibly stamped. And then hot anger shook her. Fifteen years of her life wrecked, and look at Dannie! That was Jimmy Malone's work.

Over and over, throughout the winter, she had planned this home-coming as a surprise to Dannie. Book-fine were the things she intended to say to him. When he opened the door, and stared at her and about the altered room, she swiftly went to him, and took the bundles he carried from his arms.

"Hurry up, and unhitch, Dannie," she said. "Your supper is waiting."

And Dannie turned and stolidly walked back to his team, without uttering a word.

"Uncle Dannie!" cried a child's voice. "Please let me ride to the barn with you!"

A winsome little maid came rushing to Dannie, threw her arms about his neck, and hugged him tight, as he stooped to lift her. Her yellow curls were against his cheek, and her breath was flower-sweet in his face.

"Why didn't you kiss Aunt Mary?" she demanded. "Daddy Dolan always kisses mammy when he comes from all day gone. Aunt Mary's worked so hard to please you. And Daddie worked, and mammy worked, and another woman. You are pleased, ain't you, Uncle Dannie?"

"Who told ye to call me Uncle?" asked Dannie, with unsteady lips.

"She did!" announced the little woman, flourishing the whip in the direction of the cabin. Dannie climbed down to unhitch. "You are goin' to be my Uncle, ain't you, as soon as it's a little over a year, so folks won't talk?"

"Who told ye that?" panted Dannie, hiding behind a horse.

"Nobody told me! Mammy just SAID it to Daddy, and I heard," answered the little maid. "And I'm glad of it, and so are all of us glad. Mammy said she'd just love to come here now, whin things would be like white folks. Mammy said Aunt Mary had suffered a lot more'n her share. Say, you won't make her suffer any more, will you?"

"No," moaned Dannie, and staggered into the barn with the horses. He leaned against a stall, and shut his eyes. He could see the bright room, plainer than ever, and that little singing bird sounded loud as any thunder in his ears. And whether closed or open, he could see Mary, never in all her life so beautiful, never so sweet; flesh and blood Mary, in a dainty dress, with the shining, unafraid eyes of girlhood. It was that thing which struck Dannie first, and hit him hardest. Mary was a careless girl again. When before had he seen her with neither trouble, anxiety or, worse yet, FEAR, in her beautiful eyes?

And she had come to stay. She would not have refurnished her cabin otherwise. Dannie took hold of the manger with both hands, because his sinking knees needed bracing.

"Dannie," called Mary's voice in the doorway, "has my spickled hin showed any signs of setting yet?"

"She's been over twa weeks," answered Dannie. "She's in that barrel there in the corner."

Mary entered the barn, removed the prop, lowered the board, and kneeling, stroked the hen, and talked softly to her. She slipped a hand under the hen, and lifted her to see the eggs. Dannie staring at Mary noted closer the fresh, cleared skin, the glossy hair, the delicately colored cheeks, and the plumpness of the bare arms. One little wisp of curl lay against the curve of her neck, just where it showed rose-pink, and looked honey sweet. And in one great surge, the repressed stream of passion in the strong man broke, and Dannie swayed against his horse. His tongue stuck to the roof of his mouth, and he caught at the harness to steady himself, while he strove to grow accustomed to the fact that Hell had opened in a new form for him. The old heart hunger for Mary Malone was back in stronger force than ever before; and because of him Jimmy lay stretched on Five Mile Hill.

"Dannie, you are just fine!" said Mary. "I've been almost wild to get home, because I thought iverything would be ruined, and instid of that it's all ixactly the way I do it. Do hurry, and get riddy for supper. Oh, it's so good to be home again! I want to make garden, and fix my flowers, and get some little chickens and turkeys into my fingers."

"I have to go home, and wash, and spruce up a bit, for ladies," said Dannie, leaving the barn.

Mary made no reply, and it came to him that she expected it. "Damned if I will!" he said, as he started home. "If she wants to come here, and force herself on me, she can, but she canna mak' me."

Just then Dannie stepped in his door, and slowly gazed about him. In a way his home was as completely transformed as hers. He washed his face and hands, and started for a better coat. His sleeping room shone with clean windows, curtained in snowy white. A freshly ironed suit of underclothing and a shirt lay on his bed. Dannie stared at them.

"She think's I'll tog up in them, and come courtin'" he growled. "I'll show her if I do! I winna touch them!"

To prove that he would not, Dannie caught them up in a wad, and threw them into a corner. That showed a clean sheet, fresh pillow, and new covers, invitingly spread back. Dannie turned as white as the pillow at which he stared.

"That's a damn plain insinuation that I'm to get into ye," he said to the bed, "and go on living here. I dinna know as that child's jabber counts. For all I know, Mary may already have picked out some town dude to bring here and farm out on me, and they'll live with the bird cage, and I can go on climbin' into ye alone."

Here was a new thought. Mary might mean only kindness to him again, as she had sent word by Jimmy she meant years ago. He might lose her for the second time. And again a wave of desire struck Dannie, and left him staggering.

"Ain't you comin', Uncle Dannie?" called the child's voice at the back door.

"What's your name, little lass?" inquired Dannie.

"Tilly," answered the little girl promptly.

"Well, Tilly, ye go tell your Aunt Mary I have been in an eelevator handlin' grain, and I'm covered wi' fine dust and chaff that sticks me. I canna come until I've had a bath, and put on clean clothing. Tell her to go ahead."

The child vanished. In a second she was back. "She said she won't do it, and take all the time you want. But I wish you'd hurry, for she won't let me either."

Dannie hurried. But the hasty bath and the fresh clothing felt so good he was in a softened mood when he approached Mary's door again. Tilly was waiting on the step, and ran to meet him. Tilly was a dream. Almost, Dannie understood why Mary had brought her. Tilly led him to the table, and pulled back a chair for him, and he lifted her into hers, and as Mary set dish after dish of food on the table, Tilly filled in every pause that threatened to grow awkward with her chatter. Dannie had been a very lonely man, and he did love Mary's cooking. Until then he had not realized how sore a trial six months of his own had been.

"If I was a praying mon, I'd ask a blessing, and thank God fra this food," said Dannie.

"What's the matter with me?" asked Mary.

"I have never yet found anything," answered Dannie. "And I do thank ye fra everything. I believe I'm most thankful of all fra the clean clothes and the clean bed. I'm afraid I was neglectin' myself, Mary."

"Will, you'll not be neglected any more," said Mary. "Things have turned over a new leaf here. For all you give, you get some return, after this. We are going to do business in a businesslike way, and divide even. I liked that bank account, pretty will, Dannie. Thank you, for that. And don't think I spint all of it. I didn't spind a hundred dollars all togither. Not the price of one horse! But it made me so happy I could fly. Home again, and the things I've always wanted, and nothing to fear. Oh, Dannie, you don't know what it manes to a woman to be always afraid! My heart is almost jumping out of my body, just with pure joy that the old fear is gone."

"I know what it means to a mon to be afraid," said Dannie. And vividly before him loomed the awful, distorted, dying face of Jimmy.

Mary guessed, and her bright face clouded.

"Some day, Dannie, we must have a little talk," she said, "and clear up a few things neither of us understand. 'Til thin we will just farm, and be partners, and be as happy as iver we can. I don't know as you mean to, but if you do, I warn you right now that you need niver mintion the name of Jimmy Malone to me again, for any reason."

Dannie left the cabin abruptly.

"Now you gone and made him mad!" reproached Tilly.

During the past winter Mary had lived with other married people for the first time, and she had imbibed some of Mrs. Dolan's philosophy.

"Whin he smells the biscuit I mane to make for breakfast, he'll get glad again," she said, and he did.

But first he went home, and tried to learn where he stood. WAS HE TRULY RESPONSIBLE FOR JIMMY'S DEATH? Yes. If he had acted like a man, he could have saved Jimmy. He was responsible. Did he want to marry Mary? Did he? Dannie reached empty arms to empty space, and groaned aloud. Would she marry him? Well, now, would she? After years of neglect and sorrow, Dannie knew that Mary had learned to prefer him to Jimmy. But almost any man would have been preferable to a woman, to Jimmy. Jimmy was distinctly a man's man. A jolly good fellow, but he would not deny himself anything, no matter what it cost his wife, and he had been very hard to live with. Dannie admitted that. So Mary had come to prefer him to Jimmy, that was sure; but it was not a question between him and Jimmy, now. It was between him, and any marriageable man that Mary might fancy.

He had grown old, and gray, and wrinkled, though he was under forty. Mary had grown round, and young, and he had never seen her looking so beautiful. Surely she would want a man now as young, and as fresh as herself; and she might want to live in town after a while, if she grew tired of the country. Could he remember Jimmy's dreadful death, realize that he was responsible for it, and make love to his wife? No, she was sacred to Jimmy. Could he live beside her, and lose her to another man for the second time? No, she belonged to him. It was almost daybreak when Dannie remembered the fresh bed, and lay down for a few hours' rest.

But there was no rest for Dannie, and after tossing about until dawn he began his work. When he carried the milk into the cabin, and smelled the biscuit, he fulfilled Mary's prophecy, got glad again, and came to breakfast. Then he went about his work. But as the day wore on, he repeatedly heard the voice of the woman and the child, combining in a chorus of laughter. From the little front porch, the green bird warbled and trilled. Neighbors who had heard of her return came up the lane to welcome a happy Mary Malone. The dead dreariness of winter melted before the spring sun, and in Dannie's veins the warm blood swept up, as the sap flooded the trees, and in spite of himself he grew gladder and yet gladder.

He now knew how he had missed Mary. How he had loathed that empty, silent cabin. How remorse and heart hunger had gnawed at his vitals, and he decided that he would go on just as Mary had said, and let things drift; and when she was ready to have the talk with him she had mentioned, he would hear what she had to say. And as he thought over these things, he caught himself watching for furrows that Jimmy was not making on the other side of the field. He tried to talk to the robins and blackbirds instead of Jimmy, but they were not such good company. And when the day was over, he tried not to be glad that he was going to the shining eyes of Mary Malone, a good supper, and a clean bed, and it was not in the heart of man to do it.

The summer wore on, autumn came, and the year Tilly had spoken of was over. Dannie went his way, doing the work of two men, thinking of everything, planning for everything, and he was all the heart of Mary Malone could desire, save her lover. By little Mary pieced it out. Dannie never mentioned fishing; he had lost his love for the river. She knew that he frequently took walks to Five Mile Hill. His devotion to Jimmy's memory was unswerving. And at last it came to her, that in death as in life, Jimmy Malone was separating them. She began to realize that there might be things she did not know. What had Jimmy told the priest? Why had Father Michael refused to confess Jimmy until he sent Dannie to him? What had passed between them? If it was what she had thought all year, why did it not free Dannie to her? If there was something more, what was it?

Surely Dannie loved her. Much as he had cared for Jimmy, he had vowed that everything was for her first. She was eager to be his wife, and something bound him. One day, she decided to ask him. The next, she shrank in burning confusion, for when Jimmy Malone had asked for her love, she had admitted to him that she loved Dannie, and Jimmy had told her that it was no use, Dannie did not care for girls, and that he had said he wished she would not thrust herself upon him. On the strength of that statement Mary married Jimmy inside five weeks, and spent years in bitter repentance.

That was the thing which held her now. If Dannie knew what she did, and did not care to marry her, how could she mention it? Mary began to grow pale, and lose sleep, and Dannie said the heat of the summer had tired her, and suggested that she go to Mrs. Dolan's for a weeks rest. The fact that he was willing, and possibly anxious to send her away for a whole week, angered Mary. She went.

CHAPTER XI

THE POT OF GOLD

Mary had not been in the Dolan home an hour until Katy knew all she could tell of her trouble. Mrs. Dolan was practical. "Go to see Father Michael," she said. "What's he for but to hilp us. Go ask him what Jimmy told him. Till him how you feel and what you know. He can till you what Dannie knows and thin you will understand where you are at."

Mary was on the way before Mrs. Dolan fully finished. She went to the priest's residence and asked his housekeeper to inquire if he would see her. He would, and Mary entered his presence strangely calm and self-possessed. This was the last fight she knew of that she could make for happiness, and if she lost, happiness was over for her. She had need of all her wit and she knew it. Father Michael began laughing as he shook hands.

"Now look here, Mary," he said, "I've been expecting you. I warn you before you begin that I cannot sanction your marriage to a Protestant."

"Oh, but I'm going to convart him!" cried Mary so quickly that the priest laughed harder than ever.

"So that's the lay of the land!" he chuckled. "Well, if you'll guarantee that, I'll give in. When shall I read the banns?"

"Not until we get Dannie's consint," answered Mary, and for the first her voice wavered.

Father Michael looked his surprise. "Tut! Tut!" he said. "And is Dannie dilatory?"

"Dannie is the finest man that will ever live in this world," said Mary, "but he don't want to marry me."

"To my certain knowledge Dannie has loved you all your life," said Father Michael. "He wants nothing here or hereafter as he wants to marry you."

"Thin why don't he till me so?" sobbed Mary, burying her burning face in her hands.

"Has he said nothing to you?" gravely inquired the priest.

"No, he hasn't and I don't belave he intinds to," answered Mary, wiping her eyes and trying to be composed. "There is something about Jimmy that is holding him back. Mrs. Dolan thought you'd help me."

"What do you want me to do, Mary?" asked Father Michael.

"Two things," answered Mary promptly. "I want you to tell me what Jimmy confissed to you before he died, and then I want you to talk to Dannie and show him that he is free from any promise that Jimmy might have got out of him. Will you?"

"A dying confession—" began the priest.

"Yes, but I know—" broke in Mary. "I saw them fight, and I heard Jimmy till Dannie that he'd lied to him to separate us, but he turned right around and took it back and I knew Dannie belaved him thin; but he can't after Jimmy confissed it again to both of you."

"What do you mean by 'saw them fight?'" Father Michael was leaning toward Mary anxiously.

Mary told him.

"Then that is the explanation to the whole thing," said the priest. "Dannie did believe Jimmy when he took it back, and he died before he could repeat to Dannie what he had told me. And I have had the feeling that Dannie thought himself in a way to blame for Jimmy's death."

"He was not! Oh, he was not!" cried Mary Malone. "Didn't I live there with them all those years? Dannie always was good as gold to Jimmy. It was shameful the way Jimmy imposed on him, and spint his money, and took me from him. It was shameful! Shameful!"

"Be calm! Be calm!" cautioned Father Michael. "I agree with you. I am only trying to arrive at Dannie's point of view. He well might feel that he was responsible, if after humoring Jimmy like a child all his life, he at last lost his temper and dealt with him as if he were a man. If that is the case, he is of honor so fine, that he would hesitate to speak to you, no matter what he suffered. And then it is clear to me that he does not understand how Jimmy separated you in the first place."

"And lied me into marrying him, whin I told him over and over how I loved Dannie. Jimmy Malone took iverything I had to give, and he left me alone for fiftane years, with my three little dead babies, that died because I'd no heart to desire life for thim, and he took my youth, and he took my womanhood, and he took my man—" Mary arose in primitive rage. "You naden't bother!" she said. "I'm going straight to Dannie meself."

"Don't!" said Father Michael softly. "Don't do that, Mary! It isn't the accepted way. There is a better! Let him come to you."

"But he won't come! He don't know! He's in Jimmy's grip tighter in death than he was in life." Mary began to sob again.

"He will come," said Father Michael. "Be calm! Wait a little, my child. After all these years, don't spoil a love that has been almost unequaled in holiness and beauty, by anger at the dead. Let me go to Dannie. We are good friends. I can tell him Jimmy made a confession to me, that he was trying to repeat to him, when punishment, far more awful than anything you have suffered, overtook him. Always remember, Mary, he died unshriven!" Mary began to shiver. "Your suffering is over," continued the priest. "You have many good years yet that you may spend with Dannie; God will give you living children, I am sure. Think of the years Jimmy's secret has hounded and driven him! Think of the penalty he must pay before he gets a glimpse of paradise, if he be not eternally lost!"

"I have!" exclaimed Mary. "And it is nothing to the fact that he took Dannie from me, and yet kept him in my home while he possessed me himsilf for years. May he burn——"

"Mary! Let that suffice!" cried the priest. "He will! The question now is, shall I go to Dannie?"

"Will you till him just what Jimmy told you? Will you till him that I have loved him always?"

"Yes," said Father Michael.

"Will you go now?"

"I cannot! I have work. I will come early in the morning."

"You will till him ivirything?" she repeated.

"I will," promised Father Michael.

Mary went back to Mrs. Dolan's comforted. She was anxious to return home at once, but at last consented to spend the day. Now that she was sure Dannie did not know the truth, her heart warmed toward him. She was anxious to comfort and help him in the long struggle which she saw that he must have endured. By late afternoon she could bear it no longer and started back to Rainbow Bottom in time to prepare supper.

For the first hour after Mary had gone Dannie whistled to keep up his courage. By the second he had no courage to keep. By the third he was indulging in the worst fit of despondency he ever had known. He had told her to stay a week. A week! It would be an eternity! There alone again! Could he bear it? He got through to mid-afternoon some way, and then in jealous fear and foreboding he became almost frantic. One way or the other, this thing must be settled. Fiercer raged the storm within him and at last toward evening it became unendurable.

At its height the curling smoke from the chimney told him that Mary had come home. An unreasoning joy seized him. He went to the barn and listened. He could hear her moving about preparing supper. As he watched she came to the well for water and before she returned to the cabin she stood looking over the fields as if trying to locate him. Dannie's blood ran hotly and his pulses were leaping. "Go to her! Go to her now!" demanded passion, struggling to break leash. "You killed Jimmy! You murdered your friend!" cried conscience, with unyielding insistence. Poor Dannie gave one last glance at Mary, and then turned, and for the second time he ran from her as if pursued by demons. But this time he went straight to Five Mile Hill, and the grave of Jimmy Malone.

He sat down on it, and within a few feet of Jimmy's bones, Dannie took his tired head in his hands, and tried to think, and for the life of him, he could think but two things. That he had killed Jimmy, and that to live longer without Mary would kill him. Hour after hour he fought with his lifelong love for Jimmy and his lifelong love for Mary. Night came on, the frost bit, the wind chilled, and the little brown owls screeched among the gravestones, and Dannie battled on. Morning came, the sun arose, and shone on Dannie, sitting numb with drawn face and bleeding heart.

Mary prepared a fine supper the night before, and patiently waited, and when Dannie did not come, she concluded that he had gone to town, without knowing that she had returned. Tilly grew sleepy, so she put the child to bed, and presently she went herself. Father Michael would make everything right in the morning. But in the morning Dannie was not there, and had not been. Mary became alarmed. She was very nervous by the time Father Michael arrived. He decided to go to the nearest neighbor, and ask when Dannie had been seen last. As he turned from the lane into the road a man of that neighborhood was passing on his wagon, and the priest hailed him, and asked if he knew where Dannie Macnoun was.

"Back in Five Mile Hill, a man with his head on his knees, is a-settin' on the grave of Jimmy Malone, and I allow that would be Dannie Macnoun, the damn fool!" he said.

Father Michael went back to the cabin, and told Mary he had learned where Dannie was, and to have no uneasiness, and he would go to see him immediately.

"And first of all you'll tell him how Jimmy lied to him?"

"I will!" said the priest.

He entered the cemetery, and walked slowly to the grave of Jimmy Malone. Dannie lifted his head, and stared at him.

"I saw you," said Father Michael, "and I came in to speak with you." He took Dannie's hand. "You are here at this hour to my surprise."

"I dinna know that ye should be surprised at my comin' to sit by Jimmy at ony time," coldly replied Dannie. "He was my only friend in life, and another mon so fine I'll never know. I often come here."

The priest shifted his weight from one foot to the other, and then he sat down on a grave near Dannie. "For a year I have been waiting to talk with you," he said.

Dannie wiped his face, and lifting his hat, ran his fingers through his hair, as if to arouse himself. His eyes were dull and listless. "I am afraid I am no fit to talk sensibly," he said. "I am much troubled. Some other time——"

"Could you tell me your trouble?" asked Father Michael.

Dannie shook his head.

"I have known Mary Malone all her life," said the priest softly, "and been her confessor. I have known Jimmy Malone all his life, and heard his dying confession. I know what it was he was trying to tell you when he died. Think again!"

Dannie Macnoun stood up. He looked at the priest intently. "Did ye come here purposely to find me?"

"Yes."

"What do ye want?"

"To clear your mind of all trouble, and fill your heart with love, and great peace, and rest. Our Heavenly Father knows that you need peace of heart, and rest, Dannie."

"To fill my heart wi' peace, ye will have to prove to me that I'm no responsible fra the death of Jimmy Malone; and to give it rest, ye will have to prove to me that I'm free to marry his wife. Ye can do neither of those things."

"I can do both," said the priest calmly. "My son, that is what I came to do."

Dannie's face grew whiter and whiter, as the blood receded, and his big hands gripped at his sides.

"Aye, but ye canna!" he cried desperately. "Ye canna!"

"I can," said the priest. "Listen to me! Did Jimmy get anything at all said to you?"

"He said, 'Mary,' then he choked on the next word, then he gasped out 'yours,' and it was over."

"Have you any idea what he was trying to tell you?"

"Na!" answered Dannie. "He was mortal sick, and half delirious, and I paid little heed. If he lived, he would tell me when he was better. If he died, nothing mattered, fra I was responsible, and better friend mon never had. There was nothing on earth Jimmy would na have done for me. He was so big hearted, so generous! My God, how I have missed him! How I have missed him!"

"Your faith in Jimmy is strong," ventured the bewildered priest, for he did not see his way.

Dannie lifted his head. The sunshine was warming him, and his thoughts were beginning to clear.

"My faith in Jimmy Malone is so strong," he said, "that if I lost it, I never should trust another living mon. He had his faults to others, I admit that, but he never had ony to me. He was my friend, and above my life I loved him. I wad gladly have died to save him."

"And yet you say you are responsible for his death!"

"Let me tell ye!" cried Dannie eagerly, and began on the story the priest wanted to hear from him. As he finished Father Michael's face lighted.

"What folly!" he said, "that a man of your intelligence should torture yourself with the thought of responsibility in a case like that. Any one would have claimed the fish in those circumstances. Priest that I am, I would have had it, even if I fought for it. Any man would! And as for what followed, it was bound to come! He was a tortured man, and a broken one. If he had not lain out that night, he would a few nights later. It was not in your power to save him. No man can be saved from himself, Dannie. Did what he said make no impression on you?"

"Enough that I would have killed him with my naked hands if he had na taken it back. Of course he had to retract! If I believed that of Jimmy, after the life we lived together, I would curse God and mon, and break fra the woods, and live and dee there alone."

"Then what was he trying to tell you when he died?" asked the bewildered priest.

"To take care of Mary, I judge."

"Not to marry her; and take her for your own?"

Dannie began to tremble.

"Remember, I talked with him first," said Father Michael, "and what he confessed to me, he knew was final. He died before he could talk to you, but I think it is time to tell you what he wanted to say. He—he—was trying—trying to tell you, that there was nothing but love in his heart for you. That he did not in any way blame you. That—that Mary was yours. That you were free to take her. That——"

"What!" cried Dannie wildly. "Are ye sure? Oh, my God!"

"Perfectly sure!" answered Father Michael. "Jimmy knew how long and faithfully you had loved Mary, and she had loved you——"

"Mary had loved me? Carefu', mon! Are ye sure?"

"I know," said Father Michael convincingly. "I give you my priestly word, I know, and Jimmy knew, and was altogether willing. He loved you deeply, as he could love any one, Dannie, and he blamed you for nothing at all. The only thing that would have brought Jimmy any comfort in dying, was to know that you would end your life with Mary, and not hate his memory."

"Hate!" cried Dannie. "Hate! Father Michael, if ye have come to tell me that Jimmy na held me responsible fra his death, and was willing fra me to have Mary, your face looks like the face of God to me!" Dannie gripped the priest's hand. "Are ye sure? Are ye sure, mon?" He almost lifted Father Michael from the ground.

"I tell you, I know! Go and be happy!"

"Some ither day I will try to thank ye," said Dannie, turning away. "Noo, I'm in a little of a hurry." He was half way to the gate when he turned back. "Does Mary know this?" he asked.

"She does," said the priest. "You are one good man, Dannie, go and be happy, and may the blessing of God go with you."

Dannie lifted his hat.

"And Jimmy, too," he said, "put Jimmy in, Father Michael."

"May the peace of God rest the troubled soul of Jimmy Malone," said Father Michael, and not being a Catholic, Dannie did not know that from the blessing for which he asked.

He hurried away with the brightness of dawn on his lined face, which looked almost boyish under his whitening hair.

Mary Malone was at the window, and turmoil and bitterness were beginning to burn in her heart again. Maybe the priest had not found Dannie. Maybe he was not coming. Maybe a thousand things. Then he WAS coming. Coming straight and sure. Coming across the fields, and leaping fences at a bound. Coming with such speed and force as comes the strong man, fifteen years denied. Mary's heart began to jar, and thump, and waves of happiness surged over her. And then she saw that look of dawn, of serene delight on the face of the man, and she stood aghast. Dannie threw wide the door, and crossed her threshold with outstretched arms.

"Is it true?" he panted. "That thing Father Michael told me, is it true? Will ye be mine, Mary Malone? At last will you be mine? Oh, my girl, is the beautiful thing that the priest told me true?"

"THE BEAUTIFUL THING THAT THE PRIEST TOLD HIM!"

Mary Malone swung a chair before her, and stepped back. "Wait!" she cried sharply. "There must be some mistake. Till me ixactly what Father Michael told you?"

"He told me that Jimmy na held me responsible fra his death. That he loved me when he died. That he was willing I should have ye! Oh, Mary, wasna that splendid of him. Wasna he a grand mon? Mary, come to me. Say that it's true! Tell me, if ye love me."

Mary Malone stared wide-eyed at Dannie, and gasped for breath.

Dannie came closer. At last he had found his tongue. "Fra the love of mercy, if ye are comin' to me, come noo, Mary" he begged. "My arms will split if they dinna get round ye soon, dear. Jimmy told ye fra me, sixteen years ago, how I loved ye, and he told me when he came back how sorry ye were fra me, and he—he almost cried when he told me. I never saw a mon feel so. Grand old Jimmy! No other mon like him!"

Mary drew back in desperation.

"You see here, Dannie Micnoun!" she screamed. "You see here——"

"I do," broke in Dannie. "I'm lookin'! All I ever saw, or see now, or shall see till I dee is 'here,' when 'here' is ye, Mary Malone. Oh! If a woman ever could understand what passion means to a mon! If ye knew what I have suffered through all these years, you'd end it, Mary Malone."

Mary gave the chair a shove. "Come here, Dannie," she said. Dannie cleared the space between them. Mary set her hands against his breast. "One minute," she panted. "Just one! I have loved you all me life, me man. I niver loved any one but you. I niver wanted any one but you. I niver hoped for any Hivin better than I knew I'd find in your arms. There was a mistake. There was an awful mistake, when I married Jimmy. I'm not tillin' you now, and I niver will, but you must realize that! Do you understand me?"

"Hardly," breathed Dannie. "Hardly!"

"Will, you can take your time if you want to think it out, because that's all I'll iver till you. There was a horrible mistake. It was YOU I loved, and wanted to marry. Now bend down to me, Dannie Micnoun, because I'm going to take your head on me breast and kiss your dear face until I'm tired," said Mary Malone.

An hour later Father Michael came leisurely down the lane, and the peace of God was with him.

A radiant Mary went out to meet him.

"You didn't till him!" she cried accusingly. "You didn't till him!"

The priest laid a hand on her head.

"Mary, the greatest thing in the whole world is self-sacrifice," he said. "The pot at the foot of the rainbow is just now running over with the pure gold of perfect contentment. But had you and I done such a dreadful thing as to destroy the confidence of a good man in his friend, your heart never could know such joy as it now knows in this sacrifice of yours; and no such blessed, shining light could illumine your face. That is what I wanted to see. I said to myself as I came along, 'She will try, but she will learn, as I did, that she cannot look in his eyes and undeceive him. And when she becomes reconciled, her face will be so good to see.' And it is. You did not tell him either, Mary Malone!"

Made in the USA
Monee, IL
21 March 2020